Désirée

ANNEMARIE SELINKO

Désirée

William Morrow & Company · New York

The publishers wish to acknowledge the special assistance of Joy Gary in the preparation of the final American version of this novel.

Translated from the German.

To the memory of
my sister, Liselotte,
to her joyous spirit,
her greatness of heart.

⤜ Contents ⤛

PART I

THE DAUGHTER OF A SILK MERCHANT
OF MARSEILLES

PART II

MARSHAL BERNADOTTE'S LADY

Part III

OUR LADY OF PEACE

ix

Part IV

THE QUEEN OF SWEDEN

Part One

THE DAUGHTER OF A SILK MERCHANT
OF MARSEILLES

Marseilles, at the beginning of Germinal, Year II
(The end of March, 1794, by Mama's
old-fashioned reckoning)

A woman can usually get what she wants from a man if she has a well-developed figure. So I've decided to stuff four handkerchiefs into the front of my dress tomorrow; then I shall look really grown up. Actually I *am* grown up already, but nobody else knows that, and I don't altogether look it.

Last November I was fourteen, and Papa gave me this lovely diary for my birthday. It's a shame to spoil these beautiful white pages with writing. There's a little lock at the side of the diary, and I can lock it up. Even my sister Julie won't know what I put in it. It was my last present from dear Papa. My father was the silk merchant François Clary, of Marseilles; he died two months ago, of congestion of the lungs.

"What shall I write in that book?" I asked in perplexity when I saw it on the table among my presents. Papa smiled and kissed me on the forehead. "The story of Citizeness Bernardine Eugénie Désirée Clary," he said, and suddenly he looked sad.

I am starting my future history tonight, because I'm so excited I can't get to sleep. So I slid softly out of bed, and I only hope Julie, over there, won't be awakened by the flickering of the candle. She'd make a frightful scene.

The reason why I'm excited is that tomorrow I'm going with my sister-in-law Suzanne to see Deputy Albitte and ask him to release

Etienne. Etienne is my brother, and his life is in danger. Two days ago the police suddenly came to arrest him. Such things do happen these days; it's only five years since the great Revolution, and people say it's not over yet. Anyhow, lots of people are guillotined every day in the Town Hall square, and it's not safe to be related to aristocrats. Fortunately, we haven't any fine folk among our relatives. Papa made his own way, and he built up Grandpa's little business into one of the biggest silk firms in Marseilles. Papa was very glad about the Revolution, though just before it he had been appointed a Purveyor to the Court and had sent some blue silk velvet to the Queen. Etienne says the velvet was never paid for. Papa almost cried when he read to us the first broadside giving the Rights of Man.

Etienne has been running the business since Papa died. When Etienne was arrested, Marie, our cook, who used to be my nurse, said quietly to me, "Eugénie, I hear that Albitte is coming to town. Your sister-in-law must go to see him and try to get Citizen Etienne Clary set free." Marie always knows what's going on in town.

At supper we were all very dismal. Two places at the table were empty—Papa's chair next to Mama and Etienne's next to Suzanne. Mama won't let anyone use Papa's chair. I kept thinking of Albitte and crumbling my bread into little balls. That annoyed Julie. She is only four years older, but she wants to mother me all the time and it makes me wild.

"Eugénie," she said, "it's bad manners to crumble your bread." I stopped making bread balls and said, "Albitte is in town."

The others took no notice. They never do when I say anything. So I said it again. "Albitte is in town."

At that Mama said, "Who is Albitte, Eugénie?"

Suzanne was not listening, she was sobbing into her soup.

"Albitte," I said, proud of my knowledge, "is the Jacobin Deputy for Marseilles. He is staying a week and will be in the Town Hall every day. And tomorrow Suzanne must go to see him; she must ask him why Etienne has been arrested, and insist that it must be a misunderstanding."

"But," Suzanne sobbed, looking at me, "he wouldn't receive me!"

"I think—I think it might be better," said Mama doubtfully, "for Suzanne to ask our lawyer to see Albitte."

Sometimes my family make me sick. Mama won't have a jar of marmalade made at home unless she can give it a stir. And yet she will leave a matter of life and death to our silly old lawyer. I expect many grown-ups are like that.

"We must see Albitte ourselves," I said, "and Suzanne, as Etienne's wife, is the one who should go. If you're scared, Suzanne, *I'll* go, and I'll ask Albitte to release my big brother."

"Don't you dare go to the Town Hall!" said Mama at once. Then she went on with her soup.

"Mama, I think . . ."

"I do not wish to discuss the matter further," said Mama, and Suzanne began sobbing into her soup again.

After supper I went upstairs to see whether Persson had got back. You see, in the evening I give Persson French lessons. He has the sweetest old horse-face imaginable. He's terribly tall and thin, and he's the only fair-haired man I know. That's because he is a Swede. Heaven only knows where Sweden is—somewhere up by the North Pole, I think. Persson showed me once on the map, but I forget where. Persson's papa has a silk business in Stockholm, and the business is somehow connected with ours here. So Persson came to Marseilles for a year to be an assistant in Papa's business. Everyone says you can only learn the silk trade in Marseilles. So one day Persson came to our house. At first we couldn't make out a word of what he said. He declared that he was talking French, but it didn't sound like French at all. Mama got a room ready for him on the top floor, and said that in these unsettled times it was better for Persson to live with us.

I found Persson had come in; really he is such a respectable young man, and we sat down in the parlour. Usually he reads to me from the newspapers, and I correct his pronunciation. And once more, as so often, I got out the old broadside about the Rights of Man that Papa had brought home, and then Persson and I listened to each other reciting it, because we wanted to learn it all by heart. Persson's old horse-face grew quite solemn, and he said he envied me because

I belonged to the nation that had presented these great thoughts to the world. "Liberty, Equality, and the Sovereignty of the People," he declaimed, sitting next to me.

Then he said, "Much blood has been shed to establish these new laws, so much innocent blood. And it must not have been shed in vain, mademoiselle."

Of course, Persson is a foreigner, and he always calls Mama "Mme Clary," and me "Mlle Eugénie," though that is forbidden; we are both just "Citizeness Clary."

Suddenly Julie came into the room. "Would you come for a moment, Eugénie?" she said, and took me to Suzanne's room.

Suzanne was sitting hunched up on the sofa, sipping port wine. Port is supposed to be strengthening, but I am never given a glass, because young girls do not need strengthening, Mama says. Mama was sitting next to Suzanne, and I could see that she was trying to look energetic. When she does that, she looks more frail and helpless than ever; she hunches up her narrow shoulders, and her face looks very small under the little widow's cap she has worn for two months. My poor mama reminds you much more of an orphan child than a widow.

"We have decided," said Mama, "that tomorrow Suzanne will try to see Deputy Albitte. And," Mama added, clearing her throat, "you are to go with her, Eugénie!"

"I am afraid to go alone, among all the crowds of people," Suzanne murmured. I could see that the wine had not strengthened her, only made her drowsy. And I wondered why I was to go with her, and not Julie.

"Suzanne has made this decision for Etienne's sake," said Mama, "and it will be a comfort to her, my dear child, to know that you are with her."

"Of course you must keep your mouth shut, and let Suzanne do the talking," Julie hastened to add.

I was glad that Suzanne was going to see Albitte. That was the best thing to do, the only thing, in my opinion. But they were treating me, as usual, like a child, so I said nothing.

"Tomorrow will be a very trying day for us all," said Mama, getting up. "So we must go to bed soon."

I ran into the parlour and told Persson that I had to go to bed. He picked up the newspapers and bowed. "Then I wish you good night, Mlle Clary," he said. I was at the door when he suddenly murmured something else.

I turned back. "Did you say something, M. Persson?"

"It's only—" he began. I went over to him and tried to see his face in the dusk; I did not bother to light the candles as we were going to bed. I could only just see Persson's pale face.

"I only wanted to say, mademoiselle, that I—yes, that I shall soon be going home."

"Oh, I am sorry, monsieur. Why?"

"I haven't told Mme Clary yet. I did not want to trouble her. But you see, mademoiselle, I've been here for a year and more, and they want me in the business, in Stockholm. And when M. Etienne Clary comes back everything will be in order here. I mean, in the business as well; and then I will go back to Stockholm."

It was the longest speech I had ever heard Persson make. I couldn't quite understand why he told me before the others. I had always thought he didn't take me any more seriously than the others do. But now, of course, I wanted us to go on talking. So I went over to the sofa and indicated with a very ladylike gesture that he was to be seated next to me. When he sat down, his tall frame folded up like a pocketknife. He rested his elbows on his knees, and I could see he didn't know what to say next.

"Is Stockholm a beautiful city?" I asked politely.

"To me it is the most beautiful city in the world," he answered. "Green ice floes sail about in the Mälar, and the sky is as white as a sheet that has just been washed. That is in the winter, but our winter is very long."

His description didn't make me think Stockholm particularly beautiful. I wondered, too, where it was that the green floes were drifting about.

"Our business is in the Västra Långgatan. That is the most modern business center in Stockholm. It is just by the Royal Palace," Persson added proudly.

But I was not really listening. I was thinking about tomorrow, and how I must stuff some handkerchiefs into the front of my dress and . . .

"I wanted to ask you a favour, Mlle Clary," I heard Persson saying.

I must look as pretty as I can, I was thinking, so that for my sake they will release Etienne. But I asked politely, "What is it, monsieur?"

"I should like so much," he faltered, "to keep the broadside about the Rights of Man, the one M. Clary brought home. I know, mademoiselle, that it is a presumptuous request."

It was indeed. Papa had always kept the broadside on his little bedside table, and after his death I had taken it for myself.

"I shall always treasure it and revere it, mademoiselle," said Persson.

Then I teased him for the last time. "So you've become a Republican, monsieur?"

And once more he wouldn't say. "I am a Swede, mademoiselle," he replied, "and Sweden is a monarchy."

"You may keep the broadside, monsieur," I said, "and show it to your friends in Sweden."

At that moment the door flew open, and I heard Julie's voice, shrill with anger. "When are you coming to bed, Eugénie? . . . Oh," she added, "I didn't know you were sitting here with M. Persson. Monsieur, the child must go to bed. Come along, Eugénie!"

Julie was still scolding me when I had put almost all my paper curlers into my hair and she was in bed. "Eugénie, your behaviour is scandalous. Persson is a young man, and it's not proper to sit in the dark with a young man. You forget that you are a daughter of François Clary. Papa was a highly respected citizen, and Persson can't even speak decent French. You will disgrace the whole family!"

What rubbish, I thought, as I blew out the candle and got into bed. What Julie needs, I decided, is a husband; if she had one my life would be easier.

I tried to sleep, but I could not stop thinking about tomorrow's visit to the Town Hall. And I kept thinking, too, of the guillotine. I see it so often, close up, when I am trying to get to sleep, and then I dig my head into the pillow to drive away that memory, the memory of the knife and the severed head.

7

Two years ago our cook Marie took me secretly to the square before the Town Hall. We pushed our way through the crowd that swarmed around the scaffold. I wanted to see everything, and I clenched my teeth because they were chattering so badly. The red cart brought up twenty gentlemen and ladies. They all wore fine clothes, but dirty bits of straw clung to the gentlemen's silk breeches and the ladies' lace sleeves. Their hands were bound with rope behind their backs.

Sawdust is spread on the scaffold around the guillotine, and every morning and evening, immediately after the executions, fresh sawdust is put down. Nevertheless the sawdust is always a terrible reddish-yellow mess. The whole square smells of dried blood and sawdust. The guillotine is painted red like the carts, but the paint is peeling off; for the guillotine has been there for years.

On that afternoon the first person brought in was a young man who was accused of being in secret correspondence with enemies abroad. When the executioner jerked him onto the scaffold his lips were moving; I think he was praying. He knelt, and I shut my eyes; I heard the guillotine fall.

When I looked up, the executioner was holding a head in his hand. The head had a chalk-white face; the eyes were wide-open and staring at me. My heart stood still. The mouth in the chalky face was wide-open as though about to scream. There was no end to that silent scream. I could hear confused voices around me. Someone sobbed, and a woman gave a harsh giggle. Then the noises seemed to come from far away, everything went black before my eyes, and—well, yes, I was horribly sick.

I felt better then, but people were shouting at me for being sick: I had spoiled someone's shoes. I kept my eyes shut so as not to see the bleeding head. Marie was ashamed of my behaviour, and took me out of the crowd; I heard people abusing us as we passed them. And ever since then I often can't sleep for thinking of the dead staring eyes and the silent scream.

When we got home I cried and cried. Papa put his arms around me and said, "The people of France have suffered for hundreds of years. And two flames rose from the suffering of the oppressed—the flame of Justice, and the flame of Hatred. The flame of Hatred will burn down and be extinguished in streams of blood. But the other flame, the sacred flame, little daughter, can never again be completely extinguished."

"The Rights of Man can never be annulled, can they, Papa?"

"No, they can never be annulled. But they can be temporarily abrogated, openly or secretly, and trodden underfoot. But those who trample on them will incur the deepest blood-guilt in all history. And whenever and wherever in days to come men rob their brethren of their rights of Liberty and Equality, no one can say for them, 'Father, forgive them, for they know not what they do,' because, little daughter, after the Declaration of the Rights of Man they will know perfectly well what they are doing!"

When Papa said that, his voice was quite changed. It sounded— yes, really, it sounded just as I should expect the voice of God to sound. And the longer the time that has passed since that talk with Papa, the better I have understood what he meant. I feel very close to him tonight. I am afraid for Etienne, and a little afraid of the visit to the Town Hall. But at night we are more easily frightened than in the daytime.

If only I knew whether my life's story will be happy or sad! I want ever so much to have some experience out of the ordinary. But first I must find a husband for Julie. And, above all, Etienne must be got somehow out of prison.

Good night, Papa! You see I have begun to write down my story.

Twenty-four hours later

I am the disgrace of the family.

On top of that, so much has happened I've no idea how to get it all down. First of all—Etienne has been released, and is sitting downstairs in the dining room with Mama, Suzanne, and Julie, and he is eating away as if he'd been kept a month on bread and water. Actually he was in prison only three days!

Secondly, I have met a young man with a very interesting face and the most unpronounceable name—Boonopat, or Bonapart, or something like that. Thirdly, downstairs they're all furious, they call me a disgrace to the family, and they have packed me off to bed.

They are celebrating Etienne's return, and even though it was my idea to see Albitte, I am being scolded and scolded, and there's no one I can talk to about the future and this Citizen Bounapar. Impossible name, I'll never remember it! There's simply no one I can talk to about this new young man. But my dear good papa must have foreseen how lonely you can be if you are misunderstood by the people around you, and that is why he gave me this diary.

Today began with one row after another. First Julie told me Mama had decided I was to wear my horrid grey frock, and that *of course* I must wear a lace fichu tight around my neck. I fought against the fichu, but Julie shrieked, "Do—you—think we shall let you go in a low-necked dress like a—like a girl from the port? Let you go to a government office without a fichu?"

As soon as Julie had gone I quickly borrowed her little pot of rouge. For my fourteenth birthday I had got a pot of my own, but I hate it, it's such a childish pink. Julie's "Cerise" suits me much better. I dabbed it on carefully, and I thought how difficult it must have been for the great ladies in Versailles who used thirteen different shades one on top of another to get the right effect. I read about it in the newspaper, in an article on the Widow Capet, our Queen who was guillotined.

"My rouge! How often must I tell you not to use my things without first asking my permission!" said Julie crossly as she came back into the bedroom. I quickly powdered my whole face; then I smoothed my eyebrows and eyelids with a dampened forefinger— they look much nicer when they are a little shiny. Julie sat on the bed and watched me critically. I began to take the paper curlers out of my hair, but they got caught in my curls. I have such horrid, stubborn natural curls it's a terrible business to coax them into smooth ringlets hanging down to my shoulders.

We heard Mama's voice outside. "Isn't that child ready yet, Julie? We must dine now if Suzanne and Eugénie are to be at the Town Hall by two o'clock."

I tried to hurry, but that only made me clumsier than ever, and I simply could not get my hair right.

"Julie, can't you help me?"

Honour to whom honour is due. Julie has the light touch of a fairy. She finished doing my hair in five minutes.

"In one of the papers I saw a drawing of the young Marquise de Fontenay," I said. "She wears her hair in short curls and brushes it down onto her forehead. Short hair would suit me, too."

"She just does it to remind everyone that she was only rescued from the guillotine in the nick of time! But she wouldn't have cut off her hair till she left the prison. She must have had long hair when Deputy Tallien first saw her there. But," Julie added like an old maiden aunt, "I should advise you, Eugénie, not to read news-paper articles about the Fontenay."

"You needn't be so condescending and superior, Julie. I'm no longer a child, and I know quite well why Tallien got a pardon for the beautiful Fontenay, and what he was after. And so—"

"You are impossible, Eugénie! Who tells you all these things? Marie in the kitchen?"

"Julie, where *is* that child?" Mama called. She sounded annoyed.

I pretended to be tidying my fichu, and stuffed the four handker-chiefs into my frock. Two on the right and two on the left.

"Take out those handkerchiefs at once! You can't go out like that," Julie said, but I pretended not to hear her, and impatiently pulled open one drawer after another looking for my Revolutionary cockade. Naturally I found it in the last drawer I opened, and I fastened it onto what seemed to me a very well-rounded handkerchief bosom. Then I ran downstairs to the dining room with Julie.

Mama and Suzanne had begun to eat. Suzanne, too, had put on her cockade. At the beginning of the Revolution everyone wore a cockade, but now they are worn only by Jacobins, or by people like us who are going to see someone in a government office or a deputy. Naturally when times are unsettled, for example last year when the Girondists were being persecuted, and there were wholesale arrests, no one dared to go out without the blue-white-red rosette of the Republic. At first I loved these rosettes showing the national colours of France. But now I don't like them any longer. I think it's undignified to pin one's convictions onto one's frock or coat lapel.

After dinner Mama got out the cut-glass decanter of port wine. Yesterday only Suzanne had a glass, but today Mama poured out two glasses and gave Suzanne one and me one.

"Drink it slowly," she told me. "Port wine is strengthening."

I took a big gulp; it tasted sticky and sweet, and all of a sudden it made me tingle. It made me very cheerful, too. I smiled at Julie, and then I saw there were tears in her eyes. She actually put her arm around my shoulder and pressed her face against my cheek. "Eugénie," she whispered, "take care of yourself."

The wine was making me very lively. For fun I rubbed my nose against Julie's cheek and whispered, "Perhaps you're afraid Deputy Albitte might seduce me!"

"Can't you ever be serious?" Julie was plainly shocked. "It's not just a game going to the Town Hall, with Etienne under arrest. You know they—" she stopped short.

I took a last good gulp of port. Then I looked straight at her. "I know, Julie, I know what you mean. Usually the close relatives of arrested men are arrested, too. Naturally Suzanne and I are in danger. You and Mama are in danger, too, but you two are not going, so you may not be noticed. And . . ."

"I wish I could go with Suzanne." Her lips were trembling, but she controlled herself. "But then if anything does happen, Mama will need me."

"Nothing will happen to us," I said. "But if it did, I'd know you were looking after Mama, and that you'd try to get me out. We two must always stick together, mustn't we, Julie?"

Suzanne did not speak on our way into the center of the town. We walked very fast, and she did not look to right or left even when we went past the fashion shops in the rue Cannebière. When we reached the large square in front of the Town Hall she suddenly took my arm. I tried not to see the guillotine, but the square still smelled of fresh sawdust and dried blood. We met Citizeness Renard, who has made Mama's hats for years. The citizeness looked around timidly before nodding to us. She had evidently heard that a member of the Clary family had been arrested.

A great crowd hung about the entrance to the Town Hall. When we tried to push our way through, someone caught hold of Suzanne's arm. Poor Suzanne shook with fear and turned very pale.

"What do you want, citizeness?"

"We wish to speak to Citizen Deputy Albitte," I said quickly in a loud voice.

The man—I decided he was the porter—let go of Suzanne's arm. "Second door on the right," he said.

We pressed on through the dimly lit entrance, found the door, opened it, and were assaulted by a confused roar of voices and a horribly stuffy atmosphere.

At first we did not know what to do. So many people were sitting and standing in the narrow waiting room that one could hardly move. At the far end of the room there was another door, at which a young man in the uniform of the Jacobin Club stood guard. He wore a high collar, a huge black cocked hat with a cockade, and a silk coat with very fine lace cuffs; he had a walking stick under his arm. I thought he must be one of Albitte's secretaries, so I caught hold of Suzanne's hand and tried to push through to him. Suzanne's hand was trembling and as cold as ice, but I could feel beads of perspiration on my forehead, and I was vexed with the handkerchiefs inside my dress, for they made me hotter than ever.

"We want to see Citizen Deputy Albitte, please," Suzanne murmured when we came up to the young man.

"What?" he shouted at her.

"To see Citizen Deputy Albitte," Suzanne stammered.

"Everyone in this room wants to see him. Have you sent in your name, citizeness?"

Suzanne shook her head. "How do we do that?" I asked.

"Write your name and business on a chit," he said. "People who can't write get me to do it for them. That costs—" He glanced appraisingly at our clothes.

"We can write," Suzanne said.

"Over there on the window ledge the citizeness will find paper and a quill," said the Jacobin youth. He might have been an archangel at the gates of Paradise.

We pushed through to the window ledge. Suzanne quickly filled out a form. Names? Citizeness Suzanne Clary and Citizeness Bernardine Eugénie Désirée Clary. Purpose of visit? We stared at each other in perplexity.

"Write the truth," I said.

"Then he won't see us," Suzanne whispered.

"He'll make inquiries anyhow before he sees us," I urged. "Things are not exactly simple here."

"Simple, no, indeed!" Suzanne moaned as she wrote, "Purpose of visit: Concerns arrest of Citizen Etienne Clary."

We then struggled back to our Jacobin archangel. He glanced casually at the paper, barked, "Wait," and disappeared behind the door. He was gone, it seemed to me, for an eternity. But at last he came back and said, "You may wait. The Citizen Deputy will receive you. Your name will be called out."

Soon afterward the door was opened, someone gave the archangel instructions, and he shouted, "Citizen Joseph Petit." I saw an old man with a little girl get up from the bench by the wall, and I quickly pushed Suzanne toward the two empty places. "We had better sit down. It'll be hours before it's our turn."

Our situation had improved a great deal. We leaned back against the wall, closed our eyes, and wriggled our toes in our shoes. Soon I began to look about, and I noticed our shoemaker, old Simon. I remembered his son, young Simon with the bowlegs, and how gallantly those bowlegs had marched in that procession eighteen months ago.

At that time, eighteen months ago, I saw the beginning of it all, and I shall never forget it as long as I live. Our country was being attacked on all sides by enemy armies. The other countries would not tolerate our proclamation of the Republic. It was being said that our armies would not be able to hold out much longer against those superior forces. But one morning I was awakened by singing under our windows. I jumped out of bed, and ran onto the balcony, and I saw marching past the *Volontaires* of Marseilles. They were taking three cannon from the fortress with them, because they did not intend to appear empty-handed before the Minister of War in Paris.

I knew many of the marchers. There were the apothecary's two nephews, and, heavens! shoemaker Simon's bowlegged son, outdoing himself to keep pace with the others! And there was Léon, the assistant from our own shop—he had not even asked permission, but had simply joined up and gone off. And behind Léon I saw three dignified young men with dark eyes and black hair, Banker Levi's sons. The Rights of Man had given them the same civil liberties as all other Frenchmen. Now they had put on their Sunday best to go to war for France. "Au revoir, M. Levi," I shouted, and all three of them looked up and waved. The Levis were followed by our butcher's sons, and then came in serried ranks the workmen from the docks. I recognized them by their blue linen tunics and the clatter of their clogs. And they were all singing *"Allons, enfants de la patrie,"* the new song, which was to become famous overnight, and I sang with them. Suddenly Julie was standing next to me. We gathered roses from the ramblers growing around the balcony and threw them down.

"Le jour de gloire est arrivé," roared up to us, and the tears ran down our cheeks. And below, Franchon, the tailor, caught two of the roses and looked up, laughing. Julie waved back at him with both her hands and called excitedly, *"Aux armes, citoyens, aux armes!"*

They still looked like ordinary citizens in their dark coats or blue linen tunics, their leather boots or wooden shoes.

In Paris only some of them were given uniforms, because there were not enough to go around. But with or without uniforms, they beat back the enemy and won the battles of Valmy and Wattignies —the Simons and Léons and Franchons and Levis. And now the song they sang as they marched to Paris is being played and sung all over France. It is called "La Marseillaise," because it was carried through the land by the men of our city. . . .

While I was thinking of those scenes, the old shoemaker had pushed his way through to us. He shook hands with us eagerly but with embarrassment, and we felt that he wanted to express his sympathy. Then he turned hastily to the subject of leather soles, which now are almost impossible to be obtained, and he went on to the tax relief which he wants to discuss with Albitte, and to his bowlegged son, from whom he has had no news. Then his name was called out, and he took leave of us.

We waited for many hours. Sometimes I closed my eyes and leaned against Suzanne. Every time I opened them the rays of the sun shone at a sharper angle and a little redder through the window. Now there were fewer people in the room. Albitte seemed to be cutting short the interviews, for the archangel was calling out new names more often. But plenty of people who had been here before us were still waiting.

"I must find a husband for Julie," I said. "In the novels she reads the heroines fall in love when they are eighteen at the latest. Where did you meet Etienne, Suzanne?"

"Don't bother me now," Suzanne said. "I want to concentrate on what I must say in there." She glanced at the door.

"If I ever have to receive people, I shall not keep them waiting. I'll give them definite times to come, one after another, and receive them at once. This waiting is awful!"

"What nonsense you talk, Eugénie. As if you would ever in your life—what did you call it?—be receiving people."

I fell silent, and grew sleepier still. Port wine makes you gay at first, I reflected, then sad, and finally tired. But it is certainly not strengthening.

"Don't yawn. It's very rude," Suzanne was saying.

"Oh, but we are living in a free republic," I murmured sleepily.

Then I woke up with a start because another name had been called out. Suzanne put her hand on mine. "It's not our turn yet," she said. Her hand was still cold.

At last I really fell fast asleep. I slept so soundly that I thought I was in bed at home. Suddenly I was disturbed by the light. I did not open my eyes. "Julie," I seemed to be saying, "let me sleep, I'm tired." A voice said, "Wake up, citizeness." But I took no notice until someone shook me by the shoulder.

"Wake up, citizeness. You can't go on sleeping here!"

"Oh, leave me alone," I grumbled, but then I was suddenly wide-awake. Startled, I pushed the strange hand from my shoulder. I had no idea where I was. I was in some dark room, and a man with a lantern was bending over me. For heaven's sake, where was I?

"Don't be alarmed, citizeness," the strange man said. His voice was soft and pleasant, but he spoke with a foreign accent, which made me sure I was having a bad dream. I said I wasn't afraid, but, I thought, where am I, and who are you?

The strange man stopped shining the lantern in my face, and now I could see his features more clearly. He was a really handsome young man, with kind dark eyes, a very smooth face, and a charming smile. He was wearing a dark suit and a coat over it.

"I'm sorry to disturb you," the young man said politely, "but I'm going home, and I'm closing Deputy Albitte's office."

Office? How had I got to an office? My head ached and my legs felt like lead. "What office? And who are you?" I stammered.

"It's Deputy Albitte's office. And my name, as this seems to interest the citizeness, is Citizen Joseph Buonaparte, secretary to the Committee of Public Safety in Paris, seconded to Deputy Albitte as his secretary during his journey to Marseilles. Our office hours were over a long time ago; I must lock up, and it's against the law for anyone to spend the night in the Town Hall. I must therefore ask the citizeness very kindly to wake up and leave."

Town Hall, Albitte! Now I knew where I was, and why. But where was Suzanne? I was at a loss.

"Where is Suzanne?" I asked the friendly young man.

At that his smile broadened into a laugh. "I have not had the privilege of meeting Suzanne," he said. "I can only tell you that the last people who came to see Citizen Albitte left two hours ago. I am the only person in the office. And I am going home now."

"But I must wait for Suzanne!" I insisted. "You must excuse me, Citizen Bo—ma—"

"Buonaparte," said the young man, politely helping me out.

"Well, Citizen Bonapat, you must excuse me, but here I am, and here I stay until Suzanne comes back. Otherwise there'll be a frightful row when I get home alone and confess that I lost her in the Town Hall. You can understand that, can't you?"

He sighed. "You're awfully persistent," he said. He put the lantern on the floor and sat down next to me on the bench. "What is this Suzanne's surname, and why did she want to see Albitte?"

"Her name is Suzanne Clary, and she is my brother Etienne's wife," I told him. "Etienne was arrested, and Suzanne and I came to ask for his release."

"Just a moment," he said. He got up, took the lantern, and disappeared through the door where the archangel had stood guard. I followed him. He was bending over a large desk and looking through some files of papers.

"If Albitte received your sister-in-law," he explained, "your brother's file must be here. The Deputy always asks for the papers in the case before talking to the relatives of arrested men."

I did not know what to say, so I murmured, "The Deputy is a very just and kind man."

He glanced up at me mockingly. "Above all a kind man, citizeness. Perhaps too kind. And that's why Citizen Robespierre of the Committee of Public Safety commissioned me to assist him."

"Oh, so you know Robespierre," I said without thinking. Heavens, here was someone who knew Deputy Robespierre, who will arrest his best friends to serve the Republic!

"Ah, here we are! 'Etienne Clary,' " the young man exclaimed in satisfaction. " 'Etienne Clary, silk merchant of Marseilles.' Is that right?"

I nodded eagerly. "But in any case," I said, "his arrest was a misunderstanding."

Citizen Buonaparte turned to me. "What was a misunderstanding?"

18

"Whatever it was that led to his arrest."

The young man looked severe. "I see. And why was he arrested?"

"Well, that we don't know," I admitted. "But at any rate I can assure you that it was a misunderstanding." Then I thought of something. "Listen," I said eagerly, "you said you know Citizen Robespierre, of the Committee of Public Safety. Perhaps you can tell him that Etienne's arrest was a mistake and—"

My heart stood still. For the young man shook his head slowly and seriously. "I can do nothing about this case. There is nothing more to be done. Here—" he solemnly picked up a document— "here is the decision, entered by Deputy Albitte himself."

He held the sheet out to me. "Read it for yourself!"

I bent over the document. Though he was holding the lantern quite close, I could make nothing out. I saw a few hastily written words, but the letters danced before my eyes.

"I am so troubled, please read it to me," I said, close to tears.

" 'The matter has been fully explained,' " he read, " 'and he has been set free.' "

"Does that mean—" I was trembling all over—"does that mean that Etienne—?"

"Of course! Your brother is a free man. He probably went home to his Suzanne long ago, and is now sitting with the rest of the family enjoying his supper. And the whole family are making a fuss over him and have entirely forgotten you. But—but—what's the matter, citizeness?"

I had begun to weep helplessly. I couldn't stop, the tears ran down my cheeks, and I cried and cried; and I simply could not understand why I was crying, for I wasn't sad, I was terribly happy, and I didn't know you can weep for joy.

"I am so glad, monsieur," I sobbed, "so glad!"

It was obvious that the scene was making the young man uncomfortable. He put down the file and busied himself with things on the desk. I dug down into my "Pompadour" handbag and looked for a handkerchief, but I found I had forgotten to put one in. Then I remembered the handkerchiefs in the front of my dress, and I reached down inside the open neck. At that moment the young

19

man looked up, and he could hardly believe his eyes. Two, three, four little handkerchiefs came out of my frock, just as if I was a conjurer.

"I put them there so that everyone would think I was grown-up," I murmured, thinking I owed him an explanation. I was terribly ashamed. "You see, at home they treat me like a child."

"You are no longer a child, you are a young lady," Citizen Boonopat assured me at once. "And now I'll take you home. It's not pleasant for a young lady to walk through the city alone at this time of night."

"It is ever so kind of you, monsieur, but I cannot accept—" I began to stammer in embarrassment. "You said yourself that you wanted to go home."

He laughed. "A friend of Robespierre permits no contradiction. We'll each have a sweet, and then go."

He opened a drawer in the desk and held out a bag to me. In it were cherries dipped in chocolate. "Albitte always keeps sweets in his desk," he told me. "Take another chocolate cherry. Good, isn't it? Nowadays only deputies can afford sweets like these." The last sentence sounded a little bitter.

"I live on the other side of the city; it would be very much out of your way," I said guiltily, as we were leaving. But I did not want to refuse his offer to escort me, for it's quite true that young ladies cannot be out alone in the evening without being molested. Besides, I did so like him.

"I am so ashamed of having cried," I said a little later.

He pressed my arm reassuringly. "I understand how you felt. I have brothers and sisters, too, and I love them. And, also, sisters of about your age."

After that I no longer felt in the least shy. "Marseilles isn't your home, is it?" I asked him.

"Yes, it is. All my family, except one brother, live here now."

"I thought— Well, your accent is different from ours."

"I am a Corsican," he said, "a Corsican refugee. We all came to France a little over a year ago—my mother, my brothers and sisters, and I. We had to leave everything we owned in Corsica, and escaped with our bare lives."

It sounded wildly romantic. "Why?" I asked, breathless with excitement.

"Because we are patriots," he said.

"But doesn't Corsica belong to Italy?" I inquired. My ignorance is beyond belief.

"How can you ask such a thing?" he replied indignantly. "For twenty-five years Corsica has belonged to France. We were brought up as French citizens, patriotic French citizens! That's why we couldn't possibly come to terms with the party that wanted to hand Corsica over to the English. Then a year ago English warships suddenly appeared off our coast. You must have heard about it—didn't you?"

I nodded. Probably I had heard about it at the time, but I had forgotten all about it now.

"We had to flee. Mama and all of us." His voice was grim. He was like a real hero in a novel—a homeless refugee.

"And have you friends in Marseilles?"

"My brother helps us. He was able to get Mama a small government pension, because she had to flee from the English. My brother was educated in France. In Brienne, in the Cadet College. He is a general."

"Oh," I said, speechless with admiration. One really should say something when told that a man's brother is a general, but I couldn't think of a thing and he changed the subject.

"You are a daughter of the late silk merchant Clary, aren't you?"

I was startled. "How did you know that?"

He laughed. "You needn't be surprised. I might tell you that the eyes of the law see everything and that I, as an official of the Republic, am one of those many eyes. But I'll be honest, mademoiselle, and admit that you yourself told me. You said you were Etienne Clary's sister, and I learned from the documents that Etienne Clary is the son of the late François Clary."

He spoke quickly, and when he does that he is liable to roll his *r*'s like a real foreigner. But, after all, he is a Corsican.

"By the way, mademoiselle," he said suddenly, "you were right. Your brother's arrest was indeed due to a misunderstanding. The

warrant for the arrest was actually made out in your father's name—
François Clary."

"But Papa is no longer alive!"

"Quite so, and that explains the misunderstanding. It's all down
in your brother's file. Recently an examination of certain pre-Revo-
lution documents revealed that the silk merchant François Clary had
petitioned to be granted a patent of nobility."

I was astonished. "Really? We knew nothing about that. And
I don't understand it. Papa never had any liking for the aristocracy.
Why should he have done that?"

"For business reasons," Citizen Buonaparte explained, "only for
business reasons. I suppose he wanted to be appointed a Purveyor to
the Court?"

"Yes, and once he sent some blue silk velvet to the Queen at
Versailles—to the Widow Capet, I mean. Papa's silks were famous
for their excellent quality," I added proudly.

"His petition was regarded as—well, let us say as entirely unsuited
to the times. That's why a warrant for his arrest was issued. And
when our people went to his address they found only the silk merchant Etienne Clary, and so they arrested him."

"I'm sure that Etienne knew nothing about that petition," I declared.

"I assume that your sister-in-law Suzanne convinced Deputy Albitte of her husband's innocence. That is why your brother was
released. Your sister-in-law must have hurried to the prison at once
to fetch him. But all that is over and done with. What interests
me," he continued, and his voice was soft, almost tender, "what interests me is not your family, mademoiselle, but you yourself, little
citizeness. What is your name?"

"My name is Bernardine Eugénie Désirée. They call me Eugénie.
But I should much prefer Désirée."

"All your names are beautiful. And what shall I call you, Mlle
Bernardine Eugénie Désirée?"

I felt myself blushing. Thank goodness it was dark, and he could
not see my face. I had a feeling that the conversation was taking a
turn which Mama would not have approved.

"Call me Eugénie as everyone else does. But you must come to see us, and in front of Mama I'll suggest that you call me by my Christian name. Then there won't be a row, because I believe that if Mama knew—"

I stopped short.

"Are you never allowed to take a walk with a young man?" he inquired.

"I don't know. So far, I've never known any young man," I said without thinking. I had completely forgotten Persson.

He pressed my arm again and laughed. "But now you know one —Eugénie!"

"When will you call on us?" I asked.

"Shall I come soon?" he rejoined, teasing.

But I did not answer at once. I was full of an idea that had occurred to me a little earlier—Julie! Julie, who so loves reading novels, would adore this young man with the strange foreign accent.

"Well, what is your answer, Mlle Eugénie?"

"Come tomorrow," I said, "tomorrow after the shop has been closed for the day. If it is warm enough we can sit in the garden. We have a little summer house—it's Julie's favourite spot in the garden." I considered that I had been extremely diplomatic.

"Julie? So far I have only heard about Suzanne and Etienne, not Julie. Who is Julie?"

We had already reached our road, and I had to talk quickly. "Julie is my sister," I said.

"Older or younger?" He sounded keenly interested.

"Older. She is eighteen."

"And—pretty?"

"Very pretty," I assured him eagerly, but then I wondered whether Julie would really be considered pretty. It is so difficult to judge one's own sister.

"You swear it?"

"She has lovely brown eyes," I declared, and so she has.

"Are you sure your mother would welcome me?" he asked with diffidence. He did not seem at all certain that Mama would be glad to see him, and, quite frankly, I wasn't sure either.

"I am sure she would welcome you," I insisted, determined to give Julie her chance. Besides, there was something I wanted myself.

23

"Do you think you could bring your brother, the General?" I asked.

Now M. Buonapat was quite eager. "Of course. He would be delighted, we have so few acquaintances in Marseilles."

"You see, I've never seen a real general close up," I confessed.

"Well, then you can see one tomorrow. True, at the moment he has no command, he is working out some scheme or other. Still, he is a real general."

I tried in vain to imagine what a real general would be like. I was sure that I had never met a general, and, as a matter of fact, I had not seen one even at a distance. And the pictures of the old generals in the days of the *Roi Soleil* are all of old gentlemen with huge wigs. After the Revolution, Mama took down those portraits, which had been in the parlour, and stored them in the attic.

"There must be a great difference in age between you and your brother," I said, for M. Bunapat seemed very young.

"No, not much difference. About a year."

"What?" I exclaimed. "Your brother is only a year older than you, and a general?"

"No, a year younger. My brother is only twenty-four. But he is aggressive, and full of astonishing ideas. Well, you'll see him tomorrow yourself."

Our house was now in sight. Lights shone from the ground-floor windows. No doubt the family had been at supper for some time.

"That is where I live, in that white house."

Suddenly M. Bunapat's manner changed. When he saw the attractive white house he was less sure of himself, and quickly said good-by. "I mustn't keep you, Mlle Eugénie. I'm sure your family is anxious about you. Oh, no, don't thank me. No trouble at all. It was a great pleasure to escort you, and, if you really meant it, I shall take the liberty of calling tomorrow in the late afternoon, with my young brother. That is, if your mother does not object, and we would not be disturbing you."

At that moment the house door was opened, and Julie's voice pierced the darkness. "There she is, by the garden gate!" Then she called out impatiently, "Eugénie, is that you, Eugénie?"

"I'm coming in a moment, Julie," I called back.

24

"Au revoir, mademoiselle," M. Bunapat said as I ran up to the house.

Five minutes later I was informed that I was a disgrace to the family.

Mama, Suzanne, and Etienne were at the dining table; the meal was over and they were having coffee when Julie brought me in in triumph. "Here she is!"

"Thank God," Mama said. "Where were you, my child?"

I glanced at Suzanne reproachfully. "Suzanne forgot all about me," I informed them. "I went to sleep and—"

Suzanne was holding her coffeecup in her right hand, and with her left she was clinging to Etienne's hand. She put down her cup indignantly. "Well, I never! First she went so sound asleep in the Town Hall that I couldn't arouse her, and I had to see Albitte alone. I couldn't keep him waiting until Mlle Eugénie condescended to wake up. And now she dares—"

"When you left Albitte I think you must have hurried to the prison and forgotten all about me!" I said. "But I'm not cross with you, really."

"But where have you been all this time?" Mama asked anxiously. "We sent Marie to the Town Hall, but the building was closed and the porter said that there was no one there except Albitte's secretary. Marie came back half an hour ago. Great heavens, Eugénie, to think that you walked through the town alone, at this late hour. When I think what might have happened to you!"

Mama took up the little silver bell which always stands at her place and rang it vigorously. "Bring the child her soup, Marie!"

"But I did not walk through the town alone," I said. "Albitte's secretary accompanied me."

Marie put down the soup in front of me. But before I could get the spoon to my mouth Suzanne burst out, "The secretary? That rude fellow who stood guard outside the door and called out the names?"

"No, he was only a guard. Albitte's real secretary is a very nice young man who knows Robespierre personally. At least he says he does. By the way, I have . . ."

But they would not let me finish. Etienne, who had not been able

25

to shave in prison but otherwise was quite unchanged, interrupted me. "What is his name?"

"A complicated name. Hard to remember, Boonapat or something like that. A Corsican. By the way, I have . . ."

Again they would not let me finish.

"And you walked about the town alone with this strange Jacobin in the evening?" Etienne shouted at me. He imagined that he was taking Papa's place.

Some families are quite incapable of logical thinking. First they had fussed because they thought I had walked home alone, and now they were outraged because I had not been alone, but instead had had excellent male protection.

"He is not a complete stranger; he introduced himself to me. His family live in Marseilles. They are refugees from Corsica. By the way, I have . . ."

"Have your soup before you go on, or it will be cold," said Mama.

"Refugees from Corsica?" said Etienne contemptuously. "Probably adventurers who were involved in political intrigues at home, and are trying their luck under the protection of the Jacobins. Adventurers, nothing but adventurers!"

I put down my spoon to defend my new friend. "I think he has a very respectable family," I said. "And his brother is a general. By the way, I have . . ."

"What is his brother's name?"

"I don't know I suppose it's Bunapat, too. By the way, I . . ."

"Never heard the name," Etienne growled. "But then most of the officers of the old régime have been dismissed, there aren't enough young ones, and promotions have been granted indiscrimininately. The new generals have no manners, no knowledge, and no experience!"

"They can all get experience enough. After all, we're at war," I interrupted. "By the way, I wanted to say . . ."

"Go on with your soup!" Mama insisted.

But I refused to be interrupted again. "I have been trying to say that I have invited them both here tomorrow."

Then I started quickly on my soup, because I knew that they would all be looking at me in horror.

"Whom have you invited, my child?" Mama asked.

"Two young gentlemen. Citizen Joseph Bonpat or whatever his name is, and his young brother, the General," I answered stoutly.

"You will have to cancel that invitation," said Etienne, banging the table. "Times are too unsettled to offer hospitality to two escaped Corsican adventurers no one has ever heard of!"

"And it's not proper for you to invite a gentleman you met by chance in a government office. That is not the way to behave. You are no longer a child, Eugénie!" This from Mama.

"That is the very first time anyone in this house has admitted that I am no longer a child," I remarked.

"Eugénie, I am ashamed of you," said Julie, in tones of deep sorrow.

"But these Corsican refugees have so few friends in the town," I ventured. I hoped to appeal to Mama's soft heart.

"People whose origins Mama and I know nothing about? Out of the question. Don't you ever consider your sister's and your own good name?" This from Etienne.

"It won't hurt Julie," I murmured, and glanced at her. I hoped she would help me. But she remained silent.

Etienne's experience during the last few days had destroyed his self-control. "You are a disgrace to the family!" he shouted.

"Etienne, she is only a child and does not know what she has done," said Mama.

At that, unfortunately, I, too, lost my temper. I was burning with rage. "Once and for all, I wish to have it understood that I am neither a child nor a disgrace!"

For a moment there was silence. Then Mama commanded, "Go to your room at once, Eugénie!"

"But I'm still hungry, I've only begun my meal."

Mama's silver bell rang violently. "Marie, please serve Mlle Eugénie's meal in her room." And to me, "Go along, my child, have a good rest and think about your recent behaviour. You have caused your mother and your good brother Etienne great anxiety. Good night."

Marie brought my supper up to the room I share with Julie. She sat down on Julie's bed. "What happened?" she demanded at once. "What's wrong with them all?"

When we are alone Marie always speaks to me informally: she is my friend and not a servant—after all, she came to us years ago when I needed a wet nurse, and I believe she loves me as much as her own natural child, Pierre, who is being brought up somewhere in the country.

I shrugged my shoulders. "It's all because I've invited two young men here tomorrow."

Marie nodded thoughtfully. "Very clever of you, Eugénie. It's time Mlle Julie met some young men."

Marie and I always understand each other.

"Shall I make you a cup of chocolate?" she whispered. "From our private store?" For Marie and I have a private store of delicacies which Mama doesn't know about. Marie gets the things from the larder, without asking.

After I had drunk the chocolate, when I was alone, I began to write everything down. It's now midnight and Julie is still downstairs. It's hateful of them to leave me out.

Now Julie has come in and is beginning to undress. Mama has decided to receive the two gentlemen tomorrow—the invitation could hardly be cancelled. This Julie has reported with feigned indifference. "But I am to tell you that it will be their first and last visit."

Julie is standing in front of the mirror rubbing cream on her face. The cream is called Lily Dew. Julie read somewhere that even in prison the Du Barry always used Lily Dew. But Julie hasn't it in her to become a Du Barry! Now she is asking whether he is handsome.

"Who?" I asked, pretending to be stupid.

"This gentleman who brought you home."

"Very handsome by moonlight. Very handsome by lantern light. But I've not yet seen him by daylight."

That's all that Julie is getting out of me.

Marseilles, at the beginning of Prairial
(*The lovely month of May, says Mama,*
is almost over)

His name is Napoleone.

When I wake up in the morning and think of him, with my eyes closed so Julie will think I'm still asleep, my heart feels heavy with the weight of my love. I never knew you really feel love, I mean all through you. But now love has tight hold of my heart.

I had better tell it all just as it happened, beginning with the afternoon when the two Buonapartes came to see us. As I had arranged with Joseph Buonaparte, they came the day after my unfortunate call on Deputy Albitte. They came late in the afternoon. Etienne is not usually home by then, but he had closed the shop and was waiting in the parlour with Mama, so that the young men should see at once that our home is not without manly protection.

Nobody had spoken more than a few words to me during the day, and I could see they were still vexed with my improper behaviour. After dinner Julie disappeared into the kitchen; she had decided to make a cake. Mama said there was no need; she was still full of Etienne's idea of "Corsican adventurers."

I went out into the garden. Spring was in the air already, and I found the first buds on the lilac trees. Then I asked Marie for a duster and did some dusting in the summer house—it was better to be prepared, I thought. When I went in with the duster I saw Julie, taking a cake tin out of the oven; her face was burning, her forehead damp with perspiration, and her hair was a mess.

"You're going about things the wrong way, Julie," I blurted.

"Why? I kept exactly to Mama's recipe, and you see if our guests don't like it."

"I didn't mean the cake," I said. "I meant your face and your hair. You'll smell of the cooking when the gentlemen come, and—"

29

I paused—"do please give it up, Julie, and go and powder your nose. That's much more important than baking cakes."

"Will you listen to the child, Marie!" cried Julie, irritated.

"If you ask me, Mlle Julie, I think the child is quite right," said Marie as she took the cake tin from her.

In our room Julie did her hair and carefully put on some rouge, while I looked out the window.

"Aren't you changing?" Julie asked in surprise. I really didn't see any point in it. Of course I quite liked M. Joseph, but in my mind I had already betrothed him to Julie. As for his brother, the General, I couldn't imagine him taking any notice of me. Nor had I any idea what you talk about to a General. I was interested only in his uniform, though I hoped he would tell us about the fighting at Valmy and Wattignies. I do hope, I was thinking all the time, that Etienne will be courteous and friendly to them, and that it has a happy ending. While I was looking out of the window I got more and more apprehensive. Then I saw them coming. They were having a lively discussion as they came along. And was I disappointed!

If you can imagine it, he was a small man, smaller than M. Joseph, who is only middle-sized. And nothing glittered on him, not a single star, or ribbon of any Order. Only when they reached the gate did I see his narrow gold epaulettes. His uniform was dark green, and his top boots weren't polished and didn't even fit well. I couldn't see his face because it was hidden by an enormous hat, with nothing on it but the cockade of the Republic. I didn't dream that a general could look so shabby. I was horribly disappointed.

"He looks very poor," I murmured.

Julie had joined me at the window, but she kept behind the curtain. I suppose she didn't want the two citizens to see how curious she was.

"Why do you say that?" she said. "He looks very handsome. You can't expect a secretary at the Town Hall to be immaculately turned out."

"Oh, you mean M. Joseph! Yes, he looks quite elegant; anyway, someone seems to brush his boots regularly. But look at his little brother, the General!" I shook my head and sighed. "Such a let-down! I had no idea that there were such undersized officers in the Army."

"What did you think he would be like?" Julie asked.

I shrugged my shoulders. "Why, like a general. Like a man who gives you the feeling that he can really command."

To think that all that happened only two months ago! It seems an eternity since the first time I saw Joseph and Napoleone in our parlour. When Julie and I went in, they both jumped up and bowed almost too politely, not only to Julie but to me, too. Then we all sat, stiff and strained, around the oval mahogany table. Mama was on the sofa, with Joseph Buonaparte next to her. On the other side of the table sat the poverty-stricken General, on the most uncomfortable chair in the house, with Etienne next to him. Julie and I were between Mama and Etienne.

"I have just been thanking Citizen Joseph Buonaparte," said Mama, "for his kindness yesterday in seeing you home, Eugénie."

At that moment Marie came in with liqueur and Julie's cake. While Mama filled the glasses and cut the cake, Etienne tried to make conversation with the General. "Is it indiscreet, Citizen General," he asked, "if I inquire whether you are in our city on official business?"

Joseph answered at once for the General. "Not at all. The Army of the French Republic is a people's army, and is maintained by the citizens' taxes. Every citizen, therefore, has the right to know what is being done by our army. Am I not right, Napoleone?"

The name Napoleone sounded very foreign. We couldn't help all staring at the General.

"You may ask anything you like, Citizen Clary," the General replied. "I, at all events, make no secret of my plans. In my opinion the Republic is only wasting its resources in this endless defensive warfare on our frontiers. Wars of defence merely cost money and bring in neither glory nor the means of replenishing our exchequer. . . . Thank you, Mme Clary, thank you very much." Mama had handed him cake on a plate. He turned again at once to Etienne. "We must pass on, of course, to offensive warfare. It will help our finances, and will show Europe that the people's army has not been defeated."

I had paid attention—but not to the words. His face was no longer concealed by his hat, and though it's not a handsome face, it seems to me more wonderful than any face I have ever seen or dreamt of. And suddenly I understood why on the day before I had been attracted to Joseph Buonaparte. The brothers are like each other, but Joseph's features are not so strong and not so compelling as Napoleone's. They had only suggested the existence of a stronger face for which I had seemed to be longing. Napoleone's face fulfilled my expectations.

"Offensive warfare?" I heard Etienne ask in dismay. We all sat in dead silence, and I realized that the young General must have said something startling. Etienne was looking at him open-mouthed. "Yes, but, Citizen General, has our army, with very limited equipment, as we are given to understand . . ."

The General waved his hand and laughed. "Limited? *That's* not the word! Our army is a beggars' army. Our soldiers at the frontiers are in rags; they march into battle in wooden shoes. And our artillery is so wretchedly equipped that you might think Carnot, our Minister of War, planned to defend France with bows and arrows."

I leaned forward and looked hard at him. Afterward Julie told me my behaviour had been *dreadful*. But I couldn't help it. I particularly wanted to see him laugh again. He has a thin face with tightly drawn skin, very sunburned, and surrounded by reddish-brown hair. His hair comes down to his shoulders; it is not dressed or even powdered. When he laughs his drawn face suddenly becomes very boyish, and he looks much younger than he really is.

I pulled myself together because someone was saying to me, "Your health, Mlle Clary." They all had their glasses and were sipping the liqueur. Joseph had put his glass close to mine; his eyes were sparkling, and I remembered what we had arranged the day before. "Oh," I told him, "call me Eugénie as the others do." Mama raised her eyebrows, but Etienne was too engrossed in his conversation with the General to hear.

"And on what front could an offensive operation be successfully carried out?" he wanted to know.

"On the Italian front, naturally. We will drive the Austrians out of Italy. A very cheap campaign. Our troops can easily take care of themselves in Italy. So rich and fertile a country!"

"And the Italian people? They are still loyal to the Austrians."

"We will liberate the Italian people. In all the provinces we conquer we shall proclaim the Rights of Man." Though the subject seemed to interest the General very much, I could see that Etienne's objections bored him.

"Your garden is wonderful," Joseph Buonaparte said to Mama, looking through the glass door.

"It's too early yet," Julie ventured, "but when the lilac is out, and the climbing roses around the summer house—"

She stopped in confusion. I could see she was disconcerted; lilac and rambler roses do not bloom at the same time.

"Have the plans for an offensive operation on the Italian front taken definite shape?" Etienne gave him no peace. The thought of offensive action seemed to fascinate him.

"Yes. I've practically completed the plans. At present I am inspecting our fortifications here in the south."

"But Government circles are still determined on an Italian campaign?"

"Citizen Robespierre personally entrusted me with this tour of inspection. It seems to me imperative before our Italian offensive begins."

Etienne clicked his tongue, a sign that he was impressed. "A great plan," and he nodded, "a bold plan." The General smiled at Etienne, and that smile seemed to captivate my brother, that hard-headed businessman. Etienne said eagerly, stammering like a schoolchild, "If only that great plan succeeds, if only it succeeds!"

"Have no fear, Citizen Clary, it will succeed," the General replied, getting up. "And which of the two young ladies will be so kind as to show me the garden?"

Julie and I both jumped to our feet. And Julie smiled at Joseph. I don't know just how it happened, but two minutes later we four found ourselves—without Mama and without Etienne—in the garden.

Because the gravel path to the summer house is very narrow we had to go two by two. Julie and Joseph went ahead, and I walked with Napoleone, racking my brains for something to say to him. I wanted terribly to make a good impression on him. He seemed not to notice our silence and to be buried in his thoughts. He walked so slowly that Julie and his brother got farther and farther away from us. Finally, I began to think he was deliberately dawdling.

"When do you think my brother and your sister will be married?" he said, all of a sudden.

I thought at first that I couldn't have heard him properly. I looked at him astounded, and I could feel that I was blushing.

"Well," he repeated, "when will they be married? Soon, I hope."

"Yes, but," I stammered, "they have only just met. And after all, we don't know—"

"They are made for each other," he declared. "You know that, too."

"I?" I looked at him with round astonished eyes, the way I look at Etienne when I have a guilty conscience and don't want him to find me out. Etienne usually mutters something about "Eyes of a child" and isn't mad at me any more.

"Please don't look at me like that!" He was not impressed.

I thought I'd surely sink through the earth. But I was angry, too.

"You yourself were thinking yesterday evening that it would be a good thing for your sister to marry my brother," he declared. "After all, at her age young ladies usually are betrothed."

"I thought nothing of the sort, Citizen General!" I felt that in some way I had compromised Julie. I was no longer angry with Napoleone, only with myself.

He stopped, and looked me in the face. He was only half a head taller than I, and he seemed pleased to have found somebody he could tower over. It was getting dark, and the light-biue spring twilight lowered like a screen between us and Julie and Joseph. The General's face was so close to mine that I could still see his eyes; they were sparkling, and I was also surprised to find that men can have long eyelashes.

"You must never have any secrets from me, Mlle Eugénie. I can see deep into the hearts of young ladies. Besides, Joseph told me last night that you had promised to introduce him to your elder sister.

You also told him that your sister was very pretty. That's not true, and—you must have had good reason for your little white lie."

"We must hurry," I said to that. "The others must be in the summer house already."

"Hadn't we better give your sister a chance to get better acquainted with my brother before she becomes betrothed to him?" he asked softly. His voice sounded very gentle, almost—yes, almost caressing. His accent quite often seems less foreign than his brother's.

"Joseph will very soon be suing for your sister's hand," he told me then quite forthrightly. It was so dark now that I could see his face only dimly, but I could tell he was smiling.

"How do you know that?" I asked, puzzled.

"We talked about it last night," he replied, as if that were the most natural thing in the world to do.

"But last night your brother had never met my sister," I retorted, outraged.

Then he very gently took my arm, and I could feel his nearness all through me. We went slowly on, and he spoke so tenderly and trustingly that we might have been friends for years.

"Joseph told me of his meeting with you, and also that your family are very well-to-do. Your father is no longer living, but I assume that he left a considerable dowry for you and your sister. Our people are very poor."

"You have sisters, too, haven't you?" I remembered that Joseph had mentioned sisters of my age the day before.

"Yes, three young sisters and three young brothers," he said. "And Joseph and I have to provide for Mama and all of them. Mama has a very small pension from the State, because she's considered a persecuted patriot since fleeing from Corsica. But the pension doesn't even pay the rent. You have no idea, Mlle Eugénie, how expensive a life is now in France."

"So your brother only wants to marry my sister for her dowry?" I tried to sound cool and wise, but my voice shook with indignation and dismay.

"How can you say that, Mlle Eugénie! I think your sister is a lovely girl—so friendly, so modest, with such pretty eyes—I am quite sure that Joseph finds her charming. They will be very happy together."

He began to walk faster. To him the subject was settled. "I'm going to tell Julie everything you've said," I warned him.

"Of course. That's why I've explained it so carefully. Yes, tell Julie, so that she'll know that Joseph will soon be suing for her hand."

I was horrified. How shameless, I thought; and I imagined Etienne sneering, "Corsican adventurers!" "May I ask," I said coldly, "why you are so concerned about your brother's marriage?"

"Sh! Don't shout! You must realize, Mlle Eugénie, that before I take over as commander in chief in Italy I want to see my family well settled. Joseph is interested, too, in politics and literature, and he may be able to do well in one or the other of those fields if he no longer has to accept subordinate posts. After my first Italian victories, I will of course look after my whole family." He paused. "And—believe me, mademoiselle, I shall look after them well!"

We had come to the summer house. "Where have you been so long with the child, General?" Julie asked. "We waited a long time for you and Eugénie." But we could see that she and Joseph had completely forgotten us. They were sitting close together on a little bench, though there were plenty of other places to sit. They were also holding hands but I suppose they thought no one could see them in the twilight.

We all four went back then to the house, and both the brothers Buonaparte said they must be going. But at that Etienne spoke up. "My mother and I would be honoured if the Citizen General and Citizen Joseph Buonaparte would stay to supper with us. It's been a long time since I've had an opportunity to participate in such interesting conversation." With this, he looked quite appealingly at the General; he paid no attention to Joseph.

Julie and I hurried to our room to do something about our hair. "Thank goodness," she said, "they both made a good impression on Mama and Etienne."

"I must tell you," I said, "that Joseph Buonaparte will soon ask for your hand. And mostly because—" I stopped, my heart was beating so—"because of the dowry!"

36

"How can you say such a hateful thing!" Julie's face was flaming. "He told me how poor his family is, and—" she put two little black velvet bows in her hair—"and naturally he couldn't marry anyone without a dowry because he has only a small salary and has to help his mother and the younger children. I think that's very fine of him. Otherwise . . . Eugénie!" she exclaimed. "I won't have you constantly using my rouge!"

"Has he told you already that he wants to marry you?" I asked.

"Whatever put that idea into your head? Why, we just discussed things in general, and his little brothers and sisters."

On our way down to the dining room, where they were all crowded around our two guests, Julie suddenly put her arm around my shoulders and pressed her cheek to mine. Hers was very hot. "I don't know why," she whispered, and she kissed me, "but I'm so happy!"

I took her hand. In spite of her burning cheeks, her fingers were ice-cold. I suppose that's love. For myself, I wasn't hot or cold but I had that queer heaviness around my heart. Napoleone—a queer name. So that's what it's like to be in love. Napoleone . . .

That was all two months ago.

And yesterday I was kissed for the first time and Julie was betrothed. The two events belong together somehow, for while Julie and Joseph were sitting in the summer house Napoleone and I were standing by the hedge at the bottom of the garden, so as not to disturb the others. Mama has told me always to spend the evenings in the garden with Julie and Joseph, because Julie is a young lady of good family.

Since that first visit the two brothers have been to see us almost every day. Etienne—who could have believed it? Wonders will never cease—invited them to come. He never gets enough of his talks with the young General. (Poor Napoleone, how terribly they must bore him!) Etienne is one of those people who values a person according to his success. When I first said that the two Buonapartes were Corsican refugees, he refused to have anything to do with them, and called them "adventurers." But ever since Joseph showed him the clipping from the December *Moniteur* in which his brother was gazetted Brigadier General, Etienne has been fascinated with Napoleone.

Napoleone had driven the English out of Toulon. This is how it happened. The English, who are always meddling with our affairs, were enraged at our condemning our King to death (though Napoleone says it's only a hundred and fifty years since they did the same thing to their own king). So they, the English, formed an alliance with the Royalists of Toulon, and occupied the town. Then our troops besieged Toulon. Napoleone was ordered there, and in no time succeeded where his superiors had failed. Toulon was stormed, and the English routed. Then for the first time the name Buonaparte appeared in the Army Orders, and Napoleone was promoted to Brigadier General. Etienne, of course, pestered him for the whole story of the siege of Toulon; but Napoleone says there was no trick to it, merely a matter of a few cannon, and he, Napoleone Buonaparte, understands thoroughly how and where to put cannon to the best advantage.

After his success at Toulon, Napoleone went to Paris to try to see Robespierre. Robespierre is the most powerful man in the Committee of Public Safety. That committee is our Government. To get to the great Robespierre he had first to see the younger Robespierre, the great man's brother. Robespierre—the right one—thought Napoleone's plans for a campaign in Italy were excellent, discussed them with the Minister of War, Carnot, and asked him for permission to entrust the preparations to Napoleone. Napoleone says that Carnot gets furious whenever Robespierre interferes with his Ministry, because it's really none of his business. But nobody dares to contradict Robespierre, because he has only to sign a warrant and off one goes to the guillotine. That's why Carnot received Napoleone with such a show of friendliness and accepted his Italian plans. "First," said Carnot, "inspect our fortresses in the south; I will give your ideas careful attention, Citizen General." But Napoleone is quite sure that his plans lie pigeonholed in the Ministry of War. Robespierre, however, will soon arrange, Joseph thinks, for Napoleone to be given the supreme command in Italy.

Etienne and all our friends hate this Robespierre. But they don't say so aloud; that would be too dangerous. It is said that Robespierre has made the members of the Revolutionary Tribunal give him secret reports on the opinions of all the officials in the State service. Even the private life of every single citizen, they say, is watched. Robespierre has declared that every genuine Republican has a duty to live a moral life and to despise luxury. Recently, he actually had all the brothels in Paris closed. I asked Etienne whether brothels were a luxury, but he said angrily that I mustn't talk about such things. And no dancing in the streets is allowed any longer, though that was a pleasure everybody enjoyed on public holidays. Etienne has absolutely forbidden us ever to criticize Robespierre in front of the two Buonapartes.

Etienne talks to Napoleone of practically nothing but the Italian plans. "It is our sacred duty," says Napoleone, "to instil into all the European peoples the idea of Liberty, Equality, and Fraternity. And if necessary—with the help of cannon!" I always listen to these talks just to be near Napoleone, though they weary me terribly. The worst is when Napoleone begins to read the *Handbook of Modern Artillery* to my brother. That sometimes happens and Etienne, that dolt, imagines that he understands it a bit. I think Napoleone is a complete spellbinder.

But when we are alone he never talks about cannon. And we are often alone. After supper Julie always says, "Don't you think we ought to take our guests into the garden for a bit, Mama?" Mama says, "Go along, children!" and we four, Joseph and Napoleone and Julie and I, disappear in the direction of the summer house. But before we get there, Napoleone generally says, "Eugénie, what do you say to a race? Let's see which of us can get to the hedge first!" Then I lift up my skirt and Julie cries, "Ready—set—go!" and Napoleone and I run like two possessed for the hedge. While I run to it with my hair flying and my heart beating wildly and a stitch in my side, Joseph and Julia disappear into the summer house.

Sometimes Napoleone wins the race, and sometimes I do; but if I get there first, I know that Napoleone has purposely let me win. The hedge is just chest-high. Usually, we lean close together against the foliage; I rest my arms on it and look up at the stars; and then Napoleone and I have long talks. Sometimes we talk about *The Sorrows of Werther*, a very popular novel by an unknown German writer named Goethe. I had to hide the book, because Mama won't let me read love stories. I didn't like it much, anyway. It is the story, sad beyond belief, of a young man who shoots himself because the young lady whom he loves marries his best friend.

Napoleone is quite enthusiastic about the book. I asked him whether he could imagine himself committing suicide because he was crossed in love. "No, because a girl whom I love will marry no other," he said and laughed. Then he became suddenly serious and looked at me, and I quickly changed the subject.

Often we just lean against the hedge and watch the quiet meadow beyond. The less we talk, the nearer together we seem. Then I imagine that we can hear the grass and the wild flowers breathing. Now and then a bird somewhere sings a melancholy song. The moon hangs in the sky like a golden lantern, and while I look at the slumbering meadow I think, Dear Lord, let this evening last forever, let me go on forever close to him. For, although I've read that there are no supernatural powers and the Government in Paris has set up an altar to Human Reason, when I am very sad or very happy I always think, Dear Lord. . . .

Yesterday Napoleone unexpectedly asked, "Are you never afraid of your destiny, Eugénie?" When we are alone with the sleeping meadow, sometimes he uses the familiar *tu*, although not even betrothed lovers or married couples do that nowadays.

. "Afraid of my destiny? No—" I shook my head—"I am not afraid. No one knows what's in store for him. Why should one be afraid of what one doesn't know?"

"It's strange that most people say they don't know their destiny," he said. His face was very pale in the moonlight, his eyes stared far away. "I am my destiny. I know my fate."

"And are you afraid of it?" I was amazed.

He seemed to think it over. Then quickly, in jerks, "No. I know I shall do great things. I was born to build states and to rule them. I am one of the men who make world history."

I stared at him, dumfounded. It had never occurred to me that anyone could think or say such things. Suddenly I laughed. At that he drew back and his face was distorted. He turned on me.

"You laugh, Eugénie?" he almost whispered. "Eugénie—you laugh?"

"Forgive me—please forgive me," I said. "It was only because—I was afraid of your face, it was so white in the moonlight, and—so strange. When I'm afraid, I always try—to laugh."

"I don't want to shock you, Eugénie," he said, and his voice was tender. "I can understand your being frightened. Frightened—of my great destiny."

We were silent again for a while. Then a thought occurred to me. "Well, I too shall make world history, Napoleone!"

He looked at me in astonishment, but I went right on. "World history consists, after all, of the destinies of all people, doesn't it? Not only men who sign death warrants or know where to put cannon and how to fire them make history. I think that other people, I mean those who are beheaded or shot at, and—every man or woman who lives and hopes and loves and dies makes world history."

He nodded slowly. "Quite right, my Eugénie. But I shall influence all those millions of destinies of which you speak. Do you believe in me, Eugénie? Do you believe in me, whatever happens?"

His face was so near, so near that I trembled and involuntarily closed my eyes. Then I felt his mouth hard on my lips. Suddenly—I don't know how it happened, I knew Julie wouldn't approve and it was certainly not what I meant to do, but—my lips parted.

That night, long after Julie had put out the candle, I couldn't get to sleep. Julie's voice came out of the dark: "Can't you sleep either, little one?"

"No. It's so hot in the room."

"I've something I must tell you," Julie whispered. "A tremendous secret, you mustn't tell anyone. Anyhow, not till tomorrow afternoon. Will you promise?"

"Yes, I promise," I said, wildly excited.

"Tomorrow afternoon, M. Joseph Buonaparte is coming to speak to Mama."

I was astonished. "Speak to Mama? Whatever about?"

Julie was annoyed. "You certainly are stupid! About us, naturally, about him and me. He wants—well, what a child you are! He wants to sue for my hand!"

I sat up in bed. "Julie! That means you are betrothed!"

"Sh! Not so loud! Tomorrow afternoon I shall be betrothed. If Mama makes no objection."

I leapt out of bed and ran over to her, but I bumped into a chair and hurt my toes. I yelled.

"Sh, Eugénie! You'll wake the whole house." But I kept going. Quickly I snuggled under the covers and excitedly shook her shoulder. I didn't know how to show her how glad I was.

"Now you are a fiancée, nearly a bride. Has he kissed you yet?"

"People don't ask such questions," Julie explained severely. Then it seemed to occur to her that she must be a good example to her little sister. "Listen to this," she continued. "A young lady allows herself to be kissed only after her mother approves the betrothal. But you are still too young to understand such things."

I think I'm tipsy, just a little tipsy, and it's very nice, very pleasant. Julie became betrothed to Joseph, and Mama sent Etienne down to the cellar for champagne. Champagne that Papa bought years and years ago, to be saved for Julie's betrothal. They are all still sitting on the terrace, discussing where Julie and Joseph will live. Napoleone has just gone to tell his mother all about it. Mama has invited Mme Letizia Buonaparte and all the children for tomorrow evening. Then we'll meet Julie's new family. I do hope Mme Letizia will like me; I hope . . . No, I mustn't write it, or it won't happen! Only pray for it and secretly believe it.

We ought to have champagne often. Champagne prickles on your tongue and tastes sweet, and after the first glass I always laugh and don't know why. After my third glass Mama said, "Nobody must give the child any more!" Suppose she knew I had already been kissed!

This morning I had to get up very early, and till now I've had no chance to be alone. As soon as Napoleone went away I hurried to my room, and now I am writing in my book. But my thoughts are running about and bumping into each other like so many ants; and like ants they're carrying a little load. Ants carry pine needles, twigs, or a grain of sand; my thoughts carry dreams of the future. I keep dropping my load because I have been drinking champagne and can't concentrate properly.

I don't know how it happened, but in the last few days I had quite forgotten that our Swede, M. Persson, was going away today. Since the Buonapartes have been coming to see us I haven't had much time for him. I don't think he likes Joseph and Napoleone. When I asked him what he thought of our new friends, he only said that he found them difficult to understand because they talked so much and so fast; and besides, their accent was different from ours. I can well understand that the Corsican accent is too much for him.

Yesterday afternoon he told me that he had packed his things and was leaving by the mail coach at nine in the morning. I decided, naturally, to see him off; first, because I really like old horse-face; and secondly, it's fun seeing the mail coach off. You always see different people there, and sometimes ladies in Paris gowns. But then, of course, I forgot Persson and his journey because, after all, I had my first kiss to think about.

Luckily I remembered Persson's departure the moment I woke up this morning. I jumped out of bed, put on my chemise and my two petticoats, scarcely gave myself time to tidy my hair, and ran down to the dining room. There I found Persson having his farewell breakfast. Mama and Etienne were hovering round him and urging him to eat as much as possible. The poor man has a frightfully long trip ahead of him. First to the Rhine and then through Germany to Lübeck, and from there by boat to Sweden. I don't know how many times he has to change mail coaches to get to Lübeck. Marie had given him a picnic basket with two bottles of wine, and a roast chicken, and hard-boiled eggs, and preserved cherries. Finally Etienne and I took M. Persson between us and marched him to the mail coach. Etienne carried one of the travelling bags and Persson struggled with a big parcel, the other bag, and the picnic basket. I begged him to let me carry something, and at last he reluctantly gave me the parcel, saying that it contained something very precious. "The most beautiful silk," he confided to me, "that I have ever seen in all my life. Silk which your dear papa himself bought and at that time intended for the Queen at Versailles. But events prevented the Queen . . ."

43

"Yes, really royal silk," said Etienne. "And in all these years I have never offered that brocade to anyone. Papa always said that it was only suitable for a court dress."

"But the ladies in Paris are still elegantly dressed," I objected.

Etienne sniffed contemptuously. "The ladies in Paris are no longer ladies! On the contrary, they prefer transparent muslins. If you call that elegant! No, heavy brocade is no longer worn in France today."

"And so," said Persson to me, "I have been permitted to buy the silk. I have been able to save a great part of my salary from the firm of Clary, and I am glad that I could use it for this. A reminder—" he sort of gulped. "A reminder of your dead papa and the firm of Clary."

I was surprised at Etienne. Since he couldn't sell this heavy brocade, which is certainly very valuable but at the moment unfashionable in France, he had worked it off on Persson—for a lot of money, of course. The firm of Clary did very well on this transaction.

"It wasn't easy for me to dispose of this material," Etienne said candidly. "But in M. Persson's country there is a royal court, and Her Majesty the Queen of Sweden will need, I hope, a new State robe and will appoint M. Persson a Purveyor to the Court."

"You mustn't keep brocade too long, silk goes to pieces," I informed Persson—from head-to-toe the daughter of a silk merchant.

"This material won't rot," declared Etienne. "There are too many gold threads woven in."

The parcel was quite heavy and I held it in my two arms, clasped to my breast. Although it was still early, the sun was hot and my hair stuck damply to my forehead when at last we reached the mail coach. We were rather late and couldn't spend long in farewells. The other passengers had already taken their seats in the coach. Etienne, with a sigh of relief, hoisted the travelling bag he'd been carrying and set it down on the toes of an elderly lady; and Persson almost dropped the picnic basket while he shook hands with Etienne. Then he got into an excited discussion with the postillion, who had placed his luggage on the roof of the coach. Persson told him that he would not let the big parcel go out of his sight and would hold it on his knees the whole time. The postillion objected, but in the end the driver lost patience and shouted, "Take your seats!" The postillion sprang to the box beside him and blew his horn. At last Persson got awkwardly into the coach with his parcel. The coach door was shut but Persson opened it again. "I shall always hold it in honour, Mlle Eugénie," he shouted. Etienne, with a shrug of his shoulders, asked, "Whatever does that crazy Swede mean?"

"The Rights of Man," I replied, surprised at myself because my eyes were wet. "The broadside on which the Rights of Man are printed." As I said it I thought how pleased Persson's parents would be to see his horse-face once more, and I thought that a fine man was vanishing forever from my life.

Etienne went back to the shop and I went with him. I always feel quite at home in the Clary silk shop. As a little girl I had often gone there with Papa and he had always told me where the different bolts of silk came from. I can also distinguish the various qualities and Papa always said that it was in my blood because I am a true silk merchant's daughter. But I think it is just because I so often watched Papa and Etienne take a piece of material between their fingers, apparently crumpling it and then looking with appraising eyes to see whether it would crush easily, whether it was new or old material, and whether there was any danger of its soon becoming brittle.

Although it was early in the morning, there were already customers in the shop. Etienne and I greeted them courteously, but I knew right away that these weren't important customers, only citizenesses who wanted muslin for a new fichu or cheap taffeta for a coat. The ladies from the great houses nearby, who used to give us big orders at the opening of the Versailles season, are no longer to be seen. Some have been guillotined, many have fled to England, but most have gone "underground"—that means they are living under false names in some place where they are not known. Etienne often says that it is greatly to the disadvantage of all merchants that the Republic does not arrange balls or receptions. For that, the dreadfully stingy Robespiere is to blame.

I busied myself in the shop for a while, helping the customers feel the different materials and persuading them to buy harsh green silk ribbons, because I felt that Etienne would like to get rid of them.

Finally I went home, thinking as always of Napoleone and wondering whether he would wear a gala uniform when we celebrated Julie's betrothal.

At home I found Mama in an awful state. Julie had announced that Joseph was coming that afternoon to speak to her, and she just didn't feel up to it. At last, in spite of the heat, she went into the town to consult Etienne. When she came back she had a headache, lay on her sofa, and asked to be called as soon as Citizen Joseph Buonaparte arrived.

Julie, however, really acted crazy. She stalked around the parlour and groaned. Her face, too, was quite green and I knew she was ill. Julie always suffers from stomach-ache when she gets excited. In the end I took the distracted girl into the garden with me and sat with her in the summer house. The bees hummed in the rambler roses and I felt sleepy and very contented. Life is so simple, I thought, when you really love a man. Then you belong only to him. If I were forbidden to marry Napoleone, I should just run away with him.

At five o'clock there arrived a gigantic bouquet, with Joseph hidden behind it. The bouquet and Joseph were escorted to the parlour by Marie; then Mama was informed and the door of the parlour closed behind them both. I pressed my ear to the keyhole to find out what Joseph and Mama were murmuring, but I couldn't hear a single word.

"A hundred and fifty thousand francs in gold," I said to Julie, who was leaning against the door with me. She pulled herself together.

"What? What are you talking about?"

"Papa left a hundred and fifty thousand francs in gold for your dowry, and a hundred and fifty thousand for mine. Don't you remember that the lawyer read that when Papa's will was opened?"

"That's not at all important," said Julie, peevishly, pulling out her handkerchief and wiping her forehead. A bride-to-be can certainly be funny.

"Well, are we to congratulate you?" laughed someone behind us. Napoleone! He'd just arrived and he leaned against the door with us. "May I, as a future brother-in-law, share the intolerable suspense?"

46

Julie's patience collapsed. "Do what you like, but leave me in peace!" she sobbed. At that Napoleone and I went on tiptoe to the sofa and sat down silently. I was fighting against hysterics; the whole situation was absurdly idiotic. Napoleone poked me gently in the side, "A little more dignity, if I may say so, Eugénie!" he whispered, and made a terrible, silly face.

Suddenly Mama came to the door and said in a shaky voice, "Julie, please come in."

Julie dashed into the parlour like a mad thing, the door closed behind her and Mama, and I—yes, I threw my arms around Napoleone's neck and laughed and laughed.

"Stop kissing me," I protested, because Napoleone had immediately seized this opportunity. But in spite of that, I didn't let him go —until I thought of the gala uniform. I drew away a little and looked at him reproachfully. The same threadbare green uniform as always.

"You might have worn your gala uniform, respected General," I said. I immediately regretted my words. His tanned face grew quite red.

"I have none, Eugénie," he confessed. "I have never had enough money to buy myself one and all we get from the State is a tunic— the field uniform I have on. We have to pay for the gala uniform with our own money, and you know—"

I nodded enthusiastically. "Of course, you are helping your mama and your brothers and sisters. And a second uniform would be quite superfluous, wouldn't it?"

"Children, I have a great, a very great surprise for you!" Mama stood before us, laughing and crying at the same time. "Julie and Joseph—" Her voice quivered. Then she pulled herself together. "Eugénie, call Suzanne! And go and see if Etienne is home yet. He promised me he'd be here punctually at half-past five."

I rushed up the stairs and told them both.

And then we all drank champagne. It was getting dark in the garden, but Joseph and Julie no longer bothered about the summer house, but kept talking about the home they would have in one of the suburbs. Part of Julie's dowry was to go for buying a nice villa.

Napoleone left to tell his mother all about it. And I came up to my room to write it all down. . . .

My nice little tipsiness is all gone. I'm only tired and a little bit sad. For now I'll soon be alone in our white room and I'll never be able to use Julie's rouge again and surreptitiously read her novels. But I don't want to be sad; I want to think about something cheerful. I must find out when Napoleone's birthday is. Perhaps the allowance I've saved will be enough for a gala uniform. But—where do you buy a gala uniform for a General?

Marseilles, middle of Thermidor
(*Beginning of August, Mama says*)

Napoleone has been arrested.

I have been living in a bad dream since last evening. Except for me, the whole town is wild with joy. People are dancing in front of the Town Hall, bands march by one after another, and the mayor is planning a ball, the first in two years. On the ninth of Thermidor Robespierre and his brother were deprived of their civil rights by the other deputies, arrested, and the next morning hauled off to the guillotine. Everyone who had anything whatsoever to do with Robespierre is afraid now of being arrested. Joseph has already lost the post he got through Napoleone's friendship with Robespierre's younger brother. So far, more than ninety Jacobins have been executed in Paris. Etienne says he will never forgive me for bringing the Buonapartes to our home. Mama insists that Julie and I attend the mayor's ball. It would be my first ball, but I won't go. I can hardly laugh and dance when I don't know where they've taken Napoleone.

Until the ninth of Thermidor—no, actually until the tenth—Julie and I were very happy. Julie was working eagerly on her trousseau and embroidered hundreds of times the letter *B* on pillow slips, table cloths, towels and handkerchiefs. The wedding is to be in about six weeks. Joseph came to see us every evening, often with his mother and his brothers and sisters. If Napoleone wasn't inspecting some fortification or other, he appeared at all hours of the day; and sometimes his handsome adjutants, Lieutenant Junot and Captain Marmont, came, too. But the interminable talk about politics didn't interest me at all. That's why I've just learned that about two months ago Robespierre instituted a new method of voting. It seems that from now on even deputies can be arrested at the order of a member of the Committee of Public Safety. They say that lots of deputies have guilty consciences because they've got rich on bribes. Deputies Tallien and Barras are rumoured millionaires. Robespierre also unexpectedly arrested the beautiful Marquise de Fontenay, whom Deputy Tallien had previously released from prison and who, since then, has been his mistress. Why Robespierre arrested her, no one knows—perhaps only to annoy Tallien. Many believe there really was something against Fontenay, while others believe that Tallien and Barras were afraid of being arrested themselves because they took bribes—in any event, they organized a great conspiracy, secretly, with a certain Fouché.

At first we could hardly believe these rumours. But when the first newspapers arrived from Paris, the whole town changed with a bang. Flags were hung from the windows, the shops were closed, and everyone called on everyone else. The mayor didn't wait for instructions from Paris; he simply released all the political prisoners. Fanatical members of the Jacobin Club, however, were quietly arrested. The mayor's wife is making a list of prominent Marseilles citizens who will be invited to the ball at the Town Hall.

Napoleone and Joseph came to see Etienne. They seemed very worried and shut themselves up with him in the parlour. Afterward, Etienne was angry. He told Mama that "these Corsican adventurers" would land us all in jail. Napoleone sat for hours in our summer house and told me that he would have to take up a new profession. "You don't really think," he said, "that an officer in whom Robespierre was interested will be kept on in the Army." For the first time I saw him take snuff Every day Junot and Marmont met Napoleone secretly at our house. Neither of them could imagine

49

that his name would ever be dropped from the list of officers. When I repeated to him what Marmont and Junot had said, and tried to comfort him, he shrugged his shoulders contemptuously. "Junot is an idiot," he declared. "Entirely loyal, but an idiot."

"But you've always said he was your best friend?"

"Of course. Entirely loyal even unto death, but without a brain in his head. None. An idiot."

"And—Marmont?"

"Marmont—that's something else again. Marmont is loyal because he believes that eventually my Italian plans must succeed—*must* succeed, do you understand?"

Then everything turned out quite differently from what we had expected. Last evening Napoleone was having supper with us. Suddenly we heard marching feet. Napoleone jumped up and rushed to the window, because he can't bear to see even four marching soldiers without wanting to know their regiment, where they come from, where they're going, and the name of their sergeant. The marching stopped in front of our house, we heard voices, then crunching on the gravel path, and finally a loud knock on our door. We all sat there petrified. Napoleone had turned from the window and stared, as though he'd been turned to stone, at the door. He crossed his arms over his chest; his face was very white. The door flew open. Marie and a soldier burst into the room together.

"Mme Clary . . ." Marie began.

The soldier interrupted her. "Is General Napoleone Buonaparte in your house?" He seemed to know the name by heart for he rolled it off without hesitation. Napoleone quietly stepped out from the bay of the window and went over to him. The soldier clicked his heels together and saluted.

"Warrant for the arrest of Citizen General Buonaparte!"

Simultaneously he handed Napoleone a piece of paper. Napoleone lifted this nearer his eyes, and I leapt up and said, "I'll get a light."

"Thank you, my dear, I can read the command very well," said Napoleone.

Then he let the paper drop, considered the soldier carefully, went straight to him and tapped his top button. "Even on a warm summer evening, the uniform of a sergeant in the Republican Army should be buttoned according to regulations!" While the embarrassed soldier fumbled with his uniform, Napoleone turned to Marie. "Marie, my sword is in the hall. Please be kind enough to hand it to the sergeant!" And with a bow to Mama: "Excuse the interruption, Citizeness Clary."

Napoleone's spurs clanked. The sergeant stamped out of the room behind him. We didn't stir. Outside, we heard again crunching on the gravel path in the front garden, the marching steps thundered down the road and died away. Finally Etienne broke the silence. "Let's finish our meal, we can't help—" His spoon clinked. We were eating the roast when my brother exclaimed, "What have I said from the start? An adventurer who tried to make a career with the help of the Republic." When we got to dessert, he added, "Julie, I regret that I ever gave my consent to your betrothal to Joseph."

After the meal, I crept out by the back door. Though Mama had frequently invited the Buonaparte family to our home, Mme Letizia had never returned the invitation. I could readily imagine why she hadn't. The family lived in the poorest quarter of the town, behind the fish market, and Mme Letizia was probably ashamed to ask us there. But now I was on my way there. I had to tell her and Joseph what had happened and to see what we could do to help Napoleone.

I shall never forget that trip through the dark narrow streets behind the fish market. At first I ran; I felt that I mustn't waste a minute. I never slowed up until I got to the Town Hall square. My damp hair clung to my forehead and my heart hammered painfully. People were dancing in the square; and an emaciated man, with his shirt open, grabbed hold of my shoulder and laughed coarsely when I pushed him away. Again and again some creature or other stood in my way; I felt clammy fingers snatching at me.

Suddenly I heard a girlish giggle: "Well, I never, it's the little Clary girl!" It was Elisa Buonaparte, Napoleone's eldest sister. Actually, Elisa is only seventeen; but that evening she was so heavily rouged and so dressed up, with dangling earrings, that she looked much older. She was leaning on the arm of a young man whose fashionably high collar hid half his face. "Eugénie—" she called after me, "Eugénie, can't my young man treat you to a glass of wine?" But I kept on and disappeared in the narrow unlit alleyways on the way to the fish market. There I was submerged in leering, creaking, simmering darkness. Terms of endearment and curses fluttered down from the doors and windows, and in the alley lovesick cats meowed. I breathed more freely when I reached the fish market where there were a few lanterns. I was suddenly ashamed of being afraid, and I was also somehow ashamed of my own beautiful white villa with the lilac bushes and rambler roses. I crossed the fish market and asked a man where the Buonapartes lived. He pointed to a dark, narrow cavern of a street. The third house on the left. Joseph had once mentioned that they lived in a cellar. I saw a narrow staircase and stumbled down the stairs, pushed open a door and found myself in Mme Buonaparte's kitchen. It was a large room which I couldn't see clearly because there was only one miserable candle, standing in a cracked teacup. The smell was frightful. Joseph, wearing a crumpled shirt and no tie, sat at the table reading a newspaper by candlelight. Nineteen-year-old Lucien, opposite him, was leaning over the table and writing. Between them were plates with remains of food on them. In the dark recess of the kitchen, someone was washing clothes. *Schrum, schrum*—I could hear hands moving up and down with fanatical energy on the washing board; there was a sound of gurgling water; and it was so hot that I almost suffocated.

"Joseph," I said, so he'd notice me. Joseph was startled.

"Has someone come in?" This was Mme Buonaparte speaking in her broken French. The *schrum, schrum* at the washing board stopped. Napoleone's mother stepped into the circle of candlelight, drying her hands on her large apron.

"It's I," I said, "Eugénie Clary."

Whereupon Joseph and Lucien exclaimed together, "In the name of God, what's happened?"

"They've arrested Napoleone," I said.

For a moment there was deathly silence. Mme Buonaparte groaned, "Holy Mary, Mother of God." Joseph's voice choked as he cried, "I've seen it coming, I've seen it coming!" Lucien managed a broken, "How awful!"

They asked me to sit down on a wobbly chair and tell them all about it. Brother Louis—sixteen years old and very fat—came out of the adjoining room and listened with no change of expression. I was interrupted by a terrible scream; the door was flung open and little Jérôme, Napoleone's ten-year-old brother, rushed into the kitchen, followed by twelve-year-old Caroline. She was shouting horrible waterfront curses. And then they began to struggle for something he was trying to stuff into his mouth. Mme Buonaparte slapped Jérôme, reprimanded Caroline in Italian and took away whatever it was Jérôme was trying to swallow. When she discovered that it was a bar of marzipan, she broke it in two and gave Jérôme and Caroline each a piece. She shouted, "Be quiet! We have a guest!"

When Caroline noticed me, she said, "Oh, la, la—one of the rich Clarys!" Then she came over to the table and sat on Lucien's lap.

A horrible family, I decided, but I was ashamed of thinking so. They can't help it that there are so many of them. They can't help being so poor and not having any living room except the kitchen.

In the meantime, Joseph had begun to question me. "Who arrested Napoleone? Are you sure they were soldiers—not the police?"

"They were soldiers," I answered.

"Then he is not in prison but under some sort of military arrest," Joseph concluded.

"What difference does that make?" Mme Buonaparte moaned.

"A tremendous difference," Joseph declared. "The military authorities would never execute a general without a trial; he'll come before a court martial."

"You've no idea how dreadful this is for us, *signorina*," Mme Buonaparte remarked. She pulled up a kitchen stool, sat down beside me and placed her damp work-worn hand on mine. "Napoleone is the only one of us who earns a regular income. And he has always been industrious and economical, and gives me half of his pay for the other children. It's a pity, what a pity!"

"Well, at least, if he's arrested he can't force me to join the Army," fat Louis commented. He sounded positively triumphant.

"Shut up!" Lucien shouted at the fat boy. Louis is sixteen years old but he has never done a day's work in his life, and Napoleone wanted him to join the Army so that his mother would have one less mouth to feed. I can't imagine how flat-footed Louis could ever march anywhere. But perhaps Napoleone wanted him to join the cavalry.

"But why have they arrested him?" Mme Buonaparte asked.

"Napoleone knew Robespierre," Joseph muttered. "And he had the bad luck to submit his crazy plans to the Minister of War through Robespierre. What madness!" The corners of Joseph's mouth twitched nervously.

"Politics, these dreadful politics!" Mme Buonaparte moaned. "*Signorina*, I assure you that politics are my family's misfortune. The father of my children—God rest his soul—devoted his life to politics, lost his clients' cases and left us nothing but his debts. And what do my sons talk about all day long? 'One must make useful contacts, one must meet Robespierre, it would be a good thing if we knew Barras—' That's how they carry on. And where does it all lead to?" She pounded the table furiously. "To being arrested, *signorina*."

I bowed my head. "Your son Napoleone is a genius, madame," I said softly.

"Yes—unfortunately," she answered irritably, staring into the flickering light of the candle.

I sat up straight. "We must find out where they have taken Napoleone and then try to help him," I said, looking at Joseph.

"But we are poor people, we don't know anyone who would help us," Mme Buonaparte lamented.

I never took my eyes off Joseph.

"The Military Commandant of Marseilles must know where they have imprisoned Napoleone," Lucien said. By his family, Lucien is considered a budding poet and a dreamer; nevertheless, he made the first practical suggestion.

"What's the name of the Military Commandant of Marseilles?" I asked.

"Colonel Lefabre," Joseph said, "and he can't bear Napoleone. Only a little while ago Napoleone told the old man what he thought of him because the local fortifications are in such terrible condition."

"I'll go to see him tomorrow," I suddenly heard myself saying. "Mme Buonaparte, will you pack up a nice parcel of linen for him and perhaps a little food, and send it to me tomorrow morning? I'll take it to this colonel and ask him to give it to Napoleone. And I'll ask him . . ."

"Grazie tanto, signorina, grazie tanto," Mme Buonaparte spoke with an effort. At the same time we heard a piercing shriek, water squirted on the floor and Caroline shouted gleefully, "Mama, Jérôme has fallen into the washtub."

While Mme Buonaparte pulled her youngest out of the tub, and then slapped him, I stood up. Joseph went to get his coat, to take me home. Lucien declared, "You are very kind, Mlle Eugénie; we shall never forget what you are doing for us." Then I realized how much I dreaded calling on this Colonel Lefabre.

When I said good-by to Mme Buonaparte she assured me, "I'll send Paulette to you tomorrow morning with the parcel." She thought of something else: "Now where is Paulette? She said that she and Elisa were going to see a friend across the road and be back in half an hour. And here they're out again till all hours."

I remembered Elisa's rouged face. I supposed that Elisa was by now enjoying herself with her young man in some tavern. And Paulette? Paulette is exactly as old as I.

Joseph and I walked in silence through the town. I remembered the evening when he had taken me home for the first time. Could that have been only four months ago? That was the beginning—then, I was still a child, though I thought myself grown up. Today I know that one is not really grown up until one loves a man with all one's heart.

"They simply can't send him to the guillotine," Joseph said as we approached our villa. He'd clearly been thinking, too, during our long silence. "The worst they could do—that's a military regulation —the worst they could do would be to shoot him."

"Joseph!"

His features were sharply drawn in the moonlight. He does not love him, I realized with a shock—no, he does not love his brother; in fact, he hates him. Because Napoleone is younger and yet was able to get him a post, because Napoleone urged him to marry Julie, because Napoleone . . .

". . . But we belong together," Joseph was saying, "Napoleone and I and our brothers and sisters, we belong together, and we must stick together in good times and bad."

"Good night, Joseph," I said.

"Good night, Eugénie."

I got into the house unnoticed. Julie was in bed but the candle on her dressing table was still lit. She had been waiting for me. "You went to see the Buonapartes, didn't you?" she asked.

"Yes," I answered, as I quickly began to undress. "They live in a frightful cellar, and late in the evening Mme Letizia washes their clothes, and Jérôme, that terrible child, fell into the washtub, and I think that the two girls—Elisa and Paulette—spend their evenings somewhere with men. Good night, Julie—sleep well."

At breakfast Etienne announced that Julie must postpone her wedding as he did not want a brother-in-law whose brother had been arrested because of his Jacobin opinions. It would be a family disgrace and bad for the business as well. Julie began to sob. "I refuse to postpone my wedding." Then she locked herself up in our room. No one discussed the matter with me because, except for Julie, no one has any idea that Napoleone's concerns are mine. Well, perhaps Marie knows. I believe that Marie knows everything. After breakfast Marie came into the dining room, beckoned to me, and I went out into the kitchen where I found Paulette with the parcel.

"Come on," I said to her, "let's go quickly before anyone notices us." For Etienne would be wild with rage if he knew that I intended to call on an official with a parcel of underdrawers for Napoleone Buonaparte, who was under arrest.

I have spent my whole life in Marseilles, and Paulette came here only a year ago; but she knows her way about far better than I do. She knew exactly where to find the Military Commandant. She never stopped talking as we walked there. She swayed her hips as she walked, and her shabby, bright blue skirt swung back and forth. She held herself very erect and pushed out her bosom—it's much larger than mine though we are the same age—and every few minutes she passed her pointed red tongue over her lips to keep them shiny. Paulette's nose is narrow like Napoleone's; her dark blonde hair, done up in a thousand tiny ringlets, is tied together with a blue ribbon. She has plucked her eyebrows so that only a thin line remains, and this she blackens with charcoal. I think that Paulette is very beautiful, but Mama doesn't like her looks and doesn't wish me to be seen with her.

Paulette kept coming excitedly back to the former Marquise de Fontenay, the new Mme Tallien. "People in Paris are mad about her. They call her 'nôtre dame de Thermidor.' She was carried in triumph out of prison on the ninth of Thermidor, and Deputy Tallien married her at once. And just imagine—" Paulette opened her eyes wide and took a deep breath "—just imagine, she doesn't wear petticoats under her frock. She goes out in a transparent sort of undergarment—and one can see everything! I tell you—everything!"

"Where did you hear that?" I asked, but Paulette ignored me.

"Her hair is coal black and so are her eyes; and she lives in a house called 'La Chaumière,' in Paris, and inside it the walls are all lined with silk. Every afternoon she receives all the famous politicians there and—yes, and I've heard that if one wants a favour from the Government one need only tell her about it. I've been talking to a gentleman who arrived only yesterday from Paris, and this gentleman—" she stopped suddenly.

"And this gentleman?" I asked expectantly.

"I met him. You know how one meets people, don't you? He was standing in the Town Hall square, looking at the Town Hall, and I happened to be passing. And—well, we suddenly got into conversation. But you must keep your mouth shut about this. Swear you will?" I nodded. "All right," Paulette continued, "swear by all the saints in heaven. You see, Napoleone is furious when I talk to strange gentlemen. He's such an old maid about such things. . . . By the way, do you think that your brother Etienne would give me some material for a new dress? I've been thinking that some transparent material in rose might be nice, and—" she broke off. "There, over there is the Military Commandant's office. Do you want me to go in with you?"

I shook my head. "I think it's better for me to see him alone. You'll wait for me, won't you? And cross your fingers to wish me luck?"

She nodded seriously and crossed her fingers. "And I'll recite the Lord's Prayer—it can't hurt anything," she said.

I held the parcel close and walked briskly toward the Military Headquarters. I heard my own voice, sounding rather hoarse and strange, asking the guard on duty to announce me to Colonel Lefabre.

When I was conducted into the bare room and saw the huge desk and the foursquare Colonel my heart beat so violently that at first I couldn't speak. The Colonel had a square red face with grey stubbles of hair on it, and he wore an old-fashioned pigtail wig. I put the parcel on the desk, swallowed desperately and didn't know what to say.

"What is in that parcel, citizeness? And who are you?"

"Undergarments, drawers, Citizen Colonel Lefabre, and my name is Clary."

His watery blue eyes studied me from head to toe. "Are you a daughter of the late silk merchant, François Clary?"

I nodded.

"I used occasionally to play cards with your papa. A very honourable man, your papa." He continued to stare at me. "And what do you want me to do with these drawers, Citizeness Clary?"

"The parcel is for General Napoleone Buonaparte. He has been arrested. We don't know where he is. But you, Colonel, must know where he is. There's probably a cake in the parcel, too. Clean linen and a cake—"

"And what has François Clary's daughter to do with this Jacobin, Buonaparte?" the Colonel asked me slowly.

I felt very hot. "His brother Joseph is engaged to my sister Julie," I said, and considered my answer a stroke of genius.

"And why hasn't his brother Joseph, or your sister Julie come to see me?"

The watery eyes were very serious and continued to gaze at me intently. I had the feeling that he knew everything. "Joseph is afraid. The relatives of arrested men are always afraid, aren't they?" I spoke with difficulty. "And Julie has her own worries at the moment. She is crying because Etienne—that's our older brother—has abruptly refused to allow her to marry Joseph Buonaparte. And we've had all this trouble because—" I was by then so furious that I couldn't control myself—"all because you, Citizen Colonel, have arrested the General."

"Sit down," was all he said.

I sat down on the edge of a chair beside his desk. The Colonel took a pinch of snuff. He looked out the window. He seemed to have forgotten me completely. Suddenly he turned and faced me. "Listen to me, citizeness—your brother Etienne is quite right. A Buonaparte is not a suitable match for a Clary—a very honourable and respected man, your late papa."

I said nothing.

"I don't know this Joseph Buonaparte. He's not in the Army, is he? But as far as the other brother is concerned, this Napoleone Buonaparte . . ."

"General Napoleone Buonaparte!" I interrupted, tossing my head.

". . . As for this General, it was not I who had him arrested. I only carried out orders received from the Ministry of War in Paris. Buonaparte has Jacobin sympathies, and all such officers—I mean all the extreme elements in the Army—have been arrested."

"And—what will happen to him?"

"I've not been informed about that."

And as the Colonel made a gesture indicating that it was time for me to leave, I stood up. "The linen and the cake," I said pointing to the parcel, "perhaps you could give him these things?"

"Nonsense. Buonaparte isn't here any longer. He was taken to Fort Carré in Antibes."

I had not been prepared for this blow. They had dragged him away, I couldn't reach him . . . "But he must have some clean laundry so that he can change," I said awkwardly. The red face before me was blurred; I wiped away my tears, but fresh tears came. "Can't you send him the parcel, Citizen Colonel?"

"But, my dear child, do you think I have nothing better to do than spend my time looking after the underclothing of an uncouth youngster who is allowed to call himself a general?"

I sobbed loudly. He took another pinch of snuff; the scene obviously embarrassed him greatly. "Do stop crying," he said.

"No," I sobbed.

He came around his desk and stood next to me. "You stop crying, I say!" he shouted at me.

"No," I sobbed again. Finally I wiped my eyes and looked at him. He was standing close to me, his watery blue eyes glittering helplessly.

"I can't stand tears," he said. At that I began to cry again. "Stop it," he shouted. "Stop it! . . . Well—if you won't leave me in peace—all right, I'll send one of my soldiers to Fort Carré with the parcel and ask the Commandant there to give it to this Buonaparte. Are you satisfied now?"

I tried to smile but the tears were in my way and I sniffled. I was at the door before I remembered that I hadn't thanked him. I turned. The Colonel was standing beside his desk, looking gloomily at the parcel. "Thank you very much, Citizen Colonel," I whispered.

He glanced up, cleared his throat and said, "Listen to me, Citizeness Clary, I will tell you two things in confidence. First, this will not cost this Jacobin general his head. Second, a Buonaparte is not a suitable match for a daughter of François Clary. Good-by, citizeness."

Paulette walked part of the way home with me. She babbled like a waterfall. Rose-coloured silk. Mme Tallien always wears flesh-coloured silk stockings. Napoleone will be pleased to have the cake. There are almonds in it. Do I like almonds? Is it true that Julie's dowry is large enough for her to buy a villa for herself and Joseph? When will I ask Etienne about the silk, and when can she come to the shop to fetch it . . . ?

I didn't really listen to her. Like a rhyme it went through my head: A Buonaparte is no match for a daughter of François Clary.

When I reached home I learned that Julie had got her way. Her wedding is not to be postponed. I sat with her in the garden and helped her embroider initials on her napkins. A beautifully rounded *B*—

B, B, and again *B.*

⌣⌣

Marseilles, end of Fructidor
(Middle of September)

I don't know how Julie spent her wedding night. The night before, at any rate, was terribly exciting, at least for me.

Julie's wedding was to be a very quiet affair, only our family and the innumerable Buonapartes had been asked. Mama and Marie had, naturally, been baking cakes and stirring fruit creams for days; and the evening before the wedding Mama almost collapsed, she was worried that it wouldn't go well. Mama always worries before a big party but so far everything always has gone well. It was decided that we should all go to sleep early, and before going to bed Julie was to take a bath. We bathe oftener than other people because Papa had very modern ideas, and Mama wants us to conduct our lives according to his ideas. So we have a bath almost every month in a large wooden tub which Papa installed especially for this purpose in the laundry. And since it was the evening before Julie's wedding, Mama decided to pour some jasmine scent into the water; and Julie felt like Mme Pompadour herself.

We went to bed but neither Julie nor I could sleep, so we discussed Julie's new home. It's outside Marseilles, but no more than half an hour by carriage from our villa. Suddenly we stopped talking and listened. ". . . *Le jour de gloire est arrivé*," someone was whistling underneath our window. I sat up. The second line of our Marseilles song. And also—Napoleone's signal. Whenever he comes to see us he announces his approach to me from afar by this whistle. I jumped out of bed, pulled aside the curtains, tore open the window and leaned out. It was a dark and oppressively sultry night. A storm hung in the air. I pursed my lips and whistled. Very few girls can whistle well. I'm one of them, but unfortunately people don't appreciate this gift much and even consider it ill bred.

"Le jour de gloire . . ." I whistled.

". . . *est arrivé*," came from below. A figure which had been standing close to the house emerged from the darkness and stepped out onto the gravel path.

I forgot to close the window, I forgot to put on my bedroom slippers, I forgot to take a coat with me, I forgot that I was wearing only a nightgown, I forgot what's proper and what isn't—I ran down the stairs like one possessed, opened the house door, felt the gravel under my bare feet, and felt his mouth on the tip of my nose. It was so dark, and in the darkness one can't be sure where a kiss will land! In the distance it thundered, and he held me close and whispered,

"Aren't you cold, *carissima"*— And I said, "Only my feet—I have no slippers on." He lifted me up and carried me to our doorstep. We sat there and he took off his coat and wrapped it around me. "When did you get back?" I asked.

And he said that he hadn't actually been home yet, he was on the way then to his mother's. I put my cheek against his shoulder, felt the rough material of his uniform and was very happy. "Was it very bad?" I asked.

"No, not at all. However, many thanks for the parcel. It reached me along with a letter from Colonel Lefabre. He wrote that he was sending it only to please you." I could feel his lips on my hair.

Suddenly he said, "I asked to be tried by a court martial, but they would not grant me even this."

I raised my head and looked at him, but it was so dark that I could see only the outlines of his face. "Court martial?" I asked. "But wouldn't that have been terrible!"

"Why so? Then I would have had an opportunity to explain my plans to some senior officers. The plans I allowed to be submitted to this idiot of a War Minister through Robespierre. A court martial would at least have attracted attention to me. But as it is—" he moved away from me and rested his head on his hand— "But as it is, my plans are collecting dust in some archive or other, and Citizen Carnot continues to be proud and satisfied because our armies are able, with a great effort, to defend our frontiers."

"And what will you do now?" I inquired.

"They released me because there is no evidence against me. But I am very unpopular with the gentlemen at the Ministry of War. Unpopular, do you understand? And they will send me off to one of the dullest sectors of the front and . . ."

"It's raining," I interrupted. The first heavy drops of rain were falling on my face.

"That doesn't matter!" he said and went right on explaining to me what can happen to a general whom the authorities want out of the way. I tucked up my legs and wrapped the general's coat more closely around me. We could hear thunder again, and a horse was neighing. "My horse. I tied him to your garden fence," he remarked casually.

62

It began to rain harder. There was a flash of lightning. The thunder was frightening and the horse was neighing desperately. Napoleone shouted at the horse.

Above us a window rattled. "Is anyone there?" Etienne called down.

"Come in the house, we'll get so wet," I whispered to Napoleone.

"Who is there?" Etienne shouted. At the same time we could hear Suzanne's voice, "Shut the window, Etienne, and come to me—I'm frightened—" Etienne's again: "There is someone in the garden. I must go down and look."

Napoleone got up, stood under the window and said, "M. Clary —it's me." There was a flash of lightning. For a fraction of a second I could see the small slender figure in the tight-fitting uniform. Then it was pitch dark again. Thunder crashed, the horse neighed wildly, the rain splashed.

"Who is there?" Etienne shouted into the rain.

"General Buonaparte!" Napoleone called back.

"But you are still in prison!" Etienne roared. "And anyway what are you doing in the middle of the night, in this weather, in our garden, General?"

I jumped up, clutching the uniform coat which went down to my ankles, and stood next to Napoleone. "Sit down again and wrap your feet in the coat. Do you want to be sick?" Napoleone whispered to me.

"With whom are you talking?" Etienne called down.

The rain was slackening, so I could hear well enough now to tell that Etienne's voice was trembling with rage.

"He's talking to me," I called. "Etienne—it's I, Eugénie."

It had stopped raining. To my horror, because of my compromising situation, a very pale moon shone timidly between the clouds and showed us Etienne, his nightcap on his head.

"General—you owe me an explanation." The nightcap fairly quivered.

"I have the honour to request the hand of your younger sister in marriage, M. Clary," Napoleone called up to him. He had put his arm around my shoulder.

"Eugénie, come into the house at once," commanded Etienne.

Behind him Suzanne's head appeared. She was wearing a lot of curlers in her hair and this made her look very weird.

"Good night, *carissima*, we'll meet tomorrow at the wedding party," Napoleone said and kissed my cheek. His spurs clanked down the gravel path. I slipped into the house, forgetting to return his coat to him. At the open door of his bedroom stood Etienne in his nightgown and holding a lighted candle. I crept past him, barefooted and wrapped in Napoleone's coat.

"If Papa had lived to see this—" snarled Etienne.

In our room Julie sat straight up in bed. "I heard everything," she said.

"I must wash my feet, they're muddy," I said. And I took the jug and poured water into the washbasin. When I had washed I went to bed and spread the uniform coat over me. "It's his coat," I said to Julie, "and I'm sure I'll have happy dreams because I'm covered up with his coat."

"Mme General Buonaparte," Julie murmured thoughtfully.

"If I'm lucky, he'll be dismissed from the Army," I said.

"That would be perfectly terrible," Julie answered.

"Do you think I want a husband who'll spend his life roaming about at some front or other, who comes home only now and then and always wants to talk to me about battles? No, I'd much rather they made him leave the Army and then perhaps I could persuade Etienne to give him a job in the shop."

"You'll never persuade Etienne to do that," Julie declared, and blew out the candle.

"I don't think so either. A shame, because Napoleone is a genius," I said thoughtfully. "But I fear he's not very interested in the silk trade. . . . Good night, Julie."

Julie was almost too late at the registry office. We couldn't find her new gloves and Mama says that one can't be married without gloves. When Mama was young everyone was married in church, but since the Revolution people must be married in a registry office, and not many couples have a church ceremony afterward; it's not easy to find one of the few priests who have taken the oath of allegiance to the Republic. Julie and Joseph didn't want a priest; and for days Mama had talked of nothing but her own white bridal veil which she would like Julie to wear, and about the organ music which "in her day" was part of every wedding service. Julie has a rose-coloured dress with real Brussels lace, and she wore red roses, and Etienne managed to get her some rose-coloured gloves from a business acquaintance in Paris. And we could not find these gloves. The marriage was arranged for ten o'clock in the morning, and just five minutes before ten I found the gloves under Julie's bed. At last Julie hurried off, and in her wake followed Mama and Julie's two witnesses, Etienne and Uncle Somis. Uncle Somis is Mama's brother, who appears whenever there is a family funeral or a wedding. At the registry office Joseph and his two witnesses, Napoleone and Lucien, were waiting for Julie.

I hadn't really had time to dress for I had been off on the glove hunt. So I stood at the window of our room and shouted "Good luck" after Julie, but she didn't hear me. The carriage, decorated with fading white roses from the garden, didn't look in the least like an ordinary hired carriage.

I successfully begged Etienne for some sky-blue satin for a new dress from the shop. And then I insisted that Mlle Lisette, the dressmaker who makes all our clothes, was not to cut the skirt too full. But I'm sorry to say the skirt is not as close-fitting as the skirts in the Paris fashion plates, and I'm laced around the waist and not under my bosom like Mme Tallien in the pictures of her as "Mme de Thermidor," the Goddess of the Revolution. But I think my new dress is very grand; I felt like the Queen of Sheba, dressed up to impress King Solomon. But after all, I'm almost a bride, too, though so far Etienne acts as if my betrothal were merely a disturbance in our garden in the middle of last night.

The guests came before I was ready. Mme Letizia in dark green, her hair, without a trace of white, combed straight back like a peasant's and caught at the nape of her neck; Elisa, thick-set, painted like a tin soldier and wearing all the ribbons she's been wangling out of Etienne for weeks. Beside her Paulette looked like a dainty ivory carving in rose muslin. (Heaven knows why Etienne gave her this material, the most fashionable in the shop.) And Louis, unkempt and obviously in a bad temper; Caroline clean and with her hair carefully done for once; and that dreadful child, Jérôme, who immediately demanded something to eat. Suzanne and I served liqueurs to every Buonaparte over fourteen, and Mme Letizia said she had a surprise for us all.

"A wedding present for Julie?" Suzanne asked quickly. For so far, Mme Letizia had not given Julie anything. Of course she is terribly poor, but I think she might at least have done a bit of embroidery for her. However, Mme Letizia shook her head, smiled mysteriously and said, "Oh, no."

We guessed this and that, wondering what she could have brought. At last the secret was out, the surprise was yet another member of the Buonaparte family! Mme Letizia's stepbrother, an uncle called Fesch, only thirty years old, formerly a priest. But this Uncle Fesch is not a martyr, and in these anticlerical times he has left religion and has become a businessman. "Does he do well in business?" I inquired. Mme Letizia shook her head regretfully and intimated that if Etienne made a great effort, her brother might be willing to consider a post with the firm of Clary.

Soon afterward Uncle Fesch arrived. He had a round merry face and a clean but shabby coat. He kissed Suzanne's hand and mine and praised our liqueur.

Then they came! First the carriage with the white roses, and Julie and Joseph and Mama and Napoleone got out. In the second carriage were Etienne, Lucien and Uncle Somis. Julie and Joseph ran over to us, Joseph embraced his mother, and all the other Buonapartes rushed over to Julie. Uncle Fesch hugged our mama, who had no idea who he was, and Uncle Somis gave me a resounding kiss on the cheek, and patted Elisa; and all the Clarys, and all the Buonapartes formed such a confused cluster of people that Napoleone and I had a chance to kiss each other very thoroughly until someone cleared his throat indignantly near us—Etienne, of course.

At the table the bridal couple sat between Uncle Somis and Napoleone, while I found myself wedged in between Uncle Fesch and Lucien Buonaparte. Julie was so excited that her cheeks were pink and her eyes were shining, and for the first time in her life she was really pretty. Immediately after the soup Uncle Fesch tapped his glass because, as a former abbé, he had an awful urge to make a

66

speech. His speech was very long and very serious and very dull; and as he considered it politically unwise to mention the Lord, he confined his laudatory remarks to "Providence." He said that we were indebted to Providence for this great happiness and this good dinner and this harmonious family party; we owed all this to the good, the great, the omnipotent—Providence. Joseph winked at me and then Julie smiled, too. Napoleone's eyes twinkled. He laughed. And Mama, growing increasingly tearful as Uncle Fesch's sermon continued, looked at me deeply moved.

Etienne, on the contrary, gave me a look of sheer outrage because the "Providence" that had brought Joseph and Julie together and bound the Clary and Buonaparte families so intimately together was, undoubtedly, I.

After the roast Etienne made a speech which was short and bad, and then we drank Julie's and Joseph's health.

We had got to Marie's wonderful marzipan cake, with the sugared fruits, when Napoleone rose quickly, without first politely tapping his glass, and thundered, "Quiet for a moment." We flinched like frightened recruits. And Napoleone declared abruptly that he was glad to take part in this family celebration; he did not, however, owe his good fortune to Providence but to the Ministry of War in Paris, which had released him from prison without any explanation. Then he paused. I think he hoped to imply that, as a son once believed lost forever but now returned to his family, he had expected to be welcomed more warmly. So far, of course, the young couple had been the centre of attention. After his impressive pause, Napoleone looked at me and I knew what was coming and I was frightened of Etienne.

"And so I want to take this opportunity, while the Clary and Buonaparte families are together on this joyful occasion, to inform—" again he paused. Then his voice softened, everyone was quiet, and it was clear that they were all trembling with emotion. "—inform you that last night I asked for Mlle Eugénie's hand in marriage and that Eugénie has consented to be my wife."

A storm of good wishes burst from the Buonapartes and I found myself in Mme Letizia's arms. But I glanced over at Mama. Mama looked as though she'd been hit over the head. No, she was not at all pleased. She turned toward Etienne and Etienne shrugged his

67

shoulders. But at that moment Napoleone, glass in hand, stepped over to him and smiled—and the power Napoleone has over people is astonishing. For Etienne's thin lips parted, he smirked and touched Napoleone's glass with his. Paulette embraced me and called me sister, M. Fesch said something to Mme Letizia in Italian and she happily answered, *"Ecco."* I think he asked her whether my dowry was as large as Julie's. Everyone was so excited that no one had taken any notice of Jérôme, the youngest Buonaparte, who had been stuffing himself with all the food he had room for, and more. Suddenly Mme Letizia shrieked, and I saw her leading a chalk-white Jérôme out of the room. I conducted mother and son to the terrace, and here Jérôme disgorged. After that he felt better, but we couldn't have our coffee on the terrace as we had planned.

Soon Julie and Joseph left and got into the gay carriage to drive to their new home. We all walked to the garden gate with them. I put my arm around Mama's shoulder and told her there was no reason to cry. Then more liqueur and cake were served. And Etienne tactfully explained to Uncle Fesch that he would not be needing new employees in the business as he had already promised to find work in the shop for Joseph and perhaps Lucien, too. Finally all the Buonapartes except Napoleone left. We walked in the garden; and Uncle Somis, who as I said appears only for weddings and funerals, asked me when I was to be married. In answer to this Mama, for the first time in her life, became truly energetic. She turned to Napoleone and placed both her hands pleadingly against his chest.

"General Buonaparte, promise me one thing—wait for the wedding until Eugénie is sixteen, will you?"

"Mme Clary—" Napoleone smiled. "It's not for me to decide this, but for you yourself, M. Etienne and Mlle Eugénie."

But Mama shook her head. "I don't know what it is about you, General Buonaparte—you are very young, and yet I have the feeling—" she hesitated, looked at him and smiled sadly—"I have the feeling that people usually do as you wish. At least your own family does; and since we've known you we, too, seem to. So I am appealing to you. . . . Eugénie is still very young. Please wait until she is sixteen."

Whereupon Napoleone kissed Mama's hand, and without another word I knew this was a promise.

The very next day Napoleone was ordered to report for duty in the Vendée, where he was to command an infantry brigade under General Hoche. I squatted on the grass in the warm September sun and watched him pace up and down before me, pale with fury. He poured forth a stream of words to explain to me how disgracefully he was being treated. To the Vendée! To track down hidden Royalists! A few starved aristocrats with their fanatically loyal peasants! "I am an artillery expert and not a policeman," he shouted at me. And as he spoke, he rushed up and down, up and down, his hands clasped behind his back. "They begrudge me the triumph of a court martial; they'd rather bury me in the Vendée—as though I were a colonel overdue for retirement. Keep me away from the front, let me be forgotten—!" When he was angry, his eyes showed a yellowish glint and were as transparent as glass.

"You can ask for your discharge," I ventured quietly. "With the money Papa left me I could buy a little country house and perhaps a few acres with it. If we managed it well and . . ."

He stopped with a jolt and stared at me.

"But if this idea doesn't appeal to you, you might join Etienne in the firm—" I continued quickly.

"Eugénie, are you mad? Or do you seriously believe that I would settle down in a farmhouse and keep chickens? Or sell silk ribbons in your brother's little shop?"

"I had no intention of offending you, I only thought this might be a solution."

He laughed. His laughter was shrill and he was shaking unnaturally.

"A solution! A solution for the best artillery general in France! Or do you realize that I *am* the best general in France?"

With that he rushed up and down again, this time in silence. Suddenly, "I leave tomorrow!"

"To the Vendée?"

"No, to Paris. I'll talk to the gentlemen in the Ministry of War."

"But isn't that—I mean, isn't it a serious offense in the Army if an officer disobeys orders?"

"Yes, it is. If one of my recruits disobeys, I have him shot. Perhaps I'll be shot, too, when I get to Paris. I'll take Junot and Marmont with me."

Junot and Marmont, his personal adjutants since the action in Toulon, were still in Marseilles. They considered his destiny theirs.

"Can you lend me some money?"

I nodded.

"Junot and Marmont haven't enough to pay the bill for their room. Like me they've had no pay since the day of my arrest. I must bail them out of their inn. How much can you lend me?"

I had been saving up for his dress uniform. Ninety-eight francs were hidden under the nightgowns in my dresser. "Give me all you have," he said and I ran up to my room and fetched the money.

He put the money in his pocket, then took it out again, counted it carefully and said, "I owe you ninety-eight francs." Then he grasped my shoulders and held me close. "You'll see, I'll convince everyone in Paris. They must give me the supreme command in Italy, they must give it to me."

"When are you going?" I asked.

"As soon as I've got my adjutants out of their inn. And don't forget to write to me often. Send your letters to the Ministry of War in Paris; they'll forward my post to the front. And don't be sad—"

"I shall have a lot to do," I said. "I'll be embroidering the initials on the linen for my trousseau."

He nodded eagerly. *"B, B,* and again *B!* Mme General Buonaparte—"

And then he untied his horse which, to Etienne's annoyance, he had again hitched to our garden fence, and rode off toward the town. As he disappeared down the quiet street of villas he looked small and very lonely.

Paris, twelve months later—Fructidor, Year III

Nothing is more unpleasant than running away from home.

For two nights I've not seen a bed. My back aches badly because I've been sitting continuously in a travelling coach for four days. And I think the part of me I sit on must be black and blue—ordinary travelling coaches have very bad springs. And I've no money for my return journey. But I shan't need it; I have run away; I'll never go back.

I arrived in Paris two hours ago. It was almost evening and in the dusk all the houses looked alike: grey houses, one next to the other, with no front gardens. Houses and more houses. I had no idea that Paris was so vast. I was the only one in our coach who had never before been in Paris. Wheezing M. Blanc, who joined us two days ago and has business in Paris, took me to a hackney carriage. I showed the coachman the slip of paper on which I had written the address of Marie's sister. I gave the coachman all the money I had, but he was rude because I had nothing over for a tip. The address was right and Marie's relatives, the Clapains, were at home, fortunately. They live in the rear building of a house in the rue du Bac. I've no idea in what district of Paris the rue du Bac is; not far from the Tuileries, I think. We drove past the Palace, which I recognized from the pictures I've seen. I keep pinching myself to make sure that I'm not dreaming. I am really in Paris, I've really seen the Tuileries, I really ran away from home.

Marie's sister, Mme Clapain, was very kind to me. At first she was embarrassed and went on drying her hands on her apron, because I am the daughter of Marie's "gentry." But when I told her that I'd come secretly to Paris to arrange a certain matter, and because I have no money, Marie said that perhaps—well. Marie's sister was no longer embarrassed and said I could spend the night with her. Was I hungry? And how long did I want to stay? I said that I was hungry and gave her my bread ration ticket, for since the bad harvest, bread is strictly rationed and food is terribly expensive. I said I didn't know how long I'd stay. Perhaps one night, perhaps two. I began to eat and then M. Clapain came home. He is a carpenter and told me that this flat is in the rear building of a mansion which belonged to an aristocrat. The mansion was confiscated by the government but because of the housing shortage this building has been turned into flats for families with many children.

The Clapains have an enormous number of children. Three little children were crawling about on the floor; two more came running in from the street, wanting something to eat. So many diapers are hanging up to dry in the kitchen where we eat that it's like being in a Bedouin's tent. Immediately after the meal, Mme Clapain said she'd like to take a walk with her husband; she so seldom has a chance to because someone always has to look after the children. But now I'm here; and she will put the children to bed and leave without worry. The children were stuffed two into each of the beds, and the youngest was in a cradle in the kitchen. Mme Clapain put on a little hat with a frayed ostrich feather, M. Clapain poured the entire contents of a small bag of powder into his thinning hair, and off they went.

I felt terribly alone and strange in this huge city until I rummaged in my travelling bag and found a few familiar objects. At the last moment I had put in my diary. At first I turned back the pages and read how everything had happened. And now, with a split quill which I found next to the dusty bottle of ink on the kitchen dresser, I am trying to explain why I ran away from home.

I've not written in my diary for a whole year.

But nothing happens in the life of a grass widow—I should say a grass fiancée—whose fiancé is in Paris. Etienne got me some cambric for handkerchiefs and nightgowns, and damask for tablecloths, and linen for sheets. He deducted the price of these things from my dowry. I embroidered one rounded *B* after the other, constantly pricked my fingers and called alternately on Mme Letizia in her basement flat and Julie and Joseph in their charming little villa. But Mme Letizia talked of nothing but inflation and the high cost of living and complained that Napoleone hadn't been able to send her any money. Julie and Joseph, on the other hand, never stopped gazing at each other and making remarks which no outsider could understand. They giggled and seemed brazenly happy and at the same time somewhat idiotic. Nevertheless, I went to see them often because Julie wanted to know what Napoleone had written to me, and I wanted to read his letters to Joseph.

Unfortunately we all have the impression that my fiancé is having a bad time in Paris. A year ago he arrived there with his two adjutants and with fat Louis, whom he took with him at the last moment so that Mme Letizia would have one mouth less to feed at home. As was to be expected, there was a fearful row at the Ministry of War because he had disobeyed the orders to go to the Vendée. Naturally Napoleone discussed his Italian plans again; and to get rid of him, the Minister of War sent him to the Italian front—on an inspection tour; no mention of a supreme command. Napoleone departed; and when he got there the generals on the southern front either did not receive him, or told him not to interfere with the commands of other officers. Then he came down with malaria and returned to Paris with a yellow face and wearing his old shabby uniform. When he reappeared at the Ministry of War, the Minister was furious and ordered him out. In the beginning Napoleone still got half his monthly pay, the first of every month; but later he was discharged from the Army without a pension. A terrible situation. . . . We don't know what he's been living on. By pawning his father's watch, he could survive about three days! He made Louis join the Army, since he couldn't support him any longer. From time to time, Napoleone has an assistant's job in the Ministry of War. He draws military maps and is ruining his eyes at this work. His torn trousers were a great anxiety. His journey to Italy finished off his threadbare uniform and he tried to mend the trousers himself, but the seams burst open. Naturally he sent in a request for a new uniform but the State does not grant uniforms to unemployed generals. In his despair he went where they all go when they want to get something done—to "La Chaumière," home of the beautiful Mme Tallien.

We now have a government called a "directorate," administered by five directors. However, according to Joseph, only one of our directors has real authority and that is Director Barras. Whatever happens in our country, Barras swims to the top. (Like a piece of garbage in the harbour, I think. But perhaps that's not the proper thing to say about the head of a state—one of the five heads of state.) Barras was a count by birth, but this did him no harm because he became a fanatical Jacobin at the right time. Then, with the help of Tallien and a deputy called Fouché, he brought about the fall of Robespierre and saved the Republic from the "tyrants." He moved into an official apartment in the Palais Luxembourg and is now one of our five directors. These directors receive all important persons; and as Barras is unmarried, he has asked Mme Tallien to act as his hostess every afternoon and to receive his guests and those of the French Republic (the same people). One of Etienne's business friends told us that champagne flows like water at Mme Tallien's and that her drawing rooms are crowded with war profiteers and with men speculating in houses. These men buy confiscated aristocratic homes at a low price from the State and sell them at a huge profit to the nouveaux riches. There one can also meet very amusing ladies, friends of Mme Tallien. The two most beautiful women, however, are Mme Tallien herself and Josephine de Beauharnais. Mme de Beauharnais is Barras' mistress and she always wears a narrow red ribbon around her neck to show that she is related to "a victim of the guillotine." It is no longer considered a disgrace, but rather a distinction to claim such a relationship. (This Josephine is the widow of the General de Beauharnais who was beheaded, and therefore she is a former countess.) Mama asked Etienne's friend whether there were no virtuous women left in Paris. And Etienne's friend said, "Well, yes, there are but they are very expensive." He laughed and Mama quickly asked me to get her a glass of water from the kitchen.

Napoleone called one afternoon on the ladies Tallien and Beauharnais and introduced himself. They both thought it perfectly horrid of the Minister of War to refuse him a new pair of trousers and the supreme command in Italy. They both promised to get him at least a new pair of trousers. But, they said, he must change his name. Napoleone sat down at once and wrote to Joseph, "I have decided to change my name—it will be legal, shortly—and I advise you to do the same. No one in Paris can pronounce Buonaparte. From now on I call myself Bonaparte—and Napoleon instead of

Napoleone. Please address my letters accordingly and inform the whole family of my decision. We are French citizens and I want my name to be French when it is written in the book of history."

Therefore: no longer Buonaparte, but Bonaparte. His trousers are in shreds, his father's watch pawned, but he still and always thinks of making world history. Joseph, this copycat, naturally calls himself Bonaparte, too. And so does Lucien, who has found a post in St. Maximin as manager of a military depot, and who has begun to write political articles. Joseph sometimes drives about the country as Etienne's travelling salesman. He makes good contracts for the business and Etienne says that he does quite well out of the commissions. But Joseph dislikes being called a traveller in silks.

During the last few months I've had very few letters from Napoleon. But he writes to Joseph twice a week. Nevertheless, I've finally sent him my portrait for which he asked me shortly before he left. It is a hideous portrait. My nose is certainly not turned up as much as that. But I had to pay the painter in advance, so I accepted the portrait and sent it to Paris. Napoleon did not thank me for it. His letters no longer say anything. As usual they still begin *"mia Carissima,"* and end by saying that he presses me to his heart. Not a word about when we'll be married. Not a word to show that he knows that in two months I'll be sixteen. Not a word to say that wherever he may be we belong together. But to his brother Joseph he writes pages and pages about the fashionable ladies he meets at Mme Tallien's reception. "I have learned to appreciate the role distinguished women can play in the life of a man," Napoleon assures his brother, enthusiastically, "women with understanding, women of the great world—"

I simply can't describe how sick these letters to Joseph make me.

A week ago Julie decided to accompany Joseph on a long business journey. And as it was the first time that one of her children was to be away from Marseilles for any length of time, Mama wept and wept; and to distract her, Etienne arranged for her to spend a month with her brother, our uncle Somis. Mama packed seven travelling bags and I took her to the coach station. Uncle Somis lives four hours' drive from Marseilles. After the visit, Mama discovered that "her health was impaired" and she gave Etienne no peace until he

agreed to take her to a watering place. That is why I was unexpectedly alone in the house with Marie.

My decision was made one afternoon when I was sitting in the
summer house with Marie. The roses had faded long ago, the twigs
and leaves were sharply silhouetted against the glassy blue of the
sky. It was one of those early autumn days on which one is deeply
conscious that something is about to die. And perhaps that was why
not only the outlines of objects but my thoughts, too, seemed particularly sharp and clear. And suddenly I dropped the towel on which
I was embroidering a *B*.

"I must go to Paris," I said. "I know it's a crazy thing to do and
the family would never allow it, but—I must go to Paris."

Marie, who was shelling peas, did not look up. "Well, if you
must go to Paris," she said, "then go to Paris."

I mechanically watched a dung beetle moving in a green-gold
glimmer across the table. "It would be quite simple," I said. "After
all, we two are alone in the house. I could take the coach to Paris
tomorrow."

"You have enough money?" Marie said, pressing open a fat pod
between her thumbs. The pea exploded with a tiny bang, but the
beetle continued its way undisturbed across the table.

"Yes, probably enough for the journey there. If I don't stay at an
inn more than two nights, I can spend the other two nights in the
taproom at the coach station. Perhaps there'll be a bench or a sofa
in the waiting rooms."

"I thought you'd saved more money than that," Marie said, looking up at me for the first time. "Under your nightgowns—in the
chest of drawers."

I shook my head. "No, I—I lent someone quite a lot of money."

"And where will you spend the night in Paris?"

The beetle had reached the edge of the table. I picked it up
carefully, turned it around, and watched it begin to walk back across
the table.

"In Paris?" I considered. "I haven't really thought about that.
Well, that depends, doesn't it?"

"You both promised your mama to postpone your wedding until
you were sixteen. And yet you want to go to Paris now?"

76

"Marie, if I don't go now it may be too late. Then there may not be any wedding." I spoke without thinking. For the first time I put into words what so far I had dared only to think.

Marie's pea pods went on popping. "What is her name?" she inquired.

I shrugged my shoulders. "I'm not quite sure. Perhaps it's Mme Tallien; but it may be the other one, Barras' mistress. Her name is Josephine, she was once a countess. But I don't know anything definite—and, Marie, you mustn't think horrid things about him. After all, he hasn't seen me for a long time. And when he sees me again . . ."

"Yes," Marie said, "you are right. You must go to Paris. My Pierre was called up for military service when he left me—and he never came back to me; though our little Pierre was born in the meantime, and I wrote to him that the child was with a foster mother, and that I'd been obliged to take service as a wet nurse with the Clarys because I had no money. My Pierre never even answered this letter. I should have tried somehow to go to see him."

I knew Marie's story. She has told it to me so often that I practically grew up with her unhappy love affair. The story about faithless Pierre is as familiar to me as an old song.

"You couldn't go to him, it was too far away," I said. The beetle had again reached the edge of the table. It was crawling about in despair, thinking that it had reached the end of the world.

"You will go to Paris," Marie said. "You can spend the first few nights at my sister's. After that you can decide what to do next."

"Yes, then I shall see," I said and got up. "I'm going in to town to find out what time the coach leaves tomorrow."

I took the beetle off the table and put it down on the grass.

In the evening I packed a travelling bag. As the whole family was away, I found only an old and very shabby bag. I stuffed in the blue silk dress I'd got for Julie's wedding. My most beautiful dress. I'll wear it, I thought, when I go to Mme Tallien's house to see him again.

Next morning Marie took me to the coach station. I walked through the familiar streets as in a dream, a very very lovely dream in which one is sure that one is doing the only right thing. At the last moment Marie handed me a large gold medallion. "I haven't any money. I send all of my wages to little Pierre," she murmured, "so take the medallion. It's real gold and your mama gave it to me the day I stopped feeding you. You can easily sell it, Eugénie."

"Sell it?" I asked astonished. "But why?"

"So that you'll have some money for the return journey," Marie said and turned away abruptly. She did not want to see the coach drive off.

For one day, two, three, four days I was shaken about in the coach along a dusty interminable road. Every three hours the coach gave a lurch—and I fell either against the bony shoulders of the lady in mourning at my right, or against the fat stomach of the man at my left. Then the horses were changed and we jolted on once more. And I was continuously imagining what it would be like to go to Mme Tallien's house and ask for General Bonaparte. I imagined myself standing in front of him and saying, "Napoleone—" no, of course I must call him Napoleon—"Napoleon, I've come to you because I know you have no money to pay for the journey to come to me. And we belong together!"

Will he be happy when he sees me? There are strange shadows in Marie's sister's kitchen and I can't recognize them because I've never seen the place by daylight. Of course, he'll be happy to see me. He'll take my arm and introduce me right away to his grand new friends. And then we'll leave them, to be by ourselves. We'll take a walk because we have no money to spend in a coffee house. Perhaps he has some friends with whom I can stay until we've written to Mama and get her consent to my marriage. And then we'll be married and . . .

I hear them coming home. M. and Mme Clapain. I hope they have a halfway comfortable sofa on which I can stretch out, and tomorrow—dear Lord, how happy I am about tomorrow!

Paris, twenty-four hours—no, an eternity—later

It is night and I am again sitting in Mme Clapain's kitchen. Perhaps I've not really come back nor ever been away. Perhaps today was only a bad dream—perhaps I'll wake up. But didn't the waters of the Seine close over me? The water was so near; the lights of Paris danced on the ripples—danced and called out to me; and I leaned over the cold stone parapet of the bridge. Perhaps I really did die and was carried away by the current across Paris, floating, spinning, feeling nothing any more. I would much rather be dead.

Instead I am seated at a wobbly kitchen table and my thoughts go around in circles. I can hear every word that was said, and the rain beats against the windows. It has rained all day long. I got very wet on my way to Mme Tallien's. I wore the lovely blue silk dress. But walking through the Tuileries Gardens and along the rue Honoré I discovered that for Paris my dress is very unfashionable. Here the ladies wear dresses that look like chemises; they are very close fitting, not tied at the waist, but bound with a silk ribbon under the breast. They don't wear fichus; instead, though it's autumn, they wear transparent shawls around their shoulders. My tight elbow-sleeves, bordered with lace, are quite impossible. No one wears sleeves any more, only shoulder straps. I was embarrassed because I looked like a country bumpkin.

It was not difficult to find "La Chaumière" in the allée des Veuves. Mme Clapain had told me exactly how to get there; and though, despite my impatience, I peeked at the shop windows in the Palais Royal, it took me only half an hour to reach my destination. The outside of the house is not particularly striking; it's not much larger than our villa at home and built in country style, with a thatched roof. But brocade curtains shimmer behind the windows. It was still early in the afternoon but I wanted to prepare for my great surprise and to be waiting in one of the drawing rooms when Napoleon arrived. As he calls on Mme Tallien almost every afternoon, her house is the best place to meet him. And he had written to Joseph that anyone can go to "La Chaumière" because Mme Tallien keeps open house.

A number of people were hanging about the entrance, staring critically at the guests entering the house. I looked neither left nor right but walked straight toward the doorway. I lifted the latch, the door opened, and there was a lackey. He wore a red livery with silver buttons and looked exactly like the lackeys of the aristocracy before the Revolution. I had not known that Republican dignitaries are allowed to employ liveried servants. Deputy Tallien, by the way, was himself formerly a valet. The haughty lackey looked me up and down and asked condescendingly, "What do you want, citizeness?"

I had not expected this question. So I stuttered, "I want to go in."

"That's obvious," the lackey said. "Have you an invitation?"

I shook my head. "I thought—well, I thought everyone could go in."

"I suppose that would suit this little woman." The man grinned, and stared at me more insolently. "Ladies like you must keep to the rue Honoré and the Palais Royal."

I blushed furiously. "What—what do you mean, citizen?" I spoke with an effort and was so ashamed that I could hardly speak. "I must go in, because there's someone in the house I must see."

But he simply opened the door and pushed me out. "Mme Tallien's orders—citizenesses are not invited unless they have a gentleman escort. Or—" he glanced at me contemptuously— "or are you perhaps a personal friend of madame?"

He forced me out and slammed the door in my face.

I joined the curious crowd in the road. The door was opened and shut continually, but some of the girls had pushed themselves in front of me and I could not see Mme Tallien's guests. "It's a new regulation. A month ago we all got in without any trouble," a heavily rouged girl remarked, and winked at me. "But some foreign paper published an article saying that Mme Tallien's house was run like a brothel—" The girl giggled and showed gaps between her teeth behind her purple-painted lips.

"She herself doesn't care, but Barras makes her keep up appearances," another girl said. And I moved away from her, horrified because loathsome pustules could be seen through her chalky-white face powder. "You're new here, aren't you?" she asked, glancing pityingly at my old-fashioned dress.

"That Barras!" the girl with the purple lips remarked in a trembling voice. "Two years ago he was still paying Lucille twenty-five francs a night, and today he can afford to keep the Beauharnais!" Repulsive little bubbles appeared at the corners of her mouth. "That old goat! Day before yesterday Rosalie got in with her new friend, that wealthy Ouvrard, and she told me that the Beauharnais now has taken up with a very young fellow, an officer who likes squeezing a woman's hands and gazing into her eyes—"

"I wonder why Barras stands for that," the girl with the pustules on her face remarked.

"Barras? Why, he asks her to sleep with the officers. Barras wants to be on good terms with men in uniform because heaven knows when he may need them. Besides, he's probably sick to death of her already—Josephine who always wears those white frocks! She's an old she-goat with grown-up children . . ."

"The children are twelve and fourteen, that's not very old," a young man interrupted. "By the way, the Tallien spoke at the National Convention again today."

"You don't say, citizen!" At once the two girls concentrated their attention on the young man. But he leaned down and spoke to me, "You are from the provinces, citizeness? But you've surely seen that the beautiful Thérèse is the first woman to speak in the National Convention? Today she discussed necessary reform in the education of young girls. Are you interested in these problems too, citizeness?" He smelled horribly of wine and cheese, and I moved away from him.

"It's raining, we should go to a coffee house," the girl with the purple lips suggested, and she glanced invitingly at the young man with the horrid breath. "It's raining, citizeness," the young man said to me.

Yes, it was raining. My blue dress was getting wet. Besides, I was cold. The young man touched my hand as though by chance. At that moment I knew: I can't stand this another moment.

Another hackney carriage rolled up. I elbowed my way through the crowd, rushed over to the carriage like a madwoman, and bumped into an officer's coat. The man wearing the coat had just left the carriage. He was so terribly tall that I had to look way up to see his features clearly. But his cocked hat was pressed far down on his forehead and I saw only a huge jutting nose.

"I beg your pardon, citizen," I said because the giant recoiled when I rushed at him. "I beg your pardon, but I should like to belong to you."

"What do you want?" the giant asked, startled.

"Yes—for a few moments I'd like to belong to you. You see, ladies aren't allowed to go into Mme Tallien's house without an escort. And I must get in, I must—and I have no escort!"

The officer looked me up and down and didn't seem particularly pleased; but, suddenly making up his mind, he offered me his arm and said, "Come along, citizeness."

The lackey in the hall recognized me at once. He glanced at me indignantly, bowed deeply to the giant and took his coat. I went over to a tall mirror, pushed the soaking strands of hair out of my face and realized that my nose was shiny. But as I was taking out my powder puff, the giant said impatiently, "Well, are you ready, citizeness?"

I turned quickly. He was wearing a beautifully tailored uniform with heavy gold epaulettes. When I looked up at him again, I noticed that the narrow mouth under the huge nose was closed tight in disapproval. He was obviously annoyed because he had given way and had brought me in with him. And it occurred to me that he probably thought me one of the street girls who were hanging about outside. I was quite hot with shame. "Please excuse me, I didn't know what else to do," I whispered.

"When we get inside, you must behave decently and don't disgrace me," he said severely as he bowed stiffly and offered me his arm. The lackey opened a white folding door. We found ourselves in a large room in which there were a great many people. Another servant seemed to shoot up out of the floor and he looked at us questioningly. My companion turned to me brusquely. "Your name?"

No one must know that I am here, I thought quickly. "Désirée,"

I whispered. "Désirée—and what next?" my escort asked irritably. I shook my head desperately. "Please—no other name."

Whereupon the lackey was instructed to announce, "Citizeness Désirée," and "General Jean-Baptiste Bernadotte."

"Citizeness Désirée and Citizen General Jean-Baptiste Bernadotte," the servant shouted. The people standing near us turned around. A black-haired woman in a yellow veil-like gown left a group and glided toward us.

"What a pleasure, Citizen General! What a charming surprise—" she twittered, holding out both hands to the giant. A critical glance from very large dark eyes swept over me and rested for the fraction of a second on my filthy shoes.

"You are too kind, Mme Tallien," the giant said, bowing over her hands and kissing—no, not the hands but her white wrists. "My first outing—as usual when a poor soldier from the front has some leave—is to find the magic circle of Thérèse."

"The poor soldier from the front is flattering, as usual! And yet he has already found companionship in Paris—?" Again the dark eyes studied me critically. I tried to achieve some sort of bow. Thereupon Mme Tallien lost the slight interest she had shown in my insignificant person and calmly stood between me and the General. "Come with me, Jean-Baptiste—you must speak to Barras. The Director is in the garden room with that dreadful Germaine de Staël—you know whom I mean—old Necker's daughter, the one who writes one novel after another. We must relieve the Director of her company. He'll be charmed that you . . ."

And then I saw the yellow veil-like material over her entirely naked back, and also the back of my giant. Other guests came in between them and me and I found myself left all alone in Mme Tallien's glittering salon.

I concealed myself as best I could in the bay of a window overlooking the huge room, but I couldn't see Napoleon anywhere. True, I saw a lot of uniforms but none of them was as shabby as my fiancé's. The longer I stayed the more closely I pressed against the window. Not only was my dress impossible; my shoes, too, seemed ridiculous, for the ladies were not wearing real shoes, only thin soles without heels. These soles were attached to the feet with narrow gold or silver straps; the toes were visible, and the toenails were polished pink or in a silvery colour. In one of the adjoining rooms someone was playing the violin, and lackeys in red livery, balancing huge trays with liqueurs and various delicacies, circled among the guests. I gulped down a roll with salmon on it, but I did not enjoy it because I was too excited.

Then two gentlemen came over and stood beside me in the bay of the window. They chatted to each other and took no notice of me. They said that the people of Paris won't tolerate the increasing living costs much longer and that social unrest is inevitable. "If I were Barras, I'd simply shoot down this rabble, my dear Fouché," one of them said languidly, taking some snuff. The other replied, "Well, first he'd have to find a man willing to do the shooting!" In reply, the other, between two sneezes, managed to say that he had that very afternoon seen General Bernadotte among the guests. But the one called Fouché shook his head. "That man? Never on your life." Then he continued, "But what about that little wretch who is running after Josephine?"

At that moment someone in the room clapped his hands and I heard Mme Tallien's twittering voice above the murmuring of the crowd. "Please, all come into the green drawing room—we have a surprise for our friends."

I moved along into the next room with the others, but it was so crowded that I couldn't see what was happening. I only saw that the walls were covered with white and green striped silk. Glasses of champagne were passed around; I had one, too, and then we crowded together more closely still to make way for the hostess. Thérèse passed near me, and I could see that she had nothing on under the yellow veils; the dark-red points of her breasts were clearly visible— it was most indecent. She had taken the arm of a gentleman in a lavender dress coat covered with gold embroidery. He was holding a lorgnon to his eye and looked extremely arrogant. Someone whispered, "Good old Barras is getting fat." So I knew that one of the five directors of France was walking past me.

"Form a circle around the sofa," Thérèse called out and we obediently placed ourselves around it. Then I saw him!

Right on the sofa. With a lady in white. He was wearing his

worn old shoes, but he had beautifully pressed trousers and a new uniform tunic; without insignia of rank or decorations. His thin face was no longer tanned, but unhealthily pale. He sat there very stiffly, staring at Thérèse Tallien as though he expected her to save his soul. The lady next to him was leaning back, resting her arms along the back of the sofa. Her tiny head, with brushed-up curls, was thrown back. Her eyes were half-open; her eyelids were painted silver, and a narrow red velvet ribbon around her neck made it look provocatively white. I knew who she was, the widow Beauharnais, Josephine. Her closed lips smiled derisively and we all followed the direction of her half-closed eyes. She was smiling at Barras.

"Have you all champagne?" That was Tallien's voice. The slender figure in white stretched out a hand, someone gave her two glasses and she offered one to Napoleon. "General—your glass." Now she was smiling at him; a very intimate, slightly pitying smile.

"Citizens and citizenesses, ladies and gentlemen, I have the great honour to make an announcement here among our friends, an announcement concerning our beloved Josephine—"

Thérèse's voice was shrill whenever she spoke loudly. How she was enjoying the scene! She remained near the sofa, still holding up her glass. Napoleon had risen and seemed terribly embarrassed. Josephine had again thrown back her childlike curly head, and her silver eyelids were very noticeable. "Our beloved Josephine has decided once more to enter the holy state of matrimony—" Suppressed giggles were audible, while Josephine absent-mindedly played with the red ribbon around her neck. "As I say, holy matrimony—" Thérèse stopped to heighten the effect of her words, glanced at Barras; he nodded—"Josephine has become engaged to Citizen General Napoleon Bonaparte."

"*No!*"

I heard the scream as distinctly as the others did. The scream seemed to pierce the room and hang loosely in the air. A deadly silence followed. I realized a second later that it was I who had screamed.

By that time I was standing in front of the sofa, saw Thérèse Tallien move away in terror, was conscious of her sweetish scent, and realized that the other woman—the one in white on the sofa—was staring at me. I myself, however, looked only at Napoleon. His eyes were like glass, translucent and without expression. A vein was throbbing at his right temple. We stood opposite each other for an eternity—he and I; but perhaps it was only a fraction of a second. Then I looked at the woman—shining silvery eyelids, tiny wrinkles around her eyes, lips rouged a dark red. How I hated her! I flung my champagne at her feet. The champagne squirted over her dress; she screamed hysterically.

I was running along a rainy wet street. I ran and ran. I don't know how I left the green drawing room and the white drawing room and got to the hall, where I passed the horrified guests who shrank away from me and the lackeys who tried to snatch hold of my arm. I know only that suddenly I was in wet darkness and that I was running by a row of houses, and then turned into another street; that my heart was pounding and that I instinctively found my way to where I wanted to go. I was on a quay, running and stumbling through the rain. I slipped, ran on again and finally reached the bridge. The Seine, I thought—now everything will be all right. I walked slowly along the bridge, leaned against the parapet and saw many lights dancing in the water. They swayed, up and down—looking so gay. I leaned over farther, the lights danced closer; the rain was rustling down, and I was more alone than I had ever been in all my life. I thought of Mama and of Julie, and that they would forgive me when they knew everything. Napoleon will surely write tonight to his mother or to Joseph to tell them about his engagement. That was my first rational thought. It hurt me so that I could not bear it. So I placed my hands on the parapet and tried to pull myself up and . . .

At that very moment, someone with an iron grip grabbed my shoulders and pulled me back. I tried to shake off the strange hands and shouted, "Leave me alone! Let me go!" But he was holding both my arms and pulling me firmly away from the parapet. I kicked him in self-defence. In spite of all my efforts, I was dragged away. It was so dark that I couldn't see who he was. I heard myself sobbing in despair and I was choking; and I hated the masculine voice, louder than the rain, "Calm yourself. Don't be foolish—here is my carriage."

There was a carriage on the quay. I kept on struggling wildly, but the stranger was much stronger than I and he pushed me into the carriage. Then he sat down next to me and called to the coachman, "Drive on—it doesn't matter where, but drive on."

I moved away as far as I could from the stranger. Suddenly I noticed that my teeth were chattering, from wetness and excitement; and small streams of water were falling from my hair, over my face. A hand reached for mine, a large warm hand. I sobbed, "Let me get out! Leave me!" Yet at the same time I clutched at this strange hand because I was so thoroughly miserable.

"You yourself asked me to escort you," came from the dark depths of the carriage. "Don't you remember, Mlle Désirée?"

I thrust away his hand and said, "I—I want—to be alone now—"

"Oh, no, you asked me to be your escort at Mme Tallien's. And now we two are staying together until I've seen you home."

His voice was soft and quite attractive. "Are you this General—this General Bernadotte?" I asked. Then everything came back to me and I screamed, "Leave me alone! I simply can't bear generals. Generals have no hearts."

"Well, there are generals—and generals," he said and laughed. I heard a rustle in the dark and a coat was laid across my shoulders.

"I'll get your coat wet," I said. "In the first place, I'm soaked through with rain; and in the second place, I can't stop crying."

"It doesn't matter," he said. "I expect that. Wrap yourself up in the coat." A memory flashed through my mind of another general's coat, on another rainy night. That time, Napoleon was holding my hand. . . . The carriage rolled along. Once the coachman stopped and asked a question, but the strange general called out, "No, just go on. I don't care where you go!"

So we drove on and on and I sobbed into the strange coat. "What a coincidence that you happened to be passing on the bridge," I said. And he answered, "No coincidence at all. I felt responsible for you because it was I who took you to the reception. And when you left the drawing room so precipitately, I followed you. But you ran so fast that I preferred to pursue you in a hired carriage. Besides, I wanted to leave you alone as long as possible."

"And why were you mean enough not to leave me alone altogether?" I demanded.

"It was no longer possible," he replied quietly, putting his arm around my shoulder. I was dead tired, nothing mattered anyway, I felt so exhausted. Just drive on, I thought; on, never to have to stop; never to have to see or hear or speak; just to drive on. . . . I put my head on his shoulder and he held me a little closer to him At the same time, I tried to remember what he looked like. But his face was blurred with the many other faces I had seen. "Forgive me for having disgraced you," I said.

"It's all right," he said. "I'm only sorry—for your sake—"

"I poured the champagne over her white dress on purpose. Champagne leaves spots," I murmured. Suddenly I began to cry again. "She is far more beautiful than I am—and a great lady—"

He held me close and with his free hand pressed my face against his shoulder. "Just cry yourself out," he said. "Just cry."

I cried like I've never cried before. I couldn't stop. At times I screamed, and then again I gasped; and all the time I burrowed against the roughness of his uniform. "I'm getting your shoulder pad wet," I sobbed.

"They're already soaked. But don't mind that—go on crying," he said.

I think we drove through the streets for hours, until I had no more tears left. I had cried myself empty "Now I'll take you home. Where do you live?" he asked

"Just let me out here, I can get home," I said, and thought of the Seine again.

"Then we'll drive some more," he said. I sat up. His shoulder was so wet that it was no longer comfortable.

In a little while I asked, "Do you know General Bonaparte personally?"

"No, I saw him once, casually, in the waiting room of the Ministry of War. I don't like him."

"*Why?*"

"I don't know. One can't explain the attraction or antipathy one feels for people. You, for example, I find attractive."

We were silent again. The carriage rolled on through the rain.

Whenever we passed a street lantern, the pavement glistened in many colours. My eyes were burning, so I closed them and leaned back my head. "I believed in him as I have never believed in any other human being," I heard myself saying. "More than in Mama; more than in—no, it was different with Papa. So I simply cannot understand—"

"There's a lot you can't understand, little one."

"We were to have been married in a few weeks. And now without a word he . . ."

"He would never have married you, little girl. He has been engaged for a long time, to the daughter of a wealthy silk merchant in Marseilles."

I pulled away. His warm protecting hand found mine again. "You didn't know that either, did you? The Tallien told me about it this afternoon. 'Our little general is sacrificing a large dowry to marry Barras' discarded mistress,' is literally what the Tallien said. Bonaparte's brother is married to this Marseilles fiancée's sister. At the moment, a faded countess with useful connections in Paris is more important to Bonaparte than a dowry in Marseilles. So you see, my child—he would not have married you in any case."

His voice was calm, almost comforting in the darkness. At first I didn't understand what he meant. "What are you talking about?" I asked, rubbing my forehead with my left hand to help me think more clearly. My right hand still held tight to his; it was then the only bit of warmth in my life.

"My poor child—forgive me for hurting you, but it is better for you to face the facts. I know how hard it is—but now you know the worst. That's why I told you what the Tallien said. First, it was a wealthy merchant's daughter; now, a countess who has useful connections because she slept with one of the directors, and before that with two gentlemen in the Army's supreme command. You, on the other hand, my little girl, have no connections and no dowry."

"How do you know that?"

"One can tell by looking at you," he said. "You are only a little girl, a very good little girl. You don't know how great ladies behave or how social life is conducted in drawing rooms. And you obviously have no money or you would have slipped a note to the Tallien's lackey and he would have admitted you. Yes, you are an upright little thing and—" he paused. Suddenly he burst out, "And I should like to marry you."

"Let me get out! Don't make fun of me," I said. I leaned forward and knocked against the glass. "Coachman, stop the carriage at once!" The carriage stopped. But the General shouted, "Drive on immediately!" And the carriage drove on through the night.

"Perhaps I did not express myself very well," came from the darkness. "You must forgive me but I've never had an opportunity to meet young girls like you. And, Mlle Désirée, I mean it—I'd like very much to marry you."

"In Mme Tallien's drawing room there were crowds of ladies who seem to have a preference for generals," I said. "I have not!"

"You don't think I would marry one of those cocottes—forgive the word, mademoiselle—one of those ladies, I mean."

I was too tired to answer, much too tired to think. I could not understand what this Bernadotte, this tower of a man, wanted of me. My life was over anyway. I felt cold despite his large coat, and my silk shoes were soaked through and felt like lead on my feet.

"Without a revolution, I wouldn't be a general; not even an officer, mademoiselle. You are very young but perhaps you've heard that before the Revolution no bourgeois was ever promoted beyond the rank of captain. My father was a clerk in a lawyer's office and came of a family of craftsmen. We are simple people, mademoiselle. I worked my way up. I joined the Army when I was fifteen and then for a long time I was a noncommissioned officer; and gradually— well, now I am a general commanding a division, mademoiselle. But perhaps I am too old for you?"

"You will believe in me—whatever may happen," Napoleon once said to me. A great lady with useful connections and silver eyelids . . . Of course, I understand you, Napoleon—but it is shattering me.

"I have a very important question to ask you, mademoiselle."

"Forgive me, I didn't hear you. What did you ask me, General Bernadotte?"

"Whether I am too old for you?"

"I don't know how old you are. And it doesn't matter, does it?"

"But it does. It's very important. Perhaps I really am too old; I am thirty-one."

"I'll soon be sixteen," I said. "And I'm very tired; I'd like to go home now."

"Yes, of course. Forgive me, I am very inconsiderate. You live—?"

I told him the address and he gave it to the coachman.

"Will you consider my proposal? In ten days I must return to the Rhineland. Perhaps you could give me an answer by then?" He spoke slowly and added more quickly, "My name is Jean-Baptiste, Jean-Baptiste Bernadotte. For years I have been saving part of my pay; I could buy a little house for you and the child."

"For what child?" I asked involuntarily. He became more than ever incomprehensible.

"For our child, naturally," he said promptly—and reached for my hand but I quickly pulled it away. "I want so much to have a wife and a child. For years I've wanted them, mademoiselle."

I lost my patience. "Listen to me, you don't know me at all."

"Yes, I do—I know you well," he said and he sounded as though he did. "I think I know you far better than your family does. I have so little time to think about my own life; I'm almost always at the front, and so I couldn't come visit your family for weeks—and take walks with you and do whatever a man is supposed to do before he can make a proposal of marriage. I have to decide quickly—and I have decided."

He was serious. He wanted to use his leave to get married, to buy a house—and a child . . . "General Bernadotte," I said, "in the life of every woman there is only one great love."

"How do you know?" he asked quickly.

"It's so—" How *did* I know this? "It says so in all the novels and it must be true," I said.

At that moment the carriage creaked to a stop. We had arrived at the Clapains' house in the rue du Bac. He opened the carriage door and helped me out. A lantern hung over the house door. I stood as I had at Mme Tallien's, on tiptoe, so that I could see his face. He had beautiful white teeth and a huge nose. I handed him the key which Mme Clapain had lent me and he unlocked the door. "You

live in a very fine house," he remarked. "Oh—we live in the building at the back," I said. "And now good night and many thanks,
truly many thanks for—everything."

But he didn't move. "Go back to the carriage, you'll get all wet,"
I said. Then I remembered something and smiled. "Don't worry,
I'll stay here," I assured him.

"That's a good girl," he said. "Good night—and when may I
come for your answer?"

I shook my head. "In the life of every woman . . ." I began
again. But he raised his hand warningly. Instead, I said, "It wouldn't
do, General, really not. It isn't that I'm too young for you, but you
can see yourself—I'm much too short for you!" With that, I quickly
closed the door behind me.

When I came into the Clapains' kitchen, I was no longer tired—
only utterly exhausted. I can't sleep now—can never sleep again.
So I am sitting at the kitchen table writing and writing. The day
after tomorrow this Bernadotte will come here to inquire after me,
but I will certainly not be here. I don't know where I'll be the day
after tomorrow.

Marseilles, three weeks later

I have been very ill.

Cold in the head, sore throat, very high fever, and what the poets
call a broken heart. In Paris I sold Marie's gold medallion for just
enough assignats to pay for my journey home. Marie put me right
to bed and called the doctor because I had such a high fever. He
couldn't understand where I could have caught cold—it hadn't rained
for days in Marseilles. Marie also sent a messenger to Mama, who
returned at once to nurse me. So far, no one has discovered that I
have been in Paris.

Now I am lying on the sofa on the terrace. They have covered me up with many blankets, and they say that I am very pale and fright-fully thin. Joseph and Julie returned from their journey yesterday and are coming to see us this evening. I hope I shall be allowed to stay up.

Marie has just come running out to the terrace. She is flourishing an extra broadside and seems very excited.

Gen. Napoleon Bonaparte has been appointed Military Governor of Paris. Hunger riots in the capital have been suppressed by the National Guard.

At first the letters danced before my eyes. Now I have become more accustomed to them. Napoleon is the Military Governor of Paris. The broadside reports that mobs of rioters stormed the Tuiler-ies and wanted to tear the deputies to pieces. In his distress Barras entrusted Gen. Napoleon Bonaparte, a former officer, with the com-mand of the National Guard. Whereupon, this general demanded unrestricted powers from the National Convention and was actually granted these powers. He ordered a young cavalry officer named Murat to assemble some cannon, which were placed at the north, west and east sides of the Tuileries. These cannon covered the rue Saint-Roche and the Pont Royal. But the mob pressed forward, until a voice cut through the air: "Fire!" A single cannon shot was enough to drive back the crowd. Order has been re-established. The di-rectors, Barras, Larevellière, Letourneur, Rewbell, and Carnot, are grateful to this man who has saved the Republic from further chaos, and appoint him Military Governor of Paris.

I am trying to think all this out. I remember a conversation over-heard in the bay of the window at Mme Tallien's: "If I were Barras, I'd shoot down the rabble, dear Fouché." . . . "But he would have to find someone willing to shoot." One cannon shot was enough; Napoleon let it be fired! Napoleon fired off a cannon—into the rabble, the broadside reports. Rabble—probably people living in cellars and unable to pay the high price of bread! Napoleon's mother, too, lives in a cellar. "Your son is a genius, madame." . . . "Yes, unfortunately!"

I was interrupted again and now I'm writing in my own room.

While I was thinking about the broadside, I heard Joseph and Julie come into the parlour. The door to the terrace is not quite closed. So they didn't wait until evening to call!

Joseph said, "Napoleon has sent a courier with a long letter for me and a lot of money for our mama. I have sent a messenger to our mama asking her to come here at once. Is that all right, Mme Clary?"

Mama said it was quite all right. She said she would be glad to see Mme Letizia, and didn't Julie and Joseph want to speak to me; I was on the terrace and still very weak. But Joseph hesitated, and Julie began to cry, and she told Mama that Napoleon had written to Joseph that he was engaged to General de Beauharnais' widow. And they were to tell me that he would always be my best friend. Mama wailed, "The poor, poor child!" Then I heard Mme Letizia, Elisa and Paulette come in and they all talked at once, until Joseph began to read something out loud, undoubtedly the letter from the new Military Governor of Paris.

Much later he and Julie came out to the terrace and sat down beside me, and Julie stroked my hand. Joseph was obviously ill at ease and he said that the garden looked rather autumnal already.

"I should like to congratulate you on your brother's appointment," I said, pointing to the letter which he was nervously kneading between his fingers.

"Thank you very much. I regret to say that I have something to tell you, Eugénie, and—both Julie and I are—very upset—"

I interrupted him. "Never mind, Joseph—I know." And when I saw his puzzled face, I added, "The door to the parlour was open and I heard everything you said."

At that moment, in came Mme Letizia. Her eyes flashed. "A widow with two children! Six years older than my boy. How dares Napoleon bring me such a daughter-in-law!"

In my mind I saw Josephine—silver eyelids, childlike curls, supercilious smile. And before me stood Mme Letizia with the red, workworn hands and the wrinkled neck of a woman who all her life has washed laundry and scolded children. Her rough hands grasped a pile of bank notes. The Military Governor of Paris had already sent his mother part of his salary.

Later I was settled on the sofa in the parlour and listened to the others discussing the great event. Etienne got out his best liqueur and said that he was very proud to be related to General Bonaparte. Mama and Suzanne bent low over their embroidery. "I feel much better now," I said. "Won't you bring me some of the linen I was initialling? I'd like to finish embroidering the monograms for my trousseau."

No one contradicted me. But when I began to stitch a *B, B,* and another *B,* there was an embarrassed silence. Suddenly I realized that a part of my life was over. "From now on," I announced, "I no longer wish to be called Eugénie. My name is Eugénie Bernardine Désirée and I prefer Désirée. Please call me Désirée."

They looked at each other anxiously. I think they doubted my sanity.

Rome, three days after Christmas in the Year V
(Here in Italy they still use the pre-Revolutionary
calendar: December 27, 1797)

They have left me alone with the dying man.

His name is Jean-Pierre Duphot and he is a general on Napoleon's staff. He came to Rome today to ask me to marry him. Two hours ago a bullet struck him in the stomach. We laid him down on the sofa in Joseph's study. The doctor said he could not help him.

Duphot is unconscious. He breathes in gulps, a thin thread of blood oozes from the corners of his mouth, and I have put some cloths around his chin. His eyes are half-open, but they see nothing. I can hear low voices in the next room—Joseph, Julie, the doctor and two secretaries of the Embassy. Julie and Joseph left the room because they were afraid of seeing a man die. The doctor followed them. This doctor is Italian and considers it more important to get to know His Excellency, the Ambassador of the French Republic in

Rome, whose brother conquered Italy, than to watch over the death of an insignificant member of the General Staff. I don't know why, but I have a feeling that Duphot will regain consciousness; though I also feel that he is already far away. I have got out my diary and have begun to write in it again after all these years. Now I don't feel quite so alone. My pen scratches, and the rattling gasps are no longer the only sound in this terrible, huge room.

I have not seen Napoleone—only his mother still calls him that; the whole world talks of Napoleon Bonaparte and of practically nothing else—since that moment in Paris. My family still knows nothing of that encounter. He married Josephine the following spring. Tallien and Director Barras were their witnesses, and Napoleon immediately paid the widow Beauharnais' dressmakers' bills. He left for Italy two days after the wedding; he was entrusted by the Government with the supreme command! He won six battles within fourteen days.

The breathing of the dying man has changed. It is quieter. And his eyes are wide open. I have called his name, but he cannot hear me.

Yes, in two weeks Napoleon won six battles; and then the Austrians evacuated northern Italy. I often think of our evening conversations by the garden hedge. Napoleon actually has founded new states. He called his first Lombardy, and his latest is the Cisalpine Republic. He chose Milan as the capital of Lombardy and selected fifty Italians to govern this State in the name of France. Overnight the words "Liberty, Equality, Fraternity" were inscribed on all public buildings. The people of Milan were forced to surrender a large sum of money, three hundred carriage horses, and their most beautiful art treasures. Napoleon sent everything to Paris. First, however, he deducted the pay for his troops from the Italian money; ordinarily the Directorate remained in debt to the Southern Army! Barras and his associates in Paris didn't know what was happening to them: money in the national treasury; Italy's most beautiful horses drawing their carriages; and valuable works of art in their drawing rooms. Napoleon particularly recommended one picture to the Parisians' attention; it is called *La Gioconda* and is the work of a certain Leonardo Da Vinci. A lady, apparently named Mona, is smiling with closed lips. Her smile reminds one of Josephine's. Perhaps she had bad teeth, like the widow Beauharnais. . . .

Finally something has happened which no one would have thought possible. The French Republic broke with the Church of Rome and for years Roman Catholic priests have fled to sanctuary beyond our borders. Now the Pope himself has suggested a peace treaty with France and has approached Napoleon, victor in Italy.

This delighted Etienne, who spent days telling everyone who came to his shop how years ago Napoleon had spoken to him of his Italian plans. And Etienne always says that he is not only Napoleon's brother-in-law, but his best friend as well.

I've been sitting with Duphot a long time, and I've even held up his head. But it doesn't help! His breathing is no easier, he struggles for air. I wiped some of the bloody foam from his mouth. His face is like wax. I called in the doctor. "Internal bleeding," he explained in broken French, and immediately returned to Joseph and Julie. I'm sure they were discussing tomorrow's ball.

The Government in Paris was worried long before the agreement with the Vatican was concluded; for Napoleon by himself wrote and signed, quite independently, all the treaties with the various parts of Italy he had liberated. He never inquired whether the Government in Paris agreed. This goes beyond the powers of a supreme commander, the directors grumbled; this has nothing to do with the conduct of the war; this is foreign policy of the greatest significance. . . . But Napoleon ignored these objections and did not trouble to answer the Government's communications. He simply continued to send money to Paris. Occasionally he asked for more troops, but he specified exactly from which sector these troops were to be taken; showing how familiar he is not only with his own Southern Front but with conditions on all the other French fronts as well. When it was suggested in Paris that a diplomatic adviser be assigned to Napoleon, and that embassies should be accredited to the new Italian States, he finally wrote to the Government. He listed several names; these were the gentlemen to be chosen as ambassadors of the Republic and sent to him. At the head of the list was his brother Joseph.

So Joseph and Julie came to Italy; first to Parma, then as French Ambassador to Genoa, and finally to Rome. Moreover, they did not come directly from Marseilles but from Paris. As soon as Napoleon was appointed Military Governor of Paris, he wrote Joseph that he would have far greater opportunities in the capital than in Marseilles. Whatever happens, Napoleon always finds a post for his brother Joseph. He began as a modest secretary in the Town Hall in Marseilles. In Paris, Napoleon introduced Joseph to Barras and other politicians and also to army contractors, and to the nouveaux riches speculating in houses. Joseph began to prosper. He bought some of the property confiscated from the aristocrats when it was sold at low prices by the Government, and then resold these houses at far higher prices. Etienne explained to us that, because of the housing shortage, speculations of this kind were very profitable. Within a short time Joseph could afford to buy a small house for himself and Julie in the rue du Rocher.

When the Italian victories were reported—Millesimo, Castiglione, Arcola, Rivoli—Joseph became a very important man in Paris. He was the elder brother of Bonaparte, whom the foreign press called "the strong man of France" and our own papers praised as "the liberator of the Italian people" and whose thin face can be seen in shop windows, on coffeecups, flower vases or snuffboxes. On one side is Napoleon's face and on the other the French flag. . . .

No one was surprised when the French Government at once acceded to the request of their most successful general, and Joseph became an ambassador. Joseph and Julie moved into their first Italian marble palace, and Julie was very unhappy and wrote desperate letters asking me to come and stay with her. So Mama let me go. Since then I have been wandering with her and Joseph from one palace to another; I live in horrible high rooms, with black and white tile floors; and I sit in pillared halls in which various weird bronze fountains spout water from all likely, and sometimes quite unlikely, openings. Our present palace is called Palazzo Corsini. We are surrounded by the clanking of spurs and the rattling of swords because the staff of Joseph's embassy consists chiefly of officers.

Tomorrow evening Joseph is giving the largest ball yet arranged by the Embassy; he wants Julie and himself to be presented to the three hundred and fifty most prominent Roman citizens. Julie hasn't been able to sleep for a week; she is very pale and has circles under her eyes. Julie is one of those women who go all to pieces if they're having four guests for dinner. Here we always have at least fifteen, and any moment Joseph is apt to arrange a reception for a few hundred people. Although a small army of lackeys, cooks and chambermaids buzz around us, Julie feels personally responsible for the whole circus and clings to me sobbing and moaning that things will "go badly." She inherited this unfortunate attitude from Mama and even talks like her.

Duphot has moved again. I had hoped that he would regain consciousness; for a moment he looked at me quite clearly, but then his half-open eyes no longer focussed; he struggled for breath, spat blood, and sank down more deeply into the pillow. Jean-Pierre Duphot, I'd give a great deal to be able to help you. But there is nothing I can do. . . .

In spite of battles and victories and peace treaties and newly formed States, Napoleon finds time to take care of his family. From the beginning, couriers from Italy arrived in Marseilles with letters and money for Mme Letizia. She moved to a more respectable flat, and the irrepressible Jérôme was sent to a good school. Caroline went to the same fashionable boarding school in Paris as Hortense Beauharnais, Napoleon's stepdaughter. The Bonapartes have really risen in the world! Napoleon was furious because his mother allowed Elisa to marry a certain Felix Bacciochi. "Why this sudden marriage?" he wrote, "and why on earth to this worthless music student, Bacchiochi?"

Elisa had been running around with Bacciochi for a long time, hoping that he would marry her. When news of the first Italian victories was received, Bacciochi asked at once to marry her and he was promptly accepted. After the wedding, Napoleon was afraid that Paulette, too, might bring someone of whom he disapproved into the family; so he arranged for Mme Letizia and Paulette to visit him at his headquarters in Montebello. There he married her off with lightning speed to a General Leclerc whom none of us know.

Unpleasant and incomprehensible as it may seem, and in spite of all the world history Napoleon has been making, he has not forgotten me. He is apparently determined to make amends to me for something; so with Julie's and Joseph's approval, he sends me one eligible bachelor after another. The first was Junot, formerly his personal adjutant in the Marseilles days. Junot, tall and blond and amiable, appeared in Genoa, urged me to join him in the garden, clicked his heels together and declared that he had the honour to ask for my hand in marriage. I thanked him but refused. But these were Napoleon's orders, Junot remarked artlessly! I remembered Napoleon's opinion of Junot: loyal unto death, but an idiot! I shook my head, and Junot rode back to Montebello. The next candidate was Marmont, whom I had known in Marseilles. Marmont did not ask me directly but with artful insinuations. I remembered what Napoleon had once said to me about this friend—"intelligent, will stand by me for the sake of his career!" So—he hopes to marry Joseph Bonaparte's sister-in-law, kept running through my head. By marrying me he would be related to Napoleon, could do Napoleon a favour, and at the same time acquire a considerable dowry. I countered Marmont's delicate approach with an equally tactful "no." Then I went to Joseph and asked him if he couldn't write Napoleon and ask him to spare me further offers of marriage from his officers.

"Can't you understand that Napoleon considers it an honour to his generals when he suggests them as husbands for his sister-in-law?"

"I am not an order or a decoration to be awarded to some deserving officer," I said. "And if I'm not left in peace, I'll go back to Mama."

I hope this will convince him.

Meanwhile, in spite of the cooler weather, Julie and I sat in the courtyard this morning. In the centre here, there's a fat bronze lady holding a dolphin in her arms and this dolphin continuously spits out water. We were studying the names of the aristocratic Italian families who will be represented at the Embassy tomorrow. In came Joseph with a letter in his hand. His Excellency first talked of this and that, as he always does when he has something unpleasant on his mind, and finally said, "Napoleon has arranged for us to have a new military attaché, Gen. Jean-Pierre Duphot, a very charming young man—"

I looked up. "Duphot? Didn't a General Duphot call on you once in Genoa?"

"Yes, of course." Joseph was obviously delighted. "And I see he made an impression on you, didn't he. Fine! Napoleon writes that he hopes, Eugénie—you must excuse him but he always says Eugénie instead of Désirée—will be particularly kind to Duphot. He is a very lonely young man, Napoleon says. And so . . ."

I rose. "A new marriage prospect? No, thank you. I thought we were through with this foolishness." At the door, I turned around. "Write to Napoleon at once that this Duphot—or whatever his name is—is not to be sent here."

"But he has already arrived. He came a quarter of an hour ago and brought me this letter from Napoleon."

I slammed the door angrily. It gave me particular pleasure to do this, for in a marble palace the slamming of a door sounds like an explosion.

To avoid Duphot, I did not appear at dinner; but I came down for supper, as I find it boring to eat alone in my room. Naturally they had seated Duphot next to me—Joseph obeys Napoleon's wishes slavishly. I glanced casually at the young man. Medium height, very dark, a lot of white teeth in a wide mouth—that was my impression of him. I was especially irritated by the flashing teeth, as he grinned at me continually.

Our table talk was frequently interrupted. We are used to hearing crowds around the Embassy shouting, "Evviva la Francia! Evviva la libertà!" Sometimes there are shouts of "A basso la Francia!" Most Italians are enthusiastic about the ideas of the Republic, but many of them seem embittered by the heavy cost to them of our occupation and the fact that Napoleon selects all of their officials. Today the shouting around the palace gate was somehow different; louder—and threatening.

Joseph explained why. Last night a few Roman citizens were arrested as hostages because a French lieutenant had been killed in a tavern brawl. A deputation from the Roman City Council was outside the palace; these men had asked to speak to Joseph. And a great crowd had collected to see what was happening.

"Why don't you receive the gentlemen; we can wait dinner," Julie said.

But Joseph declared—and the other embassy gentlemen nodded in agreement—that this was out of the question. He would not receive them; it had nothing to do with him. From the very beginning, it had been the responsibility of the Military Governor of Rome.

In the meantime the noise outside grew louder; they were storming the outer gate.

"My patience is exhausted!" Joseph shouted. "I'll have the square cleared!" He turned to one of his secretaries. "Go over at once to the Military Commander's office and tell him that the square in front of the Embassy is to be cleared at once. This noise is unbearable!" The young secretary turned to go. "It would be safer to leave by the back door," General Duphot called after him.

We continued our meal in silence. Before our coffee was served, we heard the clattering of horses' hooves. Someone had sent a battalion of hussars to clear the square! Joseph rose, and we went with him to the first-floor balcony. The square below was like a witches' cauldron. A surging sea of faces, a cacophony of voices, an occasional scream. We couldn't see the deputation from the City Council; the crowd had pushed them flat against the entrance gates to our palace. The two guards in front of the Embassy stood motionless at their post, and it looked as if at any moment they would be trampled to death. Joseph pulled us back from the balcony quickly, but he could still peer out of the windows. My brother-in-law was deathly pale and gnawing his underlip; the hand with which he kept smoothing his hair was trembling with rage.

The hussars had surrounded the square. They sat on their horses like statues, ready to charge, awaiting a command. But their commanding officer apparently could not bring himself to give the order. "I'll go down and try to bring these people to their senses," Duphot said.

"General, you must not expose yourself to this danger! It would be madness! Our hussars will soon . . ." Joseph said imploringly.

Duphot flashed his white teeth. "I am an officer, Your Excellency," he interrupted, "and am therefore accustomed to danger. I should prefer to prevent unnecessary bloodshed."

Spurs jingling, he walked over to the door, turned around and sought my eyes. I turned quickly toward the window. So he was acting the role of a brave man for my sake; to impress me, he was dashing down alone and unarmed into the furious mob. It's so silly, I thought; Junot, Marmont, Duphot—what do they want of me?

The next minute, the gate below was swung wide. We opened the window a crack so that we could hear better. The roaring shouts decreased in intensity, changed into a threatening murmur. A high-pitched voice yelled, "*A basso!*" and again, "*A basso!*" At first we couldn't see Duphot, but then the crowd moved back from the gate and made way for him. As he raised his hands, entreating the people to be quiet so that he might be heard, a shot was fired. Immediately afterward came the first salvo by the hussars.

I plunged down the stairs and wrenched open the gate. The two guards had lifted up General Duphot and were holding him under his arms; but his legs dangled helplessly from his body, his face hung to one side, his mouth was distorted. His perpetual smile had frozen into a terrible grin. He was unconscious. The two guards dragged him into the hall, his lifeless legs trailing across the marble tiles, and his spurs clanking against the stone. The two soldiers looked up at me helplessly.

"Upstairs—" I heard myself saying. "We must lay him down somewhere upstairs." We were surrounded by scared, white faces. Joseph. Julie. The fat Councillor of Embassy. Julie's maid, Minette. They all drew back as the two soldiers carried Duphot up the stairs. Outside, in the square in front of the Embassy, it was as still as death. Two salvos had been enough.

I opened the door to Joseph's study, which is the room nearest the staircase. The soldiers laid Duphot on a sofa, and I pushed pillows under his head. Joseph stood next to me and said, "I've sent for a doctor. Perhaps it's not so bad."

The stain on the front of the dark-blue uniform spread. "Open his uniform, Joseph," I said; and Joseph fumbled awkwardly with the gold buttons. The spot of blood on the white shirt was bright red. "A stomach wound," Joseph said. I looked at the General's face. He had turned very yellow. From his wide-open mouth came sobs in fits and starts. At first I thought he was weeping; I soon realized he was struggling for breath.

The thin little Italian physician, when he finally arrived, was even more agitated than Joseph. It was such a wonderful opportunity for him, to be called to the French Embassy. He was a great admirer of the French Republic and of Gen. Napoleon Bonaparte. While he opened Duphot's shirt he expressed regret for the trouble in the city and stammered something about "irresponsible elements." I interrupted him to ask whether he needed anything. He looked at me, startled, and remembered what he was doing. "Oh, yes, some lukewarm water. And perhaps a clean cloth."

He began to wash out the wound. Joseph had stepped over to the window; and Julie leaned against the wall, struggling not to be sick. I took her outside and then told Joseph he'd better look after her. Joseph was obviously delighted to leave the room. "A blanket," the doctor said to me, "can you get a blanket? He's very cold, he's bleeding so much—internally, mademoiselle, internally—"

We spread a blanket over Duphot. "I'm afraid there's nothing more to be done, mademoiselle. What a terrible thing—such an important man!" The doctor's eyes rested briefly on Duphot's gold epaulettes, then he hurried to the door behind which Joseph had disappeared. I went into the next room with him. Joseph, Julie, the Councillor of Embassy and a few secretaries sat whispering around a large table; and a lackey was serving port wine to strengthen them. Joseph jumped up, offered the doctor a glass; and I could see that at this manifestation of the Bonaparte courtesy the little Italian was practically walking on air. He stammered, "Oh, Excellency—oh, brother of our great Liberator—"

I returned to Duphot. At first I was busy; I fetched clean cloths and wiped the blood that trickled down his chin. I soon gave this up, because it came constantly in an unbroken flow. Finally I just spread out cloths under his chin. I tried in vain to attract the attention of the glazing eyes. At last I fetched my diary and began to write.

I believe that many hours have passed; the candles are nearly burned out. But I can still hear a soft murmur of voices in the next room. No one is going to bed until . . .

He recovered consciousness once.

I heard him moving, knelt down beside him and raised his head onto my arm. He looked at me. Again and again. He wasn't sure where he was. "You are in Rome, General Duphot," I said, "in Rome, in the home of Ambassador Bonaparte."

He moved his lips and spat out bloody foam. I wiped his face with my free hand. "Marie—" he was able to whisper, "I want to go to Marie—"

"Where is Marie? Quickly—tell me where is Marie?"

His eyes cleared and he recognized me; still his eyes were questioning. So I repeated, "You are in Rome. There were riots. You have been wounded—a shot in the stomach."

He nodded almost imperceptibly. He understood me. My thoughts ran on: he was beyond help, but perhaps Marie . . .

"Marie. What is her surname? And where does she live?" I whispered urgently.

His expression was anxious. "Don't tell—" his lips shaped the words—"Don't tell—Bonaparte—"

"I won't tell him anything," I promised. "But if you are ill a long time we must tell Marie, mustn't we? Napoleon Bonaparte won't ever know anything about it." I smiled at him confidentially.

"The sister-in-law—I'm to marry Eugénie, the sister-in-law," he managed to say. "Bonaparte proposed it and—" I couldn't understand the rest. Then he said softly, "You must be sensible, little Marie—I'll always look after—you and little George—dear, dear Marie—"

His hand slid to one side, he tried to kiss my arm. He thought I was Marie. He had explained to Marie exactly why he was deserting her—her and the little son—to marry me, Bonaparte's sister-in-law. Such a marriage would mean promotion and undreamed-of opportunities. . . .

His head, resting on my arm, was as heavy as lead. I raised it a little. "Marie's address—I'll write to her," I said, trying to catch his eye again.

For the fraction of a second he was completely conscious. "Marie

Meunier—rue de Lyon—thirty-six—in Paris—" His features had sharpened, his eyes lay in deep hollows, and his breathing sounded like stifled hiccups. He was sweating profusely.

"Marie and little George will always be well provided for," I said. He didn't hear me. "I promise," I repeated. His eyes glittered at nothing, his lips were contorted.

I jumped up and ran to the door. At that moment he sighed. His long sigh trembled through the room and was gone. "Come at once, doctor," I heard myself calling.

"It's all over," the little Italian answered, after bending casually over the sofa. I went to the window and drew back the curtains. The morning crept grey and leaden into the room. I put out the low-burning candles.

In the next room they still sat at the table. The lackeys had brought fresh candles; the whole room, so bright and festive, seemed like another world.

"You must call off the ball, Joseph," I said.

Joseph sat up, startled. He had apparently been asleep, his chin resting on his chest. "What—what did you say? Oh, I see it's you, Désirée."

"You must call off the ball, Joseph," I said again.

"That's impossible. I have particularly ordered . . ."

"But there is a dead man in your house," I explained.

He stared at me, frowning. Then he rose quickly. "I'll consider the matter," he murmured, going toward the door.

Julie and the others followed him. In front of their bedroom Julie stopped. "Désirée, may I lie down in your room. I'm afraid to be alone!"

I said, "But, of course. You can use my bed, I'll be writing in my diary—"

"You don't still keep your diary! How funny—" She smiled a tired smile.

"Why funny?"

"Because everything is so different. So very different." She sighed and lay down, fully dressed, on my bed.

Julie slept until noon and I didn't awaken her. In the course of the morning I heard hammering, went down and saw that they were building a platform in the great hall. Joseph stood in one corner and gave the workmen directions in Italian. At last he had a chance to use his mother tongue. When he saw me he stepped over to me quickly. "That's the platform for the ball. Julie and I will stand on it and watch the dancing."

"For the ball?" I asked astonished. "But you can't go on with the ball!"

"No, you are right, not with a dead man in the house; so we have removed—the body of—the late Duphot."

Joseph continued zealously, "I have given orders that Duphot is to be laid out in state in a mortuary chapel. It's to be done as beautifully as possible, because he was a general in the French Army. But the ball is absolutely essential; it's more important than ever to have this ball, because we must prove to everyone that peace and quiet prevail in Rome. If I were to postpone it, people would say that we are not masters of the situation; and, after all, the whole affair was merely an insignificant though regrettable incident. You understand that, don't you?"

I nodded. General Duphot had deserted his mistress and his son to marry me; the General had rashly exposed himself to an infuriated mob in order to impress me; the General had been shot—an insignificant though regrettable incident. "It is most urgent that I talk to your brother, Joseph," I said.

"Which one? Lucien?"

"No, your famous brother. The General. To Napoleon—"

Joseph tried to conceal his astonishment. The family knows that heretofore I have always avoided meeting Napoleon. "It concerns General Duphot's survivors," I said brusquely and left the hall. The workmen were hammering like mad.

When I got back to my room I found a tearful Julie in my bed. I sat down beside her, and she put her arms around my neck and sobbed like a child. "I want to go home," she sobbed. "I—don't want to live in these strange palaces—I want to have a home like everyone else. What are we doing in this foreign country where people want to shoot us? And in these draughty palaces—with great high ceilings like a church. . . . We don't belong here. I want to go home—"

I held her close. General Duphot's death had made Julie realize how unhappy she is here.

A little later a letter came from Mama in Marseilles. We sat together on my bed and read the news Mama had written, in her neat slanting handwriting. Etienne and Suzanne had decided to move to Genoa, where he was opening a branch of the Clary firm. French businessmen have splendid opportunities in Genoa now and Italy is the centre of the silk trade. And as Mama does not wish to remain alone in Marseilles, she is moving to Genoa with Etienne and Suzanne. She assumes that for the present I shall be staying with Julie. And she prays to God that soon I shall find a dear, kind husband; but, for heaven's sake, I must never be rushed into anything! Yes— and Etienne wants to sell our house in Marseilles.

Julie had stopped crying. We stared at each other, horrified. "That means that we have no home," she whispered.

I swallowed hard. "But in any case you would never have gone back to our villa in Marseilles," I said.

Julie stared out the window. "I don't know. No, of course not," she said, "but it was lovely to think about the house and the garden and the little summer house. You know, in all these months while we've been moving from palace to palace, and I've been so dreadfully unhappy, I've always thought about them; never about Joseph's little house in Paris, but always about Papa's villa in Marseilles . . ."

At that moment there was a knock at the door. Joseph came in and brought the tears back again. "I want to go home—" Julie cried. He sat down beside us on the bed and took her in his arms. "And so you shall," he said tenderly. "Tonight there is the big ball, and tomorrow we leave. Back to Paris. I've had enough of Rome."

He pressed his lips together and settled his chin down onto his neck, where it became two chins—however, he thought this pose gave him an extremely distinguished appearance. "I shall request the Government to give me a new and perhaps more important post. Are you glad to be returning to our home in the rue du Rocher, Julie?"

"If Désirée comes with us—" Julie sobbed.

"I'm coming with you," I said. "Where else could I go?"

Julie raised a tear-stained face to mine. "We'll have a very good time in Paris, we three—you and Joseph and I. And you have no idea, Désirée, how wonderful Paris is. Such a huge city. And the lovely parks—and so many lights . . . But, of course, you have never been there and can't possibly imagine it."

Julie and Joseph left my room to make arrangements for tomorrow's journey, and I sank down on my bed. My eyes stung from lack of sleep. I imagined the conversation I would have with Napoleon and tried to remember his face. But when I closed my eyes all I could see was the unreal, supercilious features which nowadays smile out from so many coffeecups, flower vases, or snuffboxes. Soon these porcelain faces vanished, and I remembered the lights that dance at night on the ripples of the Seine—and which I can never forget.

Paris, end of Germinal, Year VI
(*Except in our Republic, where everyone calls it*
April, 1798)

I have seen him again.

We were invited by him to a farewell reception; he is practically immediately sailing with his armies for Egypt. He told his mother that with the pyramids as a base, he intends to unite the East and the West, and to turn our Republic into a world empire. Mme Letizia listened quietly, but later she asked Joseph whether Napoleon ever suffered from feverish attacks of malaria and whether this illness was being kept secret from her. Her poor boy did not seem quite right in the head. Joseph explained to her, and to Julie and me, exactly how Napoleon plans to destroy the British. He will smash their colonial empire.

Napoleon and Josephine live in a small house in the rue de la Victoire. The house formerly belonged to Talma, the actor; and

Josephine bought it from his widow in the Barras days when she glittered in the salon of Thérèse Tallien. At that time the street was called rue Chântereine. After Napoleon's Italian victories, the Paris Town Council decided to change the name in his honour and now it is called the rue de la Victoire.

It is unbelievable how many people crowded into this small and rather insignificant house yesterday. It has only two tiny drawing rooms and a dining room. I still feel dizzy when I think of all those faces and voices! During the morning, Julie made me sick with her affectionate anxiety. "Are you excited? Do you feel anything for him?" I was excited but I didn't know whether I felt anything for him. When he smiles he can do what he likes with me, I thought. I clung to the hope that he and Josephine would still be furious because of the scene I had made that day at the Tallien's. He would, I thought, dislike me and would not smile at me, and I almost hoped that he would hate me.

I had a new dress and naturally I wore it. It was a gold dress with a rose petticoat, and I used a bronze chain I had bought in an antique shop in Rome for a belt. The day before yesterday I had my hair cut. Josephine was the first Parisienne with short hair, but now other fashionable women are imitating her childish curls brushed up high on the head. My hair is so thick and heavy that it will take time to train properly. Meanwhile, I brush up my short hair and tie it up on my head with a silk ribbon. Whatever I wore, I'll look, I thought, like a country bumpkin compared to Josephine. My new dress is cut very low in the neck, but for a long time I've not needed to put in handkerchiefs; on the contrary, I've decided to eat fewer sweets or I shall be too fat. My nose is still turned up and will be, I suppose, until the end of my days. This is particularly unfortunate because since the conquest of Italy "classical profiles" are the rage.

We left at one o'clock to drive to the rue de la Victoire, where the small drawing room was already swarming with Bonapartes. Mme Letizia and her daughters now live in Paris. All the members of the family see each other constantly; but whenever the Bonapartes meet, everyone kisses everyone else. First I was pressed to Mme Letizia's bosom, and then madly embraced by Mme Leclerc. Mme Leclerc is little Paulette, who said before her marriage, "Leclerc is the only officer we know with whom I'm not the tiniest bit in love." But Napoleon decided that her many love affairs were bad for the Bonaparte family's reputation, and he insisted on the marriage. Leclerc has short legs, he is fat and very energetic and never laughs, and he looks much older than Paulette. Elisa—still painted like a tin soldier —with her Bacciochi husband was at the reception, too, and boasted about the wonderful position Napoleon had got for her musical husband in one of the ministries. Caroline, and Josephine's daughter, the square, blonde Hortense, had been allowed to leave their fancy boarding school for one day so that they could wish their brother and stepfather a successful journey to the pyramids. Now they sat on a small delicate chair and giggled about Mme Letizia's new brocade dress, which reminded them of the curtains in the dining room.

Among the loud and forward Bonapartes I noticed a slender, blond and very young officer with an adjutant's sash, whose blue eyes stared helplessly at Paulette. I asked Caroline who he was, and she nearly died laughing before she was able to say, "Napoleon's son!"

The young man sensed what I had asked; he came over to me and presented himself, shyly: "Eugène de Beauharnais," he said, "Personal Adjutant of General Bonaparte."

The only members of the family who had not appeared were our host and hostess, Napoleon and Josephine.

At last a door opened and Josephine called, "Sorry, my dears, excuse us—we just got home! Joseph, come here a minute; Napoleon wants to talk to you. Make yourselves comfortable, all of you. I'll be right out."

She disappeared. Joseph followed her, and Mme Letizia shrugged, petulantly. We all began to talk again, but we were suddenly silenced—someone had apparently gone crazy in the next room. Something crashed on the top of a table or a chimney tile and a lot of glass broke. At this moment Josephine came in.

"How nice that the whole family is here," she said, and smiled and then went over to Mme Letizia. Her white dress clung to her slender figure, a shawl of red velvet edged in ermine was draped around her shoulders; and when the shawl slipped—just so—her neck looked unbelievably white. We could hear Joseph saying something in the next room.

"Lucien—have you a son called Lucien, madame?" Josephine asked Mme Letizia.

"My third eldest son—what about him?" Mme Letizia glared at Josephine. This daughter-in-law—who didn't take the trouble to learn by heart the names of her brothers and sisters-in-law!

"He has written Napoleon that he is married," Josephine said.

"I know he has." Mme Letizia's eyes narrowed. "Is my second eldest son by any chance dissatisfied with his brother's choice?"

Josephine shrugged her slender shoulders and smiled. "It seems he is—listen to him!"

The raving in the next room seemed to amuse her. The door flew open, and there was Napoleon. His thin face was red with fury. "Mother, did you know that Lucien has married an innkeeper's daughter?"

Mme Letizia looked Napoleon up and down; her look travelled from his tangled reddish-brown hair, hanging untidily down to his shoulders, to his impeccable uniform made by the best military tailor in Paris, and at his highly polished and elegant small boots. "What don't you like about your sister-in-law, Christine Boyer from St. Maximin, Napoleone?"

"You don't understand! The daughter of an innkeeper, a village lout who every evening serves the local peasants in his tavern? Mother, I can't comprehend you!"

"Christine Boyer is, as far as I know, a fine girl with an excellent reputation," Mme Letizia said; and she looked casually at Josephine's narrow white figure.

"Unfortunately," Joseph interrupted, "we cannot all marry former countesses."

Josephine's nostrils dilated; she smiled, but it seemed a little forced. Her son, Eugène, blushed.

Napoleon whirled around and stared at Joseph. That small vein hammered in his right temple. He passed his hand over his forehead, glared at Joseph and said, "I have the right to demand suitable marriages from my brothers. Mother, I want you to write to Lucien at once that he is to get a divorce or to have his marriage annulled. Write him that these are my orders. . . . Josephine, can we dine now?"

At that moment he noticed me. For a second we looked straight at each other. This was it—this meeting, so long feared, so hateful and so longed for. Quickly he came forward, pushing aside the four-square Hortense, who stood in his way, and took both my hands in his. "Eugénie! I'm so pleased you came."

His eyes never left my face. He smiled, and his thin face was young and carefree, as it was when he promised Mama to wait until my sixteenth birthday for the wedding. He said, "You have become very beautiful, Eugénie." And—"Grown up, quite grown up."

I withdrew my hands. "After all, I'm almost nineteen." It sounded gawky and naive. "And we've not seen each other for a long time, General." That was better.

"Yes, it's been a long time—too long, Eugénie, hasn't it? The last time—where did we last meet?" He looked at me and laughed. Lights danced in his eyes as he remembered our last meeting and found it funny. "Josephine, Josephine, you must meet Eugénie, Julie's sister! I've told you so much about Eugénie—"

"But Julie tells me that Mlle Eugénie prefers to be called Désirée." The slender white figure came closer to Napoleon. Nothing in her mysterious smile showed she recognized me. "It is very good of you to have come, mademoiselle."

"I must talk to you, General," I said quickly. His smile froze. A scene, he undoubtedly thought; my God—a sentimental, childish scene! "I have to talk to you about a very serious matter," I added.

Josephine took his arm. "We can dine now," she said hastily. "Please—dinner."

At the table I sat between the boring Leclerc and the shy Eugène de Beauharnais. Napoleon talked incessantly, addressing his remarks chiefly to Joseph and Leclerc. We had finished our soup before he began his. In Marseilles he rarely talked this much; and when he did, he spoke in short, broken sentences illustrated with dramatic gestures. Now he spoke fluently, very sure of himself and not in the least interested in any other ideas. When he started on "our archenemies, the British—" Paulette groaned, "Oh, no—not that again!" We were told, with all the trimmings, why he had decided against the invasion of the British Isles. He had, he informed us, closely examined the coast around Dunkerque; he had also considered the construction of flat invasion barges which could land in small British fishing harbours; because the larger ports, which were accessible to warships, were too strongly fortified for an invasion landing.

"We've finished our soup; do eat yours, Bonaparte." He ignored Josephine's quiet voice. They called each other *vous,* and she called him Bonaparte, I noticed; probably this use of the surname was customary in aristocratic families. Undoubtedly in the old days she had addressed Count de Beauharnais as *vous.*

"But by air—" Napoleon spoke loudly, leaning forward and staring at General Leclerc opposite him. "Imagine, General Leclerc—one battalion after another transported by air across the Channel and these troops occupying strategic points in England! Troops equipped with very light artillery!"

Leclerc's mouth, open to contradict him, snapped shut.

"Don't drink so much—or so rashly, my boy." Mme Letizia's deep voice echoed through the room. Napoleon put down his wine glass at once and began to eat. For a few seconds there was silence, interrupted only by the senseless giggles of that half-grown schoolgirl, Caroline.

"It's a shame that your grenadiers can't grow wings," Bacciochi spoke into the silence that made him uncomfortable.

Napoleon ignored him and turned to Joseph: "Perhaps later I'll be able to organize an attack by air. A few inventors have shown me their designs; huge balloons, constructed to carry three or four men and remain in the air for hours. Very interesting, fantastic possibilities—"

He had finally finished his soup. Josephine rang the bell.

While we were eating chicken with asparagus sauce Napoleon explained to the girls, Caroline and Hortense, what pyramids are. The rest of us were informed that from his Egyptian base he intended not only to destroy England's colonial power but to liberate Egypt.

"My first order of the day to the troops—" *Bang!* His chair had toppled over, he had jumped up, run out of the room and returned immediately with a closely written sheet of paper.

"Here—you must hear this: 'Soldiers—forty centuries are gazing down upon you—'" He broke off and said, "You see, that's the age of the pyramids, and I intend to issue this order of the day in the shadow of the pyramids. . . . Well, listen, the order continues: 'The people here are Mohammedans! The creed of this people is, "God is God, and Mohammed is his Prophet—" ' "

"Mohammedans call God 'Allah,' " Elisa interrupted; for in Paris she had begun to read many books, and she was proud of her knowledge. Napoleon frowned and flicked his hand as though he were removing a fly.

"I'll look into that. But here is the important part: 'Don't argue with this creed. Treat them'—I mean the Egyptian people—'as you have treated Jews and Italians. Show their Muftis and Imams as much respect as you have shown to priests and rabbis—' " Napoleon paused and looked at each of us, one after the other. "Well, and—? "

"It's lucky for the Egyptians that the laws of the Republic force you to liberate them, in the name of the Rights of Man," said Joseph meaningly.

"What do you mean by that?"

"That your order of the day is based on the Rights of Man. And you did not invent them," Joseph declared. His face was expressionless. For the first time in years I recalled what I had realized so long ago in Marseilles: Joseph hates his brother.

"You have written it very well, my boy," Mme Letizia said soothingly.

"Please finish your dinner, Bonaparte; we are expecting guests after dinner," Josephine said. Napoleon obediently began to shovel in the good food. I happened to glance at Hortense. The child— no, at fourteen one is no longer a child, my own experience has taught me that—well, this squarely built young girl, who does not in the least resemble her charming mother, was listening to Napoleon; and her protruding, watery blue eyes were enthralled. Small red patches had appeared on Hortense's cheeks. It can't be, I thought, but Hortense is in love with her stepfather. It wasn't funny, it was sad and awful.

"Mama wants to drink your health," Eugène de Beauharnais interrupted my thoughts. I reached for my glass. Josephine smiled at me very slowly; she raised her glass to her lips; and as she put it down again, she winked at me. So Josephine remembered. . . .

With a "Coffee in the drawing room," Josephine rose. In the next room several guests were already waiting to wish Napoleon a successful journey. It seemed as though everyone who used to call on Mme Tallien now crowded into Josephine's small house in the rue de la Victoire. I saw a great many uniforms and managed to avoid my former suitors, Junot and Marmont, who were laughingly assuring the ladies that in Egypt they intended to have their hair cut short.

"We'll look like Roman heroes—and not have any lice," they told the ladies. "Incidentally—one of your son's ideas, madame," said a very smart officer with dark curly hair, sparkling eyes and a flat nose, to Mme Letizia.

"I don't doubt it, General Murat; my son has many queer ideas." Mme Letizia smiled. She seemed to like this young officer. He was bedecked in gold braid and wore a blue tunic and trousers embroidered in gold. Mme Letizia has a weakness for bright tropical colours.

An honour guest apparently arrived, because Josephine drove three young people from the sofa. And whom did she seat on the sofa? Barras, Director of the French Republic, in gold-embroidered lilac, and holding his lorgnon to his eye. Napoleon and Joseph immediately sat down on either side of him; and a thin man, whose pointed nose I had seen somewhere, stood behind them, leaning well forward. I remembered: He was one of the two gentlemen I had seen in the bay of the window at Mme Tallien's—Fouché, I think, was his name.

Eugène—small drops of perspiration glistening on his forehead—felt responsible for seating the many guests. He steered fat Elisa and me to two chairs which he placed directly opposite the sofa on which Barras was enthroned. Then Eugène moved up a gilded chair and asked Police Director Fouché to be seated. But when we were joined by an elegant young man with a slight limp, and hair powdered in the old-fashioned manner, Fouché jumped up quickly.

"Dear Talleyrand—do join us!"

The gentlemen were discussing our ambassador in Vienna, who is on his way home. Something very exciting had apparently happened in Vienna. I gathered from the conversation that on some Austrian national holiday our ambassador had hoisted our French Republican flag; and that the Viennese had stormed the Embassy and had tried to pull it down. I never have a chance to see the newspapers because Joseph takes them to his study as soon as they are delivered.

"You should not have appointed a general as ambassador in Vienna, Minister Talleyrand, but a professional diplomat," Joseph was saying.

Talleyrand raised his eyebrows and smiled. "Our Republic has not yet a sufficient number of professional diplomats, M. Bonaparte. We must do the best we can. You yourself helped us out in Italy, did you not?"

That did it. Joseph was merely a "substitute diplomat" in the opinion of this Minister Talleyrand, who seemed to be in charge of our foreign affairs.

"And besides—" this was Barras' nasal voice—"besides, this Bernadotte is one of the most able men at our disposal, don't you agree, General Bonaparte? I remember that when you were in urgent need of reinforcements in Italy, the Minister of War ordered Bernadotte to join you with the best division in the Rhine Army. With a whole division, during the worst part of the winter, this man crossed the Alps in ten hours—ascent, six hours; descent, four hours. If I correctly recall the letter you sent us at the time, General, you were profoundly impressed."

"The man's undoubtedly an outstanding general, but—" Joseph shrugged—"diplomat? Or politician?"

"I believe that it was right to raise the Republican flag in Vienna. Why should the French Embassy not do so when all the other embassies were?" Talleyrand spoke thoughtfully. "And after this infringement of our extraterritorial rights, this offence against our Embassy, General Bernadotte left Vienna at once. But I think that an apology from the Austrian Government will reach Paris before he does."

Talleyrand studied the polished fingernails of his extraordinarily narrow hands. "At any rate," he concluded, "we could not have found a better man to send to Vienna."

An almost imperceptible smile passed over Barras' swarthy face and slightly blurred features. "A man of vision—with political foresight as well." The Director dropped his lorgnon and looked with naked eyes at Napoleon. Napoleon's lips had narrowed, the vein was beating at his temple. "A convinced Republican," Barras continued, "who is determined to destroy enemies of the Republic either at home or abroad."

"And his next appointment?" That from Joseph, whose jealousy of the Ambassador in Vienna had caused him to lose his self-control.

The lorgnon was glittering once more. "The Republic needs reliable men. And I can imagine why a man who began his military career as a simple recruit enjoys the confidence of the Army. And as this man has also justified the Government's confidence, it would be only natural. . . ."

"Our future Minister of War!" Pointed Nose, Police Director Fouché, had spoken.

Barras adjusted his lorgnon and considered with interest Thérèse Tallien's Venetian lace chemise—heaven knows it was only a chemise —which had appeared before us. "Our beautiful Thérèse." He smiled as he rose heavily.

But Thérèse restrained him. "Do stay, Director. And here is our Italian hero. . . . A delightful afternoon, General Bonaparte. Josephine looks charming—and what is this I hear? You are taking little Eugène to the Pyramids as Adjutant? May I present Ouvrard to you; he is the man who supplied your Italian Army with ten thousand pairs of boots. . . . Ouvrard, here he is in person—'the strong man of France'!" The round little man following in her wake bowed down almost to the floor.

Elisa nudged me. "Her latest friend! Army Contractor Ouvrard. She's been living with Barras again until recently. She gave him up for a time to Josephine, you know; but at present the old fool Barras prefers fifteen-year-olds—it's so unrefined, I think; his hair is dyed, of course; no one has natural hair that black—"

I suddenly felt that I could not stand another minute of the sweating, sweetly scented Elisa. I jumped up, walked quickly to the door and looked for a mirror in the hall where I could powder my nose. The hall was almost dark. Before I got as far as the candles flickering before the tall mirror, I jumped back in surprise. Two people who had been pressed close together in a corner sprang apart. I saw a shimmering white dress.

"Oh— I beg your pardon." I spoke involuntarily.

The white figure stepped swiftly forward into the candlelight. "But why?" Josephine casually tidied her childlike curls. "May I present to you M. Charles. Hippolyte, this is my brother-in-law Joseph's charming sister-in-law—we are both his sisters-in-law, so we are related, are we not, Mlle Désirée?"

A very young man, no more than twenty-five, bowed gracefully before me. "This is M. Hippolyte Charles," Josephine said, "one of our youngest and most successful . . . What do you do, Hippolyte? . . . Yes, of course, one of our most successful army contractors—"

Josephine laughed softly, and obviously considered the whole episode a great joke. "Mlle Désirée is one of my former rivals, Hippolyte," she added.

"A victorious or defeated rival?" M. Charles immediately asked.

There wasn't time to answer; spurs jingled and Napoleon shouted, "Josephine—Josephine, where are you hiding? Our guests are asking for you."

"I was just showing Mlle Désirée and M. Charles the Venetian mirror you presented to me in Montebello, Bonaparte." Josephine was unperturbed. She took Napoleon's arm and guided him toward M. Charles.

"I want you to meet one of our young army contractors. . . . And now, M. Charles, you shall have the wish of your heart. You may shake hands with Italy's liberator." Josephine's laugh was charming and quickly dissipated Napoleon's irritation.

"You wanted to talk to me, Eugé—Désirée?" Napoleon turned to me.

Josephine put her hand on Hippolyte Charles' arm. "Come with me—I must look after my other guests."

We stood opposite each other, alone in the flickering candlelight. I began to rummage in my handbag. Napoleon had stepped over to the mirror and was staring at his reflection. In this light, deep shadows ringed his eyes, and his thin cheeks were hollow.

"You heard what Barras said?" he asked abruptly. He was so

absorbed in his thoughts that he couldn't have noticed that he had called me *tu,* as he had when we were such great friends.

"Yes, I heard him; but I didn't understand," I said. "I don't know anything about politics."

He kept staring into the mirror. " 'Enemies of the Republic inside France.' Lovely expression. He meant me. For he is quite aware that today I could—" He stopped studying the twitching shadows in the mirror and gnawed his underlip. "We generals saved the Republic. And we generals hold it together. We might suddenly wish to form our own Government. They beheaded the King. Since his death the kingly crown has been in disrepute, like something tossed in the gutter. One need only bend down and pick it up."

He spoke as in a dream. And again I felt as I had near the hedge in our garden: first frightened, and then with a childish desire to laugh away this fear. He turned abruptly; his voice was sharp: "But I am going to Egypt. Let the directors go on quarreling with political parties, and selling out to army contractors, suffocating France in worthless assignats. I am going to Egypt, where I shall raise the flag of the Republic . . ."

"Forgive me for interrupting you, General," I said. "I have written down a lady's name for you, and will you please see that she is provided for."

He took the slip of paper out of my hand and moved closer to the candlesticks. "Marie Meunier—who is that?"

"The woman who had been living with General Duphot; the mother of his son. I promised Duphot that they would both be cared for."

Napoleon dropped the hand holding the slip of paper. His voice was gentle and pitying. "I was sorry, very sorry. You were engaged to Duphot, Désirée?"

I wanted to scream at him, to tell him once and for all that I'd had enough of this wretched comedy. "You know quite well that I hardly knew Duphot." I spoke hoarsely. "I don't know why you torment me, General."

"How, little Désirée?"

"With these offers of marriage! I've had enough of it; I want peace."

"Believe me, only in marriage can a woman find the real meaning of her life," Napoleon said unctuously.

"I—I should like to throw these candlesticks at your head," I burst out, digging my fingernails into my palms to keep from snatching the candlesticks. He came to me and smiled. That irresistible smile which had once meant heaven and earth and hell to me!

"We are friends, aren't we, Bernardine Eugénie Désirée?" he asked.

"Promise me that this Marie Meunier will be given a widow's pension? And the child an orphan's allowance?"

"Oh, there you are, Désirée—get ready, we must be going." It was Julie, who had come in with Joseph. They both stopped in surprise when they saw Napoleon and me. We stood stiffly opposite each other but then suddenly smiled.

"Do you promise, General?" I repeated.

"I promise, Mlle Désirée." Casually he lifted my hand to his lips. Then Joseph stepped between us and with many pats on the shoulder took leave of his brother.

Paris, four weeks later

The happiest day of my life began like all other days in Paris. After breakfast I took the small green watering can to water both dusty palms which Julie brought from Italy in two pots and keeps in the dining room. Joseph and Julie sat across from each other at breakfast; Joseph was reading a letter, and I only half-listened to what he said.

"There, you see, Julie—he has accepted my invitation!"

"For heaven's sake, we've made no preparation—and whom else do you want to invite? Shall we try to get spring chickens? And as a first course, trout in mayonnaise? Though trout is frightfully dear at the moment. You should have given me warning, Joseph!"

"I wasn't sure whether he'd come. He's only been back in Paris a few days and he is overwhelmed with invitations. Everyone wants to hear right from him what actually happened in Vienna."

I left the room to refill the watering can. The dusty palms need a lot of water. When I returned, Joseph was saying, ". . . wrote to him that my honoured friend, Director Barras, and my brother Napoleon had told me so many splendid things about him that I should be most happy to welcome him in my own home for a modest meal."

"Strawberries with Madeira sauce for dessert," Julie considered out loud.

"And he accepted! Do you know what that means? A personal contact with France's future Minister of War established, Napoleon's express wish fulfilled. Barras makes no secret of the fact that he will entrust him with the Ministry of War. With old Scherer, Napoleon could do what he liked; but we don't know about this new one. Julie, the meal must be especially good and . . ."

"Whom else shall we ask?"

I took the bowl with the early roses from the centre of the dining room table and carried it out to the kitchen to change the water. When I came back Joseph was saying, "An intimate little family dinner party—that will be best! Then Lucien and I can talk to him undisturbed. So—Josephine, Lucien and Christine, you and I." He looked at me. "Yes, and of course the child. Make yourself beautiful; tonight you will meet the future War Minister of France."

How they bore me, these "intimate family dinner parties" which Joseph loves giving for some deputy, general or ambassador. "Family dinners" arranged only so that Joseph can learn some behind-the-scenes political secrets and pass them on in long letters sent by special couriers across the seas to Napoleon, who is on his way to Egypt. So far Joseph has not accepted or been offered a new post as ambassador. He apparently prefers to live in Paris, "focus of political interests"; and since the last elections he has been a Corsican deputy; for Napoleon's victories have made the island, naturally, terribly proud of the Bonapartes.

Independent of Joseph, Lucien was a candidate for Corsica in the elections; and he, too, was elected to the Council of the Five Hundred. A few days ago, shortly after Napoleon's departure, he and his Christine moved to Paris. Mme Letizia found them a place to live and they manage to get along somehow on Lucien's small salary as a deputy. Lucien belongs to the extreme Left. When he was told that Napoleon expected him to divorce the innkeeper's daughter, Lucien was convulsed. "My military brother seems to have gone mad! What doesn't he like about my Christine?"

"Her father's inn," Joseph tried to explain.

"Well, our mama's father has a peasant's farm on Corsica," Lucien laughed, "and it's a small farm at that."

But Lucien suddenly frowned, stared at Joseph and said, "Napoleon has some very remarkable ideas, for a Republican."

Lucien's speeches are printed in the newspapers almost every day. This young man, thin, with dark-blond hair, and blue eyes that sparkle when he gets excited, is a talented public speaker. I don't know whether or not Lucien enjoys Joseph's "intimate family dinners" at which everyone tries to make so-called useful contacts; perhaps he comes only so as not to hurt Julie's and Joseph's feelings.

While I was putting on my yellow silk dress, Julie slipped into my room. After her usual "If only everything will go well," she sat down on my bed. "Do tie the brocade ribbon in your hair, it's so becoming," she suggested.

"I'll ruin it—and anyway no one is coming who could possibly interest me," I said, rummaging in my ribbon-and-comb box.

"Joseph heard that this future War Minister has said that Napoleon's Egyptian campaign is pure madness and that the Government shouldn't have allowed him to go," Julie said.

I was in a bad humour and finally decided not to wear any ribbon in my hair but just to sweep my curls up and try to keep them there with two combs. "These political dinners bore me beyond belief," I grumbled.

"Josephine didn't want to come at first," Julie said. "Joseph had to give her a long explanation about how important it is for Napoleon to stand in well with this coming man. She recently bought that country house, Malmaison, you know, and she had planned to drive out there with some friends for a picnic."

"She's right," I answered. "The weather is so glorious." I looked out of the window at the pale blue evening. Through the open window wafted the fragrance of lime blossoms. I began positively to hate this unknown guest of honour. We heard a carriage drive up to the door, and with a last "If only it goes well," Julie hurried off.

I didn't feel in the least like going down to greet the guests. And I didn't, until the babble of voices was very loud and I felt that everyone had arrived and that Julie was probably waiting for me before having dinner announced.

It occurred to me that I might go to bed and say I had a headache, but I was already at the drawing room door. The very next moment I would have given anything in the world if I actually had gone to bed with a headache.

He stood with his back to the door; nevertheless, I recognized him at once—a tower of a man in a dark-blue uniform with vast gold epaulettes and a broad sash in the Republican colours. The others— Joseph and Julie and Josephine and Lucien and his Christine—stood in a semicircle around him, toying with small glasses. It was not my fault that I remained paralyzed at the door, staring horrified at that broad-shouldered back. But the semicircle found my behaviour peculiar. Joseph stared at me over his guest's shoulder, the others followed his glance, and finally the huge tall man realized that something unusual was going on behind his back.

He stopped talking and turned around.

His eyes went wide with astonishment. I could hardly breathe, my heart beat so hard. "Désirée—come along, we're waiting for you," Julie said.

At the same time Joseph came over, took my arm and said, "And this is my wife's little sister, General Bernadotte; my sister-in-law, Mlle Désirée Clary."

I couldn't look at him. I concentrated on one of his gold buttons, was aware as in a dream that he kissed my hand, and then heard Joseph say, from somewhere far away, "We were interrupted, dear General. You were saying that . . ."

"I—I've quite forgotten what I was saying."

Among a thousand voices, I would have known his. It was the voice of the rain-drenched bridge, the voice in the dark corner of the carriage, the voice at the door of the house in the rue du Bac.

"Please come to dinner," Julie said; but General Bernadotte didn't budge. "Please come to dinner," Julie repeated, going over to him. At last he offered her his arm; Joseph and Josephine, Lucien, his chubby Christine and I followed.

This "intimate family dinner party" given for political reasons was different—oh, so different from what Joseph had expected. Joseph had planned for General Bernadotte to sit between his hostess and Gen. Napoleon Bonaparte's wife. Lucien was on Josephine's other side so that he himself would be opposite General Bernadotte. Joseph thought this arrangement would enable him to direct the conversation successfully.

But General Bernadotte seemed a trifle absent-minded. He busied himself mechanically with the terrifically expensive trout, and Joseph had to raise his glass twice before the General noticed. I could see that he was working on some problem. I suppose he was trying to remember what he had been told that evening in the Tallien's drawing room: "Napoleon has a fiancée in Marseilles, a young girl with a large dowry. His brother is married to this girl's sister. Napoleon is leaving this girl, and the dowry, in the lurch—"

Joseph had to remind General Bernadotte three times before he realized that we were waiting to drink to our guest of honour. Hastily he raised his glass. Then he seemed to remember his dinner partner and his duties as a guest. He turned to Julie abruptly: "Has your sister been living in Paris very long?"

The question was so unexpected that it startled Julie, and she didn't understand it.

"You are both from Marseilles, aren't you. I know that, but has your sister been in Paris long?" he persisted.

Julie pulled herself together. "No, she's been here only a few months. It's the first time she's ever been in Paris. And you like it here very much, don't you, Désirée?"

"Paris is a lovely city," I recited, stiff as a schoolgirl.

"Yes, when it's not raining," he said, and his eyes narrowed.

"Oh—even in the rain." Christine, the innkeeper's daughter from St. Maximin, spoke eagerly. "Paris is a fairy-tale city, I think."

"You are right, madame. Fairy tales can happen even in the rain," he replied seriously.

Joseph was getting restless. He hadn't written those persuasive letters—in an effort to secure the presence of the future Minister of War in his home—merely to discuss the weather and its influence on fairy tales.

"Yesterday I had a letter from my brother Napoleon," Joseph said meaningfully. But it seemed that Bernadotte was not at all interested. "My brother writes that his journey is progressing according to plan and that so far he has not seen the British Fleet under Nelson."

"Then your brother has good luck," Bernadotte said goodnaturedly and raised his glass to Joseph. "To the good health of General Bonaparte. I am greatly indebted to him."

Joseph didn't know whether to be offended or pleased. But there was no doubt that Bernadotte considered his rank quite equal to Napoleon's. True, Napoleon had been given a supreme command in Italy; but Bernadotte in the meantime, had been an Ambassador; and he knew he was to get the Ministry of War.

It happened while we were eating the spring chickens. Josephine —yes, oddly enough it was Josephine, Napoleon's wife, who precipitated it. For some time I'd noticed that she was looking curiously from me to General Bernadotte and back to me. I don't suppose anyone is more aware than Josephine of the feeling of tension and the subtle vibrations between a man and a woman. So far she hadn't said much. But at Julie's, "It's her first visit to Paris," Josephine raised her thin plucked eyebrows and glanced at Bernadotte with interest. It is possible, very possible, that she recalled seeing Bernadotte at the Tallien's that afternoon. And at last she had an excuse to put an end to Joseph's military-political talk and to introduce a subject which interested her more. She bent her childlike curly head slightly to one side, twinkled at Bernadotte and asked, "It can't have been easy for you as an Ambassador in Vienna. I mean because you are unmarried, General Bernadotte. Did you not often miss the presence of a lady at the Embassy?"

Bernadotte firmly put down his knife and fork. "How right you are, dear Josephine—and I may call you Josephine, may I not, as I did in the old days at your friend Mme Tallien's? And I cannot tell you how unhappy I've been not to be married. But—" he turned to

126

the others at the table—"but I ask you, ladies and gentlemen, what am I to do?"

No one knew whether he was joking or in earnest. Everyone was ill at ease and remained silent until Julie finally said, with forced politeness, "I suppose you haven't found the right lady yet, General."

"But yes, madame, I have found her. But she simply vanished and now—" He shrugged his shoulders in a comic gesture of embarrassment and looked at me. His whole face was gay with laughter.

"And now you must look for her and ask her to marry you," cried Christine. She was enjoying the conversation and didn't think it at all odd. At home in the taproom at St. Maximin the young men, drinking their glass of wine, had always talked about their love affairs.

"You are quite right, madame," Bernadotte said seriously. "I shall ask her to marry me!"

With that he jumped up, pushed back his chair and spoke to Joseph. "M. Joseph Bonaparte, I have the honour to ask for the hand of your sister-in-law, Mlle Désirée Clary."

He sat down again, calmly, and continued to look steadily at Joseph.

Deathly silence. A clock ticked and I was sure they could also hear my heart pounding. I stared at the white tablecloth in despair.

"I don't quite understand, General Bernadotte. . . . Are you serious?" I heard Joseph ask.

"Very serious."

Deathly silence again.

"I—think you must give Désirée time to consider your honourable offer," Joseph said.

"I have given her time, M. Bonaparte."

"But you've only met her for the first time!" Julie's voice trembled with excitement.

I raised my head. "I should be very happy to marry you, General Bernadotte."

Was that my voice? A chair crashed over backward as someone jumped up in surprise. All these astonished faces—I simply couldn't stand it. I don't know how I got out of the dining room, but suddenly I was upstairs on my bed and weeping.

Then the door opened and Julie came in and held me close and tried to soothe me. "You don't have to marry him unless you want to, dear. Don't cry, don't cry—"

"But I can't help crying," I sobbed, "I can't help it; I'm so terribly happy that I have to cry."

Though I washed my face in cold water and powdered profusely, Bernadotte said at once, when I reappeared in the drawing room, "I see you have been crying again, Mlle Désirée!"

He was sitting next to Josephine on a small sofa; but Josephine got right up and said, "Désirée must sit next to Jean-Baptiste."

So I sat next to him, and they all began to talk quickly to cover their embarrassment. Joseph had brought the champagne we had not drunk at the table into the drawing room, and Julie gave us each a small plate.

"We forgot the dessert," she said. So the strawberries with Madeira sauce were served and helped us through these awkward moments. Afterward, Bernadotte, who was not in the least disconcerted but in exuberant spirits, asked Julie politely, "Madame, would you object if I invited your sister for a little drive?"

Julie nodded understandingly. "Of course not, dear General. When? Tomorrow afternoon?"

"No, I thought—right now," Bernadotte said.

"But it's already dark!" Julie was horrified; it wasn't considered proper for a young girl to drive with a gentleman late in the evening.

I rose firmly. "Only a short drive, Julie," I said. "We'll be back soon." With that I ran out of the room so quickly that Bernadotte hardly had a chance to make his farewells to the others.

His carriage stood outside the house. It was open, and we drove through the fragrance of lime blossoms and the dark blue spring evening. But as we approached the centre of the city, the lights of Paris were so bright that we could no longer see the stars. So far we hadn't said a word to each other. As we drove along beside the Seine, Bernadotte called out to the coachman. The carriage stopped at a bridge.

"This is the bridge," Bernadotte said; and we walked close together to the centre, where we leaned over the parapet and watched the lights of Paris dancing on the water.

"I called at the rue du Bac several times and asked about you, in the rear building; but no one would give me any information."

I nodded. "They knew that I had come to Paris secretly."

When we walked back to the carriage he put his arm around my shoulder. My head reached just to his epaulettes.

"You said that you were too small for me," he said.

"Yes, and I've grown smaller, for at that time I was still wearing high heels. But they aren't fashionable now. Perhaps it doesn't matter."

"What doesn't matter?"

"That I'm so small."

"No, not at all. On the contrary."

"Why on the contrary?"

"I like you the way you are."

On the drive home he put his arm around me. I pressed my cheek against his shoulder, but the gold wire epaulettes scratched my face. "These horrible gold things bother me," I murmured.

He laughed softly. "I know you can't bear generals."

It suddenly occurred to me that he is the fifth general who has asked me to marry him: Napoleon, Junot, Marmont, Duphot—I pushed the thought aside and went on happily scratching my cheek on the epaulettes of a general named Bernadotte.

When we returned to the drawing room, the other guests had already gone. Julie and Joseph greeted us. "I hope we shall see you here often, General," Joseph said.

I began, "Every day, won't we—" and paused. Then, for the first time, I said, "Won't we—Jean-Baptiste?"

"We have decided to be married very soon, if you approve," Bernadotte told Joseph—though actually we hadn't discussed the wedding at all. But I want to marry him very, very soon.

"Tomorrow I'll begin looking for a nice little house; and as soon as I find one that Désirée and I like, we'll be married."

Like a beloved, far-off melody the memory sang in my heart, "I have saved part of my pay for years; I can buy a little house for you and the child—"

"I'll write Mama tonight. Good night, General Bernadotte," I heard Julie saying. And Joseph—"Good night, dear brother-in-law! My brother Napoleon will be delighted with this news."

As soon as Joseph was alone with Julie and me he said, "I can't understand it at all. Bernadotte isn't a man who makes rash decisions."

"Isn't he too old for Désirée? He is at least . . ."

"Middle thirties, I should say," said Joseph to Julie. And to me —"Tell me, Désirée, do you realize that you are marrying one of the most distinguished men in the Republic . . ."

"The trousseau—" Julie interrupted. "If Désirée really is to be married soon, we must begin to worry about the trousseau!"

"This Bernadotte must have no occasion to say that the trousseau of a sister-in-law of a Bonaparte is not perfect," Joseph insisted. "How long will it take you to have everything ready?"

"We can buy everything quickly," Julie said, "but embroidering the monograms takes time."

For the first time, I joined this lively conversation. "The trousseau is ready in Marseilles. We need only have the boxes sent here. And I finished the monograms ages ago."

"Yes, yes, of course," Julie said, her eyes open wide with surprise. "Yes, Désirée is right—the monograms are done. B—"

"B, B, and again B." I smiled and went to the door.

"The whole affair strikes me as very peculiar," Joseph muttered suspiciously.

"If she'll only be happy," Julie whispered.

I am happy. Dear Lord in Heaven, dear lime trees outside along the road, dear roses here in the blue vase—I am so *completely* happy.

Part Two

MARSHAL BERNADOTTE'S LADY

Sceaux, near Paris, autumn of
Year VI (1798)

I married General Jean-Baptiste Bernadotte on the thirteenth of
Thermidor in the sixth year of the Republic at seven o'clock in the
evening, at the registry office in the Parisian suburb of Sceaux. My
husband's witnesses were his friend, Captain of Cavalry Antoine
Morien, and M. Francois Desranges, Notary of Sceaux. I had my
uncle Somis, without whom no family wedding could ever seem quite
complete, and of course Joseph. At the last moment Lucien Bonaparte also appeared at the registry office, so I marched up with three
witnesses.

After the ceremony we all drove to the rue du Rocher where Julie
had prepared a veritable banquet. (Everything went off well, but
Julie had worried so about it she hadn't slept for three nights.) So
as not to hurt anyone's feelings, Joseph had rounded up every last
Bonaparte living in Paris or anywhere near. Mme Letizia kept saying
how disappointed she was that her step-brother Fesch, who has returned to his church, couldn't be there. Mama originally hoped to
come up from Genoa, but she has been sick and decided the journey
in the summer heat would be too strenuous. Jean-Baptiste hates
family gatherings, and since he has no relatives in Paris anyway, he
asked only his old comrade Morien.

My wedding was, therefore, completely dominated by Bonapartes.
My easygoing, countrified uncle Somis could hardly be expected to
compete with them. To my surprise, Joseph also invited General

Junot and his Laura—at Napoleon's request Junot recently married Laura Permon, the daughter of a Corsican friend of Mme Letizia. Junot is attached to Napoleon's staff in Egypt and was in Paris only to report to the Government on Napoleon's entry into Alexandria and Cairo and on his victorious Battle of the Pyramids.

I was frightfully bored at my wedding. Our dinner party began very late because it's now fashionable to be married in the evening, and so Joseph decided that we shouldn't go to the registry office until seven o'clock. Julie wanted me to stay in bed all day to look as rested and pretty as possible. Naturally, I had no time for that; I had to help Marie arrange our new dishes in the kitchen cupboard. And there are many other things to do to get the house ready.

Two days after Jean-Baptiste and I became engaged—Julie still hadn't recovered from the shock—the General arrived with the news that he had found a suitable house. "Désirée," he urged, "come look at it right away."

Our little house is in the rue de la Lune in Sceaux. Number three. On the ground floor we have a kitchen, a dining room, and a small room in which Jean-Baptiste has his desk and his books. Every day he brings more books; and we call this little room "the study."

On the floor above there's a beautiful bedroom with a tiny dressing room. Jean-Baptiste had the attic rebuilt into two small bedrooms for Marie and Fernand. Of course I brought my Marie and Jean-Baptiste his Fernand.

Mama wanted to take Marie with her to Genoa, but Marie refused to go. She said nothing about her plans for the future, but rented a single room in Marseilles and supported herself by cooking on special occasions for people who were proud to employ "Mme Clary's former cook." Though Marie never said so in her letters, I knew that she was waiting in Marseilles. The day after my engagement I wrote her a short note: "I am engaged to the General B. of the Bridge, the one I told you about. We'll be married as soon as he finds a suitable house. If I know him, he will find this house within twenty-four hours. When can you come to me?" I got no answer to this letter. A week later Marie was in Paris.

"How do you think your Marie and my Fernand will get on together?" Jean-Baptiste asked.

"Who is your Fernand?" I asked uneasily.

It seems that Fernand comes from Pau, Jean-Baptiste's home town in Gascony, that they were schoolmates, and then joined the Army at the same time. Jean-Baptiste got one promotion after another, but Fernand was always on the verge of being thrown out altogether. Fernand is small and fat; and whenever he had to march, his feet hurt; and every time an attack was ordered, Fernand had a stomach-ache. So of course he couldn't do anything and it was all very unpleasant for him. Nevertheless, he wanted to remain a soldier to be near Jean-Baptiste. He has a passion for polishing boots and can get the worst grease spots off a uniform, like magic. Two years ago Fernand was honourably discharged from the Army and now devotes his full time to the boots, grease spots and every last wish of Jean-Baptiste.

"I am my General's valet and former schoolmate," he said when he was presented to me.

Fernand and Marie immediately began to quarrel. Marie claimed that Fernand stole food from the pantry, while Fernand accused Marie of taking his shoe brushes—he has twenty-four of them—and the General's laundry, which she had decided to wash without asking him.

The first time I saw our little house I said to Jean-Baptiste, "I must write Etienne to send you my dowry right away."

Jean-Baptiste's nostrils quivered in contempt. "What do you take me for? Do you think I would furnish my home with my bride's money?"

"But Joseph used Julie's dowry—" I began.

"Please don't compare me with the Bonapartes," he said sharply. But then he put his arm lovingly around me and laughed. "Little girl, little girl—today Bernadotte can afford to buy you only a doll's house in Sceaux! But if you crave a castle, well . . ."

I quickly exclaimed, "Oh, please—not that! Promise me that we'll never have to live in a castle."

With horror I recalled the long months in those Italian palaces, and also that Bernadotte was called "the coming man." His gold epaulettes glittered dangerously.

"Promise me: never a castle!" I implored.

He looked at me. "We belong together, Désirée," he said and he was no longer smiling. "In Vienna I lived in a palace of sorts. Tomorrow I could be at the front, camping in the open. Day after tomorrow my headquarters may be in a castle and I would, of course, ask you to join me. Would you refuse?"

We were standing under the big chestnut tree in our future garden. We would be married soon, and then I would try to be a good housewife; to make the house attractive, the rooms tidy, and keep it neat. I wanted to belong here—in this tiny house, in this garden with the old chestnut tree and the neglected flowerbeds. But now the picture was spoiled by memories of ghostly, high-ceilinged halls, spurs clanking on marble tiles, and lackeys in everyone's way.

"Would you refuse?" Jean-Baptiste repeated.

"We will be very happy here," I whispered.

"Would you refuse?" he persisted.

I put my cheek on his shoulder; by this time I was used to the gold epaulettes scratching my face. "I will never refuse," I said, "but I would not be happy."

On the morning of my wedding day, Marie and I were kneeling in front of the kitchen cupboards, putting away the white china, decorated with tiny flowers, that Jean-Baptiste and I had picked out together. Marie asked, "Are you excited, Eugénie?"

A few hours later, while Julie's maid was curling my unruly hair with an iron, in an effort to arrange it in Josephine-ringlets, Julie said, "I think it's funny that you don't seem a bit excited."

I shook my head. Excited? Since that wretched moment in the dark carriage, when Jean-Baptiste's hand embodied all the warmth in my life, I should have known that I belonged to him. In a few hours I would sign a piece of paper at the Sceaux Registry Office and thereby confirm what seems so right. No, I was not excited in the least.

The ceremony was followed by the dinner party at Julie's at which I was so bored.

Except for a toast to the bridal couple, launched by my perspiring uncle Somis, and a passionate outburst from our orator, Lucien Bonaparte, in honour of two children of the Revolution—he meant Jean-Baptiste and me—the conversation was chiefly about Napoleon's

Egyptian campaign. Joseph was determined to convince my poor Jean-Baptiste, who already is sick of the subject, that the conquest of Egypt is fresh proof of Napoleon's genius. And Lucien, who envisions his brother Napoleon proclaiming the Rights of Man all over the world, supported Joseph.

"I think it's impossible," Jean-Baptiste said, "for us to hold Egypt for long. The English also believe we can't, and that's why they refuse to involve themselves in our colonial war."

"But Napoleon has already conquered Alexandria and Cairo," Joseph insisted, "and won the Battle of the Pyramids."

"That doesn't worry the English particularly. After all, Egypt is under Turkish rule. The English consider our troops on the Nile a temporary danger."

"The enemy casualties were twenty thousand in the Battle of the Pyramids; ours less than fifty. Magnificent," Joseph declared.

Jean-Baptiste shrugged his shoulders. "Magnificent? The glorious French Army, commanded by their brilliant General Bonaparte and equipped with modern heavy artillery, killed twenty thousand half-naked Africans, who didn't even have shoes on their feet. I would call it a magnificent victory of cannon over spears and bows and arrows!"

Lucien opened his mouth to contradict, but changed his mind. His blue, childishly radiant eyes clouded. "Perished in the name of the Rights of Man," said he, finally.

"The end justifies the means. Napoleon will drive deeper into Africa and drive the English from the Mediterranean," Joseph declared.

"The English have no idea of fighting us on land. Why should they? After all, they have their fleet; and not even you will deny that the English fleet is far superior to ours. And as soon as they have destroyed our ships which carried Bonaparte's armies to Egypt—" Jean-Baptiste looked around the table. "Don't you see what's in the cards? Every hour, the French Army is in greater danger of being cut off from the Motherland; when this happens, your brother and his—victorious—regiments will be caught in the desert like mice in a trap. This Egyptian campaign is a wild gamble and the stake is too high for our Republic!"

I realized that Joseph and Junot would immediately write Napoleon that my husband had called him a gambler. What I didn't yet know, and what no one in Paris would have believed, was that exactly sixteen days ago the English Fleet, under the command of a certain Admiral Nelson, had attacked the whole French Fleet in the Bay of Aboukir and practically destroyed it. And that General Bonaparte was desperately trying to establish contact with France, while he paced restlessly up and down in front of a tent and realized that he and his troops might die there in the burning desert sand. Surely, on the night of my wedding, no one suspected that Jean-Baptiste Bernadotte had predicted precisely what had already happened.

I yawned for the second time—it's not quite the thing for a bride to do; but, after all, I'd never been married before so how could I know how a bride should behave—anyway, I yawned and Jean-Baptiste got up and said quietly, "It's late, Désirée. We must go home."

It sounded so intimate—"We must go home." 'Way down the table those schoolgirls, Caroline and Hortense, nudged each other and giggled. My jovial uncle Somis winked at me confidentially and patted my cheek when I said good night. "Don't be afraid, my child. Bernadotte won't bite off your head."

We drove to Sceaux in an open carriage through the hot, still, summer night. The stars and a round yellow moon seemed close enough to touch, and it seemed quite appropriate that we lived in the rue de la Lune. When we reached our house, we found the dining room all lighted up. Tall candles shone out from the heavy silver candlesticks Josephine had given us from herself and Napoleon for a wedding present. A gleaming white damask cloth, champagne glasses, a dish of grapes, peaches, and marzipan cakes were on the table; and in the wine cooler, a bottle of champagne. We saw no one, and the house was silent.

"Marie did it," I said delightedly.

But Jean-Baptiste said, "No, it was Fernand."

"But I know Marie's marzipan cakes," I insisted, as one melted in my mouth.

Jean-Baptiste warily examined the champagne botttle. "If we

drink any more tonight," he said, "we'll both have horrible headaches in the morning."

I nodded and opened the door to the garden. In wafted the fragrance of fading roses; sharp-etched chestnut leaves were rimmed with silver. Behind me, Jean-Baptiste blew out the tall candles.

Our bedroom was pitch-dark; but I groped my way to the window, pulled the curtains aside, and let in the silver moonlight. I heard Jean-Baptiste go into the next room and bustle about in there. Probably he wants to give me time to undress and go to bed, I thought, and appreciated his thoughtfulness. I quickly slipped off my dress and went over to the big double bed where my nightgown was laid out on the silk coverlet. I put on the nightgown, slid under the blanket—and shrieked.

"For God's sake, Désirée—what's wrong?" Jean-Baptiste stood beside the bed.

"I don't know, something stabbed me." I moved. "Ouch—there it is again!"

Jean-Baptiste lit a candle, I sat up and threw back the blanket: *Roses!* Roses and more roses—with sharp thorns!

"What idiot—?" exclaimed Jean-Baptiste while we both gaped in astonishment at the bed of roses. I began to collect them; Jean-Baptiste spread out the wide blanket. I kept fishing more roses out of the bed.

"Undoubtedly Fernand," I said. "He wanted to surprise us."

"You're unfair to the lad; it was your Marie, of course," Jean-Baptiste replied immediately. "Roses—I ask you, roses in a soldier's bed!"

The roses I had fished out of the soldier's bed were now strewn on the night table, and their fragrance filled the room. Suddenly I realized that Jean-Baptiste was looking at me and that I had only a nightgown on. I quickly sat down on the bed and said, "I'm cold, give me the blanket." With that he dropped the blanket completely over me. I almost suffocated; but I stuck my nose out, closed my eyes tight, and didn't see him blow out the candle.

Next morning we discovered that Marie and Fernand had finally agreed about something: It was their joint idea, to decorate our

bridal bed with roses; and, in complete accord, they had both forgotten the thorns.

Jean-Baptiste had taken two months' leave so that he could spend
the first few weeks of our marriage with me undisturbed. But the
moment we heard about the destruction of our fleet at Aboukir, he
had to report every morning at the Luxembourg Palace and take part
in the directors' consultations with the Minister of War.

He had rented a stable near our little house and kept two saddle
horses there; and whenever I think now of my honeymoon, I always
see myself, late every afternoon, standing at the garden gate waiting
for Jean-Baptiste. When I heard the distant *clop-clop-clop* of horses'
hooves, my heart beat faster because I knew that any minute Jean-
Baptiste would appear on the good-natured brown horse or the unfriendly sorrel, that I was actually married to him for always—and
not dreaming. . . . Ten minutes later we would sit under the chestnut tree drinking coffee, and Jean-Baptiste would tell me the news
—which wouldn't be published in the *Moniteur* for a day or two—
and other things which, "for God's sake," I "mustn't mention."
And I blinked contentedly at the sinking sun and played with the
big shiny chestnuts that had fallen on the grass.

The defeat at Aboukir was like a signal to the enemies of our
Republic. Russia started arming; and the Austrians, who only a short
time before had apologized to our Government for their insult to
our flag in Vienna—those same Austrians were on the march again.
They were approaching our frontiers from Switzerland and northern
Italy.

The Italian States under French rule, which Napoleon had so
proudly set up, welcomed the Austrians with open arms; and our
generals retreated in a panic.

One afternoon Jean-Baptiste came home unusually late.

"They have given me the supreme command in Italy; I've been
ordered to stop the rout of our troops and at least hold Lombardy,"
he told me as he jumped from his horse.

It was already dark when we finished our coffee. He brought a
candle and a large sheaf of paper into the garden and began to write.

"Will you accept the supreme command?" I asked. A terrible fear lay like a cold hand on my heart.

Jean-Baptiste looked up. "What's that? Will I accept the supreme command in Italy? Yes, if they meet my conditions; I'm listing them now."

His pen raced like a hunted thing over the white paper. Later we went into the house, and Jean-Baptiste went on writing in his study. I put his supper on the desk, but he paid no attention. He wrote and wrote. A few days later I learned by chance from Joseph that Jean-Baptiste had turned over to Barras a plan of action for the Italian Front. First question: How many troops would be necessary to hold this front by maintaining effective garrisons from which they could counterattack?

But the directors couldn't meet Jean-Baptiste's conditions. True, new recruits of various age groups were called up, but there were not enough uniforms or arms to equip them. Jean-Baptiste declared that under these circumstances he must decline to assume the responsibility for the Italian Front; and Scherer, the Minister of War, took over the supreme command himself.

Two weeks later Jean-Baptiste came home at noon. I was helping Marie preserve plums and ran out through the garden to meet him. "Don't kiss me," I warned him, "I smell just like the kitchen. We're making plum jam—so much that you can have it every morning for breakfast all winter."

"But I won't be here to eat your jam," he said calmly and walked toward the house. "Fernand! Fernand—get my field uniform ready, pack the saddlebags as usual. I leave tomorrow morning at seven. You and the luggage at nine—" I heard no more for Jean-Baptiste had disappeared upstairs. I stood paralyzed at the front door.

We spent all afternoon alone in the garden. The sun no longer warmed us, the lawn was covered with dead leaves. Overnight, it was autumn. I folded my hands in my lap and listened to Jean-Baptiste. Occasionally I missed the point of what he was saying, but I heard his voice. At first he spoke to me as though I were a mature human being, and then softly and tenderly as to a child.

"You've always known that I would go to war again, haven't

you? You are married to an officer, you are a sensible young woman. You must pull yourself together and be courageous—"

"I don't want to be courageous," I said.

"Pay attention—Jourdan has assumed the supreme command of three armies: the Danube Army, the so-called Swiss Army, and the Army of Observation. Massena will try, with the Swiss Army, to hold back the enemy at the Swiss frontier; I will command the Army of Observation and march with my troops to the Rhine. I will storm the Rhine at two points: near Fort Louis du Rhin, and near Speyer and Mayence. For the conquest and occupation of the Rhineland and the adjacent German territories, I have asked for thirty thousand men. These have been promised me, but the Government cannot keep this promise. Désirée, I go to cross the Rhine with a sham army, and I must throw back the enemy with it. . . . Are you listening to me, little one?"

"There is nothing you can't do, Jean-Baptiste," I said, and I loved him so much that tears came to my eyes.

He shrugged his shoulders. "The Government, unfortunately, seems to agree with you and will allow me only an inadequate complement of raw recruits to attack the Rhineland."

" 'We generals saved the Republic, we generals will keep it intact,' " I murmured. "Napoleon once said that to me."

"Of course. That's why the Republic pays its generals. There's nothing strange in that."

"The man I bought the plums from this morning was very put out with the Army and the Government. He said, 'As long as General Bonaparte was in Italy, we had one victory after another; and the Austrians were begging for peace. But as soon as he left there and went off, for the glory of our country, to the Pyramids, things went from bad to worse.' It's funny—the impression Napoleon's campaign has made on ordinary people."

"Yes, but it never occurred to the plum dealer that Napoleon's defeat at Aboukir was the signal for our enemies to resume the attack. Nor does the plum dealer realize that although Napoleon won many victories, he never permanently fortified the conquered territory. As a result, we are now obliged to defend the frontiers with ridiculously small forces while Comrade Bonaparte, with his

141

splendidly equipped army, suns himself on the banks of the Nile. And this is 'the strong man.' "

" 'A royal crown lies in the gutter. One need only bend down and pick it up,' " I said.

"Who said that?" Jean-Baptiste shouted.

"Napoleon."

"To you?"

"No, to himself. He was looking at himself in a mirror. I happened to be watching him."

We didn't speak for a long time. It was so dark that I couldn't see Jean-Baptiste's face clearly.

There was a sudden cry of rage from Marie. "No pistols on my kitchen table! Get out—and be quick about it!"

And Fernand, plaintively, "Let me at least clean them here—I'll load them outside."

And Marie, "Out of my kitchen with those firearms, I say!"

"Do you use your pistols in battle?" I asked Jean-Baptiste.

"Very seldom, now that I'm a general," came out of the darkness. Then we got up and went into the house.

It was a long, long night. For many hours I lay alone in our wide bed and counted the hours as the clock struck in our little church in Sceaux. I knew that Jean-Baptiste was downstairs in his study, poring over maps and drawing thin lines and little crosses and tiny circles. Finally I must have dozed off for I suddenly awoke in terror, certain that something terrible had happened. Jean-Baptiste was asleep beside me. But I had awakened him. "Is something wrong?" he murmured.

"I had a terrifying dream," I whispered, "that you were riding off—to war."

"I really am riding off to war tomorrow," he answered. He must have acquired the habit in those long years at the front: Jean-Baptiste can be fast asleep, but he wakes up instantly and completely. "I'd like to discuss something with you," he continued. "I've thought about this several times. . . . Tell me, Désirée—what do you do with yourself all day long?"

"Do with myself? What on earth do you mean? Yesterday I helped Marie with the plums; day before yesterday I went with Julie

142

to see Mme Berthier, the dressmaker. She's the one who fled to England with the aristocrats, but now she's come back. And last week I . . ."

"But what particularly interests you, Désirée?"

"Well, nothing really," I confessed in confusion. He put his arm under my head and drew me closer. It was wonderful to rest my cheek against his shoulder without being scratched by an epaulette.

"Désirée, I don't want the days to seem long for you while I am away, and so I thought you should take some lessons."

"Lessons? But, Jean-Baptiste, I haven't learned anything since I was ten years old."

"That's just it."

"I went to school when I was six, at the same time as Julie. The nuns taught us. But when I was ten, all the convents were dissolved. Mama wanted to teach Julie and me herself, but she never got around to it. How long did you go to school, Jean-Baptiste?"

"From the time I was eleven until I was thirteen. Then I was expelled from school."

"Why?"

"One of our teachers was unfair to Fernand."

"And so you told the teacher what you thought of him?"

"No, I boxed his ears."

"That was the only thing to do," I said, leaning against his shoulder. "I thought you'd been at school for years and years, you know so much. And you read so many, many books—"

"At first I just read to make up for the lessons I'd missed. Later I studied hard at the officers' school. But now I want to learn many other things. When, for example, one is called upon to govern occupied territory, shouldn't one have some idea of trade policies, law and . . . But you needn't bother with these things, little girl. I thought you might take lessons in music and deportment."

"Deportment? Do you mean dancing? I know how to dance; I danced at home, on the anniversary of every Bastille Day, in the square in front of the Town Hall."

"I don't mean only dancing," he explained. "Many young girls used to be taught a number of things; for example, how to curtsy, the gestures with which a lady invites her guests to move from one room to another . . ."

"But, Jean-Baptiste, we have only the dining room! I needn't acquire elaborate gestures to show a guest the way from the dining room to your study."

"If I should be appointed Military Governor anywhere, you would be the First Lady of the district and would have to receive innumerable dignitaries in your salon."

"Salon!" I was outraged. "Jean-Baptiste, are you talking about palaces again?" I laughed and bit his shoulder.

"Ouch—stop that!" he yelled. I let go.

"You can't imagine how eagerly the Austrian aristocrats and the foreign diplomats in Vienna waited for the ambassador of our Republic to make a fool of himself. They positively prayed that I'd eat my fish with a knife. We owe our Republic impeccable manners, Désirée." After a while he added, "It would be lovely, Désirée, if you could play the piano."

"I don't think it would be lovely."

"But you are musical?" he asked hopefully.

"I don't know whether I am or not. I like music very much. Julie plays the piano, but it sounds awful. It's a crime to play badly."

"I want you to take piano lessons and study singing." I gathered that he didn't wish to be contradicted. "I have told you about my friend, the violinist, Rodolphe Kreutzer. Kreutzer accompanied me to Vienna when I went there as Ambassador. And he brought a Viennese composer to see me at the Embassy. His name was Beethoven. M. Beethoven and M. Kreutzer played together many evenings, and I was sorry I had not learned to play some instrument when I was a child. But—" he laughed suddenly out loud—"but my mama was pleased when she had enough money to buy me a new pair of Sunday trousers!"

Unfortunately, he got serious again immediately. "I insist that you take music lessons. I asked Kreutzer yesterday to write down for me the name of a music teacher. You'll find the slip of paper in my desk drawer. Begin the lessons and write me regularly about your progress."

Again a cold hand clutched at my heart. "Write to me regularly," he had said. "Write to me—" Letters, nothing but letters would be left. A leaden grey morning came in through the curtains. I stared at the curtains, my eyes wide open. I could see the blue of the curtains distinctly; gradually I could distinguish the little bouquets of flowers in their design. Jean-Baptiste had gone to sleep again.

A fist hammered on our door. "It's half-past six, General," Fernand announced.

Half an hour later we were sitting at the breakfast table, and for the first time I saw Jean-Baptiste in his field uniform. Neither orders, nor decorations, nor sash brightened the severe dark blue of his tunic. I had no more than started my breakfast when the dreaded farewells began—horses neighed; someone knocked on the door; I heard men's voices; spurs clanked and Fernand rushed outside. "Sir, the gentlemen are here."

"Ask them to come in," said Jean-Baptiste; and our room was full of officers, ten, twelve—I don't know how many. They clicked their heels together and their swords rattled. Jean-Baptiste waved casually toward them.

"The gentlemen of my staff."

I smiled mechanically.

"My wife is extremely pleased to meet you," explained Jean-Baptiste, smiling graciously, and he jumped up.

"I am ready. We can go now, gentlemen." And to me, "Good-by, my darling one, write me regularly. The Ministry of War will send me your letters by special courier. Good-by, Marie, take care of madame."

He was already out the door, and the officers with the rattling swords disappeared with him. I wish I'd kissed him again, I mused. Suddenly the room, grey in the morning light, spun around me; the yellow flames of the candles behaved very oddly—they twitched and flickered and then everything went black.

When I came to, I was lying on my bed. The room reeked of vinegar. Marie's face floated above me.

"You fainted, Eugénie," Marie said.

I pushed the cloth with the vinegar smell off my forehead. "I wanted to kiss him again, Marie," I said wearily. "—In farewell, you know."

Sceaux, near Paris, New Year's Eve
(The last year of the eighteenth century begins)

Bells ringing in the New Year woke me from my nightmare, bells
nearby in the village church at Sceaux and from faraway Notre-Dame
and other churches in Paris. In my dream I was sitting in the little
summer house in Marseilles, talking to a man who looked exactly
like Jean-Baptiste—though I knew that it was not Jean-Baptiste, but
our son.

"You missed your deportment lesson, Mama, and M. Montel's
dancing class," my son said in Jean-Baptiste's voice. I wanted to
explain that I had been too tired. But at that moment something
awful happened: my son shriveled up before my eyes; he got smaller
and smaller until he was a dwarf only up to my knee. This dwarf,
whom I knew was my son, clung to my knee and whispered, "Cannon
fodder, Mama—I am only cannon fodder and will be ordered to the
Rhine. I myself seldom use my pistol, but the others shoot—piff-
paff, piff-piff!"

At that, my son shook with laughter. An uncontrollable fear
seized me. I wanted to hold the dwarf, to protect him, but he always
eluded me. Finally he ducked under the white garden table. I
stooped, but I was so tired, so terribly tired and sad. Suddenly
Joseph was standing beside me, holding out a glass. "Long live the
Bernadotte Dynasty," he said with a wicked laugh. I looked at him
but saw Napoleon instead. Then the bells pealed and I awoke.

Now I am sitting in Jean-Baptiste's study and have moved aside
the heavy books and maps to make room on the desk for my diary.
From the street I can hear merry voices and laughter and drunken
singing. Why is everyone so happy when a new year begins? I am
unutterably sad.

146

In the first place, I have quarrelled with Jean-Baptiste by letter. Secondly, I am afraid of this new year.

The day after Jean-Baptiste left, I obediently drove to the music teacher's, the one Rodolphe Kreutzer recommended. He is a spindly little man and his breath smells very bad. He lives in an untidy room in the Latin Quarter, and his walls are decorated with dusty laurel leaves. He told me at once that he gave lessons only because of his gouty fingers; otherwise, he would be giving concerts. Could I pay him for twelve lessons in advance? I paid him. Then I had to sit down at a piano and learn what the notes are called, and which key belongs to which note. As I drove home from my first lesson I felt dizzy and I was afraid I might faint again. Since then I've driven to the Latin Quarter twice a week, and I've rented a piano so I can practice at home. Jean-Baptiste wants me to buy a piano but I think it would be a waste of money.

I'm always reading in the *Moniteur* of Jean-Baptiste's victorious progress in Germany. But, though he writes to me almost every day, he never mentions the war in his letters. Instead, he asks incessantly how my lessons are going. I am a very bad correspondent and my letters to him are always too short and never say what I really want to tell him—that I am very unhappy without him and long for him terribly. His letters, on the other hand, sound like an elderly uncle —how important it is for me to continue "my studies"; and when he found out that I hadn't even begun taking dancing and deportment lessons, this is word for word what he wrote: "Though I long to see you again, it means a great deal to me to have you complete your education. A knowledge of music and dancing is important; I recommend a few lessons from M. Montel. I see I am giving you too much good advice and am therefore closing as I kiss your lips. Your J. Bernadotte, who loves you."

Is that a letter from a lover? I was so angry that in my next letter I never referred to his good advice at all, nor did I tell him that I had actually begun lessons with this M. Montel. Heaven knows who recommended this perfumed ballet dancer, this cross between an archbishop and a ballerina. He teaches me how to curtsy "gracefully" to invisible dignitaries, and he slithers around behind me to see if I look equally charming from the rear when I advance to meet—also

147

invisible—old ladies, to escort them to a—praise be, visible—sofa. One would think M. Montel was grooming me to be received at some royal court. Me, a confirmed Republican, who at my grandest might expect to dine at Joseph's and sit next to Chief of State Paul Barras, who, they say, pinches young girls.

Since I never wrote about my deportment lessons, a courier brought me the following letter from Jean-Baptiste: "You do not mention the progress you are making in dancing, music and the other subjects. I am far away and I am glad that my little friend is making such good use of her lessons. Your J. Bernadotte."

This letter arrived one morning when I was particularly miserable, and I didn't feel in the least like getting up. I lay alone in the wide double bed and had no desire to entertain either Julie, who had come to see me, or my own thoughts. Then the letter came. Even Jean-Baptiste's private correspondence is marked *République Française* and below this, *Liberté-Egalité*. I gnashed my teeth. Why should I, the daughter of a respectable silk merchant in Marseilles, be trained to be a "great lady"? Jean-Baptiste is a general, of course, and probably one of the "coming men"; but he, too, comes of a simple family, and, anyway, in the Republic all citizens are equal, and I have no wish to know the kind of people who direct their guests from one room to another with affected gestures.

I got up and wrote him a long, long letter. While I wrote I cried and made blots. I had not married an old sermonizer, I said, but a man who—I thought—understood me. The little man with the bad breath who gives me finger exercises, and that perfumed M. Montel, could both go to the devil—I had had enough of them, more than enough. I sealed the letter quickly without reading it over and had Marie call the carriage and take the letter to the Ministry of War for immediate forwarding to General Bernadotte's headquarters.

The next day, of course, I was terrified that Jean-Baptiste might be really angry. I drove to monsieur's to take my lesson, and afterward I sat for two hours at the piano practicing scales and the little Mozart minuet I want to surprise Jean-Baptiste with when he comes home. Inside, I felt as grey and gloomy as the garden and the leafless chestnut tree. A whole week crept by and at last came Jean-Baptiste's answer:

"I do not yet know, my dear Désirée, what was in my letter that wounded you so. I have no wish to treat you as a child, but as a loving and understanding wife. Everything I say should convince you of this fact. . . ." And then he began all over again to discuss the progress of my education, and remarked unctuously that knowledge can be acquired only "with hard and persistent labour." Finally he demanded, "Write and tell me that you love me."

Up to now I have not answered his letter. And now something else has happened which makes further letter writing impossible.

Yesterday morning I was sitting, as I often do, alone in Jean-Baptiste's study, twirling the globe which stands on a little table and thinking of the many countries and continents about which I know nothing. Marie came in and brought me a cup of broth. "Drink this," she said. "You need nourishment."

"Why? I'm very well. Except I'm too fat. My yellow silk dress is too tight," I said, pushing the cup away. "Besides, that greasy soup is revolting."

Marie started toward the door. "You must make yourself eat; you know quite well why."

"Why?"

Marie smiled, came over and put her arms around me. "You really do know, don't you?"

I thrust her aside and shouted, "No, I don't know . . . and it's not true, it can't be true!" I tore upstairs, locked the door, and flung myself down on my bed.

Of course I had known, but I had refused to believe it. It's just not possible—because it would be awful! It's perfectly natural to skip a month, or two or even three. . . . I hadn't said anything to Julie because she would have insisted I see a doctor; and I didn't want to be examined—I didn't want to be sure . . .

So Marie knows. I stared up at the ceiling and tried to imagine what it would be like. It's quite normal, I said to myself; all women want children. Mama and Suzanne—and Julie has already been to two doctors because she wants a child so much and hasn't had any. But children are a terrible responsibility; one must always sound so wise and plausible in explaining to them what one should and shouldn't do, and I'm so ignorant. . . . A little boy with black curls like Jean-Baptiste . . . Except that nowadays they're calling up the sixteen-year-olds. A little boy like Jean-Baptiste, to be murdered in Italy or the Rhineland—or to kill other women's sons.

I laid my hands tentatively where he was. A young new human being—in me? It seemed incredible. *My* little human being, I suddenly thought, part of myself. Fleetingly I was entirely happy; but— *my* little human being? No one belongs to anyone else. And why should my small son always understand me? I certainly consider Mama's ideas old-fashioned. How often I've had to tell her white lies. My son will surely do exactly the same—he'll lie to me and find me old-fashioned and be annoyed with me. . . . I never asked for you, little stranger within me, I thought angrily.

Marie knocked on the door but I didn't open it. I heard her go back down to the kitchen. After a while she came back and knocked again. Finally I let her in.

"I warmed up the soup for you," she said.

"Marie, when you were expecting your little Pierre, were you very happy?"

Marie sat down on the bed and I stretched out again. "Naturally not. I wasn't married."

"I've heard that when—I mean if you don't want a child, you can —there are women who can help—" I said hesitantly.

Marie looked at me speculatively. "Yes," she said slowly, "I've heard that, too. My sister went to one of those women. You see, she'd already had so many children she didn't want another. Afterward she was ill for a long, long time. Now she can never have more children—nor will she ever be really well again, either. But the fashionable ladies—like the Tallien or Mme Josephine—I am sure they know a good doctor who would help. Of course it's illegal—" She paused. I lay there, my eyes closed, my hands on my stomach. It was quite flat. I heard Marie ask, "So you want an abortion?"

"No!"

I'd shouted "no" without thinking. Marie got up, seeming very pleased. "Come, eat the soup," she said tenderly, "and then sit down and write to the General. Bernadotte will be delighted."

I shook my head. "No, I cannot write about things like that. I wish I could talk to him."

I drank the soup, dressed, drove to M. Montel's and learned a new quadrille.

This morning I had a great surprise—Josephine came to see me! She's been only twice before, and each time with Julie and Joseph; but no one would have known that her sudden visit was at all unusual. She was beautifully dressed—a white dress of thin wool; a short, fitted ermine jacket; and a high black postillion hat with a white ostrich feather. But the grey wintry morning wasn't kind to her—when she smiled, the many small wrinkles around her eyes showed, and her lips must have been very dry, for her rose-coloured lipstick stuck to them unevenly.

"I wanted to see how you were doing as a grass widow, madame," she said—and added, "We grass widows must stick together, mustn't we?"

Marie brought us "grass widows" hot chocolate, and I asked politely, "Do you hear regularly from General Bonaparte, madame?"

"Irregularly," said she. "Bonaparte has lost his fleet, and the English are blockading his lines of communication. Now and then a small vessel gets through."

I couldn't think of anything else to say. Josephine saw the piano. "Julie tells me you are taking piano lessons, madame," she remarked.

I nodded. "Do you play?"

"Yes, of course—since I was six years old," replied the former Countess.

"I am also taking dancing lessons from M. Montel," I announced. "I don't want to disgrace my Bernadotte."

"It's not so simple, being married to a general—I mean a general off at the front," Josephine said, nibbling a marzipan cake. "Misunderstandings can occur so easily."

They certainly can, I silently agreed, and thought of my nonsensical correspondence with Jean-Baptiste. "You can't always write what you mean," I confessed.

"That's true," Josephine agreed. "And other people meddle in matters that aren't any of their business and write malicious letters."

She drank her chocolate. "Joseph, for instance. Our mutual brother-in-law—"

She took out a lace handkerchief and dabbed her lips. "Joseph intends to write Napoleon that yesterday he came to see me at Malmaison and found Hippolyte Charles there. You remember Hippolyte, the charming young army contractor? And also, that Hippolyte was in his dressing gown. Imagine his bothering Napoleon with such a trivial matter, when he has so many other things to worry about."

"Why ever was M. Charles walking around in a dressing gown at Malmaison?" I really couldn't understand why he didn't dress more suitably for his visits.

"It was only nine o'clock in the morning," Josephine said, "and he hadn't finished dressing. Joseph arrived very unexpectedly." That floored me.

"I need companionship, I can't bear to be alone so much; I've never been alone in my whole life." Josephine's eyes filled with tears. "And since we grass widows must stick together against our mutual brother-in-law, I thought you could tell your sister. Julie might persuade Joseph not to write to Bonaparte."

So that was it—that's what Mme Josephine wanted from me. "Julie has no influence on Joseph's actions," I replied truthfully.

Josephine's eyes were those of a terrified child. "You won't help me?"

"Tonight I'm going to Joseph's for a small New Year's dinner, and I'll speak to Julie," I said. "But you mustn't expect too much, madame."

Josephine stood up, obviously relieved. "I knew you would understand my position. And why do I never see you at Thérèse Tallien's? Two weeks ago she produced a little Ouvrard. You must come see him."

And again at the door, "You're not bored in Paris, madame? We must go to the theatre together soon. And please tell your sister that naturally Joseph can write whatever he likes to my Bonaparte; he's just to leave out the dressing gown."

I drove half an hour earlier than I'd planned to the rue du Rocher. Julie, in a new red dress that was very unbecoming because it made her naturally colourless face look even paler, fluttered excitedly around, rearranging the little silver horseshoes with which she had decorated the table and which were supposed to bring us all happiness in the new year.

"I've given you Louis Bonaparte as a dinner partner; the fat boy is such a bore, I can't very well inflict him on anyone else," she said.

"I'd like to ask you something," I said. "Can you ask Joseph not to write Napoleon anything about the dressing gown—I mean the dressing gown M. Charles was wearing at Malmaison?"

"The letter to Napoleon has already gone off. Any further discussion is superfluous," said Joseph at that very moment. I hadn't heard him come into the dining room; but there he was, standing by the sideboard, pouring himself a drink of brandy. "I'd like to bet Josephine came to you today and asked you to intercede for her. Didn't she, Désirée?"

I shrugged.

"But why you want to help her instead of us is beyond me," Joseph continued indignantly.

"What do you mean by 'us'?" I demanded.

"Me, for example, and Napoleon, of course."

"It's none of your business. And Napoleon, off in Egypt, can't undo what's done. It will only make him unhappy. Why trouble him?"

Joseph looked at me with interest. "Still in love with him? How touching—" he mocked. "I thought you had forgotten him long ago."

"Forgotten?" I was astonished. "No one can ever forget his first love." Napoleon . . . I hardly ever think of him. But how my heart beat then, and that special happiness—and my heart-sickness afterward; that I'll never forget.

"And therefore you want to spare him this great disillusionment." Joseph seemed to enjoy this conversation. He poured himself another brandy.

"Of course. I know what disillusionment can mean."

Joseph grinned. "But my letter is already on the way."

"So there's no point in discussing it further," I said.

Joseph, meanwhile, had filled two more glasses. "Come, Julie,

Désirée, we three must wish each other Happy New Year. Have to be in the right mood—our guests will be here any minute."

Dutifully, Julie and I each took a glass. I hadn't even taken a sip when I suddenly felt wretched. The smell disgusted me, and I hastily put the glass back on the sideboard.

"Aren't you well? You're green in the face, Désirée," cried Julie.

I felt beads of sweat on my forehead, fell into a chair and shook my head. "No—no, it's nothing—it often happens." With that I closed my eyes.

"Perhaps she's expecting a baby," I heard Joseph say.

"Impossible, or I'd know about it," Julie declared.

"If she's ill, I must write to Bernadotte right away," Joseph said eagerly.

I quickly opened my eyes. "Don't you dare, Joseph. You will not write him a word about this. I want to surprise him!"

"What with?" asked Joseph and Julie simultaneously.

"With a son," I announced, suddenly proud.

Julie fell to her knees and hugged me. Joseph said, "But perhaps it will be a daughter."

"No, it will be a son. Bernadotte wouldn't want a daughter." I stood up. "And now I'm going home. Don't be hurt, but I'd rather go to bed and sleep over the New Year."

Joseph had poured still more brandy, and he and Julie drank to me. Julie's eyes were wet.

"Long live the Bernadotte Dynasty," Joseph laughed.

I enjoyed this jest. "Yes, a toast to the Bernadotte Dynasty," I said.

Then I drove home.

But the church bells didn't let me sleep over the New Year. Now at last they are silent, and we're already in the Year VII. Somewhere in Germany Jean-Baptiste drinks with his staff officers. Perhaps they drink to the health of Mme Bernadotte. But I am facing this New Year all alone. No, not quite alone. . . . We'll face the future together—you little unborn son. And we'll hope for the best, won't we? For the Bernadotte Dynasty!

Sceaux, near Paris, 17 Messidor, Year VII
(To Mama, probably July 4, 1799)

Eight hours ago I had a son.

He has dark silky down on his head, but Marie says this first hair will probably fall out. He has dark-blue eyes, but Marie says that all new babies have blue eyes.

I'm so weak that everything swims before my eyes; and they would be very upset if they knew that Marie gave in and secretly brought me my diary. The midwife is sure that I am going to die, but the doctor thinks he can pull me through. I've lost a lot of blood, and now they have somehow raised the foot of the bed to help stop the hemorrhage.

I hear Jean-Baptiste's voice out in the living room. Dear, dear Jean-Baptiste. . . .

Sceaux, near Paris, a week later

Now not even the giantess, my pessimistic midwife, thinks I'm going to die. I lie propped up with pillows while Marie brings me all my favourite food. In the morning and at night the War Minister of France sits on my bed and discourses at length on the raising of children.

Jean-Baptiste came back very unexpectedly about two months ago. After New Year's Day I pulled myself together and wrote him again; but only short letters, and not at all affectionate, because I longed for him so terribly and at the same time I was angry with him. I read in the *Moniteur* that he captured Philippsburg with three hundred men—the town was defended by fifteen hundred— and then set up his headquarters in a place called Germersheim.

From there he went on to Mannheim, captured the town and became Governor of Hesse. He ruled over the German inhabitants in accordance with the laws of our Republic; forbade punishment by whipping and abolished the ghettos. The Universities of Heidelberg and Giessen wrote him enthusiastic letters of thanks. I think Germans are peculiar people: Until their cities are conquered, they consider themselves—for some unfathomable reason—braver and better than everyone else on earth; as soon as they've been right royally beaten, a howling and gnashing of teeth goes up all through Germany and the Germans declare that they have always secretly sided with their enemies.

Next, Jean-Baptiste got word from Barras to come to Paris, and he turned over the command of his army to General Masséna. One afternoon I was sitting as I often did at the piano, practicing the Mozart minuet. It went quite well except for one part I spoil regularly. The door behind me opened. "Marie, that's the minuet I've learned as a surprise for our General. Does it sound all right?"

"It sounds wonderful, Désirée; and it's an enormous surprise for your General!" Jean-Baptiste took me in his arms, and after two kisses it was as though we'd never been separated.

While I set the coffee table I racked my brains about how to tell him our son was on the way. But my hero's eagle eye misses nothing. Jean-Baptiste asked, "Tell me, little girl, why didn't you write me that we're expecting a son?" (The possibility of a daughter never occurred to him either.)

I stood still, frowned, and tried to look furious. "Because I didn't want to cause my old sermonizer any trouble. You were already beside yourself anytime anything forced me to interrupt my education." Whereupon I went to him. "But calm yourself, you great big General; your son has already begun his lessons in correct deportment at M. Montel's, tucked under his mother's heart."

Jean-Baptiste forbade me to go on with my lessons; he hardly wanted me to leave the house, so anxious was he about my health.

Meanwhile, all Paris talked of nothing but a domestic crisis, and dreaded riots—some organized by the Royalists who, gaining strength again, were openly corresponding with *émigré* aristocrats, and other riots organized by the extreme Left, the austere Jacobins. I didn't pay much attention. The white tapering blossoms of our chestnut trees were out, and I sat under its broad branches, hemming diapers. Julie, beside me, was bending over a baby pillow she was making for my son. She came to see me every day, hoping I'd "infect" her— she wanted a child so much. And it would make no difference to her whether it was a boy or a girl, she says, she'd take whatever came. So far, unfortunately, nothing's come.

In the afternoon Joseph and Lucien Bonaparte often called, and both talked earnestly to my Jean-Baptiste. It seems that Barras had made him some sort of offer which Jean-Baptiste had indignantly refused. We have five directors, but only Barras has any real power. Every party in the Republic is unanimously dissatisfied with our more or less corrupt heads of state, and Barras hoped to exploit this discontent and get rid of three of his fellow directors. He would like to carry on the Directorate with just the collaboration of the old Jacobin, Sieyès.

Since Barras was afraid that the coup d'état he was planning might result in riots, he had asked Jean-Baptiste to stand by him as his military adviser. Jean-Baptiste refused. Barras should obey the Constitution; and, if it needed changing, he should ask the deputies.

Joseph thought my husband was crazy. "You could be the Dictator of France tomorrow, with the support of your troops," cried Joseph.

"Quite so," answered Jean-Baptiste quietly, "and that must be avoided. You seem to forget, M. Bonaparte, that I am a confirmed Republican."

"But perhaps it's in the best interests of the Republic to have a military man head of the Government in time of war, or—let's say— firmly behind the Government," Lucien said, reflectively.

Jean-Baptiste shook his head. "A change in the Constitution is the responsibility of the people. We have two chambers—the Council of Five Hundred, to which you yourself belong, Lucien, and the Council of Ancients, to which you probably will belong when you reach the proper age. The deputies must decide these things, and certainly not the Army or one of its generals. But I'm afraid we're boring the ladies. What's that funny-looking thing you're sewing, Désirée?"

"A little jacket for your son, Jean-Baptiste."

Nearly three weeks ago, on 30 Prairial, Barras succeeded in forcing his three fellow directors to resign. Now he and Sieyès are at the head of the State. The Parties of the Left, who were the most prominent, demanded the appointment of new ministers. Talleyrand was replaced as Foreign Minister by our minister in Geneva, a M. Reinhart; and M. Cambacérès, our most famous lawyer, and gourmet, was named Minister of Justice. However, since we're conducting a war on all fronts, and the Republic couldn't shoulder this risk unless conditions in the Army were improved, everything depended on the choice of a new Minister of War.

Early in the morning of 15 Messidor, a messenger arrived from the Luxembourg Palace: Jean-Baptiste was urgently requested to confer with the two directors immediately. Jean-Baptiste went right to town, and I sat under the chestnut tree all day, feeling annoyed with myself. The evening before, I had eaten a whole pound of cherries at one sitting, and these cherries were rumbling around in my stomach; I felt more and more uncomfortable. Suddenly, pain stabbed through me like a knife. It lasted only a fraction of a second, but afterward I sat paralyzed. How terribly it had hurt.

"Marie," I called. "Marie!"

Marie came, gave me one look and said, "Up to the bedroom. I'll send Fernand for the midwife."

"But it's only the cherries from last night."

"Up to the bedroom." Marie took my arm and pulled me up. The knife didn't stab again and, relieved, I ran up the stairs. I heard Marie dispatch Fernand. (Fernand had come back from Germany with Jean-Baptiste.)

"At last that fellow is good for something," Marie said, when she came up to the bedroom. She spread three sheets over the bed.

"It's just the cherries," I insisted. At that moment the knife jabbed again; this time from behind and right through me. I screamed; and when it was over, I began to cry.

"Aren't you ashamed? Stop crying at once!" Marie commanded, and I knew she was worried.

"Julie—I want Julie," I moaned. Julie would pity me, she'd pity me terribly; and I so longed to be pitied.

Fernand came back with the midwife and was sent off to fetch Julie.

The midwife! There never was such a midwife! She had examined me several times in the last few months and always gave me the creeps. Now she reminded me of a giantess in some gruesome fairy tale. The giantess had huge red arms and a broad red face with a real moustache. The most unwholesome thing about this female grenadier, however, was that her lips, under her moustache, were smeared with lipstick; and on her tangled grey hair she wore a coquettish white lace cap.

The giantess gazed at me observantly and, it seemed to me, with considerable contempt.

"Shall I undress and get in bed?" I asked.

"There's plenty of time. It's going to take you forever," she prophesied.

In a minute Marie said, "I have boiling water ready in the kitchen."

The giantess turned on her, "No hurry about that. Better start some coffee."

"Of course, strong coffee. To cheer up madame?" Marie inquired hopefully.

"No, to cheer me up," replied the giantess.

An endless afternoon turned into an endless evening; the evening, into a long, long night; a dusky dawn dragged into a sticky hot morning which went on and on. Then it was afternoon again, another evening and another night. By then I could no longer tell one time of day from another. Incessantly the knife thrust through me; and far away I heard someone screaming, screaming, screaming. Sometimes everything went black; then brandy was poured down my throat, I threw up and couldn't breathe, sank into nothingness and was roused by a fresh pain. Occasionally I sensed Julie's nearness; someone kept wiping my forehead and cheeks, the sweat flowed in streams, my nightgown stuck to me. I could hear Marie's quiet voice, "You must help, Eugénie, help—"

Like a monster, the giantess stood over me; her shapeless shadow danced along the wall, many candles flickered—was it already dark again, or still . . .

"Go away—leave me alone," I moaned, lashing out. They went away and then Jean-Baptiste was sitting on my bed, holding me in his arms. Again the knife turned inside me but Jean-Baptiste didn't let me go.

"Why aren't you in Paris—at the Luxembourg Palace—they sent for you?" The pain was ebbing but my voice sounded strange and gasping.

"It is night," he said.

"You don't have to go to war again?" I whispered anxiously.

"No, no. I'm staying here. I am now . . ."

I heard no more, for the knife thrust through me and I was drowning in a sea of pain.

. . . The pain had stopped. Soon I felt quite well again. I was too weak to think any more.

As I lay gently cradled by the waves, feeling nothing, seeing nothing, hearing . . . Yes, I heard . . .

"Isn't the doctor here? If he doesn't come soon, it will be too late." A voice, high-pitched in agitation, that I didn't recognize. Why a doctor? I felt so well now, rocking with the waves, the Seine with its many lights . . . Burning hot, bitter coffee was poured into me. I blinked.

"If the doctor doesn't come soon—" That was the giantess. How funny—I couldn't believe this high, excited voice was hers. Why had she lost her head? Soon it would all be over. . . .

But it wasn't over. It was only beginning.

Men's voices at the door.

"Wait in the living room, Mr. War Minister, sir. Be calm, sir. I assure you, Mr. War Minister—"

What Minister of War? How did a Minister of War get into my room?

"I beg of you, Doctor—" That's Jean-Baptiste's voice. Don't leave me, Jean-Baptiste . . .

Something stuck me. An injection, I found out later. The doctor gave me camphor drops and instructed the giantess to lift up my shoulders. I was conscious again. Marie and Julie stood at either side of the bed, holding candlesticks. The doctor was a short thin man in a black suit. His face was in shadow. Something shone, flashed between his hands. "A knife!" I screamed. "He has a knife!"

"No, only forceps," Marie said. "Don't scream so, Eugénie."

But perhaps it was a knife, after all, for the pains shot through me again, as before, except oftener, ever oftener, finally without a break. I was ripped to pieces; ripped, torn—until I fell into a deep pit and knew no more.

The voice of the giantess again, rough and indifferent: "The end is near, Dr. Moulin."

"Perhaps she'll pull through, citizeness, if only the hemorrhage stops."

Something whimpered in the room—high and squally. I tried to open my eyes but my lids were like lead.

"Jean-Baptiste—a son, a wonderful little son," Julie was sobbing.

After a while I could open my eyes, wide—as wide as they went. Jean-Baptiste has a son. Julie held a small bundle of white cloth in her arms, and Jean-Baptiste stood beside her.

"How small a small child is," he said in surprise. He turned and came over to the bed. He knelt down and took my hand and laid it against his cheek, his completely unshaven cheek—and wet, too. Do generals also weep?

"We have a fine son, but he's still very small," he reported.

"They're always small at the beginning," I said. My lips were so bitten that I could hardly talk. Julie showed me the bundle. A crab-red little face peeped out of the wrappings. The little face had scrunched-up eyes and looked offended. Perhaps he hadn't wanted to be born.

"I must ask you all to leave the room. The wife of our Minister of War needs rest," announced the doctor.

"The wife of our Minister of War? Does he mean me, Jean-Baptiste?"

"I have been the French Minister of War since the day before yesterday," Jean-Baptiste said.

"And I haven't yet congratulated you," I murmured.

"You were very busy." He smiled.

Julie laid the little bundle in the cradle; and they all, except the doctor and the giantess, left the room and I went to sleep.

Oscar! An entirely new name, one I had never heard before. Os-car. . . . It sounded rather pretty. Apparently a Nordic name. My son will have a Nordic name and be called Oscar. It was Napoleon's idea, and Napoleon insists on being his godfather. The name "Oscar" occurred to him because out there in the desert he's been reading *Ossian*. When he learned, from one of Joseph's long-winded letters, that I was expecting a son, he promptly wrote, "If it's a son, Eugénie must call him Oscar. And I want to be his godfather."

Of Jean-Baptiste—who, after all, also has something to say in this matter—not a word. When we showed Jean-Baptiste this letter, he laughed. "We mustn't offend your old admirer, little girl. As far as I'm concerned, he can be the boy's godfather; and Julie can represent him at the christening. The name Oscar . . ."

"It's a hideous name," said Marie, who happened to be in the room.

"The name of a Nordic hero," Julie, who had delivered Napoleon's letter, contributed.

"But our son is neither Nordic nor heroic," I said, and considered the tiny face of the bundle I held in my arms. The little face was no longer red but yellow. My son had jaundice, but Marie claimed that most newborn babies get jaundice when they are a few days old.

"Oscar Bernadotte sounds distinguished," Jean-Baptiste said. And that settled the matter for him. "We'll move in fourteen days, if that's all right with you, Désirée."

In two weeks we are moving to another house. A minister of war must live in Paris, and therefore Jean-Baptiste has bought a small villa in the rue Cisalpine, around the corner from Julie, between the rue Courcelles and the rue du Rocher. It's not much larger than our little house in Sceaux; but at least we'll have a real nursery next to the bedroom, and a dining room as well as a drawing room where Jean-Baptiste can receive the officials and politicians who often call on him in the evening. At the moment, all this takes place in the dining room.

I myself am doing marvellously. Marie cooks my favourite dishes, and I'm not so weak any more—I can sit up by myself. Unfortunately, I have callers all day long and this makes me tired. Josephine came, and even Thérèse Tallien; and also that woman writer with the pug-face, this Mme de Staël, whom I know only slightly. On top of everything, Joseph solemnly presented me with his novel. For he has perpetrated a book and now considers himself a writer, heaven-sent. The book is called *Moina, or the Peasant Girl of Saint Denis* and is so boring and sentimental that I go to sleep every time I try to read it. And along comes Julie, with, "Isn't it wonderful?"

Actually, I know quite well that the many callers don't come to see either me or my yellow son Oscar, but the wife of Minister of War Bernadotte. This woman with the ugly pug-face, who is married to the Swedish Ambassador but doesn't live with him because she's a writer—and to write she needs stimulation which she finds among wild-haired, wild-eyed, adolescent poets with whom she is in love— As I was saying, this Mme de Staël told me that France had at last found the one man who can restore order; and that everyone considers my Jean-Baptiste the real head of the Government. I have also read the proclamation which Jean-Baptiste sent to all his soldiers on the day of his appointment as Minister of War. It is so beautiful that tears came to my eyes. He wrote, "Soldiers of France! I have witnessed your terrible sufferings; indeed, as you know, I have participated in them. I swear that I shall never rest until I have provided you with bread, clothing, and arms. And you, comrades, you must swear that once again you will defeat this powerful coalition that threatens France. We are bound by the oaths we have sworn."

Jean-Baptiste gets home from the Ministry of War at eight o'clock, has a small meal served at my bedside, and then goes down to his study to dictate to a secretary half the night. He goes off at six o'clock in the morning to the rue Varenne, where the Ministry is now. And Fernand says that the camp bed, which Jean-Baptiste has put up in the study, is often unused. It is dreadful that my husband all alone has to save our Republic. And also, the Government hasn't enough money to buy arms and uniforms for the ninety thousand recruits whom Jean-Baptiste is having trained, and there have been some wild scenes between him and Director Sieyès.

If only Jean-Baptiste were left alone in the evening to work at home in peace; but I constantly hear people coming and going. Jean-Baptiste told me only yesterday that members of various political parties are trying very hard to persuade him to side with them. Just now, as—rushed and exhausted—he was shovelling in his supper, Fernand announced that a "M. Chiappe," who wouldn't say what he wanted, was waiting downstairs. Jean-Baptiste wiped his mouth, jumped up and hurried downstairs to get rid of this mysterious M. Chiappe. A quarter of an hour later, Jean-Baptiste returned to my room. His face was red with rage.

"This Chiappe has been sent to me by the Duke of Enghien. Such insolence, such Bourbon insolence—!"

"And who is the Duke of Enghien, if I may ask?" I inquired.

"Louis de Bourbon Condé, Duke of Enghien. The most able member of the Bourbon family, in the pay of England, now somewhere in Germany. If I can seize the power, and then give France back to the Bourbons, they will make me High Constable, and God knows what else! What insolence!"

"What did you answer?"

"I threw him out, and told him to inform his principals that I am a firm Republican."

"Everyone says that today you really govern France. If you wanted to, could you overthrow the directors and become Director yourself?" I asked cautiously.

"Of course," Jean-Baptiste said quietly. "In fact, the Jacobins proposed that I do so—some Jacobins and some of our generals, too. If I wished, I could be named Director with far greater powers than the directors have today."

"And you have refused?"

"Naturally. I support the Constitution."

At this moment Fernand announced that our brother-in-law, Joseph, wished to see Jean-Baptiste.

"The last person I wanted to see today," grumbled Jean-Baptiste. "Let him come up, Fernand."

Joseph appeared. First he leaned over the cradle and declared

164

that Oscar was the most beautiful child he had ever seen; then he wanted Jean-Baptiste to go down to the study with him.

"I must ask you something, and our conversation will bore Désirée," he ventured.

Jean-Baptiste shook his head. "I have so little opportunity to be with Désirée, I would rather stay with her. Sit down, and make it brief, Bonaparte. I have a long evening's work ahead of me."

They both sat beside my bed. Jean-Baptiste sought my hand; peace and strength flowed from his nearness as my hand lay safe in his. I closed my eyes.

"It's about Napoleon," I heard Joseph say. "What would you say if Napoleon decided to return to France?"

"I would say that Napoleon cannot return unless the Minister of War recalls him from Egypt."

"My dear brother-in-law, we need not pretend with each other. In Egypt, a supreme commander of Napoleon's stature is now superfluous. Since the destruction of our fleet, our operations there are more or less at a standstill. And the Egyptian campaign can therefore . . ."

". . . be regarded as a fiasco, as I predicted it would be."

"I wouldn't express it so baldly. Still, as we can expect no decisive developments in Egypt, my brother's talents could be used to greater advantage on another front. Napoleon is not only a military strategist; you yourself know of his interest in administration. He could be of the utmost service to you here in Paris in the reorganization of the Army. In addition—"

Joseph hesitated and waited for some comment; Jean-Baptiste made none. His hand still lay protectingly on mine. "You realize," Joseph continued, "that there are already several conspiracies against the Government."

"As Minister of War I could hardly be unaware of it. But what has that to do with the supreme commander of our Egyptian Expeditionary Force?"

"The Republic needs a—yes, it needs many strong men. In wartime, France cannot afford these party intrigues and domestic political differences."

"So you suggest that I should recall your brother to put down these various conspiracies? Do I understand you correctly?"

"Yes, I thought that . . ."

"It's up to the police to expose conspiracies. No more, no less."

"Of course, if these conspiracies are against the State. But I can confidentially advise you that influential circles are considering a consolidation of the powerful political forces."

"What do you mean by that?"

"For example, if you yourself and Napoleon, the two most capable . . ." Joseph got no further.

"Stop that drivel. Come to the point: To free the Republic from party politics, certain people want a dictator; your brother, Napoleon, wishes to be recalled from Egypt in order to compete for the position of Dictator. Be frank with me, Bonaparte!"

Joseph nervously cleared his throat. "I spoke to Talleyrand today. The ex-Minister thinks that Director Sieyès might not be averse to supporting a change in the Constitution."

"I am familiar with Talleyrand's point of view. I am also cognizant of the aims of various Jacobins. I can inform you, too, that the Royalists are concentrating all their hopes on a dictator. As far as I am concerned, I have sworn loyalty to the Republic and under all circumstances will uphold our Constitution. Is this answer clear enough?"

"You realize that this lack of activity in Egypt can drive any man of Napoleon's ambition to desperation. Besides, my brother has important private matters to settle in Paris. He intends to get a divorce. Josephine's unfaithfulness was a great blow to him. Supposing that in his despair my brother came to the conclusion that he must return —what then?"

Jean-Baptiste's hand gripped mine like iron, but just for a moment. He relaxed, and I heard him say quietly, "As Minister of War I should be obliged to place your brother before a court martial; and I assume that he would be condemned and shot as a deserter."

"But Napoleon, as a passionate patriot, can no longer remain in Africa . . ."

"A supreme commander's place is with his troops. He led these troops into the desert, and he must remain with them until a way has been found to bring them back. Even a civilian like yourself must see this, M. Bonaparte."

The silence got increasingly oppressive.

"Your novel is so exciting, Joseph," I said finally.

"Yes, everyone has congratulated me," Joseph answered—with his usual modesty—and at last rose to go. Jean-Baptiste accompanied him downstairs.

I tried to sleep. Half-asleep, I remembered a little girl who had raced with a scrawny, insignificant-looking officer all the way to a hedge. The distorted face of the officer was frightening in the moonlight. "I, for example—I know my destiny," the officer had said. The girl had laughed. "You will believe in me, Eugénie, whatever happens?"

He would come back from Egypt. I know him; he will come back and destroy the Republic if he has a chance. He cares nothing for the Republic, or for the rights of its citizens; nor could he understand a man like Jean-Baptiste. He never knew a man like him. . . . "My little daughter, whenever and wherever in the future men may seek to deprive their brothers of liberty and equality, no one can say of them: 'Father forgive them for they know not what they do.'" Jean-Baptiste and Papa would have understood each other.

When the clock struck eleven, Marie came in, lifted Oscar from his cradle and put him at my breast. Jean-Baptiste came up, too; he knows when I give Oscar his night feeding.

"He will come back, Jean-Baptiste," I said.

"Who?"

"The godfather of our son. How will you handle it?"

"If I have the authority, I shall have him shot."

"And—if not?"

"Then he will probably seize the authority and have me shot. Good night, my darling."

"Good night, Jean-Baptiste."

"But don't worry about it, little one. I'm only joking."

"I understand, Jean-Baptiste. Good night."

Paris, 18 Brumaire of the Year VII
(*In other countries: November 9, 1799.*
Our Republic has a new Constitution)

He has come back.

And today he succeeded in his coup d'état, and, for the last few hours, has been head of the State. Several deputies and generals have been arrested. Jean-Baptiste says that any moment we may expect the state police to search our house. It would be unspeakably awful for me if Police Director Fouché, and then Napoleon, got hold of my diary. The two of them would die laughing at me. . . . So I am quickly, tonight, writing down what has happened. Then I shall lock the book and give it to Julie for safekeeping. Fortunately Julie is the sister-in-law of our new ruler and so, let us hope, Napoleon will never let the police rummage through her bureau drawers.

I'm sitting in the salon of our new home in the rue Cisalpine. I can hear Jean-Baptiste walking up and down in the dining room next to the salon. Up and down, up and down.

"If you have any compromising papers, give them to me and I'll take them to Julie in the morning with my diary," I called out to him. But Jean-Baptiste shook his head. "I have nothing—what did you call it?—compromising. And Bonaparte knows very well already what I think about his treason."

Fernand busied himself around the room, and I asked him if there were still as many people, in silent groups, in front of our house. He said there were. "What do they want, all these people?"

Fernand put a fresh candle in my candlestick and said, "They want to see what happens to our General. The rumour is that the Jacobins have asked him to take over command of the National Guard, and—" Fernand scratched his head ostentatiously while he decided whether or not to tell me the truth. "Yes, and the people think that our General will be arrested. General Moreau has been already."

I got ready for a long night. Jean-Baptiste still paced up and down. While I write, the hours tick away, and we wait.

Yes, he suddenly came back as I was sure he would. Four weeks and two days ago at six o'clock in the morning, an exhausted messenger dismounted in front of Joseph's house, and reported, "General Bonaparte, accompanied only by his secretary Bourienne, has landed at the port of Fréjus. He arrived in a small merchant vessel that eluded the British. He has hired a special coach and will be in Paris at any moment."

Joseph dressed hurriedly, got Lucien up, and the two brothers stood watch in the rue de la Victoire. Their voices woke Josephine. When she heard the news, she grabbed her newest dress from the wardrobe, packed her cosmetics with trembling hands and ran frantically to her carriage. Then she tried to intercept Napoleon south of the city. Not till she was under way did she remember to put on her rouge. The divorce must be stopped; Napoleon must talk to her himself before Joseph influenced him. However, Josephine's carriage was hardly out of sight before Napoleon's post horses galloped into the rue de la Victoire. The two carriages had passed each other. Napoleon alighted quickly, his brothers ran forward to greet him, everyone patted everyone else's shoulders. Then the three retired to one of the small drawing rooms.

At noon an exhausted Josephine returned. And opened the drawing room door. Napoleon examined her critically from head to toe.

"Madame, we have no more to say to each other. Tomorrow I start divorce proceedings, and I would appreciate your moving to Malmaison immediately. In the meantime I shall look for a new house for myself."

Josephine sobbed loudly. Napoleon turned his back on her, and Lucien escorted her to her bedroom. The three Bonaparte brothers continued their conference. Later, Talleyrand, the former Minister, joined them. Meanwhile the news spread like wildfire through Paris. General Bonaparte had returned victorious from Egypt. Curious people gathered around his house. Enthusiastic recruits joined the crowd shouting, "Long live Bonaparte!" and Napoleon showed himself at the window and waved to the people below.

During all this, Josephine sat on her bed upstairs dissolved in tears, while her daughter Hortense tried to interest her in a cup of camomile tea. Not until evening were Bourienne and Napoleon alone. Napoleon began dictating letters to countless deputies and generals to advise them personally of his safe return. Then Hortense appeared—as always gawky and thin, still colourless and shy, but already dressed like a young lady. Her long, hooked nose made her look old for her age.

"Couldn't you speak to Mama, Papa Bonaparte?" she pleaded. But Napoleon brushed her aside like a troublesome fly. He didn't dismiss Bourienne until midnight. As he was considering on which of the fragile gold sofas to spend the night, since Josephine was in the bedroom, there was loud sobbing outside the door. He went right over to the door and locked it. Josephine stayed outside sobbing for two whole hours. At last he opened it. Next morning he woke up in Josephine's bedroom.

I got all this straight from Julie, who heard it from Joseph and Bourienne.

"And do you know what Napoleon said to me?" Julie added. "He said, 'Julie, if I divorce Josephine, all Paris will know that she was unfaithful to me and laugh at me. But if I stay with her, everyone will be convinced that I have no reason to doubt my wife, and that the stories about her were merely malicious gossip. I never, under any circumstances, want to be laughed at.' . . . A worthy point of view, don't you agree, Désirée?" Julie babbled along, "Junot is also back from Egypt. And Eugène de Beauharnais. Officers of the Egyptian Army are landing almost daily in France. Junot told us that Napoleon left a blonde mistress behind in Egypt. A certain Mme Pauline Fourès, whom he calls 'Bellilot.' She's the wife of a young officer and secretly accompanied her husband to Egypt. Imagine— disguised in a man's uniform. When Napoleon first heard from Joseph about Josephine, he paced back and forth in his tent like a madman. Later he summoned this Bellilot and had supper with her."

"What's become of her now?" I asked.

Julie shrugged her shoulders. "They say—Junot, Murat and the others—that Napoleon turned her over to his next in command."

"And how does he look?"

"Who? The next in command?"

"Don't be silly, I mean Napoleon, of course."

Julie was thoughtful. "Yes—he has changed. Perhaps it's his hair. He had it cut in Egypt, and his face looks fatter and his features less irregular. But it's not only that—no, I'm sure it's not. Anyway you'll see him yourself on Sunday; you're dining at Mortefontaine, aren't you?"

Prominent Parisians have a country house, and poets and writers some sort of garden where in the shade they can relax. So since Joseph now considers himself both a prominent Parisian and a writer, he has bought the charming Villa Mortefontaine with its huge park. It's an hour's drive from Paris. And next Sunday we are to dine there with Napoleon and Josephine.

There certainly would never have been a coup d'état today if Jean-Baptiste had still been Minister of War when Napoleon returned. But shortly before, he had again quarrelled violently with Director Sieyès, and was so angry that he resigned. Now, thinking it all over and realizing that Sieyès supported Napoleon, it seems probable to me that this director foresaw Napoleon's return and intentionally quarrelled with Jean-Baptiste so as to force his resignation. Jean-Baptiste's successor dares not have Napoleon court martialled because some of the generals, and the clique of deputies who are supporting Joseph and Lucien, rejoiced too much over Napoleon's return.

During those autumn days Jean-Baptiste had many callers. General Moreau came almost daily and declared that the Army must intervene if Napoleon dared a coup d'état. A troop of Jacobin city councillors from Paris marched in and asked if General Bernadotte would take over command of the National Guard if there was trouble. Jean-Baptiste replied that he would gladly take over this command, but he must first be accredited to it. This only the Government, that is the Minister of War, can authorize. With that the City Councillors departed disappointed.

On the Sunday morning we were to drive to Mortefontaine, I suddenly heard a well-known voice in our drawing room: "Eugénie—I must see my godson!" I dashed downstairs. There he was, his face tanned, his hair shorn. "We wanted to surprise you and Bernadotte. Since we're all invited to Mortefontaine, Josephine and I thought we'd drive by and take you. I must meet your son, and admire the new house, and I've not yet seen Comrade Bernadotte since my return."

"You look wonderfully well, my dear," said Josephine, standing slender and graceful at the terrace door. Jean-Baptiste appeared, and I departed for the kitchen to ask Marie to make some coffee and serve liqueur. When I came back, Jean-Baptiste had brought Oscar down, and Napoleon was bending over our little bundle, going "ti-ti-ti" and trying to tickle its chin. Oscar didn't care for any of this and began to cry shrilly.

"A new recruit for the Army, Comrade Bernadotte." Napoleon laughed and clapped Jean-Baptiste genially on the shoulder. I rescued our son from the arms of his father, who held him stiffly away from him and asserted that Oscar was undoubtedly damp.

While we drank Marie's bittersweet coffee, Josephine entangled me in a discussion of roses. Roses are her passion and I have heard that she's laid out a magnificent rose garden at Malmaison. She'd noticed the few miserable little rosebushes planted in front of our terrace, and asked me if and how I cared for them. So I didn't hear the conversation between Jean-Baptiste and Napoleon. But Josephine and I were suddenly silent because Napoleon said, "I'm told that if you were still Minister of War, Comrade Bernadotte, you would have me court martialled, and shot. What particularly have you against me?"

"I think you know our service regulations as well as I do, Comrade Bonaparte," Jean-Baptiste answered, and, with a smile, "Far better than I. You had the advantage of attending the War College, and of beginning your active service as an officer. I, as you probably know, served for a long time in the ranks."

Napoleon leaned forward toward Jean-Baptiste. At that moment the change in him I'd noticed before was startlingly apparent. His short hair made his head seem rounder and his gaunt cheeks fuller. I'd never noticed before how sharply defined his chin was. It jutted out practically square. All this merely emphasized the change; it wasn't the cause of it.

Even his smile was different. This smile I had once loved so much, and later feared, that before rarely and fleetingly transformed his whole stern face was now fixed, compelling and—solicitous. Why this set smile—and for whom? Jean-Baptiste, of course. Jean-Baptiste was to be won over as a friend, a confidante, an enthusiastic ally.

"I have returned from Egypt to place myself again at the disposal of our country, for I consider my Egyptian assignment completed. You say that our frontiers are now secured, that as Minister of War you attempted to set up an army of a hundred thousand infantrymen and forty thousand cavalry. The few thousand men I left behind in Africa can, therefore, mean nothing to the French Army which you have expanded to one hundred and forty thousand men. While a man like me, in the Republic's present desperate situation, could . . ."

"The situation is not desperate," Jean-Baptiste said calmly.

"No?" Napoleon smiled. "From the moment of my return people on all sides have told me that the Government is no longer in control. The Royalists are active once more in the Vendée, and some of them in Paris are corresponding openly with the Bourbons in England. The Manège Club, on the other hand, is preparing for a Jacobin revolution. You must be aware, Comrade Bernadotte, that the Manège Club plans to overthrow the Directorate?"

"You are certainly better informed about the aims and intentions of the Manège Club than I." Jean-Baptiste spoke slowly. "Your brothers, Joseph and Lucien, founded this club and conduct its meetings."

"In my opinion it is the duty of the Army and its leaders to consolidate all our positive forces to maintain civil peace and discipline, and to set up a form of government worthy of the ideals of the Revolution," Napoleon declaimed.

The conversation bored me so I turned again to Josephine. To my surprise she was watching Jean-Baptiste intently as though his answer were of vital importance.

"I would consider any intervention by the Army or its leaders as high treason," Jean-Baptiste declared.

Napoleon kept on smiling fixedly. At the word "high treason," Josephine raised her plucked eyebrows. I poured fresh coffee.

"If men of all parties—I emphasize all parties—came to me and asked for a coalition of all the positive forces in the country, and, with the help of men of integrity, wanted me to draft a new constitution, one setting forth the inalienable rights of the people, would you stand by me, Comrade Bernadotte? Could those who want to realize the ideals of the Revolution count on you? Jean-Baptiste Bernadotte—may France count on you?"

Napoleon's glistening grey eyes stared at Jean-Baptiste. With a bang Jean-Baptiste set down his cup.

"Listen to me, Bonaparte. If you are here, not for a cup of coffee, but to ask me to commit high treason, I must ask you to leave my house."

Away went the ingratiating look in Napoleon's eyes. His mechanical smile was weird and uneasy.

"You would also take arms against those of your comrades who might be entrusted by the nation to save the Republic?"

A roar of laughter suddenly broke the tension. Jean-Baptiste shook with hearty and uncontrolled mirth. "Comrade Bonaparte, Comrade Bonaparte! While you were sunning yourself in Egypt, it was suggested to me not once, but at least three or four times, that I play the strong man and, protected by the bayonets of our troops, bring about—how do you and your brothers say it?—a coalition of all the positive forces in the country. I refused. Our Government consists of two chambers with many members, and if these gentlemen and their constituents are dissatisfied, they can ask for a change in the Constitution. I personally believe that, with the present Constitution, we can keep peace at home and defend our frontiers. Should the deputies, however, without undue pressure, decide to change our form of government, this concerns neither me nor the Army."

"But if there should be such pressure, Comrade Bernadotte, if force had to be used, where would you stand?"

Jean-Baptiste rose, strode to the terrace door and gazed out as though reaching for words in the grey autumn sky. Napoleon's look almost bored a hole in the back of his dark uniform. The familiar little vein throbbed at his right temple. Jean-Baptiste turned abruptly, came over to Napoleon and dropped his hand heavily on Napoleon's shoulder.

"Comrade Bonaparte—I have served under your command in Italy, I have seen how you plan a campaign. I assure you France boasts no better commander in chief. You can take an old sergeant's word for this. But what the politicians suggest is unworthy of a general of the Republican Army. Don't do it, Bonaparte!"

Napoleon was apparently engrossed in the marguerites I had embroidered on the tablecloth. His face was expressionless. Jean-Baptiste let his hand slip from Napoleon's shoulder, and quietly returned to his place. "If you persist in this, however, I shall fight you and your followers by force of arms, provided . . ."

Napoleon glanced up. "Provided—what?"

"Provided I am ordered by the recognized Government to do so."

"How stubborn you are," Napoleon murmured. Whereupon Josephine suggested that we ought to start for Mortefontaine.

Julie's house was full of guests. We met Talleyrand and Fouché there, and naturally Napoleon's personal friends, General Junot, Murat, Leclerc and Marmont. They were all pleasantly surprised when Napoleon and Jean-Baptiste arrived together.

After dinner Fouché remarked to Jean-Baptiste, "I didn't know that you and General Bonaparte were friends."

"Friends? In any case we are related by marriage," Jean-Baptiste said.

Fouché laughed. "Some people are unusually wise in their choice of relatives."

Jean-Baptiste smiled good-naturedly. "As for me, God knows I didn't choose this relationship."

In the days following all Paris spoke of nothing but whether or not Napoleon would dare try a coup d'état. Once I happened to be driving through the rue de la Victoire and saw many young men standing in front of Napoleon's house beating time and shouting in chorus to the closed windows above, "Vive Bonaparte!"

Fernand claims the youths are paid for these demonstrations, but Jean-Baptiste says that many Parisians remember with enthusiasm the large sums of money Napoleon extorted from the conquered Italian states and sent back to Paris.

When I came down early yesterday to the dining room, I knew somehow: Today. Today would be the day. Joseph, clutching one of Jean-Baptiste's uniform buttons, was talking to him feverishly. He wanted Jean-Baptiste to go with him immediately to see Napoleon. "But you must at least hear what he has to say; then you can see for your-self that he only wants to save the Republic," Joseph said.

Jean-Baptiste answered, "I know his plans, and they have nothing to do with the Republic."

And Joseph, "For the last time—do you refuse to support my brother?"

"For the last time—I refuse to take part in any form of high treason."

Joseph turned to me. "Make him listen to reason, Désirée!" And I, "May I bring you a cup of coffee, Joseph? You seem upset." Joseph refused and departed, and Jean-Baptiste stood at the terrace door, staring at the empty autumn garden.

An hour later, General Moreau, M. Sazzarin, Jean-Baptiste's former secretary, and several other gentlemen from the War Ministry descended on us like an avalanche. They insisted that Jean-Baptiste should take command of the National Guard to prevent Napoleon's entry into the Senate, the Council of Five Hundred.

"Any such order must come from the Government," Jean-Baptiste stood firm.

In the midst of this discussion, in burst more city councillors—the same ones who had been here earlier—and sided with the others' request. Jean-Baptiste patiently explained all over again, "I cannot possibly act under orders from the Paris Municipal Council. Nor from my comrade, dear Moreau. I must be empowered to act by the Government itself. If the directors are no longer in office, my orders must come from the Council of Five Hundred."

Late that afternoon I saw Jean-Baptiste in civilian clothes for the first time. He wore a dark-red coat, too tight and too long for him, a funny high hat, and an artfully tied yellow neckcloth. My General seemed to be dressed for a masquerade.

"Where are you going?" I naturally wanted to know.

"For a walk," Jean-Baptiste replied, "only for a walk."

Jean-Baptiste's walk lasted for hours. In the evening Moreau and his other friends returned and waited for him. It was pitch dark when he finally got here. "Well?" we all demanded.

"I went to the Luxembourg and the Tuileries," he reported. "Large concentrations of troops are everywhere, but everything is quiet. Most of the soldiers are veterans of the Italian campaigns; I recognized some of them . . ."

"Napoleon has undoubtedly made them many promises," Moreau said.

Jean-Baptiste smiled bitterly. "He made them these promises long ago through their officers, who are now suddenly all back in Paris. Junot, Masséna, Murat, Marmont, Leclerc—the whole clique around Bonaparte."

"Do you believe that these troops are ready to march against the National Guard?" Moreau inquired.

"They have no idea of it," Jean-Baptiste said. "I went as a simple curious civilian, and talked a long time with an old sergeant and some of his men. The soldiers believe that Napoleon will be given command of the National Guard. That's what their officers have told them."

Moreau was furious. "That's the most outrageous lie I've ever heard."

"I think that tomorrow Napoleon will demand from the deputies command of the National Guard," Jean-Baptiste said evenly.

"And we shall insist you share this command with him," Moreau shouted. "Are you prepared to do so?"

Jean-Baptiste nodded. "Submit this request to the Minister of War. If Napoleon is given command of the National Guard, then Bernadotte, as the Ministry's trustee, is to share it with him."

I couldn't sleep all night. From downstairs came the sound of voices. I could distinguish Moreau's light, angry tones and Sazzarin's bass. That was yesterday, only yesterday. . . .

Throughout the day a continuous stream of messengers arrived, officers of all ranks, finally a recruit. The recruit, sweating profusely, leapt from his horse and cried, "Bonaparte is First Consul. First Consul!"

"Sit down, man," Jean-Baptiste said calmly. "Désirée, give him a glass of wine." But before the soldier had pulled himself together enough to speak sensibly, a young captain hurried into the room. "General Bernadotte, the Consular Government has been proclaimed. Bonaparte is the First Consul!"

During the morning Napoleon had gone first to the Senate where he asked to be heard. The Senate, consisting chiefly of venerable and chronically sleepy lawyers, had listened, bored, to his impassioned speech. Napoleon talked some drivel about a conspiracy against the Government, and asked that he be granted in this hour of national peril unrestricted powers to act. The chairman of the Senate explained in a tortuous speech that he must come to some agreement with the Government. Accompanied by Joseph, Napoleon then went to the Council of Five Hundred. Here the atmosphere was very different. Each individual deputy knew exactly what Napoleon's appearance meant, but at first they clung tenaciously to the day's agenda. Soon, however, the chairman of the council—the young Jacobin, Lucien Bonaparte—pulled his brother up on the rostrum. "General Bonaparte has an announcement of decisive importance to the Republic."

"Hear, hear . . ." from the Bonaparte clique, and a concert of whistles from their opponents. Napoleon began to speak. All who heard him agree that he stuttered, that he mumbled something about an intrigue against the Republic and a conspiracy against his own life, but by then there was so much noise he couldn't be heard.

A general uproar followed. The Bonaparte contingent forced their way to the rostrum; their opponents—and these were members of all parties—jumped up, made their way to the exits and found them blocked by troops. Who ordered these troops into the Chamber to "protect" the deputies has not been explained. However, General Leclerc, Paulette's husband, was seen at their head. The National Guard, normally responsible for the safety of the representatives, lined up with the others. Soon the whole Chamber boiled like a witches' brew! Lucien and Napoleon stood close together on the speaker's rostrum; a voice shouted, "Vive Bonaparte!"—ten voices joined in, then thirty, then eighty. The gallery, where Murat, Masséna and Marmont had unexpectedly turned up among the journalists, roared, too. And the deputies, surrounded on all sides by muskets, their toes trampled by grenadiers' boots, cheered helplessly.

The troops withdrew to the far corners of the Chamber and to the gallery. Police Director Fouché arrived with some men in civilian clothes and discreetly requested those members who, it was feared, might disturb the new "peace and order," to follow him. The

Chamber, which now had great gaps, sat for hours, deliberating a new constitution. The chairman read the proposals for the formation of a new Government, to be headed by three consuls. General Napoleon Bonaparte was unanimously elected as First Consul, and at his request the Tuileries were placed at his disposal as his official residence.

During the evening, Fernand brought us the special editions, damp from the news presses. In enormous type the name *Bonaparte* hit us in the eye. In the kitchen with Marie I said, "Do you remember that other news sheet? Bonaparte was appointed Military Governor of Paris and you brought it to me on the terrace, at home in Marseilles. . . ."

Marie was carefully filling a bottle with the diluted milk Oscar still has to drink because his mama is very inefficient and can't produce enough for him. "And tonight he's moving to the Tuileries. Perhaps he'll sleep in the same room the King used to," I added.

"That would be just like him," Marie growled, and handed me the bottle.

While I sat in the bedroom with my child in my arms and watched how greedily he swallowed and smacked his lips, Jean-Baptiste came up and sat beside me. In stamped Fernand with a slip of paper. "Reporting, sir. This note has just been delivered by an unknown female."

Bernadotte glanced at the paper, and held it up for me to read. In shaky script it said, "General Moreau has just been arrested. . . ."

"A message from Mme Moreau brought by her kitchen maid," Jean-Baptiste decided. Oscar was asleep so we went downstairs, and ever since have been waiting for the state police. I began to write in my diary.

There are nights which never end.

Suddenly a carriage stopped in front of our house. Now they have come to take him away, I thought. I jumped up and ran into the salon. Jean-Baptiste was standing motionless in the centre of the room, listening tensely. I went to him, and he put his arm around me. Never in my life have I been so close to him.

Once, twice, three times—the door knocker banged. "I'll open it," Jean-Baptiste said and let go of me. At the same time we heard voices. First a man's voice, and then a woman's laugh. My knees gave way and I fell into the nearest chair, and suddenly found myself crying. It was Julie. Dear Lord, only Julie. . . .

We were all in the salon. Joseph and Lucien and Julie. With trembling fingers I put fresh candles in the holders, and all at once the room was very bright. Julie was wearing her red evening dress and had apparently drunk too much champagne. Small red spots blotched her cheeks, and she giggled so much she could hardly speak. We assumed that all three had come direct from the Tuileries. Discussions had been going on there all night, details of the new Constitution gone over, and a provisional list of new ministers compiled. Finally Josephine, who was unpacking in the former quarters of the royal family, had decided that they really must celebrate. A state carriage had been sent to fetch Julie, Mme Letizia and Napoleon's sisters, and Josephine had had a room in the Tuileries festively lighted. "We drank much too much, but after all it's a big day. Napoleon will govern France, Lucien is Minister of the Interior, and Joseph is to be Foreign Minister—at least he's on the list—" Julie prattled on. "You must forgive us for waking you, but as we drove past your house I said we could at least say good morning to Désirée and Jean-Baptiste . . ."

"You didn't wake us up; we haven't slept," I said.

". . . and the three consuls will be advised by a State Council consisting of real experts. You may be chosen for this council, Bernadotte," Joseph was saying.

"Josephine wants to do over the Tuileries," Julie continued. "I can understand that, everything looks so dusty and old-fashioned. Her bedroom will be decorated in white. . . . And imagine—he says she must have a regular court household. She is to engage a reader, and three lady companions who will really be ladies-in-waiting. Foreign countries shall see that the wife of our new head of State understands such matters." Still Julie rambled on.

"I insist on the release of General Moreau," I heard Jean-Baptiste say.

"Protective custody and nothing more, I assure you—to protect Moreau from the mob. No one knows what the people of Paris might do in their wild enthusiasm for Napoleon and the new Constitution. . . ." This from Lucien.

A clock struck six. "We must go. She is waiting outside in the carriage for us. We only wanted to say a quick good morning to you," cried Julie.

"Who is waiting outside in the carriage?" I asked.

"Mama-in-law. Mme Letizia was too tired to come in. We promised to drive her home."

I suddenly longed to see Mme Letizia after this night. I went out. The air smelled of fog, and as I reached the street several figures slipped back into the half-light. Did people always stand in front of our house and wait?

I opened the carriage door. "Mme Letizia," I called into the darkness. "It's I—Désirée. I want to congratulate you."

The figure in the corner of the carriage moved, but it was too dark for me to see her face. "Congratulate me? Why, my child?"

"Because Napoleon is our First Consul, and Lucien is Minister of the Interior, and Joseph says that he . . ."

"The children shouldn't get so involved with politics," came out of the dark. This Mme Bonaparte will never really learn French. She speaks not one syllable better than on the day I met her in Marseilles. I remembered the horrible reeking cellar where they lived then. And now they'd like to redecorate the Tuileries.

"I thought that you'd be very pleased, Mme," I concluded awkwardly.

"No. Napoleon doesn't belong in the Tuileries. It's not for him," came firmly from the dark carriage.

"We live in a republic," I remonstrated.

"Call Julie and the two boys. I'm tired. You'll see, in the Tuileries he will get bad ideas, some very bad ideas!"

They appeared finally, Julie, Joseph, Lucien. Julie embraced me, and pressed her hot cheek against mine. "It's so wonderful for Joseph," she whispered. "Come and have dinner with me. I must talk with you."

At that moment Jean-Baptiste came out to show our guests to their carriage. Suddenly out of the fog sprang the lurking figures—these unknowns who with us had waited through the endless night. "Vive

Bernadotte!" someone shouted. The voice quivered. "Vive Bernadotte, Vive Bernadotte!" There were only three or four voices. And
it was ridiculous for Joseph to cringe with terror.

A grey rainy day has begun. An officer of the National Guard has
just left the following message: "Order from the First Consul—
General Bernadotte is to report to him at eleven o'clock in the Tuileries." I am closing and locking my diary. I shall take it to Julie.

Paris, March 21, 1804
(Only the Magistrates stick to the Republican calendar,
and write today: 1 Germinal of the Year XII)

It was mad of me to drive alone at night to the Tuileries to see
him.

I realized this from the start. Nevertheless, I climbed into Mme
Letizia's carriage, still trying to decide what to say to him. Somewhere a clock struck eleven. I would walk through the long empty
corridors of the Tuileries, slip into his study, stand in front of his
desk, and explain to him that . . .

The carriage rolled along beside the Seine. In the course of years,
I've become familiar with most of the bridges. But whenever I come
to a certain bridge, my heart starts pounding. I always have to stop,
get out and walk. On my bridge. . . . It was one of the very first
spring nights of the year. Spring hadn't really quite come, but the
air was soft and sweet. It had rained the whole day, but now the
heavy clouds were breaking and the stars were out. He cannot have
him shot, I thought. On the rippling waters of the Seine the stars
danced with the lights of Paris. He cannot have him shot!

Cannot?

He can do anything.

On the bridge I walked slowly up and down, meditating on all these years I've lived through without respite. Danced at weddings, curt-sied to Napoleon in the Tuileries as though to royalty, celebrated the victory of Marengo at Julie's and drunk so much champagne that the next morning Marie had to hold my head over the washbasin. I have bought a yellow silk evening dress, and a silver one embroidered with rose pearls, and a white one with green velvet bows. Those were minor events. The big ones—Oscar's first tooth, Oscar's first "Mama" and Oscar who for the first time without my help on chubby, unsteady little legs has walked from the piano to the chest of drawers.

And now I've been thinking over these past years. Remembering them and trying desperately to put off the moment when I intended to force my way into the presence of the First Consul. Julie returned my diary just a few days ago.

"I was tidying up my chest of drawers, that mahogany monster I brought from Marseilles," she said. "It's in the nursery now; the children have so many things they really need it. And so I found your book. I don't have to take care of it any longer, do I?"

"No, no longer," I said. "Or, perhaps, not yet."

"You'll have a lot to catch up on." Julie laughed. "I don't suppose you've even mentioned that I have two daughters."

"No, I gave you the diary during the night after the coup d'état. But now I'll write down that you went regularly to take the cure at Plombières and took your Joseph with you, that over two and a half years ago Zenaïde Charlotte Julie was born, and thirteen months later Charlotte Napoleone. And that you still read innumerable novels and were so thrilled by some story about a harem that Miss Daughter Number One was christened Zenaïde."

"I hope she'll forgive me that," Julie said remorsefully.

I took the diary from her. I must, first of all, I thought, write that Mama is dead. It was last summer. I was sitting with Julie in our garden and suddenly Joseph rushed in with Etienne's letter to us. Mama died in Genoa after a heart attack. "Now we are all alone," Julie said. "You have me," Joseph insisted. He didn't understand us. Julie belongs to him and I to Jean-Baptiste, but since Papa's death, we have had only Mama who remembered how everything was when we were children.

On the evening of this sad day, Jean-Baptiste said to me, "You know that we must all abide by the laws of Nature. This law of Nature is that we do not outlive our children. It would be unnatural if we did. We must accept the laws of Nature philosophically." He wanted to comfort me. Every woman who has endured the pain of childbirth is told that she is sharing the fate of all mothers. But it's not much comfort, I find.

From my bridge, Mme Letizia's carriage loomed up like a black monster lying in wait for me. On Napoleon's desk lies a sentence of death, and I will say to him . . .

Yes, what will I say to him?

One may no longer talk with him as with other people, one may not even sit down unless he suggests it. The morning after that endless night of waiting for Jean-Baptiste's arrest words flew between him and Napoleon.

"You have been elected to the State Council, Bernadotte. You will represent the Ministry of War in my State Council," the First Consul told him.

"Do you think I've changed my mind in one night?" asked Jean-Baptiste.

"No. But, during this same night I have become responsible for the Republic, and I cannot afford to lose one of her ablest men. Will you accept, Bernadotte?"

Jean-Baptiste told me that there was a long pause. A pause in which he first inspected the huge room in the Tuileries, with its enormous desk resting on gilded lions' heads. A pause in which he then looked out of the window and down on the soldiers of the National Guard with their blue-white-red cockades. A pause in which he told himself that the directors had resigned and had recognized the Consular Government. That the Republic had delivered itself up to this man to avert civil war.

"You are right, the Republic needs each of her citizens, Consul Bonaparte. I therefore accept."

Early the next morning Moreau and all the arrested deputies were set free. Moreau, what's more, was given a command. Napoleon was preparing a new Italian campaign, and appointed Jean-Baptiste supreme commander of our Army of the West. Jean-Baptiste forti-

fied the Channel coast against English attacks, and commanded all
the garrisons from Brittany to the Gironde. He has to spend most
of his time at his headquarters in Rennes, and he wasn't home when
Oscar had whooping cough. Napoleon won the Battle of Marengo,
and Paris went mad celebrating. Today our troops are scattered all
over Europe, because, in his negotiations for peace, Napoleon demanded the surrender to France of innumerable provinces, which
the Republic is now occupying.

So many lights are dancing on the Seine, many more than before.
Then I thought there could be nothing more cynical and more mad-
dening than Paris. But Jean-Baptiste says that Paris today is a hundred times more full of fight than before and that I was hardly in
a position to judge. Napoleon has allowed the exiled aristocrats to
come back. In the Faubourg St. Germain there's intrigue again, confiscated gardens have been returned, torch bearers flank the light carriages of the Noailles, the Radziwills, the De Montesquieus, and the
Montmorencys. With grace and dignity the former great of Versailles
have moved through the rooms of the Tuileries and curtsied before
the Leader of the Republic, bowed over the hand of the erstwhile
Widow Beauharnais who never left the country and never went
hungry either. Instead, M. Barras paid her bills and she danced with
the ex-lackey Tallien at the ball for "Relatives of Victims of the
Guillotine." Sometimes it's more than I can manage to keep straight,
the titles of all these princes, counts, and barons who are introduced
to me.

"I'm afraid of him. He has no heart." I heard her voice distinctly
that early spring night on the bridge. Christine. Christine, the peasant girl from St. Maximin, the wife of Lucien Bonaparte. Hundreds,
thousands of witnesses saw how Lucien pulled his brother up to the
rostrum, and with shining eyes brought forth the first "Vive Bonaparte." A couple of weeks later the walls of the Tuileries trembled
because they quarrelled so terribly. Minister of the Interior Lucien
Bonaparte and First Consul Napoleon Bonaparte. First they argued
about the censorship of the press which Napoleon had introduced.
Then about banishing of writers. And constantly about Christine,
the innkeeper's daughter, who had been forbidden to enter the
Tuileries. Lucien didn't last long as Minister of the Interior. Nor

did Christine continue as a cause of family disagreement. The plump peasant girl with the apple-red cheeks and dimples began, after a miserable wet winter, to cough blood. One afternoon I was sitting with her, and we talked about next spring and read the fashion magazines. Christine wanted a dress with gold embroidery.

"In this dress," I said, "you will drive to the Tuileries and be presented to the First Consul, and you will be so beautiful that he will envy Lucien."

Christine's dimples disappeared. "I'm afraid of him," she said. "He has no heart."

Finally Mme Letizia insisted that Christine be received at the Tuileries. Napoleon heeded this and a week later casually told his brother, "And don't forget to bring your wife to the opera tomorrow evening and to present her to me."

Lucien answered simply, "I'm afraid my wife will be unable to accept this honourable invitation."

Napoleon's lips were a thin line. "It is not an invitation, Lucien, but a command from the First Consul."

Lucien shook his head. "My wife cannot comply with a command, even from the First Consul. My wife is dying."

The most expensive wreath at Christine's funeral was inscribed, "To my beloved sister-in-law Christine—N. Bonaparte."

The Widow Jouberthou has red hair, an ample bosom, and dimples which remind one a little of Christine. She had been married to some unknown little bank clerk. Napoleon demanded that Lucien marry the daughter of one of the repatriated aristocrats. But Lucien turned up at the registry office with the Widow Jouberthou. Whereupon Napoleon signed an expulsion order against the French Citizen Lucien Bonaparte, former member of the Council of Five Hundred, former Minister of the Interior of the French Republic. Lucien paid us a farewell visit before he left for Italy.

"Back there in Brumaire," he said, "I wanted to do the best thing for the Republic. You know that, don't you, Bernadotte?"

"I know that," answered Bernadotte, "but you made a grave mistake—back there in Brumaire."

It was about two years ago that Hortense cried so loudly in her room in the Tuileries that the guards kept looking up at her windows in alarm. Napoleon had betrothed his stepdaughter to his brother Louis. Louis, the fat, flat-footed youth, had no interest whatsoever in colourless Hortense. He preferred the actress at the *Comédie Française*. But Napoleon feared another *mésalliance* in the family. So Hortense locked herself in, and simply screamed. She refused to let her mother in. Finally they sent for Julie. Julie hammered with her fists on Hortense's door until the girl opened it.

"Can I help you?" Julie asked. Hortense shook her head. "You love someone else, don't you?" Julie said. Hortense's weeping ceased, and her thin figure stiffened. "You love someone else," Julie repeated. Hortense nodded almost imperceptibly. "I'll talk to your stepfather," Julie said. Hortense shrugged her shoulders hopelessly. Julie continued. "Is the other man one of the First Consul's group? Would your stepfather consider him eligible?" Hortense didn't answer. Tears flowed from her wide-open eyes. "Or—is this other man already married?" Hortense's lips parted. She started to smile, then suddenly laughed. Laughed and laughed—shrill and wild, like one gone mad.

Julie grabbed her shoulders. "Stop that! Pull yourself together! If you don't I'll have to call the doctor—" But Hortense couldn't stop laughing. That finished my patient Julie. Without thinking she slapped Hortense hard.

Hortense was struck dumb. She closed her big mouth and took a couple of deep breaths. When she was calmer, "I love—*him*," she said softly.

Julie hadn't thought of this possibility. "Does he know?" she asked.

Hortense nodded. "There are very few things he doesn't know. And the rest he finds out from our Minister of Police, M. Fouché." She sounded bitter.

Julie stood up and took Hortense's hand. "You'd better marry Louis. Louis is his favourite brother. . . ."

The nuptials were celebrated a few weeks later. Paulette was held up to Hortense as an example. How she fought against her marriage. Napoleon practically had to push her into marrying General Leclerc. And ho   she wept because Napoleon ordered her to accompany Leclerc to San Domingo. She finally embarked with him, tears streaming down her face. Leclerc died in San Domingo of yellow fever. And Paulette was so disconsolate that she cut off her honey-coloured hair and laid it in his coffin. To the First Consul this was undying proof of Paulette's devotion to the late lamented. I once disagreed with him. "On the contrary, it proves that she never loved him. And that therefore she must at the last make a show of love."

Paulette's hair grew back into shoulder-length ringlets, and Napoleon decided that she should hold these curls up with some valuable pearl combs. These combs are part of the family jewels of the Borghese family. The Borghese are old Italian nobility related to all the ruling houses of Europe. Napoleon practically shoved the aging Count Camillo Borghese, with his weak knees and trembling hands, at his favourite sister Paulette. That's a laugh—the Countess Pauline Borghese. Paulette in her soiled finery, picking up men on the street. . . .

They're all so changed, I thought. I took a last look at the lights dancing on the ripples. Why only I, why do they think I'm the only one who can, perhaps, succeed?

I walked back to the carriage. "To the Tuileries."

I thought over my project with some despair. This Bourbon, the Duke of Enghien, who is apparently in the pay of the English, and who keeps threatening to restore the Republic to the Bourbons, has been arrested. He wasn't arrested on French soil. They didn't find him in France but in a small town called Ettenheim in Germany. Four days ago Napoleon ordered an unexpected attack against this little town. Three hundred dragoons crossed the Rhine, snatched the Duke out of Ettenheim, and dragged him to France. Now he's waiting in the fortress at Vincennes for his fate to be decided. Today a court martial condemned him to death for high treason and for an alleged attempt to assassinate the First Consul. The death sentence has been sent to the First Consul. Napoleon will either confirm it, or pardon the culprit.

The old nobility, now frequent visitors at Josephine's, have naturally implored her to beg Napoleon for clemency. They were all at the Tuileries while foreign diplomats besieged Talleyrand. Napoleon received no one. Josephine tried to get a word in at lunch. With a "Please don't bother me," he shut her up. Toward evening,

Joseph had himself announced. Napoleon asked what he wanted. Joseph explained to the secretary, "An appeal in the name of justice." The secretary was told to inform Joseph that the First Consul was not to be disturbed.

At supper Jean-Baptiste was unusually quiet. Suddenly he banged his fist on the table. "Do you realize what Bonaparte has done? With the help of three hundred dragoons he seizes a political enemy in a foreign country. Brings him to France and is holding him here for a court martial. To any man with even a spark of decent feeling this is a slap in the face!"

"And what will happen to the prisoner? He can't have him shot." I was horrified.

Jean-Baptiste was clearly appalled. "And he's under oath to the Republic: he swore to uphold the Rights of Man."

We said no more about the Duke. But I kept thinking about the death sentence that was right now on Napoleon's desk waiting for a stroke of his pen.

"Julie told me that Jérôme Bonaparte has agreed to divorce his American wife," I said, to relieve the depressing silence. Jérôme, once such a dreadful child, was now a naval officer and on one of his voyages he had almost been captured by the English.

To escape them he was landed at an American port, and had married a Miss Elizabeth Patterson, a young lady from Baltimore. This naturally made Napoleon furious. Now Jérôme was on his way home, and, to please his distinguished brother, he had agreed to divorce the former Miss Patterson. "But she is very rich," had been Jérôme's only written protest to Napoleon.

"The family affairs of the First Consul really do not interest me," remarked Jean-Baptiste. At that very minute we heard a carriage drive up.

"It's after ten," I said. "Much too late for callers."

Fernand stamped in and announced, "Mme Letizia Bonaparte."

I was astonished. Napoleon's mother never just dropped in. Now she was right behind Fernand. "Good evening, General Bernadotte! Good evening, madame."

In recent years Mme Letizia hasn't aged, she seems younger. Her face that used to be drawn and careworn is fuller, the wrinkles round her mouth are gone. There's a little silver in her black hair, which she still wears peasant fashion, combed back and knotted at the back of her neck. A few Parisian curls hang down on her forehead and are very unbecoming.

We steered her into the drawing room, and she sat down and slowly drew off her light-grey gloves. I couldn't help staring at her hands and the large cameo ring Napoleon had brought her from Italy. I kept thinking of those red chapped hands that in the old days were always washing clothes.

"General Bernadotte, do you believe it possible that my son will have this Duke of Enghien shot?" she asked immediately.

"Not the First Consul but a court martial condemned the Duke to death," Jean-Baptiste answered cautiously.

"The court martial acts according to my son's wishes. Do you believe it possible that my son will have the sentence carried out?"

"Not only possible, but very probable. I don't see why else he would even have ordered the Duke's arrest and court martial in the first place. He wasn't even on French soil."

"I thank you, General Bernadotte." Mme Letizia studied her cameo ring. "Do you know on what grounds my son took this step?"

"No, madame."

"Can you imagine?"

"I'd rather not say, madame."

Again she was silent. She sat on the sofa, leaning forward, her legs a little apart—like a peasant woman who is very tired and dares rest only for an instant.

"General Bernadotte, do you understand the full meaning of this death sentence?"

Jean-Baptiste gave no answer. He ran his hand through his hair, and I could see how painful this conversation was to him.

Mme Letizia lifted her head. Her eyes were wide. "Murder! Low, common murder!"

"You mustn't be so upset, madame . . ." Jean-Baptiste began in distress, but she raised both hands and cut him off.

"Not be upset, you say? My son is about to commit murder, and I—I, his mother, should remain aloof?"

I went over and sat down beside her on the sofa and took her hand. Her fingers trembled. "Napoleon could have political reasons," I whispered.

"Shut up, Eugénie," she snapped. She looked Jean-Baptiste straight in the eye. "There is no excuse for murder, General. Political reasons are . . ."

"Madame," Jean-Baptiste said quietly. "You sent your son for many years to the military academy and there he was trained to be an officer. It could be, madame, that your son places less value on the life of one man than you do."

She shook her head in desperation. "This isn't a question of the life of one man in battle, General. This concerns a man who was dragged to France by force to be shot. With this shot France will lose the respect of other nations. I won't have Napoleon become a murderer. I will not have it, do you understand me?"

"You should speak to him, madame," Jean-Baptiste suggested.

"No, no, signor—" Her voice shook and her mouth worked frantically. "That would do no good. Napoleon would say, 'Mama, you don't understand, go to sleep, Mama; shall I increase your monthly allowance?' She must go, signor—she, Eugénie."

My heart stood still. I began to shake my head desperately.

"Signor General—you don't know it, but before when my Napoleone was arrested, and we were afraid that he'd be shot, she—the little girl, Eugénie—rushed to the authorities and helped him. Now she must go to him—and she must remind him, and ask him . . ."

"I don't believe it would make any impression on the First Consul," said Jean-Baptiste.

"Eugénie—pardon, Signora Bernadotte—madame, you don't want your country exposed to the whole world as a republic in which murder is condoned. You don't, do you? People have told me—oh, so many people came to me today with stories of this Duke. They told me that he has an old mother and a young fiancée. . . . Madame, take pity on me, help me, I don't want my Napoleone—"

Jean-Baptiste was wandering aimlessly about the room.

Mme Letizia didn't give up. "General, if your son, your little Oscar, were about to sign this death sentence . . ."

"Désirée, get ready and drive to the Tuileries." Jean-Baptiste spoke calmly but very firmly.

I got up. "You'll come with me, won't you, Jean-Baptiste. You will come with me?"

"You know very well, little one, that that would deprive the Duke of his last chance." Jean-Baptiste smiled bitterly. He took me in his arms and held me tight. "You must speak to him alone. I fear you won't have much success, but you must try, darling." His voice was full of pity.

I still objected. "It wouldn't look well for me to go to the Tuileries alone at night," I ventured. "So many women go there alone late at night." I didn't care whether Mme Letizia heard me or not. "Yes, alone, to the First Consul."

"Put on your hat, take a wrap, and go," Jean-Baptiste said.

"Use my carriage, madame. And, if you don't mind, I'll wait here till you come back," Mme Letizia said. I nodded mechanically. "I won't disturb you, General. I'll sit here by the window and wait." Whereupon I hurried to my room and with shaking fingers tied on my new hat with the pale pink roses.

Since an infernal machine exploded close behind Napoleon's carriage four years ago on Christmas Eve, hardly a month goes by that Police Chief Fouché doesn't foil some plot against the First Consul. Now, no one can enter the Tuileries without being stopped every ten steps and asked what or whom one wants there. Nevertheless everything went more smoothly than I had expected. Each time I was challenged I said, "I wish to speak to the First Consul," and was allowed to pass. No one asked me my name. Nor was I asked the purpose of my visit. The soldiers merely smiled surreptitiously, stared at me curiously, and undressed me in their imagination. The whole thing was painfully embarrassing.

I finally reached the door from which it is possible to see into the anteroom of the office of the First Consul. I had never been here before since the occasional family parties I'd been invited to in the Tuileries had all been held in Josephine's apartments. The two soldiers of the National Guard, standing guard at this door, asked me nothing at all. So I opened the door and went in. A young man in civilian clothes sat at a desk writing. I cleared my throat twice before he heard me. When he did he shot up as though he'd been bitten by a tarantula. "What do you want, mademoiselle?"

"I want to speak to the First Consul."

"You've made a mistake, mademoiselle. These are the First Consul's offices."

I had no idea what the young man was talking about.

"Do you mean that the First Consul has already gone to bed?" I asked.

"The First Consul is still in his office."

"Then take me in to him."

"Mademoiselle—" It was really funny. The young man, who up to then had been concentrating on my feet, blushed and, for the first time, looked at my face. "Mademoiselle, Constant, the valet, must have told you that he is waiting for you at the back entrance. These rooms—are only offices."

"But I wish to speak to the First Consul, and not to his valet. Go in and ask the First Consul if he can be disturbed for a moment. It is—yes, it's very important."

"But mademoiselle—" the young man implored me.

"And don't call me mademoiselle, but madame. I am Mme Jean-Baptiste Bernadotte."

"Mademoi—oh, madame—oh, your pardon—" The young man goggled at me as though I were the ghost of his great-grandmother. "It was a mistake," he said.

"Mistakes can happen. But now will you finally show me in?"

The young man disappeared, and returned immediately.

"May I ask madame to follow me. The First Consul is in conference. The First Consul begs madame to be patient for a minute. Only a minute, the First Consul said."

He took me to a small salon with dark-red brocade chairs grouped sternly around a marble-topped table. A salon obviously used just to wait in. But I didn't wait long. A door opened and three, four backs, reverently bowing low to someone I couldn't see, were wishing him "a pleasant rest, a very fine rest." The door closed behind them. The gentlemen—each held a stack of files under his arm—steered a course through the anteroom while the secretary scurried past them and disappeared into the First Consul's office. He'd hardly closed the door when he popped out again and solemnly announced:

"Mme Jean-Baptiste Bernadotte—the First Consul will see you."

"This is the nicest surprise I've had for years," Napoleon said as I went in. He had waited for me right at the door. He took my hands and raised them to his lips. And—really kissed them. Cool, damp lips first on my right hand and then on my left. I withdrew my hands quickly, and didn't know what to say.

"Sit down, dearest! Sit down. And tell me how you are. You look younger every year."

"I do not," I said. "Time goes so fast. By next year we'll have to find a tutor for Oscar."

He urged me into the armchair beside his desk. He himself didn't sit opposite me at the desk, but paced restlessly up and down all around the room, and I had to crane my neck to keep him in sight. It was a very large room with a great many small tables, all loaded with books and papers. On the large desk, however, everything was in two neat piles. Both these piles were in wooden boxes that looked like narrow drawers. Between the two narrow boxes—right in front of the armchair behind the desk—I noticed a single document with a blood-red seal. In the fireplace there was a roaring fire. It was unbearably hot.

"You must see this. The first copies off the press—here." He held a few sheets, cluttered with print, under my nose. I saw it was in paragraphs. "The Civil Code is completed. The *Code Civil* of the French Republic. The laws for which we fought the Revolution —worked out, written down and printed. And valid, valid forever. I have given France a new civil code!"

Year after year he'd shut himself up with our leading experts on civil law, compiling France's new civil code. Now it was finished and ready to be enforced.

"The most humane laws in the world," he said. "Read this—here —this applies to children. The oldest son has no more rights than his brothers and sisters. And here: Parents are required to support their children. And see this—" He picked up some other pages from one of the tables and began to leaf through them. "The new marriage laws. They make possible not only divorce but also separation. And here—" He held up another page. "This will surprise the aristocracy. Hereditary titles have been abolished."

"People already call your *Civil Code* the *Code Napoleon*," I remarked. I wanted him to keep in good humour. Besides, it was true. He tossed the sheets of paper on the mantelpiece.

"Excuse me, I'm boring you, madame," he said coming closer. "Take off your hat, madame."

"No, no—I'm only staying a minute. I just wanted . . ."

"But it's unbecoming, madame. It doesn't suit you at all. May I remove your hat?"

"No. And furthermore it's a new hat, and Jean-Baptiste says it looks very well on me."

He retreated quickly. "Of course, if General Bernadotte says so. . . ." He began to stride up and down behind my back. Now, I've annoyed him, I thought miserably, and hastily untied the ribbons on my hat.

"May I ask to what I owe the honour of this late visit, madame?" His voice was sharp.

"I have taken off my hat," I said. I realized he had stood still. Then he came over close behind me again. I felt his hand touch my hair very lightly. "Eugénie—" he murmured, "little Eugénie—"

I quickly ducked my head to shake off his hand. His voice was as it had been on that rainy night when we became engaged.

"I wanted to ask you something." I could hear my voice tremble.

He crossed the room, away from me, and leaned against the mantelpiece. The glow of the flames was reflected in his shiny boots.

"Naturally," he said.

"Why naturally?" I asked without thinking.

"I hadn't expected you to come to me unless you wanted something," he said cuttingly. And while he knelt to put another large log on the fire, continued, "Most people who come to see me have a favour to ask. A man in my position is used to that. Now, what can I do for you, Mme Jean-Baptiste Bernadotte?"

His sneering superiority was more than I could bear. Except for his short hair and his beautifully tailored uniform, he looked very much as he had in our garden in Marseilles.

"Had you perhaps flattered yourself that I would call on you in the middle of the night, unless I had an important reason to?" I spat out.

My rage seemed to amuse him. He cheerfully rocked back and

forth, heel and toe, toe and heel. "No, I never expected that, Mme Jean-Baptiste Bernadotte, but—perhaps I secretly hoped you might. May one still hope, madame?"

This isn't getting me anywhere, I thought desperately. I can't even make him take me seriously. My fingers plucked at the silk roses on my new hat.

"You are ruining your new hat, madame." I didn't look up. I swallowed and gulped and a tear escaped and trickled down my cheek to my lips. I put out my tongue to catch it.

"What can I do to help you, Eugénie?"

There he was again—the Napoleon of the old days. Tender, sincere.

"You say that many people come to ask you something. Do you usually grant their requests?"

"If I can justify it, of course."

"Justify it to whom? You—you yourself are the most powerful man in France, aren't you?"

"Justify it to myself, Eugénie. Well—tell me what you want."

"I beg you to reprieve him."

Silence. The fire crackled.

"You mean the Duke of Enghien?"

I nodded.

I waited for his answer, and he let me wait. I tore one petal after another out of the silk roses on my hat.

"Who sent you to me with this request, Eugénie?"

"That's not important. Many people have made this request. I am only one of them."

"I must know who sent you." He spoke sharply.

I plucked at the roses.

"I asked who sent you? Bernadotte?"

I shook my head.

"Madame, I am accustomed to having my questions answered."

I looked up. His head was thrust forward, his mouth distorted, and there was saliva at the corners of his mouth.

"You needn't shout at me, I'm not afraid," I said. And I really wasn't afraid of him any more.

"I remember that you like to play the role of the courageous young lady. I remember that scene in the Tallien's salon—" He hissed the last part.

"I am not at all courageous," I said. "I'm actually a coward. But if there's a great deal at stake, I can pull myself together."

"And that day, in Mme Tallien's salon, you had a great deal at stake, didn't you?"

"Everything," I said simply, and waited for the next sneering remark. He made none. I lifted my head and sought his eyes.

"But before that I had once been very courageous. That was when my fiancé—you know I was once engaged, long before I met General Bernadotte—when my fiancé was arrested after the fall of Robespierre. We feared he might be shot. His brothers considered it very dangerous but I went to the Military Commandant of Marseilles with a parcel of underclothes and a cake . . ."

"Yes. And that's precisely why I must know who sent you here tonight."

"What has that to do with it?"

"I'll explain it to you, Eugénie. The person or the persons who have sent you to me know me very well. They have found a possible way to save this Enghien's life. I said only—a possible way. I am curious to know who knows me well enough and is smart enough to exploit it. And yet is obviously opposed to me politically. Well?"

I smiled. How he complicated everything, how politically involved everything appeared to him.

"Try, madame, to see the situation through my eyes. The Jacobins reproach me for allowing the *émigrés* to return, and say that I favour them socially. At the same time, they spread the rumour that I intend to turn over the Republic to the Bourbons. Our France—this France which I have created, the France of the *Code Napoleon!* Doesn't that sound like madness?"

At the last word he went over to the desk and picked up the document with the red seal. He stared at the short text on the document. Then he put it back on the desk, and turned again to me:

"If this Enghien is executed, I shall have proved to France and to the world that I condemn all the Bourbons as dangerous traitors. Do you understand me, madame? After that I will settle my accounts with the others—" In a few rapid strides he moved round the desk,

stood before me, and rocked back and forth triumphantly on his toes
—his heels—his toes again—and his heels. "With the plotters, the
chronic complainers, the writers of broadsides, with all the chuckle-
heads who call me a tyrant. I'll drive them from the community of
French people. And protect France from her enemies at home."

"Enemies at home" . . . Where had I heard that before? Barras
had used it long ago, and, as he spoke, he had looked at Napoleon.
The gilded clock on the mantelpiece, its face set between two hideous
lions, showed one o'clock. I stood up.

"It is very late," I said. But he pulled me back into the armchair.

"Don't go yet, Eugénie—I am so glad you came to see me. And
the night is long . . ."

"But you must be tired yourself," I interrupted.

"I sleep badly. And very little. I—" A hidden door covered with
wallpaper, that I hadn't noticed before, opened a crack. Napoleon
didn't see it. "The camouflaged door is opening," I said. Napoleon
turned. "What is it, Constant?"

A little man in lackey's uniform appeared in the doorway gesticu-
lating frantically. Napoleon stepped nearer him.

"—won't wait any longer. I can't keep her quiet."

"Tell her to get dressed and go home," I heard Napoleon say.
The door closed softly. It was Mlle George of the *Théâtre Français,*
I decided. All Paris knows that Napoleon had been unfaithful to
Josephine with Mme Grassini, the singer; now it's his "Georgina,"
the sixteen-year-old actress, Mlle George.

"I mustn't disturb you any longer," I said and rose.

"I've sent her away, you can't leave me alone," he said, and sat
me back down again. His voice was gentle. "You asked me a favour,
Eugénie. For the first time in your life you asked me a favour."

I closed my eyes, exhausted. The quick changes in his tone of
voice were breaking me down. The heat in the room was unbearable.
On top of all that he positively exuded a restlessness that made me
almost ill. Strange that after so many years I could still sense this
man's every mood, every feeling. He was thinking it over, I knew,
trying to decide and fighting with himself. I dared not leave. Perhaps he'll relent, perhaps he'll give in. . . .

"You don't realize what you're demanding, Eugénie. Enghien

himself is not important. I must once and for all prove to the Bourbons, prove to the whole world, how France feels. The French people must choose their ruler themselves—"

I raised my head.

"Free citizens of a free republic will go to the polls." Was he reciting a poem, or rehearsing a speech?

He was standing in front of the desk holding the document in one hand. The seal on it looked like a huge drop of blood.

"You asked me who sent me here tonight." I spoke loudly. "Before you make a decision I will answer your question."

He did not look up. "Yes? I hear you."

"Your mother."

He lowered his hand, slowly; went over to the fireplace, bent down and picked up a log. "I didn't know my mother was interested in politics," he murmured. "I suppose people have been pestering her to intervene . . ."

"Your mother doesn't consider this death sentence a political issue."

"But?"

"Murder."

"Eugénie—now you have gone too far!"

"Your mother fervently begged me to talk to you. It's not exactly a pleasure."

The shadow of a smile flitted over his face. He fumbled among the files and documents piled high on the small tables. Finally he found what he wanted. He unrolled a large piece of drawing paper and held it under my nose.

"How do you like this? I haven't shown it to anyone yet."

In the top corner was a drawing of a large bee. In the centre a square buzzing with little bees, spaced out at regular intervals. "Bees?" I asked, startled.

"Yes, bees." He beamed happily. "Do you know what they mean?"

I shook my head.

"It's an emblem," said Napoleon.

"An emblem? Where will you use it?"

Expansive arm-waving. "Everywhere. On the walls, carpets, cur-

199

tains, liveries, court carriages, the coronation robes of the Emperor—"

I gasped. He hesitated, looked at me. His eyes bored into mine.

"Do you understand me—do you, Eugénie?"

My heart was pounding. He was already unrolling another sheet. Lions this time, in all possible positions—sleeping lions, leaping lions, lions crouched, lions attacking. Across this sheet Napoleon had written, "An eagle with outspread wings."

"I've commissioned David, the painter, to design a coat of arms."

The lions were carelessly cast on the floor, and he now had the drawing of an eagle with outspread wings.

"I've decided on this one. Do you like it?"

The room was so hot I could hardly breathe. The eagle swam before my eyes, enormous and menacing.

"My coat of arms. The coat of arms of the Emperor of the French."

Had I dreamed these words? I gave a start and found the drawing in my shaking hands. I hadn't realized he'd handed it to me. Napoleon stood at the desk again, staring at the document with the red seal.

He stood motionless, his lips so tight together that his chin jutted out squarely. I felt small beads of perspiration on my forehead. He never looked at me. He leaned over, grabbed the pen, wrote a single word on the document and poured sand over it. Then he shook the bronze bell on his desk violently. On the bell there was a bronze eagle with outspread wings.

The secretary hurried in. Napoleon carefully folded up the document. "Sealing wax!" The secretary brought over wax and a candlestick. Napoleon watched him with interest.

"Drive to Vincennes immediately and deliver this to the commandant of the fortress. You are responsible for seeing that this is given to the commandant in person."

With his back to the door, and after three deep bows, the secretary managed to leave the room.

"I would like to know what you have decided." My voice was hoarse.

Napoleon went down on his knees before me and began to gather up the silk rose petals.

"You've ruined your hat, madame," he remarked and gave me a handful of torn petals. I got up, put the drawing of the eagle on a small table and the pieces of torn silk on the fire.

"Don't worry about it," he added. "The hat wasn't really becoming to you."

Napoleon escorted me through the empty corridors. I noticed the walls. Bees ran through my head, bees, to decorate the Tuileries. I was jumpy because every few moments we passed a guard who saluted noisily. He took me right to the carriage.

"Your mother's carriage. She's waiting for my return. What shall I tell her?" He bowed over my hand. But this time he didn't kiss it. "Wish my mother a pleasant good night. And I thank you kindly for your visit, madame."

In our parlour I found Mme Letizia right where I had left her, in the armchair at the window. The sky was already light. Sparrows twittered cheerily in the garden. Jean-Baptiste was at work on his documents, writing.

"Forgive me for staying away so long, but he wouldn't let me go. He chatted about all sorts of things," I said. A lead ring seemed clamped around my temples.

"Did he send a message to Vincennes?" Mme Letizia asked.

I nodded. "Yes, he did, but he wouldn't tell me what he had decided. He told me to wish you a pleasant good night, madame."

"Thank you, my child," Mme Letizia answered and rose. At the door she turned. "In any event—thank you."

Jean-Baptiste took me in his arms and carried me up to the bedroom. He slipped off my dress and my underclothes. He tried to put on my nightgown, but I was too tired to raise my arms, and he simply wrapped a blanket round me.

"Did you know that Napoleon intends to be crowned Emperor?" I murmured.

"I've heard the rumour, but I believe that's being spread by his enemies. Who told you?"

"Napoleon himself."

Jean-Baptiste stared at me. Then he left me abruptly, and went into the dressing room. I heard him pacing up and down in there for a long time. I couldn't get to sleep until finally I felt him next to me, and I could bury my face in his shoulder. I slept until late in the morning, but I was terribly unhappy in my sleep. I dreamed of a white sheet of paper over which crawled blood-red bees.

Marie brought me my breakfast in bed and a late edition of the *Moniteur*. On the first page I read that this morning at five o'clock in the fortress at Vincennes the Duke of Enghien had been shot.

A few hours later Mme Letizia left Paris to join her exiled son Lucien in Italy.

Paris, May 20, 1804
(1 Prairial of the Year XII)

"Her Imperial Highness, the Princess Joseph," Fernand announced.

And in swished my sister Julie.

"Madame la maréchale, I trust you slept well," Julie said, the corners of her mouth twitching. Was she laughing or crying?

"Very well, thank you, from the bottom of my heart, Imperial Highness," I replied with the deep curtsy M. Montel had taught me.

"I've come early—let's sit in the garden a little while," said my sister, Her Imperial Highness, Princess of the French.

Our garden is small, and despite Josephine's good advice, our rosebushes have not flourished under my care, and there is no tree which could possibly mean as much to me as the old chestnut tree in Sceaux. But when the lilac blooms and the two apple trees Jean-Baptiste planted on Oscar's first birthday are in blossom, there's no sweeter spring scene than our little garden in the rue Cisalpine.

Julie carefully dusted off the garden bench with a handkerchief before she sat down in her dark blue satin dress. This set the blue ostrich feathers in her hair to waving solemnly. Marie brought us lemonade, and looked at Julie critically.

"Her Imperial Highness should use some rouge," she remarked. "Madame la maréchale looks much better."

202

Julie tossed her head irritably. "The Marshal's wife has an easier life. I'm so worried by this big move. We're moving over to the Luxembourg Palace, Marie."

"The lovely villa in the rue du Rocher is no longer good enough for the Princess Julie," Marie remarked sarcastically.

"But, no, Marie," Julie said. "You're unjust. I hate palaces. It's only because the heirs to the French throne always have lived in the Luxembourg."

Julie, wife of the heir apparent to the throne of France, looked thoroughly miserable. But Marie had no sympathy. "The late M. Clary wouldn't have approved, not at all," she grumbled. She put her hands on her hips. "Your late papa was a real Republican."

Julie was terribly uncomfortable. "I can't help it, Marie."

"Leave us alone awhile, Marie," I begged, and as soon as she was out of hearing, "Pay no attention to the old dragon."

"But I really can't help it," Julie moaned. "Moving's no pleasure, and all these ceremonies make me sick. Yesterday, at the appointment of the marshals of France, we had to stand for three solid hours, and today in the Dôme des Invalides . . ."

"We will sit," I declared. "Drink your lemonade."

The lemonade was just like the last few days: sweet—bittersweet. We've been overwhelmed with congratulations. My Jean-Baptiste has been made a marshal of France. This is every soldier's dream, whether he's a recruit or a general. And now for my husband the dream's come true. Only not at all in the way we'd imagined it.

Soon after my nocturnal visit to the Tuileries, George Cadoudal, the Royalist leader, was arrested. After the execution of the Duke of Enghien no one doubted the outcome of Cadoudal's trial. I was worried about Jean-Baptiste when General Moreau, General Pichegru and certain other officers were also arrested and accused of conspiring with Cadoudal. We expected the state police any hour. Instead Jean-Baptiste, just as before, was summoned to the Tuileries by the First Consul.

"The French nation has chosen me. You will not oppose the Republic?"

"I have never opposed the Republic, and I cannot imagine ever doing so," answered Jean-Baptiste quietly.

"We will appoint you a marshal of France," Napoleon declared.

This was too much for Jean-Baptiste.

"We?" he demanded.

"Yes. We. Napoleon I, Emperor of the French."

Jean-Baptiste was dumfounded. This so delighted Napoleon that he roared with laughter, slapped his knees, and danced happily around the room.

General Moreau was found guilty of high treason, but not condemned to death, only exiled. He sailed for America, wearing his French general's uniform. His sword, on which, according to custom among all officers, were the names and dates of the victories he'd participated in, accompanied him. The last meticulously engraved inscription was *Hohenlinden*.

Then everything happened in rapid succession. Day before yesterday, the First Consul went to St. Cloud to hunt. There he allowed himself to be surprised by the decision of the Senate to elect him Emperor of the French. Yesterday, against the back drop of an imposing military parade, he presented marshals' batons to the eighteen most famous generals in the French Army. A week before, Jean-Baptiste had been instructed in strictest confidence to order a marshal's uniform from his tailor. A detailed drawing of this new uniform had been sent him from the Tuileries. After the batons had been distributed, each of the new marshals made a short speech. All eighteen addressed Napoleon as "Your Majesty."

During the speeches of Murat and Masséna, Napoleon half-closed his eyes. One could see how tiring the last few days had been for him. However, when Jean-Baptiste began to speak, thanking him for the honour, Napoleon's face was transfigured with a look of eager interest and a smile—that solicitous, compelling smile. He advanced on Jean-Baptiste, seized his hand and urged him to consider him "not only as Emperor," but also his friend. Jean-Baptiste stood at attention and never moved a muscle.

I watched this ceremony from a platform erected for the wives of the eighteen new marshals. I held Oscar by the hand although it had been made quite clear he wasn't invited. "Madame la maréchale," said a master of ceremonies, "suppose the child cries and interrupts His Majesty's speech." But I thought Oscar should see his papa made a marshal of France. When the thousands of spectators cheered, *"Vive l'Empereur!"* because Napoleon shook Jean-Baptiste's hand, Oscar waved the little flag I'd bought for him in great excitement.

Julie was on another platform. The exclusive one for the Imperial family. Since an emperor must have a distinguished family, Napoleon had designated his brothers, with the exception of Lucien, of course, Imperial princes, and their wives Imperial princesses. Joseph will be recognized as the successor to the throne until Napoleon has a son. Mme Letizia's title raised quite a problem. Napoleon couldn't call her "Empress-Mother," because she never was an empress, but only the wife of the obscure Corsican lawyer, Carlo Buonaparte. Napoleon and his brothers and sisters often speak of her as "Madame Mère," so finally he decided to present her to the nation as "Madame Mère." Madame Mère, incidentally, is still in Italy with Lucien. Hortense, the wife of His Imperial Highness, the flat-footed Prince Louis, has now become a princess by marriage. Eugène de Beauharnais, son of Her Majesty, the Empress Josephine, will also be called Prince.

Although Napoleon's sisters had, within twenty-four hours, ordered themselves gowns, embroidered all over with bees, the *Moniteur* didn't even mention their elevation to Imperial princesses. Caroline, who just before the fall of the Directorate had married General Murat, stood next to me during the ceremony, being like me a madame la maréchale. We'd read in the *Moniteur* that the marshals were to be addressed as "monseigneur." Caroline asked me in all seriousness if I intended to call my husband "monseigneur" in public. I couldn't resist answering such nonsense with some of my own—"No, I'll say 'monseigneur' only in our bedroom. In public I'll call him Jean-Baptiste."

After the ceremony the eighteen marshals and their wives dined with the Imperial family in the Tuileries. The walls, carpets and curtains swarmed with gold embroidered bees. Many hundreds of sewing women must have worked day and night to finish these decorations in time. At first I couldn't think what this bee pattern reminded me of. But after I'd drunk more and more champagne, and the bees seemed to stand on their heads, I recognized it: The Lily.

Napoleon's bees are the Bourbon fleur-de-lis upside down. This is no accident, I thought. I wanted to ask Napoleon whether I was right. But I was sitting too far away from him. Now and then I heard him laugh boisterously, and once, in a sudden silence, he addressed his youngest sister Caroline across the table as madame la maréchale. . . .

"Where will it all end—" said I tactlessly to Julie, sitting on our garden bench.

"But everything has only just begun," Julie whispered, holding her bottle of smelling salts to her nose.

"Aren't you well?" I asked anxiously.

"I can't sleep properly any more," she admitted. "Suppose the Emperor leaves no son and Joseph and I succeed—" She began to shake all over and flung her arms around my neck. "Désirée, you are the only person who understands me. . . . I'm still only the daughter of the silk merchant Clary from Marseilles; I can't—"

I disentangled her arms from my neck. "You must pull yourself together, Julie. Show them who you really are, show all Paris, show all France."

"Who am I really?" Julie's lips trembled.

"The daughter of the silk merchant François Clary," I said earnestly. "Don't forget it, Julie Clary. Head up, don't be ashamed."

Julie got up and I guided her to my bedroom. The ostrich feathers in her hair were crooked, and her nose was red from weeping. She let me fix her hair, put on some rouge and powder her face without a murmur. Suddenly I burst out laughing.

"Julie," I finally managed to say, "it's no wonder you are tired and worried. The ladies of old aristocratic families are always very fragile, and so Princess Julie of the high-born House of Bonaparte is naturally less robust than Citizeness Bernadotte."

"You're making a great mistake, Désirée, not to take Napoleon seriously," Julie said.

"You forget that I was the very first person under the sun who ever did take him seriously," I told her. "But now we must hurry. On the way to the cathedral I want to see the procession of senators."

Policemen cleared the way to the Luxembourg Palace for Julie's carriage. Here we heard Napoleon solemnly proclaimed Emperor of the French. At the head of the procession rode a regiment of dra-goons. Twelve perspiring city councillors followed on foot. It was no picnic for these pot-bellied gentlemen to have to march clear across Paris in parade formation. Behind them trailed the two pre-fects in gala uniform. And then—greeted by roars of laughter from the spectators—old Fontanes, President of the Senate, on horse-back. They had strapped Fontanes onto a brown horse, gentle as a lamb, and led by a groom. Nevertheless, it looked as though the President of the Senate would fall from his horse any minute. In his left hand he held a parchment roll; with his right he clutched his saddle desperately. Behind him the rest of the senators marched in orderly ranks. Then came a band playing an ear-shattering cavalry march, which made Fontanes on his horse even more nervous. The highest officers of the Paris garrison and four cavalry squadrons brought up the rear.

The procession stopped in front of the Luxembourg. A bugler stepped forward, trumpeted a signal in all directions. Old Fontanes righted himself, unrolled his parchment. He then announced that the Senate had decided to elect Consul General Napoleon Bonaparte Emperor of the French.

The crowd listened in silence to the old man's trembling voice and when he'd finished there were a few cries of *"Vive l'Empereur!"* The band played "La Marseillaise," and the procession moved on. Fontanes read his proclamation again on the place du Corps Legisla-tif, the place Vendôme, the place du Carrousel, and in front of the City Hall.

Julie and I told the coachman to drive us as quickly as possible to the Dôme des Invalides. It would have caused a terrible scandal if we hadn't turned up punctually there. We were shown to our places in the gallery which had been reserved for the Empress, the ladies of the Imperial family, and the marshals' wives. And we got there only just in time. Julie slid quickly into her seat on Josephine's left. I was put in the second row, and almost dislocated my neck trying to see, what with Julie's ostrich feathers and Josephine's high-combed childish curls with pearls scattered through them. Below surged a sea of uniforms. Seven hundred retired officers in shabby uniforms, hung with orders and faded ribbons, sat in the first few rows. Right behind them, slender and frozen-stiff, were two hundred students from the Polytechnical School. Eighteen gilded chairs had been set in front of the pews. Here it was all dark blue and gold: the marshals. While retired officers and the future technicians were so awe-struck they could hardly breathe, the marshals seemed to be bearing up nicely. I saw Jean-Baptiste talking zealously to General Masséna. General Junot kept looking up at us and waving to his wife. At that Josephine snapped open her fan and held it in front of her face to show Junot his behaviour was unseemly.

The marshals stopped talking. The Cardinal approached the altar, knelt and prayed silently. At the same time we heard the sound of bugles outside and many voices shouting, *"Vive l'Empereur!"* The Cardinal rose and walked slowly toward the door, followed by ten church dignitaries. Here he received the Emperor of the French.

Napoleon was escorted by Joseph and Louis and his ministers. Both princes wore most peculiar costumes. In their wine-red velvet waistcoats, wide knee-breeches, and white silk stockings, they looked like—yes, like actors portraying lackeys in a performance at the *Théâtre Français*. The procession of clerical and secular dignitaries which had now reached the altar was arrayed in all the colours of the rainbow. Napoleon and the Cardinal were in the lead. Napoleon—an inconspicuous dark-green silhouette against this display. "He is mad, he's wearing a colonel's uniform without orders or decorations," Caroline whispered in exasperation. She sat next to Princess Hortense. Hortense jabbed her with her pointed elbow and hissed, "Ssst."

With deliberation Napoleon mounted the three steps to the gilded throne at the left of the altar. I assume it was a throne, although I'd never seen one before. There he sat—a small lonely figure in a colonel's field uniform. I strained my eyes to make out the emblem on the high back of the gilded chair. It was an *N*. A large *N*, encircled by a laurel wreath.

Not until there was a great rustling of silk dresses around me did it occur to me that we were supposed to kneel and that the Cardinal had already begun to read the Mass. Napoleon had risen, and walked down two of the steps. "He refused to go to confession first, although Uncle Fesch told him to," Caroline was whispering to

Paulette. Hortense hissed "Ssst" again. Josephine covered her face with her folded hands and looked as though she were seriously praying.

Uncle Fesch—the chubby abbé, who during the Revolution resigned to become a travelling salesman and asked Etienne for a job in the Clary firm, had long since returned to his church. From the day the French troops entered Rome, and Napoleon dictated peace conditions to the Vatican, Uncle Fesch had been sure of a cardinal's hat.

And now Uncle Fesch, in the purple of a cardinal, held the golden pyx on high. On their knees before him were the marshals, on their knees the retired officers, who in the hour of need had led the peasants, labourers, fishermen, bank clerks, and recruits to the defence of the Republic's frontiers. On their knees were the young pupils of the Polytechnical School. On her knees was Josephine, the first Empress of the French, and beside her the whole Bonaparte family. On their knees were the high dignitaries of the Church. Napoleon remained standing on the first step to the throne, and bowed his head as he waited.

The last organ note died away. Like a gentle breeze a sigh of relief soughed through the cathedral. Then thousands held their breath. Napoleon removed a paper from his breast pocket and began to speak. But he didn't unfold the paper. He spoke without notes, and he spoke quietly, but clear as a bell his voice vibrated through the cathedral.

"He took elocution lessons from some actor," Caroline whispered. "No, from an actress," Paulette giggled. "Mlle George." "Ssst," hissed Hortense.

As he reached the final sentence, Napoleon stepped down from the first step to his throne. He stood by the altar, his right hand raised for the oath.

"And now you swear to preserve the principles of freedom and equality, on which are based all of our rights, with all the power which in you rests. Do you so swear?"

Every hand went up. Mine, too. A chorus of voices chanted the oath, the sound swelled, soared to the dome, and died away.

The *Te Deum* started. Slowly Napoleon went back to the throne, sat down and never took his eyes off the congregation. The organ played louder.

Escorted by his eighteen gold-bedecked marshals, Napoleon left the cathedral. Dark green pinpointed against all this splendour. In front of the cathedral he mounted his white horse and rode at the head of his guard back to the Tuileries. The crowd cheered. A woman with crazy eyes held up an infant and screamed, "Bless him, bless him!"

Jean-Baptiste waited for me at our carriage. On the way home I said, "You sat in the front row, so you could see everything clearly. How did his face look when he sat so still on the throne?"

"He smiled. With his mouth, but not with his eyes."

And since he didn't go on, but stared straight ahead, I asked, "What are you thinking about, Jean-Baptiste?"

"About the collar of my marshal's uniform. I can hardly bear the prescribed height. Besides, it's too tight and makes me uncomfortable."

He looked very elegant to me. His white satin vest and dark-blue coat were embroidered all over with oak leaves in real gold threads. His blue velvet cape, lined with white satin, was trimmed with gold braid. Around the hem were enormous golden oak leaves.

"Your former fiancé knows how to be comfortable. He laces us up in gold oak leaves while he wears a colonel's field uniform," said Jean-Baptiste. He sounded bitter.

When we got out of the carriage at our house, a group of young men in shabby clothes immediately descended on us. "Vive Bernadotte!" they shouted. "Vive Bernadotte!"

Jean-Baptiste hesitated a fraction of a second. "Vive l'Empereur," he finally answered. "Vive l'Empereur."

When we were alone together at dinner, he casually remarked, "You will be interested to hear that the Emperor has given the Police Minister confidential instructions to watch over not only the private lives, but also the private correspondence of his marshals."

"Julie told me that in the winter he will be really crowned," I said while I thought this over.

Jean-Baptiste laughed. "By whom? Does he perhaps plan to have his uncle Fesch set the crown on his head, accompanied by organ music, in Notre-Dame Cathedral?"

"No. The Pope is to crown him."

Jean-Baptiste set his wine glass down so hard that the wine spilled. "But that is—" He shook his head. "Désirée, I consider that impossible. He wouldn't go on a pilgrimage to Rome to be crowned."

"Of course not. He will have the Pope come to Paris for the occasion."

At first I couldn't understand why Jean-Baptiste found this idea so unbelievable. But he explained to me that the Pope never leaves the Vatican to crown anyone in a foreign country. "I'm not too well versed in history," he concluded, "but I don't think anything like that has ever happened."

I was frantically pouring salt on the tablecloth, hoping this would make the stain wash out better.

"Joseph says that Napoleon will force the Pope to come here," I said.

"God knows, I'm not a faithful son of the Holy Roman Church. That would be too much to expect of a former Revolutionary sergeant. But neither do I think he should badger the old gentleman to come over those bad roads from Rome to Paris," Jean-Baptiste said.

"And they must somehow find an old crown, and a sceptre, and an imperial orb; and we're all supposed to take part in the ceremony. Joseph and Louis want to do it up Spanish style. I can't see flat-footed Louis in any such rig."

Jean-Baptiste stared straight ahead. Suddenly he said, "I will ask him for some independent administrative post, preferably far away from Paris. I would prefer command of an entire province. Not only military command, do you understand? I have worked out a new system of licensing and toll-collecting, and I believe I could make any province prosper."

"But then you'd have to go away again," I objected in despair.

"I have to in any event. Bonaparte will bring about new French peace negotiations, but no lasting peace. And we marshals will be riding all over Europe with our armies until—" he paused—"until we have killed ourselves with victories."

As he spoke, Jean-Baptiste began to loosen his collar. I watched him. "The marshal's uniform is too small for you," I said.

"That's true, my little girl. The marshal's uniform *is* too small for me. And therefore Sergeant Bernadotte will soon be leaving Paris. Come, finish your drink. It's time to go to bed."

Paris, 9 Frimaire of the Year XII
(*By the Church calendar: November 30, 1804*)

The Pontiff actually came to Paris to crown Napoleon and Josephine.

And Jean-Baptiste made a terrible scene with me because he is jealous of him. (Not of the Pope but of Napoleon.) This afternoon, in the Tuileries, we rehearsed the Empress' coronation procession. My head is still spinning and in addition I am very worried because of Jean-Baptiste's jealousy. Between the two I can't get to sleep, so I'm sitting at Jean-Baptiste's large desk, with his many books and maps, writing in my diary. Jean-Baptiste has gone out—I don't know where. . . .

The coronation will be in two days. For months Paris has talked of nothing else. It's to be the most brilliant event of all time, Napoleon says. And the Pope was persuaded to come to Paris, to convince the whole world, particularly the Bourbon adherents, that Napoleon was properly crowned and anointed in Notre-Dame. The erstwhile great at the court of Versailles, who are all devout Catholics, had all been betting with each other on whether the Pope would come or not. Most of them considered it highly unlikely. And who should arrive in Paris a few days ago with a retinue of six cardinals, four archbishops, six prelates and a whole army of personal physicians, secretaries, soldiers of the Swiss Guard, and lackeys? Pius VII.

Josephine gave a great banquet in his honour in the Tuileries. But the Pope left early; he was offended because she had thought he would enjoy a ballet after supper. She really meant well. "Now that the old gentleman is in Paris—" Josephine explained to Uncle Fesch. But Uncle Fesch, now a cardinal from head to toe, only shook his head angrily.

Members of the Imperial family have been rehearsing for the coronation for weeks either in Fontainebleau or in the Tuileries. This afternoon, we, too, the wives of the eighteen marshals, were ordered to the Tuileries. The coronation procession of the Empress was to be rehearsed. When I got to the Tuileries with Laura Junot and Mme Berthier, we were shown in to Josephine's white salon. Most of the members of the Bonaparte family were already assembled and quarrelling.

Joseph is responsible for directing the coronation festivities, but details are being decided on by Master of Ceremonies Despréaux, who will be paid two thousand four hundred francs for his services. Despréaux is also the stage manager and his assistant is that frightful M. Montel from whom I once learned proper deportment. We marshals' wives huddled together in one corner and tried to find out what the quarrelling was about.

"But it is His Majesty's expressed wish," cried Despréaux in despair.

"And if he throws me out of France, like poor Lucien," yelped Elisa Bacciochi, "I won't do it."

"Carry her train indeed. Don't make me laugh," indignantly from Paulette.

"But Julie and Hortense have to carry the train, too, and aren't objecting although they're both Imperial Highnesses." Joseph tried to calm his sisters. His thinning hair, usually slicked firmly back, was every which way.

"Imperial Highnesses," hissed Caroline. "And why weren't we, the Emperor's own sisters, called Highnesses, if I may ask? Are we perhaps not as good as the silk merchant's daughter and . . ."

I felt my face reddening with rage.

". . . and Hortense, the daughter of this—this—" Caroline groped for an insulting word for Her Majesty, the Empress Josephine.

"Ladies, I implore you," moaned Despréaux.

"It's about the coronation robe with the enormous train," Laura Junot whispered to me. "The Emperor wants his sisters and Princess Julie and Hortense to carry it."

"Now—can we begin the rehearsal?" Josephine had entered by a side door. She looked very peculiar. To her shoulders were fastened two sheets sewn together to represent the coronation robe which hadn't been finished. We all sank down in a court curtsy.

"Please line up for Her Majesty's coronation procession," Joseph called.

"She can walk on her hands for all of me. I'm not carrying the train." Elisa Bacciochi quivered with fury.

Despréaux sidled over to us. "The eighteen marshals' wives will unfortunately be seventeen," he announced mysteriously. "For, as a sister of the Emperor, Mme Murat will help carry the train."

"She wouldn't dream of it," Caroline shouted clear across the room.

"Now, I don't see how these seventeen ladies can go two by two," Despréaux mused. "Montel, have you any idea how seventeen ladies can form nine pairs to precede Her Majesty with grace and dignity?"

Montel tripped up and down, frowning anxiously. "Seventeen ladies—in couples—none may walk by herself—"

"May I help you work out this difficult strategic operation?" asked someone right behind us. We turned around and sank again into a deep court curtsy. "I suggest that only sixteen marshals' wives lead Her Majesty's procession. Then will follow, as arranged, Securier with Her Majesty's ring, Murat with her crown, and finally one of the marshals' wives carrying—a cushion with one of Her Majesty's lace handkerchiefs. It will be a very poetic touch."

"A stroke of genius, Your Majesty," exclaimed Despréaux, deeply moved, and practically bent double in one of his best bows. Montel, too, bowed down to the ground.

"And this lady with the lace handkerchief—" Napoleon peered reflectively from Mme Berthier to Laura Junot, from Laura Junot to plain Mme Lefèbvre. I already knew but for once I held my tongue and looked right past him. I wanted to be one of the sixteen. The wife of Marshal Bernadotte. No more and no less, I didn't want to be singled out, I didn't want . . .

"We will ask Mme Jean-Baptiste Bernadotte to assume this responsibility. Mme Bernadotte will look charming. In sky blue, perhaps?"

"Sky blue isn't becoming to me!" I put in quickly, remembering the blue silk dress I'd worn at the Tallien's.

"In sky blue," the Emperor repeated, undoubtedly also remembering that unfortunate dress, and turned aside.

He went over to his sisters and Paulette started right in, "Sire, we do not wish . . ."

"Madame, you forget yourself," came like the crack of a whip from Napoleon. No one may address the Emperor without his speaking first. Paulette shut her mouth. Napoleon turned to Joseph. "More trouble?"

"The girls don't want to carry the Empress' train," Joseph complained, pushing back his few damp strands of hair.

"Why not?"

"Sire, the ladies Bacciochi and Murat, and the Princess Borghese feel . . ."

"Then Their Imperial Highnesses, the Princesses Julie and Hortense Bonaparte, will carry the train alone," Napoleon decided.

"The train is much too heavy for two alone," said Josephine, gathering her sheets around her, and going over to Napoleon.

"If we can't have the same privileges as Julie and Hortense, we won't take on the same duties," Elisa burst out.

"Shut up!" Napoleon shouted. And to Paulette, whom he prefers, "What exactly do you want?"

"We have as much right to the rank of Imperial Highness as those two." Paulette jutted her chin at Julie and Hortense.

Napoleon raised his eyebrows. "One would think I'd inherited the crown from our common father, and were cheating my sisters in distributing our inheritance. My sisters seem to forget that any distinctions they receive depend on my bounty. So far a very generous bounty, don't you think?"

In the deafening silence Josephine's voice rippled like a gentle melody. "Sire, I beg that in your graciousness you raise your sisters to Imperial Highnesses."

She needs allies, went through my head; she's afraid. Perhaps the rumours are true, perhaps he really is considering a divorce. . . .

Napoleon began to laugh. The scene apparently amused him enormously and we realized that it had all along.

"All right," he said to his sisters, "if you promise to behave, I'll grant you . . ."

"Sire!" screamed Elisa and Caroline delightedly. Paulette relapsed into, *"Napoleone, molti grazie!"*

"I would like to see Her Majesty's coronation procession. Proceed!" Napoleon looked at Despréaux.

A very inferior piano, representing the organ, tinkled out a solemn march. Despréaux arranged the sixteen marshals' wives in eight couples and Montel showed them how to walk gracefully, lightly, and above all joyously. This the ladies seemed unable to do because the Emperor stared stonily at their feet. They stumbled in deadly embarrassment around the room, and Paulette bit her hand to keep from laughing. Finally Serurier and Murat were summoned. Both joined the march of the marshals' wives solemnly carrying a sofa cushion on their outstretched palms. This was how the Empress' insignia were to be borne at the coronation. After them I pranced in alone, also armed with a sofa cushion. Finally came Josephine, her trailing sheets cheerfully carried by the two newly created Imperial Princesses and Julie and Hortense.

In this order we marched up and down the room four times, stopping only when Napoleon turned to leave. At that, of course, we sank into another deep court curtsy. But Joseph ran after his brother like a madman. "Sire, I beg of you—Sire!"

"I really haven't time," said Napoleon impatiently.

"Sire, it's about the virgins," Joseph explained and beckoned to Despréaux, who scampered over.

"The virgins are a very serious problem," Despréaux said. "We can't find any."

Napoleon heroically suppressed a smile. "Why must you have virgins, gentlemen?" he asked.

"Your Majesty has perhaps forgotten—in the account of the medieval coronation ceremony in Rheims, on which ours is modelled, twelve virgins, with two candles each, walk to the altar after the anointment of Your Majesty. We have considered a cousin of Mme Berthier, and one of my aunts on my mother's side," Despréaux stammered, "but both ladies already are—they are not—"

"They are undoubtedly virgins, but well over forty," thundered Murat's voice from the background. Murat, the cavalry officer, had forgotten his courtly dignity.

"I have repeatedly asked that members of the old aristocracy take part in the coronation, an event which concerns the entire French people. I'm convinced, gentlemen, that around the Faubourg St. Germain you will find plenty of suitable young girls." With that we curtsied again and Napoleon really did leave.

Then refreshments were served and Josephine sent a lady-in-waiting to ask me over to her sofa. She wanted me to know that she was pleased about my distinguished new duty. She sat between Julie and me and gulped champagne. Her slender face seemed to have got smaller in the last few months. Her eyes, under the silver lids, looked unnaturally large, and the remarkable layers of enamel on her cheeks had cracked up during the long afternoon. Two fine lines, from the sides of her nose to the corners of her mouth, deepened whenever she tried to smile. But the childish curls, piled high on her head, looked, as always, young and carefree.

"Le Roy won't be able to whip me up a sky-blue ensemble in two days," I said.

Josephine, after the long hours she'd spent in the morning having her coronation robes fitted, must have been too tired to be discreet about her past. She said, "Paul Barras once gave me a pair of sapphire earrings. If I can find them, I'll gladly lend them to you."

"Madame is too kind, but I think . . ."

That's as far as I got because we were interrupted. Joseph stood before us. "What's happened now?" Josephine demanded.

"His Majesty requests Your Majesty to come to his study at once," Joseph said.

Josephine raised her thin eyebrows. "New difficulties about the coronation, dear brother-in-law?"

Joseph could contain himself no longer. "The Pope has just informed us that he refuses to crown Your Majesty," he said with considerable relish.

Josephine's small rouged mouth smiled derisively. "And on what grounds does the Holy Father refuse?"

Joseph looked discreetly in every other direction. "Tell me. No one can hear us but Princess Julie and Mme Bernadotte, and they're both in the family, after all," said Josephine.

Joseph pulled in his chin, doubling it. "The Pope has learned that His Majesty and Your Majesty were not married in a church, and has declared . . . pardon me, madame, these are the words of the Holy Father—that he cannot crown the concubine of the Emperor of the French."

"And where did the Holy Father discover that Bonaparte and I had only a civil marriage ceremony?" Josephine asked him calmly.

"That's what we have to find out," Joseph replied.

Josephine thoughtfully studied her empty glass. "And how has His Majesty decided to answer the Holy Father?"

"His Majesty will probably argue with the Pope."

"There's one very simple solution." Josephine smiled and rose. She handed Joseph the empty champagne glass. "I will speak to Bona—I will discuss it with the Emperor." And, on her way out, "We'll even be married in church. Then everything will be in order."

While Joseph gave the empty glass to the nearest lackey and dashed after Josephine so as not to miss her conversation with Napoleon, Julie said thoughtfully, "I wonder if she didn't tell the Pope herself."

"Yes, or else she would have been more surprised," I said.

"I'm actually sorry for her," Julie said, inspecting her hands. "She's so afraid of a divorce, and it would be horrid of him to leave her now. Just because she can't have any more children. Don't you think so?"

I shrugged my shoulders. "He's having this entire farce of a coronation in the style of Charlemagne combined with the ceremonial at Rheims to impress on the whole world that he's founding an hereditary dynasty. I don't see any point in it, when only Joseph, if he outlives him, will become Emperor, or one of the little sons of Louis and Hortense."

"But he can't send Josephine away," Julie practically wept. "She got engaged to him when he couldn't even afford new trousers. She's kept up with him step by step and always tried to help him in his career. And anyway, her crown has been delivered, and the whole world recognizes her as Empress and . . ."

"He can't play Charlemagne and be crowned by the Pope, and, at the same time, be involved in a divorce case like an ordinary citizen," I said. "But if even I realize this, Josephine, who is a hundred times cleverer than I, has known it a long time. Napoleon must be counting on her coronation, and he'll surely make it all right with the Church."

"And after the church ceremony, it won't be so easy for him to get a divorce, will it? Josephine is counting on that?"

"Yes, of course."

"He does love her. In his own way, but he really loves her and he can't let her down."

"No?" I said. "He can't? Believe me, Napoleon can . . ."

There was a rustle of gowns all through the room. Everyone curtsied. The Empress had returned. On her way in, Josephine took a glass of champagne from the tray and said to Despréaux, "We can go over my coronation procession again." She came over to Julie and me. "Tonight Uncle Fesch is going to marry us quietly in the palace chapel," she said, taking a couple of quick sips of champagne. "Isn't that funny, after almost nine years of marriage? So— madame la maréchale, have you decided to borrow my sapphires?"

On the way home, I decided not to let Napoleon make me wear a blue dress. Tomorrow my rose-coloured dress—all the marshals' wives are to wear rose—will be delivered by Le Roy, and I shall wear rose when I carry Josephine's handkerchief through Notre-Dame.

Jean-Baptiste waited for me in the dining room. He looked like a hungry lion. Anyway, he looked as fearsome as I suppose a hungry lion does. "What kept you so long in the Tuileries?" he demanded.

"I listened to the Bonapartes quarrel with each other. Then we rehearsed. And I've been given a special part. I don't have to dance in with the other marshals' wives. I come in all alone after Murat carrying a handkerchief for Josephine on a cushion. Isn't that an honour?"

219

Jean-Baptiste thought that one over. "I don't want you to take a special part. Joseph and that ass Despréaux made it up just because you're Julie's sister. And I forbid it."

I sighed. "That won't make any difference. Joseph and Despréaux have nothing to do with it. The Emperor wishes it."

I would never have believed that anything could so upset Jean-Baptiste. His voice was almost shrill. "What did you say?"

"The Emperor wishes it. I can't do anything about it."

"And I can't endure it. My wife can't expose herself before the whole world." Jean-Baptiste shouted so he made the glasses on the table jingle. I had no idea he was that furious.

"Why are you so angry?" I asked.

"They'll point at you. The fiancée, they'll say, Mme Jean-Baptiste Bernadotte, the Emperor's young love, whom he cannot forget. His little Eugénie who will show off at his coronation. Now as before— his little Eugénie. And I'll be the laughingstock of Paris."

Disconcerted, I just gaped at Jean-Baptiste. No one knows as well as I how strained his relationship with Napoleon is. How he is tortured by the constant feeling that he has betrayed the ideals of his youth. How impatiently he waits for approval of his request for an independent command far away from Paris. And Napoleon lets him wait, wait, and wait. But I certainly never expected this miserable waiting to lead to a jealous scene. I went to him and put my hands on his breast. "There's no sense letting a whim of Napoleon's upset you, Jean-Baptiste."

But he pushed my hands away. "You know exactly what's happening," he declared. "You know very well. People are to think he's granting a special favour to his little fiancée of long ago. But I assure you, he's quite forgotten this 'long ago.' As a man I know he has. Only the present interests him. He's in love with you. He wants to make you happy so that you . . ."

"Jean-Baptiste!"

He put his hand to his forehead. "Forgive me, it's not your fault," he murmured. At that moment Fernand appeared and set the soup tureen on the table. Silently we took our places. Jean-Baptiste's hand, raising the spoon to his mouth, shook.

"I won't take any part in the coronation ceremonies. I'll stay in bed and be sick," I said. Jean-Baptiste didn't answer. After dinner he left the house.

Now, sitting at his desk writing, I'm trying to decide whether Napoleon really is in love with me again. That interminable night in his office, before the Duke of Enghien was shot, he spoke to me in his long-ago voice, "Take your hat off, madame. . . ." And a little later: "Eugénie—little Eugénie . . ." Mlle George was sent home. I believe that night he remembered the hedge in our garden in Marseilles. And the sleeping meadows and the stars that were so near. How strange that in two days the little Bonaparte of the hedge will be crowned Emperor of the French. And that there was a time in my life when I didn't belong to my Bernadotte.

The clock in the dining room just struck midnight. Perhaps Jean-Baptiste is calling on Mme Récamier. He speaks of her so often. Juliette Récamier is married to a rich old bank director and reads all the books that are published and some that aren't, and lies all day long on a sofa. She fancies herself as the Muse of all famous men, but she kisses none of them. Not even her own husband, Paulette maintains. Jean-Baptiste often discusses books and music with his bosom friend. And sometimes she sends me a boring novel and asks me to read the masterpiece. I hate and admire the Récamier very much.

One-thirty. Now Napoleon and Josephine are undoubtedly kneeling in the chapel in the Tuileries, and Uncle Fesch is performing the marriage ceremony. How easily I could explain to Jean-Baptiste why Napoleon can't forget me, but it would only annoy him. I am a part of Napoleon's youth. And no one forgets his youth, even though he seldom thinks about it. If I walk in the coronation procession in sky blue, I am no more than a memory to Napoleon. But it is quite possible that Jean-Baptiste is right and Napoleon would like to refresh this memory. A declaration of love from Napoleon would be balm on a long-healed wound. Tomorrow I'll stay in bed with a terrible cold, and the next day, too. His Majesty's sky-blue memory has the sniffles and begs to be excused. . . .

Last night—no, it was already today—I fell asleep over my diary. I woke up only when someone took me in his arms and carried me to the bedroom. The gold braid on the epaulettes scratched my cheeks as usual. "You were with your soul-mate. It makes me sick. . . ." I muttered sleepily.

"I was at the Opera, little girl, and all alone. I longed to hear some good music. Then I dismissed the carriage and walked home."

"I love you very much, Jean-Baptiste. And I'm seriously ill with a cold in the head and a sore throat and can't take part in the coronation ceremony."

"I will convey Mme Bernadotte's regrets to the Emperor." And after a while, "You must never forget, little one, that I love you very much. Do you hear me or are you already asleep?"

"I was dreaming, Jean-Baptiste. What happens when someone puts balm on a wound healed years ago?"

"One laughs at that someone, Désirée."

"Yes, I'm laughing at him, the mighty Emperor of the French."

Paris, at night after Napoleon's coronation
December 2, 1804

Impressive and occasionally comical was the coronation of my former fiancé as Emperor of the French. As Napoleon was sat on the throne, the heavy gold crown on his head, our eyes suddenly met. I stood behind the Empress in front of the altar the whole time holding a velvet cushion with a lace handkerchief.

Things naturally didn't happen at all as I'd planned. Day before yesterday, Jean-Baptiste explained to the Master of Ceremonies that to my horror and despair a heavy cold and high fever would keep me from the coronation. This was too much for Despréaux since the other marshals' wives would have staggered from their deathbeds to appear in Notre-Dame. Why shouldn't I? "Madame la maréchale," Jean-Baptiste told the shocked Despréaux, "would drown out the organ music with her sneezing."

I actually stayed in bed all day. At noon, Julie, who had heard of my sudden illness and was quite worried, came and fixed me hot milk and honey. It tasted very good, and I didn't have the nerve to tell her that I wasn't sick at all. But yesterday morning I got so bored in bed, I dressed and went to the nursery, and Oscar and I killed a National Guardsman—I mean a toy one. We wanted to see what the head was stuffed with. It turned out to be sawdust which spewed out all over the floor so that we had to slide quickly around the room to clean it up. Both Oscar and I are afraid of Marie, who gets stricter with us every year.

Suddenly the door opened and Fernand announced Napoleon's personal physician. Before I could say that I would receive Dr. Corvisart in my bedroom in five minutes, Fernand, the clumsy fool, had him in the nursery. Dr. Corvisart put his black bag on the saddle of the rocking horse, and bowed to me politely.

"His Majesty has asked me to inquire about madame la maréchale's health. I am glad I can inform His Majesty that madame has recovered."

"Doctor, I still feel very weak," I said hopelessly.

Dr. Corvisart raised his odd triangular eyebrows that look as though they'd been pasted on his pale face. "I believe I can reconcile with my conscience as a physician the opinion that madame is strong enough to carry Her Majesty's lace handkerchief at the coronation." And with another bow and without cracking a smile, "His Majesty has given me very detailed instructions."

I gulped, and realized that with a stroke of his pen, Napoleon could reduce Jean-Baptiste in rank. How powerless we are, I thought.

"If you advise me, Dr. Corvisart—" I said.

Dr. Corvisart bowed over my hand. "I urgently advise you to be at the coronation, madame," he replied earnestly. He picked up his black bag and left the nursery.

In the afternoon, Le Roy delivered my rose-coloured dress and the white ostrich feathers to wear in my hair. At six o'clock a sudden cannon blast set our windows rattling. I ran to the kitchen and asked Fernand what was wrong.

"Every hour, from now until midnight, salutes will be fired, and Bengal lights will light up all the squares. We ought to take Oscar to town so he can see the lights."

Fernand went on polishing Jean-Baptiste's sword with fanatical zeal.

"It's snowing too hard," I replied. "And the child seemed hoarse this morning."

I went up to the nursery and sat by the window with Oscar on my lap. It was already dark, but I lighted no candles. Oscar and I watched the snowflakes dancing in the lantern light in front of our house.

"There is a city," I said, "where the snow falls every winter for many months. Not just for a few days, as it does here. And the whole sky looks all freshly washed."

"And then?" Oscar said.

"That's all," I said.

"I thought you were going to tell me a new story."

"It's not a story. It's true."

"What's the city called?" Oscar asked.

"Stockholm."

"Where is Stockholm?"

"Far, far away. Near the North Pole, I think."

"Does Stockholm belong to the Emperor?"

"No, Oscar. Stockholm has its own king."

"What's his name?"

"I don't know, darling."

Again the cannon roared. Oscar was scared, and flung his arms around me. "You mustn't be afraid, they're only cannon saluting the Emperor."

Oscar looked at me. "I'm not a bit afraid of cannon, Mama. And someday I'll be a marshal of France, like Papa."

I watched the snowflakes. They reminded me of Persson. "Perhaps you'll be a good, honest silk merchant like your grandpapa," I said.

"But I want to be a marshal. Or a sergeant. Papa told me he was a sergeant. And Fernand was, too." He was excited. Something very important had occurred to him. "Fernand says I can go to the coronation with him tomorrow."

"Oh, no, Oscar, children aren't allowed in the church. Mama and Papa weren't sent a ticket for you."

"But Fernand will take me to the door of the church. There we can see the whole procession, Fernand says. The Empress and Aunt Julie and—" he took a deep breath—"and the Emperor with his crown, Mama. Fernand promised."

"It's much too cold, Oscar, you can't stand for hours in front of Notre-Dame. And in that tremendous crowd a little man like you would be mashed to pieces."

"Please, Mama—please, please."

"I'll tell you all about it, Oscar. I promise you."

Two small arms hugged me and I got a sweet, very damp kiss. "Please, Mama! If I promise to drink all my milk every day?"

"You can't go, Oscar, really you can't. It's so cold, and you're coughing again. Be reasonable, darling."

"If I drink the whole bottle of that horrid cough medicine today, then could I, Mama?"

"In this city, Stockholm, near the North Pole, there is a wide river, green chunks of ice—" I began, hoping to divert him. But Stockholm no longer interested him.

"I want to see the coronation, Mama, I want to terribly," he sobbed.

"When you are bigger, you may see a coronation," I heard myself saying.

"But will the Emperor be crowned again later?" asked Oscar skeptically.

"No, not that. But we will go to another coronation, Oscar, both of us. Mama promises you. And it will be a much more beautiful coronation than the one tomorrow. Believe me, far more beautiful . . ."

"Madame la maréchale shouldn't tell the child such tales." Marie's voice came from the darkness behind us. "Come, Oscar, you must drink your milk now and take that good cough medicine Uncle Doctor gave you."

Marie lit the nursery candles, and I left my place at the window. I couldn't see the dancing snowflakes any more.

Later Jean-Baptiste came up to tell Oscar good night. Oscar immediately complained, "Mama won't let me stand outside the church with Fernand to see the Emperor with his crown."

"I won't allow it either," Jean-Baptiste declared.

"Mama says that she'll take me to another coronation, later, when I am grown up. Will you come, too, Papa?"

"Who's to be crowned then?" Jean-Baptiste asked.

"Mama, who will be crowned?" Oscar demanded shrilly.

And, since I didn't know what to say, I tried to look mysterious. "I won't tell. It will be a surprise. Good night, darling, and sweet dreams."

Jean-Baptiste carefully tucked the covers around our little son and blew out the candles.

For the first time in ages I prepared our evening meal myself. Marie, Fernand, and the kitchen maid were all out. Free performances were being given at every theatre. Yvette, my new lady's maid, had vanished at noon. Julie had explained to me that a marshal's wife can neither do her own hair nor sew on buttons, so I finally gave in and hired this Yvette, who before the Revolution had powdered some duchess's hair and naturally considers herself far grander than I.

After supper, we went to the kitchen. I washed the dishes and my marshal put on Marie's apron and dried them. "I always used to help my mother," he remarked. And, with a little laugh, "She'd have loved our crystal glasses." His smile faded. "Joseph told me the Emperor's personal physician came to see you," he said.

"In this city everyone knows everyone else's business." I sighed.

"No," said Jean-Baptiste, "not everyone, but the Emperor knows a great deal about a great many people. That's his system."

As I dropped asleep I heard the cannon thunder again. Really, I would have been quite happy in a country house near Marseilles, I thought. A country house with a nice neat poultry run. But neither Napoleon, Emperor of the French, nor Bernadotte, Marshal of France, has any interest in chickens. . . .

I woke up because Jean-Baptiste was shaking me. It was still dark. "Must we get up already?" I asked uneasily.

"No, but you were crying so hard in your sleep, I had to wake you. Did you dream something terrible?"

I tried to remember. "I went with Oscar to a coronation." I struggled to reconstruct the dream. "We had to get in the church,

226

but there were so many people at the portal we couldn't get through. We were pushed and buffeted about, the crowd got bigger. I held Oscar's hand and—suddenly there weren't any people at all, but a flock of chickens running between our legs, cackling dreadfully—" I moved closer to Jean-Baptiste.

"And was that so awful?" was all he asked, but his voice was gentle and comforting.

"Yes, it was terrible. The chickens cackled like—exactly like nervous people. But that wasn't the worst. The worst was the crowns."

"The crowns?"

"Yes, Oscar and I were wearing heavy crowns. I could hardly hold my head up, but I knew my crown would fall off if I didn't. And Oscar—yes, Oscar's crown was much too heavy for him, too. I saw his thin little neck stiffen under it, and I was afraid the child would collapse. And—then you woke me up. It was a dreadful dream. . . ."

Jean-Baptiste slipped his arm under my head and held me close. "It's quite natural for you to dream about a coronation. In two hours we must get up and dress for the ceremony at Notre-Dame. But what about the chickens?"

I didn't answer. I tried to forget my hateful dream and go back to sleep.

It had stopped snowing, but it was colder than last night. We heard later that the people of Paris had waited since five o'clock that morning in front of Notre-Dame and along the route for the golden carriages of the Emperor, the Empress and members of the Imperial family. Jean-Baptiste and I had to go to the Archbishop's palace, where the coronation procession was forming. While Fernand helped Jean-Baptiste into his uniform, breathing hard on the gold buttons and giving each a final fillip with his polishing cloth, Yvette arranged the white ostrich feathers in my hair. I sat at my dressing table and stared in horror at the mirror. With this headdress I looked like a circus horse. Every few minutes Jean-Baptiste called from the next room, "Aren't you ready yet, Désirée?" But the ostrich feathers just wouldn't set right.

Finally Marie flung open the door. "This has just been delivered for madame la maréchale. By a lackey in the livery of the Imperial household."

Yvette took the little package and laid it before me on the dressing table. Marie naturally didn't leave but kept staring curiously at the red leather box I unpeeled from the paper. Jean-Baptiste shoved Fernand aside and stood over me. I looked up and met his eyes in the dressing table mirror. Napoleon has surely thought up some-thing dreadful and Jean-Baptiste will be furious, I thought. My hands shook so I couldn't open the leather box. "Let me," said Jean-Baptiste. He pressed the lock and the box flew open.

"Oh—" breathed Yvette. "Mmm," from Marie, while Fernand gasped. Inside was a small jewel box of sparkling gold. On the lid hovered an eagle with outstretched wings. My eyes popped.

"Open it," Jean-Baptiste ordered.

I fumbled at it and finally I got a good hold on the eagle between its outspread wings and pulled. The lid came off. The box was lined with red velvet, and on the velvet sparkled—gold pieces. I wheeled around and looked at Jean-Baptiste. "Can you understand it?" There was no answer. Jean-Baptiste looked like he'd seen a snake. His face was very pale. "They're gold francs," I murmured, and absent-mindedly sifted the top coins through my fingers. Then I spread them out on the dressing table beside my powder box, hair brushes and jewelry. Something rustled. I pulled out a piece of paper from among the gold pieces. Napoleon's handwriting. His large uneven letters. First they danced before my eyes, then finally formed words.

"Madame la maréchale, in Marseilles you were kind enough to lend me your secret savings so that I might travel to Paris. This journey has brought me good fortune. It is an obligation which I take pleasure in meeting today, and thank you. N." And a post-script: "The amount involved at the time was 98 Fr."

"There are ninety-eight gold francs, Jean-Baptiste," I said.

I was greatly relieved when Jean-Baptiste smiled. "I had saved up my pocket money to buy the Emperor a decent uniform, his old one was so shabby, but he needed the money to pay his debts, and to get Junot and Marmont out of the inn," I explained with a rush.

We arrived at the Archbishop's palace shortly before nine o'clock. We were shown to a large room on the upper floor where we greeted the other marshals and their wives, and were served hot coffee. We all crowded near the windows. At the portals of Notre-Dame there was a milling throng. Six grenadier battalions, aided by hussars of the guard, struggled to maintain order. Although the doors of the cathedral had been opened for the invited guests since six o'clock in the morning, men were still working feverishly inside on the decorations. A double line of National Guardsmen pushed back the curious crowd.

"Eighty thousand men are guarding the Emperor's coronation procession," Murat confided to Jean-Baptiste. As Governor of Paris Murat is responsible for all such things. All of a sudden the Prefect of Police stopped all traffic to Notre-Dame, so the specially invited ladies and gentlemen arrived at the door on foot. Only those of us taking part in the procession were allowed to leave our wraps at the Archbishop's palace. The other guests had to go coatless to the cathedral, and it made me shiver just to see the ladies who had left their carriages and scurried through the cold in thin silk dresses. Then something funny happened. A group of these ladies chanced to meet the procession of High Court Judges. The judges were wearing long red robes. They gallantly opened their enormous robes, and the freezing ladies crept in gladly. Though our windows were closed tight, we could hear the crowd laughing at these unlikely couples.

A few carriages drove up anyway—foreign princes invited as guests of honour. "Third sitting," muttered Jean-Baptiste. "Napoleon's paying all their expenses. There's the Margrave of Baden and over here the Prince of Hesse-Darmstadt, and right behind him the Prince of Hesse-Homburg."

Jean-Baptiste pronounces these impossible Germanic names so easily. How does he do it? I left the window, stood by the fireplace and finally got a second cup of coffee. Meanwhile, some sort of altercation was going on near the door. But I hadn't noticed it particularly until Mme Lannes dashed over and said, "I think it's about you, dearest Mme Bernadotte."

And it was. A gentleman in a tobacco-brown coat, his lace cravat askew, was arguing with the sentries at the door who refused to let him in. "Let me go to my little sister—Mme Bernadotte—Eugénie—"

The gentleman in brown was Etienne. When he saw me he screamed like a drowning man. "Eugénie—Eugénie—help me!"

"Listen here, why won't you let my brother in?" I asked the sentries, and pulled Etienne into the room. The sentries mumbled something about, "Orders to admit only ladies and gentlemen in the coronation procession." I called Jean-Baptiste, and we urged the sweating Etienne into an armchair. He'd travelled day and night from Genoa to Paris to be at the coronation. "You know, Eugénie," he said, "how close I am to the Emperor. The friend of my youth, the man on whom I've set my hopes for years—" Etienne paused for breath. He looked miserable.

"Then what's bothering you? The friend of your youth will be crowned Emperor any minute. What more do you want?"

"To be there," Etienne said. "To be at the ceremony."

"You should have come to Paris earlier, dear brother-in-law," Jean-Baptiste said sensibly. "All the tickets have been spoken for."

Etienne, who has gotten quite fat, mopped his brow. "In this awful weather my coach was delayed even more than usual."

"Perhaps Joseph can help him," I whispered to Jean-Baptiste. "We can't do any more now."

"Joseph is in the Tuileries with His Majesty, and can't see anyone, I've already been told," Etienne said unhappily.

"Listen, Etienne, you never liked Napoleon so you can't care that much about seeing his coronation," I said, trying to calm him.

But that really started Etienne off. "How can you say such a thing! Don't you remember that in Marseilles I was the Emperor's closest confidant, his best friend?"

"I know you were horrified when I became engaged to him," I said.

Whereupon Jean-Baptiste slapped Etienne on the back. "Really? You opposed this engagement? Brother-in-law Etienne, you're a man after my own heart. If I have to hold you on my knees in that crowded cathedral—I'll get you in somehow." Still beaming, he turned and called, "Junot, Berthier. We must smuggle M. Etienne Clary into the cathedral. Come, we've fought harder battles in our day."

So from the window I watched my brother Etienne, hidden by three marshals' uniforms, swept into Notre-Dame.

After a while the three marshals' uniforms reappeared, and reported that Etienne was sitting with the diplomatic corps. "He's next to the Turkish Minister," Jean-Baptiste informed me, "who is wearing a green turban and—" He stopped as the Pope's procession came into view, a battalion of dragoons in front and the Swiss Guard following.

Presently we saw a monk riding on a mule and holding a cross in his upraised hands. "The mule had to be hired and Despréaux says its costs sixty-seven francs a day," Marshal Berthier said. Jean-Baptiste laughed. Then came the Pontiff's carriage. It was drawn by eight grey horses, and we immediately recognized the Empress' gala coach that had been placed at the Pope's disposal. The Pope came into the Archbishop's palace, but we had no chance to welcome him. He donned his vestments in a downstairs room, left the palace at the head of the highest ecclesiastical dignitaries, and walked slowly to the portal of Notre-Dame.

Someone opened a window. The crowd kept silent. Only a few women knelt as the Pope passed while most of the men didn't even take off their hats. Suddenly the Pope stopped, said something to a young man in the front row, his head held high, and made the sign of the cross. We later heard that Pius VII had noticed this young man and so many others still standing, and had smilingly remarked, "I believe the blessing of an old man can do no harm." Twice more the Pope made the sign of the cross in the clear frosty air, then the white figure disappeared through the portals of Notre-Dame, and, like a red wave, the ranks of cardinals closed in behind him.

"What happens now in the cathedral?" I asked.

Someone explained to me that at the Pope's entrance the choir of the Imperial Chapel began the *Tu es Petrus,* and that the Pope would then be seated on the throne at the left of the altar.

"And it's time right now for the Emperor's arrival," he continued. But the Emperor kept the people of Paris, the marching regiments, the distinguished guests, and the head of the Holy Roman Church waiting for him another whole hour.

At last a salvo of cannon proclaimed that the Emperor had left the Tuileries. I don't know why, but suddenly we were all silent. Wordlessly we walked in front of the large mirrors on the ground floor. Silently the marshals checked on the stars of their orders and straightened their blue-and-gold backs. Valets handed them their blue capes which they flung over their shoulders. As I powdered my face, I was astonished to find that my hands were trembling.

It sounded like a rumbling storm—first far away, then louder and louder, finally raging close by, *"Vive l'Empereur—Vive l'Empereur. . . ."*

First came Murat, on horseback, in the gold-laden uniform of the Governor of Paris. Behind him thundered the dragoons. Then mounted heralds: in lilac velvet embroidered with golden eagles. The heralds carried staffs embellished with gold bees. Such lilac splendour dumfounded me. And once, I thought, I saved my pocket money to buy him a new uniform, because his old one was so shabby. One gilded carriage after another passed, each drawn by six horses. Despréaux alighted from the first, the Emperor's aides from the second, then the ministers. And finally, in a coach covered with gold bees, the Imperial princesses. The princesses were all in white, and wore coronets in their hair. Julie came over to me quickly and squeezed my hand. "If only everything goes well," she said in exactly Mama's tone of voice.

"Yes, but fix your coronet, it's crooked," I whispered back.

Like the sun suddenly emerging on this grey wintry day came the Emperor's carriage. It was gilded all over and decorated with a frieze of bronze medallions, representing the various Departments of France, joined with golden palm leaves. On top of the carriage gleamed four enormous bronze eagles, their claws clutching laurel branches. In their midst lay a large golden crown. The coach was lined with green velvet, the Corsican colour. Eight horses with white feather plumes snorted to a stop in front of the palace.

We went outside and instinctively lined up.

In the right-hand corner of the carriage sat the Emperor. Napoleon was dressed in purplish-red velvet, and when he alighted, we saw he wore wide trunk-breeches, and white silk stockings embroidered with jewels. In this costume he looked very strange, like an opera star with too short legs. And why Spanish trunk-breeches, Napoleon, why trunk-breeches?

The Empress, on the other hand, sitting at his left, looked more beautiful than ever before. In her childlike curls shone the largest diamond I had ever seen. Although Josephine was heavily rouged, I felt at once that her smile—radiant and young, how very young— came from her heart. The Emperor had had a religious marriage ceremony performed, she could be crowned, she had nothing more to worry about. . . .

When Joseph and Louis, who had been seated facing Napoleon in the Emperor's coach, went by me, I couldn't believe my eyes. They were both formidably decked out. In white from head to foot. Their shoes were white satin with gold rosettes, and I noticed that Joseph had acquired a little paunch. While he grinned just like my Oscar's freshly painted rocking horse, Louis looked glum as he flat-footed it into the palace.

In the palace, Napoleon and Josephine quickly put on their corona-tion robes. For a second Josephine's mouth tightened with the strain of standing erect under the weight of her purple robe. But then Julie and Hortense, Elisa, Paulette and Caroline picked up the train, and Josephine gave a deep sigh of relief. As Napoleon laboriously pulled on a pair of gloves, the fingers stiff with gold embroidery, he looked toward us for the first time. "Can we begin?"

Despréaux had already distributed all our paraphernalia. Now we awaited his signal to take up our rehearsed positions. But the signal wasn't given. Despréaux whispered to Joseph, and Joseph shrugged his shoulders. Napoleon had turned away and was studying himself in a mirror. Not a muscle in his face moved, but his eyes narrowed suddenly as he tried to view himself objectively. He saw a not quite middle-sized man. The ermine collar of his coronation robe reached nearly up to his ears. . . . *The crown of France lies in the gutter, one need only lean down to pick it up.* . . . Well, Napoleon had leaned and fished the crown out of the gutter. The Imperial crown.

Our embarrassed whispers and aimless standing about reminded me of a funeral. I looked for Jean-Baptiste. He was with the other marshals, holding the velvet cushion with the Emperor's Chain of the Legion of Honour he had to carry in the procession. He was thoughtfully gnawing his underlip. Now we carry the Republic to its grave, I thought. Papa, your son Etienne has a ticket of admission, and your daughter Julie is a princess and wears a small gold crown. . . .

"What are we waiting for, Despréaux?" Napoleon sounded impatient.

"Sire, wasn't it decided that Madame Mère was to lead the coronation procession, and Madame Mère is . . ."

"Mother isn't here," said Louis. His voice reverberated with malicious pleasure. Napoleon had sent one courier after another to Italy to ask his mother surely to be in Paris for the coronation. Finally Mme Letizia could no longer ignore his urgency. She'd taken leave of her exiled son Lucien and set off.

"We regret her absence greatly," Napoleon said expressionlessly. "Despréaux, we will go to the cathedral."

Fanfares blared forth. Slowly and solemnly the heralds in lilac and gold moved toward the cathedral. Pages in green followed them closely. Then came Despréaux, Master of Ceremonies, and behind him, in pairs and stiff as marionettes, tripped the sixteen marshals' wives. Then along came Serurier and Murat, Serurier with a cushion on which rested the Empress' ring, Murat with Josephine's crown. The air was icy cold when I emerged, holding the cushion with the lace handkerchief like some sacrificial offering. Passing by the crowds, held back by an impenetrable cordon of soldiers, I heard occasional shouts, "Vive Bernadotte—Bernadotte—" I stared straight ahead at Murat's gold-embroidered back. As I carried Josephine's handkerchief through Notre-Dame, music from the organ and the smell of incense wiped out all thought.

Not until we had come to the choir did Murat stop and step aside. I saw the altar and the two gold thrones. On the throne at the left sat, still as a statue, a little old gentleman in white. Pius VII had waited for Napoleon nearly two hours. . . . I stepped up beside Murat and looked around. Saw Josephine approaching the altar, her eyes wide open, shiny with tears and smiling ecstatically. At the lowest step to the double throne at the right of the altar, she paused. Right in front of me now stood the Imperial princesses with her train. I craned my neck to see Napoleon's entrance. First came

Kellermann with the large Imperial crown. After him Perignon with the sceptre and Lefèbvre with Charlemagne's sword. Then Jean-Baptiste with the Chain of the Legion of Honour, next Eugène de Beauharnais with the Emperor's ring, and finally Berthier with the Imperial orb, and the lame Foreign Minister Talleyrand with a gold wire contraption into which, in the course of the ceremony, the Emperor was to let fall his robe.

The exultant notes of "La Marseillaise" poured triumphantly from the organ. Napoleon walked slowly up to the altar, with Joseph and Louis carrying the train of his purple robe. Finally Napoleon stood beside Josephine. His brothers and the marshals lined up together behind him. The Pope rose and said the Mass.

Then Despréaux gave Marshal Kellermann an almost imperceptible signal. Kellermann stepped forward and held out the crown to the Pope. It seemed to be very heavy because the delicate hands of the Pope could hardly hold it up. Suddenly Napoleon let the purple robe slip from his shoulders. His brothers caught it and passed it to Talleyrand. The organ music stopped. Clearly and solemnly the Pope pronounced the blessing. Then held high the heavy crown to set it on Napoleon's bowed head. But Napoleon's head wasn't bowed. His hands in the gold-embroidered gloves reached up and impetuously seized the crown. For a short second Napoleon held the crown above his head. Then he slowly put it on.

Not only was I startled but all the others, too. Napoleon had violated all the rituals of coronation and crowned himself.

The organ swelled, Lefèbvre presented the Emperor with the sword of Charlemagne, Jean-Baptiste dropped the Chain of the Legion of Honour around his neck, Berthier turned over the orb, and Perignon the golden sceptre. Finally Talleyrand put the purple robe over his shoulders, and the Emperor slowly ascended the steps to his throne. Joseph and Louis picked up the train, and then stood, one on each side of the throne. *"Vivat Imperator in aeternum,"* proclaimed the Pope.

Thereupon Pius VII made the sign of the cross before Josephine's face and kissed her on the cheek. At this point Murat was to have handed him Josephine's crown. But Napoleon had already covered the short distance from his throne and held out his hands for her crown. So Murat gave the crown not to the Pope but to Napoleon. For the first time that day the Emperor smiled. Carefully, very carefully so as not to disarrange her hair, he set the crown on Josephine's childish curls. Escorted by Napoleon, Josephine took a step toward the throne, then jerked to a stop and practically went over backward. Elisa, Paulette and Caroline had dropped the train *on purpose*. They wanted Josephine to fall, to make her ridiculous at the moment of her greatest triumph. But by main force, Julie and Hortense managed to hang on to the heavy train. Napoleon took Josephine's arm and supported her. No, she didn't fall. She just stumbled on the first step to the throne.

While young girls of the old French aristocracy—the virgins who had caused Despréaux such anxiety—walked toward the altar with their candles, the Pope and his entourage withdrew to the crypt. Napoleon, his face expressionless, sat next to Josephine on the throne. He stared straight ahead with half-closed eyes. Since he'd mounted the throne, I'd been standing between Murat and Talleyrand in the front row below. What does a man think about who has just crowned himself Emperor of the French? I couldn't take my eyes off his set face. Now—now a muscle twitched near his mouth, he clamped his lips together firmly and—suppressed a yawn. Suddenly he caught sight of me. The half-closed eyes opened and he smiled for the second time that day; not tenderly, as he had when he crowned Josephine, but easily, happily—yes, as he used to; the way he had when we'd raced to the hedge and just for fun he'd let me win.

"I told you so," said his eyes. "Long ago at the hedge. You didn't believe me. You hoped so much that I'd be discharged from the Army, because you wanted to make a silk merchant out of me." . . . We kept looking right at each other. There he sat, the ermine collar practically up to his ears, and the heavy crown on his shorn hair; and yet for a moment he looked just as he once had. I remembered the Duke of Enghien; and Lucien, the first to be banished; and Moreau and the others—known and unknown French citizens who followed after him. I forced myself to look away and didn't look at the throne again until I heard the voice of the president of the Senate.

The Senate president stood before Napoleon, unfurling a parchment roll. With one hand on the Bible, the other raised, the Emperor repeated the oath after him. His voice rang clear and cold as though he were giving orders. Napoleon I swore to preserve for the French people religious, political and civil liberties.

The clergy returned to escort the Imperial couple out of the cathedral. For a moment Cardinal Fesch stopped next to Napoleon. Laughing, Napoleon poked his uncle in the side with the sceptre. But the Cardinal's round face looked so horrified at his nephew's thoughtless gesture that Napoleon moved on with a shrug of his shoulders. The very next minute, Joseph, who was still carrying the purple train, called out loudly to Napoleon, "What would our father have said if he'd seen us here?"

Walking out behind Murat, I looked for the green turban of the Turkish Minister so I could find Etienne. I was lucky.

Etienne had his mouth open and seemed transported with rapture. He still gazed in adoration after his Emperor although by this time many backs blocked his view.

"Does the Emperor wear his crown in bed at night?" Oscar asked as I put him to bed that evening.

"No, I don't think so," I said.

"Perhaps it's too heavy," Oscar decided. (Julie had recently given him a bearskin cap which was much too heavy for him.)

I had to laugh. "Too heavy? No, darling, Napoleon doesn't find the crown the least bit heavy; quite the opposite."

"Marie says that many people who shout 'Vive l'Empereur' in the street are paid for it by the police," Oscar reported. "Is that true, Mama?"

"I don't know; but you oughtn't to say such things."

"Why not?"

"Because—" I bit my lips. I wanted to say, "Because it's dangerous." But Oscar should be able to say anything that pops into his head. On the other hand, the Minister of Police forbids people who say everything they think to live in Paris or anywhere near the capital. Just a little while ago, the authoress, Mme de Staël, Juliette Récamier's best friend, was exiled.

"Your grandfather Clary was a complete Republican," I said softly and kissed my son on his clean little forehead.

"I thought he was a silk merchant," replied Oscar.

Two hours later I danced a waltz for the first time in my life. Brother-in-law Joseph, His Imperial Highness, gave a really large reception and invited all the foreign princes and diplomats, also all the marshals, and Etienne because, after all, he's Julie's brother.

Marie Antoinette had once tried to introduce the Viennese waltz to Versailles. But only the best people, those whom she received, learned it. During the Revolution, of course, everything was forbidden that reminded anyone of the Austrian. But now these sweet three-quarter-time tunes from abroad are accepted in France. Although I'd also practiced waltz steps at M. Montel's, I didn't really know how to dance it. But Jean-Baptiste, who before our marriage was our Ambassador in Vienna, showed me. He held me very close and counted in his sergeant's voice, "One, two three—one, two three —" At first I felt like a recruit. But he gradually relaxed, and we turned and twisted around and around. The ballroom in the Luxembourg seemed a surging sea of lights, and I felt him kiss the top of my head.

"The Emperor flirted with you during the coronation—one, two three—I saw him distinctly," Jean-Baptiste whispered.

"I had the feeling that his heart wasn't in it," I said.

"In what? Flirting with you?" Jean-Baptiste wanted to know.

"Don't be horrid. I mean the coronation, naturally," I said.

"You must keep time, little one."

"A coronation should touch a man's heart," I insisted. "For Napoleon, it was only a formality. He had himself crowned an Emperor —and took the oath of the Republic. . . . One, two three—"

Someone shouted, "A toast to the Emperor!" Glasses clinked.

"That was your brother Etienne," said Jean-Baptiste.

"Let's go on dancing," I whispered, "on and on—"

Jean-Baptiste kissed my hair again. The crystal chandeliers sparkled in a thousand colours and seemed to sway. The whole ballroom revolved around us. As though from far away, I heard the voices of the many guests, sounding like cackling hens. One, two three—don't think back, but only of Jean-Baptiste's lips and dancing the waltz. . . .

On our way home we drove past the Tuileries. They were brilliantly lighted in honour of the occasion. Pages with glowing red torches were on guard. Someone told us that the Emperor had dined all alone with Josephine. Josephine had to keep her crown on because he thought it very becoming to her. After the meal, Napoleon retired to his study and unrolled general staff maps. "He's working on his next campaign," Jean-Baptiste explained to me. It had begun to snow and many of the torches died out.

Paris, two weeks after the Emperor's coronation

A few days ago the Emperor distributed the eagle to every regiment. We all had to assemble on the champ de Mars. Napoleon wore his coronation robe again and put on the large crown. Each regiment held a standard on which perched a golden eagle. Under the eagle flew the tricolour. These eagles must never fall into enemy hands, the Emperor said, and promised our troops new victories. We stood for hours on a platform and watched the regiments pass by. Etienne, next to me, shouted himself hoarse and almost deafened me in his enthusiasm. It started to snow again, the parade seemed endless, and we all got wet feet. I had time to think over the preparations for the marshals' ball.

The Master of Ceremonies had hinted to the marshals that they arrange a ball in honour of the Emperor. It was to be the most magnificent ball ever, and they had requisitioned the Opera House for the occasion.

We marshals' wives held many meetings and checked the guest list so no one would be forgotten and offended. M. Montel lectured us on how we were to advance to greet the Imperial couple and how to escort Napoleon and Josephine to the ballroom. Despréaux informed us that the Emperor would offer his arm to one of the marshals' wives, and one of the marshals would escort the Empress to her throne. We debated for hours on end which marshal and which wife were worthy of this honour. Finally Murat, as the husband of an Imperial princess, was selected to accompany the Empress. As to which lady was to take the Emperor's arm, however, they vacillated between Mme Berthier, the oldest marshal's wife, and me, the sister of the Imperial Princess Julie. But I succeeded in convincing the others that fat Berthier was the only proper person to welcome the Emperor. I was actually furious with Napoleon because he was still letting Jean-Baptiste wait for the independent command far away from Paris.

The afternoon of the ball, Paulette called on me unexpectedly, flanked by an Italian violin virtuoso and a French captain of dragoons. She sat them both down on the sofa in my salon, and then came back upstairs with me to the bedroom.

"Which of them do you think is my lover?" she asked and laughed. Gold powder glittered in her dark-blond hair under a little black velvet hat. Emeralds, from the Borghese family jewels, sparkled in her tiny ears. Her light-green velvet skirt fitted snugly across her hips, and the black velvet jacket showed off, with startling frankness, the points of her breasts. Her eyebrows were as black as when she was fifteen, but she now used a fine pencil instead of pieces of coal from her mother's kitchen. Under her lustrous eyes, which always reminded me of the eyes of Napoleon, there were deep shadows.

"Well, which of them is my lover?" she asked again. I didn't know. "Both of them," cried Paulette triumphantly and sat down at my dressing table. The gold jewel box was still there.

"Who had the bad taste to send you a jewel box decorated with these dreadful Imperial eagles?" she demanded.

"Now, you must guess," I replied.

Paulette frowned. This guessing game intrigued her. She racked her brains. Suddenly she gasped, "Was it—tell me, was it—?"

I didn't move a muscle. "I have the infinite graciousness of our sovereign to thank for the box."

Paulette let out a long low whistle. Then, excitedly, "What do you know! At the moment, he's supposed to be cheating on Josephine with Mme Duchatel—you know, the lady-in-waiting with the violet eyes and the long nose."

I blushed. "On the day of his coronation, Napoleon paid back an old debt from the Marseilles days. Nothing more."

Paulette stretched out her small hands, loaded with diamonds also from the house of Borghese. "God forbid, little one—naturally nothing more." She paused, then looked thoughtful. "I want to talk to you about Mother," she began, in a conciliatory tone. "Mother arrived yesterday. Secretly. I don't think even Fouché knows she's in Paris. She's staying with me. And you must help them."

"Help whom?" I asked in bewilderment.

"Both of them—Madame Mère and Napoleon, too—her royal son and heir." Paulette laughed, but it didn't ring true.

"I'm worried," she continued. "Napoleon insists she stand on ceremony and wait upon him at the Tuileries to advise him of her arrival. Just imagine—Mother curtsying and all those grand opera goings-on—" I tried in vain to visualize Mme Letizia bowing low in a court curtsy before Napoleon. "You see, he's angry because she purposely travelled in slow stages so as not to be here for the coronation." Paulette gnawed her lower lip. "And he's hurt because Mama didn't want to see his triumph. He truly longs to see her and— Eugénie, Désirée, madame la maréchale, please get them together. As though by chance, you understand? And leave them alone at the moment of meeting so it won't matter whether there's any ceremony or not. Can you fix that?"

"You really are a dreadful family!" I exploded.

But Paulette didn't turn a hair. "You've always known that. And do you know I'm the only one of his brothers and sisters Napoleon really likes?"

"Yes, I know," I said, and thought of an afternoon when Paulette went with me to see the Commandant of Marseilles.

"The others only want to be his heirs," Paulette remarked, and began to polish her nails. "Joseph, by the way, isn't recognized as successor to the throne now that Napoleon has adopted Louis and Hortense's two little boys. Josephine nagged him night and day to make her grandchildren crown princes. And do you know the lowest thing?" Paulette's eyes widened in indignation. "She tells him he's to blame for their childless marriage! I ask you—Napoleon!"

"I'll bring Mme Letizia and the Emperor together," I said quickly. "At the marshals' ball. I'll send word to you by Marie. You have only to see that your mother comes to the box I choose."

"You are a darling, Eugénie. Am I relieved!"

She ran her finger around my small jar of pomade and began earnestly dabbing it on her upper lip. Then she pressed her lips together to colour the lower lip, too.

"The other day," she said, "an English newspaper published a scandalous article about me. My little long-haired violinist translated it for me. The English call me 'the Napoleon of Love.' Such nonsense." She turned to me. "We have an entirely different technique, Napoleon and I; he wins offensive wars—I lose my defensive battles." A forlorn little smile flickered over her face. "Why does he always make me marry men who don't interest me? First, Leclerc; and then Borghese. Both my sisters have it easier; and, besides, they're ambitious. They don't care anything about people except as useful connections. Elisa can't forget that horrible cellar and is beset with fears of being poor again. So she grabs everything she possibly can. Caroline, on the other hand, was so young when we lived in the cellar she doesn't remember it at all. And to wear a crown on her head, Caroline's ready to stoop to any meanness. Now I . . ."

"I think your two cavaliers must be getting impatient," I said.

Paulette jumped right up. "You're right, I must go. I'll wait for your message and then send our *madre* to the opera. Agreed?"

I nodded. "Agreed!"

What if my own little rascal, my Oscar, should ever demand a court curtsy of me!

Allons enfants de la patrie,
Le jour de gloire est arrivé. . . .

The voices of the violins were drowned out by the jubilant wind instruments. On Jean-Baptiste's arm, I slowly descended the stairs to the bottom step where I was to welcome the Emperor of the French as a guest of his marshals.

Aux armes citoyens!
Formez vos bataillons!

The anthem. The song of Marseilles, song of my girlhood. Once
I stood in my nightgown on the balcony of our white villa and tossed
roses down to our volunteers; to Franchon, the tailor, and to the
shoemaker's bowlegged son, and the Levi brothers in their Sunday
suits—citizens all, marching away to defend the young Republic
against the whole world; the Republic which then hadn't money
enough to buy boots for her soldiers.

Formez vos bataillons!
Marchons, marchons. . . .

Silk trains rustled, dress swords clanked, we bowed down to the
ground; Napoleon appeared. When I first saw Napoleon, I couldn't
understand why the Army accepted such short officers. Now he had
played up his small stature, had surrounded himself with the very
tallest aides he could find, and wore a simple, general's uniform.

Josephine dropped his arm, the diamond tiara nodded in greeting.
Murat bowed over her hand.

"How are you, madame?" said the Emperor to the fat Berthier
and, without giving her time to answer, turned to the next marshal's
wife. "I'm delighted to see you, madame. You should always wear
nile green. The colour suits you. However, the Nile isn't really
green at all but yellow. Yellow ochre—it flows in my memory."

On the cheeks of the lady addressed burned hectic red blotches.
"Your Majesty is too kind," she lisped. I wondered if all crowned
heads were as crushing as Napoleon, or if he uses these short, curt
sentences because he assumes this is how monarchs habitually converse with their subjects.

Josephine, meanwhile, had turned her artfully painted smile on
the marshals' wives. "How are you? . . . Your little daughter has
whooping cough? I was so upset when I heard it—" Every single
one got the impression that the Empress, with every fibre of her
being, had been waiting for days just to see her. In Josephine's wake
came the Imperial Princesses: Elisa and Caroline, their eyes in arro-

gant slits; Paulette, slightly drunk after some supper party or other; Hortense, tense but making an anxious effort to be friendly. And my Julie, pale and fighting desperately against her shyness.

Then Murat and Josephine walked slowly through the ballroom. Napoleon followed, Mme Berthier, panting with excitement, on his arm. We others closed in behind. A thousand silk skirts rustled as the women curtsied. Josephine stopped constantly to say a few friendly words to someone. Napoleon addressed his remarks chiefly to the gentlemen. Innumerable officers from the provinces had been invited to represent their regiments. Napoleon questioned them about their garrisons. He seemed to know the number of lice in every single military barracks in France! How could I lure him to Box 17, I wondered hopelessly. First he must drink a few glasses of champagne, I decided. Then I would dare it—

Champagne was passed around. Napoleon refused. He stood on the stage next to his chair of state, letting Joseph and Talleyrand talk to him.

Josephine called me over to her and said, "I couldn't find the sapphire earrings the other day. I'm so sorry."

"Your Majesty is very kind, but I couldn't wear blue, anyway."

"Are you satisfied with Le Roy's gowns, madame?"

I didn't answer the Empress. In the crowded room, I'd spotted a square red face. I knew that face. The short neck above the collar of a colonel's uniform.

"With the gowns of Le Roy's?" the Empress repeated sharply.

"Yes, of course, very satisfied," I said. Next to the square red face was a lady's head with hair dyed lemon yellow and an impossible coiffure. Provinces, I thought; a colonel from some provincial garrison, whose wife I don't know, but the man himself . . .

Later on I succeeded in crossing the ballroom alone. Not recognizing the colonel bothered me, and I decided to try to move inconspicuously a little closer to them. All the guests stood respectfully aside for me and whispered, "Madame la maréchale Bernadotte." Officers bowed deep, ladies smiled fixedly. I smiled back, smiled and smiled until my mouth ached. By this time, I was quite near my colonel, and I heard the lady with the unbelievable coiffure whisper to him, "It is, too, the little Clary." All at once I knew who the colonel was. He had discarded the wig with the pigtail, but otherwise the years seemed to have rolled uneventfully over him. He was probably still Commandant at Marseilles. The little Jacobin general, whom he had arrested ten years ago, in the meantime had become Emperor of the French.

"Do you remember me, Colonel Lefabre?" I heard myself ask.

The woman with the extraordinary hair bowed awkwardly. "Madame la maréchale," she whispered.

"François Clary's daughter," Square Face said at the same time. Then they both waited, embarrassed, for my next remark

"I haven't been in Marseilles for a very long time," I said.

"Madame would be very bored there, a dull provincial hole," said the lady with the hair, shrugging her scrawny shoulders.

"If you want to be posted elsewhere, Colonel Lefabre—" I began, looking into his watery blue eyes.

"Could you speak to the Emperor about us?" cried Mme Lefabre, all excited.

"No, but to Marshal Bernadotte," I answered.

"I knew your papa very well—" the Colonel murmured.

At that moment, I pulled myself together. The Polonaise!

I forgot the Lefabres and without a word gathered up my train and scurried away. Looking scandalized, people frowned as they made way for me. Once again I was behaving impossibly.

Murat was opening the Polonaise with Julie. The Emperor had escorted Mme Berthier through the ballroom and I should have been with Prince Joseph. The dance had already begun. Joseph stood by himself on the stage near the chairs of state, waiting for me.

"I couldn't find you, Désirée," he hissed angrily.

"Forgive me," I murmured as we hurried to join the other couples. From time to time my brother-in-law scowled at me.

"I'm not used to waiting," he growled.

"Do smile," I whispered angrily. "Smile!" So many eyes were on the oldest brother of the Emperor and the wife of Marshal Bernadotte.

After two contradances, the guests swooped down on the buffet. Napoleon had retired to the back of the stage and was talking to

Duroc. I waved to a lackey passing around champagne and approached the Emperor.

Napoleon immediately interrupted his conversation. "I have something to tell you, madame."

"A little refreshment?" I asked, waving toward the champagne, with one of M. Montel's fanciest gestures. Napoleon and Duroc each took a glass.

"*A votre santé, madame,*" the Emperor said politely, took a tiny sip and put his glass back. "What I started to say, madame—" Napoleon stopped and looked me up and down. "Have I ever told you, madame la maréchale, that you are very pretty?"

Duroc smiled broadly, clicked his heels together and said, "If Your Majesty will permit, I should—"

"Go along, Duroc, devote yourself to the ladies!" the Emperor called after him. Then he began again to appraise me, in silence. Slowly a smile played around his mouth.

"Your Majesty had something to tell me?" I said, and plunged on, "If I may ask it, I'd be very grateful to Your Majesty if we could meet in Box Seventeen."

It was apparent that Napoleon at first thought he couldn't have heard me correctly. He leaned forward, raised his eyebrows and repeated, "Box Seventeen?"

I nodded eagerly.

Napoleon glanced at the other people on the stage. Josephine was chattering to hordes of ladies, Joseph was holding forth to Talleyrand and the peevish Louis. The marshals' uniforms gleamed among the dancers.

"Would that be proper, little Eugénie?"

"Sire, please don't misunderstand me."

"Box Seventeen—the meaning's clear, isn't it?" Then quickly, "Murat will escort us, it looks better."

Murat, like the rest of the Emperor's entourage, had been watching us every minute out of the corner of his eye. One wave and he came on the double.

"Mme Bernadotte and I wish to be together in a box. Show us the way."

A trio, we left the stage. We passed through the respectful lines that automatically form whenever the Emperor approaches. On the landing, as we neared the box, several couples leapt hastily apart. Young officers sprang from an embrace to rigid attention. I found it very funny, but Napoleon remarked, "The younger generation have no morals. I shall discuss this with Despréaux. I want only those beyond reproach around me." The next minute we were at the locked doors of the boxes. "Thank you, Murat." Murat's spurs jingled and he disappeared. Napoleon kept looking for the number.

"Your Majesty had something to tell me," I said. "Is it good news?"

"Yes, we have approved Marshal Bernadotte's request for an independent command with widespread civil responsibilities. Tomorrow your husband will be appointed Governor of Hanover. I congratulate you, madame. It is an important and very responsible post."

"Hanover—" I whispered, having no idea where Hanover was.

"When you visit your husband in Hanover, you will live in a royal palace and be the First Lady of the land. And here we have Box Seventeen."

It was only a few steps to the door of the box. "You go in first and be sure the curtains are drawn," Napoleon said. I opened the door and closed it behind me swiftly. I knew quite well that the curtains were drawn.

"Well, my child?" Mme Letizia said as I came in.

"He's outside. And he doesn't know that you're here, Madame Mère."

"Don't get so excited. It doesn't mean your head," said Mme Letizia firmly.

No, but it could mean Jean-Baptiste's appointment, I thought. "I'll call him now, madame," I said softly.

"The curtains are drawn," I announced outside, at which I'd hoped to let the Emperor go first into the box and for me to disappear. But Napoleon shoved me into the little room. I flattened out against the side wall to let him by. Mme Letizia had risen. Napoleon stopped, as though he'd taken root at the door. Through the heavy curtains wafted strains of a sweet Viennese waltz.

"Son, won't you say good evening to your mother?" asked Mme

Letizia quietly. She took a step toward him. If she only bows the least bit, I thought, everything will be all right. The Emperor didn't budge. Mme Letizia took another step.

"Madame Mère, what a beautiful surprise," Napoleon said, not moving.

A last step, and now Mme Letizia stood before him. She bowed her head slightly—and kissed his cheek. Disregarding court etiquette, I slid past the Emperor. Brushing by him, I may have given him a tiny push which landed him, quite naturally, in his mother's arms.

As I re-entered the ballroom, Murat came right over. Like a bloodhound on the trail, he sniffed. "Back so soon, madame?" I looked surprised. "I told the Empress that Bernadotte would be pleased if she would have a word with him, and I gave Bernadotte the wink that the Empress wanted to see him. So neither of them suspected what was going on in the box." Murat grinned.

"Going on in the box? What *do* you mean, Marshal Murat?"

Murat was so intent on our conversation that he didn't notice the astonished outcry throughout the room. "I meant a very special box. The box to which you took His Majesty," he said confidentially.

"Oh, Box Seventeen! But why shouldn't Jean-Baptiste and the Empress know what happened in this box? The entire ballroom knows by now." I laughed.

The sheepish look on Murat's face was priceless. He raised his head, followed the eyes of the other guests and saw—yes, saw the Emperor pull aside the curtains of Box 17. Right beside him was Mme Letizia. Despréaux signalled to the orchestra, a loud "Hush!" echoed through the hall, followed by wild applause.

"Caroline didn't know her mother was back in Paris," said Murat, obviously bewildered, and looked at me anxiously.

"I believe Madame Mère will stand by the son who needs her most," I said thoughtfully. "First the exiled Lucien and now the reigning Napoleon. . . ."

We danced until dawn. While Jean-Baptiste waltzed me around, I asked, "Where is Hanover?"

"In Germany," he answered. "The English royal family came from Hanover. The population suffered terribly during the war."

"Do you know who's to rule in Hanover? As French Governor?"

"No idea," said Jean-Baptiste. "And it—" He stopped, smack in the middle of a three-quarter beat. He bent his head so that he looked straight into my eyes. "Is that true?" is all he asked.

I nodded.

"Now I'll show them!" he muttered, and danced on.

"Whom will you show what?"

"How to run a country. I'll show the Emperor and all his generals. Especially the generals. And Hanover will like it."

Jean-Baptiste spoke very quickly and I knew that he was happy, happy for the first time in so many long years. Strange that at this moment he didn't think about France at all, but only about—Hanover. Hanover—somewhere in Germany.

"You'll live in the royal palace," I said.

"Naturally, that should be the best quarters," he said indifferently. He wasn't a bit impressed.

I suddenly realized that to Jean-Baptiste the best quarters are only just good enough for him; the English King's palace in Hanover is only just good enough for former Sergeant Bernadotte. Why does it all seem to me so monstrous? "I'm dizzy, Jean-Baptiste, I'm dizzy —" But Jean-Baptiste didn't stop dancing until the violinists packed up their instruments and the marshals' ball was over.

Before Jean-Baptiste left for Hanover, he granted my wish and had Colonel Lefabre come to Paris. The story of Napoleon's underdrawers gave him the idea of assigning the Colonel to the Quartermaster's department. Here Lefabre was responsible for the uniforms, boots and underclothing of our troops. The Colonel and his wife called to thank me. The Colonel, of course, rumbled, "Knew your papa very well. A very honourable man, your papa—"

My eyes filled, but I smiled. "You're right, Colonel. 'A Bonaparte is no match for a daughter of François Clary—' "

His wife sucked in her breath in horror. *Lèse-majesté!* The Colonel turned purplish-blue in embarrassment but he met my eyes. "You're right, madame la maréchale," he mumbled. "Your late father would have preferred Bernadotte."

Napoleon always knew of the promotion of senior officers; and when he saw Colonel Lefabre's name on a list, he thought for a moment, then laughed aloud. "Overlord of the Underwear! Bernadotte has made him supervisor of all the underclothing worn in the Army. To please his wife. Murat, he is the Overlord of the Underwear."

Murat spread the Emperor's quip in strictest confidence, and to this day that's what everyone calls poor Lefabre.

In a stagecoach between Hanover in Germany
and Paris, September, 1805
(The Emperor has forbidden our Republican calendar.
My late mama would be pleased—she
never could get used to it)

We were very happy in Hanover—Jean-Baptiste, Oscar and I. The valuable parquet floor in the royal palace was the only real bone of contention. "That Oscar thinks the polished floor in the big room was built for the son of the Military Governor to slide on doesn't surprise me. He is a six-year-old child. But that you—" He'd shake his head but his eyes would smile. And every time, I'd promise never again to take a running start and slide with a swish across the shining floor in the ballrom of the former kings of Hanover, now occupied by Msgr. Jean-Baptiste, Marshal of France, Governor of the Kingdom of Hanover.

Again and again I promised and next day couldn't resist the temptation. Away we'd go sliding, Oscar and I. It was really scandalous; for, after all, I was the First Lady of the Kingdom of Hanover and had a small court consisting of a reader, a lady-in-waiting, and the wives of my husband's officers. Unfortunately, I sometimes forgot.

Yes, we were happy in Hanover. And Hanover was happy with us. That sounds odd, for Hanover was conquered territory, and Jean-Baptiste the commander of an army of occupation. From six o'clock in the morning until six in the evening, and after supper until late at night, he pored over files of documents at his desk.

Jean-Baptiste began his "rule" in this Germanic country by introducing the Rights of Man. In France much blood had flowed to establish equality among citizens. In Hanover, an enemy country, a stroke of the pen was enough: the signature *Bernadotte*. Corporal punishment was ruled out. The ghettos were abolished and the Jews permitted to choose any careers they wished. Not in vain did the Levis of Marseilles march into battle in their Sunday suits. A former sergeant knows very well what to feed the troops, so requisitions on the citizens of Hanover to maintain our troops weren't oppressive. Jean-Baptiste set the tax rate and every officer must abide by it. Besides, the citizens' earnings increased. Jean-Baptiste also did away with customs barriers; and Hanover is like an island in the middle of war-devastated Germany, trading in every direction. When the citizens of Hanover became really wealthy, Jean-Baptiste raised their taxes a little. With this extra revenue he bought grain and sent it to northern Germany where there was a famine. People of Hanover were puzzled, our own officers touched their foreheads, but no one can long resent anyone who treats him like a decent human being.

Finally Jean-Baptiste advised the Hanover merchants to get on friendly terms with the Hanseatic towns and through this friendship earn much more money. The deputation was speechless at this advice. For it's an open secret that the Hanseatic towns aren't in sympathy with the Emperor's plans for a Continental system, and that their ships go back and forth to England. But when a Marshal of France gave his poor conquered enemies this advice they got right in the swing of it and filled the State Treasury of Hanover. Jean-Baptiste was able to send large sums to the University of Göttingen, where some of the most distinguished scholars in Europe are now professors. Jean-Baptiste was naturally very proud of "his" University. And he was happy working on his documents.

Occasionally I'd also find him reading fat volumes. "How much an uneducated sergeant has to learn," he'd say, not looking up but holding out his hand. I'd go to him and he would lay his hand on my cheek. "You govern an awful lot," I'd say. But he would just shake his head. "I'm learning, little girl. And I want to do my best. It's not hard if things stay quiet—"

We both knew what Jean-Baptiste meant.

I gained weight in Hanover. We didn't dance all night nor stand for hours at parades—at least no longer than two hours. For my sake, Jean-Baptiste cut down on the parades. After supper our officers and their ladies usually sat in my salon while we discussed the news from Paris. The Emperor was apparently still preparing his invasion of England; his squadrons were at Boulogne. And Josephine was running up more debts, but this was only mentioned in whispers. Sometimes Jean-Baptiste also invited professors from Göttingen, who tried to explain their ideas to us in atrocious French. One of them read a play to us in German, by the author of that night-table novel, *The Sorrows of Werther,* which once enthralled Julie so. The author is named Goethe. I signalled to Jean-Baptiste to put us out of our misery; we understood so little German.

Another told us about a great physician in Göttingen who has restored many people's hearing. This particularly interested Jean-Baptiste because a number of our soldiers have been deafened by the booming of their own cannon. And suddenly he exclaimed, "I have a friend who must see this professor. He lives in Vienna. I'll write him, he must go to Göttingen. He can also visit us, Désirée, you must meet him. He's a musician I met in Vienna when I was Ambassador. A friend of Kreutzer—you remember him!"

This threw me into a panic, of course. Under the pretext of having so many new obligations, I'd announced to Jean-Baptiste that I had no time any more for my piano or deportment lessons. And he was too busy to make me. I don't miss the piano playing; and as for deportment, I simply sweep my guests from the dining room into the salons with the few graceful gestures M. Montel taught me. And for a silk merchant's daughter, transplanted to the royal palace at Hanover, I did it very well. Now I was horrified that I would have to play the piano for this musician from Vienna.

But it didn't happen. Never will I forget the evening the Viennese musician spent with us. The evening began wonderfully. . . .

Oscar, who gets starry-eyed whenever he hears music, plagued me so long I gave in and let him stay up. And Oscar also knew more about the imminent concert than I. The Viennese musician's name is —I thought I remembered it—a very foreign name, probably German —yes, his name is Beethoven. Jean-Baptiste had given instructions that all the members of the former royal Hanover orchestra be placed at this Beethoven's disposal and must rehearse with him three whole mornings in the great hall. On these days Oscar and I weren't permitted in the hall and therefore couldn't slide across the parquet floor. So I maintained my dignity without difficulty.

Oscar was really terribly excited. "How long may I stay up, Mama? Until after midnight? How can a deaf man write music? Do you think he never can hear his own music? Has M. Beethoven an ear trumpet? Does he ever blow on it?"

Mornings I usually went for a drive with Oscar; and in the yellow-green shade of the long lime-tree avenue from the palace to the village of Herrenhausen, I tried to answer all his questions. As I had not yet seen M. Beethoven, or whatever his name is, I knew nothing about his ear trumpet. I did assume that although he's a musician he probably used it to hear and not to blow.

"Papa says he's one of the biggest men he knows. How big can he be? Taller than a grenadier in the Emperor's bodyguard?"

"Papa doesn't mean physically big, but spiritually. He is—yes, probably he's a genius. That's what Papa means by a big man."

Oscar thought this over. Finally, "Bigger than Papa?"

I took Oscar's sticky little hand, which turned out to be clutching a half-sucked piece of candy. "That I don't know, darling."

"Greater than the Emperor, Mama?"

At that the footman, riding beside our coachman, half-turned and looked at me curiously. I didn't move a muscle. "No one is greater than the Emperor, Oscar," I said quietly.

"Perhaps he can't hear his own music—" mused Oscar.

"Perhaps," I answered, absent-mindedly, and felt suddenly sad. I wanted to bring my son up differently, I thought; as a free man, as Papa would have wished. The new tutor, whom the Emperor personally recommended and who had been with us a month, had tried to teach the child the amendment to the catechism, which is now compulsory in all French schools: "We owe our Emperor, Napoleon

I, God's image on earth, respect, obedience, loyalty, military service—"

Recently I happened to visit Oscar's schoolroom and thought at first I'd heard it wrong. But the narrow-chested young tutor, formerly head boy at the Brienne Cadet School, who folded up like a jackknife if he saw Jean-Baptiste or me (but vented his spleen on the poor puppy Fernand brought home, when he thought no one was looking)—well, this tutor, Napoleon's choice, was reciting the words. No doubt about it—"Emperor Napoleon I, God's image on earth . . ."

"I don't want the child to learn that. Leave out the amendment to the catechism," I said.

"It is taught in all the schools of the Empire. It is the law," said the young man, and chanted without inflection. "His Majesty is very much interested in the education of his godson, and I have instructions to report to His Majesty regularly. The boy is the son of a marshal of France."

I looked at Oscar. His thin little neck craned over a copybook. He was scrawling. First the nuns taught me, I thought; and then the nuns were imprisoned or thrown out. We children were told there was no God, only pure Reason. We were to worship this pure Reason, and Robespierre had an altar erected. Next came a time when no one bothered about our thoughts and everyone was allowed to think what he wished. When Napoleon became First Consul he reinstated priests, who swore allegiance not to the Republic but to the Holy Roman Church. Finally Napoleon forced the Pope to travel from Rome to Paris to crown him and made Catholicism the official state religion. And now he enforces this amendment. This amendment must be learned. . . .

Peasants' sons are called from the fields to march in Napoleon's armies. It costs eight thousand francs to buy a man out of military service, and eight thousand francs is a great deal of money for a peasant. So they hide their sons, and the police arrest wives, sisters, and fiancées as hostages. Even though French deserters are no longer a problem. France has enough soldiers. The defeated rulers must raise regiments to prove their loyalty to the Emperor. Thousands, tens of thousands, will be dragged from their beds and will march for Napoleon. Jean-Baptiste complains so often that his soldiers don't understand our language at all, and his officers must issue commands through interpreters. Why does Napoleon make them march, these young men, into still more new wars, still more new victories? The frontiers of France have not needed to be defended for a long time. France has no frontiers any more. Or is he no longer concerned about France but only about himself, Napoleon, the Emperor—?

I don't know how long we stood facing each other, the young tutor and I. I suddenly felt as though I'd sleep-walked through the last few years. I finally wheeled around and walked to the door. And said again, "Leave out the amendment to the catechism. Oscar is still too young. He doesn't know what it means." With that I closed the door behind me.

The corridor was empty. Weakly I leaned against the wall and began to cry uncontrollably. Too little, I wept, to know what it means. . . . And that's why you make the children learn it, Napoleon, that's why—you destroyer of faith! For the Rights of Man a whole nation suffered and bled; and when it was exhausted, and the Rights of Man proclaimed, you put yourself in command of the nation. . . .

I don't remember how I got to my bedroom. I only know I was suddenly lying on my bed, crying into the pillows. These proclamations! We're all used to them. They always cover the first page of the *Moniteur.* Always the same old diatribes as the one before he left for the Pyramids, that he'd tried out on us at the dinner table in Paris—high-sounding phrases that dragged the Rights of Man into every order of the day. Joseph, who really hates him, had said maliciously, "The Rights of Man weren't your invention, Napoleon. . . ." Instead, he applied them to his own devices, paying lip-service to freedom while he enslaved the nation—condoning bloodshed in the name of the Rights of Man. . . .

Someone's arms were around me; gold epaulettes scratched my cheek. "Désirée—?"

"Do you know the amendment to the catechism that Oscar has to learn?" I sobbed. Jean-Baptiste held me close. "I've forbidden it," I whispered. "Is that all right with you, Jean-Baptiste?"

"Thank you. Otherwise I would have forbidden it myself," he said. He still held me tight.

"Jean-Baptiste, I nearly married that man. Just imagine!"

His laugh released me from the prison of my thoughts. "There are things I don't want to imagine, little one."

A few days later we were ready, Oscar and Jean-Baptiste and I, for our concert by the Viennese musician. M. Beethoven is a middle-sized, thick-set man with the wildest hair ever seen in our dining room. His face is round, and tanned by the sun. He has pockmarks and a flat nose, and sleepy eyes except when anyone speaks to him. Then his eyes wake up and he pays strict attention. Since I knew the poor man was deaf, I shouted right at him how very pleased I was to have him with us. Jean-Baptiste slapped him on the back and asked him for the latest news from Vienna. He asked, naturally, only out of politeness. But the musician answered earnestly, "Vienna is prepared for war. It expects the Emperor's armies to attack Austria."

Jean-Baptiste wrinkled his brow and shook his head. He hadn't wanted to be taken so literally. "How do the musicians in my orchestra play?" he put in quickly.

The stocky man merely shrugged his shoulders. Jean-Baptiste repeated the question as loudly as possible. The musician raised his heavy eyebrows, the sleepy eyes blinked mischievously. "I understood you perfectly, Ambassador—excuse me, Marshal—you're called that now, aren't you? The members of your orchestra play very badly, Marshal Bernadotte."

"But you will, nevertheless, conduct your new symphony, won't you?" Bernadotte shouted at him.

M. Beethoven looked pleased. "Yes, because I want to know what you'll say about it, Ambassador."

"Monseigneur," screamed my husband's aide into M. Beethoven's ear.

"Just call me Herr van Beethoven, I'm no seigneur," said our guest.

"The Marshal is called 'monseigneur,'" yelled the aide desperately.

I held my handkerchief over my mouth because I had to laugh.

Our guest fastened his deep-set eyes seriously on Jean-Baptiste. "It's difficult to get all these new titles straight if one has none oneself, and is deaf besides," he said. "Thank you, *monseigneur,* for introducing me to this professor in Göttingen."

"Can you hear your music?" sang out someone close to the stranger. Beethoven looked searchingly around. He had heard the high childish voice. Someone tugged at his coat—Oscar.

I wanted to say something quickly to make him forget the heartless childish question, but the large unkempt head was already bending over. "Did you ask me a question, little boy?"

"—If you can hear your own music," Oscar shouted at the top of his voice.

M. van Beethoven nodded seriously. "Yes, very well. Here, within." He beat on his chest. "And here." He touched his wide, bulging forehead. And with a broad smile, "But I can't always hear the musicians very well who play my music. And sometimes that's fortunate; for example, when the musicians are as bad as your papa's."

After supper we all took our seats in the great ballroom. The members of the orchestra uneasily tuned their instruments and peered at us shyly. "They're not accustomed to playing a Beethoven symphony," Jean-Baptiste said. "Ballet music is simpler."

Three red silk armchairs, decorated with the gold crowns of the royal House of Hanover, had been placed in front of the regular rows of chairs. Here sat Jean-Baptiste and I, with the child between us— almost out of sight in his deep chair. Herr van Beethoven walked among the musicians, giving them final instructions in German. With vast sweeping gestures, he emphasized every word.

"What is it?" I asked Jean-Baptiste.

"A symphony he wrote last year."

At the same time, Herr van Beethoven turned from the orchestra and came over to us. "I had intended dedicating this symphony to General Bernadotte," he remarked thoughtfully, "but I now believe it might be more correct to dedicate it to the Emperor of the French. But—" He paused, stared dreamily into space, apparently forgetting us and the audience. Suddenly he remembered where he was and

257

pushed a heavy lock of hair from his forehead. "We shall see," he said and then, "May we begin, General?"

"Monseigneur," hissed Jean-Baptiste's aide, from right behind us. Jean-Baptiste smiled. "Please—do begin, my dear Beethoven."

The awkward figure climbed up on the podium. We saw only the broad back. The wide hand, with curiously slender fingers, held a baton. He rapped on the music stand. It was dead still. He spread out his arms, swung them up and—it began.

I'm no judge of whether our musicians played well or badly. I only know that that average-looking man with his outstretched arms inspired them to make such music as I have never heard before. It swelled like organ music and still was sweet as a violin, it rejoiced and shouted, it enticed and it promised. The music had nothing to do with the song of Marseilles. So must it have been before, back when they fought for the Rights of Man and France still had frontiers. Like a prayer and like a cry of triumph. . . . I leaned forward to look at Jean-Baptiste. Jean-Baptiste's face was stony. His lips were drawn tight, his nose stern and straight, his eyes shone. His right hand gripped the arm of the chair so hard the veins stood out.

None of us had noticed that a courier had appeared at the door. Nor that Colonel Villatte, the aide-de-camp, got up quietly and took a letter from the courier. Nor that the aide-de-camp looked only fleetingly at the sealed message and then went immediately to Jean-Baptiste. When Villatte tapped Jean-Baptiste's arm, my husband jumped. For a fraction of a second he looked bewildered, then he met the eyes of his aide-de-camp. Jean-Baptiste took the letter and motioned to him. Villatte stood still beside him. The music soared again, the walls of the great hall fell away. I felt myself floating, hoping, believing as I had once, holding my father's hand and having faith. . . .

In the brief silence between two movements of the symphony, we heard paper rustling. Jean-Baptiste first broke the seal and then unfolded the letter. Herr van Beethoven turned around and looked at him questioningly. Jean-Baptiste nodded. "Play on." Herr van Beethoven raised his baton, spread out his arms, the violins rejoiced.

Jean-Baptiste read. Once he looked up briefly. It was as though he longed to eavesdrop on this heavenly music. Then he took the pen his aide-de-camp offered him and wrote a few words on the pad he always carries with him. The aide-de-camp disappeared with the message. Noiselessly another officer took his place beside Jean-Baptiste.

He also vanished with a message on a piece of paper, and a third stood at attention next to the red silk armchair. This third one clicked his heels together so hard that the noise jarred the heavenly music. Jean-Baptiste's mouth twitched in irritation but he went on writing. And not until this third officer had disappeared did he listen again. Jean-Baptiste was no longer erect, his eyes shining with rapture, but stooped slightly, with half-closed eyes, and gnawing on his lower lip. Only at the end—once again the music sang of freedom, equality and brotherhood—did Jean-Baptiste lift his head and listen, not to the music, I knew very well, but to a voice within himself. I don't know what this voice said to him; it merged with Beethoven's music and Jean-Baptiste smiled bitterly.

There was a storm of applause. I took off my gloves so I could clap louder. Herr van Beethoven bowed awkwardly, obviously embarrassed, and indicated the musicians, of whom he had been so scornful. They rose with a great clatter and bowed, and we applauded some more. Beside Jean-Baptiste now stood all three aides. Their faces were terribly tense. But Jean-Baptiste walked forward and held out his hand to help Herr van Beethoven, clumsier and younger than he, down from the platform, just as he would a high dignitary.

"Thank you, Beethoven," he said. "With all my heart, I thank you."

The pock-marked face looked smoother, more composed; the deep-set eyes shone happily.

"Do you still remember, General, how one evening at your Embassy in Vienna you played 'La Marseillaise' for me?"

"On the piano, with one finger. That's all I can do," laughed Jean-Baptiste.

"That was when I first heard it. The anthem of a free people—" Beethoven's eyes never left Jean-Baptiste's face. Jean-Baptiste towered over him, and Beethoven had to look up. "I often thought of that evening while I was writing this symphony. That's why I wanted to dedicate it to you. A young general of the French people."

"I am no longer a young general, Beethoven!" When Beethoven said nothing, Jean-Baptiste shouted louder. "I said, I am no longer a young general—"

Still Beethoven didn't answer. I noted the three aides behind Jean-Baptiste begin to squirm with impatience.

"Then came a younger man who carried the message of your people beyond the frontiers," said Beethoven wearily. "So I thought I should dedicate the symphony to him. What do you think, General Bernadotte?"

"Monseigneur!" cried the three aides behind Jean-Baptiste, in unison. Jean-Baptiste waved them angrily away.

"Beyond all frontiers, Bernadotte—" Beethoven repeated seriously. His smile was sincere, almost childlike. "That evening in Vienna you told me about the Rights of Man. Before that I had known little about them. I don't concern myself with politics. But that—yes, that had nothing to do with politics—" He smiled. "You played the National Anthem for me with one finger, Bernadotte!"

"And this is what you created from it, Beethoven," said Jean-Baptiste, deeply moved. There was a short pause.

"Monseigneur—" one of the aides whispered.

Jean-Baptiste drew himself up and passed his hand across his face as though to wipe away a memory. "Herr van Beethoven, I thank you for your concert. I wish you a pleasant journey to Göttingen and sincerely hope that the professor will not disappoint you."

He turned toward our guests, the officers of the Hanover garrison with their wives and the social leaders of Hanover. "I must bid you farewell—tomorrow morning early I ride with my troops to the front." Jean-Baptiste bowed and smiled. "The Emperor's orders. Good night, ladies and gentlemen."

He offered me his arm.

Yes, we were happy in Hanover. The yellow light of the candles fought back the grey of the dawn when Jean-Baptiste took leave of me.

"You and Oscar must return to Paris today," he said.

Fernand had long since packed Jean-Baptiste's field kit. The gold-embroidered marshal's uniform was carefully laid between special covers in his big travelling bag. He travels with table silver for twelve people, and a wretchedly narrow camp cot. Jean-Baptiste wore the plain field uniform with the general's epaulettes.

I held his hand against my face. "Little girl, don't forget to write often. The Ministry of War will . . ."

"—Forward my letters. I know," I said. "Jean-Baptiste, will this never end? Will it always go on, always and always?"

"Give Oscar a big kiss from me, little one!"

"Jean-Baptiste, I asked you whether this would go on forever."

"The Emperor's orders: to conquer and occupy Bavaria. You are married to a marshal of France, it shouldn't surprise you." His voice was expressionless.

"Bavaria— And when you've conquered Bavaria? Do you come back to me in Paris, or do we both return to Hanover?"

A big shrug. "From Bavaria, we march against Austria."

"And then? There are no more frontiers to defend. France has no more frontiers, France—"

"France is Europe," said Jean-Baptiste, "and France's officers march, my child. The Emperor's orders."

"When I remember how often they asked you to take control. If you had only . . ."

"Désirée!" He was cross, forbidding. Then more gently, "My darling, I began as an ordinary recruit and never attended the War College, but I could not imagine ever fishing a crown out of the gutter. I don't fish in the gutter. Don't forget that, never forget it!"

He blew out the candles.

Just before I climbed into my travelling carriage, Herr van Beethoven was announced. I already had my hat on my head and Oscar was beside me, proudly clasping his own little travelling bag. Beethoven moved toward me slowly. His walk was awkward and he bowed clumsily.

"I'd be pleased if you—" he stuttered a little but soon he pulled himself together "—would tell General Bernadotte that I cannot, after all, dedicate the new symphony to the Emperor of the French. Him least of all." He paused. "I will call the symphony *Eroica*—to the memory of a hope which was never fulfilled." He sighed. "General Bernadotte will understand."

"I'll tell him, and I'm sure he'll understand," I said, and held out my hand to him.

"Do you know, Mama, what I want to be?" asked Oscar, as our coach rolled along the endless country roads. "I want to be a musician."

"I thought a sergeant, or a marshal like your papa. Or a silk merchant like your grandpapa," I said absently. At last I had my diary out and, bracing it against my knees, was writing.

"I've thought it over. I want to be a musician, a composer like this Herr van Beethoven. Or—a king!"

"Why a king?"

"Because a king can do good for a lot of people. One of the lackeys at the palace told me so. They used to have a king in Hanover. Before the Emperor sent Papa there. Did you know that?"

Now even my six-year-old son has discovered how uneducated I am.

"A composer or a king," he persisted.

"Better be a king," I advised. "It's easier."

Paris, June 4, 1806

It's spring and Jean-Baptiste still hasn't come home. His letters are short and tell me nothing. He's governing in Ansbach and trying to introduce there the reforms he did in Hanover. I was to join him as soon as Oscar was all well, but when he recovered from whooping-cough, he came down with measles. He still has them. Josephine called on me once. She said I was neglecting my roses and sent me her gardener from Malmaison. The gardener demanded enormous wages and attacked my roses so viciously there is almost nothing left of them. In between Oscar's illnesses, Hortense invited him to play with her two sons. Since Napoleon adopted these sons, Hortense and Louis Bonaparte are counting on the older boy's inheriting Napoleon's Imperial crown. Joseph is equally sure that he's the heir to the throne. (Why Joseph should be expected to survive his younger brother, and why Napoleon doesn't choose a son of his own as his heir, I'll never understand. Only last December, Josephine's reader, Eléonore Revel, "very quietly," but with a lot of talk, gave birth to little "Léon." Perhaps the Empress may yet succeed; she did in her first marriage. Fortunately it's none of my business.)

Every day was just like every other. Until the moment Julie took me unawares. Since Oscar caught the measles, she hadn't even come as close as the dining room. Instead she was always sending her maid over to ask how we were. One spring afternoon, however, there she was in the salon in a great state of excitement. I appeared at the door that leads out into the garden, but she quickly clamoured: "Don't come any nearer—you'll infect me. And my children are so delicate. I only want to be the first to tell you the big news. It's unbelievable—"

Her hat was crooked, tiny beads of perspiration dampened her forehead, she was very pale.

"What on earth has happened to you?" I asked in alarm.

"I have become a queen. Queen of Naples," said Julie tonelessly. She looked as though she'd seen a ghost.

First I thought, she's sick. She's feverish. She's already caught the measles somewhere, but definitely not at our house. "Marie!" I called. "Marie—come quickly, Julie isn't well."

Marie hurried to her but Julie pushed her away. "Leave me alone. There's nothing wrong with me. I only have to get used to the idea. A queen. I am a queen. The Queen of Naples. Naples is in Italy, as far as I know. My husband—His Majesty, King Joseph. And I am Her Majesty, Queen Julie. . . . Oh, Désirée, it's terrible. We'll have to go to Italy again and live in one of those monstrous marble palaces . . ."

"Your late papa, bless him, wouldn't have approved of this at all, Mlle Julie," Marie scolded.

"Shut up, Marie!" Julie said angrily. I had never heard Julie speak like that to our Marie. Marie snapped her mouth shut and stamped out of the room. The door slammed behind her. The next moment, however, it opened again and in came my long-lost companion. Mme la Flotte wore her best dress, and sank into a court curtsy before Julie, as before the Empress. . . . "May I congratulate Your Majesty?"

Julie had collapsed when Marie left the room in a fury. Now she sat bolt upright, with her hand to her forehead. Her mouth twitched. Then she got control of herself and made a face like a bad actress trying to put on a queenly act.

"Thank you. How did you know what has happened?" Julie said in a new, strange voice.

My companion was still crouched in front of Julie. "They talk of nothing else in the city, Your Majesty." And quite irrelevantly, "Your Majesty is too kind."

"Leave me alone with my sister," Julie commanded in the same queer new voice. Whereupon my companion, with her back to the door, tried to find the way out. I watched this maneuver with interest.

When she finally managed to wiggle out of the door, I remarked, "She seems to think she's at court."

"In my presence, from now on, people are expected to conduct themselves as at court," said Julie. "This afternoon Joseph is assembling a retinue." Julie huddled her narrow shoulders as though she were freezing. "Désirée, I'm so scared."

I tried to cheer her up. "Nonsense, you won't change."

But Julie shook her head and hid her face in her hands. "No, no, it's no use, you can't talk me out of it. I've actually become a queen."

She began to cry harder, and I went over to comfort her. "Don't touch me, go away—measles!" she shouted.

I went to the garden door. "Yvette, Yvette!" My maid appeared. When she saw Julie, she, too, sank into a court curtsy. Fortunately Julie was too busy weeping to notice. "Bring us a bottle of champagne, Yvette."

"I'm just not equal to the task," Julie said. "More receptions, more court balls, and in a foreign country. We'll have to leave Paris—"

Yvette returned with champagne and two glasses, and another

court curtsy. I waved her out of the room; then filled a glass for Julie and one for myself. Julie took hers and began to drink in hasty, thirsty gulps.

"To you, my dear. I take it congratulations are in order," I said.

"It's all your fault. You brought Joseph to our house in the first place," and she smiled at me. I laughed, too, through my tears.

I thought of the whispered rumours that Joseph is unfaithful to Julie. Little affairs, nothing serious. "I hope you're happy with Joseph," I said.

"I rarely see him alone," Julie replied, staring past me into the garden. "I suppose I'm happy. I have the children—my Zenaïde, and little Charlotte Napoleone. . . ."

"Your daughters are princesses now, and everything will be for the best." I smiled and I also tried to imagine it all. Julie is a queen, her daughters are princesses, and Joseph, the little secretary in the Town Hall, who married Julie for her dowry, is King Joseph I of Naples.

"The Emperor has decided to change the occupied territories into independent states that can be ruled by the Imperial princes and princesses. These states will, of course, be bound to France by treaties of friendship. We—Joseph and I—will rule Naples and Sicily. Elisa is Duchess of Lucca. And Louis, King of Holland. Murat, just imagine, Murat will be Duke of Cleve and Berg."

"Do the marshals have a turn, too?" I asked, horrified.

"No, but Murat is married to Caroline, and Caroline would be offended if she didn't get the revenue from some country or other." I sighed with relief. "Someone has to rule these countries we've conquered," said Julie.

"Who's conquered them?" I asked pointedly.

Julie didn't answer. She poured herself another glass of champagne, gulped it, and said, "I wanted to be the first to tell you all about it. I have to go now. Le Roy is making my robes of state. So much purple—"

"No—" I was very firm— "You can't. It won't be becoming to you. Let them make you a green coronation robe. Not purple."

"And I must pack. I want to look glamourous to Joseph, in Naples," she moaned. "Will you come with me?"

"No, I must get my child well, and besides—" Why pretend to Julie? "And besides, I'm waiting for my husband. Sometime he has to come home, doesn't he?"

I heard no more about Julie for days. But then on the society page in the *Moniteur* appeared all kinds of accounts of balls, receptions, and *bon voyage* parties for Their Majesties, the King and Queen of Naples. This morning Oscar was allowed to get up for the first time and sit by the open window. It was an enchanting May morning and my garden was beautiful even though my rosebushes had very few buds. In my neighbour's garden the lilac was in bloom. Lilacs, and my longing for Jean-Baptiste, made me feel empty and heavy of heart.

A carriage drove up. My heart stopped as it does every time an unexpected carriage stops in front of my house. But it was only Julie.

"Is madame la maréchale at home?"

The salon door flew open, my companion and Yvette collapsed into a court curtsy. Marie, who had wanted to dust the salon, marched out into the garden with an uncompromising look. She doesn't want to see Julie any more.

Julie's regal twist of the wrist—undoubtedly learned from M. Montel—encompassed the room. Oscar got up and ran to her. "Aunt Julie, I'm well again." Without a word, Julie took the child in her arms. She hugged him, then looked at me over his curly head. "Before you read it in the *Moniteur*—and it will be announced tomorrow morning—I wanted to tell you, Jean-Baptiste has been made Prince of Ponte Corvo. Congratulations, Princess!" She smiled. "Congratulations, little Crown Prince of Ponte Corvo!" She kissed Oscar.

"I don't understand. Jean-Baptiste is not a brother of the Emperor." It was the first thing I thought of.

"But he's governing Ansbach and Hanover so magnificently, the Emperor wants to honour him," exulted Julie. She let Oscar go. "Aren't you pleased, Highness? You—Princess, you!"

"I suppose . . ." I interrupted myself. "Yvette, champagne!" Yvette danced in. "I get a little drunk if I drink champagne in the morning," I remarked. "But since you made Marie so mad she never serves any chocolate when you come to see me. So—and now tell me, where is Ponte Corvo?"

Julie looked blank. "Stupid of me, I should have asked Joseph! I don't know, darling—but what does it matter?"

"Perhaps we'll have to go there and rule it," I suggested. "That would be awful, Julie."

"The name sounds Italian, so it must be near Naples," said Julie hopefully. "Then you'd at least live near me. But—" Her face fell. "Too good to be true," she said. "Your Jean-Baptiste is still a marshal, the Emperor needs him for his campaigns. No, you'll surely be allowed to stay here, and I have to go to Naples alone with Joseph."

"Someday these dreadful wars must surely end," I said. "We are killing ourselves with 'victories.'" Who told me that? Jean-Baptiste. France has no more frontiers to defend. France is practically all Europe. And is ruled by the Emperor and by Joseph, by Louis and Caroline and Elisa. And now the marshals, too.

"Good health, Princess!" Julie raised her champagne glass.

"Good health, Majesty." I smiled back.

Tomorrow it will all be in the *Moniteur*. The champagne prickles, pleasantly sweet. Where is Ponte Corvo? And when will my Jean-Baptiste ever come home?

Summer, 1807, in a travelling coach
somewhere in Europe

Marienburg—my destination's called, but unfortunately I'm not sure where Marienburg is. However, a colonel, assigned to me by the Emperor, is sitting next to me with a map on his knees. From time to time he calls directions to the coachman, so I assume we'll ultimately reach Marienburg. Marie, sitting opposite, grumbles continually about the muddy roads in which we often get stuck. I think we're driving straight through Poland. When we stop to change horses, I hear a language that doesn't sound German. "A short cut," the colonel told me. "We could drive through North Germany but it would be roundabout and Your Highness is in a hurry. . . ."

Yes, I'm in a hurry, a very great hurry.

"Marienburg is not far from Danzig," the colonel informed me. That tells me very little because I don't know where Danzig is.

"They were fighting on these roads just a few weeks ago," the colonel said. "But now, of course, we're at peace."

Yes, Napoleon has once again concluded a peace treaty. This time in Tilsit. Led by the Prussians, the Germans had risen and tried to drive our troops from their country. And the Russians supported the Germans. The *Moniteur* had told us all about our glorious victory at Jena. And Joseph told me privately that Jean-Baptiste had refused to obey the Emperor's orders. For "strategic reasons." And he then told the Emperor he could go on and have him court martialled. But before it came to that, Jean-Baptiste had encircled General Blücher with his army in Lübeck (wherever that is) and taken the town by storm.

Then followed the endless winter when I had so little news from him. Berlin fell and the enemy troops were pursued across Poland. Jean-Baptiste commanded the left wing of our army. At Mohrungen he won a great victory although his troops were greatly outnumbered. With this he not only inflicted a final defeat on the enemy, but saved face for the Emperor as well. This personal success so impressed the enemy's high command that they sent back his travelling bag with his marshal's uniform and his camp cot, both of which they'd captured. All this was months ago. Again and again Jean-Baptiste's regiments threw back flank attacks against our army. The Emperor won the Battles of Jena and Eylau and Friedland, collected representatives of the European States in Tilsit and dictated his peace conditions to them. Then, quite unexpectedly, Napoleon returned to Paris. And it was somewhat surprising, too, when his lackeys in their green uniforms—green is the Corsican colour, as Mme Letizia explained—rode from house to house inviting people to attend a huge victory celebration at the Tuileries.

I took my new dress from Le Roy—rose-coloured satin, dark-red scalloped roses—out of my wardrobe, Yvette arranged my unruly hair and I wore the pearl and ruby tiara Jean-Baptiste had sent by special messenger last August on our wedding anniversary. It's so long since we've seen each other—such a terribly long time.

"Your Highness will have a wonderful time," my companion said enviously, staring at the gold jewel box with the eagle in which I kept my jewels. The jewel box I was presented on Coronation Day.

I shook my head. "I'll feel very lonely in the Tuileries without Queen Julie." Impossible! Julie is now in Naples, as lonely as can be.

The reception in the Tuileries was not at all what I'd expected. We assembled in the great ballroom, of course, and waited until the folding doors were opened and "La Marseillaise" trumpeted forth. At that we curtsied low and the Emperor and the Empress entered. Napoleon and Josephine made the rounds slowly, engaging some guests in conversation and making others miserable by ignoring them.

At first I couldn't see Napoleon very well. His tall gold-encrusted aides surrounded him. But suddenly he stopped near me to speak to some Dutch dignitaries, as I remember it.

"Evil tongues, I hear, are saying that my officers send their troops into the front lines while they themselves stay behind the lines—" he began. And thundered: "Well—is that not what you say in Holland?"

I'd heard that the Dutch are very dissatisfied with the French Government in general, and especially with sluggish Louis and his melancholy Queen Hortense. I, therefore, rather expected the Emperor to scold the Dutch so I hardly listened to him. Instead I studied his face. Napoleon had changed a great deal. The sharp face under the short hair had filled out, the smile on his pale mouth was no longer both solicitous and demanding, but only supercilious. Besides, he'd put on weight, I noticed, and looked as though he had been laced into his trim general's uniform. He wore no decorations except the Order of the Legion of Honour which he had founded himself. He was definitely getting fat. This rotund image of God on earth spoke with sweeping gestures except now and then when he folded his hands behind his back as he used to in moments of great stress.

His supercilious smile was disdainful. "Gentlemen, I think our Grand Army has given outstanding evidence of bravery. One of our highest ranking officers voluntarily risked his life. In Tilsit, I was informed that one of the marshals of France had been wounded."

Did anyone hear my heart thud in the deep silence?

After an effective pause, Napoleon said, "It is the Prince of Ponte Corvo."

"Is—that—true?" My voice cut through the fog of etiquette that blankets the Emperor. A frown, so deep it started at his nose, furrowed his face. One doesn't shout in the presence of His Majesty. One . . . well, well, there's Marshal Bernadotte's little wife. . . . The frown disappeared, and at that moment I knew Napoleon had already seen me before. This was the way he wanted me to hear the news; in the presence of a thousand strangers. He wanted to punish me. For what?

"My dear Princess," he began, and I dipped into a deep curtsy. He took my hand and drew me up. "I deplore the necessity of imparting such sad news to you," he said, looking beyond me and over my head. "The Prince of Ponte Corvo, who has distinguished himself repeatedly during the campaign, and whose conquest of Lübeck we admired enormously, was slightly wounded in the throat at Spandau. I hear that the Prince is already much improved. I beg you, dear Princess, not to worry."

"And I beg for the opportunity to go to my husband, Sire," I said faintly. Only then did the Emperor actually look at me. Marshals' wives just don't follow their husbands to their headquarters.

"The Prince has been transferred to Marienburg for better nursing care. I advise you, Princess, not to undertake this journey. The roads through North Germany, and especially in the Danzig district, are very bad. Also very recently there's been fighting in these provinces. It is not a sight for beautiful women. . . ." He spoke coolly, but he watched me all the time with interest. This is his revenge, I thought, because I went to him the night before the execution of the Duke of Enghien. Because I eluded him that night. Because I love Jean-Baptiste. Jean-Baptiste, a general he hadn't chosen for me.

"Sire—I beg you with all my heart, for permission to go to my husband. I haven't seen him for nearly two years."

Napoleon's eyes never left my face. "Nearly two years . . . You see, gentlemen, that the marshals of France do sacrifice themselves for their country. If you wish to venture on this journey, dear Princess, you will be provided with a pass. For how many persons?"

"For two. I'll take Marie with me."

"I beg your pardon, Princess—who?"

"Marie. Our faithful Marie from Marseilles. Your Majesty may perhaps still remember her," I flung back.

At last. The marble mask vanished, and an amused smile took its place. "Of course, the faithful Marie—Marie of the marzipan cakes."

And to one of his aides, "A pass for the Princess of Ponte Corvo and one woman companion." He looked searchingly around, and his eyes lighted on a tall grenadier colonel. "Colonel Moulin! You will escort the Princess and be responsible to me for her safety." And then to me, "When do you plan to leave?"

"Tomorrow morning, Sire."

"Please convey my warm regards to the Prince and tell him you bring a gift from me. In recognition of his services in this victorious campaign—" Napoleon's eyes glistened, his smile was almost a sneer. Here it comes, I thought. "I present him with the residence of the former General Moreau in the rue d'Anjou. I recently bought it from his wife. I'm told that the general has chosen America for his exile. It's a pity, a capable soldier, but unfortunately a traitor to France. A great pity. . . ."

As I curtsied I saw only his back. The hands clasped convulsively behind his back. The house of General Moreau, that Moreau who, just like Jean-Baptiste, would not betray the Republic on the eighteenth of Brumaire, and who was arrested five years later in connection with a Royalist conspiracy and sentenced to two years' imprisonment. It was ridiculous to arrest this faithful general of the Republic as a Royalist. The First Consul changed his sentence to exile for life. And now the Emperor has bought his house and is giving it to Moreau's best friend, Jean-Baptiste, whom he hates but cannot do without.

That's how I come to be travelling along country roads, through battlefields strewn with horses, their stomachs distended and all four legs sticking out stiffly. Past little mounds of earth on which are warped, hastily put together wooden crosses. It's raining, raining all the time.

"And they all have mothers," I said irrelevantly.

The colonel beside me, who had been asleep, sat up. "Who? Mothers?"

I pointed to the mounds of earth on which the rain rustled down. "The dead soldiers. They're all sons!"

Marie drew the curtains in front of the carriage windows. In bewilderment the colonel peered from one to the other of us. We were silent. He shrugged and closed his eyes again.

"I miss Oscar," I said to Marie. I have left Oscar for the first time since he was born. In the early morning hours before my departure, I drove with the child to Mme Letizia in Versailles. The Emperor's mother lives in the Trianon. She had just returned from early Mass.

"I'll take good care of Oscar," she promised. "Remember, I've brought up five sons."

Brought up—but badly, I thought. But one doesn't say any such thing to the mother of Napoleon. She stroked the child's forehead with her rough hand which, in spite of care and creams, will never lose the traces of heavy housework. "Go without anxiety to your Bernadotte, Eugénie. I'll take good care." Oscar—I feel cold without my little son. When he's sick, he always sleeps in my bed.

"Should we not stop at an inn?" asked the colonel. I shook my head. It was now late night and Marie put a bottle, filled with hot water at a coach station, under my feet. The rain rattled on the carriage roof. The soldiers' graves and their poor crosses were drenched. And so we drove toward Marienburg.

"Now I've seen everything," popped out as our carriage finally drew up in front of Jean-Baptiste's headquarters. I'd gradually got used to palaces, but the Marienburg is no palace. It's a fortress. A medieval, grey, hideous castle, dilapidated and unhomelike. Soldiers swarmed around the entrance. Such heel-clicking and excitement when Colonel Moulin showed my pass. The Marshal's wife in person.

"I want to surprise the Prince; please don't announce me," I said as I alighted. Two officers led me through the gateway and into a badly paved courtyard. I looked in horror at the thick, crumbling walls, and expected any moment to meet minnesingers, knights and their ladies. But I saw only soldiers from the different regiments.

"Monseigneur is nearly well. Monseigneur usually works at this hour and doesn't like to be disturbed. What a surprise!" said the younger of the two officers and laughed.

"Couldn't you find any better headquarters than this?" I asked tactlessly.

"At the front, the Prince doesn't care where he lives. And here we at least have room for our offices. This way, if you please, Princess."

He opened an unimpressive door, and we walked along a cold and stuffy corridor. Finally we came to a little anteroom, and Fernand hurled himself at me. *"Madame!"*

I almost didn't recognize him, so splendidly was he turned out. A wine-red lackey's uniform with huge gold buttons adorned with a strange coat of arms.

"How elegant you've become, Fernand." I laughed.

"We are now the Prince of Ponte Corvo," he explained solemnly. "Please look at these buttons, madame." He stuck out his stomach to show me all the buttons on his coat. "The Ponte Corvo coat of arms. Madame's coat of arms!" he announced proudly.

"At last I have a chance to see it," I said as I studied the intricate design with interest. "How is my husband, Fernand?"

"We are now quite well again, but the new skin over our wound still itches," Fernand informed me. I put my finger on my mouth. "Shh." Fernand understood and very quietly opened the door.

Jean-Baptiste didn't hear me. He was sitting at the desk, chin in hand, studying a huge volume. The candle beside the book cast a light only on his forehead. His forehead was clear and very calm. I looked around. Jean-Baptiste was surrounded by a strange confusion of familiar objects. In front of the fireplace with a crackling fire stood the desk with files and leather volumes. Next to the fireplace hung a huge map, on which the flickering flames cast red lights. In the background I saw Jean-Baptiste's narrow camp cot, a table with his silver washbowl, and bandage material. Otherwise the big room was empty. I went a little nearer. The log in the fireplace crackled so Jean-Baptiste didn't hear me. The collar of his dark-blue uniform was open, and he was wearing a white neckcloth. Under his chin the cloth was loose, and I saw a white bandage. He turned a page in the fat volume and made a note in the margin.

I took off my hat. It was very warm beside the fireplace, and for the first time in days I felt warm and safe. But I was tired, so dreadfully tired. But that didn't matter now. I was at last at my destination.

"Your Highness," I said. "Dear Prince of Ponte Corvo . . ."

At the sound of my voice, he jumped up. "My God—*Désirée!*" He was beside me in two rapid strides.

"Does the wound still hurt?" I asked between kisses.

"Yes, especially when you press against it so hard," he admitted ruefully. Alarmed, I let my arms fall. "I'll kiss you without putting my arms around you," I promised.

"Could you? Splendid—"

I sat on his lap. I pointed to the heavy volume on his desk. "What are you reading?"

"Law. An uneducated sergeant must learn many things if he's to administer all of North Germany and the Hanseatic towns," he said. "And don't forget that I'm also to continue governing Hanover and Ansbach."

I closed the book and clung to him desperately. "Oscar was ill," I whispered. "And you left us alone. You were wounded, and far away—"

His mouth was gentle. "Little girl, little girl—" he said and held me close.

Until the door suddenly was flung open. It was definitely embarrassing. Naturally I sprang from his lap, and smoothed my hair. In the doorway stood only Marie and Fernand.

"Marie asks where the Princess will sleep. She wants to unpack the travelling bags," Fernand said accusingly. I realized he resented my bringing Marie.

"My Eugénie can't spend the night in this bug-infested fortress," cried Marie.

"Bugs? Not one," Fernand cried back. "These damp walls kill all animal life. In the quartermaster's stores there are beds, even princely beds with canopies," he declared.

"Bug-burg," Marie replied bitterly.

"Hearing those two quarrel takes me right back to the rue Cisalpine." Jean-Baptiste laughed. With a shock I remembered the Emperor's gift. After supper I would tell him we're to take over Moreau's house. First we'll dine and wine—and then—

"Fernand, you are to see that, within half an hour, a bedroom and a salon are ready for the Princess," Jean-Baptiste ordered. "And not with that damp furniture from the store. The aide on duty is to requisition furniture for the Princess from the surrounding estates. Good furniture."

"Without bugs," Marie hissed.

"The Princess and I wish to dine alone. Here in my room—in an hour."

We heard them quarrelling a little while longer in the anteroom. We remembered the bridal bed adorned with roses and thorns. We laughed a great deal. I sat on his lap again and told him a wild mixture of news: Julie's queenly qualms, Oscar's whooping cough and measles, and Beethoven's message.

"I was to tell you that he cannot, after all, dedicate the new symphony to the Emperor. He is simply calling it 'Eroica.' In memory of a hope which he once had," I said.

"Which we all once had." Jean-Baptiste nodded. "Eroica. Why not?"

Fernand set a small table. While we supped—Jean-Baptiste's cook at the Bug-Burg served us a delicious spring chicken, and Fernand poured heavy Burgundy into our glasses—I substantiated something. "You've bought some new silver—with the initials of the Prince of Ponte Corvo. At home I'm still using ours with the simple *B*."

"Have the *B* removed and the new coat of arms engraved on it, Désirée. You needn't economize, darling. We are very rich."

Fernand finally left us alone. I took a deep breath.

"We are wealthier than you know," I began. "The Emperor has given us a house."

Jean-Baptiste raised his head. "You have many messages for me,

little one. My old friend Beethoven calls a buried hope 'Eroica.'
My old enemy, the Emperor, gives me a house. Which house?"

"General Moreau's house. In the rue d'Anjou. He bought it from
Mme Moreau."

"I know. For four hundred thousand francs. Several months ago,
and it's been much discussed among the officers."

Jean-Baptiste slowly peeled an orange. This orange had travelled
through all of Europe. It might very well have been grown in the
kingdom of my sister—to become a tiny part of the rations of the
Grand Army now occupying the whole Continent. I drank a liqueur.
Jean-Baptiste seemed suddenly depressed.

"Moreau's house," he murmured. "Comrade Moreau has gone
into exile. To me, on the contrary, the Emperor gives fine presents.
I had a letter today in which the Emperor informs me he will present
me with estates in Poland and Westphalia which will guarantee me
an annual income of over three hundred thousand francs. He did not
mention Moreau's house or your visit. It's not easy to take the joy
out of a man's reunion with his wife. But the Emperor of the French
has done it."

"He said he greatly admired your attack on Lübeck."

No answer. Jean-Baptiste frowned.

"I'll get the new house all ready and comfortable. You have to
come home. The child always asks for you," I said helplessly.

"Moreau's house will never be home to me, merely quarters, where
I sometimes visit you and Oscar. . . ." He stared into the fire, then
he smiled. "I shall write Moreau."

"You can't get in touch with him. We have the Continental system," I said.

"The Emperor assigned me to administer the Hanseatic towns.
From Lübeck one can write to Sweden. And Sweden wants to stay
neutral. From Sweden letters are sent on to England and to America.
And in Sweden I have friends."

My memory stirred, a memory half-forgotten but suddenly very
clear. Stockholm up near the North Pole, the sky like a white
sheet . . . "What do you know about Sweden?"

Jean-Baptiste roused from his reverie, and spoke with animation,

"When I took Lübeck, I found Swedish troops in the town. A squadron of Swedish dragoons."

"Are we at war with Sweden, too?"

"With whom are we not at war? That is, since Tilsit established so-called peace. But at that time the Swedes were fighting with our enemies. Their mad young King thought himself chosen by God to destroy Napoleon. A religious maniac."

"What's his name?"

"Gustavus—the Fourth, I think. In Sweden all the kings are either Charles or Gustavus. His father, the third Gustavus, had so many enemies that he was killed by his own nobles at a masked ball."

"Oh, how horrible. And barbaric—at a masked ball."

"Once upon a time our guillotine took care of such things," said Jean-Baptiste ironically. "Is that any less barbaric? It's hard to judge, but harder to condemn." He gazed again into the fire, his happier mood returned. "The son of this murdered Gustavus—another Gustavus, the Fourth—also sent his dragoons to fight against France, and that's how I happened to find a Swedish squadron in Lübeck. Sweden interests me for a very particular reason, and I seized this opportunity to learn more about it. I invited the captured officers to supper, and that's how I met Mörner and—" He stopped. "Wait, I wrote down the names somewhere." He walked over to the desk.

"It's not important—" I said. "Go on with the story."

"No, it *is* important. I must know the names."

He rummaged in a drawer, found a piece of paper, and came back to me. "They were Mssrs. Gustav Mörner, Flach, De la Grange, and the Barons Leijonhjelm, Banér and Friesendorff."

"No one can pronounce such names."

"These officers explained the situation to me. Gustavus broke with us in this war against the will of his people. He probably counted on winning the Tsar's support by this move. The Swedes are always afraid Russia might take Finland away from them."

"Finland? Where is Finland?" I asked, confused again.

"Come here, I'll show you the whole thing on the map," said Jean-Baptiste, and so I had to look at the map. He held up the candlestick. "There you have Denmark, connected with the mainland by Jutland. Geographically it can never be defended against attacks from the Continent, so the Danes have made a pact of friendship with the Emperor. You understand, don't you?"

I nodded.

"Here you have the strait called Öresund. Here Sweden begins. Sweden doesn't want to ally itself with the Emperor. Up to now Sweden could count on the Tsar's help. Now it's too late. By the treaty of Tilsit the Tsar joined with the Emperor. And Napoleon is leaving the Tsar a free hand in the Baltic States. What do you think this Gustavus is up to now?"

I had no idea, naturally.

"This madman has declared war on Russia, because of Finland. See—here, on the map: There you have Finland. Finland belongs to Sweden . . ."

"How could the Swedes ever hold Finland if the Tsar decides to occupy it?" I was studying the map.

"You see, even an ignorant little girl like you asks this question. Naturally they couldn't hold Finland. The Finns, and with them the Swedes, will be bled to death in such a struggle. Finland will, of course, be ceded to Russia. And so—" Jean-Baptiste tapped the map— "And so Sweden should try to unite with Norway. It could be achieved with comparatively little difficulty."

"Who rules Norway?"

"The King of Denmark. But the Norwegians don't like him. These Norwegians must be peculiar people. No nobles, no court. The Norwegians are now more discontented than ever because, since the Danish King is also the King of Norway, Norway is considered committed to Napoleon. If I were asked to advise the Swedes, I would suggest ceding Finland to Russia, and working toward union with Norway. Such a union would at the very least have a sound geographical basis."

"Did you explain this to the Swedish officers in Lübeck?"

"Very clearly. At first they wouldn't hear of ceding Finland. None of their reasons seemed to me well-founded. Finally I said, 'Gentlemen, I am entirely objective. A Frenchman, who studies the map, a marshal who knows something of strategy, tells you that Russia needs Finland to safeguard her frontiers. If you really have the interests of the Finnish people at heart, work for an independent

Finland. But I have the impression that you're not actually concerned about the Finns but for the Swedes who live in Finland. Even so, it must be clear to you that the Tsar will secure his frontiers, and that your country will be ravaged if you don't give in on the question of Finland. As to your second enemy, the Emperor of France, I can assure you that we will very soon be sending French troops into Denmark. Whether Sweden can defend herself against these troops depends on you yourselves. Norway, on the contrary, can be conquered by Napoleon only through Sweden. Save your country by armed neutrality! And if you want a union of states, gentlemen, stand by Norway.' "

"You expressed it very well, Jean-Baptiste. How did the Swedes reply?"

"By staring at me as though I'd invented gunpowder. 'Don't look at me,' I said, 'but at the map.' " Jean-Baptiste paused. "Next morning I sent them home. Now I have friends in Sweden."

"Why do you need friends in Sweden?"

"Friends are useful everywhere and at all times. And if the Swedes don't stop fighting both France and Russia, I will have to occupy their country. We expect the English to seize Denmark and then attack us from there. That's why Napoleon is sending French troops to Denmark. Since I'm to govern the Hanseatic towns, the Emperor will also give me command of our troops in Denmark. And if the Swedish Gustavus continues to feel he's an instrument of God destined to destroy Napoleon, the Emperor will one day take the obvious step. He'll order the conquest and occupation of Sweden. From Denmark I simply cross the narrow strait, Öresund, and land in Schonen, in southern Sweden. Come, look at the map again."

Once more I had to trot over to the map. But I didn't look. I'd been travelling day and night to take care of my husband, and instead I had to have a geography lesson.

"The Swedes can't defend Schonen. Strategically untenable. I assume that here—" he beat on the map—"they would fight, and hope to hold."

"Tell me, did you tell these Swedish officers that you would probably be conquering their country? And that, since they can't hold—

what is it—Schone or Skone, they'd better take a stand farther north?"

"Yes. You can't imagine how nonplussed they were when I did. Especially one of them, this Mörner, with the round face and long curls. He got very excited. 'You're betraying your secret plans, monseigneur,' he kept saying. 'How can you divulge your plans to us?' Do you know what I said?"

"No," I said, getting a little closer to the narrow camp cot. I was so tired I could hardly keep my eyes open. "What did you say, Jean-Baptiste?"

" 'Gentlemen, I can't believe Sweden can be defended if it's attacked by a marshal of France.' That's what I said. Little girl, are you asleep?"

"Almost—" I murmured and tried to make myself comfortable on the narrow camp cot.

"Come, I've had a bedroom prepared for you. I suppose everyone else has gone to bed. I'll carry you to your room; no one will see us," Jean-Baptiste whispered.

"But I don't want to get up, I'm so tired—"

Jean-Baptiste leaned over me. "If you want to sleep here, I can go back to my desk. I have so much to do."

"N-no, you're wounded, you must lie down—" I muttered. Hesitantly Jean-Baptiste sat down on the edge of the bed. "You must take off my shoes and my dress—I'm so tired—" I said.

"I believe that the Swedish officers will speak to their ministers and give them no rest until the Swedish King abdicates. His uncle would succeed him—"

"A Gustavus—"

"No, a Charles. Charles the Thirteenth. This uncle has, unfortunately, no children. He's also said to be somewhat senile. Why are you wearing three petticoats, darling?"

"Because it rained all the time during the journey. I was cold. Poor Mörner. Senile and childless . . ."

"No, not Mörner, the thirteenth Charles of Sweden."

"If I make myself as thin as possible and get 'way over to one side, there'd be room for both of us in the camp cot. We could try—"

"Yes, we could try, my darling."

Sometime during the night I woke up. I lay on Jean-Baptiste's arm.

"Are you uncomfortable, little girl?"

"I'm marvellously comfortable. Why aren't you asleep, Jean-Baptiste?"

"I'm not tired. So many thoughts are going through my head. But you must sleep, darling."

"The Mälar flows through Stockholm, and on the Mälar float green ice floes," I said softly.

"How do you know that?"

"I just know it. I knew a man named Persson. Hold me closer, Jean-Baptiste, so I'm sure I'm really with you. Otherwise I'll think it's all a dream. . . ."

Not until autumn did I return to Paris. Jean-Baptiste and his officers went to Hamburg, and his administration of the Hanseatic towns began. He also planned to visit Denmark and inspect the fortifications on the Danish coast opposite Sweden.

I had good weather on my return trip. Hot bottles were not necessary. A tired autumn sun shone on our carriage, and on the highways and the fields, from which this year there was no harvest. We saw no more dead horses. And only a few graves. The rain had beaten down the mounds of earth and the crosses had been knocked down by the wind. One could forget that the route led across battlefields. One could forget that here thousands of men lie buried. But I did not forget.

Somewhere Colonel Moulin got hold of an old copy of the *Moniteur*. We discovered that Napoleon's youngest brother Jérôme —that dreadful child who ate too much at Julie's wedding and threw up his insides—had become a king. The Emperor had united several of the conquered German principalities and established the Kingdom of Westphalia. Jérôme I, King of Westphalia. Besides, Napoleon managed to marry off twenty-three-year-old Jérôme I of Westphalia to the daughter of an ancient German dynasty. Catherine of Württemberg was now Julie's sister-in-law. Does Jérôme ever let himself remember the Miss Patterson in America whom he so cheerfully divorced on Napoleon's orders?

"Marie, the Emperor's youngest brother has become a king!"

"Now he can eat too much every day, if no one's watching him," Marie said. Colonel Moulin stared at her in horror. It was not the first *lèse-majesté* she'd committed in his presence. I dropped the old number of the *Moniteur* out of the carriage window to flutter over the recent battlefields.

In our new home in the rue d'Anjou
in Paris. July, 1809

The church bells woke me up. Tiny dust particles danced in the rays of the sun, slanting into the room through the closed shutters. It was awfully hot although it was still very early. I tossed off the covers, crossed my hands behind my head and remembered. The bells of Paris. . . .

Perhaps it's the birthday of one of the many kings in the Bonaparte family. Napoleon has, of course, allowed all his relatives to rule something. Joseph, incidentally, isn't King of Naples any more but of Spain. Julie has been on her way to Madrid for months. Literally months.

The Spaniards wanted no part of Joseph so they ambushed his troops, encircled and annihilated them. Therefore, instead of King Joseph, the opposition entered Madrid. At which point the Emperor dispatched fresh troops to rescue Joseph's people from these misguided patriots. Murat, however, is ruling peacefully in Naples with Caroline. That is, Caroline is ruling since Murat is also a marshal and finds himself constantly at some front.

Caroline doesn't bother much with her kingdom or her son. She prefers to visit Elisa, Napoleon's oldest sister, who rules in Tuscany, gets fatter every year and at the moment is having an affair with a court musician, a certain Paganini. Julie told me all about it when she spent a few weeks here before leaving for Spain so she could have some new clothes made. Purplish-red, of course, to please Joseph. The church bells. . . .

Which Bonaparte could be having a birthday? Not King Jérôme, nor Eugène Beauharnais, Viceroy of Italy. That backward young man has changed since his marriage. Napoleon married him to a daughter of the King of Bavaria, and Eugène now opens his mouth occasionally in society. I suppose Eugène is happy.

Again the bells. The deep voice of Notre-Dame. When is King Louis's birthday? He'll probably last forever, he only imagines he's sick. Except for his flat feet he's perfectly healthy. Napoleon has taken good care of this brother from the very beginning. Put him in the Army so he'd have a profession, then appointed him his aide, and married him to his stepdaughter Hortense. Finally he installed dear old Louis on the Dutch throne— What do they call the Dutch adherents who persist in rebelling against Louis and his troops? Oh, yes, *Saboteurs*—because they wear "sabots," shoes made of wood like our fishermen's in Marseilles. They hate Louis mainly because Napoleon made him King of Holland. They couldn't possibly know that Louis can't stand his brother. Louis closes both eyes when merchant ships secretly leave his home port for England. Actually Louis is a super-saboteur when it comes to annoying Napoleon. Napoleon should at least have allowed him to choose his own wife. Who was just talking about Louis to me? Paulette, yes, Paulette. The only Bonaparte who doesn't care a fig for politics, but only for her amusement and her lovers. On Paulette's birthday no bells are rung. Nor on Lucien's. Lucien is still in exile, although Napoleon offered him the Spanish crown. Naturally, on condition that he leave his red-haired Mme Jouberthou. Lucien sensibly ducked that and tried to take his family to America. But en route his ship was captured by the English. Now Lucien lives as an "enemy alien" in England. Always watched but still—free. He recently wrote just that to his mother in a letter he had smuggled into France. And that's Lucien who once helped Napoleon to the Consulate to save the Republic of France. Lucien, the blue-eyed idealist. No bells for Lucien. . . .

The door opened a crack. "I thought the bells might have wakened you. I'll have your breakfast brought up," Marie said.

"Why are the bells ringing, Marie?"

"Why are they ever rung? The Emperor has won a great victory."

"Where? When? Is there anything in the paper?"

"I'll send you your breakfast and your reader," said Marie. "No, first your breakfast, then the fine young lady who reads to you."

Marie is always amused because, like the other court ladies, I must employ the young daughter of an old impoverished aristocratic family to read the *Moniteur* and novels to me. I'd rather read them alone and in bed. The Emperor insists that we marshals' wives be waited on as if we were all eighty years old. I am twenty-nine.

Yvette brought my morning chocolate. She opened the windows and sun and the fragrance of roses filled the room, although I've only three rosebushes. The garden here is very small, the house is right in the city. Most of Moreau's furniture we found here I gave away and bought some new—white-gold, luxurious, terribly expensive. In the salon there was a bust of the former owner. At first I didn't exactly know what I ought to do with it. I couldn't leave it in the salon. Our friend Moreau is unfortunately in disgrace these days. But I didn't want to throw it out. I finally put it in the hall.

In the salon opposite I had to hang a portrait of the Emperor. I succeeded in getting a copy of the portrait showing Napoleon as First Consul. In it the face of God's image on earth is thin and tense as before in Marseilles. The hair is long and tangled the way it was then, and the eyes are neither hard as glass nor unnaturally glittering. The eyes lost in thought but intelligent have a faraway look, and the mouth is that of the youthful Napoleon who once leaned against a summer hedge and said that there were men destined to make world history.

The bells. . . . They still give one a headache, although we're well used to victory chimes. "Yvette," I asked between two sips of chocolate, "what have we won, where, when?"

"At Wagram, Princess, on the fourth and fifth of July."

"Send in Mademoiselle and Oscar."

The child and my reader came at the same time. I arranged my pillows, and Oscar sat beside me. "Mademoiselle will read to us from the *Moniteur*. We've had another victory."

That's how Oscar and I learned a great battle had been fought at Wagram near Vienna. An Austrian army of seventy thousand men was completely destroyed. Only fifteen hundred Frenchmen were killed and three thousand wounded. Details followed. The names of most of the marshals were given. Jean-Baptiste wasn't mentioned. And yet I knew that he and his troops were in Austria. Napoleon had given him command of all the Saxon regiments in his army.

"If only nothing terrible has happened."

"But, Princess, I've just been reading that it was a very great victory," Mademoiselle assured me.

"Isn't there anything about Papa in the paper?" asked Oscar.

Mademoiselle studied the report again. "No, nothing at all," she said finally. At that moment there was an urgent knock at the door. Mme la Flotte poked her bewitchingly painted face in.

"Princess, His Excellency, Minister Fouché, begs to be received!"

Police Minister Fouché had never before called on me. The victory bells are silent at last. Perhaps I misunderstood Mme la Flotte.

"Whom did you announce?"

"M. Fouché! His Excellency, the Minister of Police," Mme la Flotte repeated. She tried to seem casual, but her pop eyes practically rolled out of her head from excitement.

"Run along, Oscar. I must dress quickly. Yvette—Yvette!" Yvette was already beside me with the lilac-coloured day dress. Yvette is right, lilac looks well on me. "Mme la Flotte, show His Excellency into the little salon."

"I have already taken him to the little salon."

"Mademoiselle—go down and ask His Excellency to wait a minute. I'm still dressing, but I'll soon be ready. Tell him that. Or no—tell him nothing. Give him the *Moniteur* to read."

A smile flitted across Mme la Flotte's pretty face. "Princess, the Minister of Police reads the *Moniteur* before it goes to press. It's part of his job."

"Yvette, we have no time to fix my hair. Get me the rose-coloured muslin scarf, tie it like a turban around my head."

The La Flotte and the reader vanished.

"Mme la Flotte—" There she was again. "Tell me, does this turban make me look like poor Mme de Staël? The author, the one the Minister of Police banished from Paris?"

"Princess, the De Staël is pug-faced and the Princess isn't."

"Thank you, Mme la Flotte. Yvette, I can't find my rouge."

"In a drawer of the dressing table. The Princess uses it so seldom."

"Yes, because I'm already too rosy-cheeked for a princess. Princesses are pale. It's more genteel. But right now I am too pale. Is it really so hot today or is it just me?"

"It's very hot, Princess. It's always hot in Paris in midsummer," Yvette said.

With which I went reluctantly downstairs. Fouché— Someone called him the bad conscience of the nation. People fear him because he knows too much. During the Revolution, they named him "Bloody Fouché," because no other deputy signed so many death sentences. He finally got too bloodthirsty for even Robespierre.

Fouché has his own idea of the responsibilities of a Minister of Police. Offices and ministries, officials and ministers, officers and civilians all come under his observation. This is not too difficult if one's generous. And the Minister of Police has a secret fund out of which he pays his spies. Who is in his pay? Or rather—who is not?

"What does he want from me?" I asked myself for the last time as I stood at the door of my little salon. The mass-murderer of Lyons, Etienne had called him when the death sentences he'd ordered in Lyons during the Revolution were discussed. How silly to think of that now. He doesn't look a bit like a murderer. I met him often at receptions in the Tuileries. Fouché is always carefully turned out and strikingly pale. Probably anemic. He speaks courteously and softly with his eyes half-closed. . . . The communiqué doesn't mention Jean-Baptiste, I know perfectly well what's happened. But I have no guilty conscience, M. Fouché! I'm just worried, terribly worried.

When I came in he jumped right up. "I come to congratulate you, Princess—we've won a great victory, and I read that the Prince of Ponte Corvo and his Saxon troops were the first to storm Wagram.

I also read that the Prince, with seven—nearly eight thousand soldiers beat back forty thousand men to do so."

"Yes, but—there was nothing about it in the paper," I stammered, and asked him again to be seated.

"I only said that I had read it, dear Princess, not where I read it. No, it's not in the newspaper, but in an Order of the Day your husband addressed to his Saxon troops, praising them for their valour."

Fouché paused, selected a piece of candy from a Dresden china box on a little table between us. He looked at the box thoughtfully. "Incidentally, I have read something else. The copy of a letter from His Majesty to the Prince of Ponte Corvo, in which the Emperor expresses his complete disagreement with the Prince's Order of the Day. His Majesty explains that this Order contains many things contrary to fact. For instance, Oudinot seized Wagram, and the Prince of Ponte Corvo could not possibly have been the first to storm the town. Furthermore the Saxons under your husband's command could hardly have distinguished themselves since they did not fire a single shot. In conclusion the Emperor made the statement that the Prince of Ponte Corvo is to be informed that in this campaign he in no way distinguished himself."

"That— Has the Emperor written that to Jean-Baptiste?" I asked, considerably upset.

Fouché carefully put the bonbon dish back on the table. "No doubt about that. A copy of his letter was enclosed in a note to me. I have received an order to—" Again that ominous pause. He looked me right in the eye, in what I suppose he thought was a friendly way. "—to watch the movements of the Prince of Ponte Corvo and censor his correspondence."

"That will be difficult, Your Excellency. My husband is still with his troops in Austria."

"You are mistaken, dear Princess. The Prince of Ponte Corvo is expected momentarily in Paris. After this exchange of letters with the Emperor, he resigned command of his troops and, because of his health, requested leave. Leave for an indefinite period has been granted him. I congratulate you, Princess. You haven't seen your husband for a long time and in a very short time he'll be here."

Why not play out the comedy? That's what they all do. What can you lose? "May I think a moment?"

He looked amused. "Think about what, honoured Princess?"

I put my hand to my head. "Everything. I'm not very clever. Your Excellency—please don't contradict—I must think about what's happened. You say that my husband writes his Saxon troops distinguished themselves—is that right?"

"They faced the enemy bold as brass. At least so the Prince wrote in his Order of the Day."

"And why does this annoy the Emperor?"

"In a secret circular letter to all his marshals, the Emperor explained, 'His Majesty the Emperor personally commands his troops, and it is his prerogative to praise any of them. Besides, our French Army is responsible for our victories and not any foreign troops. It would not otherwise be consistent with our politics or our honour.' Anyway, that's the way it went in the Emperor's letter to the marshals."

"Someone or other just told me that my husband had complained to the Emperor because he's always assigned these foreign troops. Jean-Baptiste has always wanted to command French troops and not these poor Saxons."

"Why—poor Saxons?" demanded Fouché.

"The King of Saxony sends them into battles they care nothing about. Why, as a matter of fact, are the Saxons fighting at Wagram?"

"They are allies of France, Princess. Don't you see yourself how wise the Emperor was to put the Prince of Ponte Corvo in command of these Saxon troops?"

I didn't answer.

"They held like iron. The Saxons, I mean, under your husband's command, Princess. Or so at least says their supreme commander, the Prince of Ponte Corvo."

"But the Emperor says it's not true?"

"No, the Emperor merely says that he alone has the right to commend the troops. And that it's politically unwise and inconsistent with our honour to praise foreign troops. You didn't pay proper attention, Princess."

I must get his rooms in order, I thought, he's coming home. I stood up. "Excuse me, Your Excellency, I want to get things ready for Jean-Baptiste's return. And thank you so much for your call. I don't quite know—"

He was very close to me. Of medium height, narrow-chested, a little stooped. The long pointed nose with the sort of bloated nostrils seemed to sniffle. "What don't you know, dear Princess?"

"Why you ever came to see me. Did you want to tell me that you have my husband under observation? I can't stop you. It's not important anyway, but—why have you told all this?"

"Can't you really guess, honoured Princess?"

A thought. I suppose I turned red with rage, but my voice was loud and clear.

"Your Excellency, if you thought I would help you spy on my husband, you made a great mistake." I wanted to make a marvellous grandiose gesture, flick my hand and shout, "Get out." Unfortunately I just don't have it in me.

"If I thought so, I was indeed mistaken, that's all," he said calmly. "Perhaps I did think so, perhaps not. At this moment, Princess, I'm not sure myself."

What's it all about, I wondered—why has he come? If the Emperor wants to exile us, he will exile us. If he wants to court martial Jean-Baptiste, he will court martial him. If he wants grounds for anything, his Minister of Police will provide them. . . .

"Most women have unpaid bills at their dressmakers," Fouché ventured quietly.

I lost my temper. "Now you have gone too far, monsieur."

"Our revered Empress, for example, always has overdue bills at Le Roy. I am naturally at Her Majesty's service at all times."

What? Is he implying that he—pays the Empress? For what services? It's unbelievable, I thought. And knew of course that it was true.

"Sometimes it is not unrewarding to read a man's correspondence. There are frequent surprises. Surprises that don't interest me, but perhaps a wife . . ."

"Don't go to too much trouble," I said in disgust. "You will find that for years Jean-Baptiste has been writing to Mme Récamier, and receives affectionate letters from her. Mme Récamier is a clever, well-read woman, and for a man like my Jean-Baptiste it's a treat to correspond with her."

I'd give a lot to be able to read the intellectual love letters Jean-Baptiste must write to Mme Récamier, I suddenly realized.

"And now you must really excuse me. I must straighten up Jean-Baptiste's room."

"Just a moment, honoured Princess. Would you be kind enough to give the Prince a message from me?"

"Certainly. What about?"

"The Emperor is at Schönbrunn in Vienna. It is clearly impossible to warn him that the English troops are massed, ready to land at Dunkerque and in Antwerp. From the Channel coast they plan to march directly to Paris. I have therefore, on my own responsibility and solely for the defence of the country, decided to call up the National Guard. I want Marshal Bernadotte, as soon as he returns, to assume command of these forces and to defend France. That is all, madame."

My heartbeats slowed down. I tried to imagine what it might be like. Landing by the English. Attack by the English. March to Paris. All the marshals are at some foreign front. For all practical purposes there are no troops in France. And England is attacking France. . . .

Fouché toyed with the bonbon dish again. I said, "The Emperor distrusts him—and you—you would give him command of the National Guard which must defend our frontiers?"

Fouché shrugged his shoulders. "To whom should I give the command, Princess? I am a former mathematics teacher and was never a —sergeant. Heaven sent me a marshal to Paris, and heaven be praised. Will you deliver my message to the Prince?"

I just nodded, saw him to the door. Suddenly I had a new idea. Fouché is so sly, perhaps the whole thing is a trap. "But I don't know whether my husband will consider this command if it's without the knowledge of His Majesty," I said.

Fouché stood all too close to me. He must have stomach trouble, his breath is awful. "Don't worry, madame, if it involves the defence of France, Marshal Bernadotte will accept the command." And, very quietly, "As long as he is a Marshal of France."

Whereupon he kissed my hand and departed.

That same evening Jean-Baptiste's coach stopped before our house. Jean-Baptiste was accompanied only by Fernand. He hadn't even brought his personal aides. Two days later away he went again. Headed for the Channel coast.

Villa la Grange, near Paris. Autumn, 1809

I have very little time to write anything in my diary. I spend the whole day with Jean-Baptiste and try to cheer him up.

Fouché didn't exaggerate the danger back in July. The English really did land on the Channel coast and took Vlissingen. Within a few days Jean-Baptiste accomplished a miracle. He fortified Dunkerque and Antwerp so well that not only were all the English attacks beaten off, but countless English soldiers and quantities of booty fell into his hands. But the English rallied with courage and dispatch and got their ships out of Dunkerque.

This news reached the Emperor at Schönbrunn and infuriated him. In his absence, a minister had dared to call up the National Guard, and to name as supreme commander the very marshal who was under police supervision. At the same time Napoleon had to acknowledge publicly that Fouché with the help of Jean-Baptiste had defended France. Without this unanticipated mobilization and without the foresight of a marshal who made an army out of untrained peasant boys who for over ten years had never handled firearms, France would have been lost.

Fouché has been elevated to the aristocracy, and is now Duke of Otranto. That sounds almost as romantic as Ponte Corvo and Fouché is about as familiar with his duchy as we are with our Italian principality. The Emperor of course couldn't forgo the pleasure of personally designing Fouché's coat of arms: a gold column with a snake coiled around it.

The gold column caused great merriment. The former president of the Jacobin Club, who used to confiscate as anti-Republican every fortune he heard about, is today one of the richest men in France. One of his best friends is Thérèse Tallien's former lover, Ouvrard, the arms contractor. Ouvrard is also a banker, and often goes security for Fouché. Under the circumstances, no one mentions the snake coiling around the column. Napoleon is indebted to his Minister of Police and he's also seized this opportunity to tell him what he thinks of him.

Naturally everyone waited to see if Jean-Baptiste would be honoured, and perhaps given a new high command. But the Emperor didn't even write him a word of thanks.

"Why should he? I didn't save France for him," said Jean-Baptiste.

We now live in La Grange, a great big beautiful villa near Paris, which Jean-Baptiste has bought. He hates the house in the rue d'Anjou. Even though I had the rooms freshly papered, he says "shadows" lurk in every corner.

"Is it all right with you to put Moreau's bust in the hall?" I asked cautiously when Jean-Baptiste first saw the house.

Jean-Baptiste looked at me. "You couldn't have found a better place. I want all our guests to realize as soon as they enter that we will never forget we live in Moreau's former house. Strange that you always anticipate my every wish, little one."

"Why strange? I love you." I enjoy each single day that Jean-Baptiste is out of favour and we can be together quietly in the country. From Julie, of course, I hear what's going on in the big outside world.

She and Joseph have returned. The Emperor had sent Junot and his armies to Spain to help Joseph finally get to Madrid. Junot's army was practically annihilated by the Spanish patriots, backed by the English. Junot blames Joseph for this disaster because as King of Spain he assumed entire command and wouldn't listen to Junot's advice. Things have come to a pretty pass if Joseph can command armies. Only to prove to Napoleon that he can fight as well as "my little brother, the General."

Odd that Julie hasn't yet seen through Joseph. I wonder whether they would all desert Napoleon, as they did in Marseilles, if things went badly for him? No, not all of them. Josephine would be loyal. But he will soon leave her, I hear. The rumour is that he intends to divorce her. Because he hopes to found a dynasty with the help of an Austrian archduchess, a daughter of the Emperor Franz. Poor Josephine, she's been unfaithful to him but she would never desert him.

Yesterday we had an unexpected visitor: Count Talleyrand, Prince of Bénévent. The Prince called it a "neighbourly call," and laughed, The duchy of Bénévent lies next to Ponte Corvo. Talleyrand and we were presented with our small principalities at the same time. After Fouché, Talleyrand is the most powerful man in the service of Napoleon. A year ago Talleyrand resigned as Minister of Foreign Affairs, presumably after a heated argument with Napoleon, during which Talleyrand warned against further wars. It seems, however, that Napoleon cannot forgo his diplomatic services. Talleyrand was appointed Grand Seigneur of the Empire, and is consulted before any important decision is made by the Ministry of Foreign Affairs.

I'm really fond of the lame "Grand Seigneur." He's witty and charming and never talks to ladies about war and politics. I can hardly realize he was once a bishop. He was the first bishop to take the oath to the New Republic. But because he comes from an old aristocratic family even that wouldn't have saved him from arrest by Robespierre if he hadn't fled to America in time. A few years ago Napoleon forced the Pope to excommunicate Talleyrand. Napoleon wanted him to marry and disapproved of his changing mistresses so often (Napoleon has become somewhat strait-laced, especially about members of his court). But Talleyrand always excused himself by saying he really couldn't marry, he had to remain celibate. However, his excuses were finally of no avail and he had to marry his last mistress. As soon as he married her, he was never seen with her again. I would never expect this from a former bishop. However that may be, this influential man was our unexpected caller yesterday. "Why haven't I seen you in Paris for so long a time, dear Prince?" he asked.

And Jean-Baptiste politely, "That shouldn't surprise Your Excellency. You may have heard that, because of my health, I am on leave."

Talleyrand nodded seriously, and asked solicitously whether Jean-Baptiste was feeling any better. And as Jean-Baptiste rides for hours every day, and is very tanned, he had to admit that his health was considerably better.

"Have you recently had any interesting news from abroad?" Talleyrand next inquired. That was a foolish question. In the first place, Talleyrand knows better than anyone else what is happening abroad. And secondly . . .

"Ask Fouché, he reads all my mail. Before I do," Jean-Baptiste said quietly. "However, I haven't heard anything worth mentioning."

"Not even greetings from your Swedish friends?"

I saw nothing peculiar in this question. Everyone knows that Jean-Baptiste very magnanimously sent some Swedish officers home from Lübeck instead of imprisoning them there. Naturally, he now and then gets letters from them, these people with the unpronounceable names. Nevertheless the question did seem to be significant. Jean-Baptiste looked at Talleyrand and nodded, "Yes, I've had greetings. Hasn't Fouché shown you the letter?"

"The erstwhile mathematics teacher is a very conscientious man and has naturally shown me the letter. But I wouldn't call the greetings exactly casual. Nor on the other hand particularly promising."

"The Swedes last March deposed their mad King Gustavus and proclaimed his uncle, the thirteenth Charles, King," Jean-Baptiste remarked.

This began to interest me. "Really? This king destined by heaven to defeat the Emperor has already been deposed?"

I got no answer. Talleyrand and Jean-Baptiste still looked each other straight in the eye. The silence was oppressive. "Don't you believe, Excellency, that this Gustavus is really mad?" said I, to break the silence.

"It's hard to be sure from here," and Talleyrand smiled at me. "But I've been told that his uncle is very important to the future of Sweden. This uncle is old and sickly. And childish, isn't he, if I'm not mistaken, Prince?"

294

"He has adopted a young relative to succeed him. Prince Christian Augustus von Holstein-Sonderburg-Augustenburg."

"How easily you speak these foreign names," mused Talleyrand.

"I lived long enough in the North to accustom myself to these names," Jean-Baptiste replied.

"Have you interested yourself in the Swedish language, my friend?"

"No, Excellency, I've had no occasion to do so."

"I wonder . . . A year ago when you were stationed in Denmark with your troops, the Emperor left to your discretion the invasion of Sweden. I remember writing to you about it. But you were satisfied just to look from Denmark across to Sweden—and do nothing. Why was this? I've wanted to ask you for some time.'

"You've said yourself that the Emperor left it up to me. At that time, he wanted to help the Tsar conquer Finland. Our help was not needed. It was enough, as you so rightly pointed out, Excellency, to look across at Sweden from Denmark."

"And—the lookout? How did you like what you saw, dear friend?"

Jean-Baptiste shrugged his shoulders. "On clear nights one can see the lights along the Swedish coast. But the nights were mostly misty. I seldom saw the lights."

Talleyrand leaned forward and tapped his chin speculatively with the gold top of the cane he always carries because of his lameness. Why this conversation amused him, I couldn't imagine. "Were there many lights in Sweden, dear friend?"

Jean-Baptiste cocked his head to one side and smiled. He, too, seemed entertained by the conversation. "No, very few lights. Sweden is a poor country. A great power of day-before-yesterday."

"Perhaps also a great power of—tomorrow?"

Jean-Baptiste shook his head. "Not politically. But perhaps in other ways. I don't know. Every nation has potentialities if it can bring itself to forget its great past."

Talleyrand smiled. "Every man has potentialities too, if he—can forget his less influential past. We know examples, dear Prince."

"Things have been easy for Your Excellency. You come of an aristocratic family, and in your youth were allowed to study many subjects. Easier, far easier for you than for the examples to which you refer."

That struck home. Talleyrand suddenly stopped smiling. "I deserved that reprimand, my Prince," he said quietly. "The former bishop offers his apologies to the former sergeant." Was he waiting for Jean-Baptiste to smile? Probably. But Jean-Baptiste leaned forward in his chair, his chin in his hand, and didn't even look up.

"I'm tired, Excellency," he said, "tired of your questions, tired of the Police Minister's observation, tired of suspicion. Tired, Prince of Bénévent, very tired."

Talleyrand immediately stood up. "Then I shall make my request quickly and go."

Jean-Baptiste had risen, too. "A request? I can't imagine what a marshal, fallen into disfavour, could do for the Foreign Minister."

"Look here, dear Ponte Corvo—it concerns Sweden. Curious coincidence that we have just been talking about Sweden. . . . I learned yesterday that the Swedish Council of State has sent some gentlemen to Paris to discuss the resumption of diplomatic relations between their country and ours. And it was to further this mission that the Swedes exiled their young and doubtless mad King, and put his decrepit and doubtless senile uncle on the throne. These gentlemen—I don't know whether their names mean anything to you—a M. von Essen and a Count Peyron—asked after you in Paris at once."

Jean-Baptiste frowned deeply. "These names mean nothing to me. Nor do I know why the gentlemen asked about me."

"The young officers with whom you supped after the conquest of Lübeck speak of you often. You are considered a friend of—mm—of the Far North, dear Ponte Corvo. And these gentlemen, in Paris as Sweden's representatives, probably hope that you will say a good word for their country to the Emperor."

"As you see, people in Stockholm are ill-informed," Jean-Baptiste murmured.

"I should like to ask you to receive these gentlemen," said Talleyrand evenly.

Jean-Baptiste's frown deepened. "Why? Can I help these gentlemen with the Emperor? No. Or do you want to persuade the Emperor to ask me to interfere in foreign affairs which are none of my business? I'd appreciate it, Your Excellency, if you would come right out with what you want."

"It's very simple," Talleyrand said calmly. "I should like you to receive these Swedish gentlemen and say a few friendly words to them. The choice of these words I naturally leave to you. Is that too much to ask?"

"I don't think you realize what you're asking," said Jean-Baptiste tonelessly. I'd never heard him speak quite like that before.

"I shouldn't like the Swedes to get the idea that the Emperor is at present not—let's say—not availing himself of the services of one of his most famous marshals. It would create an impression abroad that the Emperor's close associates are not in complete accord. You see, the reason for my request is very simple."

"Too simple," Jean-Baptiste said. "Far too simple for a diplomat like you. And—far too complicated for a sergeant like me." He seemed troubled. "I don't understand you. I really don't, Excellency." With that he put his hand on Talleyrand's shoulder. "Do you mean to tell me that a former bishop is less eager to do his duty than a former mathematics master?"

Talleyrand with an elegant gesture pointed his stick at his stiff foot. "The comparison limps, Ponte Corvo. Just as I do. It's only a question of to whom one feels duty-bound."

Then Jean-Baptiste laughed. Heartily and much too loud for a prince, the laugh of his young army days. "Don't tell me that you feel any obligation to me. That I couldn't believe."

"Of course not. Allow me to think on a somewhat grander scale. . . . You know that we former bishops really didn't have an easy time during the Revolution. I escaped these perilous difficulties by going to America. This journey taught me to think not only of separate states, but of whole continents. I feel in duty bound to one continent. And that is ours, dear Ponte Corvo. To Europe as a whole, and naturally especially to France. I kiss your hand, beautiful Princess. Good-by, dear friend—it was a very stimulating conversation!"

Jean-Baptiste spent all afternoon riding. In the evening he helped Oscar with his arithmetic and had the poor child multiplying and adding until his eyes ached, and I tried to carry my tired youngster off to bed. But Oscar has grown so much I can't carry him any more. . . . We didn't mention Talleyrand's visit again, because before we went to bed we had an argument over Fernand. Jean-Baptiste said, "Fernand complains that you are too open-handed with tips. He says you give him money every few minutes."

"You told me your own self that we're rich now and I don't have to be so economical. And if I want to give pleasure to Fernand, your old school friend, truest of the true, why should he complain to you behind my back that I'm extravagant?"

"No more tips. Fernand gets a monthly salary from Fouché, and so earns more than enough."

"What—" I was dumfounded. "Has Fernand given you something to make you tipsy?"

"Little girl, Fouché asked Fernand to keep an eye on me, and Fernand accepted because he thought it would be silly to lose the money. But he came right to me and told me how much Fouché is paying him, and suggested that I give him that much less. Fernand is the most decent fellow under the sun."

"And what does he tell the Minister of Police about you?"

"Every day there's something to report. Today, for instance, I helped Oscar with his arithmetic. Very interesting for the former mathematics master. Yesterday . . ."

"Yesterday you wrote to Mme Récamier and I don't like it." We were off on a familiar theme.

So we spoke no more of Talleyrand.

Paris, December 16, 1809

It was horrible.

Painful and embarrassing for all who had to be there. The Emperor ordered his entire family, his government, his court, and his marshals to assemble. In their presence he yesterday divorced Josephine.

For the first time in ages Jean-Baptiste and I were asked to appear at the Tuileries. We were to be in the throne room at eleven o'clock in the morning. At half-past ten I was still in bed. I had decided that come what might, I would not move from my pillow. It was a cold, grey day. I closed my eyes and pretended to be asleep. Come what might . . .

"What does this mean? Still in bed?" Jean-Baptiste's voice. I opened my eyes and saw the dress uniform. The high gold-embroidered collar gleamed, the stars of his orders shone.

"I've caught cold. Apologize for me to the Master of Ceremonies."

"Like before the Coronation. The Emperor will send you his personal physician. Get up at once and get ready. We're already late."

"I don't think the Emperor will send his personal physician this time." I wasn't worried. "Josephine might happen to look up as she reads out her consent to the divorce. And she might see me. I think the Emperor would at least want to spare her that." I looked at Jean-Baptiste imploringly. "Don't you understand? This—this hateful, this horrible cheap triumph I simply cannot bear."

Jean-Baptiste nodded. "Stay in bed, little one, you have a bad cold. And take care of yourself."

I looked up as the blue velvet cape, hanging in deep folds from his shoulders, disappeared. Then I closed my eyes again. When eleven o'clock struck, I pulled the quilt up to my chin. I, too, shall grow older, I thought, with wrinkles around my eyes, and no longer able to bear children. . . . In spite of the eiderdown I was chilly. I called Marie and asked for some hot milk. I felt as though I might really have a cold. She brought the milk, sat down on my bed, and held my hand. Before the clock struck twelve, Jean-Baptiste was back, and Julie came with him.

Jean-Baptiste promptly loosened his high embroidered collar and muttered, "The most painful scene I have ever witnessed. The Emperor expects too much from his marshals." With that he left my bedroom. Marie followed, because Julie had come in. Marie has never forgiven Julie. She is always horrid to her, though Julie is now a queen without a country. The Spaniards have thrown King Joseph out for good. But no one in Paris dares say so.

Julie told me what had happened. "We all had to stand in the throne room," she said. "Each person was assigned a place according to rank. We—I mean the Imperial family—were close to the thrones. The Emperor and the Empress came in together, behind them the Grand Chancellor and Count Regnaud. Count Regnaud remained close to the Empress. The Empress wore white as usual. And she had powdered herself pale. Exactly right for a martyr . . ."

"Julie, don't be so unkind, it must have been terrible for her."

"Of course it was. But I never did like her; I can never forgive her on your account for . . ."

"She had never even heard of me, and it wasn't her fault," I said quickly. "And what happened next?"

"It was deathly still. The Emperor began to read a document. Something about the dear Lord alone knowing how hard this step was for him, but that no sacrifice was too great if made for the sake of France . . . And that Josephine, for thirteen years, had made his life beautiful, that he had crowned her with his own hands, and that she was always to keep the title of an Empress of the French."

"What did he look like while he was reading?"

"You know how he always looks at official functions. Carved in stone. Talleyrand calls it his 'Caesar mask.' He'd put on the mask of Caesar and read so fast it was difficult to follow. He wanted it over with as quickly as possible."

"And then what happened?"

"That's when it got so dreadfully painful. Someone handed the Empress a document, and she began to read aloud. At first her voice was so low that no one could hear a word. Suddenly she burst into tears, and handed Regnaud the sheet. He had to read it for her. It was an awful moment . . ."

"What did her document say?"

"That, with the permission of her beloved husband, she hereby declared she could bear no more children. And that, for the sake of France, the greatest sacrifice was being demanded of her that any woman would ever be asked to make. That she thanked Napoleon for his goodness, and is convinced that this divorce is necessary so that France can someday be ruled by direct descendants of the Emperor. But the dissolution of her marriage could in no way change the dictates of her heart. . . . Regnaud read all this about as passionately as though he were reading a prescription. And all the time she was sobbing her heart out. . . ."

"And afterward?"

"Afterward all of us, members of the family, went to the Emperor's large study. Napoleon and the Empress signed the divorce decree and then we signed as witnesses. Hortense and Eugène led their weeping mother away, and Jérôme said, 'I'm hungry.' The Emperor looked at him as though he'd enjoy boxing his ears in front of us all. But he only turned around and said, 'I believe that a luncheon has been prepared for my family in the great hall. I beg you to excuse me.' Whereupon he disappeared and the others all rushed to the buffet. That's when I saw Jean-Baptiste leaving. Naturally I asked where you were. He told me you were sick and I came home with him—" Julie paused.

"Your crown is crooked, Julie." As always on official occasions she wears a tiara in the shape of a crown, and as always it was on a slant. She sat down at my dressing table, tidied her hair, powdered her nose, and chattered on, "Tomorrow morning she leaves the Tuileries and goes to Malmaison. The Emperor has given her Malmaison and paid all her debts. Besides, she's to get an annual pension of three million francs; two million must be paid by the State, and one million by the Emperor. Napoleon has also given her two hundred thousand francs for the new plants she has already ordered for Malmaison, and four hundred thousand francs for the ruby necklace a jeweller is making for her."

"Will Hortense go with her to Malmaison?"

"She will probably drive with her there tomorrow. But Hortense is keeping her apartments in the Tuileries."

"And Josephine's son?"

"Eugène will continue as Viceroy of Italy. It seems he asked to resign, but the Emperor didn't let him go. After all, he adopted Josephine's children long ago. And imagine, Hortense still believes that her oldest son will be heir to the throne. She's furious. The

Hapsburg Princess, whom the Emperor is marrying, is eighteen years old, and will have masses of princes. The Hapsburgs are so horribly prolific. . . ." Julie stood up. "I must go now, dear."

"Where?"

"Back to the Tuileries. The Bonapartes wouldn't like it if I didn't celebrate with them." She put her crown on straight. "Au revoir, Désirée, get well soon."

I lay a long time with my eyes closed. A Bonaparte is not a suitable match—for one of François Clary's daughters. Julie is used to the Bonapartes and their crowns. She's changed a great deal. How very much she's changed! Am I to blame? I brought the Bonapartes to our home. To the home of honest, simple Citizen Clary. Papa, I never knew, I've thought so often, I never dreamed it would be like this.

A small table was set up by my bed. Jean-Baptiste wished to dine with his sick wife. I was told to stay in bed all day, and went to sleep very early. So I had quite a shock when Marie and Mme la Flotte suddenly appeared at my bedside. "Queen Hortense begs to be received."

"Now? What time is it?" I was utterly confused.

"Two o'clock in the morning."

"What does she want? Didn't you tell her I'm sick, Mme la Flotte?"

La Flotte's voice cracked, she was so excited. "Of course. But the Queen of Holland won't be turned away. She asks you to see her regardless."

"Sh—not so loud. You'll wake up the whole house." I rubbed the sleep out of my eyes.

"The Queen of Holland is very upset and weeping," La Flotte informed me. She wore a very expensive dressing gown, the sleeves adorned with ermine. Perhaps Fouché pays her tailor's bills, shot through my mind.

"Marie, give the Queen of Holland a cup of hot chocolate; that'll calm her down," I said. "Mme la Flotte, tell the Queen that I'm not feeling well enough to receive her."

"Yvette has already prepared chocolate for the Queen," said Marie, and pulled the dark woollen coat she'd flung over her peasant-like linen nightshirt together at her neck. "And you get up now. I have told the Queen you will receive her right away. Come, I'll help you, don't keep her waiting, she—is crying."

"Tell Her Majesty I'll hurry," I said to La Flotte.

Marie brought me a plain blue dress. "Better get properly dressed," she declared. "She will ask you to go with her."

"Where?"

"Get dressed, you're probably needed in the Tuileries," Marie said firmly.

"Princess, my mother sent me to ask you to have pity, and to come to her at once," Hortense wept when we met. Tears streamed down both sides of her long nose, her nose was red from crying, and pale blonde locks of hair fell over her forehead.

"I can't help your mother," I said, sitting down beside her.

"That's what I told Mama but she insisted that I ask you."

"Me?" I was really astonished.

"Yes, only you. I don't know why either—" sobbed Hortense into her chocolate cup.

"And now—in the middle of the night?"

"The Empress can't get to sleep," Hortense moaned. "And she won't see anyone— Just you."

"All right, I'll drive there with you, madame." I sighed. Marie was already at the door, holding out my hat, coat, and muff.

The Empress' apartments were only dimly lighted. Shadows danced, I bumped into furniture. But when Hortense opened the door to Her Majesty's bedroom the light nearly blinded us.

On every table, on the mantelpiece, even on the floor stood candlesticks. Wide-open, half-packed trunks gaped at us. Everywhere lay clothes, hats, gloves, robes of state, and negligees in wild disorder. Someone had been rummaging in a jewel box. A diamond tiara glittered under an armchair. The Empress was alone. She lay with outstretched arms on the wide bed, her thin shoulders shook convulsively as she sobbed into the pillow. We could hear hushed women's voices from the next room. Probably they were packing in the dressing room. Josephine, however, was all alone.

"Mama, I've brought the Princess Ponte Corvo," said Hortense.

Josephine didn't stir. She just dug her fingernails deeper into the silk coverlet. "Mama," Hortense repeated, "the Princess Ponte Corvo."

With quick decisive steps I went over to the bed. Grabbed the shoulders shaking with sobs and turned Josephine over. Now she lay on her back, staring at me with swollen eyes. She's become an old woman, I realized with a start. In this one night she's become an old woman. . . .

"Désirée—" Her lips moved. Then fresh tears started. Unchecked, they streamed down her unrouged cheeks. I sat on the side of the bed and tried to take her hands in mine. She twined her fingers around mine immediately. Her pale mouth was half-open. I saw gaps in her teeth; her cheeks were crinkly as tissue paper. She'd cried away her enamel make-up so I saw the large pores. Her childlike curls were very loose and damp on her temples. And the chin, her girlish, utterly charming and somewhat pointed chin had gone slack, showing the beginning of a double chin. Pitilessly the many candles bathed her poor face in uncompromising light. Had Napoleon ever seen her not carefully made up? "I've been trying to pack," wept Josephine.

"Your Majesty needs sleep above everything," I said. And to Hortense, "Blow out all these candles, madame." Hortense obeyed, slipping like a shadow from light to light. Finally only a very small night light flickered. Josephine's tears dried up. Short, hard sobs shook her. It was worse than the weeping. "Your Majesty must go to sleep," I repeated, trying to get up.

But she wouldn't let me go. "You must stay with me tonight, Désirée," her lips trembled. "You know best how much he loves me —as he loves no one else, doesn't he? Only me, only me . . . ."

So that's why she wanted to see me. Because I know better than anyone else how much he loves her. If only I could help her . . . "Yes, only you, madame. When he met you, he forgot everyone else. Me, for example. Madame remembers?"

An amused smile played around her mouth. "You threw a champagne glass at me. The spots could never be removed. It was a dress of transparent muslin, white with a red glow—and I had made you very unhappy, little Désirée. Forgive me, I didn't mean to."

I stroked her hand and let her go on about earlier times. How old was she then? Not much older than I am today.

"Mama, you'll like it at Malmaison. You've always considered Malmaison your real home," from Hortense.

Josephine winced. Who'd interrupted her memories? Oh, yes, her daughter. "Hortense is staying in the Tuileries," Josephine remarked, trying to catch my eye. The amused smile had gone, she looked old and tired. "Hortense still hopes Napoleon will name one of her sons his successor. I should never have permitted her marriage to one of his brothers. The child has had so little out of life—a husband she hates and a stepfather whom she . . ."

"—whom she loves," Josephine would have said. She never got that far. With a hoarse scream Hortense flung herself at the wide bed. I pushed her back. Was she going to strike her mother? Hortense began to sob helplessly. This just couldn't go on, I thought. Hortense was weeping already and the Empress would soon tune up again. "Hortense, get up immediately and pull yourself together." I had absolutely no right to order around the Queen of Holland, but the Queen obeyed instantly. "Your mother must rest. And you, too. When does Her Majesty leave for Malmaison?"

"Bonaparte wants me to drive there early in the morning," Josephine whispered. "He has already told the workmen that my rooms —" The rest of her sentence got drowned out with sobs.

I turned to Hortense. "Didn't Dr. Corvisart leave a sleeping draught for Her Majesty?"

"Of course. But Mama won't take it. Mama's afraid someone will poison her."

I looked at Josephine. She lay on her back again, and the tears were flowing down her swollen face. "He's always known I couldn't have another child," she moaned. "I told him so. Because once I was pregnant and Barras—" She stopped, then suddenly shrieked, "And that fool of a doctor Barras sent me to ruined me. Ruined, ruined—"

"Hortense, ask someone to bring a cup of hot tea immediately. And then get some rest yourself. I'll stay here until Her Majesty is asleep. Where is the sleeping draught?"

Hortense fumbled among the bottles and jars on the dressing

table and finally handed me a small bottle. "Five drops, Dr. Corvisart said."

"Thank you. And good night, madame."

I took off Josephine's crumpled white dress, slipped the gold sandals from her tiny feet, and covered her up. A maid brought in the tea. I took the cup and sent her right away. Then I carefully dripped the contents of the bottle into the tea. There were six drops; all the better, I decided. Josephine sat up obediently and drank in thirsty, greedy gulps. "Like everything else in my life—very sweet, with a bitter aftertaste." She smiled and reminded me of the Josephine I'd always known before. Then she fell back into the cushions. "You weren't there this morning—for the official ceremony," she said drowsily.

"No, I thought you'd prefer me not to be."

"I did." A brief pause. She breathed more regularly. "You and Lucien are the only Bonapartes who weren't there."

"I'm no Bonaparte," I said. "My sister Julie is married to Joseph. That's as far as the relationship goes."

"Don't desert him, Désirée!"

"Who, Your Majesty?"

"Bonaparte."

The drops had apparently confused her. But they were calming her. I stroked her hand slowly and, without thinking, stroked a hand with swollen veins, the hand of a delicate aging woman. . . .

"When he loses his power—and why shouldn't he lose it?—all the men I've ever known have lost their power, some even their heads, like my late husband De Beauharnais. When he loses his power—" Her eyes closed. I let go her hand. "Stay with me—I'm frightened—"

"I'll sit down in the next room and wait until Your Majesty wakes up. Then I'll accompany Your Majesty to Malmaison."

"Yes, to Malmai—"

She was asleep. I blew out the candle and went into the next room. There it was pitch dark. All the candles had burned out. I groped my way over to the window and pulled the heavy curtains apart. A gloomy winter morning dawned. By its faint light I found a deep comfortable chair. I was dead tired, and my head throbbed as if it would burst. I took off my shoes, tucked my legs under me, and tried to sleep. The maid seemed to have finally finished packing. All was quiet.

Suddenly I sat up. Someone was coming. The light of the candle was reflected on the walls. Spurs jingled. The candlestick was on the mantelpiece. I tried to look over the high back of my chair. Who entered the bedroom of the Empress without knocking?

He. Naturally—he.

He stood in front of the mantelpiece, peering round the room. Involuntarily I stirred. He looked quickly toward my chair. "Is someone here?"

"Only me, Sire."

"Who is 'me'?" He sounded angry.

"The Princess of Ponte Corvo," I stammered, trying to get my legs out from underneath me so that I could sit up and find my shoes. But my feet had gone to sleep and prickled something awful.

"The Princess of Ponte Corvo?" Incredulously he came closer.

"I beg Your Majesty's pardon, my feet have gone to sleep under me—I can't find my shoes—just a minute please . . ." I stammered on. Finally I found my shoes, stood up and sank down into a deep curtsy.

"Tell me, Princess, what are you doing here at this hour?" asked Napoleon.

"I wonder myself, Sire," I said, rubbing my eyes. He took my hand and drunk with sleep I steadied myself. "Her Majesty asked me to stay with her tonight. Her Majesty has at last gone to sleep," I whispered. Because he said nothing I felt I disturbed him. I continued, "I'd better leave and not disturb Your Majesty here. If I only knew how to get out—of this place. I mustn't rouse the Empress."

"You don't disturb me, Eugénie, sit down again."

It was already lighter. The grey, faint light of dawn picked up the furniture, the paintings, the pale-striped tapestries on the walls. I sat down again and tried to wake up a little more.

"I couldn't sleep, of course," he said, apropos of nothing. "I wanted to bid farewell to this salon. Tomorrow—this morning the workmen come."

I nodded. It was very embarrassing for me to have to be here at this farewell . . . "Look, there she is, don't you think she is beautiful, Eugénie?"

He held out a snuffbox on which a miniature was painted, considered it and went quickly back to the mantelpiece, fetched a candlestick and held the portrait under the flickering yellow light. I saw a young girl's round face with porcelain-blue eyes and very rosy cheeks. Above all a very rosy face. "It's hard to judge these snuffbox miniatures," I said. "They all look alike to me."

"Marie Louise of Austria is very beautiful, I'm told." He opened the box, held some snuff to his nose, took a deep breath, and pressed his handkerchief over his face—the very elegant and studied gesture of snuff-users. Handkerchief and portrait disappeared into his trouser pocket. He stared at me intently. "I still don't understand, Princess, how you happen to be here." Since he wouldn't stay sitting, I tried again to stand up. He shoved me back into my armchair. "You're exhausted, Eugénie, I can tell. But what are you doing here?"

"The Empress wanted to see me. I reminded Her Majesty—" I swallowed, it was so difficult to explain to him. "I reminded Her Majesty of the afternoon on which she became engaged to General Bonaparte. It was a very happy time in the life of Her Majesty."

He nodded, and sat down unceremoniously on the arm of my chair. "Yes, it was a happy time in the life of Her Majesty. And in yours, Princess?"

"I was very unhappy, Sire. But it's so long ago and long since healed," I replied. I was so tired and so cold that I forgot who was sitting beside me. When my head dropped to one side and onto his arm, I was startled. "I beg Your Majesty's pardon."

"Let your head stay, then at least I won't be so alone." He tried to put his arm around my shoulder and to draw me to him. But I made myself stiff and leaned my head against the back of the chair. "I've been very happy here, Eugénie." I never moved.

"The Hapsburgs are one of the oldest ruling families in the world, did you know?" he announced. "An Archduchess of Austria is worthy of the Emperor of the French." I sat up straight because

I wanted to see his face. Was he serious? That a Hapsburg princess is good enough for the son of the Corsican lawyer Bonaparte?

Again he stared off into space. Then he asked, "Can you waltz?" I nodded. "Can you show me? Everyone in Austria waltzes, I heard in Vienna. But back there in Schönbrunn I had no time to try. Show me how they waltz."

"Not now, not—here."

His face was distorted. "Now. And here."

Horrified, I pointed to the door of Josephine's bedroom. "Sire, you'll wake her."

He did not give in. Just lowered his voice. "Show me! At once! This is a command, Princess."

I rose. "It's difficult without music," I said. Then I began to revolve slowly. "One, two, three, and one, two, three—that's how one waltzes, Your Majesty."

But he wasn't watching me. He still sat on the arm of the chair, staring into space.

"And one, two, three—and one, two, three—" I said a little louder.

He looked up. His heavy face looked grey and puffy in the early light. "I was so happy with her, Eugénie."

"Is it—necessary, Your Majesty?"

"I can't make war on three fronts at the same time. In the south I must quell riots, I must defend the Channel coast, and Austria. . . ." He gnawed his lower lip. "Austria will make peace if the Emperor's daughter is married to me. My friend, the Russian Tsar is arming, dear Princess. And with my friend, the Tsar of Russia, I can cope only when Austria is finally pacified. She will be my hostage, my sweet eighteen-year-old hostage—" He took out the snuffbox again and gazed with considerable relish at the rosy portrait. He got up suddenly and surveyed the room again. "So it used to be like this," he murmured as though he wanted to impress on his memory forever the stripes in the tapestries on the wall and the shape of the lovely sofa. As he turned to leave, I curtsied low. He put his hand gently on my head and stroked my hair absent-mindedly. "Can I do anything for you, dear Princess?"

"Yes, if Your Majesty would be kind enough to send up some breakfast. Strong coffee, if possible."

He laughed. It sounded young, awakening memories. Then he quickly left the salon in rapid strides. His spurs clanking.

At nine o'clock in the morning I escorted the Empress through the back door to the Tuileries. Her carriage awaited us. She wore one of the three magnificent sables the Emperor brought back from Erfurt as gifts from the Tsar. The second the Emperor had draped around Paulette's shoulders, but no one knew what had become of the third. Josephine was very carefully rouged and thickly powdered under her eyes. Her face looked quite sweet and only a little jaded. I hurried her down the stairs. Hortense was already waiting in the carriage.

"I'd expected Bonaparte would bid me farewell," said Josephine softly, leaning forward a little to see the rows of windows in the Tuileries. The carriage started up. Behind every window there were curious faces.

"The Emperor rode to Versailles very early this morning. He's spending a few days with his mother," Hortense said.

All the way to Malmaison, not another word was said.

Paris, end of June, 1810

She looks, unfortunately, just like a sausage.

The new Empress, that is. The wedding festivities are over, and the Emperor spent five million francs without batting an eye to redecorate Marie Louise's apartments in the Tuileries. First, Marshal Berthier was sent to Vienna in March as matchmaker. Then came the proxy wedding in Vienna, at which the Emperor had the bride's uncle, Archduke Charles, whom Napoleon had once defeated at Aspern, stand in his stead. Finally, Caroline was dispatched to the frontier to welcome the Emperor's bride. Near Courcelles, the ladies' carriage was halted by two unknown horsemen. It was raining cats and dogs; the two strangers tore open the coach door and flung themselves in. Marie Louise naturally screamed, but Caroline calmed her down. "It's only your bridegroom, the Emperor, dear sister-in-law—and my husband, the considerate Murat."

They spent the night in the palace at Compiègne and next morning Napoleon breakfasted at Marie Louise's bedside. When Uncle Fesch married the Imperial couple in Paris, the wedding night had long been over.

During the first month, the Empress was not permitted to hold any big receptions. For some reason or other, Napoleon feels that women conceive more readily if they don't exert themselves. At least, that's his theory by day. But finally the receptions could no longer be postponed, and yesterday, along with all the other marshals, generals, ambassadors, dignitaries, and noble and ignoble princes, we were summoned to the Tuileries to be presented to the new Empress.

It was exactly as it had been—last time. The great ballroom, the thousand candles, the crowd of uniforms, court gowns with long trains over which people stumbled. Striking up of "La Marseillaise," flinging open of the folding doors, entrance of the Emperor and Empress.

In Austria it's apparently customary for youthful brides to wear pink. Marie Louise had been squeezed into a tight-fitting pink satin gown, hung all over with diamonds. She is much taller than the Emperor, and, in spite of her youth, she has plenty of bosom, which she obviously straps in. Her face is pink, too, and very full, and she uses almost no make-up. She looks very natural next to the painted court ladies, but a little more powder on her shiny nose and red cheeks wouldn't have hurt. Her eyes are pale blue, large, and somewhat protuberant. Her hair is lovely, golden brown, very thick, and artfully arranged. Did anyone else remember Josephine's downy-soft childlike curls?

Marie Louise smiled incessantly. Without any noticeable effort. But then she's the daughter of a genuine Emperor and probably's been brought up to smile at two thousand people all at once. She watched her father's armies march off to fight against Napoleon and lived through the occupation of Vienna. She must have hated the Emperor from childhood, but her father made her marry him. At Compiègne he was a stranger and insensitive to the feelings of a young girl brought up by elderly governesses in a palace. . . .

The Emperor and Empress stood before us. I curtsied. "And this is the Princess of Ponte Corvo, my brother Joseph's sister-in-law." Napoleon sounded bored. "The Prince of Ponte Corvo is a marshal of France."

I kissed her jasmine-scented glove. I could have sworn she would prefer jasmine to all other scents. Her pale-blue eyes met mine. They were like porcelain, and they didn't smile.

When the Imperial couple had taken their places on their thrones, the orchestra played a Viennese waltz. Julie came over to me. "Charming—" she whispered, examining my new dress critically. She wore purple velvet and the crown jewels of Spain. Naturally her crown sat on the bias. "My feet hurt," she complained. "Come on, let's go sit down in the next room."

At the door I bumped into Hortense. She now wears white, as her mother used to. Hortense was with Count Flahault, her equerry, and gazing deep into his eyes. Julie made for a sofa and straightened her crown. We thirstily lapped up the champagne some-one brought us.

"Do you suppose she realizes her aunt once lived here in the Tuileries?" I'd suddenly remembered it myself.

Julie looked startled. "Now, really, in this Emperor's entire court you'll find no one who had an aunt who ever lived in the Tuileries."

"Yes, the new Empress. She is the great-niece of Queen Marie Antoinette."

"Queen Marie Antoinette," said Julie, and her eyes opened wide.

"Yes, Julie Clary, also a queen. A toast, my dear, and don't think about her." I drank to her. Marie Louise has many reasons for hating us, I thought. "Tell me, does the Empress always smile?" I asked Julie, who had already seen her new sister-in-law several times.

"Always." Julie nodded seriously. "And I shall train my daughters always to smile, too. Real princesses never stop smiling."

A bittersweet, sophisticated perfume drifted by—Paulette. She put her arm around my shoulder. "The Emperor has decided Marie Louise is pregnant." Paulette shook with laughter.

"Since when?" Julie asked excitedly.

"Since yesterday." The exotic perfume wafted away.

Julie stood up. "I must go back to the throne room. The Emperor wants the members of his family near the thrones," she announced solemnly.

My eyes sought Jean-Baptiste. He was leaning against a window, watching the crowd indifferently. I went over to him. "Can we go home soon?" He nodded and took my arm. Suddenly Talleyrand barred our way.

"I've been looking for you, dear Prince. These gentlemen have asked me to present them to you." Behind him stood several enormously tall officers in foreign uniforms. Dark blue, with blue and yellow sashes.

"Count Brahe, a member of the Swedish Embassy. Colonel Wrede, who has recently arrived to convey to the Emperor on the occasion of his marriage the felicitations of His Majesty the King of Sweden. And Lieut. Baron Karl Otto Mörner, who arrived here from Stockholm this morning with tragic news. He is, by the way, dear Prince, a cousin of the Mörner who was once your prisoner in Lübeck. You still remember him?"

"We continue to correspond," said Jean-Baptiste quietly, glancing from one to the other of the Swedes. "You are one of the leaders of the so-called Unionist Party in Sweden, are you not, Colonel Wrede?"

The tall man bowed. Talleyrand turned to me. "You see, dear Princess, how well informed your husband is about the situation in the North. The Unionist Party is striving for a union between Norway and Sweden."

A polite smile played around Jean-Baptiste's mouth. He still held my arm. He looked contemplatively at Mörner. The dark-haired, undersized man, with his hair slicked back from his forehead and temples, caught his eye. "I am here on a tragic mission, Prince," Mörner said in fluent but rather harsh French. "I bring the news that the Swedish heir to the throne, His Royal Highness, Prince Christian Augustus of Augustenburg, has been killed in an accident."

Jean-Baptiste's fingers dug suddenly and so painfully into my arm

I wanted to scream. Only for a fraction of a second. "How terrible," he said calmly. "I extend my sincere sympathy to you gentlemen."

There was a pause. A few measures of the waltz drifted in. Why don't we leave? It has nothing at all to do with us. Now the childless Swedish King must simply look for another successor. Let's go home.

"Has a successor to the late heir already been chosen?" Talleyrand asked. He sounded casual, polite, interested.

I happened to look at Mörner. How odd: he kept staring at Jean-Baptiste with a peculiar expression. As though he wanted to work some thought-transference on Jean-Baptiste. What can they possibly want of my husband? He can't bring their dead Augustenburg back to life. The accident is no concern of his. We have enough troubles of our own; we're in disfavour here in Paris. I looked at the tall Colonel with the blue and yellow sash, this Wrede or some such name. He, too, was watching Jean-Baptiste. Finally the short man, the Baron Mörner, said, "On the twenty-first of August, the Swedish Parliament will meet to decide on a successor to the throne."

Another incomprehensible pause.

"I fear we must take leave of these Swedish gentlemen, Jean-Baptiste," I said. The officers promptly bowed.

"I beg of you again to express my sympathy to the King of Sweden, and tell him how deeply I mourn with him and his people," Jean-Baptiste said.

"Is that the only message?" Mörner burst out.

Jean-Baptiste, already turning to go, looked again first at one and then the other. Finally he considered the young Count Brahe, who couldn't have been more than nineteen years old.

"Count Brahe, I believe you belong to one of the most distinguished families in Sweden. And so I ask you to remind your friends and fellow officers that I was not always Prince of Ponte Corvo and also not always a marshal of France. In your aristocratic circles I would be called a former Jacobin general. And I began as a simple sergeant. In a word—a parvenu. I ask you to remember this, so that you—" he took a deep breath, again his fingers clutched painfully at my arm—"so that you will not reproach me later." And very hastily, "Farewell, gentlemen."

We met Talleyrand a second time that evening in a most remarkable way. By chance his carriage stopped next to ours in front of the Tuileries. Just as we were getting in, I saw him limping up to Jean-Baptiste.

"Dear Prince," he said, "the gift of speech was given man to conceal his thoughts. But you, my friend, make no use of this gift. No one could truly maintain that you concealed your thoughts from the Swedes."

"Must I then remind a former bishop that it is written in the Bible: 'But let your communication be, Yea, yea; Nay, nay: for whatsoever is more than these cometh of evil!' "

Talleyrand bit his lips. "I never knew you were a wit, Prince," he murmured. "You amaze me."

Jean-Baptiste laughed aloud. "Don't overrate the modest witticisms of a sergeant who used to sit around a campfire with his comrades." Suddenly he was serious. "Have the Swedish officers told you what member of the Swedish Royal House has been proposed as heir to the throne?"

"The brother-in-law of the deceased heir, the King of Denmark, is one candidate."

Jean-Baptiste nodded. "And who else?"

"The younger brother of the lad who was killed, the Duke of Augustenburg. Also, the former King, who now lives in exile in Switzerland, has a son. But as the father is considered mad, no one expects much of the son. So, we shall see. The Swedish Parliament will be convened. The people can decide for themselves. Good night, dear friend."

"Good night, Your Excellency."

Back home, Jean-Baptiste rushed right to his dressing room and tore open his high richly embroidered collar. "I've told you for years you should have your collars made larger, the marshal's uniform is too small for you."

"Too small," he muttered. "My dear, innocent little girl, who never knows what she's saying. Yes, much too small." Without paying any more attention to me he marched off to his bedroom.

315

I'm writing, because I can't sleep. And I can't sleep because I am worried. Very worried about something that's about to happen and that I can't run away from. Jean-Baptiste, don't you hear me, I am really anxious. . . .

Part Three

OUR LADY OF PEACE

Paris, September, 1810

Someone shone a light in my face. "Get up at once, Désirée, and dress quickly!"

Jean-Baptiste stood with a candlestick by my bed. Then he put down the candle, and began to button the tunic of his marshal's uniform.

"Have you gone mad, Jean-Baptiste? It's still night."

"Hurry, I've had Oscar waked, too. I want the child to be present."

Voices and footsteps sounded on the ground floor. Yvette shuffled in. In her haste she'd pulled her maid's dress over her nightgown. It was one of my discarded nightgowns and it trailed after her across the floor. "Hurry, please. Help the Princess," impatiently from Jean-Baptiste.

"Has something happened?" I demanded.

"Yes—and no. You'll hear it all yourself. Just hurry now."

"What shall I wear?" I asked, completely distraught.

"The most beautiful dress you own. The most fashionable, the most expensive, do you understand?"

"No, I understand nothing." I was angry. "Yvette, bring me the yellow silk, the one I wore at court the other day. Will you never tell me, Jean-Baptiste—"

But he had already left my room. With flying fingers I fixed my hair.

"The tiara, Princess?" Yvette asked.

"Yes, the tiara," I said indignantly. "Bring me my jewel box."
I'll wear everything I own. If no one will tell me what's going on,
how can I tell what to wear. And the child awake, in the middle
of the night . . .

"Are you ready at last, Désirée?"

"If you don't tell me, Jean-Baptiste . . ."

"A touch of rouge on the lips," Yvette whispered.

In the dressing table mirror, my sleepy face yawned at me.
"Rouge, powder, quick, Yvette."

"Come on, Désirée! We can't keep them waiting any longer."

"Whom can't we keep waiting? All I know is it's the middle of
the night, all I want is to go back to sleep . . ."

Jean-Baptiste took my arm. "Pull yourself together, little one."

"What's it all about? Will you please be kind enough to tell me?"

"The greatest moment of my life, Désirée!"

I wanted to stop and just look at him, but he had an iron grip on
my arm and propelled me down the stairs. At the door of the large
hall, Fernand and Marie shoved Oscar at us. Oscar's eyes gleamed
with excitement. "Papa, is there a war? Papa, is the Emperor coming to see us? How beautifully Mama's dressed .."

They'd arrayed the child in his best suit and flattened his stubborn
hair with water. Jean-Baptiste took Oscar by the hand.

The salon was brightly lit. Every candelabra we possess was
aglow. Several gentlemen awaited us Jean-Baptiste took my arm
and slowly, between the child and me, he approached the expectant
group.

Foreign uniforms, blue and yellow sashes, shining stars on their
orders. And a young man in a dusty tunic, his high boots spattered
from top to toe with mud. His bright hair hung all disheveled almost
to his shoulders. He held a very large sealed document in his hand.
At our entrance, the gentlemen bowed most deferentially. It was
quiet as the grave. Then the young man with the sealed document
stepped forward. He must have been riding for many days and
nights without a break. Under his eyes were deep shadows. The
hand holding the document shook.

"Gustaf Fredrik Mörner of the Upland Dragoons, my prisoner

from Lübeck," said Jean-Baptiste meditatively. "I'm happy to see you again. Extremely happy."

So this was that Mörner with whom Jean-Baptiste had discussed the future of the North a whole night through.

With a shaking hand he held out the document to Jean-Baptiste. "Your Royal Highness—"

My heart missed a beat. Jean-Baptiste let go my arm and calmly took the document.

"Your Royal Highness—as Chamberlain of His Majesty, King Charles XIII of Sweden, I have the honour to report that the Swedish Parliament has unanimously elected the Prince of Ponte Corvo heir to the throne. His Majesty King Charles XIII wishes to adopt the Prince of Ponte Corvo and to receive him in Sweden as his beloved son."

Gustaf Fredrik Mörner swayed. "Forgive me, I've been in the saddle for days," he murmured. An older man, his chest bristling with orders, leapt to support him. But Mörner rallied. "May I present these gentlemen to the Prince of Ponte Corvo?"

Jean-Baptiste nodded almost imperceptibly. "Colonel Wrede and Count Brahe I have already met."

"Our Ambassador Extraordinary in Paris, Field Marshal Count Hans Henrik von Essen."

The older man clicked his heels together, his face rigid. Jean-Baptiste nodded. "You were Governor General in Pomerania. You defended Pomerania excellently against my attacks, Field Marshal."

"Baron Friesendorff, Aide to Field Marshal Count von Essen."

"Also one of your prisoners in Lübeck, Highness." Friesendorff smiled.

Mörner, Friesendorff and young Brahe gazed with shining eyes at Jean-Baptiste. Wrede waited, looking stern. The face of Count von Essen was without expression. Only his tight-pressed lips showed his bitterness. It was so still we could hear the candles drip.

Jean-Baptiste took a deep breath. "I accept the decision of the Swedish Parliament."

His eyes fastened on von Essen, the defeated candidate, the aging servant of an aging, childless king. Deeply moved, very impressively he continued:

"I thank His Majesty, King Charles XIII, and the Swedish people for their trust in me. I swear to do everything in my power to justify this trust."

Count von Essen bowed his head. Bowed his head lower, finally really bowed from the waist. And when he did, the other Swedes bowed with him. At this moment something very strange happened. Oscar, who until then had been so quiet, stepped forward and stood alongside the Swedes. Then he turned and his little hand grasped the hand of young Brahe, who can't be more than ten years older than he. Right in the midst of the Swedes stood Oscar, bowing his head as respectfully as they, bowing to his papa and mama.

Jean-Baptiste reached for my hand, protectively his fingers covered mine. "The Crown Princess and I thank you for bringing this message directly to us."

Then many things happened fast. Jean-Baptiste said, "Fernand, bring the bottles I laid down in the cellar when Oscar was born." I tried to find Marie. The members of our household were at the door. Mme la Flotte, in an elegant negligee (paid for perhaps by Fouché), did a court curtsy. Next to her, my reader did likewise. Yvette sobbed. Only Marie seemed normal. She had on her wool dressing gown over her old-fashioned linen nightshirt. She'd dressed Oscar and had had no time to think about herself. So she stood in a corner anxiously trying to hold her dressing gown together.

"Marie—" I said in a stage whisper. "Did you hear? The Swedish people offered us the crown. It's not like Julie and Joseph. It's— entirely different. Marie—I'm frightened, Marie."

"Eugénie—" vehemently, hoarsely—and then Marie forgot to hold her dressing gown together. A tear rolled down her cheek, while she—Marie, my dear Marie—curtsied to me.

Jean-Baptiste leaned against the mantelpiece and studied the document Mörner had brought. The austere Field Marshal, Count von Essen, went over to him. "Those are the conditions, Your Royal Highness," he said.

Jean-Baptiste looked up. "I take it you yourself heard about my election less than an hour ago. You've been in Paris the whole time, Field Marshal. I regret—"

Field Marshal von Essen raised his eyebrows in astonishment. "What do you regret, Your Royal Highness?"

"That you had no time to become accustomed to the idea. I'm sincerely sorry. You have defended every policy of the House of Vasa with great loyalty and courage. That was not always easy, Count von Essen."

"It was extremely difficult. And the battle I once fought against you I have unfortunately lost, Your Royal Highness."

"We will build up the Swedish armies together," Jean-Baptiste answered.

"Before I send Prince Ponte Corvo's answer to Stockholm tomorrow morning, I must draw your attention to one paragraph in the document," said the Field Marshal. He sounded almost menacing. "It concerns nationality. The adoption requires that the Prince of Ponte Corvo be a Swedish subject."

Jean-Baptiste smiled. "Had you thought I would succeed to the throne of Sweden as a French citizen?"

An incredulous smile dawned on the face of Count von Essen. But I thought that I hadn't heard Jean-Baptiste correctly.

"Tomorrow I shall apply to the Emperor of France and ask His Majesty to allow me and my family to relinquish our French citizenship. . . . Oh, the wine! Fernand—open all the bottles!"

Triumphantly Fernand set the dusty bottles on a small table. I had shepherded these bottles from Sceaux to the rue de Rocher and from there to the rue d'Anjou.

"When I bought this wine, I was Minister of War," Jean-Baptiste said. "At that time Oscar came into the world and I said to my wife, 'We shall open these bottles on the day on which the youngster joins the French Army—'" Fernand had uncorked the first bottle.

"I'm going to be a musician, monsieur." That was Oscar's childish voice. He still clung to young Brahe's hand. "Though Mama hopes I'll be a silk merchant. Like Grandfather Clary."

Even the weary Mörner laughed. Field Marshal von Essen's face remained expressionless.

Fernand filled the glasses with the dark wine.

"Your Royal Highness will now learn his first Swedish word.

322

It's *'Skål,'* and means to your good health," said the young Count Brahe. "I should like to propose the health of His Roy . . ."

He got no further. Jean-Baptiste held up his hand. "Gentlemen, I ask you, empty this glass to the health of His Majesty the King of Sweden, my kind adopted father."

They drank slowly and seriously. I'm dreaming, I thought, and drank the superb wine. I'm lying in my bed and dreaming. Then someone shouted, "To His Royal Highness, Crown Prince Karl Johan!"

"Han skall leva—" they cried to each other. What does that mean? Is it—Swedish? I sat on the small sofa by the fireplace. They'd waked me up in the middle of the night to inform me that the Swedish King wants my husband to be his son. That makes my husband Crown Prince of Sweden. I'd always thought one could adopt only small children. Sweden, close to the North Pole! Stockholm, the city over which the sky lies like a white sheet. Tomorrow Persson will read it all in the newspaper. And won't know that the Princess of Ponte Corvo, wife of the new Crown Prince, is the little Clary girl of long ago.

"Mama, the gentlemen say that my name is now Duke of Södermanland," said Oscar, his cheeks flushed with excitement.

"Marie—the child may not have undiluted wine," I said. "Add some water to Oscar's glass." But Marie had vanished. La Flotte took Oscar's glass, with a curtsy to boot. "Why Duke of Södermanland, darling?"

"In Sweden the brother of the Crown Prince usually has this title," young Baron Friesendorff explained eagerly. "But in this case—" he stopped and blushed.

"But since the Crown Prince won't be taking his brother with him to Sweden, his son will be given this title," said Jean-Baptiste quietly. "My brother lives in Pau. I wouldn't want him to move from his home."

"I thought Your Royal Highness had no brothers," declared Count Brahe.

"I urged my brother to study law, so that he wouldn't be a clerk all his life like my late papa. My brother is a lawyer, gentlemen."

At that point Oscar asked, "Will you enjoy Sweden, Mama?"

323

Silence all around me. They all wanted to hear my answer. Waiting for me—no, they can't expect that. This is my home, I am still a Frenchwoman, I . . . Then I remembered. Jean-Baptiste wishes us to relinquish our French citizenship. I am the Crown Princess of a country I know nothing of, in which there is a very old and genuine nobility, not like the parvenus of France. I'd seen how they smiled when Oscar said my papa was a silk merchant. Only Count von Essen didn't smile, he'd been ashamed. Ashamed for the Swedish court . . .

"Tell me that you'll like it, Mama," Oscar insisted.

"I don't know Sweden yet, Oscar," I said. "But I'm looking forward to seeing it."

"The Swedish people can ask no more, Your Royal Highness," said Count von Essen gravely.

His harsh accent reminded me of Persson. I wanted so much to say something friendly. "Someone I knew in my youth lives in Stockholm. His name is Persson and he's a silk merchant. Do you happen to know him, Field Marshal?"

"I regret not, Your Royal Highness." Very curt.

"Perhaps you know him, Baron Friesendorff?"

"I deplore it, Your Royal Highness."

"Possibly Count Brahe knows a silk merchant named Persson in Stockholm?"

At least Count Brahe smiled. "Truly not, Your Royal Highness."

I persisted. "And Baron Mörner?" Mörner, Jean-Baptiste's first friend in Sweden, would surely help me.

"There are many Perssons in Sweden, Your Royal Highness. It's a very common name there."

Someone put out the candles and pulled back the curtains. The sun had long since risen. Jean-Baptiste's marshal's uniform sparkled. "I wouldn't think of signing a manifesto of any party, Colonel Wrede," he declared, "not even the Unionist Party."

Next to Wrede, stood Mörner, dirty and dishevelled. "But Your Royal Highness said in Lübeck . . ."

"Yes, that Norway and Sweden constitute a geographical entity. We must strive to achieve a union. It's the concern of the entire Swedish Government, not that of a single party. In addition, the

324

Crown Prince is above all parties. Good night, or rather, good morning, gentlemen."

I don't remember how I got up to my bedroom. Perhaps Jean-Baptiste carried me upstairs. Or Marie, with Fernand's help. "You shouldn't have spoken so gruffly to your new subjects, Jean-Baptiste."

My eyes were closed, but I sensed he was there, beside my bed. "Try to pronounce 'Karl Johan,'" he urged.

"Why?"

"That's what I'll be called. Karl after my adoptive father, the Swedish King, and Johan is the Swedish form of Jean. Charles Jean in our language." He rolled the words around on his tongue happily. "Karl Johan . . . Karl XIV Johan. On coins, it will be Karolus Johannes. And Crown Princess Desideria."

I sat up with a start. "You—that's too much! I won't be called Desideria. Under any circumstances whatever, do you understand?"

"It is the wish of the Swedish Queen, your adoptive mother-in-law. Désirée is too French for her. Besides, Desideria sounds more impressive. That you must admit."

I fell back on my pillow. "Do you believe one can suddenly forget who one is, what one was, and completely deny one's real self? Go to Sweden—and play Crown Princess? Jean-Baptiste, I think I'm going to be very unhappy."

But he wasn't listening. Just kept playing with new names. "Crown Princess Desideria— In Latin, Desideria means, the desired one. Could there be a more beautiful name for a crown princess whom the people themselves chose?"

"No, Jean-Baptiste, the Swedes didn't choose me. They need a strong man. But a weak woman, who is also the daughter of a silk merchant, and knows only a M. Persson—no, I am sure they could not want me."

Jean-Baptiste got up. "Now I'll take a cold bath and dictate my request to the Emperor." I didn't move. "Look at me, Désirée— look at me. I shall ask that my wife and my son and I be permitted to relinquish our French citizenship. In order to become Swedish subjects. You agree to this, don't you?"

I didn't answer. Didn't even look at him.

"Désirée—I won't do this if you're against it. Don't you hear me?"

I still gave no answer.

"Désirée, do you realize what's at stake?"

At that I looked at him. As though for the first time. The wise forehead, over which his dark curly hair tumbled. The large bold nose, the deep-set eyes, searching yet confident. The small passionate mouth. I thought of the leather volumes in which a former sergeant studied law, of the tariff laws in Hanover, which meant its survival.

"He fished his crown out of the gutter. Yours is offered by a nation, now ruled by a king," I said slowly. "Yes, Jean-Baptiste, I know what's at stake."

"And you will come with me and Oscar to Sweden?"

"If I'm really—desired. And—" At last I found his hand, at last I held it to my cheek. How I love him, how very much I love him! "And if you'll swear to me never to call me Desideria!"

"I swear, my darling."

"Then please permit the Crown Princess of Icicle-land to continue her interrupted night's sleep, and proceed to your cold bath, Karl Johan."

"Try Charles Jean first. I'll have to get used to Karl Johan slowly."

"If I know you, you'll get used to it quickly. And kiss me again. I'd love to know how a crown prince kisses."

"—And how does a crown prince kiss?"

"Marvellously well. Just like my old Jean-Baptiste Bernadotte."

I slept long but restlessly. And woke up feeling that something terrible had happened. Two said the clock on my night table. Two o'clock. Two o'clock at night or two in the afternoon? I heard Oscar's voice in the garden, then a strange man's voice. Through the closed shutters, daylight filtered in. Why have I slept all this time? My heart felt heavy. Something had happened but—what?

I rang. La Flotte and my reader rushed in together. Collapsed into a curtsy. "Your Royal Highness wishes?"

I remembered everything.

Go on sleeping, I thought in despair. Knowing nothing, thinking nothing, asleep.

"The Queens of Spain and Holland have asked when Your Royal Highness will receive them," said Mme la Flotte.

"Where is my husband?"

"His Royal Highness has closed himself in his study with the Swedish gentlemen."

"With whom is Oscar playing in the garden?"

"The Duke is playing ball with Count Brahe."

"Count Brahe?"

"The young Swedish Count." Mme la Flotte was smiling and obviously impressed.

"Oscar broke a windowpane in the dining room," my reader added.

"Broken glass means luck," Mme la Flotte said quickly.

"I am terribly hungry," I remarked.

My reader curtsied again and disappeared.

"What shall I tell the Queens of Spain and Holland?" Mme la Flotte persisted.

"I have a headache and I'm hungry, and I won't see anyone but my sister. So tell the Queen of Holland . . . You think of something to tell her. And now I want to be alone."

La Flotte dropped into a curtsy.

These knee-bendings drive me mad. I shall forbid them.

After breakfast or lunch, I don't know what to call a meal at this hour, I got up. Yvette bowed herself in and I said, "Get out." Then I put on the simplest dress I own, and sat down at the dressing table.

Desideria, Crown Princess of Sweden. Originally daughter of a silk merchant from Marseilles, wife of a former French general. Everything dear and familiar seems suddenly to belong to the past. In two months I will be thirty years old. Do I look it?

My face is smooth and round. Too round, maybe. I'll eat no more whipped cream. Around my eyes are tiny wrinkles. I hope they're laughter lines. I twisted my mouth in an effort to laugh. The wrinkles deepened. Desideria. I laughed. Desideria! A hideous name. I never knew my real mother-in-law. But mothers-in-law are said to be insoluble problems. Are adoptive mothers-in-law pleasanter? I don't even know my adoptive mother-in-law's name. Nor exactly why the Swedes chose Jean-Baptiste their Crown

Prince. . . . I opened the shutters and looked down into the garden.

"You're aiming directly at Mama's roses, Count," Oscar shouted.

"No, Your Royal Highness must catch the ball—here it comes!" cried young Brahe. Brahe threw hard.

Oscar lurched as he caught the ball. But—he caught it. "Do you think I'll ever win battles like Papa?" Oscar called across the lawn.

"Throw back the ball, aim straight," Brahe commanded. Oscar hurled the ball at his chest. Brahe caught it. "Your Highness throws straight," he said approvingly, and threw back the ball. It landed in my yellow roses. Huge, autumnal, fading roses, their leaves wilting. I know each rose, love them.

"Mama will be very angry," Oscar declared, and looked up anxiously at my windows. He saw me. "Slept out, Mama?"

Young Count Brahe bowed.

"I should like to talk to you, Count Brahe. Have you time?"

"We broke a windowpane in the dining room, Highness," he confessed.

"I hope the Swedish State will be responsible for the repairs," I laughed.

Count Brahe clicked his heels together. "Sad to say, the Swedish State is practically bankrupt."

"So I thought." It just slipped out. "Wait, I'll come down to the garden."

I sat between the young Count and Oscar on the little white bench in front of the arbor. The wan September sun caressed me. All at once I felt much better. Oscar asked, "Can't you talk to the Count later, Mama? We're having such fun."

"No. I want you to listen carefully." Out from the house came the sound of men's voices, Jean-Baptiste's decisive and very loud.

"Field Marshal Count von Essen, and the members of the Embassy, return to Sweden today, to deliver the answer of His Royal Highness," Count Brahe told me. "Mörner is staying here. His Royal Highness has appointed him as his aide-de-camp. Naturally, we have already sent a special courier to Stockholm."

I nodded, seeking desperately for a way to begin. But I found no inspiration and burst out with, "Please tell me honestly, dear Count, just why Sweden has offered the crown to my husband."

"His Majesty, King Charles XIII is childless, and we have for years admired the great ability and administrative powers of His Royal Highness and . . ."

I interrupted. "I've been told that one king was deposed because people believed him mad. Is he really mad?"

Count Brahe concentrated on a dying leaf and said, "We assume so."

"Why?"

"His father, King Gustavus III, had some very queer ideas. He wanted to re-establish Sweden as a Great Power, and so he attacked Russia. The nobles and all the officers were against it. And to prove to the nobility that the King alone could decide on war or peace, he turned to the—the, uh, lower classes and—"

"To whom?"

"To tradesmen, the craftsmen, the peasants. Actually to the commoners."

"He turned to the commoners. Then what happened?"

"Well, Parliament, in which only the third and the fourth estate were represented, voted him extensive powers, and the King marched again against Russia. At the time, Sweden was deeply in debt and unable to pay for all this rearming. So the aristocracy had to intervene and—" Count Brahe became quite vivacious—"and then something extremely interesting happened. At a masquerade, the King was suddenly surrounded by men in black masks, and shot. He collapsed, mortally wounded, and Field Marshal von Essen—" Brahe waved in the general direction of the hum of voices from the house—"yes, the loyal Essen caught him in his arms. After his death, his brother, our present King, became Regent. When young Gustavus IV came of age, he ascended the throne. Unfortunately, it soon became apparent that Gustavus is mad. . . ."

"This is also the King who considered himself appointed by God to destroy the Emperor of the French?"

Count Brahe nodded, and looked harder than ever at the dying leaf.

"Why didn't he revenge the murder of his papa?" Oscar inquired.

"Even a madman must realize that one doesn't seek revenge from one's own class in a time of crisis," said Brahe. "Aristocrats must stand together."

"Go on with your tale of horror, Count Brahe," I said.

He looked at me as though I'd made a joke. "Tale of horror?" But I wasn't laughing. He hesitated.

"Please tell us the rest."

"Gustavus IV interpreted Biblical passages to mean that he must destroy France—Revolutionary France, of course. That's why he allied himself with the enemies of France. Only after the Tsar made peace with the Emperor Napoleon did the King attack Russia. We marched against the strongest powers on the Continent and were almost totally destroyed. Field Marshal von Essen lost Pomerania to your husband—pardon—to His Royal Highness, the Crown Prince Karl Johan, and the Russians took Finland away from us. Our Finland—"

He paused, but briefly. "And if the Prince of Ponte Corvo, when he was with his troops in Denmark, had crossed the frozen Öresund, there would today be no more Sweden. Madame—Your Royal Highness, we are an ancient state. We are tired after so many wars, but we want to—survive."

He bit his lip. A handsome young man with regular features—this Count Brahe of ancient Swedish lineage.

"Whereupon our officers decided to end these wild political gambles. Last year—on the thirteenth of March—Gustavus IV was taken prisoner in the Royal Palace in Stockholm. Parliament met and deposed him. They crowned his uncle, who'd once been Regent. The adoptive father of Your Royal Highnesses.

"And where is he now, this—mad Gustavus?"

"In Switzerland, I believe."

"He has a son, hasn't he?"

"Yes, another Gustavus. But Parliament has deprived him, too, of all rights to the Swedish crown."

"How old is he?"

"He is Oscar's age—the age of the Heir Apparent." Count Brahe stood up, picked the leaf that had so fascinated him and crumpled it between his fingers.

330

"Come back, and do tell me what they had against this young Gustavus."

Count Brahe shrugged. "Nothing. But they had nothing in his favour, either. The people fear the bad blood in the Vasa family. It is a very old dynasty, Highness, and there's been much intermarriage."

The House of Vasa is too old for them. They want Sweden to rise again as a great power, even if it means the ruination of the Swedish people. At last they appealed to the lower classes, the so-called commoners, for support, while members of the aristocracy put on black masks and attended a ball. "Did the present King ever have any children?"

Brahe grew animated. "Charles XIII and Queen Hedwig Elisabeth Charlotte had one son, but he died many years ago. When he ascended the throne, His Majesty, of course, had to adopt a successor and chose the Prince of Augustenburg, brother-in-law of the Danish King. The Prince was also Governor of Norway. The Norwegians were very fond of him. Everyone hoped for a union between Sweden and Norway after he came to the throne. When the Prince of Augustenburg was accidentally killed last May, Parliament was convened. Your Royal Highness knows the result of that meeting."

"The result," I said softly, "but not how it was achieved. Please tell me that."

"Your Highness knows that in Lübeck the Prince—I mean the Crown Prince—took prisoner several Swedish officers."

"Naturally. Two of them are right now with Jean-Baptiste. This dishevelled Baron Mörner—has he had a bath by the way?—and Baron Frie—"

"Yes, Mörner and Baron Friesendorff." Brahe nodded. "In Lübeck the Prince of Ponte Corvo invited these young officers for supper, and casually told them where he thought lay the future of the North. As a strategist, with a map in his hand. Our officers returned to Sweden, and since then the Army has become increasingly convinced that we need a man like the Prince, if Sweden is to be saved. That's all there is to tell, Your Highness."

"You say that after the death of Augustenburg, Parliament was convened. What did the aristocracy say to that? The old Swedish

331

aristocracy which never has conceded that commoners were entitled to any rights?"

Count Brahe looked straight at me. "Most of the younger nobles are officers. We tried in vain to defend Finland, and to hold Pomerania. We were enthusiastic about the idea of Prince Ponte Corvo. We tried to win our parents over to our plan. And after the murder, it was obvious to everyone that we were lost unless we chose a strong man to succeed to the throne."

"After the murder? Not another murder?"

"Your Highness has probably not heard that at the funeral of the Prince of Augustenburg Marshal Count Axel von Fersen was murdered. In the road very near the Royal Palace."

"Fersen? Who is Count von Fersen?"

Brahe smiled. "The lover of the late Queen Marie Antoinette. The man who tried to smuggle the poor Queen and Louis XVI out of France. Their whole party was caught at Varennes. Incidentally, until his death Count von Fersen wore the Queen's ring. A very sad story. . . ."

"All the stories you've told me are sad, Count Brahe," I murmured. "The more you tell me about Stockholm, the sadder it seems." Strange that Marie Antoinette had a Swedish lover, I thought. How small the world is. "But why was this Count von Fersen murdered?"

"Because he was a fanatic enemy of the new France. And also because Augustenburg wanted peace at any price with France before Sweden was entirely destroyed. A rumour was circulated that Count von Fersen had poisoned the erstwhile Crown Prince. Nonsense, naturally—the Prince of Augustenburg fell off his horse during a parade. Anyway, the mob, who considered Fersen opposed to any peace negotiations, fell on him in the street and stoned him to death. During the funeral procession of the unlucky Augustenburg."

"Were no guards near?"

"Troops were lined up on both sides of the street. They didn't move," said Brahe with no particular emotion. "It's said the King was forewarned of this attack and did nothing to prevent it. Fersen was an enemy of our new policy of neutrality. After Fersen's murder, the Governor of Stockholm declared he could no longer guarantee law and order in the capital. So Parliament met in Orebro instead of Stockholm."

Oscar was poking holes in the sand with the toe of his boot. The conversation bored him, and he paid no attention. I'm glad he didn't hear the story of the man who was murdered while the Swedish regiments stood stolidly by.

"Since Fersen's murder the aristocracy realizes that the young officers, who wanted to call in the Prince of Ponte Corvo, are right. The old King is considered . . ."

"A murderer," he wanted to say—but he didn't say it.

"And the third and fourth estates?" I asked.

"Our unsuccessful wars depleted our treasury. Our salvation is trade with England. But only a man on good terms with Napoleon can help Sweden avoid being forced into the Continental System. The third and fourth estates are also aware of this. Besides, a poverty-stricken court is not respected by the workers. The House of Vasa will soon be too poor to pay the palace gardeners. And when the commoners were told that the Prince of Ponte Corvo is very rich, they voted for him."

"Mama, is Papa really so rich he can pay all the gardeners in Sweden?" Oscar asked.

"People often assume that self-made men are rich," I said. "The people of Sweden and its aristocracy apparently assume so."

"For years I've saved a part of my pay. I can buy a small house for you and the child," Jean-Baptiste told me that first rainy night when we drove through the streets of Paris. A little house for me and the child, Jean-Baptiste, but not this Royal Palace in Sweden where the nobles wear black masks and murder their King. Not this palace, in front of which the mob stoned a marshal of the realm, while the King's soldiers looked on. Not this palace, Jean-Baptiste . . . I buried my face in my hands and wept.

"Mama, dear Mama." Oscar put his arms tight around my neck. I wiped away my tears and saw Count Brahe's serious face. Had this young man any idea why I cried?

"Perhaps I shouldn't have told you all this, Your Royal Highness," he said. "But I think it's better for you to know."

"The aristocracy, the officers, the third and fourth estates elected my husband. And His Majesty, the King?"

"The King is a Vasa, Your Highness. A man, hardly more than sixty, who has already suffered several strokes. A man who is crippled with gout, and whose mind has become cloudy. He resisted to the end, and suggested one after another of his North German cousins, and various Danish princes. Finally he had to give in. . . ."

Finally he had to give in and adopt Jean-Baptiste as his beloved son. "The Queen is younger than His Majesty, isn't she?"

"Her Majesty is a little over fifty, and a very energetic and clever woman."

"How she will hate me," I whispered.

"Her Majesty is very happy about the little Duke of Södermanland," said Count Brahe quietly.

At that moment Mörner came out of the house. He was fresh and clean, his round boyish face beamed, he wore a dress uniform. Oscar ran to him. "I want to see the coat of arms on your buttons." He fingered one of the buttons on Mörner's uniform. "Look, Mama, three little crowns and a lion who wears a crown. What a beautiful coat of arms."

Mörner let his eyes range thoughtfully from Brahe to me. I looked weepy, and the young Count embarrassed.

"Her Royal Highness wished to hear the recent history of our Royal House," hesitatingly from Brahe. Mörner raised astonished eyebrows.

"Are we now also members of the Vasa family?" Oscar asked excitedly. "If the old King adopts Papa, that makes us all Vasas, doesn't it?"

I flinched. "Nonsense, Oscar, you stay what you are—a Bernadotte," I snapped, and stood up. "Did you want to tell me something, Baron Mörner?"

"His Royal Highness requests Her Royal Highness to come to his study."

Jean-Baptiste's study was a strange sight. Next to the desk, on which, as always, were piled all sorts of documents, stood the large mirror from my dressing room. Jean-Baptiste was trying on a new uniform. Before him knelt three tailors, their mouths full of pins.

The Swedes were piously watching the fitting. I examined the new blue coat. The high collar was simply edged in gold. None of the heavy embroidery of the marshal's uniform. Jean-Baptiste earnestly contemplated himself in the mirror. "It's tight," he said sepulchrally, "under the right arm." The three tailors jumped up simultaneously, undid the seams under the sleeve, and pinned them together again. "Can you pick any flaw in the uniform, Count von Essen?" Jean-Baptiste asked. With which all the Swedes circled studiously around him. Essen shook his head, but Friesendorff ran his hand over and then under Jean-Baptiste's shoulders.

"Forgive me, Your Royal Highness," he said, and finally solemnly announced, "It pulls under the collar." So all three tailors felt Jean-Baptiste's back, but couldn't find anything wrong. Fernand, of course, had the last word.

"Marshal, sir, the uniform fits perfectly."

"Your sash, dear Count von Essen," and Jean-Baptiste unwound the blue and yellow sash from the waist of the embittered Count and put it on. "You'll have to return to Sweden without your sash, I need it for tomorrow's audience. I couldn't get another in Paris. Send me three Swedish marshal's sashes as soon as you reach Stockholm." Just then did he notice me. "This is the Swedish uniform—is it becoming?" I nodded. "We're to see the Emperor tomorrow morning at eleven. I asked for an audience, and want you to accompany me." Then, "Essen, should the sash be worn over or under the belt?"

"Over the belt, Your Royal Highness."

"Excellent. I needn't borrow your belt. I'll wear the one from the marshal's uniform—I mean the French marshal's uniform—no one will notice. Désirée, do you really think the uniform fits well?"

At that very moment Mme la Flotte announced Julie. "I'll also need a Swedish dress sword," I heard Jean-Baptiste say as I went downstairs.

Julie looked small and lost in her heavy, elegantly draped wine-red velvet coat. She stood at the window gazing thoughtfully out into the garden. "Julie, forgive me—I've kept you waiting."

My entrance had a strange effect on Julie. Her thinnish neck stiffened, her eyes popped wide open, as though she'd never seen me before, and down she went into a deep court curtsy.

"Don't you make fun of me, I have troubles enough as it is." I was furious.

Julie replied earnestly, "Your Royal Highness, I'm not making fun of anything."

"Get up. Get up right away and stop annoying me. Since when does a queen curtsy to a crown princess?"

Julie straightened up. "If the Queen is a queen without a country, whose subjects have opposed her and the King from the very beginning, while the Crown Princess is the wife of a man unanimously elected heir to the throne by Parliament—such respect is proper. I congratulate you, darling. I congratulate you from the bottom of my heart."

"How did you hear all that? Last night was the first we knew of it ourselves." I sat down beside her on a small sofa.

"Why, all Paris is talking about nothing else. The rest of us were simply put on our thrones by the Emperor in countries he'd conquered. As his deputies, so to speak. Whereas in Sweden, Parliament selected Bernadotte. Désirée—I just can't take it in." Julie laughed. "By the way, I dined today in the Tuileries. The Emperor talked a long time about it and teased me frightfully."

"Teased you?"

"Yes, he tried to make a complete fool of me. Imagine, he tried to make me believe Jean-Baptiste is seeking his release from the French Army and wants to become a Swede. We laughed and laughed . . ."

I looked at her in astonishment. "Laughed? What's there to be funny about? I'm miserable whenever I think of it."

"Désirée—it can't be true?"

I kept still.

"But none of us ever thought of such a thing," she stammered. "Joseph is King of Spain, but still a Frenchman. And Louis King of Holland, but he wouldn't thank anyone who called him a Dutchman. And Jérôme and Elisa and . . ."

"That's the difference," I said. "You said yourself there's a great difference between us and—you others."

336

"Tell me, are you really thinking of settling in Sweden?"

"Jean-Baptiste definitely. For me—it depends."

"What does it depend on?"

"Naturally, I'll go to Sweden." I bent forward. "Imagine, they say I must call myself Desideria. In Latin that means 'Desired one.' So if I should really be desired in Stockholm, I'll stay."

"What nonsense you talk. Of course they'll want you," Julie assured me.

"I'm not so sure," I said. "The old nobility in Sweden—and my new mother-in-law—"

"Rubbish, mothers-in-law are only hateful when one takes away a son," Julie contradicted, thinking of Mme Letizia. "And Jean-Baptiste isn't the Swedish Queen's own son. And you'll have Persson in Stockholm. He'll surely remember how kind Papa and Etienne were to him. All you need do is elevate him to some aristocratic rank and you'll have a friend at court," Julie said to comfort me.

"You've got it all turned topsy-turvy," I sighed, realizing that Julie, least of all, could understand the true situation.

But her thoughts soon reverted to the Tuileries. "Something incredible has happened. The Empress is pregnant. What do you think of that? The Emperor is wild with joy. The son will be called King of Rome. Napoleon is convinced that it will be a son."

"Since when has the Empress been pregnant? Yesterday?"

"No, for three months, and—"

A knock. La Flotte announced, "The Swedish gentlemen who return to Stockholm this evening ask if they may take their leave of Your Royal Highness."

"Let the gentlemen come in."

I don't think my face betrayed to a single one of the Swedes how very much I fear the future. To Field Marshal Count von Essen, most faithful adherent of the House of Vasa, I held out my hand. "Until I see you in Stockholm, Highness," were his parting words.

As I accompanied Julie to the entrance hall, I met, to my astonishment, the young Brahe. "Aren't you leaving for Stockholm with Field Marshal Count von Essen to prepare for my husband's arrival in Sweden?"

"I have asked to be appointed, for the present, aide to Your

Royal Highness. My request has been granted. I am at your service, Your Highness."

Very tall, and boyishly slim, nineteen years old, dark eyes that shine with enthusiasm, curls like my Oscar's: Count Magnus Brahe, scion of one of the oldest and proudest families in Sweden. Personal aide to the former Mlle Clary, daughter of a silk merchant from Marseilles.

"May I request the honour of accompanying Your Royal Highness to Stockholm," he added softly. And let them dare to look down their noses at our new Crown Princess if a Count Brahe stands at her side, he clearly thought. Just let them dare.

I smiled. "Thank you, Count Brahe. But, you see, I've never had an aide, so I have no idea how to keep a young and distinguished officer occupied."

"Your Royal Highness will soon think of something," he assured me. "Until then, I can play ball with Oscar—your pardon, the Duke of Södermanland."

"As long as no more windowpanes are broken." I laughed. For the first time my awful anxiety abated a little. Perhaps it's all not so dreadful.

We'd been summoned to wait on the Emperor at eleven o'clock in the morning.

Five minutes before eleven we were in the anteroom in which Napoleon keeps diplomats, generals, princes, and ministers—foreign and domestic—waiting for hours. At our entrance there was a sudden hush. Everyone stared at Jean-Baptiste's Swedish uniform and made way for us while Jean-Baptiste instructed one of the Emperor's aides to announce the "Prince of Ponte Corvo, Marshal of France, with his wife and son."

After which we might as well have been on an island. No one wanted to recognize us, no one congratulated us. Oscar stuck close to me, his little fingers clutching my skirt. Everyone there knew what had happened. A foreign people, of their own free will, had offered Jean-Baptiste a crown. And within, on the Emperor's desk, lay Jean-Baptiste's request to resign from the Army and relinquish his French allegiance. Jean-Baptiste Bernadotte no longer wishes to be a French citizen. They looked at us furtively, we made them uneasy. At court, everyone knew that a terrible scene awaited us. One of those frenzies of the Emperor at which the walls shook and plaster crumbled. What a blessing, I thought, that he always makes people wait for hours, and looked sideways at Jean-Baptiste. He was eying one of the two guards in front of the Emperor's door. Staring at his bearskin cap as though he'd never seen one before, or ever would again. The clock struck eleven. The private secretary of the Emperor, M. Méneval, appeared. "His Majesty will see the Prince of Ponte Corvo and his family."

The Emperor's study is right beyond the waiting room. At one end is a huge desk. And an endlessly long way it seems from the door to this desk. For this reason the Emperor usually meets his friends halfway in the middle of the room. We, however, had to walk the entire length. Motionless as a statue sat Napoleon behind his desk, leaning forward slightly, waiting. . . . Jean-Baptiste's spurs jingled behind me as Oscar and I advanced toward the desk. Soon I could see his features clearly. Napoleon had put on his Caesar-mask, only his eyes glittered. Behind him stood Count Talleyrand, Duke of Bénévent, and the present Minister of Foreign Affairs, the Duke of Cadore.

Behind us Méneval tiptoed cautiously.

The three of us lined up in front of the huge desk. The child in the middle. I sank into a curtsy and bobbed up. The Emperor never stirred, just kept staring at Jean-Baptiste. In his eyes flared an evil spark. Then he jumped up, pushed back his chair, came from behind his desk and shouted, "In what uniform do you dare appear before your Emperor and Supreme Commander, Marshal?"

"The uniform is an approximation of a Swedish marshal's, Sire," Jean-Baptiste answered. He spoke very softly but to the point.

"And you dare come here in a Swedish uniform? You—a marshal of France?" A bit of plaster dropped from an ornament in the ceiling, he was screaming like a madman.

"I thought it didn't matter to Your Majesty what uniforms your marshals wore," Jean-Baptiste said placidly. "I've often seen Marshal Murat, King of Naples, in very peculiar uniforms at court."

That hit home. Baby-face Marshal Murat wears ostrich feathers in his three-cornered hat, has his uniforms studded with pearls, and gold embroidery on his riding breeches. This brother-in-law of Napoleon has a passion for fancy dress. And the Emperor laughs at him good-naturedly.

"His Majesty, my royal brother-in-law, has designed make-believe uniforms. As far as I know—they are his own invention." The suggestion of a smile hovered around his small mouth, and vanished. "But you dare to come here in a Swedish uniform. Before your Emperor."

Napoleon paused for breath and stamped his foot in anger. Oscar tried to hide behind my skirt.

"Answer me, Marshal!"

"I considered it proper to report for this audience in a Swedish uniform. It was not my intention, Sire, to offend you. Also in a way this, too, is my own invention. If Your Majesty would like to see—" Jean-Baptiste raised his sash and showed the belt. "I am wearing the belt of my old marshal's uniform, Sire."

"Stop these masquerades, Prince. To business."

The Emperor's voice was strained and he spoke very fast. The overture, arranged to intimidate us, was over. What an actor, I thought, and felt very tired. Isn't he going to ask us to sit down?

He had no intention of doing so. He just stood behind his desk and stared down at a document—Jean-Baptiste's request.

"You've submitted a very remarkable request, Prince. You mention the prospect of your being adopted by the Swedish King, and ask permission to surrender your French citizenship. A strange document. Almost incomprehensible, if one thinks back. But you're perhaps not thinking back, Msgr. Marshal of France?"

Jean-Baptiste's lips were tight-closed.

"Don't you really remember? For instance, the time when a young recruit helped defend the frontiers of a new France? Or the battlefields on which this recruit fought as sergeant, lieutenant, colonel and finally general of the French Army? Or the day on which the Emperor of the French appointed you a marshal of France?"

Jean-Baptiste was silent.

"Not so very long ago, without my knowledge, you defended the frontiers of your native land." He smiled, suddenly, the old smile.

"Perhaps you even, without my knowledge, saved France. I've already told you—it was long ago, and you may well have forgotten. I told you I cannot renounce the services of such a man as you. That was in the days of Brumaire. Perhaps you still remember? Had the Government so ordered, you and Moreau would have had me shot. The Government did not give this order. Bernadotte—I repeat, I cannot let you go."

He sat down and pushed aside the application. Looked up and said less intensely, "But since the Swedish people have chosen you—" he shrugged, laughed lightly—"heir to their throne, as your Emperor and Supreme Military Commander, I hereby give you permission to accept. And that's that."

"And I shall inform His Majesty the King of Sweden that I cannot accept. The Swedish people want a Swedish Crown Prince, Sire," said Jean-Baptiste calmly.

Napoleon jumped up. "Nonsense, Bernadotte! Look at my brothers—Joseph, Louis, Jérôme. Did any of them give up their French citizenship? Or my stepson Eugène in Italy?"

Jean-Baptiste didn't answer. Napoleon again came around from behind his desk and began to pace up and down the room. My eyes met Talleyrand's. The former bishop was leaning on his stick, tired from standing so long. His eyes twinkled. What was he thinking? That Jean-Baptiste would win out? It certainly didn't seem so.

Suddenly the Emperor stopped and confronted me. "Princess," said he softly, "I don't believe you realize that the Swedish Royal House is mad. The present King is incapable of pronouncing one coherent sentence, and his nephew had to be deposed because he was crazy! Really—cuckoo!" He tapped his forehead. "Princess, tell me, is your husband crazy? I mean crazy enough to give up his French citizenship for the Swedish succession?"

"I must ask you not to insult His Majesty, Charles XIII, in my presence," said Jean-Baptiste sharply.

"Talleyrand—are the Vasas mad, or are they not?" Napoleon asked.

"It is a very ancient dynasty, Sire. Ancient dynasties are apt to be unhealthy," Talleyrand declared.

"And you, Princess, what do you say to this? Bernadotte also asks

341

that you and the child be allowed to relinquish French citizenship."

"It's a matter of form, Sire. Without this we cannot succeed to the Swedish throne," I heard myself say. Had I given the right answer? I looked at Jean-Baptiste. But Jean-Baptiste was staring right past me. I looked around at Talleyrand. The great man nodded almost imperceptibly.

"Point two: Your resignation from the Army. That can't be done, Bernadotte, it really can't."

The Emperor was back behind the desk again, reading the application, which he must have already studied. "I can not consider doing without one of my marshals. When new wars—" He hesitated. Then rapidly, "If England doesn't surrender there will inevitably be new wars, and I will need you. You will, as always, command one of my armies. Whether you are Crown Prince of Sweden or not. Your Swedish regiments will become a part of our great army. Or do you think—" He unexpectedly smiled and looked ten years younger. "Do you think I could let anyone else command the Saxons?"

"In view of Your Majesty's Order of the Day after the battle of Wagram which stated that the Saxons had not fired a single shot, it would seem of vast unimportance who commands them. Give the command to Ney, Sire. Ney is very ambitious and has served under me."

"The Saxons stormed Wagram. And under no circumstances would I give this command to Ney. I shall permit you to become a Swede, if you remain a marshal of France. I fully understand the ambitions of my marshals. Besides, you are admirably fitted for the administration of a country. I remember Hanover and the Hanseatic towns. You are an outstanding governor, Bernadotte."

"I request you to allow me to resign from the French Army."

With that Napoleon pounded the desk with his fist. It sounded like a clap of thunder.

"My feet hurt, may I sit down, Sire?" I said. The Emperor looked at me. The glitter in his eyes dimmed, they looked grey. It was as though he looked through the wrong end of a telescope: the image grew smaller and smaller. It was as though, far distant, he saw one tiny scene: a girl in a garden, at dusk, a young girl racing to a hedge, and to please her, he let her win. . . .

"You'll have to stand on your feet for many long hours when receiving your subjects, if ever you're Crown Princess of Sweden, Eugénie," he said quietly. "Please—sit down. Gentlemen, let's all be seated."

So we gathered cozily around his desk. "Where were we? . . . You wish to leave the Army, Prince of Ponte Corvo? To fight with our armies not as a marshal of France, but as one of our allies? Do I understand you correctly?"

Only then did the Foreign Minister's face show any real interest in the conversation. So that's what Napoleon wanted, had wanted all the time. An alliance with Sweden. "If I grant your request, as you have formally presented it, it is because I naturally would not place any difficulties in the way of one of my marshals who wished to be adopted by an ancient, not very healthy royal family. It was extremely sagacious of the Swedish people to prove their friendship with France by choosing one of my marshals. Had I been asked before the election, I should, of course, have preferred one of my brothers, as an earnest of my particular interest in this alliance and my great regard for the House of Vasa. But since I wasn't consulted but only confronted with the surprising results of this election—I congratulate you, dear Prince."

"Mama—he doesn't scare me a bit."

Talleyrand bit his lip to stifle his smile, and so did the Duke of Cadore. Napoleon considered Oscar thoughtfully. "Strange that I chose a Nordic name for this particular godchild. While I was off in the hot sands of Egypt." He shook with laughter and clapped Jean-Baptiste on the shoulder. "Doesn't life play tricks, Bernadotte?" And to me, "You've probably heard, Princess, that Her Majesty is expecting a son?"

I nodded. "I rejoice with you, Sire."

Napoleon looked again at Oscar. "I understand why you must become Swedish, Bernadotte. As legally as possible. Particularly for the child. I'm told that the deposed mad King also has a son. You must never lose sight of this exiled son, Bernadotte, do you understand me?"

343

Now that he was already interfering with our future plans, I knew everything would work out well. He had accepted the situation.

"Méneval—the map of the Northern countries!"

The large globe beside the desk is no more than a toy. When decisions must be made, Méneval brings the big maps. "Come closer, Bernadotte," Jean-Baptiste sat on the arm of Napoleon's chair. The Emperor unrolled the map and spread it out on his knees. How often had the two sat thus together in the fields, I thought.

"Sweden, Bernadotte! Sweden does not observe the Continental system. Here we have Göteborg. Here English goods will be unloaded, and brought by way of Stralsund to Swedish Pomerania. From there, forwarded secretly to Germany."

"And to Russia," Talleyrand remarked quite casually.

"My ally, the Tsar of all the Russias, does not, unfortunately, pay enough attention to this problem. English goods do arrive in Russia, a country allied to us. However that may be, Bernadotte, Sweden is at the root of the problem. You will clear this up in Sweden. And if necessary, declare war on England."

Méneval had begun to take notes on the conversation. Talleyrand watched Jean-Baptiste with interest.

"Sweden's participation will complete the Continental system. I believe we can rely on the Prince of Ponte Corvo," the Duke of Cadore said with obvious satisfaction.

Jean-Baptiste was silent.

"Have you anything to add, Prince?" demanded the Emperor sharply.

Jean-Baptiste lifted his eyes from the map. "I shall, of course, serve the interests of Sweden with all the means at my disposal," he said.

"And the interests of France?"

Jean-Baptiste stood up, carefully rolled up the map of the Northern countries, and handed it to Méneval.

"As far as I know, Your Majesty's Government is negotiating a nonaggression pact with the Government of Sweden. This could be expanded into a treaty of friendship. I believe, therefore, that I will be able to serve not only Sweden, but my former country as well."

Former country—it hurt indescribably. Jean-Baptiste looked tired.

Deep furrows ran from beside his nose to the corners of his mouth.

"You are prince of a small territory under French domination," the Emperor announced coldly. "I am forced to deprive you of the principality of Ponte Corvo and its very considerable revenues."

Jean-Baptiste nodded. "In my request I specifically asked that you do so, Sire."

"Do you intend to arrive in Sweden simply as M. Jean-Baptiste Bernadotte, inactive Marshal of France? If you wish, in view of your previous services, you may keep the title of Prince."

Jean-Baptiste shook his head. "I prefer to turn back the title along with the principality. But if your Majesty wishes to reward my former services to the Republic, I would like to ask that my brother in Pau be made a baron."

Napoleon was puzzled. "Aren't you taking your brother with you to Sweden? There you could make him a count, or even a duke."

"I have no intention of taking my brother or any other member of my family to Sweden. The Swedish King wishes only to adopt me, and not all my relatives. Believe me, Sire, I know what I'm doing."

Involuntarily we all looked at the Emperor. Crowns, titles, honours he'd practically rained down on his incompetent brothers.

"I think you're right, Bernadotte," said Napoleon slowly and stood up. We also rose. The Emperor went to his desk and studied the application for the last time. "And your properties in France? In Lithuania? In Westphalia?" he asked absent-mindedly.

"I'm selling them, Sire."

"To pay the debts of the Vasa Dynasty?"

"Yes, and to maintain the court of the Bernadotte Dynasty in Sweden."

Napoleon reached for his pen. Glanced once more at Jean-Baptiste and me. "When I sign this document, Bernadotte, you, your wife and your son will cease to be French citizens. Shall I sign it?"

Jean-Baptiste nodded. His eyes were almost closed, his lips tightly pressed together.

"This signature also means that I have accepted your resignation from the Army. Shall I sign it, Bernadotte?"

Again Jean-Baptiste nodded. I groped for his hand. The clock struck twelve. A bugle call, a sentinel's signal, sounded in the courtyard. The bugle drowned out the scratching of the pen.

This time we didn't walk all the way from the Emperor's desk to the door alone. Napoleon escorted us, his hand on Oscar's shoulder. Méneval opened the door to the anteroom. Diplomats, generals, rulers, and ministers—foreign and domestic—bowed low.

"I should like you to join me in congratulating Their Royal Highnesses the Crown Prince and Crown Princess of Sweden," the Emperor said. "And my godson, the—"

"I am the Duke of Södermanland," piped up Oscar.

"And my godson, the Duke of Södermanland," Napoleon continued.

On our way home, Jean-Baptiste sat hunched up in a corner of the carriage. We didn't speak, but we understood each other perfectly. In the rue d'Anjou, a crowd of curious people had assembled. Someone shouted, *"Vive Bernadotte, Vive Bernadotte. . . ."* Just as on the night of Napoleon's coup d'état, when many people hoped Bernadotte could defend the Republic against him.

In front of our house Count Brahe, Baron Gustaf Mörner, and a few other Swedish gentlemen awaited us. The strangers had just arrived from Stockholm with important news.

"Your pardon, gentlemen. Her Royal Highness and I prefer to be alone," Jean-Baptiste murmured briefly as we went by them into the little salon. But we were not alone. Up from one of the easy chairs rose a thin figure: Fouché, the Duke of Otranto. The Police Minister has recently been in disfavour because he secretly negotiated with England, and because Napoleon found it out. Now he stood before us and held out to me a bouquet of deep red, almost black, roses.

"May I congratulate you," he lisped. "France is proud of her great son and . . ."

"That will do, Fouché. I have given up my French citizenship," said Jean-Baptiste miserably.

"I know, Highness, I know."

"Then, please excuse us. We cannot receive anyone," I said, taking the roses from him. When we finally were alone, we sat beside each other on the sofa, as tired as though we'd come a great distance. After a while Jean-Baptiste got up, went over to the piano, and absent-mindedly hit the keys with one finger. "La Marseillaise." He can play only with one finger, and only "La Marseillaise." "Today I saw Napoleon for the last time in my life," he said. And strummed on. The same tune, always the same.

Paris, September 30, 1810

This noon Jean-Baptiste left for Sweden.

He's been so busy the last few days that we had no chance for a proper good-by. The French Foreign Ministry compiled a list of Swedes, who are considered here to be particularly important. Mörner and Count Brahe briefed him on who these people are. One afternoon, Baron Alquier was announced. He wore a gold-embroidered ambassadorial uniform and the eternal smile of a courtier. "His Majesty has appointed me French Ambassador in Stockholm, and I wanted to pay my respects to Your Royal Highness before my departure."

"You needn't introduce yourself, we've known each other for years," Jean-Baptiste said calmly, but his eyes narrowed. "You were His Majesty's Ambassador in Naples when the Neapolitan Government was overthrown, and a cabinet, in accordance with His Majesty's wishes, formed."

Alquier nodded smilingly. "Wonderful scenery around Naples—"

Jean-Baptiste continued. "And you were His Majesty's Ambassador in Madrid, when the Spanish Government was forced out, and a new cabinet, complying with His Majesty's wishes, set up."

"Wonderful city, Madrid, but too hot," Alquier remarked.

"And now you are coming to Stockholm," Jean-Baptiste concluded.

"A wonderful city, but too cold, I hear," Alquier said.

Jean-Baptiste waved this aside. "Perhaps it depends on how one's received. There are warm receptions and cool ones."

Alquier continued to smile. "His Majesty, the Emperor, has assured me that Your Royal Highness will receive me very warmly. As a former, so to say—compatriot."

"When does Your Excellency leave?"

"On the thirteenth of September, Your Highness."

"We shall arrive in Stockholm at the same time."

"What a happy coincidence, Your Highness."

"Generals rarely leave anything to chance, Excellency. And the Emperor is first of all a general."

Jean-Baptiste rose. Alquier had to depart.

Messengers from Stockholm arrived constantly with reports of the magnificent preparations for Jean-Baptiste's reception. Danish diplomats called, and told us that Copenhagen, too, would welcome the Swedish Crown Prince. Every morning, the pastor of the Evangelical Community in Paris came to give Jean-Baptiste religious instruction. It has been arranged that before his arrival in Sweden, Jean-Baptiste will renounce the Roman Catholic Church and become a Protestant. This ceremony will take place in a Danish port, called Helsingör. There, in the presence of the Swedish Archbishop, Jean-Baptiste will sign the Augsburg Confession of Faith. In Sweden, Protestantism is the State religion.

"Were you ever in a Protestant church, Jean-Baptiste?" I wondered.

"Yes, twice. In Germany. It looks like a Catholic church, except that there are no holy images."

"Must I become a Protestant, too, Jean-Baptiste?"

He thought this over. "I don't think that's necessary; do as you like. But I haven't time for this nice young pastor and his daily lessons. He'd better instruct Oscar instead. Oscar must learn the Augsburg Confession by heart and, if possible, in Swedish. Count Brahe can help him."

Oscar is learning the Augsburg Confession of Faith in French and in Swedish. On Jean-Baptiste's night table is the list of important Swedes. The Court Chancellor's name is Wetterstedt. Gustaf, of course. Apparently most Swedes are called Gustaf. There are also many Löwenhjelms. One of them, a Karl Axel Löwenhjelm, is underlined on the list. He will meet Jean-Baptiste in Helsingör, and from there accompany him as Chamberlain to Stockholm. Jean-Baptiste has written "Questions of Etiquette" after his name.

"I'll leave the list for you; please, with Brahe's help, learn the names by heart," Jean-Baptiste said.

"But I can't pronounce them," I complained. "How, for example, do you say Löwenhjelm?" Jean-Baptiste couldn't pronounce it either.

"But I shall learn. One can learn anything if one wants to," he said, and added, "You must get busy on your preparations for the journey. I don't want you and Oscar to stay here any longer than absolutely necessary. As soon as I've prepared your apartments in the Royal Palace in Stockholm, you must set off. Promise me that?" He sounded very insistent. I nodded.

"By the way, I've been considering selling this house," he said thoughtfully.

"No, no—Jean-Baptiste, you mustn't do that to me," I pleaded.

He looked at me in surprise. "If you want to visit Paris any time, you can always stay with Julie. It's an unnecessary luxury to keep this house."

"It's my home. And you can't take my home away just like that. If we still had Papa's villa in Marseilles . . . But we haven't. Let me keep this house, Jean-Baptiste, let me keep it!" I implored him. "You will surely come back to Paris, too, some time. Then you'll be glad to have your house. Or would you rather stay at the Swedish Embassy?"

It was late at night, and we were sitting on Jean-Baptiste's bed, surrounded by his packed travelling bags. "If I ever do return to Paris, it will be difficult and painful," he muttered, and stared into the candlelight. "You are right, it would be best to have a place here. We'll keep the house, little one."

This morning the big coach rumbled up to the door. Fernand stowed away luggage, and stationed himself at the carriage door. As usual he wore his wine-red uniform, but he'd sewn on buttons with the Swedish coat of arms. Gustaf Mörner was waiting for Jean-Baptiste in the front hall.

Oscar and I came downstairs with him. His arm was around my shoulder. The farewell wasn't so very different from the many other times he'd left to go to the front or as a Governor.

In front of General Moreau's bust, he stopped suddenly and stared at the marble face. How they loved the Republic, these two, I thought. One of them lives in exile in America, the other has become a Crown Prince . . . "Send the bust to Stockholm with my other things," Jean-Baptiste said. He hugged Oscar and me. "You are responsible for seeing that my wife and Oscar come very soon, Count Brahe," he said hoarsely. "It could be of the utmost urgency that my family leave France very soon. Do you understand what I mean?"

Count Brahe looked straight at Jean-Baptiste. "I think so, Your Highness."

Whereupon Jean-Baptiste jumped into the travelling coach, Mörner sat next to him, Fernand closed the door, and swung up beside the coachman on the box. A few passers-by stopped to watch, a disabled soldier with medals from many campaigns on his chest shouted, *"Vive Bernadotte!"*

Jean-Baptiste quickly drew the curtains.

*Helsingör in Denmark, the night of December 21
to December 22, 1810*

I never realized that nights could be so long and so cold. To-morrow Oscar and I embark on the warship with the many pennants which will carry us across the Sund to Sweden. We will land in Hälsingborg where Sweden will welcome Crown Princess Desideria and her son, the Heir Apparent. My good little son.

Marie put four hot water bottles in my bed. Perhaps the night will go faster if I write. I have much to record. But I'm shivering in spite of the warm bottles.

I'd like to get up, put on Napoleon's sables and tiptoe into Oscar's room and sit beside his bed. I'd like to hold his hand and feel his warmth. My son, you are a part of myself. I've sat so often by your bed when I felt lonely. Those many nights in which your father fought on so many fronts. Wife of a general, wife of a marshal. . . . I never sought this, Oscar. And I never guessed a time would come when I couldn't freely go to your bedside. But you no longer sleep alone in your room. Colonel Villatte is escorting us. For many years your father's faithful aide. Your father gave orders that Villatte was to sleep in your room until we reach the Royal Palace in Stockholm. To protect you, darling. From what? From murderers, my child, from assassins who are ashamed because proud Sweden is bankrupt, her lost wars and mad kings have exhausted her. She has chosen simple M. Bernadotte Crown Prince. And young Oscar Bernadotte, grandson of a Marseilles silk merchant, to succeed him. That's why your father wants Villatte to sleep in your room, and Count Brahe in the next. Darling, we're afraid of murderers.

Marie is asleep in my dressing room. And how she snores. Marie and I have travelled a long way together. Too long, perhaps. For two days, fog has postponed our trip across the Sund. Impenetrably grey lies the future before me. I never thought it could be as cold anywhere as it is here in Denmark. But people say, "Wait till you get to Sweden, Your Highness!"

We left our home in the rue d'Anjou the end of October. I put linen dustcovers over the chairs, and draped the mirrors. Oscar and I went to Julie's at Mortefontaine to spend the last few days with her. But young Brahe and the gentlemen from the Swedish Embassy in Paris were impatient for us to leave France. I learned the reason for their impatience just yesterday. Nevertheless I couldn't go until Le Roy delivered my new court dresses.

I sat with Julie in her autumnal garden redolent of damp warm earth. Her little girls played with Oscar. They're thin and pale like Julie, and don't in the least resemble the Bonapartes. "You must come visit me soon in Stockholm, Julie," I said.

351

She shrugged her narrow shoulders. "As soon as the English are driven out of Spain, I must go to Madrid. Unfortunately I am still Queen."

She went with me for my fittings at Le Roy's. At last I could wear white dresses at court. In Paris I never did because Josephine always wore white. But in Stockholm they know very little about the former Empress and her gowns. Someone told me that Queen Hedwig Elisabeth and her ladies-in-waiting still powder their hair. I can't imagine it. Even in Sweden no one could possibly be that old-fashioned. But as I said, Brahe insisted we leave Paris. My dresses were delivered on the first of November, and on the third our travelling carriages appeared.

I was in the first carriage with Colonel Villatte, and the doctor— Jean-Baptiste had engaged a personal physician for our journey— and Mme la Flotte. The second carriage followed with Oscar, Count Brahe, Marie and Yvette. In the third was our luggage. I had planned to bring my reader, too, but she wept so bitterly at the mere thought of leaving Paris that I recommended her to Julie instead. Shall I engage a new reader? Count Brahe says that the Swedish Queen has already arranged for my royal household: ladies-in-waiting, readers, chambermaids. La Flotte, however, was all agog to come because she's in love with Count Brahe.

"That you can write I am aware. For your reports on the Crown Prince and me, written for the police, you were well paid," I told her. "But can you also read?" She blushed beet-red. "If you can also read, I shan't need to engage a new reader."

La Flotte bowed her head. "I'm looking forward so to Stockholm —the Venice of the North," she lisped.

"I would prefer the Venice of the South," I said. "I'm from the South."

All this seems very long ago, although it's really only six weeks. And in these six weeks we've sat from early until late in our carriages. And every evening there's been a banquet or a reception in our honour. In Amsterdam, in Hamburg. We stayed overnight in places with such odd names as Itzehoe and Apenrade. We made our first long halt at Nyborg in Denmark. From there, we were to travel by sea from the Island of Fünen to the Island of Seeland, on which lies Copenhagen. Here, however, a courier from Napoleon overtook us.

He was a young cavalry officer, carrying a large package, and just as we were about to embark he hailed us. He had tied his horse to a post on the quay. Panting, he dashed up with his large bundle. "Your Royal Highness, may I deliver this with highest regard from His Majesty?"

Count Brahe took the ungainly package, and Villatte asked, "Have you no letter for Her Highness?"

The young officer shook his head. "No, only this verbal greeting. When His Majesty heard that Her Highness had left Paris, he murmured, 'Terrible time of year to go to Sweden,' and looked around. His eye happened to light on me. So I was ordered to ride after Your Highness and to deliver this gift. The Emperor said, 'Hurry, Her Highness will need this gift badly.' So, Your Highness, here it is." The officer clicked his heels together.

The cold wind brought tears to my eyes. I held out my hand to him. "Thank His Majesty, and give my regards to Paris."

It was time to go on board. In the cabin we unpacked the Emperor's present. My heart stood still. A sable stole. The most magnificent sable I'd ever seen. "One of the three stoles the Tsar gave him," whispered La Flotte in awe. We'd all heard about the three sable stoles presented the Emperor by the Tsar. Josephine had one, the second went to Paulette, his favourite sister, and the third— yes, the third is now on my knees. Because I needed it so badly. Nevertheless, I'm cold. In the old days, a general's coat warmed me better. Napoleon's coat that stormy night in Marseilles. Jean-Baptiste's coat, one rainy night in Paris. They weren't so heavy with gold like generals' coats today, but rough and shabby and poorly cut. Uniforms of the gallant young Republic.

The ship pitched for three hours from Nyborg to Korsör. La Flotte was seasick and wouldn't let Count Brahe hold her head. A sure sign how much she loves him.

Tomorrow we cross over to Sweden. It's still foggy but the sea is calmer. For the last time, I studied the list of ladies and gentlemen who will receive me in Hälsingborg. My new lady-in-waiting, a Countess Carolina Lewenhaupt. Another, Mariana von Koskull.

Equerry Baron Reinhold Adelswärd; chamberlains Count Erik Piper and Sixten Sparre, and finally a new physician, whose name is Pontin.

My candles have burned low, it is four o'clock in the morning, and I must try to sleep. Jean-Baptiste did not come to meet me. I had not heard until I got here that on the twelfth of November Napoleon had sent Sweden an ultimatum: Sweden must either declare war on the English within five days, or be considered at war with France, Denmark and Russia. The State Council was convened in Stockholm. All eyes focused on the new Crown Prince.

"Gentlemen," Jean-Baptiste had said, "I ask you to forget that I was born in France, and that the Emperor holds in his power what is dearer to me than anything on earth. Gentlemen, I will not take part in this meeting of the State Council, as I do not wish, in any way, to influence your decision."

Now I understood why the gentlemen of the Swedish Embassy in Paris were anxious for Oscar and me to hasten our departure. The Swedish State Council decided to declare war against England. On November 17 the Swedes transmitted to England their declaration of war. But Count Brahe, who has talked to several Swedes here, told me, "His Royal Highness, the Crown Prince, sent a secret messenger to England, asking that this declaration of war be considered a mere formality. Sweden wishes to continue trading with England, and suggests that from now on English ships entering Göteborg harbour should fly the American flag."

I have tried in vain to understand all these developments. Napoleon could have held Oscar and me as hostages. But he let us go, and even sent me the sables. Because he thought I'd be cold. . . . Jean-Baptiste, on the other hand, requested the State Council to take no notice of his family. Sweden is more important to him. Sweden is to him the most important thing on earth.

On all sides I hear how eagerly the Swedes are waiting for our child. If only he were sleeping alone, I could go to him in my fear. I drive on through cold and fog to give up my child. And I don't even know if Oscar will be happy. Are heirs apparent usually happy?

Hälsingborg, December 22, 1810
(Today I arrived in Sweden)

The cannon on the Kronborg bastion in Helsingör thundered salutes as we embarked on the Swedish man-of-war. The crew stood at attention. Oscar's small hand touched his three-cornered hat; I tried to smile. As always it was foggy, and the icy wind brought tears to my eyes. I stayed in the cabin. Oscar, however, wanted to remain on deck to examine the cannon.

"And my husband still hasn't come?" I asked Count Brahe again and again. All forenoon small vessels with messengers from Hälsingborg had docked at Helsingör to bring detailed reports on preparations for our reception.

"Important political issues are keeping His Royal Highness in Stockholm. A new demand is expected from Napoleon."

An entire world seemed to lie between this icy fog and the gentle winter rain in Paris. Lights are dancing on the Seine. A whole world lies between Jean-Baptiste and Napoleon. And Napoleon demands . . .

My small green velvet hat with the red silk rose is becoming to me; my green velvet coat fits snugly, and makes me look taller than I am. In my green velvet muff I clutch the list of Swedish courtiers who are expecting me. The ladies-in-waiting, Lewenhaupt and Koskull, the chamberlains Piper and—I'll never learn these names. . . .

"Your Highness is not anxious?" said Count Brahe softly.

"Who is with Oscar?" I asked. "I don't want him to fall in the water."

"Your own Colonel Villatte is taking care of him," Brahe answered. The words "your own" sounded sarcastic.

"Is it true that Your Highness has put on woollen underdrawers?" Mme la Flotte was horrified. She was fighting against seasickness again. Her face, under the pink powder, had a greenish cast.

"Yes, Marie bought them in the town. It was her idea, she saw them in a shop. I think one needs warm underwear in this climate. We'll probably stand around in this ice-cold harbour for a long time listening to speeches, and no one will look under our skirts." I immediately regretted this remark. A Crown Princess doesn't say such things and Countess—I consulted my list—Countess Lewenhaupt, my new lady-in-waiting, would be shocked.

"Now we can see the Swedish coast plainly. Perhaps Your Highness would like to come on deck?" Count Brahe suggested. And waited for me to hurry on deck.

"I'm so cold and tired," I said, burrowing deeper into Napoleon's fur.

"Of course, forgive me—" murmured the young Swede.

Cannonfire. I was startled, although by now I should be used to this thunder. The first salutes came from our ship, and were answered from the coast. Yvette held up a mirror for me. I whisked the powder puff over my face. Put a little more rouge on my lips. Under my eyes were deep shadows from last night's sleeplessness.

"Your Highness looks very beautiful," Count Brahe assured me. I was so scared, I thought. People imagine a Crown Princess to be right out of a fairy tale. And I am still only the former citizeness Eugénie Désirée Clary!

While the cannon roared I went up on deck and stood next to Oscar. "Look, Mama—there's our country," the child shouted.

"Not our country, Oscar—the country of the Swedish people. Don't forget that. Never forget it." I took his hand. Snatches of military music floated out toward us. Out of the fog shone bright dresses and gold epaulettes. I saw a mass of flowers. Roses, carnations? They must cost a fortune here in winter. . . .

"As soon as we dock, I will cross the gangplank and hold out my hand to help Your Highness onto the quay. I want the Heir Apparent to stay close behind Your Highness. When we land, the Heir Apparent will take his position on the left of Your Royal Highness. I will be right behind Your Highness—" Count Brahe gave his instructions hastily. Yes, right behind me, to protect me. My young knight of ancient Swedish lineage will not let them laugh at the daughter of a simple citizen.

"Did you understand, Oscar?"

"Look, Mama, all those Swedish uniforms. A whole regiment. Just look, Mama!"

"And where shall I stand, dear Count Brahe?" asked La Flotte.

I turned to her. "Keep in the background with Colonel Villatte. I'm afraid you're not the central figure at this reception."

"Do you know what they called Count Brahe in Helsingör, Mama? Admiral Brahe," Oscar said.

Cannons crashed. "But why, Oscar? The Count is a cavalry officer."

"But they called him Admiral *de la Flotte*," Oscar shouted between salutes. "Do you understand, Mama?"

I had to laugh. I was laughing all over my face when the ship docked in Sweden.

"Kronprinsessan skall leva!" came from the fog. *"Kronprinsessan, Arveprinsen!"* Many voices, shouting rhythmically. But the fog swallowed up the faces of the people behind the cordon of soldiers. I could distinguish only the faces of the courtiers. Stiff and unsmiling, they looked me over. Looked over the child. My smile froze.

The gangplank was lowered. The Swedish national anthem, which I already knew, boomed out. Not a stirring battle song like "La Marseillaise." More of a hymn—pious, harsh, solemn.

Count Brahe hurried by me and jumped on land. His hand stretched out to me. Quickly and uncertainly I edged toward him. Then I felt his arm under mine, felt solid land under my feet, stood there first alone, and then Oscar ran up beside me. The bright blooms—they were roses—came forward. A haggard old man in the uniform of a Swedish marshal presented the flowers. "Governor General von Schonen, Marshal Johan Kristoffer Toll," Count Brahe whispered. Faded old man's eyes looked at me but gave no sign of welcome. I took the roses, and the old man bent down over my right hand. Then bowed deep before Oscar. I saw the ladies, in their silks, in their wraps trimmed with ermine and nutria, curtsy. The rear-view of uniforms as the men bowed. It began to snow. I hastily gave my hand to one after another, the foreign faces assumed forced smiles. Their smiles more natural when Oscar held out his hand to them. Marshal Toll welcomed me in his harsh French. Snowflakes whirled around us. I turned my head to look at Oscar. He was enraptured by the whirling whiteness. Again the national anthem—so strange, so solemn. Snowflakes fell on my face as I stood without moving on the pier at Hälsingborg. As the last notes died away, Oscar's voice cut the stillness: "We'll be very happy here, Mama. Look, it's snowing."

Why does my child always say or do the right thing at the right moment? Just like his father. The same old man offered me his arm to escort me to the royal carriage. Count Brahe stayed close behind me. I looked at the unfriendly old man, at the foreign faces behind him, saw the light, cold eyes, the critical expression. "I beg of you, always be good to my child," I said suddenly.

These words were not in the programme, they slipped out, probably tactlessly, and against all etiquette. Astonishment, enormous astonishment, flickered over every face, startled and condescending. I felt the snowflakes on my eyelashes and on my lips, and no one saw that I was crying.

That same evening, while I was undressing, Marie said, "Wasn't I right, Eugénie? I mean about the woollen underwear? You might have caught your death during the ceremony at the harbour."

In the Royal Palace, Stockholm
End of the interminable winter of 1811

At last the sky really was like a fresh-washed sheet, and green ice floes swam in the Mälar! The rising water roared under the green floes, the snow melted, like thunder the ice cracked apart. Strange— spring doesn't come gently to this country. But tumultuously, passionately, fighting. And at the last very slowly.

On one of these spring afternoons, Countess Lewenhaupt appeared before me. "Her Majesty invites Your Royal Highness to have a cup of tea in Her Majesty's salon."

That surprised me. Every evening, Jean-Baptiste and I dine alone with the child, and then we spend at least an hour with the Queen. The King, incidentally, is much better. Earlier he had suffered a slight stroke and the very evening he was taken ill, the Queen slipped the heavy seal ring from the King's finger and put it on Jean-Baptiste. That meant the King entrusted him with the government, but not that he has become Regent.

The King is sitting up again in his usual chair, an uneasy smile on his mouth. Only the left side pulls down slightly. But I've never called on the Queen by myself. Why should I? We have nothing to say to each other.

"Announce me to Her Majesty," I said hastily to Lewenhaupt and dashed to my dressing room. I brushed my hair, put on the fur-lined shawl Jean-Baptiste recently gave me, and walked up the icy marble staircase to Her Majesty's salon.

They were seated around a little table—all three of them. Queen Hedwig Elisabeth Charlotte, my adopted mother-in-law, who should be fond of me. Queen Sophia Magdalena, who has every reason to hate me. Her husband was murdered, her son exiled, her grandson of Oscar's age deprived of all his rights to the throne. And Princess Sofia Albertina, the lady of indefinite age. She is an old maid with a faded face, a flat bosom, a childish bow in her hair, and unattractive amber beads around her thin neck. The three ladies were bent over their needlework.

"Sit down, madame," the Queen said.

The three ladies continued to embroider. Rosebuds in a strange rose-violet colony were stretched out on their embroidery frames. Tea was served. The ladies dropped their needlework and concentrated on their tea. I took a couple of gulps and burned my tongue. The Queen motioned the lackeys out of the room. Not a single lady-in-waiting was present. "I want to talk to you, dear daughter," the Queen said.

Princess Sofia Albertina bared her long teeth in a malicious smile. The Queen Mother, on the other hand, stared indifferently into her teacup.

"I wanted to ask you, dear daughter, whether you yourself feel that you are fulfilling your duties as Crown Princess of Sweden?"

I felt myself blushing. The pale, near-sighted eyes were fixed pitilessly on my flushed face.

"I don't know, madame," I finally managed to answer.

The Queen's dark, heavy eyebrows shot up. "You don't know, madame?"

"No," I said. "I can't judge, because it's the first time I've ever been a crown princess. And I've been one for such a very short time."

Princess Sofia Albertina began to bleat. She really did, like a goat. The Queen gestured irritably, but her voice was smooth as silk. "It's extremely unfortunate for the Swedish people and for him whom the Swedish people have chosen as heir to the throne that you don't know how a crown princess should behave, madame."

The Queen took a slow sip of tea, and kept looking at me over the rim of her cup. "So I will tell you, my dear daughter, how a Crown Princess must behave."

Everything had been in vain, I thought: M. Montel's deportment lessons, my piano lessons, the graceful gestures I had practiced so diligently. And in vain, too, that I'd kept still at the court functions in Stockholm so as not to embarrass Jean-Baptiste. All, all in vain.

"A crown princess never takes a drive with one of her husband's aides without a lady-in-waiting."

What did she mean—Villatte? "I—I've known Colonel Villatte for many years; he visited us in Sceaux. We like to talk about old times," I said finally.

"At court functions crown princesses should converse graciously with everyone. You, however, act as though you were deaf and dumb."

"Speech has been given man"—the words slipped out—"to conceal his thoughts."

The virginal goat bleated shrilly. The pale eyes of the Queen opened wide in astonishment. Quickly I added, "That's not original with me but with one of our—one of the French diplomats, Count Talleyrand, Prince of Bénévent. Perhaps Your Majesty has heard . . ."

"I know quite well who Talleyrand is," said the Queen sharply.

"Madame, if one is not too clever nor too well educated, and yet must conceal one's thoughts, speech doesn't help. Therefore, I am forced—to be silent!"

A teacup rattled. The Queen Mother had put down her cup, her hand trembled so.

"You must force yourself to make conversation, madame," the Queen continued. "And besides—I cannot imagine what thoughts you wish to conceal from your Swedish friends and future subjects."

I folded my hands in my lap, and let her go on. Everything ends, and so would this tea party.

"From one of my lackeys I hear that your servant has inquired about the shop of a certain Persson. I want to make it quite clear that you are to make no purchases whatever at this shop."

I lifted my head. "Why not?"

"This Persson is not a purveyor to the court, and never will be. I have myself, since I heard about your servant's inquiries, made some myself, madame. This Persson is known to have some very revolutionary ideas."

My eyes popped. "Persson?"

"This certain Persson lived in France at the time of the Revolution. Ostensibly to learn the silk business. Since his return, he has associated with students, writers and other muddle-headed creatures, and he discusses with them the very ideas which once were the undoing of the French nation."

What did she mean? "I don't quite understand, madame. Persson once lived with us in Marseilles, he worked with Papa in the shop. In the evening I gave him French lessons, we learned the Rights of Man by heart . . ."

"Madame"—like a slap in the face—"I must insist you forget that. It is incredible that this certain Persson took lessons from you—" she was breathing hard—"or that he had anything to do with your father."

"Madame, Papa was a highly respected silk merchant, and the firm of Clary is today a very substantial one."

"I ask you to forget all that, madame. You are Crown Princess of Sweden."

A long silence followed. I looked down at my hands, trying to collect my thoughts. But my mind blurred, only my emotions were clear.

"*Jag er Kronprinsessan*—" I murmured in Swedish, and added clumsily, "I've begun to learn Swedish. I want to do my best. But obviously that isn't enough. . . ."

No answer.

I looked up. "Madame, would you have persuaded His Majesty to appoint Jean-Baptiste Regent if—if I would not then have become the Regent's wife?"

"Possibly."

"Will you have another cup of tea, madame," bleated the goat. I declined.

"I'd like you to consider seriously what I have said, dear daughter, and to act accordingly," the Queen said icily.

"I'm already considering it, madame."

"You should never for an instant forget the position of our dear son, the Crown Prince, madame," the Queen concluded. That finished me.

"Your Majesty has already reproached me because I cannot forget who and what my dead papa was. Now, madame, you tell me not to forget my husband's position. I want you to understand once and for all—I forget nothing and nobody."

Without waiting for the Queen's permission, I stood up. To the devil with etiquette. The three ladies sat up straighter—if possible —than ever. "In my home in Marseilles, madame, the mimosa is now in bloom. When it's a little warmer, I will return to France."

That worked. All three jumped. The Queen was shocked, the old goat incredulous, and even the Queen Mother looked surprised.

"You would go—back?" the Queen asked haltingly. "When did you decide this, dear daughter?"

"This instant, Your Majesty."

"It's politically unwise, definitely unwise. You must talk it over with my dear son, the Crown Prince," she said rapidly.

"I do nothing without my husband's consent."

"And where will you live in Paris, madame? You have no palace there," declared the goat happily.

"I never have had a palace there. But we kept our home in the rue d'Anjou. An ordinary house, no palace. But so beautiful to me," I told her and hurried on. "I don't need a palace. I am not used to living in palaces. I—hate palaces, madame."

The Queen had regained her poise. "Your country house near Paris might perhaps be a more suitable residence for the Crown Princess of Sweden."

"La Grange? We sold La Grange and everything else to pay Sweden's debts abroad. They were very large debts, madame."

She bit her lip. Then quickly, "No, that won't do—Crown Princess Desideria of Sweden in an ordinary Paris dwelling. And besides . . ."

"I shall discuss it with my husband. Anyway, I have no idea of travelling under the name of Desideria of Sweden."

I felt my eyes fill with tears. I mustn't cry now and give these three this satisfaction. I threw back my head.

"Desideria—'the one who is desired'! Perhaps Your Majesty will put your mind to a suitable incognito for me. Now may I go?"

And I slammed the door behind me so hard the sound echoed through the marble corridors. As I had once in Rome, the first palace into which fate tossed me.

From the Queen's salon I went directly to Jean-Baptiste's study. In the anteroom one of his aides barred the way. "May I announce Your Royal Highness?"

"No, thank you. I am accustomed to entering my husband's apartments without being announced."

"But I am obliged to announce Your Royal Highness," he insisted.

"Who obliges you to? His Royal Highness?"

"Etiquette, Your Highness. For centuries . . ."

I pushed him aside. He cringed as though I'd stabbed him. I had to laugh. "Don't worry, Baron. I won't upset your etiquette much longer." Whereupon I went into Jean-Baptiste's study.

Jean-Baptiste sat at his desk, a pile of documents before him, while he listened to Chancellor Wetterstedt and two other gentlemen. A green eyeshade cast a shadow over the upper part of his face. Fernand had already told me how greatly his eyes troubled him. Because here the days are so short, he has to read mostly by artificial light. He works every day from half-past nine in the morning until three o'clock at night, and his eyes are badly inflamed. Only the gentlemen who work with him constantly know about the green eyeshade. He has kept it a secret even from me so that I won't worry. He took it off in a hurry when I came in.

"Has something special happened, Désirée?"

"No. I just want to talk to you."

"Is it urgent?"

I shook my head. "No. I'll sit quietly in a corner and wait until you're finished with these gentlemen."

I pulled a chair up to the big round stove and warmed myself. At first, I listened. Jean-Baptiste said, "You must remember that the Swedish reichsthaler is the cheapest money in Europe." And, "We cannot squander our few English pounds, so hard earned in the secret trade with England, on any but essential supplies." And, "But I must take action. I've risked my entire private fortune to stabilize the exchange. I should mobilize, yet I cannot recruit men from our ironworks and sawmills. And I should have more artillery—or did you think modern battles were won with swords and fists?"

I began to review my own attitude toward the Queen. I convinced myself I'd been right, and became much calmer. But I felt awful, unspeakably awful. Jean-Baptiste had forgotten I was there, he'd put the eyeshade back on. He held a document up close to his eyes. "I trust the Foreign Minister fully understands the significance of this. We arrested a couple of English sailors in a tavern on the Göteborg waterfront, and England is holding three Swedes to convince France that England and Sweden really are at war with each other. Now the English Government is sending over a Mr. Thornton, one of her ablest diplomats, to discuss the exchange of prisoners. I want the Foreign Minister—Engeström himself—to confer with this Mr. Thornton."

He looked at them. "I also want Suchtelen informed. Perhaps he could take part in this conference. Unofficially, naturally."

Suchtelen is the Russian Ambassador in Stockholm. The Tsar is still formally allied with Napoleon, but he has begun to arm, and Napoleon is sending troops to Pomerania and Poland. Does Jean-Baptiste mean to effect a secret understanding between England and Russia?

"Perhaps at that time we might mention Finland to Suchtelen again," one of the gentlemen ventured.

Jean-Baptiste sighed, clearly annoyed. "You always come back to that. You'll bore the Tsar and—" He broke off. "Forgive me, gentlemen. I know what Finland means to you. We can indeed bring it up again with Suchtelen. And I will also refer to it in my next letter to the Tsar. We meet tomorrow early. I wish you good evening."

The gentlemen bowed to Jean-Baptiste and to me, and backed out of the room. The fire in the stove crackled. Jean-Baptiste had taken off the eyeshade and had his eyes shut. His mouth reminded me of Oscar asleep—tired but content. How well he rules, I thought. How well—and how wisely.

"Now, what is it, little one?"

"I'm leaving, Jean-Baptiste. When it's summer and the roads are better. I'm going home, dearest," I said softly.

At that he opened his eyes. "Have you gone mad? You are at home. Here in the royal palace in Stockholm. In the summer we'll go to Drottningholm, to our summer residence. A charming little palace, with a great big beautiful park. You'll love it."

"But I must go, Jean-Baptiste. It's the only way," I insisted. And repeated to him word for word my conversation with the Queen. He listened without comment. His perpetual frown grew deeper. And then he broke loose. Like a storm.

"And I have to listen to this nonsense. Her Majesty and Her Royal Highness cannot get along. I must say the Queen is right— you don't always behave like—what's expected at the court of Sweden. You'll learn, of course, you'll learn. But, God knows, I can't be bothered with all this now. Have you any idea what's happening in the world? And what will probably come to a head in the next few years?"

He stood up and came over to me. His voice was hoarse with excitement. "Our very existence—the existence of Europe. Napoleon's system creaks in every joint. In the south, there's been no peace for a long time. In Germany, his enemies are secretly uniting; almost daily some French soldier is shot from ambush. And in the north—" He stopped and chewed his lower lip. "Napoleon can no longer depend on the Tsar, so he will attack Russia. Do you understand what that means?"

"He's attacked and conquered so many countries," said I with a shrug. "We both know him."

Jean-Baptiste nodded. "Yes, we know him. Better than anyone else the Crown Prince of Sweden knows him. And therefore, in his hour of destiny, the Tsar of all the Russias will abide by the advice of the Swedish Crown Prince."

Jean-Baptiste took a deep breath. "And when finally there is a new coalition, under the leadership of England and Russia, then Sweden must decide. For or against Napoleon."

"Against him? That—that would mean that you would fight against France—"

"No, Napoleon and France are not the same. Not for a long time, not since the days of Brumaire, which neither he nor I have forgotten. That's also why he's concentrating troops on the frontiers of Swedish Pomerania. If he won a war against Russia, he would simply overrun Sweden, and put one of his brothers on the throne. But during a Russian war, he prefers to have me on his side. At present, he's trying to buy me: he repeatedly offers me Finland, says he will speak to the Tsar about it. The Tsar at least outwardly is still his ally."

"But you said the Tsar will never give up Finland."

"Naturally not. But the Swedes continue to hope . . . Somehow I'll make it up to them."

He smiled unexpectedly. "When Napoleon is defeated, when the great house-cleaning starts in Europe, then Napoleon's most faithful ally will pay through the nose. Denmark, of course. Denmark will then, at the suggestion of the Tsar, forgo her rights in Norway, and Norway will be united with Sweden. And that, my little girl, is not written in the stars, but on a map."

"But Napoleon isn't defeated yet," I said. "And how can you keep talking about Sweden's destiny and not realize that's exactly why I must immediately return to Paris?"

Jean-Baptiste sighed. "If you knew how tired I am, you couldn't harp so on this theme. I cannot let you go. Here you are the Crown Princess. Enough. That settles it."

"Here I can only embarrass you, but in Paris I could do a lot. I've thought everything out."

"Don't be childish. Would you perhaps spy on the Emperor for me? I have my spies in Paris, never fear. I might tell you that our old friend Talleyrand not only corresponds secretly with the Bourbons, but with me. And Fouché, now fallen into disfavour . . ."

I burst out. "I won't be a spy, Jean-Baptiste. Don't you see what will happen when—what did you call it?—when the big house-cleaning begins? Every country Napoleon has deprived of independence will throw out the Bonaparte—kings. But France herself—France, Jean-Baptiste, was a republic before Napoleon crowned himself. So much blood was shed so willingly for that republic. You say that Talleyrand corresponds secretly with the Bourbons? Can anyone force France to take back the Bourbons?"

Jean-Baptiste shrugged his shoulders.

"Depend on it, Désirée, the old dynasties cling together and will try it. But what has that to do with you and me?"

"The old dynasties might also dispute the succession of the former Jacobin General Jean-Baptiste Bernadotte to the Swedish throne. And who will remain loyal to you then?"

"I can do no more than serve Sweden with all my strength. Every franc I've saved in my life is invested in the rehabilitation of this country. Not for a second do I consider myself or my past, but only the policies which will secure Sweden's independence. If I succeed, Désirée—if I succeed, there will also be a Swedish-Norwegian union."

He had taken a chair by the stove, and his sore eyes were covered with his hand. "More than that no man can expect of anyone. And as long as Europe needs me to fight Napoleon, Europe will protect me. Who will afterward be loyal to me, Désirée?"

"The Swedish people, Jean-Baptiste. Only the Swedish people, and they're all that matters. Be faithful to the Swedes, who called you here."

"And you, my darling?"

"I am only the wife of a man who's probably a genius, and not the Desideria the Swedish nobles wanted. I lower your prestige. The aristocracy here will ridicule me and the middle classes will be ready to believe what they say about the foreigner. Let me go, Jean-Baptiste. It will strengthen your position." I smiled sadly. "Next time the King has a stroke, you will be named Regent. You can carry out your policies more easily if you have the Regency. You'll do better without me, dearest."

"It all sounds very sensible, little girl, but . . . No, no! In the first place I can't have the Swedish Crown Princess in Paris as Napoleon's hostage. My own decisions would be influenced if you were in danger, and . . ."

"But shortly before I got here you urged the Swedish State Council not to concern itself with the fate of those you loved most. At that time we were still in Paris, Oscar and I. No, Jean-Baptiste, you can't consider me. If the Swedes are to be loyal to you, you must stand by them."

I took his hand, pulled him down on the arm of my chair, and snuggled up to him. "Besides—do you seriously believe that Napoleon would ever let his brother Joseph's sister-in-law be arrested? Very unlikely, isn't it? And since he knows you, he knows that nothing would come of it. Look, he sent me a sable stole at the same time he received an unfriendly letter from the Swedish Government. No one takes me seriously, dearest, let me go."

He shook his head violently. "I work day and night. In my free time I lay cornerstones for new buildings and receive rectors of universities. At the noon hour I go to the parade ground and try to show my Swedes how Napoleon drills his soldiers. I cannot carry on if I don't know you're near me, Désirée—I need you—"

"Others need me more, Jean-Baptiste. Perhaps a day will come when my house will be the only place in which my sister and her children can take refuge. Let me go, Jean-Baptiste, I beg of you."

"You can't exploit my position in Sweden to help your family, Désirée. That I would never allow."

"It won't hurt Sweden any if I can help someone in trouble. Sweden is a small country, Jean-Baptiste, with a few million inhabitants, isn't it? Only through its humanitarianisms can Sweden become great, Jean-Baptiste."

"One might think you spent your time reading books," he said indulgently.

"I'll take the time, dearest. In Paris I'll have nothing else to do. I'll try to educate myself so that someday you won't have to be ashamed of me, you and Oscar."

"Désirée, the child needs you. Can you actually imagine not seeing Oscar? I don't know how things will work out. Perhaps you won't be able to get back for a long time. Europe will soon be one vast battlefield, and you and I . . ."

"Dearest, I couldn't go with you to the front in any case. And the child—"

Yes, the child. All the while I'd been trying to stifle this thought. The idea of being separated from Oscar was like a throbbing wound.

"The child, dearest, is still the Heir Apparent. Surrounded by three tutors and an aide-de-camp. Since our arrival in Stockholm, he has had very little time for me. I am familiar with his daily schedule, every minute is planned. At first he will miss me very much, but he'll soon realize that an heir apparent never considers his feelings. Only his duties. In this way our child will grow up like a born prince. And no one will ever call him a parvenu king, Jean-Baptiste—"

I leaned my head on Jean-Baptiste's shoulder and wept.

"You're soaking my shoulder again—as you did when I first met you. . . ."

He drew me to him.

"The material of this uniform is softer and finer, and doesn't scratch so much," I sobbed. Then I pulled myself together and got up. "I think it's time for dinner."

Jean-Baptiste stayed, poised on the arm of the chair. As soon as I got away from the stove, the icy cold that lurked in every corner of the room gripped me.

"Did you know that the mimosa is in bloom now in Marseilles?"

"The Chancellor has assured me that spring will be here in four weeks, and Wetterstedt is a reliable man," Jean-Baptiste replied.

Slowly I walked to the door. With every fibre of my being I waited for one word from him. For his decision. I would accept it as a final judgment. At the door I stood still. Whatever he decides, it will be the end of me, I felt.

"And how am I to explain your leaving to Their Majesties and

369

to the court?" It sounded so indifferent, almost meaningless. The decision was made.

"Say that my health demands I go to Plombières for the baths. And that I must spend the autumn and winter in Paris because I can't stand this cold climate," I said and I left the room quickly.

Castle Drottningholm in Sweden
Beginning of June, 1811

Like pale-grey silk the night sky is taut over the park. Midnight has long since passed and still it's not dark. Summer nights in the north stay light. I have closed the curtains, and dark draperies have been hung over my windows so I might sleep. But I've slept badly. I don't know whether this greenish twilight is to blame or my proposed departure. Tomorrow morning I start my return trip to France. . . .

Three days ago, the court moved to the summer residence, Drottningholm Castle. As far as the eye can see, there's nothing but park. Beautifully aligned linden trees, perfectly clipped hedges, and a maze of paths. But when one finally gets to the end of the huge park, one suddenly sees natural meadows, where delicate birches grow, and yellow primroses and deep-blue hyacinths. The long twilights smell very sweet. And everything seems as unreal as a dream. One doesn't sleep properly, but wanders in the half-light; it's neither night nor day. And these last days before I leave my life here are indeed a twilight interlude—the last words, unreal in their sincerity; the farewells, devastating. Yet bittersweet, because I have to go back.

I turn over the pages of my diary and think of Papa. . . . "For years I have saved a part of my pay. I can buy a small house for you and the child—" Jean-Baptiste said, and I wrote it down. Jean-Baptiste, you kept your word, you bought a little house, it was in

Sceaux near Paris and was very small and very comfortable, and we were very happy there. . . .

So, anyway, on the first of June we moved to the summer palace of Drottningholm. Jean-Baptiste, you promised me a small house, why do you give me palaces, marble staircases, pillared halls, and ballrooms? Perhaps I'm dreaming, I tell myself in the twilight of this last night in which I still call myself Crown Princess of Sweden.

Tomorrow I start off, travelling incognito as a Countess of Gotland. Perhaps I really am dreaming, and will wake up in my bedroom in Sceaux. Marie will come in and lay little Oscar in my arms. I'll open my nightgown, and put Oscar to my breast. . . .

But the array of trunks is very real. Oscar, my child, your mother isn't going to France because of her health. This is no rest cure, my child, and I won't see you again for a very long time. And when I do see you, you will no longer be a child. At least not—my child. But a real prince, a royal highness, trained to the throne. For the throne one must be either born or trained. Jean-Baptiste was born to rule. We'll have to see about you. Your mama, however, was neither born nor trained to be a queen. And that's why, in a few hours, I'll clasp you once more to my heart and leave.

For weeks, the court couldn't grasp the idea that I was actually going. They gossiped away and glanced curiously and surreptitiously at me. I had expected them to reproach me, but strangely enough they are taking it out on the Queen. The rumour is that she wasn't a good mother-in-law to me and drove me away. They would enjoy a feud between Her Majesty and Her Royal Highness. They will be disappointed tomorrow when my travelling coach sets off and an unknown Countess of Gotland leaves the country.

I came with them to Drottningholm only because I wanted to see the famous Vasa palace in which Oscar will from now on spend his summers. On the evening of our arrival, a play was presented in the little theatre. The mad Gustavus III built it and had it decorated ever so elaborately. Happy as a little lark, Mlle von Koskull sang a few arias. The King applauded enthusiastically, but Jean-Baptiste seemed quite indifferent. Odd, for a while during the long dark winter, I thought . . . But now since I've decided to leave, the great tall Koskull with the healthy teeth, the Valkyrie with the golden shield, the goddess of battle, seems to have lost all charm for Jean-Baptiste.

Dearest, though I should be far away in Paris, I'd still be deeply hurt.

Yet must I not be prepared for that? The words spoken in the twilight of this last evening were so very clear. . . .

Their Majesties gave a farewell banquet in my honour, and after dinner there was dancing. The King and Queen sat in gilded chairs with high stiff backs, and smiled graciously. That is, the King thought he was smiling graciously. But he only looked sad with his drooping mouth and vacant face. I danced with Baron Mörner, who brought us the message in the first place, and Chancellor Wetterstedt and Foreign Minister Engeström, who talks incessantly about Finland. And also with Jean-Baptiste's youngest secretary, Count Brahe. Although the bright northern nights are rather cool I said, "It's hot in here, I'd like some fresh air," and we went into the garden.

"I must thank you, Count Brahe. You have stood by me gallantly since I came here. You've done everything in your power to make things here easier for me. Forgive me for disappointing you. It's all over now."

His dark head was bowed, and he gnawed on the little moustache he's cultivating. "If Your Highness wishes . . ." he began, but I shook my head strenuously.

"No, no, dear Count. Believe me, my husband is an excellent judge of character. If, in spite of your youth he appointed you to his staff, it's only because he needs you. He needs you here in Sweden."

He didn't thank me for this compliment, but kept worrying his moustache. Suddenly he looked up desperately. "I beg Your Royal Highness not to leave—I implore you to stay."

"My decision was made weeks ago, Count Brahe, and I'm sure I'm right."

"No, no—Your Highness. Please stay, postpone your journey. It's the wrong—" He stopped again, drew his hand through his thick hair, and then exclaimed vehemently, "This is not the time for you to leave."

"Not the time? I don't understand you, Count Brahe."

He turned away. "A letter from the Tsar has come, Highness, more I dare not say."

"Then don't say it. You are one of the Crown Prince's secretaries. You should not discuss me with His Royal Highness' correspondence with ruling monarchs. I am glad that a letter has come from the Tsar. The Crown Prince depends greatly on his fine relationship with the Tsar. I hope it was a friendly letter."

"Too friendly."

I was puzzled by young Brahe's attitude. What has my departure to do with the Tsar?

"The Tsar offers the Crown Prince proof of his friendship," said Brahe earnestly, and without looking at me. "The Tsar begins his letter with 'My dear Cousin.' Your Highness will appreciate that this is considerable proof of his friendship."

Yes, considerable. The Tsar addressing the former Sergeant Bernadotte as his cousin. I smiled. "That means a great deal—for Sweden."

"It's about an alliance. Russia will give up her alliance with France, and that ends the Continental System. Now we must decide whether to ally ourselves with Russia or Napoleon. Both have suggested an alliance with Sweden."

Yes, I know. Jean-Baptiste can't get by with armed neutrality much longer.

"So that's why the Tsar writes 'My dear Cousin' to His Royal Highness, and, to strengthen his personal position in Sweden, offers him—"

"Finland?"

"No, not Finland. But the Tsar offered to make His Royal Highness a member of his family, if it would secure His Royal Highness' position in Sweden." Brahe shook his head tragically. His thin young shoulders seemed to carry the weight of the world.

I was stupefied. "What does that mean? Does the Tsar also want to—adopt us?"

"The Tsar means only—His Royal Highness." Finally Brahe turned his tormented face toward me. "There are other ways of establishing a family relationship, Your Highness. . . ."

At last I understood. There are other ways. . . . Napoleon married

373

off his stepson to a Bavarian princess. Napoleon himself is the son-in-law of the Austrian Emperor, and thus related to the Hapsburgs—closely related, in fact. A man need only marry a princess. It's that simple. An Act of State, a document; like the one Josephine had to read out. . . . . Josephine, hysterical, choking with sobs on her bed.

"That would undoubtedly secure His Royal Highness' position," I heard myself say.

"Not with us in Sweden. The Tsar took Finland away from us; we can't forget this loss so quickly. But in the rest of Europe, Your Highness . . ."

Josephine screaming on her bed. It can be done quite easily. But Josephine had no son. . . .

". . . in the rest of Europe, His Royal Highness' prestige would doubtless be increased."

But Josephine had no son. I have a son.

". . . so I would like to repeat that this is not the time for Your Highness to leave."

"Yes, Count Brahe. Right now. One day you'll understand." I held out my hand to him. "I ask you from my heart to stand by my husband loyally. My husband and I sometimes feel that our French friends and servants are frowned upon here. For that reason Colonel Villatte, my husband's oldest and most faithful aide, who fought with him on every front, is returning to Paris with me. I expect you to take his place. My husband will be very much alone. I'll see you in the morning, Count Brahe."

I did not return to the ballroom immediately, but wandered, bewildered, down to the park, past the clipped hedges. Everything here is under the pall of the past. Not twenty years ago mad Gustavus III gave his famous garden parties here. The gardeners know how dearly he loved this park, and they continue to carry out his instructions. There by the Chinese pavilion, he composed his elegies. How often he dressed up and invited his friends to a masquerade. . . .

Tonight the park seemed infinite. The murdered man's son was declared insane. And he was forced to abdicate. He was promptly brought back here—a prisoner. Here to this gay summer palace. I've been told about it often enough. He paced up and down, back and forth, along these formal paths with his keepers behind him. In his despair and madness he talked to himself and to the linden trees. And over there, near the Chinese pavilion, his mother waited for him. Mother of a man, widow of a murdered man—Sophia Magdalena.

The summer wind sang softly through the leaves. Suddenly I saw a shadow—it was moving toward me. I screamed, tried to run, but couldn't move.

"I'm sorry if I frightened you."

Close beside me on the moonlit gravel walk, stood the Queen Mother dressed all in black.

"You— Have you waited for me here, madame?" I asked, ashamed because my heart was pounding so hard I could hardly speak.

"No. I couldn't guess that you'd prefer a walk to a dance, madame," she said tonelessly. "I myself always take a walk on beautiful summer nights. I sleep very badly, madame. And this park holds so many memories. Of course, only for me, madame."

I could think of no reply to that Her son and her grandson had been exiled. My husband and my son had been called in.

"I'm saying good-by to these paths which I don't really know," I said politely. "Tomorrow morning I go back to France."

"I had not expected to see you alone, madame. I'm glad of the opportunity." We walked on, side by side. The clipped linden trees had a sweet fragrance. I wasn't afraid of her any more. Just an old lady in black.

"I think often about your leaving. And I believe I'm the only one who knows why."

"It's better not to talk about it," I replied, and began to walk faster. She took my arm. This startled me so that I jumped back.

"Are you afraid of me, child?"

Her voice took on color, but sounded deeply sad. We stood still.

"Of course not—that is—yes, I am afraid of you, madame."

"You are afraid of a sick and lonely woman?"

I nodded vehemently. "Because you hate me. Just like the other ladies of your family. Like Her Majesty, like the Princess Sofia Albertina. I disturb you, I don't belong here, I—" I paused, then

375

continued, "There's no reason to discuss it, it can't change the situation. I understand you very well, madame. Our aims are very similar."

"Please tell me what you mean by that?"

Tears welled in my eyes. This last evening had been so indescribably horrible. I sobbed, but only once, before I got myself under control. "You stay in Sweden, madame, as a constant reminder to the people of your exiled son and your exiled grandson. As long as you are here, no one can forget the last of the Vasas. Probably you would rather live with your son in Switzerland. He's known to be not too well off. You could keep house for him and darn his socks instead of embroidering roses in Her Majesty's salon." I lowered my voice and confided to her our common secret. "But—you stay here, madame, because you are the mother of an exiled king, and your staying serves his interests. Am I not right, madame?"

She didn't move—slender, very erect, a black shadow in the green twilight. "You are right. And why are you leaving, madame?"

"Because I best serve the interests of the future king by leaving."

She was silent for a long time. "That's what I thought," she said at last.

Strains of guitar music fluttered through the trees. A woman was singing. A few broken notes of her song could be heard. It was the voice of von Koskull.

"But are you also sure you're serving your own best interests, madame?" the old woman asked.

"Quite sure, madame. I'm thinking of a distant future, and King Oscar I," I answered quietly. With which I bowed deeply to her and went alone back to the palace.

Two o'clock in the morning. The birds are beginning to twitter in the park. Somewhere in this palace lives an old woman who cannot sleep. Perhaps she is still wandering around the park. She is staying, I am leaving. . . . I have described my last evening, there's nothing further to add. I still can't escape my thoughts. Has the Tsar daughters? Or sisters? Oh—I'm seeing ghosts again. My door is opening very softly, there might well be ghosts here. I feel like screaming, but perhaps I'm mistaken—no, the door is really opening. I pretend to be writing—

Jean-Baptiste.
My beloved Jean-Bap—

Paris, January 1, 1812

At the very moment all the church bells of Paris rang in the New Year, we found ourselves alone together—Napoleon and I.

Julie had surprised me completely with the invitation. "After midnight, the Emperor and the Empress are holding a reception. But the family has been asked for ten o'clock. And you must definitely come with us," the Empress said.

That day Julie and I were sitting in the parlour in the rue d'Anjou. Julie was telling me about her children, her household worries, and about Joseph. He complains constantly about the French generals who were defeated in Spain and couldn't hold his throne for him, a throne on which he's never actually sat. Julie, on the other hand, seems contented with her life. She wears purplish-red models from Le Roy's, makes doll dresses for her little girls, frequents court circles, considers the Empress truly majestic, and the little King of Rome delightful. He has blond hair, blue eyes, and two lower teeth. Napoleon crows like a cock to make his small son laugh, or meows like a cat. I tried to imagine a crowing or meowing Napoleon, but it was difficult.

Julie couldn't understand at first why I did not announce my return at the Tuileries. But I live very quietly, and see only Julie and my closest friends. That's why this invitation came as such a surprise. And I couldn't get rid of the feeling that there was some particular reason for the invitation. But what?

So it came about that for the third time in my life, I approached the Tuileries with fear in my heart. The first time was the night I begged Napoleon to spare the life of the Duke of Enghien. I had worn my new hat but my plea was in vain. The second time, I went with Jean-Baptiste when he asked to resign from the Army, and to give up our French citizenship.

This evening I wore my white-gold dress and the diamond earrings given me by the Queen Mother, Sophia Magdalena. I put on the sable stole though I wasn't cold. In Stockholm, it's freezing now at twenty to twenty-five degrees below zero. . . . The reflections of many lights were dancing in the Seine. As I entered the Tuileries, I took a deep breath. I felt—at home. The dark-grey liveries of the Emperor's lackeys, the Gobelins tapestries, and the carpets with the bees. Bees everywhere—just as he told me that night. And everywhere bright lights. No shadows, no ghosts.

The whole family had already assembled in the Empress' salon. When I came in they all wanted to welcome me at once. I had become a genuine crown princess, and even Marie Louise rose and came toward us. She was as always, or perhaps only again, wearing pink. Her porcelain eyes were expressionless, but she smiled gushingly, and immediately inquired about her "dear cousin," the Queen of Sweden. Naturally a Vasa is closer to the heart of a Hapsburg than all the parvenu Bonapartes put together. Then nothing would do but I should sit next to her on a fragile sofa. Mme Letizia admired my earrings, and wanted to know what they cost. I was glad to see the old lady again, Madame Mère, with Parisian ringlets and beautiful manicured nails.

"I can't understand what Napoleon has against my confessional chairs," she complained to the Empress. "I bought three old sentry boxes at an auction of surplus army stock and I use them in my private chapel at Versailles. They make excellent confessional chairs, and they were very cheap. Napoleon says I'm stingy. But in this household money means nothing." Mme Letizia looked disapprovingly around the Empress' salon. No, no one in the Tuileries tried to save money. . . .

"*Mama mia*—oh, *Mama mia*," Paulette laughed. The Princess Borghese is, if possible, more beautiful than ever. She still looks dainty and delicate, and around her big grey eyes are dark blue shadows. She had her champagne glass refilled again and again. Julie had told me Paulette was ill. "An illness no one mentions, and which women rarely get," Julie said, and blushed furiously. I looked at Paulette and racked my brain over what her mysterious illness could be.

"Do you remember the New Year's Eve you felt so ill? When you were expecting Oscar?" Joseph asked me. I nodded. "We drank a toast to the Bernadotte Dynasty," Joseph laughed. Not a pleasant laugh.

"King Joseph I of Spain is pale with envy," remarked Paulette, and emptied her glass.

It was after eleven. The Emperor had not yet appeared. "His Majesty is working," Marie Louise explained. The family's champagne glasses were refilled.

"When can we see the little boy?" Julie asked.

"At midnight the Emperor will welcome the New Year with the child in his arms," said Marie Louise.

"It's bad for the child's health to wake him up and show him off to so many guests," Mme Letizia scolded.

Méneval, the Emperor's secretary, had come in. "His Majesty wishes to speak to Her Royal Highness," he said.

"Do you mean—me?" I asked involuntarily.

Méneval, with a set face, repeated, "Her Royal Highness, the Crown Princess of Sweden."

Marie Louise, chatting with Julie, showed no surprise at this summons. I realized she had invited me at the express command of the Emperor. But the Bonapartes stopped talking as I made for the door.

"His Majesty expects Her Royal Highness in his small study," Méneval said as we walked through a great many rooms. My two earlier meetings with Napoleon had taken place in the large study. At our entrance, the Emperor looked up fleetingly from his papers.

"Please be seated, madame." That was all. He was being very rude. Méneval disappeared. I sat down and waited.

Before him lay a portfolio full of closely written sheets. The handwriting was so familiar to me. Probably Alquier's reports from Stockholm, I decided. The French Ambassador in Sweden is an industrious man. The clock on the mantelpiece ticked toward the New Year. A gilded bronze eagle with outspread wings supported the face of the clock. What's the stage set for, I wondered. The Emperor had sent for me to tell me something important.

"You don't need to intimidate me by keeping me waiting, Sire," I said. "I am by nature very timid, and I'm particularly afraid of you."

"Eugénie, Eugénie—" But he still didn't look up. "One waits until the Emperor speaks. Didn't M. Montel teach you that at least?"

He read on, and I had time to study him. The mask of Caesar has gotten fleshy, the hair very thin. And this face, I realized, I once dearly loved. That was long ago, but I well remember my love. Only, I had forgotten his face.

"Sire," I said impatiently. "Did you send for me to lecture me on questions of etiquette?"

"Among other things. I wish to know, madame, what brought you back to France."

"The cold, Sire."

He leaned back, crossed his arms on his chest, and twisted his mouth ironically. "So-oo. The cold. In spite of the sable I sent you, you felt the cold, madame?"

"In spite of the sable, Sire."

"And why have you not presented yourself at court since your return? The wives of my marshals regularly pay their respects to Her Majesty."

"I am no longer the wife of one of your marshals, Sire."

"Of course. I'd almost forgotten that. We are now dealing with Her Royal Highness, Crown Princess Desideria of Sweden. But you should realize, madame, that members of foreign royal houses request an audience when they visit my capital. Court courtesy, madame."

"I'm not on a visit. This is my home."

"I see. . . . This is your home—" He got up slowly, came out from behind the desk, stood before me, and suddenly shouted, "What do you mean by that? This is your home. And every day your sister and the other ladies tell you what's said here. And you sit down and write to your precious husband. Do people in Sweden consider you clever enough to send you here as a spy?"

"No, quite the opposite. It's because I'm stupid that I had to come back."

He hadn't expected this answer. He was all set to shout at me again. But instead he asked in a normal voice, "What do you mean?"

"I am stupid, Sire. Remember the Eugénie of the old days. Stupid, gauche, untrained. Unfortunately I didn't make a good impression on the Swedish court. And since it's very important that we—Jean-Baptiste, Oscar and I—be liked in Sweden, I came home. It's all very simple really."

"So simple that I don't believe you, madame." Like the crack of a whip. He began to pace up and down. "Perhaps I'm wrong, perhaps you really aren't here at Bernadotte's request. At any rate, madame—the political situation has become so extremely critical that I must ask you to leave France."

I stared at him, utterly disconcerted. Was he driving me away? Driving me out of—France?

"I want to stay here," I said softly. "If I can't stay in Paris, I'll go to Marseilles. I've often thought of buying back our old house. Papa's house. But the present owners don't want to sell. So I have no home except the house in the rue d'Anjou."

"Tell me, madame, has Bernadotte gone mad?" Napoleon asked abruptly. He pawed through the papers on his desk, and picked out a letter. I recognized Jean-Baptiste's handwriting. "I offer Bernadotte an alliance, and he replies that he is not one of my vassal princes."

"I have nothing to do with politics, Sire," I said. "And I also don't see what that has to do with my staying in Paris."

"I will tell you, madame!" He struck the desk with his fist. Plaster drifted down from the ceiling. Now he was in a frenzy, really raging.

"Your Bernadotte dares to turn down an alliance with France. Why do you think I made this offer? Well, answer me."

I didn't answer.

"Not even you, madame, can be that stupid. You must know what's common gossip in every salon. The Tsar has repudiated the Continental system, and his empire will soon cease to exist. The greatest army of all time will occupy Russia." The greatest army of all time . . . The words intoxicated him. "At our side Sweden could acquire eternal glory! Sweden could again become a great power.

I've promised Bernadotte Finland if he marches with us. Finland *and* the Hanseatic towns. Imagine, madame—Finland!"

I tried as I had so often before to imagine Finland. "I've seen it on the map, big blue spots which mean lakes," I said.

"And Bernadotte won't accept. Bernadotte is not marching with us. A French marshal not participating in this campaign!"

I looked at the clock. In a quarter of an hour a New Year would begin.

"Sire, it's nearly midnight."

He didn't hear me. He stood in front of the mirror over the mantelpiece, staring at his own face. "Two hundred thousand Frenchmen, one hundred and fifty thousand Germans, eighty thousand Italians, sixty thousand Poles, not counting one hundred and ten thousand volunteers from other countries," he muttered. "The Grand Army of Napoleon I. The largest army of all time. . . . I'll be on the march again."

Ten minutes to midnight. "Sire—" I began.

He turned, his face distorted with fury. "And Bernadotte thinks nothing of this army!"

I shook my head. "Sire, Jean-Baptiste Bernadotte is responsible for the well-being of Sweden. Whatever he does, he does solely to serve the interests of Sweden."

"Who is not for me, is against me! Madame, since you will not leave France of your own free will, I may have to arrest you as a hostage."

I didn't stir.

"It's late," he said suddenly, went back to the desk and rang a bell. Ménéval, who must have been lurking just outside the door, shot into the room.

"Here—deliver this by special courier immediately," and to me, "Do you know what it is, madame? An order. To Marshal Davout. Davout and his troops will cross the frontier and occupy Swedish Pomerania. Well, what do you say to that, madame?"

"That you're trying to cover the left flank of your great army, Sire."

He laughed out loud. "Who taught you that sentence? Have you been talking to any of my officers during the last few days?"

"Jean-Baptiste told me that a long time ago."

Napoleon's eyes narrowed. "Does he plan to defend Swedish Pomerania? It would amuse me to see him and Davout fighting each other."

"Amuse you?" I thought of the battlefields. The pathetic mounds of earth with the wind-lashed crosses. Tidy rows of mounds. And this amuses him. . . .

"Are you aware, madame, that I can have you arrested as a hostage, and thus force the Swedish Government into an alliance?"

I smiled. "My fate would not influence the decision of the Swedish Government in any way. But my arrest would prove to the Swedes that I am willing to suffer for my new country. Will you really make a martyr of me, Sire?"

The Emperor was annoyed. Even a blind chicken picks up a grain of corn occasionally. Certainly Napoleon had no wish to make a Swedish national heroine out of Mme Bernadotte. . . . He shrugged. "We force our friendship on no one. Many people strive to win our friendship."

Three minutes before midnight.

"I expect you to urge your husband to try to win our friendship." His hand was on the door handle. His eyes gleamed wickedly. "In your own interests, madame."

At that moment the bells rang. We were drowned out by the pealing of the bells. Napoleon mechanically let go the door handle. As though in a trance he stared into space. The bells of Paris proclaimed the New Year. These bells, I thought, how much I love these deep bells. "A great year in the history of France has begun," Napoleon said in a hushed voice. I turned the handle of the door.

Aides and chamberlains waited in the large study. "We must hurry, Her Majesty is expecting us," said Napoleon hastily, and began to run. His aides and chamberlains chased after him, their spurs jingling. I walked slowly with Méneval through the deserted rooms.

"Have you sent the order?" I asked. He nodded. "The Emperor's first act in the New Year," I declared, "was to disregard the neutrality of another country."

"No, Your Highness—" Ménéval corrected me. "His last act in the old year."

In the Empress' salon, I saw the little King of Rome for the first time. The Emperor held him in his arms, and the poor little thing screamed with terror. The infant wore a lace shirt and a wide sash of some order.

"Sashes of orders instead of diapers! Well, I must say . . . ." raged Mme Letizia. The Emperor, to quiet his shrieking son, tickled him tenderly. But the foreign diplomats in their court uniforms, the ladies giggling among themselves, and the members of the Bonaparte family, all of whom wanted to pet the child, scared him even more. Marie Louise, beside the Emperor, looked at the baby with some interest. Her eyes were no longer expressionless, just astonished. She seemed unable to grasp the fact that she had borne Napoleon a child.

When Napoleon saw me, he came over to me with the yelling baby. His fleshy face beamed. "You must stop crying, Sire, kings do not weep," he told the infant. Without thinking I held out my arms and took the child from him. Mme de Montesquieu, the aristocratic nurse, loped over to me. But I held the child tight. Under his lace finery he was very damp. I caressed the blond hair at the nape of his neck, he stopped crying and peered around timidly. I held him close. Oscar, I thought. Oscar is at this moment drinking champagne in the Queen's salon. . . . *Skål*—he touches his glass politely with Their Majesties', then with the scrawny Princess Sofia Albertina, and finally with the Queen Mother. The Koskull warbles an aria. In a few days Jean-Baptiste will know that Davout has marched into Swedish Pomerania, the Koskull warbles on. . . .

I kissed the silky blond hair. "A toast to His Majesty, the King of Rome," someone called. We emptied our glasses. I handed the infant to his nurse. "He is very damp," I whispered to her. She then carried the child out. The Emperor and the Empress were in a pleasant mood, and they conversed—what was it the Queen of Sweden said?—yes, graciously.

I noticed Hortense. Two months ago she had a son though she hasn't lived with Louis Bonaparte for years. Her cheeks were flushed, her eyes shone, and she leaned against her equerry, Count Flahault.

Her life has lost all meaning. Her sons will no longer be Napoleon's heirs. As usual the Emperor ignored his stepdaughter. A Count Flahault, why not?

"Your Highness will see, the Crown Prince will join Russia. And the Crown Prince is right," I heard. Had someone whispered these words—or had I only dreamed them?

Talleyrand limped by me.

I wanted to go home, I was tired. But the Emperor came up to me, the Empress on his arm. No woman with cheeks as red as hers should ever wear pink.

"And here's my hostage—my beautiful little hostage," said the Emperor amiably. The onlookers laughed, well-bred little laughs. "But, ladies and gentlemen, you don't yet know what I mean." The Emperor is sometimes annoyed when people laugh before he gets to the point of a funny story. "I fear, however, that Her Highness is not in a laughing mood. Marshal Davout has unfortunately been forced to occupy part of the northern homeland of Her Highness."

How silent the room had become.

"I take it the Tsar has more than I to offer, madame. I am told he is even offering the hand of a grand duchess. Do you suppose this might tempt our former marshal?"

"Marriage to a member of an ancient royal house is always tempting to men of simple middle-class origins," I said slowly. The bystanders were abashed.

"Undoubtedly." The Emperor smiled. "But such a temptation might endanger your own position in Sweden, madame. Therefore, as an old friend, I advise you to write to Bernadotte and urge him to conclude an alliance with France. For the sake of your own future, madame."

"My future is assured, Sire." I bowed. "At least—as Queen Mother."

He looked at me, quite startled. "Madame, until the Swedish-French alliance is concluded, I do not wish to see you at court," he said, and moved off with Marie Louise.

Marie was waiting up for me at home. I'd given Yvette and the other maids the evening off, so they could enjoy New Year's Eve.

Marie removed the diamond earrings and unclasped the gold straps over my shoulders.

"Happy New Year, Marie. The Emperor has created the largest army of all time and I'm to write to Jean-Baptiste about an alliance. Can you tell me how I got involved in world history?"

"If you hadn't gone to sleep in the Town Hall, this M. Joseph Bonaparte would not have had to wake you up. And if you hadn't set your mind on finding a fiancé for Julie . . ."

"Yes, and if I hadn't been so curious to meet his brother, the little general. How shabby he looked in his old worn-out uniform. . . ." I leaned my elbows on the dressing table and closed my eyes. Curiosity, I thought, simple curiosity was to blame for everything. But the road to Napoleon had also led to Jean-Baptiste. And I had been very happy with him.

"Eugénie," Marie said cautiously. "When are you returning to Stockholm?"

If I hurry, I thought desperately, I may be in time to celebrate my husband's engagement to a Russian grand duchess.

Marie looked at me, searched my face. "Happy New Year," she said.

The year 1812 had at last begun. I think it will be terrible.

Paris, April, 1812

Marie's son Pierre is here.

He came quite unexpectedly. He volunteered for the Grand Army, and was assigned to a regiment which will leave for the front from Paris. I have regularly paid eight thousand francs a year to buy Pierre off from military service. I've paid it gladly. I can't help it. I've always had a guilty conscience about Pierre. After his birth, Marie sent him to foster parents, so she could be my wet nurse and earn her living. I drank Pierre's mother's milk, and Marie fondled

386

me when she longed for him. Mother's milk or not—Pierre is a great tall brawny fellow, tanned by the southern sun. He has Marie's dark eyes, but a jaunty look which he must have inherited from his father. He wore a spanking new uniform, and an equally new bearskin cap. Even his blue-white-red cockade gleamed, it was so new.

Marie, as always, practically lost her mind over him. Her bony hands stroked his arms shyly. "But why?" she asked again and again. "You were so happy in the estate manager's post Her Highness got for you."

Pierre showed his startlingly white teeth. "Mama, we must do it. Join the Grand Army, conquer Russia, occupy Moscow. The Emperor has called us to arms to unite Europe at last. Think of all the possibilities, Mama. One could . . ."

"What could one do?" asked Marie sourly.

"Become a general, a marshal, a crown prince, a king—how do I know—!"

His words tumbled over each other. No, a man couldn't possibly toil in a vineyard near Marseilles when the Emperor was assembling the greatest army of all time. Day and night I see from my window the regiments on their way to Russia, their bands blaring forth. Their heavy tread shakes the houses. At the sound of drums, people rush to their windows to cheer them on.

"Mama, you must decorate my musket with roses."

The soldiers of the greatest army of all time are being decorated with flowers. . . . In the garden the first roses were in bloom. Marie looked questioningly at me. "Pick them, Marie, give them to him, see—that bud there, the dark-red one, tie that one on his musket."

Marie went into the garden, and cut the early roses. "I'll always remember that I carried on my musket roses from the wife of a marshal of France," Pierre assured me, who had cheated him of his mother's milk.

"The wife of a former marshal of France," I said.

"I would rather have fought under monsieur's command," he began.

"You'll like it just as much in Marshal Ney's army corps," I assured him.

Marie came back from the garden. We stuck roses in all Pierre's buttonholes, tied two yellow roses to the hilt of his sword, and pushed the red roses down the musket barrel. Pierre stood at attention and saluted.

"Come home safe, Pierre!"

Marie went with him to the door. When she returned, she was frowning deeply. She grabbed a polishing cloth and set to work violently on the candelabra.

Outside, a regiment again passed by with beating drums and blaring trumpets. Villatte came in. Since the mobilization of the Grand Army, he's been terribly restless.

"Why do soldiers always march into battle to music?" I asked.

"Because martial music is inspiring. It helps the men keep in step. And it also keeps them from thinking too much."

"Why must soldiers march in step?"

"Your Highness—try to imagine a battle. An order to attack. What would an attack be like if some soldiers advanced with long and others with short steps?"

I thought it over. "I still don't understand. What difference would it make if some soldiers attacked the enemy in long strides, and others in shorter ones?"

"It wouldn't look well. Besides, some of the men might be frightened at the last moment and not attack at all. Do you understand, Your Highness?"

That I understood.

"So regimental music is essential," Villatte concluded.

The music suddenly sounded hollow. Brass trumpets, drums, and more brass trumpets. It's a long time since I first heard "La Marseillaise." Without a band, only the lusty voices of dock workers, bank clerks, and craftsmen. Now thousands of trumpets pick up the melody whenever Napoleon appears.

Count Rosen came in. He had a dispatch in his hand, and said something. I couldn't hear him, the trumpets in the street were so loud. We turned from the window. "I have important news for Your Highness. On April fifth, Sweden concluded an alliance with Russia."

"Colonel Villatte—" My voice failed me. Villatte—Jean-Baptiste's comrade in 1794 when the Republic was in danger, his colleagues at the Ministry of War, aide at all his battles, the true friend who followed us to Sweden, and returned with me because Sweden disapproved of our French friends, our Villatte. . . .

"Your Highness wishes?"

"We have just learned that Sweden and Russia have become allies." The martial music had ceased, and we could hear only the marching feet. I couldn't look at Villatte but I had to say something. "You are a French citizen, and a French officer, Colonel Villatte. I think this alliance with the enemies of France will make it uncomfortable for you to remain in my house. You once asked for leave of absence from your regiment to help us and stay by my side. Now I ask you to feel free of these obligations."

How it hurt me to say that!

"Highness—I can't leave you alone now," Villatte said.

I looked at the blond Count Rosen and said, "I am not alone."

The Count stared fixedly at a corner of the room. Did he realize I must part from our best friend? "Count Rosen has been appointed my personal aide. Count Rosen will protect the Crown Princess of Sweden if it should be necessary," I continued. I didn't mind if Villatte saw the tears streaming down my cheeks. "Good-by, Colonel Villatte."

"Has the Marshal—I mean, has His Royal Highness—sent me no letter?"

"None has come. I had the news from the Swedish Embassy," Count Rosen told him.

Villatte was distraught. "I really don't know . . ."

"But I know how you feel. You must either resign from the French Army as Jean-Baptiste did. Or—" I waved toward the window, toward the marching columns, toward those long, long lines of marching men—"Or march on, Colonel Villatte."

"Not march, ride," protested Villatte, Colonel of Cavalary, indignantly.

I smiled through my tears. "Ride then, Colonel Villatte. Ride with God. And come back, safe and sound."

Paris, middle of September, 1812

I think I'd go crazy if I couldn't write everything in my diary.

I have no one with whom to share my thoughts. I am unspeakably alone in this large city of Paris. In my city, as I call it in my heart, because here I have been incredibly happy and incredibly miserable. . . . Julie asked me to spend the hot summer days in Mortefontaine, but for the first time in my life I couldn't say even to her what I think. We once shared a young girls' room in Marseilles, but now she sleeps beside Joseph Bonaparte. And Marie? Marie is the mother of a soldier marching through Russia with Napoleon. That leaves—how comical—that leaves only my Swedish aide as my confidant. Count Rosen, pure Nordic, aristocratic, blond and blue-eyed, who never gets upset. He is Swedish with every beat of his heart. For centuries Sweden has been bled by wars against Russia. Now the new Crown Prince has made a pact with the archfiend. And blond Count Rosen doesn't understand what it's all about. And can't see why I'm anxious. It is so terrible. . . .

Just a few hours ago Count Talleyrand, Prince of Bénévent and adviser to the Ministry of Foreign Affairs, and Fouché, Duke of Otranto and former Minister of Police, were here to see me. They called on me separately, and met by chance in my drawing room. Talleyrand came first. I'm not used to visitors any more. My friends live for the victories on the Russian front, and avoid me these days.

"Call Count Rosen, tell him to meet me in the drawing room," I said to Mme la Flotte. I hastily changed my gown. I couldn't think what Talleyrand wanted from me. It was still bright afternoon; had he arrived at twilight to drink a glass of champagne in the blue shadows of the garden, I would have known. . . .

Talleyrand awaited me in my salon studying with half-closed eyes the portrait of the First Consul. Before I could present Count Rosen to Talleyrand, the Duke of Otranto was announced.

"I don't understand it," I burst out.

Talleyrand raised his eyebrows. "What doesn't Your Royal Highness understand?"

"It's so long since I've had callers," I said in confusion. "The Duke of Otranto is here, too."

Fouché was certainly unpleasantly surprised to find Talleyrand with me. His nostrils flared, and he lisped, "I'm glad that Your Highness has company. I had been afraid that Your Highness would be very lonely."

"I was very lonely until this instant," said I, sitting down on the sofa under the portrait of the First Consul. The two gentlemen sat opposite me. Yvette brought in tea.

"This gentleman is France's famous police minister who, because of his health, has retired to his estates," I explained to Count Rosen who was busily passing teacups.

"Information seems to reach the Duke of Otranto's estates as readily and accurately as the Foreign Ministry in Paris," Talleyrand remarked.

"Some news travels fast," Fouché said, as he drank his tea in refined little sips.

"What are you talking about?" I asked politely. "The French victories are no secret. The bells have scarcely stopped ringing out the capture of Smolensk."

"Yes, Smolensk—" Talleyrand had finally opened his eyes, and was considering Napoleon's youthful portrait with interest. "However, Your Highness, in half an hour the bells will ring again."

"You don't say so, Your Excellency," cried Fouché.

Talleyrand smiled. "Does this surprise you? The Emperor is leading the greatest army of all time against the Tsar. The church bells will naturally soon ring again. This doesn't disturb Your Highness?"

"No, of course not. After all I am—" I broke off. I'm still a Frenchwoman, I wanted to say. But I'm no longer a Frenchwoman. And my husband has concluded a friendly alliance with Russia.

"Do you believe in the Emperor's ultimate victory, Your Highness?" Talleyrand inquired.

"The Emperor has never yet lost a war," I answered.

A strange pause ensued. Fouché stared at me curiously, while Talleyrand slowly and reflectively drank the really very good tea. "The Tsar has sought advice," he remarked at last and put down his empty cup.

I motioned to Yvette to refill it. "The Tsar will ask for peace," I said confidently.

Talleyrand smiled. "That's what the Emperor expected after his victory at Smolensk. But a courier, who arrived in Paris an hour ago to report the victory at Borodino, knows nothing about any peace negotiations. Even though this victory leaves the road to Moscow open."

Had he come to tell me this? Victories, victories, for many years nothing but victories. I must tell Marie that Pierre will soon be marching into Moscow. "Then the Russian campaign will soon be over? Have another little piece of marzipan, Excellency."

"Has Your Royal Highness heard anything from His Royal Highness, the Crown Prince, recently?" Fouché inquired.

I laughed. "That's right, you no longer read my mail. Your successor could tell you that Jean-Baptiste hasn't written me for two weeks. But I have heard from Oscar. He is well, he—" I stopped. It would bore the gentlemen if I talked about my child.

"The Swedish Crown Prince has been away." Fouché never took his eyes off me.

"Away?" I looked from one to the other in astonishment. Even Rosen, too, opened his mouth in surprise.

"His Royal Highness was in Åbo," Fouché continued.

Rosen jumped. I turned to him. "Åbo? Where is Åbo?"

"In Finland, Your Highness," Rosen replied huskily.

Finland again. . . . "Finland is occupied by the Russians, isn't it?"

Talleyrand drank his second cup of tea. "The Tsar asked the Swedish Crown Prince to meet with him in Åbo," Fouché announced triumphantly and looked at Talleyrand.

"What does the Tsar want with Jean-Baptiste?" I whispered.

"Advice," said Talleyrand. "Where would he seek advice? A former marshal, familiar with the Emperor's tactics, is the perfect adviser in a situation like this."

"And on the basis of this advice, the Tsar has sent no emissaries to the Emperor but has let our armies press forward," Fouché said.

Talleyrand looked at the clock. "At any moment now the bells will begin to ring to announce the victory of Borodino. In a few days our troops will enter Moscow."

"Has he promised him Finland?" exploded Count Rosen.

"Who has promised Finland to whom?" asked Fouché in surprise. "Finland? What are you talking about, Count?"

I tried to explain. "Sweden always hopes for the return of Finland. Finland is close—I mean—close to the hearts of my countrymen."

"And to the heart of your respected husband, Your Highness?"

"Jean-Baptiste believes that the Tsar will not give up Finland. So he is most anxious for Norway and Sweden to unite."

Talleyrand nodded slowly. "My confidential sources inform me that the Tsar has promised to support the Swedish Crown Prince in establishing this union. Naturally, after the war."

"Won't the war end when the Emperor gets to Moscow?" I asked in amazement.

Talleyrand shrugged. "I don't know what advice your husband gave the Tsar."

Silence fell, heavy as lead. Fouché ate a marzipan and smacked his lips.

"The advice which His Royal Highness is said to have given the Tsar . . ." Count Rosen began.

Fouché grinned broadly. "The French Army has marched into villages burned to the ground by the inhabitants. The French Army has found only charred granaries. The French Army is marching from victory to victory—starving. The Emperor has had to bring up provisions from the rear. He had not reckoned on this. Nor on a flank attack by the Cossacks, who were not supposed to be fighting. But the Emperor hopes to fatten up his troops in Moscow, where the Army will winter. Moscow is a wealthy city, and can supply the troops. So you see, everything depends on the entry into Moscow."

"And—do you doubt this entry?" Count Rosen asked in surprise.

"His Excellency, the Prince of Bénévent, has just said that at any moment the church bells will ring for the victory of Borodino. Beyond this, the road to Moscow lies open. By day after tomorrow, undoubtedly, the Emperor will be in the Kremlin, dear Count," Fouché explained, and grinned again.

A great fear caught at my throat. Despairingly I looked from one to another. "Please tell me frankly, gentlemen—why are you here?"

"I've wanted to call on you for a long time, Your Highness," Fouché said, "and when I heard what an important role your distinguished husband was playing in this great conflict, I had a heartfelt desire to express to Your Highness my deep sympathy, a sympathy of many years' standing, if I may say so."

Yes, for many years, Napoleon's Minister of Police spied on us. "I don't understand you," I said shortly, and turned to Talleyrand.

"Is a former mathematics master so difficult to see through, Your Highness?" Talleyrand asked. "Wars are like equations in higher mathematics. In wars, too, there's an unknown quantity. In this war, we are also dealing with an unknown quantity—but this unknown, since his meeting with the Tsar, is no longer . . . unknown. The Swedish Crown Prince has intervened, madame."

"Of what advantage is this intervention to Sweden? Instead of armed neutrality, a pact with Russia," Count Rosen said vehemently.

"I'm afraid the armed neutrality no longer impresses the Emperor. His Majesty has occupied Swedish Pomerania. You don't disapprove of your Crown Prince's policies, do you, young man?"

Talleyrand spoke kindly, but my blond young Count would not give way. "The Russians have a hundred and forty thousand men under arms, and Napoleon has . . ."

"Almost half a million—" Talleyrand nodded—"but a Russian winter without proper quarters could destroy even the biggest and best of armies, young man."

At last I understood. Without proper quarters . . . I understood, all right.

At that moment the bells started pealing. La Flotte threw open the door and shouted, "A new victory! The Battle of Borodino has been won."

We never moved. Waves of ringing bells surged over us. Napoleon wants to spend the winter in Moscow. What advice has Jean-Baptiste given the Tsar?

Fouché and Talleyrand have their spies and couriers in every camp, they'll always be on the winning side. Since they have come to see me today they believe that Napoleon will lose this war. Somehow, somewhere, while victory bells ring out in Paris. Jean-Baptiste has intervened and assured the freedom of a small country far up north. But Pierre will freeze, and Villatte will bleed to death.

Talleyrand was first to leave. Fouché, on the contrary, stayed on and on. There he sat chewing marzipan, exploring with his tongue the gaps between his long yellow teeth, gazing at Napoleon's portrait. And looking very pleased. With what? With the new victory? With himself, because he'd fallen into disfavour?

He didn't leave until the bells were silent. "The well-being of the French people is involved," he said in parting. "And the French people long for peace," he added pompously. I could find no double meaning in these empty words. "The Swedish Crown Princess and I have the same goal—peace." Fouché bowed over my hand. His lips were sticky, and I snatched back my hand.

I went out to the garden and sat down on a bench. The roses were through blooming, the grass had withered. I suddenly feared my own house and all my memories. I had understood, but I still couldn't believe it. In my restlessness I ordered the carriage sent around. As I climbed in, Count Rosen was at the carriage door. I forget so often that I have a personal aide. I really wanted to be alone. We drove along the Seine. I seemed to recall that I'd been told something about Rosen. He broke into my thoughts with, "This Duke of Otranto—he's called that, isn't he?"

"Yes, he used to be Fouché. The Emperor made him a duke. What about him?"

"This Otranto has some inside information about the conference at Åbo. He told me more about it out in the hall. His Royal Highness was accompanied by Chancellor Wetterstedt and Marshal Adlercreutz. Löwenhjelm was there, too." I nodded, these names told me so little. "At first the Tsar and His Highness were alone, later an English envoy took part in the conversations. It is assumed that His Highness will bring about an alliance between England and Russia.

The decisive alliance against Napoleon, Your Highness. It's said that Austria, too, is secretly . . ."

"But the Emperor of Austria is Napoleon's father-in-law!" I exclaimed.

"That's doesn't mean anything, Your Highness. Napoleon forced him into that. No Hapsburg would willingly have taken this parvenu into his family."

The carriage rolled along slowly. Out of the deep blue evening the steeples of Notre-Dame loomed blackly. "I was there, Count Rosen, when this parvenu, as you call the Emperor of the French, took the crown from the Pope's hands and placed it on his own head. I was standing behind the beautiful Josephine, holding a lace handkerchief on a velvet cushion. Here—in this cathedral, Count."

White pieces of torn newspaper blew into the road, extras from the *Moniteur* announcing the new victory. Tomorrow the street cleaner will sweep them into the gutter. We passed Parisians sitting placidly on their doorsteps—they are used to victories, and long only for their sons. It was the same as always except my heart was tight with sadness.

"Perhaps they'll really come back when this is all over. The Bourbons, I mean," the young blond Count said. I looked at him sideways. A classical profile, very fair skin, very light hair, slim boyish shoulders. We drove across the Pont Royal. Marie Louise's windows were all alight.

"I'll present you to the Empress Josephine, Count," I said on an impulse.

After the divorce, she wept for two days and two whole nights. And then she had a facial massage and ordered three new gowns. . . . Silver eyelids, smiles with lips closed. For her sake Napoleon robbed the Italians of the portrait of Mona Lisa. I'll show the young Swedish Count the most beautiful woman in Paris. And ask Josephine how I ought to rouge my face. If the Swedes must have a parvenue Crown Princess, she should at least be beautiful. . . .

When we got home, I went immediately to my room and began to write. How long will I be so alone? Marie has just come in and asked, "Have you heard from Colonel Villatte? And has he mentioned Pierre?" I shook my head.

"After this new victory, the Tsar will ask for peace, and Pierre will be home before winter," Marie said happily. She knelt down and removed my shoes. In her hair there is so much white, her hands are rough, all her life long she has worked hard and sent her savings to Pierre. Now Pierre is marching toward Moscow Jean-Baptiste, what will happen to Pierre in Moscow? Jean-Baptiste . .

"Sleep well, Eugénie, and pleasant dreams."

"Thank you, Marie, good night' As in my childhood. Who is putting my Oscar to bed? One, two, three aides? Or chamberlains.

And you, Jean-Baptiste? Can you hear me? Let Pierre come home safely, let him come home . . .

But you probably cannot hear me.

Paris, two weeks later

It has happened again. Once more I am the disgrace of the family. Julie and Joseph came back into town from Mortefontaine, and gave a large party to celebrate Napoleon's entry into Moscow. And I, too, was invited. But I didn't want to go, and wrote Julie that I had a cold. The very next day she came to see me.

"I'm terribly anxious to have you come," she declared. "There's so much silly talk about you and Jean-Baptiste Naturally, your husband should have joined Napoleon in his Russian campaign; then they couldn't say Jean-Baptiste had allied himself with the Tsar. I want to stop this malicious gossip . . "

"Julie, Jean-Baptiste *has* allied himself with the Tsar."

Julie looked at me unbelievably. "Do you mean to say that—that it's all true, what people say?"

"I don't know what people say, Julie. Jean-Baptiste has met the Tsar and given him advice."

"Désirée—you truly are a disgrace to the family," moaned Julie, shaking her head hopelessly.

"I've been told that before. Because I invited Joseph and Napoleon Bonaparte to our house. Long ago, when it all began. . . . The disgrace of our family. By the way, which family do you mean?"

"Naturally the Bonapartes."

"I'm no Bonaparte, Julie."

"You are a sisiter-in-law of the oldest brother of the Emperor," she declared.

"Among other things, my dear, only among other things. Above all I'm a Bernadotte; in fact the first Bernadotte woman, cofoundress of a dynasty."

"If you don't come, everyone will believe the stupid rumours that Jean Bernadotte made a secret pact with the Tsar."

"That's no secret, Julie. The French newspapers just can't write anything about it."

"But Joseph insists that you come. Don't make things hard for me, Désirée."

We hadn't seen each other all summer. Julie's face is even thinner. The lines at the corners of her mouth are deeply etched, her colourless skin is flaccid. A terrible tenderness overwhelmed me. Julie, my Julie, is a harassed, faded, and profoundly disappointed woman. Perhaps she's heard about Joseph's love affairs, perhaps he treats her badly, because he himself becomes more embittered every year and has only Napoleon to thank for his kingly crown. Perhaps she knows that Joseph never loved her and only married her for her dowry. She must realize that today this dowry means nothing to Joseph who is enormously wealthy from speculations in houses and government estates. Why does she stay with him, why torture herself with ceremonies and receptions? For love? For duty? Or sheer obstinacy?

"If it will help in any way, I'll come," I said.

She pressed her hand against her forehead. "I have another of my bad headaches. So often lately. Yes, please come. Joseph wants all Paris to know that Sweden is still neutral. The Empress will be there and the entire diplomatic corps." She stood up.

"I'll bring Count Rosen, my Swedish aide."

"Your—? Yes, of course, your aide. Do bring him, there'll be so few men. They're all away."

398

On the way out, she lingered for a moment in front of the portrait of Napoleon as First Consul. "Yes, that's how he looked then: long hair, sunken cheeks. Now . . ."

"Now he's fat," I said.

"Just imagine—the entry into Moscow. Napoleon in the Kremlin. It's enough to make you dizzy."

"Don't think, Julie. You'd better lie down. You look so tired."

"I'm worried about the party. If only everything goes well."

Disgrace of the family. I thought about Mama . . . If only everything goes well. One really never grows up until one's parents are gone. Then one can be so frighteningly alone—and un-grown up.

The high bronze candelabra in the Elysée Palace sparkled. I knew people were whispering behind my back, but my back was protected by the tall young Count Rosen. They struck up "La Marseillaise." The Empress entered and I bowed a little less deeply than the other ladies, for I am a member of a ruling house. Marie Louise—still or again in pink—stopped in front of me.

"I hear that a new Austrian ambassador has arrived in Stockholm, madame," she said. "A Count von Neipperg. Has he been presented to you, madame?"

"He must have come after I left, Your Majesty," I answered, and tried to read some meaning in her puppet-face. Since the birth of the little King of Rome Marie Louise has gained weight. She laces herself very tightly. There were beads of sweat on her short nose.

"When I was a young girl, I danced with Count von Neipperg. At my first court ball." Her smile deepened, suddenly became alive. "It was, by the way, my first and last court ball in Vienna. Shortly afterward I was married."

I hardly knew what to say. She seemed to be waiting for something and I was suddenly sad. Since she was a small child, she must have heard that Napoleon was a parvenu, a tyrant and an enemy of her country. And then all of a sudden she was forced to marry him, and be dominated by him.

"Imagine—Count von Neipperg has only one eye. He wears a black patch over the other," Marie Louise reflected. "And nevertheless—I have such pleasant memories of him. We waltzed together."

With that she left me, and I remembered the night when I had taught Napoleon the waltz. One, two, three—and one, two, three. . . .

At midnight they played "La Marseillaise" again. Joseph went over to the Empress, raised his glass of champagne:

"On September fifteenth, at the head of the most glorious army of all time, His Majesty entered Moscow, and took up his residence in the Kremlin, the palace of the Tsars. Our victorious army will spend the winter in the capital of our defeated enemy. *Vive l'Empereur!*"

I finished my drink, gulp by gulp. Talleyrand appeared beside me. "Was Your Highness forced to come?" he asked, and looked at Joseph.

I grimaced politely. "Whether I'm here or not has no meaning, Excellency. I don't understand politics."

"How strange that fate should have chosen you to play such a decisive role, Your Highness."

"What do you mean by that?" I demanded.

"Perhaps someday I'll come to you with a most important request, Your Highness. Perhaps you'll grant it. I shall make this request in the name of France."

"Do tell me—what on earth you are talking about?"

"I am very much in love, Your Highness. Forgive me, don't be shocked. You misunderstand—I am in love with France, Your Highness—our France." He rolled some champagne around on his tongue. "I recently told Your Highness that Napoleon no longer campaigns against an unknown, but against a man we know well. Your Highness remembers? And tonight we are celebrating the Emperor's arrival in Moscow. The Grand Army has at last found winter quarters in the Russian capital. Your Highness, do you believe that this has surprised the man whom we know well?"

My hand gripped the stem of my champagne glass.

"My brother should feel at home in the Kremlin. The Tsar's palace is furnished in more than oriental splendour," said someone right behind us. Joseph, King Joseph. "Sheer genius that my brother could get through so quickly. Now our troops can winter peacefully in Moscow."

But Talleyrand slowly shook his head. "Unfortunately, I can't agree with Your Majesty. A courier arrived half an hour ago. Moscow has been in flames for two weeks. Even the Kremlin is on fire."

From far away I heard the waltz tunes. The candles flickered, Joseph's face was like a mask, greenish-white, the eyes wide open, the mouth gaping with horror. Talleyrand, on the other hand, kept his eyes half-closed, was unmoved and unaffected, as though he'd expected for two weeks the news which had reached us only a half-hour before.

Moscow is on fire.

Moscow has been burning for two weeks.

"How did the fires start?" asked Joseph hoarsely.

"Incendiaries, undoubtedly. And simultaneously in various parts of the city. Our troops have tried in vain to put out the fires. Every time they think one fire is under control, a fresh blaze is reported from some other district. The inhabitants are suffering terribly!"

"And our troops, Your Excellency?"

"Will be forced to withdraw."

"But the Emperor has told me many times that under no circumstances would he lead the troops across the Russian steppes during the winter. The Emperor counted on Moscow as winter quarters," said Joseph.

"I'm only telling you what the courier reported: The Emperor cannot spend the winter in Moscow, because Moscow is burning down."

Talleyrand raised his glass to Joseph. "Don't let your face betray you, Your Majesty. The Emperor would not want the news known prematurely. *Vive l'Empereur!*"

"*Vive l'Empereur,*" Joseph repeated mechanically.

"Your Highness?" Talleyrand raised his glass to me. But I was petrified. I saw the Empress waltzing with an old gentleman crippled with gout. One, two, three—and one, two, three. . . . Joseph wiped away beads of sweat from his forehead with a lace handkerchief.

"Good night, Joseph, my love to Julie. Good night, Your Excellency," I murmured. One doesn't leave a ball before Her Majesty, has retired, but etiquette could go hang. I was tired and confused. No, no—not confused. I saw everything clearly, so terribly clearly.

Torchbearers ran along beside my carriage as always when I drive out to attend an official function. "It was an unforgettably brilliant ball," said the young Swedish Count on my left.

"Do you know Moscow, Count Rosen?"

"No, Your Highness. Why?"

"Because Moscow is burning, Count. Because Moscow has been burning for fourteen days."

"The advice of His Highness to the Tsar in Åbo. . . ."

"Don't talk any more, please don't talk any more. I'm so tired."

And Talleyrand's important request? What request—and when?

Paris, December 16, 1812

In Josephine's white-and-gold salon at Malmaison ladies rolled bandages for the wounded in Russia, and in her boudoir Josephine herself, tweezers in hand, bent over me plucking my heavy brows. It hurt, but the thin arched line made my eyes seem larger. Next she rummaged through her rouge pots and powder boxes, and found a small jar of silver make-up, rubbed a little of it on my eyelids, and studied my new face in the mirror. At that moment I noticed the morning edition of the *Moniteur* under ribbons and combs on her dressing table. It was flecked with red. I began to read. It was Emperor Napoleon's Bulletin 29, in which he openly admitted that his Grand Army lay spent, frozen, starved and buried in the snowy wastes of Russia. There was no more Grand Army. The red on the paper looked like drops of blood, but it was only lip rouge.

"You must make up like this, Désirée, when you appear in public," Josephine said. "Thin, arched eyebrows, a little green on the eyelids and, above all, the silver. When you show yourself at a window or on a balcony you must always stand on a footstool. No one will notice it, and you'll seem much taller. Believe me . . ."

"Have you read this, madame?" With shaking hands, I held out the paper to her.

Josephine gave it a fleeting glance. "Naturally. Bonaparte's first from the front in months. It just confirms what we've feared for a long time. Bonaparte has lost the war with Russia. I take it he'll soon be back in Paris. Have you ever thought of using henna when you wash your hair? Your dark hair would have a reddish cast in candlelight. It would be lovely on you, Désirée."

"This army, which on the sixth of the month had been the greatest army in history, was by the fourteenth completely demoralized. It had no cavalry, no artillery, and no transport," I read. "The enemy, apprised of the disaster which had befallen us, exploited our weakness to the full. Cossacks ambushed our columns. . ."

In these words, Napoleon informed the world that the greatest army of all times had foundered, during their retreat, in the snowy wasteland of Russia. He soberly enumerated the troop formations. Of the hundred thousand cavalrymen who had ridden off to Moscow, for example, only six hundred riders were left. Six hundred—Napoleon's cavalry! The words "exhaustion" and "starvation" appeared again and again. At first I could take it in. I read on. I read the Bulletin 29 from beginning to end. It closed with the words, "The health of His Majesty was never better."

When I looked up, a strange face confronted me in the mirror. Large, melancholy eyes under silvered lids. An upturned nose, not pink as usual, but powdered brownish. And curved lips, a deep cyclamen pink. So I, too, can look elegant, so beautiful, so unexpected. I dropped my new face over the newspaper again. "And what will happen now, madame?"

A shrug and—"There are always two possibilities in life, Désirée." Josephine kept polishing her fingernails. "Either Bonaparte will make peace, and abandon the idea of ruling all Europe. Or continue to make war. If he goes on with his wars, there are again two possibilities. He could either . . ."

"And France, madame?" I must have shouted, for she shrank back, but I couldn't help it. Suddenly I understood the Bulletin. And also the rumours. The rumours were true. Terribly true. Ten thousand men, a hundred thousand men stumbling through the snow, crying from pain like children, because their arms and legs are frozen, they suddenly fall and can't get up again. Ravenous wolves surround them. They try to shoot, but can no longer hold their muskets. The men scream in horror and the wolves slink back a little. It's getting dark. The night will be long, the wolves wait. . . .

In desperate haste the engineers build a bridge across a river, called the Beresina. Only over this bridge does the way lead back. The Cossacks pursue them closely. Any moment the bridge may be blown up, and their retreat cut off. So with a final agonizing effort, the exhausted men stagger onto the bridge. In the stampede many fall and are trampled by their comrades. The bridge sways . . . only to get across, only to live. Anyone who can't push his way through is crowded off the bridge and falls screaming among the ice floes in the river below. Tries to clutch the ice, is borne away by the current, screams, screams, screams and sinks. But His Majesty's health has never been better.

"And France, madame?" I asked again, dully.

"What about it? Bonaparte isn't France."

Josephine smiled over her shining fingernails. "Napoleon I, by the Grace of God, Emperor of the French. . . ." She winked at me "We both know how that was done. Barras needed someone to quell a hunger riot, and Bonaparte was willing to fire the cannon on the people of Paris; Bonaparte became Military Governor of Paris, Bonaparte held the high command in the south, Bonaparte conquered Italy; after that Bonaparte was in Egypt, Bonaparte overthrew the Government, Bonaparte became First Consul—" She hesitated, then added hopefully, "Perhaps she'll desert him in adversity."

"She is still the mother of his son," I protested.

Josephine tossed her childlike curls. "That doesn't mean anything. I've always been more wife than mother. And this Marie Louise—a girl from an ancient family—is probably more daughter than wife or mother. My Bonaparte crowned me himself. Marie Louise, on the other hand, was married by her papa to this Napoleon by the Grace of God. . . . Whatever happens, Désirée, don't ever forget what I've told you, will you promise?"

I looked at her, astonished.

"Just between us—there are more distinguished dynasties than the Bernadotte family, Désirée! But the Swedes themselves chose Jean-Baptiste, and he won't disappoint them. Jean-Baptiste is a born ruler, my Bonaparte has always believed so. But you, my child, will never learn how to rule. You must at least do the Swedes one favour—be beautiful! Silver grease paint and cyclamen rouge."

"But my turned-up nose?"

"We can't change that, but your nose suits you. You look so young. You'll always look younger than you are. So—let's go down to the salon and have Thérèse tell our fortune from the cards. We'll ask her about Bonaparte's star. Too bad it's raining, I wanted to show your Swedish Count the garden. The yellow roses are still in bloom. But now of course they're drowning in this rain. . . ."

On the stairs Josephine suddenly stopped. "Désirée, why aren't you in Stockholm?"

"In Stockholm there is already one queen, and one queen mother. Isn't that enough?"

"Are you afraid of your predecessors?"

My eyes filled with tears. I swallowed hard.

"Don't be silly—predecessors aren't dangerous. Only—successors," Josephine said softly, and seemed somehow relieved. "You see, I was afraid you were here for his sake. Because you still loved him—Bonaparte."

In the white-and-gold salon, the ladies were still preparing endlessly long gauze bandages. Paulette, crouched on the thick carpet in front of the fireplace, wound them into tiny rolls. Queen Hortense lay on a sofa, reading letters. A dreadfully fat lady, completely enfolded in an Oriental shawl, looked to me like a big coloured ball. The coloured ball was playing Patience. My young Count Rosen, at the window, gazed disconsolately at the rain. When we entered, the ladies bobbed up. Beautiful Paulette, however, merely shifted her weight from her left leg to her right. The coloured ball sank before me into a court curtsy.

"Perhaps Your Highness remembers the Princess de Chimay?" Josephine asked. She calls me Désirée only if we're alone. Princess de Chimay? The name of one of the very oldest, most distinguished families in France. I was sure I had never before met a member of this frightfully grand family. "Nôtre dame de Thermidor," Josephine laughed. "My old friend Thérèse!"

Josephine's friend Thérèse. The Marquise de Fontenay, who married the former valet Tallien during the Revolution to save her head. Tallien was a representative, and the lovely Thérèse became the first lady of the Directorate. And was said to have danced for her guests stark naked. And procured new trousers for Napoleon, his old pair was all worn out. I had forced my way into her house to find my fiancé. But I lost him there and found Jean-Baptiste.

She had an even worse reputation than Josephine, whom she succeeded as Barras' mistress. Napoleon refused to receive Thérèse at court. He's gotten terribly moral since he became Emperor. Poor Thérèse was sick about it because she's Josephine's bosom friend. In the end, Thérèse decided to annoy Napoleon. She married the Prince de Chimay and had seven children. Now she was round as a ball, but her black eyes laughed irresistibly. Napoleon would have liked to receive the distinguished Prince in the Tuileries, a genuine aristocrat, after all. But the Prince wouldn't come because Napoleon still refused to invite Thérèse to the court. She had danced stark naked, and Napoleon could never forget it. Undoubtedly he had watched her. . . .

"I'm glad to see you again, Princess," I said spontaneously.

"See me again?" Thérèse opened her eyes as wide as the rolls of fat on her cheeks permitted. "I've not had the honour of being presented to Your Highness."

"Désirée," came a voice from the fireplace. "The Empress has silvered your eyelids." Paulette, thin to the point of emaciation, wearing the pink pearls of the Borghese, looked me over. "But it's becoming to you. And tell me, little new Crown Princess of Sweden, is your aide there at the window deaf and dumb?"

"No, only dumb, Your Imperial Highness," spluttered Rosen angrily. And I realized that it had been a mistake to bring him here.

Quickly Josephine laid her small hand on his arm. Very lightly, but Rosen quivered. "When it stops raining," Josephine said, "I'll show you the garden. In my garden, the roses still bloom in December. You love roses, too, don't you? You even have the same name."

Josephine looked up at him mischievously, smiled without showing her bad teeth, and gazed into his eyes. Heaven knows how she managed it. Then she turned to the others. "What does Count Flahault write from Russia, Hortense?"

Hortense's lover is aide-de-camp to the Emperor. Since Hortense no longer lives with fat Louis, her relationship with Flahault has been quietly accepted in her mother's salon.

"He's marching through the snow at the Emperor's side," Hortense declared proudly.

"Bonaparte marching through the snow! He's probably driving in a sleigh, and your Flahault's letter is utter nonsense," said Josephine.

"Count Flahault tells me he has marched beside the Emperor since Smolensk. The Emperor has to walk, because nearly all the horses have frozen to death. Frozen, or been shot and eaten by the hungry troops, Mama. The Emperor wore the fur coat the Tsar once gave him, and a cap of Persian lamb. He leaned on a cane. He was accompanied by many generals who had lost their regiments. The Emperor marched between Murat and Count Flahault."

"Ridiculous. His faithful Ménéval marched beside him," said Josephine.

Hortense riffled through the pages of the long letter in her hands. "Ménéval has collapsed from exhaustion and been loaded on a wagon with the wounded."

There was dead silence in the room. A log in the fireplace crackled, but we all felt cold.

"Tomorrow I'll arrange for a service of Intercession," Josephine announced, and asked Thérèse to tell Napoleon's fortune from a large star. Thérèse very seriously shuffled her cards, divided them into two piles and said to Josephine, "Bonaparte, as always, is King of Hearts." Then Josephine had to choose cards from each pile. Thérèse wrinkled her brow solemnly, and laid out the cards in the form of a star. Josephine held her breath with excitement. Hortense came over and stood behind her, her long unpowdered nose hung sadly over her upper lip. Paulette sat close to me and looked at the young Count. Count Rosen, however, let his gaze wander, and probably doubted our sanity.

Thérèse is an artist at fortunetelling. After she had arranged the cards in a star, she stared impressively and silently into space. Finally Josephine couldn't bear it any longer and whispered, "Well?"

"The situation is ominous," intoned Thérèse, and relapsed into thoughtful silence. At last, "I see a journey."

"Naturally," Paulette said briskly. "The Emperor is coming back from Russia. He may be walking, but he's, nevertheless, on a journey."

Thérèse shook her head. "I see another journey over water. In a ship." A long pause. "No, unfortunately the outlook is not favourable."

"What about me?" Josephine inquired.

"The Queen of Spades won't accompany the Emperor. Your situation will remain unchanged. I see financial worries. But that is nothing new."

"Yes, I'm in debt again, at Le Roy's," Josephine admitted uncomfortably.

Thérèse raised her hand dramatically. "I see a separation from the Queen of Diamonds."

"That's Marie Louise," Paulette whispered to me.

"But it means nothing good. In fact, I see no favourable signs." Thérèse made her voice as mysterious as possible. "Moreover—what can the Jack of Hearts mean here? He lies between the Emperor and the Jack of Clubs. The Jack of Clubs is Talleyrand. . . ."

"The other day he was Fouché," Hortense reminded her.

"Perhaps the Jack of Hearts is the little King of Rome. Bonaparte is returning to his child," suggested Josephine.

Thérése picked up the cards and began to shuffle them madly. Then she divided them again into two piles and laid out a fresh star.

"No change. Still the sea voyage, financial worries, treachery of —" Thérése paused.

"Treachery by the Queen of Diamonds?" demanded Josephine. Thérése nodded. "And for me?" Josephine asked.

"I can't understand it. There's nothing between the Queen of Spades and the Emperor. And nevertheless—" Thérèse sighed and shook her head. "And nevertheless, he doesn't come to her. I really

don't know why, dearest Josephine. And here we have the Jack of
Hearts again! Next to the Emperor, always next to the Emperor.
The seven of Clubs and the Ace of Clubs can't get to him, because
they're held off by the Jack of Hearts. That can't be the little King
of Rome, it must mean an adult. But whom?" She looked around
the circle, perplexed. We didn't know the answer. She looked down
and pondered over the cards again. "It could also be a young woman
—a girl, for instance, whom the Emperor doesn't treat as a woman—
someone who's known him all his life, and who wouldn't leave him
in a pinch, perhaps . . "

"Désirée, of course—the Jack of Hearts is Désirée," cried Paulette.

Thérèse stared at me blankly, but Josephine nodded. "That might
be. The little comrade, a young girl he once knew. I do believe Her
Royal Highness . . ."

"Please leave me out of the game," I said hastily, embarrassed
before Count Rosen.

Josephine understood me. "Enough for today," she said, and
went over to the Count. "I think the rain has stopped I'll show you
the yellow roses and the greenhouses."

In the evening we drove back to Paris. It was raining again. "I'm
afraid you were very bored at Malmaison, Count Rosen. But I wanted
you to meet the most beautiful woman in France."

"The Empress Josephine must once have been quite beautiful,"
the young man answered politely.

She aged in a single night, I thought. I will also grow old someday, with or without silver paint on my eyelids. I hope not overnight. But that depends on Jean-Baptiste. . . .

"The ladies at Malmaison are very different from our ladies in
Stockholm," Rosen declared suddenly. "They discuss everything
from prayers to love affairs."

"People also pray and make love in Stockholm."

"Naturally. But they don't talk about it."

Paris, December 19, 1812

It has rained continuously since my visit to Malmaison. But in spite of the weather the past two days people have stood on street corners and read Bulletin 29 aloud to each other from rain-soaked newspapers, and tried to imagine their sons freezing in Russia. They wait for comfort, for further news. They wait in vain. I know of no single family who hasn't a close relative in Russia. In all the churches, services of Intercession are being held.

Yesterday evening I couldn't get to sleep. I wandered restlessly from room to room. Moreau's former house was cold and far too large for me alone. Finally I put Napoleon's sables on over my dressing gown, sat down at the desk in the little salon and tried to write to Oscar. Marie sat in a corner knitting a grey shawl. She's been knitting this shawl for Pierre ever since she heard about the icy cold of the Russian steppes. We've had no news from him. The needles clicked, Marie's lips moved silently. Now and then a newspaper rustled. Count Rosen was reading Danish newspapers, the Swedish papers haven't come for days. Now he was poring over the Danish court news. La Flotte and the staff of servants were long since asleep.

I clung to my thoughts of Oscar. I wanted to write him he should be careful ice skating so he wouldn't break his leg. If he were here —if he were here, he'd be called up for military service in a few years. How do other mothers stand it? Marie knitted, and the snow falling incessantly in Russia, white and soft, buried the sons. . . .

At that moment I heard a carriage stop in front of my house. Then a thundering knock at the door. "The servants have gone to bed," I said.

Marie put down her knitting. "The Swedish porter in the gate-house will open the door," she said.

We waited with bated breath. Heard voices in the hall. "I will speak to no one. I have already retired," I said quickly. Count Rosen left the salon.

Very soon I heard his harsh French. A door opened, and he escorted someone into the adjoining large salon. Had he gone mad? I had told him I would receive no one. "You must go at once, Marie, and say I've gone to bed."

Marie got right up and went through the connecting door into the large salon. I heard her begin a sentence and stop. There was complete silence in the next room. Incredible to admit anyone at this late hour against my express wishes. . . . I heard papers rustle, and a log fall. The coachman was lighting a fire in the big fireplace. That was the only sound I heard. Otherwise all was deathly still.

Finally the door opened. Count Rosen came in. His movements were oddly stiff and formal. "His Majesty, the Emperor."

What? I couldn't have heard correctly. "Who?"

"His Majesty accompanied by one gentleman wishes to speak to Your Royal Highness."

"The Emperor is still at the front," I declared in confusion.

"His Majesty has just returned." The young Swede was pale with excitement.

I had calmed down. Nonsense, I won't let myself be intimidated, I won't be forced into this upsetting situation, I don't want to see him again, at least not now, not alone. . . . "Tell His Majesty that I have gone to bed!"

"I've already told His Majesty that. His Majesty insists on speaking to Your Highness immediately."

I didn't move. What does one say to an Emperor who leaves his army stranded in the Russian snow? No, not stranded, there is no army any more. He lost his army. . . . And he comes first to me . . . I stood up slowly, pushed the hair back off my forehead. It occurred to me that I was wearing my old velvet dressing gown and over it the sables and must look awfully funny. Against my will, I went to the door. He must know now that Jean-Baptiste is allied with the Tsar, and had advised him how to defend Russia. He must know now that Jean-Baptiste's advice was followed. "I'm worried, Count Rosen," I murmured.

The young Swede reassured me. "I think you need have no fear, Your Highness."

The large salon was very bright. Marie was putting candles in the last of the tall candelabras. The fire flickered. On the sofa, under the portrait, sat General Caulaincourt, the Emperor's chief equerry, once eighth aide-de-camp to the First Consul. Caulaincourt wore a sheepskin coat and a woolen cap pulled down over his ears. His eyes were closed, he was apparently asleep.

The Emperor stood close to the fire, with his arms on the mantelpiece. His shoulders sagged. He seemed so tired that he had to lean against something to stay upright. A grey Persian lamb cap sat crooked on his head. He looked completely strange. Neither of them heard me come in.

"Sire—" I said softly, and went over to the Emperor.

Caulaincourt awoke, snatched off his woolen cap and stood at attention. The Emperor slowly raised his head. I forgot to bow. I stared at his face aghast. For the first time in my life I saw Napoleon unshaven.

His beard was reddish, his bloated cheeks slack and grey. His mouth was a narrow line, and his chin jutted out to a point. His eyes looked at me, but did not focus.

"Count Rosen," I said sharply, "someone forgot to take His Majesty's cap and his fur coat."

"I am cold, I'll keep my coat on," Napoleon muttered, and wearily took off his fur cap. Rosen carried out Caulaincourt's coat.

"Please come right back, Count. Marie, brandy and glasses." Marie had to play the part of a lady-in-waiting. At this hour of the night I couldn't receive gentlemen alone, even the Emperor of France. Especially not him. And Count Rosen must be a witness to our conversation.

"Please sit down, Sire," I said, and sat myself down on the sofa. The Emperor didn't budge. Caulaincourt stood indecisively in the middle of the room. Count Rosen returned. Marie brought brandy and glasses.

"Sire," I said, "a glass of brandy."

The Emperor didn't hear me.

I looked at Caulaincourt questioningly. "We've driven without stopping for thirteen days and thirteen nights," he murmured. "No one in the Tuileries knows yet that we have returned. His Majesty wanted to talk to Your Highness first."

It was fantastic. The Emperor had travelled thirteen days and thirteen nights to cling like a drowning man to my mantelpiece, and no one else knew he was in Paris. . . . I poured out a glass of brandy and took it to him. "Sire, drink this. Then you'll feel warmer." I said it very loud, and at last he raised his head and looked at me. Took in my old dressing gown and the sables he himself had given me. He swallowed the brandy in one gulp

"Do ladies in Sweden always wear fur stoles over dressing gowns?" he inquired.

"Of course not, but I was cold I am sad, and when I'm sad, I freeze. Besides, Count Rosen told you that I had already retired."

"Who?"

"My aide. Count Rosen. Come here, Count. I want to present you to His Majesty."

Count Rosen clicked his heels together The Emperor raised his glass. "Give me another brandy. I'm sure Caulaincourt wants one, too. We have a long journey behind us' He poured the whole glass of brandy down his throat. "Are you surprised to see me here, Your Highness?"

"Of course, Sire."

"Of course? But we're old friends, Highness. Very old friends, if I remember rightly. What surprises you about my visit?"

"The late hour, Sire. And the fact that you come to me unshaven."

Napoleon stroked his rough chin. A shadow of that youthful untroubled smile of the Marseilles days flitted across his slack, heavy face. "Forgive me, Highness. In the last few days I have forgotten to shave. I wanted to reach Paris as soon as possible." The suggestion of a smile vanished. "What was the effect of my last bulletin?"

"Perhaps you'll sit down, Sire?" I suggested.

"Thank you, I'd rather stand near the fire. But, please don't let it disturb you, madame. And, gentlemen, please be seated."

I sat down again on the sofa. "General Caulaincourt." I waved toward an armchair. "Count Rosen, please, here. And you must sit down, too, Marie."

"General Caulaincourt has been Duke of Vincenza for a long time," Napoleon remarked. Caulaincourt lifted his hand as though warding off my apologies. Then he fell into his chair and closed his eyes.

"May I ask, Sire—?" I began.

"No, you may not ask, madame. You most certainly may not ask anything, Mme Jean-Baptiste Bernadotte," he roared, and turned away. Count Rosen shrank back.

"I would like to know to what I owe the honour of this unexpected call, Sire," I said calmly.

"My call is no honour to you, but a disapproval. If, all your life, you hadn't been such a childish, brainless creature, you'd realize what this visit implies—Mme Jean-Baptiste Bernadotte!"

"Sit down, Count Rosen. His Majesty is apparently too tired to be courteous," I entreated my young Swede. Rosen had jumped up, and already had his hand on his sword. That would have been the last straw.

The Emperor ignored it. He came nearer and stared at the portrait above my head. The portrait of the First Consul, the portrait of the young Napoleon with the thin face, the shining eyes, and the tangled hair that hung almost to his shoulders. In a monotone he began to speak. More to the portrait than to me. "Do you know where I've come from, madame? I've come from the steppes where my soldiers lie buried. Where Murat's hussars stagger through the snow. The Cossacks have killed their horses. The men are snowblind and they whimper with pain. Do you know at all what it is, madame—snow blindness? I have come from a bridge which collapsed under Davout's grenadiers. The ice floes cracked their skulls, and the icy water turned red. At night men crawled under their dead comrades to keep warm. I have . . ."

"How can I send him this shawl?" Marie's cry cut off Napoleon's words. She leapt to her feet, rushed to the Emperor, suddenly fell on her knees before him and clutched his arm fiercely. "I am knitting a warm shawl for my Pierre. Or he can wear it over his ears, but I don't know where to send it. Your Majesty has couriers. Help a mother, Your Majesty, send a courier . . ."

Napoleon tore himself loose. His face was distorted with rage.

414

"I've written down the number of his regiment, he would be easy to find—" Marie whispered. "This shawl, this warm shawl—"

"Are you mad, woman?" Saliva oozed from the corners of Napoleon's mouth. "She asks me to send a shawl to Russia, a shawl—" He began to laugh, shook with laughter, choked with laughter, groaned with laughter. "A shawl for my hundred thousand dead, for my frozen grenadiers, a grey warm shawl for my Grand Army—" There were tears in Napoleon's eyes—from laughing.

I led Marie to the door. "Go to bed, dearest, go to bed."

Napoleon was silent, standing helplessly in the middle of the room. Then he walked with strangely stiff steps to the nearest chair and sank down into it. "Forgive me, madame, I am very tired—"

The minutes ticked away, and none of us stirred. This is the end, I thought. My thoughts wandered across a continent and over the straits to Jean-Baptiste in the royal palace in Stockholm.

A clear hard voice—"I have come to dictate to you a letter for Marshal Bernadotte, madame."

"Please have one of Your Majesty's secretaries write this letter."

"I wish you to write this letter, madame. It's a very personal letter, and not at all long. Inform the Swedish Crown Prince that we have returned to Paris to prepare the final defeat of the enemies of France."

The Emperor stood up and began pacing up and down the room, his eyes fixed on the floor as though the map of Europe were spread out on it. He tramped over this imaginary map with dirty boots. "We wish to remind the Swedish Crown Prince of the young General Bernadotte who, with his troops in the spring of 1797, rushed to the assistance of General Bonaparte. His crossing of the Alps, the most rapid crossing ever made, was the decisive factor in the victorious Italian campaign. Do you remember this, madame?"

I nodded.

The Emperor turned to Caulaincourt. "Bernadotte's classic crossing of the Alps is taught in all military colleges. A masterly achievement. Masterly . . . He brought me regiments from the Rhine Army which had fought under Moreau's command." He paused. A log on the fire cracked and dropped. Moreau, in exile. Jean-Baptiste, Crown Prince of Sweden . . .

"Remind Bernadotte first of the reinforcements he brought to me in Italy. Then of the battles in which he defended the young Republic. Finally of the song: *'Le Régiment de Sambre et Meuse, marche toujours aux cris de liberté, suivant la route glorieuse. . . .'* Write him that fourteen days ago, I heard this song in the Russian snow. Two grenadiers, who could go no farther, were digging themselves in the snow. And while they waited for the wolves, they sang this song. . . . They must have been former comrades of your husband in the Rhine Army. Don't forget to mention this incident."

My fingernails dug into my palms.

"Marshal Bernadotte advised the Tsar to secure peace in Europe by taking me prisoner during the retreat. You can tell your husband, madame, that his plan almost succeeded. But only—almost. Since I am safe in your Paris salon, madame, I myself will secure the peace of Europe. And in order finally to defeat the enemies of France— and the enemies of a permanent peace everywhere—I offer Sweden an alliance. You understand, madame?"

"Yes, Sire, you offer Sweden an alliance."

"To express myself more simply, I want Bernadotte to march with me again. Write your husband exactly that, madame."

I nodded.

"To pay for her armaments Sweden will receive from France a million francs a month. She will also receive goods to the value of six million." His eyes were fastened on young Count Rosen's face. "After the peace, Sweden will be given Finland. And Pomerania, of course."

He gestured expansively. "Write Bernadotte he is to have Finland, Pomerania, and—northern Germany from Danzig to Mecklenburg."

"Count Rosen, please get a piece of paper and write that down. It looks as though, when peace has been concluded, Sweden will have so many countries that neither of us could possibly remember them all without making a list."

"That's not necessary," Caulaincourt declared. "I have here a memorandum which His Majesty dictated to me this morning." He reached into his breast pocket and handed Rosen some closely written pages.

416

The young man skimmed them rapidly—and incredulously. "Finland?"

"We'll re-establish Sweden as a great power." Napoleon smiled at Rosen, the engaging smile of the old days. "Moreover—this will interest you as a Swede, young man. In the Kremlin archives I found a documentary record of the Russian campaign conducted by your heroic King Charles XII. I am told that in Sweden his memory is highly revered. And I wanted to learn something from this great King's success in Russia."

Count Rosen was radiant. Napoleon continued. "But unfortunately I learned that the Swedish Nation barely escaped being bled to death by his wars and impoverished by the taxes he imposed."

Napoleon smiled with bitter amusement. "Young man, I have a feeling that in the Stockholm archives, too, one can find records of the Russian venture of Charles XII. Someone has learned a great deal about it recently. Your—what do you call him?—Karl Johan. My old friend Bernadotte. . ." Napoleon shrugged his shoulders, took a deep breath, and turned on me

"Madame, you will write Bernadotte tomorrow. I must know where I stand."

So that's why he had come to see me. "You have not said, Sire, what will happen if Sweden doesn't accept this alliance?"

He didn't answer. Just looked again at his youthful portrait. "A good portrait. Did I really look like that? So—thin?"

I nodded. "By then, Sire, you had already begun to put on weight. Before, in Marseilles, for instance—you used to look desperately hungry."

"Before—in Marseilles?" He looked at me in surprise. "How do you know that, madame?"

"Yes, you did, but then . . ."

He drew his hand across his forehead. "For a moment—I had forgotten—yes, we've known each other a long time, madame."

I stood up.

"I'm tired, so terribly tired," he murmured. "I had to speak to the Crown Princess of Sweden. But you also are still Eugénie. . . ."

"Drive to the Tuileries, Sire, and have a good sleep."

"I can't, my dear. The Cossacks are on the move. And Bernadotte has established the Coalition: Russia-Sweden-England. The Austrian Ambassador in Stockholm frequently dines with Bernadotte. Do you know what that means?"

He called me Eugénie, yet seems to have forgotten I am married to this Bernadotte.

"Then what's the use of my letter, Sire?"

"Because I shall wipe Sweden off the map if Bernadotte will not march with me." He was shouting again, and then, unsteadily, he turned to go.

"You will bring your husband's answer to me personally, madame. If it should be a refusal, you part from me forever. It would no longer be possible for me to receive you at court."

I bowed. "Nor would I care to come, Sire."

Count Rosen escorted the Emperor and Caulaincourt to the door. The memorandum in Caulaincourt's neat handwriting lay on the table in front of the sofa. Finland! With an exclamation mark. And Pomerania. North Germany from Danzig to Mecklenburg. He used to appoint his marshals, now he tries to buy them. I went slowly from candelabra to candelabra, blowing out the candles.

Rosen returned. "Will Your Highness write to the Crown Prince tomorrow?"

"Yes, Count, and you will help me with the letter."

"Does Your Highness believe that the Crown Prince will answer the Emperor?"

"I am convinced of it. And it will be the last letter my husband will ever write to the Emperor." The fire in the fireplace had died down, leaving many ashes.

"I'd rather not leave Your Highness alone just now," Rosen said hesitantly.

"That's kind of you. But I am alone. Dreadfully alone, and you are too young to understand. Anyway, I'm going to Marie and comfort her."

I spent the rest of the night at Marie's bedside. I promised her I'd write to Murat and to Marshal Ney, and, of course, to Colonel Villatte, from whom I hadn't heard for weeks. I promised that in the spring I'd go with her to the Russian steppes to search for

Pierre. I promised and promised, and in her terror she was like a child and believed that I could help her.

Today special editions of the newspapers announced that His Majesty had returned unexpectedly from Russia. The health of His Majesty was never better.

Paris, end of January, 1813

At last a courier has arrived with letters from Stockholm.

"My dear Mama," Oscar writes, and his handwriting is regular and quite mature. In six months he will be fourteen. Sometimes I could scream for loneliness. His soft tanned little child's neck, the dimples in his fat little arms . . . But that was long ago. Today Oscar is a thin, awkward lad in a Swedish cadet uniform, perhaps he shaves occasionally, though this I can't imagine. . . . "My dear Mama: On January 6 we saw a wonderful performance at the Theatre Gustavus III. A famous French actress, Mlle George, who used to be in Paris at the Théâtre Français, appeared here. She played Mary Tudor, and I was with the Queen, Princess Sofia Albertina, and Papa in a box. The ladies cried because it is a frightfully sad play. I never cry at the theatre. Nor does Papa. After the play, Papa gave a supper party for Mlle George. The Queen didn't like it because Papa and the actress talked on and on about Paris and the old days. So the Queen kept interrupting the conversation, and saying 'Our dear son Karl Johan.' This made mademoiselle laugh. She finally touched the large cross of the Legion of Honour which Papa always wears, and cried: 'General Bernadotte, that I would find you again here in Stockholm, and as the son of the Queen of Sweden—I never would have believed it.' This made the Queen so angry that she sent me to bed, and retired with all the ladies. The actress drank some more coffee and liqueurs with Papa and Count Brahe. The lady-in-waiting Marianne von Koskull was so furious and jealous that she took to her bed a whole week with a cold in the head. Papa works sixteen hours every day, and looks awful ill; that theatre party for Mlle George was his first in many weeks. . . ."

I laughed. And cried a little, too, and had a great desire to spend a week in bed with a cold like Marianne von Koskull. Mlle George in Stockholm . . . Ten years ago, Josephine fussed and fumed while the First Consul played hide and seek in his study with his new sixteen-year-old mistress. Georgina, he called her, Georgina. . . . When he became Emperor, he abandoned her, because Mlle George laughs too much. "Our dear son Karl Johan." . . . I hope she laughed in the Swedish Queen's face.

Oscar had written this letter by himself without the supervision of his tutor; it folded up very small and was simply signed, "your Oscar."

My son's second letter was more studied. "A famous French authoress, exiled by the Emperor of the French because she wrote against his despotism, has arrived here, and is often received by Papa. Her name is Mme de Staël, and she calls Papa the Saviour of Europe. The lady is very fat (this word had been scratched out and "corpulent" written over it) and talks incessantly. Papa always has a headache after she has called. Papa is working sixteen hours a day, and has reorganized the Swedish Army—" Mlle George, Mme de Staël, a Russian grand duchess is waiting. . . .

Oscar's second letter was signed formally: "Your ever-loving son, Oscar, Duke of Södermanland."

I looked for a letter from Jean-Baptiste. He must have gotten my letter about Napoleon's visit and offer long ago. But I found only a few scribbled lines:

"My dearest little girl, I am overwhelmed with work, and will write more next time. Thank you for your account of the Emperor's visit. I will answer the Emperor. But I need time. My answer will not be only to him but also to the French nation and to posterity. I don't know why he wants me to send it through you. But I'll do it. I regret that you may have another difficult interview. I embrace you. Your J.-B."

A page of music fell out of the envelope. "Oscar's first composition. A Swedish folk dance. Try to play the melody. J.-B." was scrawled in the margin.

A simple melody that reminded me of a waltz. I sat right down at the piano and played it over and over. "I want to be a composer. Or a king . . ." he had said in the coach on our way from Hanover to Paris. "Why a king?" "Because a king can do so much good." Yes, Oscar, but a king must also face decisions that may break his heart, and his nation's neck. "Composer or king," my child had said . . . "Better be a king, it's easier."

I re-read Jean-Baptiste's hasty note. "My answer will not only be to him but also to the French nation and to posterity." I suddenly thought of Herr van Beethoven with the dishevelled hair: "To the memory of a hope which was not fulfilled . . ." I rang and called Count Rosen. The courier had also brought letters for him. He had a large bundle of letters in his hand "Good news from home, Count?"

"The letters are very discreet. One never knows if the French secret police will let a courier through But between the lines . . ."

"Between the lines?"

". . . I read that the Allies—Russia, England and Sweden—have asked His Royal Highness to plan the coming campaign. And Austria, represented in Stockholm by the Ambassador Count von Neipperg, is well informed, and very kindly disposed toward these plans."

So his father-in-law, too, the Austrian Emperor Francis, will fight against Napoleon.

"The occupied German territories are prepared to revolt," Count Rosen continued. "The Prussians particularly are eager to march across the Rhine, naturally."

"The Prussians are always eager to march, and always across the Rhine," I said absent-mindedly, and thought—even his father-in-law.

"The preparations for this campaign, the greatest in history, are being made secretly in Stockholm," Count Rosen whispered, his voice hoarse with excitement. "We will be a great power again. And Your Highness' son, the little Duke of Södermanland . . ."

"Oscar has sent me his first composition, I'll practice it and play it for you this evening," I said. "It's a Swedish folk dance. Why are you looking at me so oddly? Are you disappointed in my son?"

"Of course not, Your Highness. On the contrary—I was only surprised—I didn't know . . ."

"You didn't know that the Heir Apparent is musical? And you prefer to discuss the possibility that Sweden may again be a great power?"

"I was thinking of the Empire which His Royal Highness, the Crown Prince, will one day bequeath his son." His words fell over each other. "Sweden has chosen one of the greatest generals of all time to succeed to the throne. The Bernadotte Dynasty will re-establish Sweden as a great power."

"You talk like a textbook for schoolchildren, Count," I said in disgust. "The Bernadotte Dynasty—your Crown Prince will fight these battles for the people, for men's rights which we call liberty, equality and fraternity. He's fought for them since he was fifteen. That's why, at the old courts of Europe, he was privately called the Jacobin General. And later, when this is all over, and Jean-Baptiste will have won this terrible war for all Europe, they'll call him that again. Then—" I stopped, because Count Rosen looked at me uncomprehendingly. "A musician, who understands nothing of politics, once spoke of a hope which was not fulfilled," I said softly. "Perhaps this hope may yet be fulfilled, at least in Sweden. And your little country will then really be a great power, Count. But different from what you are imagining. A great power, whose kings will make no more wars, but have time to write poetry, to compose music. . . . Aren't you happy that Oscar composes?"

"Your Highness, you are the strangest woman I've ever met," exclaimed the young Count.

"You only think so because I'm the first commoner you've ever known well." I was suddenly very tired. "You've always been at court or in royal palaces. Now you are aide to a silk merchant's daughter. Try to get used to it, won't you?"

Paris, February, 1813

The letter was delivered to me at seven o'clock in the evening.

I ordered the carriage immediately, and asked Count Rosen to accompany me.

"To the Hôtel Dieu?" My Swedish coachman, unfortunately, hadn't yet learned his way around Paris.

"The Hôtel Dieu is a hospital," and because he still looked bewildered, I said, "Drive to Notre-Dame; the hospital is opposite."

The wet paving stones shimmered in many colours "I've just received a note from Colonel Villatte. He was able to get Marie's son into a load of wounded who were brought to the Hôtel Dieu. I want to take Pierre home."

"And Colonel Villatte?" Rosen asked.

"He couldn't come to Paris. He's been assigned to the Rhineland to try to assemble the survivors of his regiment."

"I am glad he's well," murmured Rosen politely.

"He's not well. He's suffering from a shoulder wound. But he hopes to see us again."

"When?"

"Sometime. When it's all over."

"An odd name—Hôtel Dieu."

"The Lord's House. A beautiful name for a hospital. The wounded used to be taken to military hospitals outside the city. But this time so few got back to Paris that military hospitals weren't needed. They simply turned over the big general hospitals."

"But there must be thousands and thousands of wounded. Where are they?"

"Why do you torment me? You've heard hundreds of times that they fell to the wolves, and their bones lie under the snow." I caught my breath.

"I beg Your Highness' pardon."

I was ashamed. One doesn't shout at an aide, aides can't talk

423

back. "The survivors were first taken to emergency hospitals in Smolensk and Wilna and other towns. Then Cossacks came and I don't know what happened to the wounded. There weren't any more wagons to bring them any farther. A few thousand are in Germany, and only one load has been brought to Paris. Somehow Villatte managed to send Pierre on this."

"What's wrong with Pierre?"

"Villatte didn't say. So I haven't told Marie anything. Well, here's the Cathedral. The hospital is to the left, coachman."

The gate was locked. Rosen pulled the bell cord. Suddenly the door opened a crack. The porter had only one arm, and I saw by his medals that he'd been wounded in the Italian campaign. "No visitors allowed," he said.

"This is Her Royal Highness . . ."

"No visitors allowed."

The door was slammed shut.

"Please knock, Count!"

Rosen knocked. He knocked loud and long. Finally it again opened a crack. I pushed Rosen aside and said quickly, "I have a permit to visit the hospital."

"Have you a special pass?" he asked skeptically.

"Yes."

We were finally admitted and found ourselves in a dark gateway lighted only by the candle in the hand of the disabled soldier. "Your pass, madame?"

"I haven't it with me. I am King Joseph's sister-in-law."

He held the candle up so that the light fell on my face.

"You will understand," I continued, "that I could have a pass at any time. But I was in such a hurry I couldn't spare the time. I've come for a wounded man," I said. And because he didn't answer, I reassured him. "I really am King Joseph's sister-in-law."

"I recognize you, madame, I have often seen you at parades. You are Marshal Bernadotte's wife."

I smiled in relief. "Have you perhaps served under my husband?"

His face didn't relax. He was silent.

"Please call someone who can show us the way to the wards," I said.

But he didn't move. The man made me uncomfortable.

"Lend us your candle, and we'll find the way ourselves," I suggested helplessly.

He handed me the candle, stepped back, and vanished in the darkness. But we heard his voice: "Marshal Bernadotte's wife," he sneered. With that he spat loudly and it spattered on the floor.

Count Rosen took the candle from me, for my hand was shaking violently. "Forget this man, we must search for Pierre," I said.

We groped our way up the broad staircase. Rosen held up the candle: a corridor with many doors. The doors were ajar. We heard moaning and sharp cries. I resolutely pushed open the first door and was assailed by a terrible stench. Blood, sweat, excrement —I rallied, and breathed deep so as not to be overcome. The moaning was close to us now, right at my feet. I took the candle from Rosen and looked down. There were beds on both sides of the room, and in the middle a row of straw mattresses. The other end of the room, where a candle and a sacred flame burned, seemed very far away. At a table with a candle sat a nun.

"Sister—"

But my voice could not be heard above the moaning and groaning. I could hardly hear the whimpering at my feet. "Water, water . . ." I lowered the candle On the straw sack lay a man with a bandaged head His mouth was wide open, and in his agony he tried to say some word, time and again. I raised my skirts so as not to brush against his poor face and groped my way forward a few steps. "Sister—" At last the nun heard me, picked up her candle and came over to us. I saw a thin expressionless face under a huge white winged cap.

"Sister, I'm looking for a wounded man named Pierre Dubois."

It didn't seem to surprise her.

"All day long women stand in front of the hospital and beg to be admitted, hoping to find their relatives or to get news of them. We let no one in. This is no sight for wives, fiancées and mothers."

"I—but I have a permit to search for Pierre Dubois," I insisted.

"We can't help you, there are so many here we don't know their names," gently, and indifferently, too.

"Then how can I find him?" I sobbed.

"I don't know," said the nun politely. "If you have a permit to search for him, you'd better search. Go from bed to bed, and perhaps you'll find him."

She turned in her soft-soled shoes and went back to her table. "Water, water—" the whimpering continued.

"Sister, can't you give the man a drink?"

She stood still. "He has a stomach wound and isn't allowed to drink. Besides, he's unconscious, the wound in his head—" She disappeared from the light thrown by my candle.

I closed my eyes for a moment. The smell of blood mingled with the stench from the pans between the beds and the sacks of straw. I shook myself. "We must go from bed to bed," I said to Rosen.

And we walked from bed to bed, from straw sack to straw sack, directing our light on every face. Irresolutely I looked down on bandaged eyes and noses, bitten, bleeding lips. Perhaps . . . No, not that one. I saw a man who hiccupped between every breath, like that General Duphot who had died in my arms many years before. I saw a smile on a waxy yellow face, and went on. The man smiled only because he had just died. His neighbour, dazzled by the light of my candle, opened his eyes wide and tried to ask me something, but I had gone on to the next one and couldn't hear his plea. This search I must spare you, Marie. This is more than a mother could bear. The bed before the last, and then the door.

Pierre was not in this ward.

We went to the next. I raised my skirt, shone the light on the face on the first straw sack, on the second, hesitated before every bandaged head, closed my eyes at the sight of a shattered chin, but forced them open again to study the face. Perhaps . . . No, definitely not Pierre.

I went on searching, searching. . . . We were nearly at the end of the room before the nun noticed us. She was still very young, her eyes were full of pity. "Are you looking for your husband, madame?" I shook my head. The light from my candle fell on an emaciated arm with a small round wound, covered with a crust. The crust moved—lice. "Wounds of this kind heal by themselves," the nun said gently, "when the soldiers get enough to eat. So many of them starved during the retreat. But perhaps you'll still find the man you're seeking, madame."

Pierre wasn't in this ward either.

In the corridor Rosen leaned suddenly against the wall. I held up the candle. Beads of sweat shone on his forehead. He turned quickly, swayed forward a few steps, and was sick. I wanted to comfort him, but that would have embarrassed him. All I could do was wait until he felt better. While I waited I noticed a sacred red flame. I went over to it slowly. It burned under a statue of the Madonna. A simple, unpretentious figure in a blue and white gown, with round red cheeks and sad eyes. The little boy in her arms was rosy and laughing. I put my candle on the floor and folded my hands. I hadn't done that for many years. The little red light flickered, from the many doors came the awful sounds. I pressed my hands together. Then I heard footsteps behind me and picked up my candle. "I humbly beg Your Highness' pardon," murmured my young Swede apologetically. I gave my Madonna one last look, her chubby face was again in shadow. We mothers, I thought, we mothers. . . .

In front of the next door, I said, "You'd better wait outside, I'll go in alone."

He hesitated. "It's my duty to stay with Your Highness until we find him," he said, a little shame-faced.

"Stay outside, Count," I said firmly, and left him.

My candle had already hovered over all the beds on the right side. At the end of the room sat an old nun reading a little black book. She, also, looked at me without surprise. "I'm looking for a certain Pierre Dubois," I said, and realized myself how hopeless my voice sounded.

"Dubois? I believe we have two Dubois here. One of them . . ." She took me by the hand and led me to a straw sack in the middle of the room. I knelt down, and my candle shone on tangled white hair, an emaciated face. His bony knuckles kneaded his stomach, his knees were drawn up, a stupefying stench rose from the straw. The nun's strong hand helped me up. "Dysentery, like most of them. They lived on snow water and raw horsemeat. Is that your Dubois?"

I shook my head.

She led me to the left bank of beds. To the last bed. At the head of the bed, I raised my candle. The dark eyes were wide open, staring at me. The swollen lips had bloody cracks. I lowered the candle. "Pierre."

He continued to stare straight ahead.

"Pierre—don't you recognize me?"

"Of course," he murmured indifferently. "Mme la maréchale."

I leaned over him. "I've come—to get you. We're taking you home, Pierre. Now. To your mother."

His face showed no emotion.

"Pierre—aren't you glad to go home?"

No answer.

I turned, perplexed, to the nun. "That's my Pierre Dubois. The one I was looking for. I want to take him home and get him well. His mother is waiting for him there. I have a carriage. Perhaps someone will help me—"

"The porters have all gone home. You must wait until tomorrow, madame."

But I didn't want to leave Pierre there another minute. "Is he very badly wounded? My ai—a gentleman is waiting for me outside the ward. Together we could help Pierre Dubois, if he can just manage the stairs . . ."

The nun lifted my hand, in which I held the candle. The light fell on the blanket. Where Pierre's legs should have been, it was flat. Quite flat. "I have a coachman downstairs who can help me," I said quietly. "I'll be right back, Sister."

A figure swayed out from the wall near the door. "Ask our coachman to come up, Count. He must carry Pierre down to the carriage. Here, take my candle. And bring all the robes we have in the carriage."

Then I waited. No more and never again will he walk, I thought. And so it is in the Dear Lord's House. One learns how to pray, another gives up. The whole world seemed like this Dear Lord's House. And we've made the world what it is. We, the mothers of sons, and you the sons of mothers.

Their footsteps echoed. I met Rosen and the coachman as they came into the ward. "Please help us, Sister, we must wrap him up warmly. And Johansson—" I nudged the coachman and he stepped forward. "And Johansson will carry him down."

The Sister lifted Pierre's shoulders, he couldn't resist. His eyes burned with hatred "Leave me in peace, madame, leave me alone—" The nun flung back the bed covering. I shut my eyes and held up my candle for her When I opened my eyes again, Pierre Dubois lay in front of me like a wrapped-up package.

That's how I brought Marie's son home to her.

Paris, beginning of April, 1813

In half an hour, I shall speak to him for the last time in my life, I thought, and put some silver paint on my eyelids.

Then this long relationship, which began as first love, will be over. . . . I painted my lips with deep red, and put on my new hat, a high tight-fitting hat, which ties under my chin with a rose bow and which I wasn't sure was becoming to me. I studied myself a long time in the mirror. So this was how he would remember me: a crown princess with silver eyelids, a violet velvet costume, a bouquet of pale violets in the low V-neck. And a new hat with a rose-coloured bow.

I heard Count Rosen in the next room ask La Flotte if I'd ever be ready. I rearranged my violets. In half an hour my personal association with my first love would be over. . . . Yesterday evening a courier from Stockholm brought me Jean-Baptiste's answer to Napoleon. The letter was sealed, but Count Brahe had enclosed an exact copy for me. Count Brahe also informed me that a copy of Jean-Baptiste's letter to Napoleon had been given all the newspapers.

I stood up and for the last time read the copy. "The sufferings of the Continent make peace imperative, and Your Majesty cannot refuse this demand for peace without increasing tenfold the sum of the crimes you have already committed. What benefits has France derived which could possibly compensate her for her enormous sacrifices? She has gained nothing but military glory and superficial fame, while misery exists everywhere within her borders. . . ."

And I'm to deliver this letter to Napoleon. Things like this only happen to me. My heart beat faster, as I read on:

"I was born in the beautiful country of France which is under your rule. Her honour and well-being can never be a matter of indifference to me. But without ceasing to pray for the prosperity and happiness of France, I shall always, to the best of my ability, defend that Nation which elected me Crown Prince, and the sovereign who adopted and recognized me as his son. In this conflict between world tyranny and freedom, I shall say to the Swedes: I am fighting with you, and for you, and all freedom-loving peoples will bless our struggle. As to my personal ambitions, I declare to you that I am ambitious, very ambitious. But my ambitions are to serve mankind, and to achieve and maintain the independence of the Scandinavian Peninsula."

This letter, addressed by Jean-Baptiste not only to Napoleon but also to the French nation, ended on a personal note: "Regardless of the outcome, whether you decide for peace or war, Sire, I shall always retain for Your Majesty the regard of a former comrade in arms."

I put the copy back on the night table. Count Rosen was waiting. I had been told to be at the Tuileries at five o'clock in the afternoon. In the next few days the Emperor and his new army leaves for the front. Russia is on the move, Prussia has joined with Russia. Napoleon made up his mind long ago. I picked up the sealed letter and straightened my hat.

Count Rosen wore the dress uniform of the Swedish dragoons and his aide's sash. "You accompany me on difficult missions, Count," I said as the carriage rolled over the Pont Royal. Since that night at the hospital, there's been a strange comradeship between us. Probably because I was there when he was sick. Somehow these things bring people close together.

We drove in the open carriage, the air smelled of spring, and the blue dusk softened the outlines of everything around us. Now one should have a rendezvous, a fleeting, secret rendezvous for which to wear violets and buy a new hat. Instead, I had to hand the Emperor of the French a letter destined for posterity from the Crown Prince of Sweden, and bring on a Napoleonic outburst of rage. A waste of this lovely twilight.

We didn't have to wait a minute. The Emperor received us in his large study. Caulaincourt and Méneval were there Count Talleyrand was over at the window and didn't turn until I was halfway to the big desk. Napoleon had no intention of sparing my spurclanking Rosen and me the well-known long, painful walk from the door to his desk. Napoleon wore the green Chasseur uniform, and with folded arms stood in front of the desk, leaning back on it, and watched me with a slightly sneering smile. I bowed, and without a word handed him the sealed letter.

The sealing wax cracked. The Emperor read it without betraying any emotion. He handed the sheets of paper, thick with Jean-Baptiste's handwriting, to Méneval. "A copy for the archives of the Foreign Ministry, the original to be kept with my private papers" And to me, "You're all dressed up, Highness. Violet suits you. But what a peculiar hat. Are high hats in style these days?"

This was worse than the outburst of fury I had expected. It was ridicule, ridicule not only of me, but also the Crown Prince of Sweden. I pressed my lips firmly together.

Napoleon turned to Talleyrand. "You know something about beautiful women, Excellency. How do you like the new hat of the Crown Princess of Sweden?"

Talleyrand kept his eyes half-closed. He seemed unutterably bored. Napoleon turned again to me.

"Have you made yourself so beautiful for me, Your Highness?"

"Yes, Sire."

"And wore violets to bring me this—" he snorted through his nose—"this scrap of paper from the former Marshal Bernadotte? Violets, madame, bloom in obscurity, and smell sweet. But this treachery, over which the English and Russian newspapers are already rejoicing, stinks to high heaven, madame!"

I bowed. "May I ask leave to withdraw, Sire?"

"You not only may withdraw, madame, you absolutely must withdraw," he roared. "Or did you think I would allow you to come and go freely at court? While Bernadotte is at war with me? And gives orders to fire on the regiments he himself has led in countless battles? And you, madame, dare come here—wearing violets . . ."

"Sire, the night of your return from Russia, you urged me to write to my husband and to bring you his answer myself. I have read a copy of his letter, Sire, and I'm sure you are seeing me for the last time. I wore violets because they look well on me. Perhaps you'll have a pleasant memory of me, Sire. May I now—for always —withdraw?"

There was a pause. A dreadfully painful pause. Count Rosen stood, stiff as a statue, behind me. Ménéval and Caulaincourt stared at the Emperor in astonishment. Talleyrand actually opened his eyes. Napoleon was definitely disconcerted, and looked around uneasily. "The gentlemen will wait here. I want to speak to Her Highness a moment alone," he said finally. "Please come with me to my study, Your Highness." He indicated the wallpapered door. "Ménéval, pour the gentlemen some brandy."

I saw Ménéval open a wall cupboard, then went into the same room where years before I had pleaded in vain for the life of the Duke of Enghien. The room was practically unchanged. The same small tables, the same piles of documents. Only probably different documents. On the carpet in front of the fireplace lay wooden blocks in various colours. The blocks were notched. Without thinking, I bent over and picked up a red one. "What's this? A toy for the King of Rome?"

"Yes—and no. I use these blocks when I'm planning a campaign. Each one represents a certain army corps. And the notches indicate the divisions at the disposal of each corps. The red block you have in your hand is the Third Army Corps—Marshal Ney's. It has five notches, that is, Ney's corps consists of five divisions. And here— the blue block with three notches is Marmont's Sixth Army Corps with three divisions. When I lay out these blocks on the floor, I can clearly visualize a battle, I have the map in my head. It's really very simple—"

"But do you also chew on the little blocks?" I'd noticed with surprise that a piece of wood had been bitten off the block in my hand.

"No, that's the little King of Rome. As soon as he's brought in here he gets out the bright little blocks; he knows where I keep them. Then, together, we build them up, my little eagle and I. And sometimes he gnaws one of them. God knows why. Mostly he chews on the corps of the worthy Ney."

I put the red block of wood back on the floor.

"You wanted to say something to me, Sire? I refuse to discuss, with Your Majesty, His Royal Highness, the Crown Prince of Sweden."

"Who wants to talk about Bernadotte," he said irritably. "It wasn't that, Eugénie, it was only—" He came close to me and stared at my face, as if he wanted to impress each feature on his memory. "Only when you said you hoped I would have pleasant memories of you, that you were saying farewell forever, I thought—" He turned away brusquely, and went to the window. "People can't part like that when they've known each other so long. Can they?"

I stood in front of the fireplace, the tips of my shoes toying with the coloured blocks of wood. Corps Ney, Corps Marmont, Corps Bernadotte? No, there is no such corps any more. Instead, he has an army, a whole army, made up of Swedish, Russian and Prussian troops. The Army Bernadotte fighting on the other side. . . .

"I said that one can't part like that, without further explanation," came from the window.

"Why not, Sire?"

"Why not? Eugénie! Have you forgotten the days in Marseilles? The hedge, the meadow? Our talks about Goethe's novel? Our youth, Eugénie, our youth. . . . You didn't understand at all why I came to you. The evening I got back from Russia. I was so terribly cold, I was so tired and so alone, and . . ."

"While you were dictating the letter to Jean-Baptiste, you had completely forgotten that you had known me as Eugénie Clary. You came to see the Crown Princess of Sweden, Sire."

I was sad. Even at our parting, he was lying, I thought.

But he shook his head emphatically. "I had been thinking about Bernadotte. That very morning. But when I reached Paris, I longed

433

to see you, only you. And then—I don't know how—I was so tired that evening, as soon as we mentioned Bernadotte I forgot Marseilles again. Can't you understand?"

It was dark. No one came to light the candles. I could no longer distinguish his features. What did he want?

"In these last weeks I have organized a new army of two hundred thousand men. By the way, England has promised Sweden one million pounds to pay for the equipment of Bernadotte's troops. Did you know that, madame?"

I didn't answer. Besides, I hadn't known it.

"Do you know who advised Bernadotte to give copies of his letter to me to the enemy press? Mme de Staël is with him in Stockholm. In the evening, she probably reads her novels to him. Did you know that, madame?"

Yes—I knew it; it doesn't matter, why does he bring it up.

"Bernadotte seems not to have found a more delectable companion."

"Yes, he has, Sire." I laughed. "Mlle George gave a command performance with great success in Stockholm and enjoyed the benevolence of His Royal Highness. Did you know that, Sire?"

"My God, Georgina, sweet little Georgina. . . ."

"His Royal Highness will soon be seeing his old friend Moreau again. Moreau is returning to Europe to fight under Jean-Baptiste's command. Did you know that, Sire?"

How lucky that the darkness lay like a wall between us.

"They say the Tsar has promised Bernadotte the crown of France," Napoleon said slowly.

That sounds mad, but it's possible. If Napoleon were defeated then—yes, then what?

"Well, madame? If Bernadotte should even play with this thought, it would be the blackest treachery ever perpetrated by a Frenchman."

"Naturally. A traitor to his own convictions. May I withdraw now, Sire?"

"If you should ever feel in personal danger in Paris, madame—I mean, if people should molest you, you must immediately seek refuge with your sister Julie. Will you promise me that?"

434

"Yes, of course. And the other way around."

"What do you mean—'the other way around'?"

"That my house is always open to Julie. That's why I'm staying in Paris."

"You, too, are reckoning on my defeat, Eugénie?" He came very close to me. "Your violets have a bewitching fragrance. . . . I should have you put out. You probably tell everyone that the Emperor will be defeated. Besides, it doesn't please me to have you go driving with that tall Swede"

"But he is my aide. I must always take him with me."

"Your mama would have disapproved. And your strict brother Etienne." He took my hand and laid it against his cheek

"Today, Sire, you have at least shaved," I said and drew my hand away.

"What a pity you're married to Bernadotte," he murmured. I groped toward the door "Eugénie!"

But I already stood in the light of the large study. The gentlemen sat around the desk, drinking brandy. Talleyrand had apparently just made a witty remark, for Méneval, Caulaincourt and my Swede were shaking with laughter.

"Let us share the joke," the Emperor said.

"We were saying that the Senate has agreed to the calling up of 250,000 recruits for the new army," Méneval said, and nearly collapsed with laughter.

"And if it goes on for two years, they'll be called up younger and younger and the recruits for the years 1814 and 1815 will be mere children," Caulaincourt continued. "The Prince of Bénévent, therefore, suggested an armistice of at least one day each year so that Your Majesty's new army can be confirmed."

The Emperor also laughed. It didn't sound entirely real. The recruits are now Oscar's age. "That isn't funny, it's sad," I said, and bowed for the last time. This time the Emperor escorted me right to the door. We didn't say another word to each other.

On the drive home, I asked Rosen if the Tsar really had offered Jean-Baptiste the French crown.

"In Sweden, that's an open secret. Did the Emperor know about it?"

I nodded.

"What else did he talk about?" Rosen asked shyly.

I thought back. Suddenly I yanked off my violet corsage and flung it out of the carriage. "About violets, Count—only about violets."

That very same evening a small parcel from the Tuileries was delivered to my house. The lackey said that it was for the Crown Prince of Sweden. I opened it and found a small gnawed block of wood. Green, with five notches. When I see Jean-Baptiste again, I'll give it to him.

Paris, summer, 1813

The coachman has carried Pierre into the garden. I am sitting at the window watching Marie bring her son a glass of lemonade. Bees buzz around the rosebushes, and there's also the sound of marching feet as the regiments pass the house. In step, always in step. . . .

Napoleon had gold bars that he'd hidden in the cellars of the Tuileries—said to be worth one hundred and forty million francs —melted down to pay for the equipment of his new regiments. How absurd that I once had to lend him my saved-up pocket money. A hundred and forty million . . . Then I wanted so much to buy him a proper general's uniform!

Of course that was long ago. Meanwhile, the sons of France have perished in Russia, and the children of France, the 1814 and 1815 recruits, are marching to war. A great many of these have been taken into the newly organized guard regiments. The Emperor assumes that every lad in France dreams of belonging to the guards. But since battles can't be fought by children who have never even seen maneuvers, the Emperor has simply assigned gunners from the Navy to the Infantry. On the Elbe the last horses still to be found on the farms of the peasants are being requisitioned, and hitched to gun carriages and wagons. Where is he getting horses for the

436

cavalry? Every French town has been ordered to send the Emperor a company of volunteers. Paris has equipped an entire regiment. Ten thousand guardsmen have paid for their own equipment. And because of the shortage of experienced fighters, the gendarmerie is sending three thousand of their number to the front as officers and noncommissioned officers. The mood of the people reminds me of the days of the young Republic when it was a question of life or death to defend our frontiers however we could. This time, too, one feels that in reality the danger extends only to our frontiers. But now children are being called up, children sing "La Marseillaise," while on every street corner one sees disabled soldiers, and the hospitals are always overcrowded. The women, with their market baskets, look grey and tired. Sleepless nights, unbearable anxiety, waiting, reunions and farewells have robbed them of the best years of their lives.

Below, in my garden—yes, Pierre has finished his lemonade. Marie has put the glass on the lawn, and she sits beside her son. Her arm supports his back. His frost-bitten left leg was amputated at the hip. We hope a wooden leg can be attached to the stump of his right, which was amputated above the knee, when the wound heals. But the wound won't heal. When Marie changes the bandages, Pierre howls in pain like an animal. I have given him Oscar's room, and Marie sleeps there with him. But I must find him a room on the ground floor, it's too difficult always carrying him up and down the stairs.

Talleyrand called on me earlier this evening. Apparently only to inquire if I didn't feel too lonely. "I would have been alone anyway this summer," I told him. "I am, unfortunately, used to having my husband at the front."

Talleyrand nodded. "Yes—at the front. Under other circumstances, Your Highness would be alone, but—not lonely."

I shrugged my shoulders. We sat in the garden, and La Flotte served us chilled champagne. Talleyrand told me that Fouché has a new post. Governor of Illyria. Illyria is an Italian state which the Emperor has just set up especially for Fouché. "The Emperor can no longer afford intrigues in Paris," Talleyrand declared. "And Fouché always intrigues."

"And you—isn't the Emperor afraid of you, Excellency?"

"Fouché intrigues to win power or to hold it. I, on the other hand, my dear Highness, want nothing but the well-being of France."

I saw the first star twinkle in the blue velvet sky. It was still so hot one could hardly breathe.

"How quickly our allies drop away," Talleyrand remarked between sips of champagne. "First the Prussians, who, by the way, are under your husband's supreme command. Your husband has established his headquarters in Stralsund, and commands the Allies' northern armies."

I nodded. Rosen had told me that. "I read in the *Moniteur*," I said finally, "that the Emperor of Austria is trying to negotiate an armistice between France and Russia."

Talleyrand held out his empty glass to Mme la Flotte. "Austria is negotiating to gain time to rearm."

"But the Austrian Emperor is the father of our Empress," said Mme la Flotte sharply.

Talleyrand ignored her. "If France is defeated, all the allied states will try to enrich themselves at our expense. Austria naturally doesn't want to be left out, so she's joining the Allies."

My mouth was dry. I had to swallow hard before I could speak. "The Austrian Emperor can't make war on his own daughter and his grandson."

"No? My dear Highness, he's already at war with them." Talleyrand smiled. "It's not yet appeared in the *Moniteur*, madame."

I didn't stir. Talleyrand's amiable voice continued. "The Allies have eight hundred thousand men under arms, and the Emperor about half that."

"But His Majesty is a genius," said Mme la Flotte with trembling lips. It sounded like a phrase learned by heart.

Talleyrand again held out an empty glass. "Quite right, madame —His Majesty is a genius."

Mme la Flotte filled his glass.

"Moreover, the Emperor has forced our allies, the Danes, to declare war on Sweden. Your husband, therefore, has the Danes at his back, Highness," Talleyrand continued pleasantly.

"He'll take care of that," I said impatiently, and thought—I must find something for Pierre to do, a real occupation. That's most important. "Did you say something, Your Excellency?"

"Only that the day may come when I shall ask a favour of you." Talleyrand stood up.

"If you see my sister, Your Excellency, give her my love. Julie can't come here any more. King Joseph has forbidden her."

Up shot his thin eyebrows. "I also miss your two faithful aides, Your Highness."

"Colonel Villatte has been on active duty for a long time, he was in Russia. And Count Rosen . "

"The tall blond Swede, I remember."

". . . told me a few days ago that, as a Swedish nobleman, he felt he must fight at the side of his crown prince."

"Nonsense. He's just jealous of Count Brahe, his personal aide-de-camp," Mme la Flotte declared

"No, he meant what he said. The Swedes are a very serious people, madame. Ride with God and come back safe and sound, I told him. Just as I told Villatte. . . . You're right, Excellency—I am very lonely."

I watched him limp away. Talleyrand limps so gracefully, so elegantly. At the same time I decided to entrust Pierre with the management of my household affairs.

I think that's a good idea.

Paris, November, 1813

At night fear takes me by the throat, for I am all alone with it. Whenever I go to sleep, I have the same dream. Jean-Baptiste rides alone across a battlefield, on which a battle was fought two

439

weeks before. Like the one I saw on my way to Marienburg. Mounds of loose earth, dead horses with bloated bellies, and deep craters where cannon balls had fallen. Jean-Baptiste rides a white horse, like that I've seen him riding at parades. He leans forward in the saddle. I cannot see his face, but I sense that he is sobbing. The horse stumbles over a fresh mound of earth. Jean-Baptiste falls to the ground and doesn't get up.

For over a week it's been rumoured in Paris that a decisive battle was fought at Leipzig. No one knows the details. Marie tells me that at the baker's they believe everything hinges on this battle. How do these women shoppers find out what's happening? Perhaps they, too, lie sleepless in their beds at night, or are haunted by bad dreams.

At first, I thought the horses I heard were part of my dream. I opened my eyes, my night light had almost burned down and I could see my clock only indistinctly. Four-thirty in the morning. A horse neighed. I sat up and listened. There came a cautious knock at the front door. So gentle, I was sure no one else heard it.

I got up, put on my dressing gown and went downstairs. In the front hall my night light went out. Again a knock—very light—so as not to frighten anyone.

"Who's there?"

"Villatte," and at practically the same time, "Rosen."

I pushed back the heavy bolt. In the light of the big lantern that hangs above the door, I distinguished two figures.

"Where have you come from?"

"From Leipzig," Villatte said.

"With messages from His Highness," Rosen added.

I went back into the hall, and, shivering, wrapped my dressing gown more tightly around me. Rosen felt his way to a candelabra and lighted a candle. Villatte had disappeared, presumably to take the horses to the stable. Rosen wore the coat and bearskin cap of a French grenadier.

"A strange uniform for a Swedish dragoon," I remarked.

"Our troops are not yet in France. His Highness told me to wear this comic coat and ridiculous cap so that I could cross the lines without trouble."

I was annoyed. "Do you think the bearskin cap of a grenadier really so funny?"

Just then Villatte returned. "We've been riding day and night," he said. His face was dirty and drawn and his unshaven beard was blue-black. He spoke indistinctly. "Besides, the decisive battle has been lost."

"Has been won—His Highness himself stormed Leipzig," Rosen declared passionately. "At the same moment His Highness entered Leipzig through the Grimma Gate, Napoleon fled from the city. His Highness fought at the head of his troops—from beginning to end."

"And why aren't you with the fleeing French Army, Colonel Villatte?"

"I am a prisoner of war, Your Highness."

"Rosen's prisoner?"

A ghost of a smile flitted over Villatte's face. "Well—that is—yes. His Highness didn't have me marched off to the prison barracks with the others, but ordered me to ride to Paris immediately to be with Your Highness until—" He gulped.

"Until?"

"Until the enemy troops enter Paris."

So that's how it is. A lonely horseman rides across a battlefield at night and weeps. "Come, gentlemen, we'll go out to the kitchen. I'll make some coffee."

"I'll wake the cook, Your Highness."

"Why, Count Rosen? I make very good coffee. Perhaps you'll be good enough to light the fire in the hearth."

Rosen clumsily pushed a few logs onto the hearth. These aristocrats, these aristocrats. . . . "Kindling first, Count, or it won't burn. Help him, Villatte. I don't think the Count has ever in his life had anything to do with a hearth."

Villatte made the fire, and I put on a kettle of water. The three of us sat down at the kitchen table and waited. The boots, the hands, and the faces of both men were spattered with mud. "The battle was fought on the seventeenth and eighteenth of October. On the morning of the nineteenth, Bernadotte stormed Leipzig," said Villatte quietly.

"Is Jean-Baptiste well? Did you see him yourself, Villatte? Is he well?"

"Very well. I saw him with my own eyes in the midst of the worst fighting—at the gates of Leipzig. It was really a terrible battle, madame, and Bernadotte was throughout extremely well."

"Did you speak to him, Villatte?"

"Yes—afterward. After the defeat, madame."

"The victory, Colonel Villatte. I won't allow—" Count Rosen's youthful voice cracked.

"How did he look, Villatte? I mean—afterward?"

Villatte shrugged his shoulders and stared into the pale oil light on the kitchen table. I got up and made the coffee. Then I set the table with the servants' heavy cups and saucers and poured it out. "Villatte, what did he look like?"

"His hair has turned grey, madame."

The coffee tasted bitter, I had forgotten the sugar. I jumped up to look for the sugar bowl. I was suddenly ashamed because I no longer knew my way around my own pantry. Finally I found the sugar and set it on the table.

"Your Highness makes wonderful coffee," said Rosen in awe.

"My husband says so, too. I always used to make black coffee for him when he worked through the night. Tell me everything you know, Count."

"If only I knew where to begin, so much has happened. I caught up with His Highness at Trachtenburg Castle. And I was there when His Highness explained his plan of campaign to the Tsar of Russia, the Emperor of Austria and the allied General Staff. The two Emperors and their generals studied the maps. But His Highness didn't need any notes. While he spoke he stared at the opposite wall, and was yet able to name tiny villages and little-known hills. His Highness' plan was unanimously accepted without discussion. His Highness suggested dividing the allied troops into three armies, which were to attack Napoleon in a half-circle. As soon as Napoleon moved toward one of the armies, the other two were to attack his flanks and cut off his line of retreat. Someone said to His Highness, 'The plan of a genius,' at which His Highness answered, 'Yes, but not original, it's based on Napoleon's tactics.' "

I poured out more coffee. A clock struck half-past five. "Go on," I urged him.

"His Highness himself commanded the Northern Army, with headquarters first in Stralsund. Then we took Berlin, and His Highness lived in Charlottenburg."

"What did His Highness say when you suddenly appeared?"

Rosen was embarrassed. "To be honest—His Highness was furious and shouted at me that he could win the war without me. And —that I should have stayed in Paris with Your Highness."

"Of course you should have stayed," Colonel Villatte said.

"What about you? You rode off, too, didn't you, to be on the spot?" Rosen parried.

"No, no, not just to be there—but to defend France. Besides, Her Highness isn't my Crown Princess, but yours. But it doesn't matter now, does it?"

"From Berlin, His Highness went to Grossbeeren where he fought his first important action. We were first attacked by Oudinot's artillery. Then Kellermann's hussars tried to break through our lines. Behind them marched an infantry division. . . ."

"Dupas' Division, madame," Villatte remarked. "Fine regiments which served for years under Bernadotte."

How had Jean-Baptiste stood it, how could he have . . .

"Then His Highness gave the order for the Cossacks to attack. They hurled themselves against the French flank—and all hell broke loose. The enemy knew on which hill His Highness was stationed. Cannon balls fell all around us. But His Highness sat motionless on his horse hour after hour, madame. In the valley below bayonets and sabres flashed while above it all the French eagles fluttered, until finally everything was obscured by clouds of smoke. One could no longer see at all, but His Highness seemed to know exactly what was happening and continued to issue orders without hesitation. Not until the Cossacks stormed the city did he order our heavy artillery to fire." Rosen stopped for breath.

"Go on," I begged.

He drew his hand across his forehead. "It began to rain. I put a cape around His Highness' shoulders, but His Highness shook it off. It had turned cool, but there were beads of sweat on His High-

ness' forehead. Toward evening, the French at last retreated. Afterward—yes, afterward, His Highness rode from one regiment to another and thanked the men. Count Brahe and I were with him.
Near the tent of the Prussian General von Bülow we saw the French
prisoners of war. Several thousand, standing at attention. The Prussians always make their prisoners stand at attention. When His
Highness saw the prisoners, he stiffened and looked as though he
wanted to turn back. But then, his lips grimly tight, he rode toward
them. He rode slowly down the line of prisoners, looking each man
in the face. Once he stopped, and assured the Frenchman nearest
him that he would see that prisoners were well treated. The man
didn't answer. His Highness rode on, but he appeared to be suddenly dead tired. He slumped forward in the saddle. Not until he
saw the eagle, did he change."

"What happened when Bernadotte saw the eagle?" Villatte asked
harshly.

"Prince von Bülow had ordered the captured flags and eagles set
up in front of his tent. It was a Prussian gesture, on his own in-
itiative. His Highness had given no specific orders on captured flags
or insignia. So the Prussians had laid them neatly in front of their
general's tent, and there they gleamed in the light of the campfires.
When His Highness saw the eagles, he stopped and dismounted.
He went right up to the eagles and saluted and stood at attention.
Two minutes, three minutes. Finally he turned abruptly away, and
rode back to his headquarters."

"And then?"

"I don't know. His Highness went to his tent, and gave orders to
admit no one. Not even Brahe. I think Fernand took him a cup of
soup."

I poured out some more coffee.

"His Highness had, of course, known all along that the decisive
battle would be at Leipzig," Rosen said, "where the three Allied
armies were to meet. The Tsar, the Austrian Emperor and the King
of Prussia were waiting for the Northern Army. On Monday, October eighteenth, His Highness had our cannon placed in position,
and the town of Schönefeld was assaulted. Schönefeld was defended
by French and Saxon regiments under Marshal Ney's command."

I tried to catch Villatte's eye. Villatte, tired Villatte, smiled. "As you see, madame, the Emperor chose his best troops to oppose Bernadotte. The Saxons, naturally, were among them. The Emperor hadn't forgotten that Bernadotte said the Saxons held like men of iron. Count Rosen, how did the Saxons stand at Leipzig?"

"If I hadn't seen it with my own eyes, Your Highness, I wouldn't have believed it. Fantastic! Before the battle began, His Highness disappeared into his tent, and appeared a little later in his parade uniform."

"Not in his field uniform?"

"No. For the first time during the entire campaign he wore his parade uniform: violet velvet coat, conspicuous from afar, and white ostrich plumes on his three-cornered hat. Not content with that, His Highness asked also for a white horse. Then he signalled to attack, spurred his white horse and galloped straight toward the enemy lines, that is, toward the Saxon regiments. And the regiments . . ."

"The regiments stood firm as iron. Not a shot was fired," laughed Villatte.

"No, not a shot. Brahe and I galloped after him. Right in front of the Saxons, His Highness reined in his horse. The Saxons presented arms. 'Vive Bernadotte!' one of them cried, and 'Vive Bernadotte!' rose in chorus. His Highness raised his baton, turned his white horse, and rode back. Behind him marched the Saxons in parade step, led by their regimental band. Twelve thousand men and forty cannon came over to us."

"And what did Jean-Baptiste say?"

"His Highness gave a brief order telling his men where to place the cannon," Rosen said. "During the battle, His Highness sat again hour after hour on his horse. From time to time, Adlercreutz, beside him, offered him a field glass, but His Highness refused it. 'I know what's happening, I know. . . . Now the Corps Regnier is falling back. Have Schönefeld occupied immediately.' And later, 'Ney has very little ammunition left, his artillery is firing only every five minutes—the guards are trying to hold out, they won't succeed —they are now seeking cover in the city of Leipzig. . . .' Early that night, His Highness suddenly declared, 'The Emperor is with his Fourth Corps. You see all those watch fires, Adlercreutz? That's where Napoleon is giving orders for the night positions.' His Highness didn't dismount until the last cannon was silent. He walked over to a campfire and warmed his hands. Suddenly he demanded the dark-blue greatcoat of his field uniform, and a three-cornered hat without plumes or insignia and a fresh horse. 'A dark horse,' he added. As he mounted, Brahe asked him if he should accompany him. His Highness looked at him blankly as if he'd never seen him before. 'Fernand is coming with me,' he murmured. Brahe was deeply hurt. Fernand is, after all, only a valet, and . . ."

"Nonsense, Fernand was Jean-Baptiste's schoolmate," I said. "Jean-Baptiste got expelled from school on his account. But what happened that night?"

"His Highness and Fernand rode off. I don't know where. They returned at dawn. Sentries saw His Highness pass, and once he dismounted and walked a bit, while Fernand held the horses. His Highness sat down beside a man who had fallen, and held his head in his lap. A sentry heard him speak to the man—the man was dead. His Highness probably didn't realize it. Next morning the sentry went to look at the dead man. He was a Frenchman."

"And—next morning?"

"We knew that His Highness had suggested to the three other sovereigns that Leipzig be stormed by his troops. The Austrian Emperor, the Tsar of Russia, and the King of Prussia were each on a separate hill, watching through their field glasses, and—by God, we did it."

Villatte, staring off into space, took up the story. "Bernadotte, at the head of his troops, stormed the so-called Grimma Gate of Leipzig. We had strong infantry positions in front of the gate, but Bernadotte had his attack covered with heavy artillery. Once more in full regalia, he himself galloped forward with his Swedish dragoons. Our French infantry hurled itself against the enemy, slashing the horses with bayonets. So then the Swedes fought on foot, with their sabres, and, madame, it was a battle such as I have never seen. Man against man, Bernadotte on his white horse, always in the middle of it all, with his white ostrich plumes, and his sabre."

"His sabre?"

"In the scabbard. He held only his field marshal's baton in his hand."

"Think of it, Villatte!"

"Finally the French fell back—put to rout," Rosen said.

"No, we were ordered to retreat," Villatte corrected Rosen. "In five days we had fired two hundred and twenty thousand rounds, and had ammunition for only sixteen thousand more. That was the only reason the Emperor ordered the retreat," said Villatte heatedly.

"When the city was stormed I saw no cannon at all. Only infantry, and we drove back the infantry," cried Rosen triumphantly.

"The infantry you saw at the Grimma Gate was there only to cover the retreat," Villatte explained quietly. "The Emperor . . ."

"Your Emperor fled through the West Gate when His Highness entered Leipzig," Rosen insisted loudly.

"The last sixteen thousand shots were fired at Bernadotte's troops. Bernadotte took Leipzig by storm with eighty-six battalions of infantry, and thirty-nine cavalry regiments."

Rosen looked surprised. "Where did you get this information, Colonel Villatte?"

Villatte shrugged his shoulders. "May I have some more coffee?"

"The pot is on the hearth, Colonel. And after that, Count Rosen?"

"His Highness rode to the market square in Leipzig and waited for the other three sovereigns. He had told them in Trachtenberg he would see them next in the market square of Leipzig, so—there he sat on his white horse and waited. . . . By chance, the French prisoners were led past him. His Highness' eyes were half-closed, I thought he wasn't watching the prisoners. But suddenly he raised his baton, and pointed at a colonel. 'Villatte, come here, Villatte.' "

"I stepped out of the ranks, madame," Villatte said, "and that's how we met again. 'Villatte, what are you doing here?' he asked. 'I'm defending France, Marshal,' I answered, and I purposely called him Marshal in a loud voice. 'Then I must tell you that you are defending France very badly, Villatte,' Bernadotte said. 'Moreover, I expected you to stay with my wife in Paris.' 'The Marshal's wife herself sent me to the front,' I said, and he didn't answer. I stood beside his horse and watched my fellow prisoners march by. Finally I thought he had forgotten me, and wanted me to leave him. But as

447

soon as I moved, Bernadotte leaned down from his horse and grabbed my shoulder. 'Colonel Villatte, you are a prisoner of war. I order you to return to Paris without delay and to take up your residence in my wife's house. Give me your word of honour as a French officer that you will not desert my wife until . . .' "

"Until?"

" 'Until I myself get there.' Those were his words. I gave him my word of honour."

I lowered my eyes. Heard Rosen's voice, "With that His Highness turned to me. 'And here's the second faithful aide to Her Highness. Count Rosen, you will accompany Colonel Villatte on his ride to Paris!' 'In my Swedish uniform?' I asked in horror. 'The allies have not yet officially marched into France.' His Highness looked at Villatte. 'Colonel, you will be responsible to me for Rosen's safe arrival in Paris, and for arranging with the proper civil authorities his right of asylum in my wife's home. And you, Rosen, are responsible for guarding our prisoner of war.' "

It all seemed very complicated to me. "Who is whose prisoner?" I asked.

Neither of them heard me. Villatte continued. " 'Then I must get him a French uniform, or I can't get him safely through our lines, Marshal,' I told Bernadotte. 'Put a bearskin cap on his head, Villatte, and you, Count Rosen, wear the bearskin cap with pride.' And before we could say any more, Bernadotte commanded, 'Forward march—au revoir, Count, au revoir, Villatte.' "

"I found a horse for Villatte, and he got me a French uniform. We had a hurried meal and rode off. We've been on the way ever since, and now—well, now we're here," Rosen concluded.

A clock struck half-past six.

"Our troops tried to escape across the Elster. That's how Marshal Pontiatowsky was drowned."

"And the Emperor?"

Villatte shrugged. "He hopes at least to hold the frontier on the Rhine. If that fails, he'll at least defend Paris."

I leaned my elbow on the kitchen table and put my hands over my eyes. The frontier on the Rhine. . . . Just as, years ago, Frenchmen answered the call to arms to hold the frontier on the Rhine. How gallantly they had held it. Jean-Baptiste was a general then.

Someone swaggered into the kitchen, shouting, "Thunderation! Without my permission, no one's allowed in my kitchen . . . Oh— I beg your pardon, Highness."

I straightened up. My fat cook stood before me. A frightened kitchen maid opened the window and let in the grey morning light. I shivered suddenly with cold. "Your Highness—a cup of hot chocolate?" the cook suggested. I shook my head. Someone helped me up. Villatte. My prisoner of war. . . .

"Go to your rooms, gentlemen. You'll find everything just as you left it," I said to my two heroes. Then I asked for a duster.

The kitchen maid looked at me in alarm. "Don't you know what a duster is?" The poor frightened thing curtsied and brought me a snow-white napkin. So that's what my kitchen maid imagines a suitable duster for a crown princess. I took it and went up to Jean-Baptiste's room. When had it been dusted last? I whisked the napkin over the dressing table and felt miserable, because the room looked so un-lived in. Jean-Baptiste long ago had all the books, all the portraits, all the busts, that meant anything to him sent to Stockholm. In this room there's nothing left he cares about.

I opened the window to air out the room. My garden looked the same as yesterday. A day like every other, I thought. Yet the Russians, the Prussians and the Austrians will soon cross the Rhine. The Russians, the Prussians, the Austrians, and the Swedes.

"Don't stand at the open window in your dressing gown. Go to your room right away, or you'll catch cold," Marie said. "What are you doing here, anyway?"

"I'm getting the room ready for Jean-Baptiste. France has been defeated. The allied troops are marching to Paris. Jean-Baptiste is coming home, Marie."

"He should be ashamed of himself—" came from between clenched teeth. I could hardly hear it. My cavalier, my poor, lonely cavalier. . . .

449

Paris, last week in March, 1814

"I hear at the baker's shop that the Cossacks rape all women, old ones, too," Marie announced excitedly.

"They prefer the old ones," I said.

"Eugénie! Don't make fun of me!"

"I'm not. The Cossacks believe that old women bring them luck."

"Nonsense."

I shrugged my shoulders. "You might as well know, Marie. . . ."

She was really angry. "Who told you that?"

"Villatte."

Marie frowned. "Couldn't you ask the Swedish Count if it's true? He's their ally, he must know."

"I can't possibly ask him that. A crown princess naturally doesn't know what ra . . ."

At that, for the first time, we heard the distant thunder.

"A thunderstorm in March?" Marie murmured in surprise.

We stared at each other. It thundered again. "Cannon at the city gates," I whispered.

That was two days ago. Since then the guns of Paris have never been silent.

We had heard so often lately that troops of the Austrian Emperor would appear any moment at our gates. That the Cossacks would storm Paris, and burn down all the houses. That the Prussians had crossed the Rhine weeks ago, shouting, "To Paris! To Paris!" Naturally Napoleon was trying to halt the allied advance. Here in Paris we knew very little about his battles. The *Moniteur* mentioned only constant victories, now here, now there. But we no longer read the *Moniteur*. Now the guns are booming at the gates of Paris. Are they our guns? Austrian, Prussian, Russian?

My days are full to the brim with anticipation. I don't know where Jean-Baptiste is. I only know that he will come. Tonight, to-morrow night. His room is ready. . . . I've had no letters for a long

time either from him or from Oscar. Germany and France lie between us and the intervening land is one huge battlefield. Now
and then a note is smuggled through to us. That's how we found
out that Jean-Baptiste, after the battle of Leipzig, refused to pursue
the French troops across the Rhine. That of all his troops only his
thirty thousand Swedes stuck by him and marched north with him.
That he went through Hanover and probably revived many memories. Was I one of your memories, Jean-Baptiste? And Herr van
Beethoven and his lost hope? Chancellor Wetterstedt and the Swedish General Staff accompanied him and tried to explain that the
Allies wanted only one thing from him, only one decision—to cross
the Rhine. But Jean-Baptiste dictated a letter to the Tsar demanding
the frontiers of France be respected. France was not Napoleon. It
was Napoleon who had been defeated. . . . Now the Prussians, the
Russians and the Austrians are marching into France. Jean-Baptiste,
meanwhile, is waging his own war. . . .

The guns seem closer. Will Marmont hold Paris? The Corps
Marmont is defending the Capital. Marmont once asked me to
marry him. What had Napoleon said about him long ago in Marseilles? Yes—intelligent, hopes to build his career along with mine.
No, Marmont won't hold Paris. At least not for Napoleon.

Jean-Baptiste marches with his Swedes toward Denmark. In September, Napoleon finally forced the Danes to declare war on Sweden.
Unhappily, very unhappily, the Danes agreed. But their king, Frederick VI, held stubbornly to his alliance with France. Why? I tried
to remember this Frederick whom I had seen only once in my life.
The son of that mad Christian and of his beautiful queen, Caroline
Matilda, born in England, who fell in love with Struensee, the chief
minister. Because of this affair Struensee was executed. The son
never mentions his mother, and stands by Napoleon to revenge himself on England, her native land. The son—the son must have
loved his mother terribly and been very jealous of her little bit of
happiness. Strange that sons judge their mothers so sternly. We
mothers. . . .

The windowpanes are rattling; the guns are very close. I must go
on writing, and not think about Jean-Baptiste . . . Jean-Baptiste is
fighting his private war, and advancing into Schleswig. It's almost

like a parade. From Kiel he sent the Danish King an ultimatum. Jean-Baptiste demanded that Norway be ceded to Sweden, and offered a million reichsthaler as compensation.

Also from Kiel a note was smuggled through to Count Rosen. Denmark has given up Norway, except for Greenland, the Färo Islands and Iceland, to Sweden. But the million thaler the Danish King has indignantly refused. The Norwegians were not for sale, he said. . . .

"Crown Princess of Sweden and Norway," said Count Rosen, looking thoughtfully at me.

I got out a map and found Norway. "And Greenland?" I asked. Rosen pointed to a large white spot on the map. "All snow and ice, Your Highness."

I'm glad that the Danes have at least kept Greenland. Jean-Baptiste is quite capable of asking me to live on a white spot on the map!

I'm writing all this down to escape my great anxiety. Jean-Baptiste is no longer in Kiel. Jean-Baptiste is . . . I don't know where he is. He disappeared three weeks ago. He finally agreed to the Allies' request and marched to the Rhine, not across the Rhine, not across the Rhine. . . . He was last seen in Liége, in Belgium. There he took a travelling coach. Count Brahe was presumably with him and he has disappeared. No one knows where he was going. Many believe that Napoleon, in desperation, secretly asked Jean-Baptiste for help. And that Jean-Baptiste has quarrelled with the Tsar, because he won't recognize the frontiers of 1794. The Paris newspapers, in the meantime, allege that Jean-Baptiste is mentally ill. Marie and Yvette hide these articles from me, but La Flotte always leaves the newspapers lying around the salon. The reports say that Jean-Baptiste's father was out of his head when he died, and that his brother has also gone crazy—no, I can't go on. Not now when no one knows where Jean-Baptiste is. Perhaps he's already in France. Perhaps he's driving along the road which was conquered mile my mile by the Russians and Prussians. Probably he's seeing the scorched earth, the ruined houses . . . I've had word from Liége, from the Chamberlain, Count Löwenstein, who asked me if I knew where His Highness might be.

I don't know, Chamberlain, but I can guess. He's coming home

452

—coming home through the ruins. And is supposed to wear his dress uniform and march in, victorious. I can't answer your question, M. Chamberlain—please, be patient. His Highness is also only human, leave him alone in these dark days and night—

Paris, March 30, 1814

Today, at seven o'clock in the morning, Marie came into my room. "You are to go to the Tuileries immediately."

I looked at her incredulously, half-awake. "To the Tuileries?"

"King Joseph has sent a carriage, you are to go to Julie at once."

I got up and dressed quickly. Joseph is Commandant of Paris, and hopes to hold the city. Julie has obeyed him, and we haven't seen each other for months. And now suddenly this urgent message.

"Shall I wake up one of your aides? And which one? The prisoner of war or the allied aide?"

Villatte is my "prisoner of war" and Rosen my "allied" aide. "I don't think I need an aide to call on Julie," I said.

"I never have understood why you always drag around an officer with you," Marie grumbled.

It was cold driving through the deserted streets. Street cleaners were sweeping away rumpled copies of a proclamation. I stopped, I had to read it. The lackey jumped down from the box and fished one out of the gutter.

Parisians surrender! Do as your brothers in Bordeaux! Recall Louis XVIII to the throne. Secure peace for France!

The proclamation was signed by Prince von Schwarzenberg, the Austrian commander in chief. The street cleaners of Paris didn't seem to think much of Louis XVIII. They were busily sweeping up the proclamations that had been secretly distributed during the night.

At the entrance to the Tuileries was a mounted cuirassier regiment,

453

motionless as statues in the pale morning light. As we drove into the courtyard I saw a mass of carriages, as if for a ball. Close to the gate were ten green carriages of state with the Imperial coat of arms. Travelling coaches and transport wagons of every kind filled the courtyard. Relays of lackeys loaded heavy iron boxes in the wagons. The crown jewels, I thought, the treasures of the Imperial family. And money chests—a great many money chests. The sentries watched, with impassive faces, the removal of the chests.

Since it was impossible to drive further, I climbed out and made my way to the door between the waiting carriages. I asked to be received by Joseph immediately. "Just tell him his sister-in-law is here," I explained to the officer on duty.

He was clearly startled. "Very well, Your Royal Highness."

They haven't forgotten me either in the Tuileries.

To my surprise I was escorted to the private apartments of the Empress. As I entered the large salon, my heart skipped a beat— Napoleon? No, only Joseph at the moment trying desperately to look like his brother. Joseph stood in front of the fireplace, his hands crossed behind him, and talked rapidly, his head thrown back. The Empress, now called the Empress Regent, because Napoleon entrusted her with absolute power to rule during his absence, sat beside Mme Letizia on a sofa. Mme Letizia wore a shawl peasant-fashion around her shoulders, while the Empress wore a travelling coat and had put on her hat. Marie Louise acted like a guest who couldn't spare the time to sit down. I noticed Méneval, now secretary to the Regent, and a few senators. Behind Mme Letizia, tall, slender and wearing a faultless uniform stood King Jérôme of Westphalia, the greedy child of long ago. The Allies long since took away his kingdom. The room was bright with many candles. Their glow blending with the grey morning dawn made the whole scene seem strangely unreal.

"Here—look—here it is all written out," said Joseph, and reached into his breast pocket for a letter. "Rheims, March 16, 1814. My verbal instructions were," Joseph read, "and so forth and so forth— Here is the passage I meant: 'Do not desert my son, and remember that I would rather see him in the Seine than in the hands of the enemies of France. The fate of Astyanax, prisoner of the Greeks, has always seemed to me the greatest tragedy of all time. Your affectionate brother.' Signed, 'Napoleon.' "

"You read that letter yesterday to the State Council. We already know what Napoleon thinks about the fate of Astyanax. What chance is there of the child falling either into the Seine or into the hands of our enemies?" demanded Jérôme. Since his sojourn in America he speaks very slowly and somewhat nasally.

"Napoleon writes," Joseph said, taking another letter from his breast pocket, " 'Stand steadfast at the gates of Paris, place two cannon at each of the gates and the National Guard on duty. At each gate station fifty men with muskets or fowling pieces, and one hundred men with lances, also two hundred fifty men at the main gate.' As if I couldn't count. He writes to me as though I were an idiot," Joseph interjected, and then continued, " 'Every day a reserve of three thousand men is being trained to muskets, fowling pieces and lances, and they should be sent, as necessary, to the battery of the Guard, or the War Academy, or elsewhere. Your devoted brother.' Signed, 'Napoleon.' "

"That's perfectly clear," Mme Letizia said calmly. "Have you carried out the orders, Joseph?"

"That's just it—I can't carry them out. We have neither muskets or fowling pieces, and the Overlord of the Underwear can't get any more. And the Guards refuse to fight against a modern army with old lances from the museum."

"Refuse?" cried Jérôme indignantly.

"Could you defend a city against cannon with lances?"

"I wouldn't know how to handle a lance. And Napoleon probably wouldn't either."

"His Majesty can do anything in the defence of France," declared Ménéval firmly. There was a slight pause.

"Well?" asked Marie Louise calmly and indifferently. "What are we to do? Shall I leave with the King of Rome or stay here?"

"Madame—" Jérôme raced to her from behind the sofa. "Madame, you've heard the oath sworn by the officers of the Guard: as long as the Empress Regent and the King of Rome are in Paris, Paris will not fall. The Guard will make a superhuman effort to protect the Regent and the Emperor's son in the Tuileries. Imagine

455

the situation—a woman, a young and beautiful woman and a helpless child on the steps of the throne of France. Every man capable of bearing arms will fight to his last drop of blood!"

"Jérôme—" Joseph interrupted. "Remember we have only lances for the arms-bearing men."

"But the Guard is still fully armed, Joseph."

"A few hundred men . . . But I can't take the responsibility alone. I realize that the presence of the Regent would inspire not only the Guard but also the people of Paris to resist to the last ditch. The departure of the Regent would be . . ."

"Flight," Jérôme shouted.

"All right—the flight of the Regent and the King of Rome would lower the morale of the people. I fear that if they left Paris—" Joseph left it hanging.

"Well?" the Empress asked.

"I must leave the decision to the Regent," said Joseph wearily, and he no longer reminded me at all of Napoleon. A fat, elderly man, helplessly stroking his thinning hair with an uncertain hand.

"I only want to do my duty, and not be reproached afterward," Marie Louise explained apathetically.

Mme Letizia recoiled as though from a blow. So this was the woman her Napoleon had married. . . .

"Madame, if you leave the Tuileries now, you may forfeit your claim to the Imperial Crown of France. You and your son," Jérôme whispered urgently. "Madame, trust the Guard, the people of Paris!"

"We'll stay here then," said Marie Louise amiably, and began to untie the ribbons of her hat.

"Madame, the letter from His Majesty," Joseph moaned. "Napoleon said he would rather see his son in the Seine, than . . ."

"Don't repeat that awful phrase," I burst out. They all turned toward me. It was dreadful. I was still near the door; I bowed hurriedly in the general direction of the Empress and murmured, "Excuse me, I won't disturb you, I only . . ."

"The Crown Princess of Sweden in the salon of the Regent? Madame, this is an impertinence that cannot be borne," roared Jérôme, and made for me like a madman.

"Jérôme, I myself asked Her Royal Highness here because, because Julie—" Joseph, utterly disconcerted, looked for support to my sister. I looked, too, and for the first time saw Julie. She sat on a sofa at the far end of the salon with her daughters. All three were blurred in the half-light.

"Please sit down, Highness," Marie Louise said graciously. I quickly betook myself to the end of the room and sat with Julie. She had her arm around Zenaïde's shoulder and was stroking the child's arm.

"Don't be so upset," I whispered.

The first rays of the sun came streaming into the room. "Jérôme, blow out the candles, we must economize," Mme Letizia said sternly. Jérôme did nothing. Julie's little daughters jumped up, delighted to have something to do.

I put my arm around Julie. "You and the children are coming home with me," I whispered. They were still arguing around the fireplace. Then Joseph came over to us.

"If the Regent and the child go to Rambouillet," he said, "I must go too."

"I thought you had the supreme command in Paris," said Julie in a low voice.

"But the Emperor wrote me that I shouldn't leave his son," Joseph said breathlessly. "The whole family will come with us. Julie, I ask you for the last time—"

Julie shook her head. Tears streamed down her cheeks. "No, no —I'm afraid we'll be chased from palace to palace, and in the end the Cossacks will get us. Let me stay with Désirée, Joseph. Her house is safe. Your house is safe, isn't it, Désirée?"

Joseph and I looked at each other. It was a long look in which we said all the things we hadn't said since that evening when we met in the Town Hall. "You can stay at my house, too, Joseph," I said at last.

He shook his head and managed a smile. "Perhaps Napoleon will come back and save Paris, then in a few days I can be with Julie again. If not—" he kissed my hand—"I thank you for everything you're doing for Julie and my children. You and your husband."

At this moment a lackey announced, "The Prince of Bénévent asks an audience."

We looked at Marie Louise. Smilingly she turned to the door. "Let him come in."

Talleyrand limped quickly toward the Empress. His face looked tired and strained, but his hair was carefully powdered. He wore the uniform of a grand seigneur of the Empire. "Your Majesty," he said, "I have spoken with the Minister of War. We have news from Marmont. The Marshal begs Your Majesty to leave Paris immediately with the King of Rome. The Marshal does not know how long he can hold the road to Rambouillet. I deeply regret being the bearer of this tragic news."

There was almost complete silence. Only the silk ribbons of Marie Louise's hat rustled as she tied them under her chin again. "Am I still to meet His Majesty in Rambouillet?" she inquired.

"His Majesty is on his way to Fontainebleau, and from there will hurry here to the defence of Paris," Joseph said.

"But I mean His Majesty, the Emperor of Austria—my papa!"

Joseph went white to his lips. Jérôme clenched his teeth, the vein on his forehead swelled. Only Talleyrand smiled pityingly and showed no surprise. Mme Letizia grabbed her daughter-in-law by the arm. "Come, madame, come with me."

At the door Marie Louise turned around once more. Her blue eyes took in the salon, lingered on the white curtains with the embroidered bees, met Talleyrand's enigmatic smile. "If only no one reproaches me later," Marie Louise said, and left.

Now we could hear the child outside crying and screaming. Instinctively I went to the door. The two governesses, Mme de Montesquieu and Mme Bouber, were trying to get the little Napoleon downstairs. They'd dressed him in a small Chasseur uniform. The child, with Marie Louise's blond curls and his father's stubborn chin, hung onto the banister. "I won't," he screamed. "I won't go." And kicked the helpless governesses in the shins.

"Come, darling, come on," Mme de Montesquieu told him in despair. "Mama is waiting downstairs in a beautiful large carriage." But the child wouldn't budge.

Suddenly Hortense took over. "I know how to deal with little boys," she said with a smile. She leaned over the boy, and with an experienced pressure sprung his fingers loose. "There, now go down like a good boy." The child was startled. For the first time, someone had taken charge.

"Are we going to Papa, Aunt Hortense?" (Kick her in the shins, I thought, give her a good kick!)

"Of course, darling," Hortense assured him, and little Napoleon obediently followed his governesses down the stairs. I looked at Hortense. She was breathing hard. Hadn't Napoleon once named her oldest son his successor? Before the birth of the King of Rome. Before . . .

"Exit Napoleon II," murmured Talleyrand beside me.

"I am sorry to be so uneducated. I don't know who this Astyanax in the Seine is, and neither do I know the word 'exit.' "

"Astyanax is a character in classical antiquity. An unfortunate boy who was taken prisoner by the Greeks and thrown from a wall. People feared he might revenge the destruction of Troy and the death of his father, Hector. But, at this moment, Highness, I can't possibly tell you the whole story of the Trojan War. 'Exit' is a Latin word which means 'he goes out.' Exit Napoleon II: Napoleon II goes out—of the Tuileries, of world history." Talleyrand looked at his watch. "I fear I must take my leave, my carriage is waiting. . . ."

He also looked back thoughtfully at the salon. His eyes also lingered on the white curtains with the embroidered bees. "A pretty pattern . . . a shame the curtains will soon be taken down."

"If they were hung upside down, the bees would stand on their heads. Then they'd look like lilies. Like Bourbon lilies," I said.

Talleyrand raised his lorgnon to his eye. "How very strange. . . . But I must go, Your Highness."

"No one is detaining you, Prince. Are you really going with the Empress?"

"Of course. But I will, unfortunately, be taken prisoner by the Russians at the gates of Paris. Therefore, I must not be late, the Russian patrol is expecting me. Au revoir, dear Highness."

"Perhaps Marshal Marmont will free you. You deserve it," I said contemptuously.

"You think so? Then you'll be disappointed. Marshal Marmont

is very busy at the moment negotiating for the surrender of Paris. But keep this news to yourself, Highness. We want to avoid unnecessary confusion and bloodshed."

How graciously he bowed, how confidently he limped away. He would certainly have the curtains hung upside down. . . .

At last I was in my carriage with Julie and her daughters, driving back to the rue d'Anjou.

And, for the first time since the day Julie became a queen, Marie spoke to her again. She put a motherly arm around Julie's thin shoulders and led her upstairs. "Marie, Queen Julie will sleep in Oscar's room, and the children can use Mme la Flotte's. Mme la Flotte must move into the guest room."

"And General Clary, M. Etienne's son?" Marie asked.

"What?"

"The General arrived an hour ago, and wants to stay here. Just for a while," Marie announced. Etienne had sent his son Marius to the War Academy instead of training him for Papa's business. And Marius, with the help of God and Napoleon, had become a general.

"The allied and the prisoner of war aides can share a room. Then General Clary can sleep in Colonel Villatte's bed," I decided.

"And the Countess Tascher?" Marie asked. The full import of this question I didn't understand until I entered the salon. There Etienne's daughter, Marcelline, who is married to a Count Tascher, flung herself, weeping, into my arms. "Aunt, I'm so frightened in my own house. The Cossacks may arrive at any moment," she sobbed.

"And your husband?"

"Somewhere at the front. Marius spent the night with me, and we decided to come here and, for the present—"

I gave her the guest room, and La Flotte will have to sleep on a divan in the dressing room.

About five o'clock in the afternoon the cannon stopped roaring. Villatte and Rosen returned from a walk and said that Blücher had taken Montmartre, and the Austrians were in Menilmontant. The Allies are demanding unconditional surrender.

"What about my children's governess?" Julie moaned. "If she

hasn't a room of her own, she'll give notice. Who's sleeping in Jean-Baptiste's bed?"

Not your governess! I thought furiously, and fled. Fled to Jean-Baptiste's empty bedroom. Sat down on the wide empty bed. Listened to the night outside, listened. . . .

Paris, March 31, 1814

At two o'clock this morning the treaty of surrender was signed. When I looked out of my window the Swedish flag waved over my front door. Count Rosen, with the help of the Swedish coachman, had hung it there. A great crowd of people waited in front of our house. Their angry mutterings carried up to my window.

"What do these people want, Villatte?"

"The rumour has gone around that His Highness will soon arrive."

"But what do these people want of Jean-Baptiste?"

The mutterings increased and sounded definitely hostile. I inquired no further.

A carriage drove up. Gendarmes held back the crowd. I saw Hortense climb out of the carriage with nine-year-old Napoleon Louis and six-year-old Charles Louis Napoleon. The babble of voices ceased. One of the children pointed to the Swedish flag and asked something. But Hortense hastily herded her boys into the house.

La Flotte appeared. "Queen Hortense wants to know if the Emperor's nephews can, for the present, remain under the protection of Your Highness. The Queen herself will go to her mother at Malmaison."

Two little boys in the house, perhaps we still have some of Oscar's toys in the attic. . . . "Tell Her Majesty I'll take good care of the children." I'll put them in Mme la Flotte's room. Marcelline can

have the dressing room, and Mme la Flotte Yvette's room, and Yvette
—I saw Hortense, below, get back in her carriage. "Vive l'Empereur!" the crowd shouted as she drove off.

Then the human wall closed in once more around my house. I no longer wait alone. Ominously, the mob waits with me.

Paris, April, 1814

On March 31, the troops of the Allies marched into Paris. The Cossacks galloped down the Champs Elysées shouting weird, incomprehensible cries. The Prussians moved forward in serried ranks; they carried captured eagles—standards and French banners through the streets, and sang songs written by their so-called Poets of Liberation.

The Austrians, on the contrary, marched to the beat of drums, and waved to the girls hanging out of the windows. They'd rolled cannon in front of the allied commanders' headquarters to protect them from the Parisians' fury. But they had no time to revenge themselves on Prince von Schwarzenberg or General von Blücher. The Parisians were lined up at the baker or begging the grocers for a small sack of flour. The granaries outside Paris had been plundered by the Allies and then burned to the ground. The roads to the southern districts are barricaded. Paris is hungry.

An April 1, a provisional government was set up to negotiate with the Allies. At the head is Talleyrand. The Tsar was quartered in the Palais Talleyrand. Talleyrand gave a great ball in his honour, attended by members of the old nobility whom Napoleon had allowed to return from exile. Champagne flowed without stint, and the Tsar produced, as if by magic, flour and meat and caviar. The guests were stuffed.

Napoleon is at Fontainebleau with five thousand guardsmen. Caulaincourt's carriage drives continuously back and forth between

Paris and Fontainebleau. Caulaincourt is negotiating in the name of
the Emperor with the Allies. The Allies are promoting Talleyrand
as head of the new Government, but France herself is supposed to
decide.

On April 4, Napoleon signed the following act of abdication:

The Foreign Powers having declared that the Emperor Napoleon was
an obstacle to the re-establishment of peace and to the territorial integrity
of France, and Whereas: being loyal to his principles, and to his promises
to further the happiness and glory of the French people in all things,
Therefore: the Emperor Napoleon declares that he is ready to abdicate
in favour of his son, and to send that Act in due form as a message to
the Senate, as soon as the Powers shall have recognized Napoleon II
together with the Constitutional Regency of the Empress. Upon this condition the Emperor will withdraw immediately to the palace which shall
be agreed. Given at our Palace of Fontainebleau, April 4, 1814.

[Signed] NAPOLEON.

Two days later the Senate announced that a Regency for Napoleon
II was out of the question. I don't know where people have suddenly found the Bourbon banners which they've hung out of their
windows. They flap, soiled and grey, in the April rain. No one
pulls them down, no one exults over them. The *Moniteur* writes
that only the restoration of the Bourbons would guarantee a lasting
peace. The police, charged with clearing the roads for the entry of
the allied troops, no longer wear blue-white-red cockades, but the
white cockades, symbol of so much bloodshed during the great Revolution.

Most of the Bonapartes fled from Rambouillet with the Empress
to Blois. The Empress won't see anyone. Safe in the arms of His
Majesty, her papa, she weepingly begs him to protect her and her
child. Her child now, only hers. The Austrian Emperor calls his
little grandson Francis. He doesn't like the name Napoleon.

Joseph has written several letters to Julie from Blois. They were
brought by peasant lads who gladly smuggled them through the
lines so they could see Paris. Julie and her children are to stay with
me until the new Government and the Allies have decided the fate
of the Bonaparte family, and the size of the "compensation for
property" to be paid them. On April 1, Julie asked me for money

to pay her governess' salary. "I haven't a sou," she said. "Joseph took all our money and the securities with him in a money chest. My jewelry, too." Pierre, as my manager, paid the governess. Then my nephew, Marius, wanted to borrow some money. I turned him over to Pierre.

Although Marcelline is afraid of the passers-by who collect in small groups outside my house, she decided to take a drive. She used my carriage with the Swedish coat of arms, and came back with two new hats. The bill she had sent to me. On the morning of April 11, Marie brought me up a cup of artificial coffee, which tastes horrible, and a piece of dry grey bread. Setting the tray on my night table, she said, "Pierre must talk to you. You have no more money."

Pierre now lives with Marie in the former porter's rooms on the ground floor. I found him at his desk. His wooden leg was leaning in a corner, he rarely uses it. The wound in his right stump hasn't yet healed. On the desk stood our money box—open and empty. Entirely empty. I sat down on the chair beside the desk. Pierre handed me a piece of paper covered with long rows of figures.

"An account of the payments I've made since the first of April— wages; purchases for the household. The sums are high, we can buy food only at exorbitant prices. Last month, at the last moment, I sold Your Highness' French Government securities, and we've been living on the proceeds. The cook could buy a veal roast today for all your guests, if I had a hundred francs. Or Swiss currency. Your Highness, we haven't a sou." He shoved the money box toward me. Yes, yes—I've seen, it's empty.

"Can Your Highness count on money from Sweden any time soon?"

I shrugged my shoulders.

"Perhaps His Highness, the Crown Prince . . ."

"But I don't know where His Highness is."

"I can, of course, borrow any amount, if Your Highness signs a promissory note. Any sum is at the disposal of the Crown Princess of Sweden. Will Your Highness sign?"

I put my hand to my head in desperation. "I can't borrow money. At least not as Crown Princess of Sweden. It would make

464

a dreadfully bad impression, and my husband wouldn't like it. No, I really can't."

Marie had come in. "You can sell some silver dishes, or pawn them," she said to me, and to Pierre, "You must wear your wooden leg, or you'll never get used to it. . . . Well, Eugénie?"

"Yes, that's one solution. But—no, Marie, that won't do either. Everything is engraved. Either with *J.B.* or the Ponte Corvo coat of arms. On the large meat platters, which might really be worth something on a loan, there's the Crown Princess' crown. All Paris would know immediately that we have no money. And that would look bad for Sweden."

"I could pawn some of Your Highness' jewelry, and no one would guess whose it was," Pierre suggested.

"And if, as Crown Princess of Sweden, I had someday to receive my mighty cousins—the Russian Tsar or the Austrian Emperor? There I'd be with a bare neck. I have so little really valuable jewelry . . ."

"Julie has always been dripping with diamonds, she . . ."

"Marie, Joseph took all of Julie's jewelry."

"How will you feed all the people under your roof?" Marie demanded.

I stared at the empty box. "Let me think, please let me think."

They let me. A hush fell over the room. "Marie, in Papa's time, the firm of Clary had a warehouse in Paris, didn't it?"

"Of course. The warehouse is still here. M. Etienne visits it whenever he comes to Paris from Genoa. Hasn't he ever mentioned it to you?"

"No, there was no reason to."

Marie raised her eyebrows. "No? Who inherited the half of the firm that belonged to your mama?"

"I don't know. Etienne never . . ."

"According to law, you, Queen Julie, and your brother Etienne each inherited a third of this half," Pierre declared.

"But when Julie and I were married we had a dowry," I argued.

"Yes, that was your inheritance from your papa. Etienne inherited one-half of the business, and your mama the other." Marie frowned. "But since your mama's death—"

"A sixth of the firm of Clary belongs to Your Highness," Pierre said, and I decided to talk it over with Julie. But Julie stayed in bed all day, and had Yvette put cold compresses on her aching head. So I couldn't suddenly burst in and say we had no money to buy dinner.

"Marie, tell the cook to buy the veal roast. The butcher will be paid this evening. And please call a carriage for me at once."

The large salon was like a madhouse. Marius and Villatte were bending over a map, and, with wonderful hindsight, winning all the battles Napoleon had lost during the last month. Julie's daughters were fighting with Hortense's sons over the contents of a very fine Sèvres porcelain candy box. La Flotte, in a flood of tears, was translating to Rosen a newspaper article in which Napoleon was denounced as a monster.

I turned to Marius. "Where is the Clary warehouse?"

Strange to say, he blushed. "You know I have nothing to do with the silk trade, Aunt. I've been an officer all my life."

This conversation was particularly embarrassing with Villatte there, but I didn't give up. "But your father is a silk merchant, and you ought to know where his warehouse is. He goes there whenever he is in Paris."

"But I've never gone with him, I—"

I looked him in the eye. He faltered. "It's in a basement in the Palais Royal, if I remember rightly," he said hastily, and gave me the address.

"Do you think your Yvette could do my hair?" Marcelline asked me at the same time, rustling in, in an expensive dressing gown. "I want to take a drive," she continued. "That is, if you don't need the carriage, Aunt."

"I don't need it. But I advise you not to take the carriage with the Swedish coat of arms."

"Oh, it's very quiet on the streets. People have got used to the change-over very quickly." Marcelline smiled. "May I?"

I nodded. "Your carriage is here," Marie whispered in my ear. No one noticed me leave.

The hired carriage stopped before a roomy, very elegant basement shop in the Palais Royal. A small sign in dignified gold letters said,

466

François Clary, silks, wholesale and retail. I had the coachman wait, went down three steps, opened a door, heard a shop bell tinkle, and stood in an office beautifully furnished with delicate chairs and little tables. Only the half-empty shelves along the walls, with large rolls of silk on them, showed what kind of business was transacted at the handsome mahogany desk. Behind the desk sat an elderly man in a well-cut business suit, the white cockade of the Bourbons in his buttonhole.

"What can I do for you, madame?"

"Are you the Paris manager of the Clary firm?"

The man bowed. "At your service, madame. White for the Restoration is in great demand. White satin is, unfortunately, sold out, but we still have a few pieces of white muslin which madame could hang over her curtains. It is very popular in the Faubourg St. Germain—"

"That's not what I want," I said sharply.

"Madame is thinking of a gown?" He looked at the shelves. "Up to yesterday we had some brocade with a woven fleur-de-lis pattern, madame, but unfortunately we're sold out, all sold out. Perhaps velour or white—"

"Business is good, monsieur—?"

"Legrand, madame, Legrand," he introduced himself.

"These white materials—brocades with embroidered fleurs-de-lis of the Bourbons, the curtain muslin for the Restoration, and the other white cloth—when did they get here? Aren't the roads from the south to Paris still closed?"

He laughed so hard that both double chins jiggled up and down in his high collar. "M. Clary shipped it from Genoa months ago. The first consignment arrived right after the Battle of Leipzig. M. Clary, the head of the firm, is politically well-informed. Madame knows who M. Clary is—" He cleared his throat impressively. "M. Clary is the brother-in-law of the victor of Leipzig. The brother-in-law of the Crown Prince of Sweden—madame will, therefore, understand . . ."

"And for weeks you have been selling white silk to the ladies of the old aristocracy?" I interrupted. He nodded proudly. I stared at the cockade in his buttonhole. "I couldn't imagine where so many white cockades came from overnight," I murmured. "The ladies of the old families whom the Emperor received at his court have also been secretly making white cockades?"

"Madame—I beg of you," he tried to soothe me, but I was angry, terribly angry. The shelves were almost empty.

"And you've sold white silk, roll after roll. While French troops fought to hold back the Allies, here you sat, coining money. Am I right, monsieur?"

"Madame, I'm merely an employee of the firm of François Clary," he said, hurt and on the defensive. "Besides, most of our accounts have not been paid. Unpaid bills, nothing but unpaid bills. The ladies who bought the white material with the fleurs-de-lis are waiting for the Bourbons' return. Then their husbands will have important positions, and the ladies can pay their bills. But the gowns for the Bourbons' reception in the Tuileries must be made first." He paused, and eyed me suspiciously. "What can I do for you, madame?"

"I need money. How much have you here?"

"Madame, I—I don't understand . . ."

"A sixth of the firm of Clary belongs to me. I am a daughter of the late founder. I need money urgently. How much have you in the cash box, M. Legrand?"

"Madame—I don't quite understand. M. Etienne has only two sisters. Mme Joseph Bonaparte, and Her Royal Highness, the Crown Princess of Sweden."

"That's right. I am the Crown Princess of Sweden. How much money have you in the shop, monsieur?"

M. Legrand groped with a trembling hand in his breast pocket, drew forth his glasses, put them on, and looked at me. Then he bowed as deeply as his fat stomach would permit. When I held out my hand to him, he began to sniffle with emotion. "I was an apprentice in your papa's business in Marseilles when Your Highness was still a child—a dear child, Your Highness, but naughty, very naughty!"

"But you didn't recognize me, did you? Not even with your glasses?" I began to cry. "I'm not naughty any more, I only try to do my best in these troubled times. . . ."

468

Legrand went swiftly to the door and locked it. "We don't want any customers now, Your Highness," he whispered.

I searched in my handbag for a handkerchief. Legrand gave me his, snowy-white, of the finest silk. "I've racked my brains figuring how I can manage without going into debt. A Clary just doesn't go into debt. I'm waiting until my husband—" In despair I crumpled up the handkerchief of our former apprentice.

"All of Paris is waiting for the gala entrance of the victor of Leipzig," Legrand assured me. "The Tsar has already arrived, and the King of Prussia. It can't be long before—"

I wiped away the last of my tears. "In all these years I've never taken my share of the firm's profits. So now I must take all you have on hand."

"I have very little on hand, Your Highness. The day before he left King Joseph asked for a large sum." My eyes widened in amazement, but he did not notice, and plunged on. "Twice a year, King Joseph drew his wife's share of our profits. When he left Paris he took all the money we'd made up to the end of March from the secret sale of white material. There's nothing left but unpaid accounts, Highness."

So Joseph Bonaparte, too, had made a profit on the white cockades! Knowingly or unknowingly, it doesn't matter now—

"Here," said Legrand, and gave me a bundle of banknotes. "This is all we have at the moment."

"It's something," I said, stuffing the money into my bag. And, decisively, "M. Legrand, we must collect the outstanding accounts immediately. Everyone says that the franc will continue to fall. My carriage is outside. Take it, drive from customer to customer, and collect. If anyone refuses to pay, make him return the goods. Will you do it?"

"But I can't leave. The apprentice—we have only one apprentice, the others were called up—I've sent the apprentice to see an old customer who needs new clothes badly. The wife of Marshal Marmont, Your Highness. And I'm expecting the buyer from Le Roy's any moment. They're working day and night at Le Roy's, and the ladies of the new court . . ."

"While you settle the accounts, I'll attend to the customers here." With that I took off my hat and coat.

Legrand stammered, "But—Highness . . ."

"Why are you surprised? As a girl I often helped in the shop in Marseilles. Don't worry, I know how to handle silk. Hurry, monsieur!"

Doubtfully, Legrand made for the door. "Monsieur, a moment." He turned. "Please take off the white cockade when you call on behalf of the firm of Clary."

"Highness, most people are wearing . . ."

"Yes, but not former apprentices of my papa. Au revoir, monsieur."

When I was alone, I sat at the desk and put my head down on my arms. I was very tired. So many nights without enough sleep. My eyes smarted from the silly tears I'd shed. Memories of Marseilles were to blame for that. A naughty child—I was a naughty and a carefree child. My papa had taken my hand and explained to me the Rights of Man. That was long ago. And will never be again.

The bell over the shop door tinkled. I leapt up. A light-blue frock coat with fancy embroidery and a white cockade. The buyer from Le Roy's. I'd always dealt with the manageress, I didn't know the buyer. "You're the buyer from Le Roy's, aren't you? I'm spelling M. Legrand. What can I do for you?"

"I'd like to speak to M. Legrand personally. . . ."

I said I was sorry. I pulled down a heavy roll of velvet from a shelf with a note on it: *Ordered by Mme Mère. Returned.* I unrolled a bit to see the right side of the material. Dark green, the Corsican colour. With embroidered gold bees.

"Here," I said. "Dark-green velvet with the Bourbon fleurs-de-lis." I struggled to turn around the heavy roll quickly, so that the bees were upside down. The buyer didn't help me. Just lifted his lorgnon and examined the velvet.

"The lilies look like bees," he objected.

"I can't help that," I snapped.

"The fleurs-de-lis remind me of Napoleonic bees," he insisted. I shrugged. "Besides," he said, "dark green is very unfashionable.

People saw too much of it during the Empire. And velvet. Velvet in the spring! Have you any pale lilac muslin?"

I looked along the shelves. Muslin—rose-coloured muslin, yellow muslin, violet muslin— Sure enough, on the top shelf. There must be a ladder somewhere, perhaps . . . Yes, there was the ladder. I leaned it against the shelves, crept shakily up and fished out the violet muslin. "The Empress Josephine has ordered a pale-lilac gown. Pale lilac is a colour of mourning. The Empress needs the gown to receive the Tsar."

I almost fell off the ladder. "She's going to—receive—the Tsar?"

"Naturally. She's looking forward to his visit, so she can discuss her financial situation with him. The financial affairs of the Bonapartes are already being negotiated. Apparently they're being generous and letting these parvenus have pensions. Have you any pale lilac muslin or not?"

I climbed down the ladder with the roll. Peeled off some of the transparent thin material for him to see.

"Too dark," he declared.

"The colour of lilac blooms," I contradicted, "and exactly right at the moment."

He looked at me disdainfully. "Why do you say that?"

"It's becoming, and slightly melancholy. Just right for Josephine. By the way—we're selling now strictly for cash."

"That's out of the question. Our customers don't pay us promptly. Naturally, as soon as the situation is clarified, mademoiselle . . ."

"The situation is clarified. The franc is falling. We sell only for cash." I took the roll from the desk and carried it back to the shelves.

"Where is M. Legrand?" Le Roy's buyer grumbled.

"I told you he isn't here."

His eyes roved hungrily over the half-empty shelves. "You've hardly anything left," he remarked.

I nodded. "Yes, we're pretty well sold out. And for cash."

He stared, as though in a trance, at a few rolls of satin. "Marshal Ney's wife," he murmured.

"Light-blue satin?" I suggested. "Mme Ney is quite ruddy and wears light blue well."

He looked at me curiously. "You're well informed, little one, well versed in the silk trade, mademoiselle—?"

"Désirée," I said amiably. "Well, how shall we dress Mme Ney for her presentation to the Bourbons in the Tuileries?"

"You sound so bitter, Mlle Désiré. You're not a secret Bonapartist?"

"Take a light blue for Mme Ney. You can have the satin at the prewar price." From the roll hung a label in Etienne's spidery handwriting. The price was on it. I named the sum.

"I'll give you a receipt," he said.

"You will pay cash or leave the satin here, I have other customers." He counted out the money on the desk.

"And the lilac muslin?" I asked, while I measured out eight metres of satin, and took the large pair of scissors from the window sill. Then, very daringly, I made a tiny incision in the material, and tore it across firmly—just as I'd seen Etienne and Papa rip off a length of silk.

"The Empress herself never pays cash," he grumbled. I ignored him. "Seven metres of muslin," he sighed.

"Take nine metres. She'll want a shawl to go with the gown," I advised him, and measured off nine metres. In the meantime he unhappily counted out the money on the desk for Josephine's melancholy dress.

"And ask Legrand to reserve the green velvet with the gold bees for us until this evening," he hurled at me as he left. That I promised him gladly.

I served three more customers, climbing constantly up and down the ladder. Finally Legrand returned. The shop happened to be empty.

"Have you collected all the accounts, monsieur?"

"Not all, but several. Here—" He handed me a leather pouch full of banknotes.

"Write it all down and I'll sign a receipt," I said.

He began to write. How long would we be able to live on this money? One week, two weeks? He shoved the slip of paper to me for my signature. I thought a minute, and wrote, *Désirée, Crown Princess of Sweden, née Clary*. He poured sand on my signature.

"From now on, I'll settle regularly with my brother, Etienne," I said. "And, M. Legrand, stock lilac muslin—the newest thing, you'll soon see. And the green velvet Madame Mère returned is reserved for Le Roy. No, I'm not joking, Le Roy really wants it. Au revoir, M. Legrand."

"Highness . . ."

The little bell over the shop door jingled again. My carriage was waiting. As I got in, the coachman wordlessly handed me a newspaper. I told him to drive to the rue d'Anjou. On the way I read the special edition. The carriage rocked, the letters danced . . .

The Allied Powers having proclaimed that the Emperor Napoleon was the sole obstacle to the establishment of peace in Europe, the Emperor Napoleon, faithful to his oath, declares that he renounces for himself and his heirs the thrones of France and Italy and that there is no personal sacrifice, even of his life, which he is not prepared to make on behalf of France.

And all that in a single sentence. . . . We'll have roast veal for dinner. I must be careful of my handbag, I had stuffed all the notes into it. The air smelt of spring. But the people in the streets looked disgruntled. People don't understand why they must still go hungry after a war. The women stood, as always, in snaky lines in front of the bakers' shops, and wore white cockades. Copies of the special edition, announcing the abdication, lay discarded in the gutters.

With a jolt, the carriage stopped. A line of gendarmes barred the entrance to the rue d'Anjou. A gendarme shouted something to the coachman. He got down from the box and opened the carriage door. "We can't drive any farther; the rue d'Anjou is cordoned off. The Tsar is expected."

"But I must go to the rue d'Anjou, I live there." The coachman explained this to the gendarme. "Persons who can prove they live in the rue d'Anjou may enter, but only on foot," I was informed. I alighted and paid the coachman.

Gendarmes were lined up on both sides of the road. There wasn't a soul in the street, my footsteps echoed. Almost at my house I was stopped. A mounted police captain trotted toward me. "You may go no farther."

I looked up at him. His face was familiar. I recognized him as the same man who for years had guarded our house on behalf of the Minister of Police. I never found out whether we were supposed to consider the man as a guard of honour or as a spy. Napoleon had the houses of his marshals watched by the police day and night.

The captain was an older man in a very down-at-the-heels uniform. On his shabby three-cornered hat there was a dark spot where, until two days ago, he'd worn a blue-white-red cockade. He had deliberately left the dark spot uncovered. Beside it was attached his white cockade, which he had to wear by decree of the new government.

"Let me through. You know I live in that house." I indicated it with a lift of my chin. In front of the entrance, gendarmes were massing.

"In half an hour, His Majesty the Tsar of Russia will call on Her Royal Highness, the Crown Princess of Sweden. I have orders to let no one pass the house," he snarled without looking at me.

So the Tsar was coming to see me, the Tsar. . . . "Then let me through quickly, I must change," I stormed.

But the shabby captain still wouldn't look at me. I stamped my foot. "Look at me, you've known me for years. You know perfectly well that I live in that house!"

"I had mistaken Your Highness for the wife of Marshal Bernadotte," he said, looking at me at last. His eyes gleamed wickedly. "I beg your pardon—a mistake. Your Highness must be ready to receive the Tsar!" Then he shouted, "Clear the way for the Crown Princess of Sweden!"

I ran the gauntlet between the rows of gendarmes. My feet were like lead. But I ran. . . . At home they'd been waiting for me frantically, the door flew open as I approached. Marie grabbed my arm. "Hurry, hurry—in half an hour the Tsar will be here."

Pierre was balancing on his crutches in the door of the porter's quarters. I tossed my handbag to him. "Here—we're out of the woods. At least for the moment," I said.

I can't remember how I got to my dressing room. Marie ripped off my clothes and flung a dressing gown around me. Yvette began to brush my hair. I closed my eyes, exhausted.

474

"Drink this, in one gulp." Marie had a glass of brandy in her hand.

"I can't, Marie. I never drink brandy."

"Drink it!"

I took the glass. My hands shook. I loathed brandy, but I drank it. It burned all the way down.

"What are you wearing?" Marie asked.

"I don't know. I haven't anything new. Perhaps the violet velvet I wore at my farewell audience with the Emperor."

Velvet in spring? Violet—becoming and melancholy. I rubbed my face with rose water, rubbed off the dust of the shop, dabbed silver paint on my eyelids—Yvette held my make-up box. There— and now rouge on my cheeks. The powder puff.

"You still have a quarter of an hour, Eugénie," Marie said, as she knelt down and took off my shoes and stockings.

"I'll receive the Tsar in the little salon, the whole family is sitting in the large one." A headache hammered at my temples.

"I've already got everything ready in the small salon—champagne and sweetmeats, don't worry." Marie put on my silver sandals.

At that instant, I saw Julie in the mirror. She had on one of her purple gowns, and held one of her small crowns in her hand.

"Shall I wear a crown or not, Désirée?"

I turned and looked at her uncomprehendingly. She was so thin that the purple gown, which was so pitifully unbecoming to her, hung in loose folds. "Why on earth should you wear a crown?"

"I thought—I mean—when you present me to the Tsar, you will surely call me by my old title. . . ."

I turned away and spoke into the mirror. "Do you really want to be presented to the Tsar, Julie?"

She nodded emphatically. "Of course. I'll ask him to protect my interests and the children's. The Tsar of Russia . . ."

"You should be ashamed of yourself, Julie Clary," I whispered. "Napoleon abdicated just a few hours ago. His family shared in his success; you got two crowns from him. Now you must wait to see what's decided about you. Your interests—" I swallowed hard, my mouth was dry. "Julie, you aren't a queen any more. You are Julie Bonaparte, née Clary. No more, but also no less."

Something clattered to the floor. Her little crown.. She slammed the door behind her. I blinked my eyes—the pain in my head was blinding. Yvette put the earrings of the Queen Mother of Sweden in my ears.

"They've been asking all day where you've been," Marie said, and helped me up.

"What did you tell them?"

"Nothing. But you stayed out a long time."

"I sent the manager around to collect outstanding accounts. So I had to stay in the shop to wait on the customers."

Take off dressing gown, put on violet velvet gown, sit down again —I went through the motions mechanically.

"Five minutes to go," Marie said. Yvette tied up my curls with a rose-coloured ribbon. Marie asked, "How is the silk business?"

"Flourishing. Satin and muslin for new court dresses for the old marshals' wives. Give me another glass of brandy, Marie."

She poured it out without a word. Without a word I drank it down. It burned, but very pleasantly. I looked in the mirror. My eyes seemed unnaturally large under the silver lids. Perhaps I should powder over the blue shadows below them? The last time I wore this dress, I had a bouquet of violets. Too bad I have none today. . . .

"By the way, Eugénie, someone sent flowers for you. Violets. They're on the mantelpiece in the little salon. It's time you went down."

I don't know whether the brandy or my fatigue was responsible —at any rate I floated down the stairs as in a dream. Below in the hall they were all assembled. Marcelline in a ball dress of Julie's. My nephew, the General, in a well-brushed dress uniform; Mme la Flotte in her best gown. Julie's daughters with purple ribbons in their hair. The small sons of Hortense all spick and span. Count Rosen in his Swedish gala-uniform with the brilliant aide's sash. Colonel Villatte, in the background, in his threadbare field uniform.

Villatte came over to me. "Your Highness, may I beg to be excused during the Tsar's visit? I'll never forget Your Highness' indulgence."

I nodded, preoccupied, and looked from one to the other of them.

476

"Please go into the large salon. I will receive the Tsar in the little salon."

Why did they stare at me in such surprise? "Count Rosen, I see you have an aide's uniform."

"His Highness sent it to me by a Russian officer."

Jean-Baptiste thinks of everything. "You will escort me to the small salon, Count."

"And we—?" Marcelline blurted out.

I was already at the door. "I wouldn't ask any Frenchman or Frenchwoman to be presented to the sovereign of an Allied Power before peace has been concluded between France and the Allies. As far as I know, the Emperor did not formally abdicate until today," I said.

Marius blushed. Marcelline seemed quite put out. La Flotte bit her lip. The children cried, "May we at least peep through the keyhole?"

The little salon was spotless. On the little table in front of the mirror there were champagne glasses and sweetmeats. On the mantelpiece, a silver basket of violets—they were pathetically small and wilted—and a sealed envelope. Then—the blare of trumpets and the sound of horses' hooves. The Tsar is, of course, always accompanied by his bodyguard. A carriage stopped. I stood stiffly erect in the middle of the room.

The door was flung open. A dazzling white uniform, sparkling gold epaulettes, a giant with a round boyish face, blond curls and an unaffected smile, and behind him, right behind him—Talleyrand. Behind them both milled many foreign uniforms. I bowed, and held out my hand for the blond giant to kiss.

"Your Highness, it is my sincere desire to pay my respects to the wife of the man who has contributed so much to the liberation of Europe," said the Tsar.

My two servants crept noiselessly around, serving champagne. The Tsar sat down beside me on the small sofa. In the armchair opposite —the embroidered frock coat of M. Talleyrand.

"The Prince of Bénévent was kind enough to place his house at my disposal." The Tsar smiled graciously. Does he always wear a gleaming white uniform? In battle, too? Nonsense, the Tsar isn't a general, but an elegant gentleman, who waits on a horse at his headquarters for reports of victories. Only Jean-Baptiste is both a prince and a general. . . . I drank champagne and smiled.

"I am exceedingly sorry that Your Highness' husband didn't enter Paris at my side." The blue eyes narrowed. "I had counted on him. We exchanged numerous letters while our troops were crossing the Rhine. We had a slight difference of opinion on the future frontiers of France."

I smiled and drank champagne.

"I wanted His Highness to take part in the deliberations over the new form of government for France. After all, His Highness is better informed about the wishes of the French people than I—or than our dear cousins, the Austrian Emperor and the King of Prussia. Besides, the individual rulers and their advisers tend to consider their own interests."

He emptied his glass in one gulp, and held it out absent-mindedly to an aide. The aide refilled it. Neither of my servants was allowed near the Tsar. I continued to smile.

"I'm awaiting impatiently for your husband's arrival, Highness. Perhaps Your Highness knows when I may expect the Crown Prince?"

I shook my head and drank champagne.

"The Provisional Government of France under the leadership of our friend, the Prince of Bénévent—" the Tsar raised his glass to Talleyrand, and Talleyrand bowed—"informs us that France longs for the return of the Bourbons, and that only the Restoration can ensure peace within the country. Personally, this surprises me. What is Your Highness' opinion?"

"I don't understand politics, Sire."

"In my various discussions with your husband, His Highness gave me the impression that the French people are not at all—do not care very much for the Bourbon Dynasty. I, therefore, suggested to His Highness—" The Tsar held out his empty glass to the aide, and looked me full in the face. "Madame, I suggested to your husband that he urge the French people to choose their great marshal, Jean-Baptiste Bernadotte, Crown Prince of Sweden, as the new King of France."

"And what did my husband answer, Sire?"

"Oddly enough, Highness, nothing. Our dear cousin, the Crown Prince of Sweden, never even answered the letter in which we made this suggestion. Furthermore, he's not arrived in Paris for this momentous occasion, and my couriers can't find him. His Highness has—vanished."

He downed his freshly filled glass, and looked at me mournfully.

"The Emperor of Austria and the King of Prussia are in favour of the Bourbon Restoration. England has already placed a man-of-war at Louis XVIII's disposal. Since the Swedish Crown Prince hasn't answered me, I shall follow the wishes of the French Government—" his glance sought Talleyrand—"and of my allies." He toyed thoughtfully with his empty glass. "Too bad," he said, and then abruptly, "What a charming room this is, madame."

We stood up, and the Tsar went to the window and looked out into the garden. I stood beside him, hardly up to his shoulder. "A lovely garden," he murmured, but he was preoccupied. My little garden looked a mess, untidy and neglected.

"This is Moreau's former house."

The Tsar closed his eyes suddenly as at a painful memory. "A cannon shot shattered both his legs. Moreau served on my general staff. He died early in September. Hadn't Your Highness heard?"

I leaned my head against the cool windowpane. "Moreau was an old friend of ours. In the days when my husband still hoped the Republic could be saved for the French people."

I spoke very softly, we were alone, over by the window, the Tsar of all the Russias and I. Not even Talleyrand could hear us.

"And it's because of this Republic that your husband didn't accept my suggestion, madame?"

I was silent.

"No answer is also an answer." He smiled.

Suddenly I thought of something and I was very indignant. "Sire—"

He leaned over me. "My dear and honoured cousin?"

"Sire, you offered my husband not only the crown of France. But also a Russian grand duchess."

"They say that walls have ears; evidently even the thick walls of

Åbo Castle—" He laughed. "Do you know what your husband said to that, Highness?"

I said nothing. I wasn't angry any more either, just tired.

" 'I'm already married,' the Crown Prince replied. And the subject was dropped. Do you feel better now, Highness?"

"I never really worried, Sire, at least not—about that. Will you have another glass of champagne, my dear—cousin?"

Talleyrand appeared and took our glasses. Talleyrand didn't leave us alone another second. "If there's anything I may do for you any time, my dear cousin, it would make me very happy," said the Tsar eagerly.

"You're very kind, Sire, but I need nothing."

"Perhaps a guard of honour of Russian officers?"

"Oh, please—not that," I entreated. Talleyrand smiled ironically.

"I understand," said the Tsar seriously. "Of course I understand, dear Cousin." He bowed over my hand. "If I had had the honour of meeting you sooner, Highness, I would never have made that suggestion to the Crown Prince. I mean the one in Åbo."

"You meant it well, Sire."

"The ladies of my family who might have been considered are, I regret, not pretty, while you, dear—very dear Cousin—I must go—"

The door had long since closed behind my royal guest and his aides-de-camp. But I still stood aimlessly in the middle of the salon. I was too tired to move. I looked around the room the Tsar had just left and thought about Moreau, who had come from America to fight for the freedom of France. He didn't live to see the white banners, the white cockades. . . . The servants began to clear away the empty champagne glasses. My glance fell on the wilted violets. "Count Rosen, where did those flowers come from?"

"Caulaincourt brought them. He came from Fontainebleau, and was on his way to Talleyrand to turn over the signed Instrument of Abdication."

I went over to the fireplace. So many violets bloom in Fontaine-bleau. The sealed envelope was not addressed. I tore it open.

A piece of paper empty except for one scrawled initial: N. I took a handful of the wilted violets out of the basket and held them against my face. They smelled very sweet, very alive, although they were already half-dead.

"Your Highness, forgive me for disturbing you," Rosen stuttered from behind me. "I'm sorry to trouble you. So far His Highness has managed somehow or other to send me my pay. But for weeks now, I've had no money, there are things I need urgently, and so—"

"Pierre, I mean the steward of my household, will give you your pay immediately—"

"But only, Highness, if you're sure you'll not be inconvenienced, Your Highness has not received any revenue either for some time."

"Of course not. That's why I'm so tired today. I've worked all day long to earn money for our household."

"Highness!" He was horrified.

"Don't be shocked. I sold silk. Nothing dishonourable, Count. One measures a few metres of satin, a few metres of muslin or velvet from a roll, cuts if off, wraps it up, and counts the money. You know that I'm the daughter of a silk merchant."

"Anyone would have lent Your Highness whatever you needed."

"Certainly, Count Rosen. But my husband has finally finished paying the House of Vasa's debts with his personal savings, I don't want to accumulate new debts for the House of Bernadotte. And now, dear Count, good night. Make my excuses to my guests, and ask Queen Julie to take my place at table. I hope you'll all enjoy the veal roast."

Marie was waiting for me at the foot of the stairs. She took my arm and helped me walk up. In my dressing room, I stumbled over something shiny, and started to pick it up. But Marie said, "Leave it, it's only one of Julie's crowns." She undressed me as if I were a child. She put me to bed, and tucked the blankets around me the way I like them.

"Imagine! The roast veal burned," she said gloomily. "The cook lingered in the driveway, hoping to see the Tsar." I closed my eyes.

I woke up in the middle of the night. Sat up with a start. It was very dark and very still. My heart was pounding. I held my head, trying to remember. . . . What had awakened me—a thought, a dream? I knew suddenly that something was going to happen, this very night, perhaps this very hour. Something I'd had a vague presentiment about all evening, but I couldn't think what. First I'd been too tired, and then the Tsar had arrived. All at once, it came to me. The abdication and the violets. The violets—

I lit the candle, and went into my dressing room. The newspaper lay on the dressing table. Slowly—word for word—I read it through. ". . . the Emperor Napoleon, faithful to his oath . . . renounces . . . the thrones of France and Italy . . . there is no personal sacrifice, even of his life, which he is not prepared to . . ."

Yes—no sacrifice, even of his life. . . . These words had awakened me. If a man feels he's reached the end of his life, he undoubtedly thinks back. To his youth, to the years of hope and expectation. He remembers a hedge, a young girl, met by chance, who leaned with him against the hedge, not so long ago he saw the girl again, wearing violets. In the park at Fontainebleau many violets are now in bloom. The soldiers of the guard stand idly in the courtyard with nothing more to do. He'll ask one of them to pick violets while he signs the Abdication. Caulaincourt can take the violets when he delivers the documents in Paris, a last greeting from a man alone with his youth. . . .

He means to take his own life, the violets prove it. I'll have Villatte ride to Fontainebleau immediately and go straight to Napoleon's bedroom. Villatte may be too late. But, nevertheless, I must call him, I must try, I must . . .

Must I? Why must I stop him? He's already at the hedge. Force him back because it's the conventional thing to do?

I slid off the chair, lay on the floor, and bit my fist to keep from screaming. I didn't want to wake anyone. The night was very long. . . .

Not until dawn did I drag myself back to bed. I ached all over and I was cold, terribly cold. After breakfast—chocolate, white rolls and sweet marmalade, for we have money again—I sent for Colonel Villatte.

"Please go to Talleyrand's office this morning, and inquire on my behalf about the health of the Emperor."

Then, with Count Rosen, I drove in a hired carriage to the warehouse for I'd heard that the Prussians in Paris were "buying" without paying, while the Russians, on the other hand, hunted for perfume.

They drink the little bottles of scent and say it tastes better than brandy.

As we entered the Clary shop, M. Legrand was struggling vainly to keep two Prussian soldiers from helping themselves to our last rolls of silk.

I quickly pushed Rosen forward in his Swedish uniform.

"Paris surrendered on condition that it would not be looted," Rosen said politely.

I prodded him in the back. "Shout at them."

Rosen took a deep breath and shouted, "I'll report this to General Blücher!"

The Prussians muttered, fingered the material again, and finally dipped into their pockets and paid for it.

When we returned to the rue d'Anjou, the gendarmes had to clear the way for us, so great was the crowd by the house. In front of the door two Russian guardsmen marched solemnly up and down. As I climbed out, they presented arms. They had full beards and looked frightening.

"A guard of honour," Count Rosen murmured.

"What are all these people waiting for? Why are they staring up at the windows?"

"They've probably heard a rumour that His Royal Highness is arriving sometime today. After all, tomorrow is the official entry of the victorious sovereigns and field marshals into Paris. It's inconceivable that His Highness will not lead the Swedish troops in the victory parade."

Inconceivable, yes, inconceivable. . . .

Before dinner, Colonel Villatte took me aside. "At first no one wanted to talk. But when I said that I asked on behalf of Your Highness, Talleyrand told me in confidence," Villatte whispered. "It's unbelievable," he concluded. With which he followed me into the dining room.

It didn't occur to me until dessert that everyone was sitting in gloomy silence. Even the children.

"Is—something wrong?" I asked.

At first no one answered. Then I saw that Julie beside me was fighting back tears.

"You act so strange, Désirée," she said miserably, "so—unapproachable, not like you used to be."

"I'm worried, and I sleep so badly, these days are so sad," I said softly.

"And you presented none of us to the Tsar," Julie sobbed. "And the children want so much to see the victory parade tomorrow, but no one dares ask you if you'll let us use the carriage with the Swedish coat of arms. In your carriage, they'd be safe—the poor, pathetic Bonaparte children."

I looked at the children. The sons of Hortense and Louis are delicate, blond and shy. They don't remind one in the least of their uncle Napoleon. Julie's Zenaïde, on the contrary, has inherited the high Bonaparte forehead. Charlotte, with her dark curls, resembles my Oscar.

"Naturally, my carriage is available to anyone who wants to see the victorious troops."

Julie touched my arm. "That's sweet of you, Désirée."

"Why? I won't need it tomorrow. I'm staying home all day."

Paris, middle of April, 1814

That night—from the twelfth to the thirteenth of April—I didn't blow out the candle on my night table. At about eleven, the murmur of voices in front of the house ebbed away. The curious crowd had scattered. It was very quiet in the rue d'Anjou. The footsteps of the two Russian sentries echoed. Midnight: still only their footsteps. The clock struck one. The day of the victory parade had dawned. Every muscle in my body was tense. I listened. I thought I would go mad. The clock struck two.

Rolling wheels shattered the silence. They rattled to a stop in front of my house. *Click-clack:* the sentries presenting arms. A hard knock on the door. Voices. Three, four—but not the voice for which I waited. I lay rigid, my eyes closed. Someone ran up the stairs. Hurried, two steps at a time. Flung open my bedroom door, kissed my mouth, my cheeks, my eyes, my forehead.

Jean-Baptiste. My Jean-Baptiste.

"You must have some warm food, you've had a long journey," I said awkwardly and opened my eyes.

Jean-Baptiste knelt beside my bed, his face on my hand. "A journey—yes, a horribly long journey," he said tonelessly.

With my free hand I stroked his hair. How light it shone in the candlelight—it had gone grey, really entirely grey. I sat up. "Come, Jean-Baptiste, go to your room and rest. I'll go to the kitchen and make you an omelette, shall I?"

But he didn't stir. Pressed his forehead against the side of my bed and didn't move.

"Jean-Baptiste, you're home, home again at last."

He slowly raised his head. The sharp lines around his mouth had deepened into furrows, his eyes were blank.

"Jean-Baptiste, get up! Your room is ready, and—"

He drew his fingers across his brow, as though he wanted to wipe away a memory. "Yes, yes—of course. Can you put them all up?"

"All?"

"I haven't come alone. I've brought Brahe as aide-de-camp, and Löwenhjelm as Chamberlain, and Admiral Stedingk, and . . ."

"It's impossible, the house is already overcrowded. Except for your bedroom and dressing room, I haven't a single room free."

"Overcrowded?"

"Julie and her children and the sons of Hortense and . . ."

He jumped up. "Do you mean to tell me you're harbouring all these Bonapartes, and supporting them at the expense of the Swedish court?"

"No, I only have Julie and various children—children, Jean-Baptiste. My house is open to them. And to the Clarys. You sent me the two aides yourself. And the household expenses, as well as the aides' salaries and the Swedish servants, I'm paying myself."

"What do you mean—yourself?"

"I'm selling silk. In a shop, you know—" I went quickly into my dressing room, and slipped into my beautiful green velvet dressing gown with the sable collar. I came back to him and continued. "The firm of Clary. . . . So now I'll make you and your gentlemen an omelette."

Then a miracle happened. He laughed. Sat on my bed and shook with laughter, and held out his arms. "My little girl—my priceless little girl. Crown Princess of Sweden and Norway—selling silk. Come, come here to me."

I went to him. "I don't see that it's anything a laugh about," I protested. "My money was gone. And everything is dreadfully expensive, you'll soon see."

"Fourteen days ago I sent a courier to you with money."

"Unfortunately, he didn't get here. Look, when the gentlemen have eaten, we must find hotel rooms for them."

He looked serious again. "The Swedish headquarters will be in a palace in the rue St. Honoré. It was requisitioned long ago. My staff can probably go right there." Then he opened the door between my bedroom and his.

I held up the candle. "Your bed is made," I said, "the bedspread has been turned back, everything's ready for you."

But he stared into his bedroom, his familiar room with the familiar furniture, as though he'd never seen it before. "I'll stay at the Swedish headquarters, too," he said without expression. And hastily, "I'll have to receive a great many people. And this wouldn't do—I can't receive them here, Désirée! Don't you understand?"

"You won't live here any more?" I was dismayed.

He put his arm around my shoulder. "I've only come back to Paris so that the Swedish troops can take part in the victory parade. Besides, I must confer with the Tsar. But I'll tell you one thing, Désirée, I'll never return to this room, never!"

"Five minutes ago you wanted to live here with your entire staff," I exclaimed angrily.

"That was before I'd seen my room again. Forgive me, it was my mistake. But there's no return from where I've come." He held me close. "There—and now let's go down. My gentlemen hope that you will welcome them. And Fernand has probably prepared a meal."

Fernand. . . . The thought of him and the roses in our bridal bed helped me back to reality. I put on rouge and powder.

Arm in arm, Jean-Baptiste and I walked into the dining room. I would gladly have kissed my erstwhile young knight, the young Count Brahe. But Löwenhjelm, who had once tried so hard to teach me Swedish etiquette, stood beside him. So I didn't dare. Admiral Stedingk, covered with orders and decorations, came up to me. And Fernand, in a brand-new livery with Swedish gold buttons.

"How is Oscar?" I asked. For months my child had lived alone among strangers in Stockholm. Jean-Baptiste extracted some letters from his breast pocket.

"The Heir Apparent has composed a regimental march," he announced proudly. For a moment my heart beat happily, the candles burned brightly: Oscar is composing.

Fernand's coffee tasted bitter and yet sweet. Like his homecoming, I thought. We sat in front of the fireplace in the large salon. The far end of the room was in darkness. But Jean-Baptiste peered into the darkness and at the portrait of the First Consul. Our conversation subsided. There was a painful silence. Suddenly Jean-Baptiste turned to me, and demanded cuttingly, "And—he?"

"The Emperor is waiting in Fontainebleau for his fate to be decided. And last night he tried to commit suicide."

"What?" they all cried together—Brahe, Löwenhjelm, Stedingk, Rosen. Only Jean-Baptiste said nothing.

"Since the Russian campaign, the Emperor has always carried poison," I said, and watched the flickering flames. "Today, or rather last night, he swallowed this poison. His valet saw him and—took action at once. That's all."

"What action?" Löwenhjelm asked in surprise.

"If you must know, the story is that Constant, the valet, stuck his finger down the Emperor's throat, and he threw up. Then he called Caulaincourt, and Caulaincourt forced the Emperor to drink some milk. The Emperor had severe cramps for a while, but this morning he got up as usual and dictated letters."

"That's grotesque," Stedingk declared, shaking his head. "Tragic and comic, too. Stuck a finger down his throat. Why didn't he shoot himself?"

I didn't answer. Jean-Baptiste gnawed on his lower lip and stared into the fire, his mind seemed far away. And again this heavy silence. Brahe cleared his throat. "Your Highness, about the victory parade tomorrow—"

Jean-Baptiste pulled himself together, and as he had before in my room drew his hand across his forehead. His absent-minded expression changed, he came over to us, and began to speak clearly and precisely. "In the first place, any possible misunderstanding between the Tsar and me must be cleared up. The Tsar, as you gentlemen know, expected me to cross the Rhine with the Prussians and the Russians. However, I led our troops northward, and took part in not a single battle on the soil of France. Should my allies take exception—" He stopped.

I looked at Brahe. Hesitantly he answered my silent question. "We've been driving around for weeks aimlessly, Your Highness, in Belgium, and in France. His Highness wanted to see the battlefields—" Brahe looked at me helplessly and added, "His Highness could agree to this trip to Paris only with a heavy heart."

"In the villages where there's been fighting, not one stone remains on another. That's not the way to make war, not that," said Jean-Baptiste between his teeth.

Then Löwenhjelm determinedly opened the portfolio he'd been carrying around the whole time. A package of letters came to view. "Your Highness, I have here all the Tsar's handwritten letters that have not yet been answered," he said loudly. "About . . ."

"Don't say it," Jean-Baptiste shouted. I'd never seen him so out of control. Then he leaned forward, and stared into the fire. The eyes of the Swedes turned on me. I was their last hope.

"Jean-Baptiste," I began. He didn't move. So I went over and knelt beside him and laid my head on his arm. "Jean-Baptiste, you must let the gentlemen speak out. The Tsar suggested that you become King of France, didn't he?"

He stiffened, but I went right on. "You haven't answered the Tsar. That's why Count d'Artois, Louis XVIII's brother, will arrive in Paris tomorrow to prepare for the return of the Bourbons. The Tsar has finally agreed to the proposals of the other Allies and Talleyrand's suggestions."

"The Tsar will never understand why I didn't cross the Rhine with him, why I wouldn't fight on French soil, why, above all, I haven't responded to his various suggestions. But Sweden can't afford a breach with the Tsar—can't you see?"

"Jean-Baptiste, the Tsar is proud to be your friend. And he understands perfectly why you couldn't accept the crown of France. I explained it all to him."

"You—explained—it all to him?" Jean-Baptiste grabbed my shoulder, looked me full in the face.

"Yes, he came to pay his respects to the wife of the victor of Leipzig."

How relieved they were, Jean-Baptiste and his Swedes. I stood up. "And now I'll wish you good night—or rather good morning, gentlemen. You'll want a few hours' rest before the victory parade. I hope by now everything has been made ready for you in the rue St. Honoré."

Then I hurried out of the salon. There are limits, and I couldn't bear to watch Jean-Baptiste leave his own home to spend the night in a palace around the corner. He caught up with me on the stairs, put his arm across my shoulders, and leaned heavily on me, all the way to my bedroom. There he dropped down on my bed. I knelt beside him and tried to take off his boots. I pulled and pulled. "You must help, Jean-Baptiste, or I'll never get them off."

"If you knew how tired I am—"

He let me undress him like a child. Finally I pulled the covers over us both, and blew out the candle. But the morning was already beginning to creep relentlessly in through the cracks in the shutters. "This damnable victory parade . . . " he mumbled. Then, "I can't march down the Champs Elysées hup-two-three-four at the head of the Northern Army—I can't."

"Of course you can. The Swedes have fought gallantly for the liberation of Europe, and naturally they want to march in the Paris parade, led by their crown prince. How long will it take? An hour, two at the most. It will be much easier than—Leipzig, Jean-Baptiste."

He moaned and put his head on my shoulder. "At Grossbeeren, he sent my oldest regiments against me. . . ."

"Forget it, Jean-Baptiste, forget it." I hated myself, but I went on, "Remember why you fought!"

"Why did I? For the Restoration of the Bourbons, perhaps, Désirée? Exactly what did you say to the Tsar?"

"That in France you're a Republican, and in Sweden a crown prince. In somewhat different words, Jean-Baptiste. But he understood me."

His breathing was quieter. "Did you tell him anything else, little girl?"

"Yes, that you didn't want the French crown, but longed with all your heart for a Russian grand duchess. So he wouldn't think you'd turn down all his suggestions!"

"Mmmm."

"Are you asleep, Jean-Baptiste?"

"Mmmm."

"The Tsar thinks you'd better stay with me. He says the grand duchesses he knows are not at all pretty."

"Mmmm."

At last he fell asleep. He slept only briefly and restlessly, as a traveller in an unfamiliar bed in a strange inn.

Marie and Fernand squabbled in my dressing room—over the large flatiron. Jean-Baptiste lifted his head from my shoulder.

"Brahe," he cried. "What's going on in front of my tent?"

"Go back to sleep, Jean-Baptiste."

"Brahe, tell Löwenhjelm . . ."

"Jean-Baptiste, in the first place, you're not in a tent, but in your wife's bedroom. Secondly, you're hearing only the usual squabble between Marie and Fernand. Go to sleep."

But Jean-Baptiste sat up. And looked thoughtfully around my room. A look of farewell, not of homecoming. Fernand's voice rose angrily, "No, your large flatiron for the dress uniform."

At that Jean-Baptiste got up and went to his dressing room. I rang, and Marie brought breakfast for two. "The Marshal should have left Fernand at home," she grumbled.

"What do you mean, at home?" I demanded.

She shrugged. "With the icicles. In Stockholm."

The door between my dressing room and Jean-Baptiste's was ajar. I heard the following conversations:

Fernand: "Brahe and Löwenhjelm have reported for duty. Your Highness, rooms in the rue St. Honoré are ready. Yesterday the Tsar moved over to the Elysée Palace, to the Russian headquarters. Mme Julie used to live there. The parade begins at two o'clock. Cannon have been placed in front of Your Highness' headquarters, for reasons of security. The rue St. Honoré will be closed off. Demonstrations, Highness, mobs . . ."

Jean-Baptiste said something I couldn't catch.

"All right—no mobs. As Your Highness commands—passers-by. Anyway, the police believe, Your Highness, that these passers-by intend to . . ."

The rest was drowned out by a splash of water. As usual every morning, Fernand was giving Jean-Baptiste a cold rub-down. "Send up Brahe and Löwenhjelm."

Brahe's voice: "Wetterstedt has arrived, with his attachés."

I mulled over Wetterstedt. Of course—Chancellor Wetterstedt.

Brahe: "Wetterstedt has already been in touch with Metternich and the English. And, what's more, our headquarters are being besieged."

Jean-Baptiste: "By the passers-by?"

"No, the street was closed long ago. Gendarmes and Cossacks are forming cordons. The Tsar has placed an entire regiment at our disposal."

Jean-Baptiste spoke very rapidly, and I could understand only a few words. "Definitely Swedish dragoons . . . under no conditions Russian sentries . . ."

Chamberlain Löwenhjelm: "Our headquarters are besieged by visitors. Talleyrand wants to welcome Your Highness in the name of the French Government. Marshals Ney and Marmont left their cards. The personal aide-de-camp of the King of Prussia called. The English Ambassador. A delegation from the citizens of Paris . . ."

Brahe: "Colonel Villatte asks to be received."

Jean-Baptiste: "Have him come in at once. I have very little time."

I tiptoed into Jean-Baptiste's dressing room. My husband stood in front of the tall mirror, buttoning the tunic of his Swedish field marshal's uniform. Fernand sprayed him with eau de cologne and then handed him the Grand Cross of the Legion of Honour. Jean-Baptiste, from long habit, took the chain and started to hang it around his neck. Suddenly he hesitated.

"Your Highness must dress for the parade now," Löwenhjelm reminded him. "After the gala breakfast of His Russian Majesty, there'll be no time to change."

So Jean-Baptiste reluctantly put on the chain, and the Star of the Legion of Honour. His eyes narrowed. "Parade—Marshal Bernadotte," he murmured to the dejected face in his mirror. Just then in came Villatte. Jean-Baptiste turned quickly, went to him, and clapped him on the shoulder. "Villatte. How happy I am to see you again."

Villatte stood at attention.

Jean-Baptiste shook his shoulder. "Well, old comrade?" But Villatte didn't budge. His face was stubborn. Jean-Baptiste's hand slipped from his friend's shoulder.

"Can I do something for you, Colonel?"

"I hear that yesterday the Allied Powers agreed to the release of all French prisoners of war. I therefore ask for—my release."

I laughed. But my laughter died. Villatte wasn't joking, his set face was deeply sad.

"Naturally, Colonel. You are entirely your own master," said Jean-Baptiste quickly. "But I'd be very glad if, for a while, you'd stay with us as our guest."

"I thank Your Highness for your friendly offer. I must, unfortunately, decline it, and beg Your Highness to excuse me." He came quickly over to me and bowed low.

Over his shoulder I saw how grey Jean-Baptiste's face was. "Villatte," I whispered, "you've gone a long way with us. Stay with us, won't you?"

"The Emperor has released his army from their oaths," Jean-Baptiste said hoarsely. "I hear that some of the marshals have called on me. So why . . ."

"That's why, Highness. Only a few guards' regiments have remained in Fontainebleau. The marshals haven't even considered it worth their while to take leave of their former commander in chief. I'm only a colonel, Highness. But I know what's right. From Fontainebleau I rejoin my regiment."

When I looked up again, Villatte had gone, and Jean-Baptiste was wrapping on his Swedish sash. "Before you go, I want to speak to you a moment alone, Jean-Baptiste," I said, and went back to my dressing room. He followed me. I waved him into the chair in front of the dressing table. "Sit down."

Then I took my little jar of rouge, and began carefully, very carefully, to paint his grey cheeks.

"You're crazy, Désirée—I won't have it," he objected.

Carefully I rubbed in the rouge, he really began to look more natural. "There—" I said with satisfaction. "You can't ride at the head of your victorious troops along the Champs Elysées with a face like death. When you come as a victor, you must also look like a victor."

He shook his head in revulsion. "I can't." It sounded like a sob. "You—I can't."

I put my hands on his shoulders. "And after the victory parade, Jean-Baptiste, you must appear at the gala performance at the Théâtre Français. You owe it to Sweden. I'm afraid you must go now, dearest."

He leaned back. His head lay against my breast, his pale lips were chapped and sore. "In all France I think there'll be only one other as lonely as I during this parade—Napoleon."

"Nonsense. You're not lonely. After all, I'm with you and not with him. Go on now, the gentlemen are waiting."

He rose obediently, and pressed my hand to his lips. "Promise me you won't watch the parade. I don't want—I don't want you to see me. . . ."

"Of course not, Jean-Baptiste. I'll be in the garden, thinking about you."

When the bells started to peal, I went out to the garden. They announced the beginning of the victory parade, and rang continuously all the while the victorious troops, led by the Tsar of Russia, the Emperor of Austria, the King of Prussia, and the Crown Prince of Sweden, marched happily through Paris.

The children had driven off with Mme la Flotte and their governess in my carriage. At the last moment, my nephew Marius, and Marcelline climbed in, too. Heaven knows how they all found room. Julie stayed in bed, and had Marie put cold compresses on her forehead. She was hurt because Jean-Baptiste had forgotten to speak to her. I had given my servants the day off. That's how I came to be sitting alone in the garden, and no one announced my unexpected caller.

This unexpected visitor had found the house door open, had come in and wandered through the deserted salons. Finally he came to the garden. I didn't notice him, because my eyes were closed and I was thinking about Jean-Baptiste. The Champs Elysées will seem endless today, Jean-Baptiste, endless.

"Highness," a voice shouted above the bells. Startled, I opened my eyes. A man was doubled over in a deep bow before me. He straightened up—a pointed nose, little eyes with pin-point pupils. So he's still around. When Napoleon discovered that his Minister of Police was negotiating secretly with the English, he threw him out. But shortly before the Battle of Leipzig, he appointed him Governor of some Italian province to keep Fouché away from Paris. The former Jacobin wore an inconspicuous frock coat, and an enormous white cockade.

Helplessly, I indicated the garden bench. In a flash, he sat down beside me and began to talk. But the bells drowned out his words. He regretfully shrugged his shoulders and smiled. I turned my head away. Jean-Baptiste, it can't go on much longer. . . .

The bells ceased.

"Forgive me, Your Highness, if I'm disturbing—"

I'd forgotten Fouché. Unwillingly, I looked at him.

"I've come with a message from Talleyrand to Mme Julie Bonaparte," he began, and took a document out of his breast pocket. "Talleyrand is very busy these days, while I—" he smiled pitifully— "unfortunately—am not. And as I wanted to call again on Your Highness in any case, I suggested to Talleyrand that I bring this document with me. It concerns the future of members of the Bonaparte family."

He handed me a copy of a long legal document. "I'll give it to my sister," I said.

He tapped the document with his forefinger. "Look at the list, Your Highness."

It read:

To the Emperor's mother: 300,000 francs; King Joseph: 500,000 francs; King Louis: 200,000 francs; Queen Hortense and her children: 400,000 francs; King Jerome and his Queen: 500,000; Princess Elisa: 300,000 francs; Princess Pauline: 300,000 francs.

"Yearly, Your Highness, yearly," Fouché explained. "The Emperor's family will receive property or revenue from the state funds, and these sums will be guaranteed them annually. Our new Government is truly generous, Your Highness."

"Where will the members of the family live?"

"Abroad, Highness, never in France."

Julie, who always felt miserable away from home—an exile. A lifelong—exile. And why? Because I once brought Joseph to our house. I must try to help her, I thought. I'll do all I can to help her.

"You will ask His Highness to do what he can for Mme Julie Bonaparte, won't you? Perhaps you yourself will go to King Louis and intercede for her. King Louis . . ." I repeated, and tried to get used to the words, at least.

"His Majesty is expected in the Tuileries within the next few days."

"What has this King Louis done with himself during the long years of his exile? How has he kept busy?" I asked. I wanted to visualize the future of the Bonaparte brothers.

"His Majesty was mostly in England, and filled his time with study. His Majesty translated Gibbon's great work, history of the *Decline and Fall of the Roman Empire,* into French."

Translated history instead of making it, I said to myself.

"Will this King Louis bring his own court to Paris?"

"Obviously. The really faithful followers of the House of Bourbon are now returning to France with him. Therefore, may I ask Your Highness—"

I looked at him in astonishment. He never noticed at all.

"—to say a good word for me. Perhaps His Majesty won't fill all the positions with Frenchmen who have lived abroad since the Revolution. If someone brought up my name . . ."

"Surely no one has forgotten you, M. Fouché. I was still only a child, but I remember distinctly the many death sentences you signed."

"Your Highness, *that* is forgotten." He straightened his white cockade. "It must be brought to mind that, in the last few years, I've secretly tried to negotiate a peace with England. General Bonaparte denounced me as a traitor. I risked my life, Your Highness."

I looked again at the document in my hand. "And—General Bonaparte?"

"Very favourable conditions. The General may himself choose a residence anywhere outside France—an island, for instance, Elba—or he can go overseas. A troop of four hundred men, whom he may choose himself, can accompany him. Besides, he may retain the title of Emperor. Generous, extremely generous, isn't it?"

"What has the Emperor decided?"

"They're discussing Elba. A charming little island, reminiscent of the Emperor's birthplace. The same vegetation as Corsica, I hear."

"And the Empress?"

"Will become Duchess of Parma. That is, if she renounces her son's right of succession. But these details will be decided in Vienna at a large congress. The formation of a new Europe. The dynasties, dispossessed by Napoleon, will return to their thrones. An acknowledgment of legitimacy, Your Highness. . . . I gather that His Highness will also go to Vienna. To press his claim to the Swedish throne." Fouché cleared his throat mildly. "I hear that, unfortunately, some of the Russians and the Austrians have declared that His Highness has no—we'd say 'legitimate'—claim. I, naturally, am at His Highness' service, to represent him in Vienna, and . . ."

I stood up. "I don't understand what you mean. I'll give the document to my sister." If he'd stayed another minute, I would have had hysterics.

Then I discovered the first daisies in the grass. And the buds on the rosebushes. Spring had come, and I hadn't noticed. How sweet the spring air was in Paris! They can't drive Julie away. . . .

Children's voices cut through the stillness. They were back from the parade, and ran to me—two tall, thin girls in little rose-coloured jackets, and two blond boys in cadet uniforms.

"Aunt Désirée, Uncle was magnificent." Charlotte was breathless with excitement. "He rode on a white horse, and wore a violet velvet coat—so elegant—'

"It wasn't a coat," her cousin, Charles Louis Napoleon, interrupted seriously, "but a cape. On his hat he had white ostrich feathers, and in his hand a silver baton"

"That's the field marshal's baton," Napoleon Louis explained.

"Uncle Marius said it was his old French marshal's baton," whispered Zenaïde

"And his face! As though it were carved out of marble, Aunt Marcelline said," from Charlotte.

"So pale?" I asked, worried.

"No—so, you know, immovable. Like a statue. . . . The Tsar smiled all the time, and the old Emperor of Austria waved to the crowd, but the King of Prussia—" The children giggled. "The Prussian King made a dreadful face and frowned. So we'd all be more afraid of him in future, Uncle Marius said."

"And the people, the other spectators. What did they say?"

"All sorts of things. There was so much to see. The foreign uniforms, and the Tsar's beautiful horse—and did you know that, besides their guns, the Cossacks carry long whips? Everyone laughed at the Prussians, they kick their legs up so high when they march in a parade, and . . ."

"And while Uncle Jean-Baptiste rode by, what did the people say?"

The children looked at each other.

"Aunt, all at once it was quiet," said Charles Louis Napoleon carefully. "Really—dead silence."

"The Swedes had captured many eagles and banners. They were carried by men right behind him," Charlotte whispered.

"Aunt, our eagles," Charles Louis Napoleon burst out indignantly.

"Now go in, children, and have Marie give you something to eat,"
I said hastily. Then I went to have a talk with Julie.

First we just tried to understand the contents of the document
which disposed of her future in such a businesslike style. Julie flung
off the compresses, buried her face in the pillows and sobbed, "But
I won't go, I won't, I won't. . . . They can't take Mortefontaine
away from me! Désirée, you must see that I stay in Mortefontaine.
With the children."

I stroked her straggly hair. "Meanwhile, you'll stay with me.
Later we'll try to get back Mortefontaine. But Joseph? What if Joseph can't get a permit to stay?"

"Joseph wrote me from Blois. He wants to go to Switzerland and
buy an estate there. And I'm to follow him with the children as
soon as possible. But I won't—I won't go. . . ." She suddenly sat
up. "Désirée, you won't desert me? You'll stand by me until it's all
settled?"

I nodded.

"You won't go to Sweden, but stay here—here in your house.
And help me?"

It's my fault she ever got mixed up with the Bonapartes, my fault
that now she had no home, I must help her, I must. . . .

"Do you promise, Désirée?"

"I'll stay with you, Julie."

Paris, early May, 1814

On the evening King Louis XVIII gave his first court ball in the
Tuileries, I had a cold. Not a real cold, of course. I went to bed,
just as I had before Napoleon's coronation, and was just as sick.
Marie brought me milk and honey. I always enjoy milk and honey.
I began to read the newspapers.

The *Moniteur* described Napoleon's departure for Elba. On April

20, the travelling coaches were drawn up in the courtyard of the *Cheval Blanc* in Fontainebleau. Not a single marshal was present. General Petit had assembled a regiment of Imperial guards in the courtyard. The Emperor came out, and General Petit held up one of the gilded eagles. Napoleon kissed the flag under the eagle. Then he got into the coach in which General Bertrand was waiting for him. That was all. At least all that the *Moniteur* reported to its readers.

In the *Journal des Debats,* however, I found an interesting article about the Crown Prince of Sweden. I read that the Crown Prince intended to divorce his wife, Désirée Clary, sister of Mme Julie Bonaparte. After the divorce the former Crown Princess of Sweden, under the name of a Countess of Gotland, would continue to live in her home in the rue d'Anjou. The Crown Prince, on the other hand . . . I took a swallow of hot milk and honey. "The Crown Prince, on the other hand, has a choice between a Russian and a Prussian princess."

Even the possibility that he might marry a Bourbon princess was explored in the *Journal des Debats.* An alliance between former Marshal J.-B. Bernadotte and one of the reigning dynasties would secure his future in Sweden.

I finished the honey and milk, but it no longer tasted sweet. And I didn't want to read any more newspapers either. I thought again about the Bourbons' first court ball. How strange that Jean-Baptiste and I had been invited. On second thought I suppose it was not so strange. Jean-Baptiste had, after all, commanded one of the three armies that liberated Europe. Besides he's the adopted son of the King of Sweden. I wonder whether Jean-Baptiste accepted the invitation. . . .

Since that first night, we've hardly been alone with each other at all. Of course, I've often visited him at the Swedish headquarters in the rue St. Honoré. Cannon are mounted out in front. Swedish dragoons, heavily armed, stand guard. Every time I've found Fouché in the anteroom. And three times, Talleyrand. Marshal Ney, too, waits around impatiently. In the main salon, on the other hand, Chancellor Wetterstedt, Admiral Stedingk and the Swedish generals seem to hold interminable conferences. Jean-Baptiste, bowed over his files, dictates letters.

This afternoon we gave a reception in the rue St. Honoré in honour of the Tsar. To my horror, the Tsar brought Count d'Artois, the brother of the new King of France. The Count has a gross, embittered face, and wears an old-fashioned peruke. The Bourbons try to pretend that the Revolution changed nothing. Although Louis XVIII had to promise to swear an oath of allegiance to the present laws of France. In short, the *Code Napoleon.*

Count d'Artois hurried over to Jean-Baptiste. "Your Highness, France will be in your debt forever. Dear Cousin!"

Jean-Baptiste went white. The Bourbon turned next to me. "Your Highness will surely be at the court ball in the Tuileries this evening?"

I held my handkerchief to my nose. "I fear a spring cold. . . ." The Tsar was most solicitous and wished me a speedy recovery.

And so I lay in bed, while the guests—so many familiar faces!— assembled in the large ballroom in the Tuileries and admired the new curtains, sky blue and white with embroidered fleurs-de-lis, and the orchestra tuned its instruments. Napoleon insisted on good dance music. . . . The folding doors are opened wide, the ladies' dresses rustle as they curtsy, but where is "La Marseillaise"? Forbidden, of course, forbidden. The eighteenth Louis leans heavily on his cane. Under the white knee breeches his swollen calves are bandaged, he suffers from dropsy and can hardly walk. The tired old gentleman surveys the ballroom. Here the Parisians beat and kicked my brother, he must be thinking, they dragged him out of this very ballroom. . . . Now the old master of ceremonies is calling out the guests' names, the old gentleman inclines his head the better to hear. First the allied sovereigns are announced. We thank them for making possible our appearance in this ballroom. And We embrace a certain J.-B. Bernadotte, fanatical Republican and the Crown Prince of Sweden, "Our esteemed cousin. The dancing will begin immediately, Your Highness—"

My thoughts were interrupted. Someone was coming up the stairs. That's odd, I thought, everyone was already asleep. Yet someone was hurrying up, two steps at a time . . .

"I hope I didn't wake you, little girl."

Neither gala uniform nor velvet cape. Only the dark-blue field uniform.

"You're not really ill, Désirée?"

"Of course not, but how about you, Jean-Baptiste? The new King invited you to the Tuileries."

"Strange that a former sergeant should have more tact than a Bourbon, don't you think?"

A pause. Then, "I'm sorry that you've gone to bed, little one. I've come to say good-by. I'm leaving tomorrow morning."

My heart hammered heavily. Tomorrow, so soon. . . .

"I've done my duty here and made my triumphal entry. What more can they expect? Besides, my agreement with Denmark has been signed by the allied commissioners. The Great Powers have recognized the ceding of Norway to Sweden. But, imagine, Désirée —the Norwegians don't want it."

So that was our farewell. I sat up in bed, a candle flickered, he talked about Norway. "Why not?" I asked.

"Because they prefer to govern themselves. In spite of my offering them the most liberal constitution in the world! And promising not to send a single Swedish administrator to Christiania. But they're convening their *Storting* . . ."

"What Ting are they convening?"

"*Storting*—the Norwegian National Assembly. They want to be independent. Perhaps even a republic."

"Then let them have it!"

I couldn't see his face, his head was sunk forward, his eyes in shadow. Jean-Baptiste—could this really be the end?

" 'Let them, let them.' How you simplify things. In the first place, Norway and Sweden are a geographical unit. Secondly, I promised Sweden this union. Third, it would console them for the loss of Finland. Fourthly, I can't afford to disappoint the Swedes. In the fifth place—I won't have it. Do you understand?"

"Afford? The Swedish Parliament elected you, once and for all, successor to their throne, Jean-Baptiste."

"And the Swedish Parliament can, once and for all, depose me— and recall the Vasa Prince. With the Bourbons back in power, my child— Away with the Jacobin general, call the old dynasties back, forget the last twenty years!"

His glance fell on the newspapers on my night table. Absent-mindedly he leafed through the *Journal des Debats*. Suddenly he began to read.

My heart lay heavy and hard as a stone in my breast. "You could marry a member of an old dynasty, Jean-Baptiste," I said. And since he kept on reading the paper, "Haven't you seen this article before?"

"No, I've really no time for scandal stories. Gossip, ridiculous court gossip . . ." He flung the paper down on the night table, and looked at me. "It's too bad. I had my carriage wait, I wanted to suggest that you . . . No, never mind, you're probably too tired."

"You came to say good-by and to suggest—" I kept my voice under control. "Tell me what you have to say to me. But say it quickly, or I'll go mad."

He looked at me in bewilderment. "It's not important. I wanted to drive with you once more through the streets of Paris. For the last time, Désirée."

"For—the last time?" I whispered.

At first I hadn't heard right. And then I began to weep.

"What's the matter, Désirée? Don't you feel well?"

"I thought—you wanted—a divorce," I sobbed, and threw back the bedclothes. "And now I'll dress quickly, and we'll drive through the streets, Jean-Baptiste, together."

The carriage rolled along beside the Seine. It was an open carriage. I put my head on Jean-Baptiste's shoulder, and felt his arm around me. The lights of Paris danced in the dark water. Jean-Baptiste had the carriage stop. We got out and strolled, arm in arm, over "our bridge," and leaned over the parapet.

"It's always the same," I said sadly. "I make a scene. First in the Tallien's salon, later in the Queen of Sweden's. Forgive me, Jean-Baptiste."

"I don't care for myself. I'm only sorry for your sake."

The same words as before. Other words of our first conversation came back to me, and I asked: "Don't you know General Bonaparte personally?"

"Yes, I do not find him attractive," he answered, as he had so long ago.

I leaned forward and spoke to the dancing lights, " 'I've earned my way, mademoiselle—I joined the Army when I was fifteen, and for a long time I was a noncommissioned officer. At present, mademoiselle, I am a divisional general. My name is Jean-Baptiste Bernadotte. For many years I have saved part of my pay, I can buy a small house for you and the child. . . .' That's what you once said, do you remember?"

"Of course. But I'd rather know how you envisage your own future, Désirée."

At first I stuttered. Then it came more easily. "If you believe it would be better for you and Oscar to divorce me, and marry a princess—then, get a divorce. I make only one condition."

"And that?"

"That I become your mistress, Jean-Baptiste."

"Out of the question. I'm not going to start keeping mistresses at the Swedish court! Besides, I can't afford a mistress, little girl. You'll just have to remain my wife, Désirée, whatever happens!"

Our Seine rippled beneath us. It was like music, like a sweet waltz. "And what if the worst happens—if you become King?"

"Yes, darling, even if I become King."

We sauntered back to the carriage. "Perhaps you could do me a favour, and refrain from selling silk personally," he remarked. Notre-Dame loomed up before us. "Stop." Jean-Baptiste stared up at the Cathedral, his mouth open as if he wanted to drink in the sight. Then he closed his eyes to impress it indelibly on his memory.

"Drive on."

"I'll have Pierre collect my share of the Clary firm's profits regularly," I said. "Pierre will stay with me as steward of my household. I'll appoint Marius Clary my equerry, and Marcelline Tascher a lady-in-waiting. I want to let La Flotte go."

"Are you pleased with Count Rosen?"

"Personally, yes, but for business, no."

"What does that mean?"

"The Count can't even tie up a package. I took him with me to the warehouse originally only to deal with the Prussians—the Prus-

503

sians were naturally looting, right under our noses. But since we had no apprentice at the time, Rosen . . ."

"Désirée! You can't change Dragoon Lieutenant Count Rosen into an apprentice!"

"Well, perhaps you could send me an aide who isn't a born count. Aren't there any parvenus at the Swedish court?"

"Only the Bernadottes," laughed Jean-Baptiste. "And Baron Wetterstedt, but he's Chancellor and I need him myself."

Jean-Baptiste leaned forward and called out an address to the coachman. We drove to Sceaux to see our first home again.

The stars were very near. Behind the garden wall the lilacs were in bloom. "I travelled this road twice a day as Minister of War," he said, and then, "When may I expect you in Stockholm, My Royal Highness?"

"Not yet." His epaulettes scratched my cheek. "The next few years will be hard enough for you. I don't want to make your life still more difficult. You know how ill-suited I am for the Swedish court."

He looked at me intently. "Do you mean to say, Désirée, that you're not going to adapt yourself to Swedish court ceremonial?"

"When I come, I'll decide all questions of etiquette myself," I said slowly. The carriage stopped at No. 3 rue de la Lune in Sceaux. Strangers live in our little house. I thought—Oscar was born upstairs there.

At that moment Jean-Baptiste said, "Imagine, Oscar already has to shave. Twice a week." We saw that the old chestnut tree in the garden had candle blossoms.

On the way home we felt so close to one another that we didn't talk at all. As the carriage drove into the rue d'Anjou, Jean-Baptiste spoke for the first time. "You have no other reasons for staying here? Really not?"

"Yes, Jean-Baptiste. Here I'm needed. There I'm superfluous. I must help Julie."

"I defeated Napoleon at Leipzig. But even so, I can't get rid of the Bonapartes."

"I'm thinking of the Clarys," I said sorrowfully. "Please—don't forget that."

The carriage stopped for the last time. Everything happened terribly fast. Jean-Baptiste got out of the carriage with me, and looked at the house. Attentively, silently. The two sentries presented arms. I held out my hand to Jean-Baptiste. The sentries were watching.

"Whatever rumours you read in the newspaper—" he drew my hand to his lips—"don't believe them, understand?"

"Too bad! I would so love to be your mistress—ouch!" Jean-Baptiste had bitten me on the finger.

The sentries, unfortunately, were watching.

To me there's nothing more disagreeable than making calls of condolence, especially on a lovely Whitmonday.

Yesterday evening a weeping ex-lady-in-waiting from Malmaison was announced. Josephine had died on Whitsunday at noon. Recently, she'd caught a heavy cold taking an evening walk on the arm of the Tsar in the park at Malmaison "The evening was quite cool, but Her Majesty absolutely refused to wear a wrap. Her Majesty wore a new muslin gown, very décolleté, with only a very light transparent scarf."

I remember that muslin, Josephine, too light for a May evening. Violet, wasn't it? Sweet, melancholy, and so becoming.

Hortense and Eugène de Beauharnais lived with their mother. The ex-lady-in-waiting handed me a note. "Bring the children with you, my one comfort," Hortense had scrawled, among other messages, all generously interspersed with dashes and exclamation marks.

So this morning, with Julie and the two sons of the former Queen of Holland, I drove to Malmaison. We tried to make the boys realize that their grandmother was dead.

"Perhaps she's not actually dead. Perhaps she's merely letting the Allies think she's dead, so she can secretly join Napoleon in Elba," Charles Louis Napoleon suggested. In the Bois de Boulogne the breeze blew a whiff of summer and of lindens into the carriage. It seemed incredible that Josephine should be dead.

In Malmaison, we found Hortense in deep black mourning, her face pale green and her nose red from crying. Solemnly she flung herself first into my arms and then into Julie's. Eugène de Beauharnais sat at a lady's tiny desk riffling through some papers. He's the erstwhile shy young man whom Napoleon appointed Viceroy of Italy, and for whom he arranged a marriage with a daughter of the King of Bavaria. He bowed stiffly over our hands. Then pointed to the pile of papers on the desk and sighed. "Unbelievable—stacks of unpaid bills. For gowns, hats, and rosebushes."

Hortense's mouth was thin. "Mama never could get along on her allowance."

"Besides the two million the State paid her every year after the divorce, Napoleon gave her one million from his civil list. And nevertheless—" Eugène smoothed his hair despairingly. "Hortense, these debts run into millions, I'd like to know who will pay them."

"The ladies aren't interested in that," Hortense said, and begged us to sit down. Stiff and silent we sat on Josephine's white salon sofa. The folding doors to the garden were open, and the fragrance of Josephine's roses wafted in.

"The Tsar of Russia came to pay Mama his respects, and Mama asked him for supper." Hortense dabbed at her now-dry eyes with her handkerchief. "I assume she wanted to ask him to protect my poor defenceless children. You know that I'm now divorced?"

We nodded politely. Hortense's lover, Count Flahault, came in. Their illegitimate son is being brought up by a Count Morny. Eugène de Beauharnais wrestled with the unpaid bills of the dead Josephine. "Mama seems not to have paid Le Roy for months. Yet she ordered twenty-six new gowns. I can't see why Mama, living in retirement, needed twenty-six gowns." He stared at the bills. His sister shrugged her shoulders contemptuously; her handkerchief hid her mouth. The one man Hortense de Beauharnais ever really loved had married her mother.

"Do you want to see her?" Hortense asked sternly.

Julie shook her head firmly. "Yes," said I, without thinking.

"Count Flahault. Take Her Royal Highness upstairs."

We went up one flight. "The dear departed is still in her bedroom," he whispered. "Here—please come in, Highness."

The tall candles burned without flickering. The shutters were closed tight. The room was permeated with incense, roses, and Josephine's heavy perfume. Gradually my eyes became accustomed to the semidarkness. Like huge black birds, the nuns knelt at the foot of the wide, low bed, and murmured prayers for the dead.

At first I shrank from looking at the dead woman. But I pulled myself together and went closer. I recognized the coronation robe which lay in gentle folds across the bed. Like a comfortable, warm coverlet. The ermine-lined cape around her breast and shoulders gleamed yellow in the candlelight, yellow like the face of the dead Josephine.

No—Josephine didn't frighten me. Nor make me want to weep. . . . Her small head lay a little to one side. Just as she often held it when she looked up at a man from under her long eyelashes. Her eyes were not quite closed, and shone under the veil of her eyelashes. Only her thin nose seemed strange and sharp. Sweeter than ever was the smile on her closed lips which not even in death betrayed the secret of her bad teeth. No, Josephine dead betrayed none of her secrets. For the last time her lady's maid had arranged the thinning hair of the fifty-one-year-old woman in childlike curls. Once more, silver paint on the eyelids, which would be closed forever, and rouge on the yellow cheeks, over which the candlelight played. How sweetly Josephine smiled in her eternal sleep, sweetly and coquettishly . . .

". . . and so charmingly," remarked a voice at my elbow. An old gentleman with bloated cheeks and lovely silvery hair. He seemed to have emerged from the darkness of a corner. "My name is Barras," he announced, and raised his lorgnon to his eye. "Have I had the honour of meeting madame?"

"Long ago," I said. "We met in General Bonaparte's salon. You were then a Director of the Republic, M. Barras."

He let the lorgnon drop. "That coronation robe. Josephine had me to thank for that, madame. 'You marry that little Bonaparte, I'll appoint him military governor of Paris, and everything will be arranged for you, dear—very dear Josephine,' I told her. As you know, madame—everything was indeed arranged for her." Barras giggled softly. "Was she close to you, madame?"

No, she only broke my heart, I thought, and I began to cry.

"A fool, this Bonaparte, a fool," the old gentleman whispered, tenderly smoothing out a crease in the purple robe. "He divorced the only woman in the world with whom a man couldn't have been bored even on a desert island."

On the ermine cape of the Empress of the French lay red roses. The warmth of the candles had wilted them, and their heavy perfume oppressed me. My knees gave way and suddenly I knelt beside Josephine's bed and buried my face in the velvet coronation robe.

"Don't cry for Josephine, madame. Josephine died as she lived. On the arm of a very powerful man who promised her one May evening among the roses at Malmaison to pay all her debts. . . . Do you hear me, dear, very dear Josephine?"

When I stood up, the old gentleman had vanished again into the darkness of his corner. Only the prayers for the dead were to be heard. So I nodded to Josephine once more. Her long eyelids seemed to flutter. She smiled sweetly, with her closed lips.

When I got downstairs, Eugène was asking Julie earnestly, "Does a dressing gown of Brussels lace with a little cap to match really cost twenty thousand francs, madame?"

I quickly walked out of the open door that led to the garden.

The sun shone so strong the air trembled. Roses bloomed in every colour. Suddenly I came upon a tiny artificial pool. On a stone bench sat a little girl watching baby ducklings swim excitedly and awkwardly behind a fat mother duck. I sat down beside the child. She had brown hair that fell in corkscrew curls to her shoulders and a white dress with a black sash. When she looked up at me sideways, my heart skipped a beat—very long eyelashes over oval eyes, a sweet, heart-shaped face. The child smiled, and she smiled with closed lips. I asked, "What's your name?"

"Josephine, madame."

She had blue eyes, and lovely pearl-white teeth. Her skin was

very fair, and in her thick hair sparkled golden lights. Josephine—
and yet not Josephine.

"Are you one of the ladies-in-waiting, madame?" she asked politely.

"No, why did you think so?"

"Because Aunt Hortense said that the Crown Princess of Sweden
was coming to call. Princesses always bring ladies-in-waiting with
them. Naturally only if they're grown-up princesses."

"And little princesses?"

"They have governesses."

The child watched the little ducks again. "The ducks are so tiny
—I think they must have come out of their mother's stomach just
yesterday."

"Nonsense. Little ducks are hatched from eggs."

The child smiled knowingly. "You mustn't tell me fairy tales,
madame."

"But they really do come out of an egg," I persisted.

She shrugged. "As you wish, madame."

"Are you the daughter of Prince Eugène?"

"Yes. But Papa probably isn't a prince any more. If we're lucky,
the Allies will give him a duchy in Bavaria. My grandfather, my
mama's papa, is the King of Bavaria."

"So you're a princess in any case," I said. "Where's your governess?"

"I ran away from her," the child said, dabbling her hand in the
water. Something suddenly occurred to her. "If you're not a lady-
in-waiting, are you perhaps a governess?"

"Why?"

"Well, you must be something."

"Perhaps I'm a princess, too."

"Impossible. You don't look like a princess." The eyelashes fluttered, she cocked her head slightly and smiled. "I really want to
know who you are."

"Really?"

"I like you. Even though you tried to make me believe that silly
story about the ducks. Have you any children?"

"A son, but he's not here."

"That's too bad. I'd rather play with boys than girls. Where is your son?"

"In Sweden. But I'm sure you don't know where that is."

"I know exactly where it is. I take geography lessons, and Papa says . . ."

"Josephine, Jo-se-phine!"

The child sighed. "My governess." She winked at me and grimaced like a street urchin. "She makes me sick! But don't tell anyone I said so, madame."

I walked back to the house reflectively. We dined alone with Hortense and Eugène. "Do you happen to know when we can send a courier to Elba?" he asked Julie as we were leaving. "I want to inform the Emperor of poor Mama's death as quickly as possible. And, yes—I'll send him the unpaid bills. What else can I do?"

We drove back through the gathering darkness. Shortly before we reached Paris something important occurred to me. I'll write it down and read it over from time to time, and never forget it. If one must found a dynasty, I thought—why not found a charming one?

"Look, a shooting star—quick, make a wish," Julie cried.

So I made a wish, quickly and probably impulsively. "The Swedes will call her Josefina," I said out loud.

"What in the world are you talking about?" Julie demanded.

"About the shooting star that's just fallen from heaven. Only about the shooting star. . . ."

Paris, late autumn, 1814

Oscar wrote to me from Norway, behind his tutor's back. I've pasted his letter in my diary so I won't lose it.

"Christiania, November 10, 1814

"My dear Mama,

"I hear that Count Brahe is sending a courier to Paris from here, so I hasten to write you. Especially since my tutor, Baron Cederström, is in bed with a cold. Cederström tries to read all my letters to you to see if I write properly. The old idiot! Dear Mama, my most affectionate congratulations—you have become Crown Princess of Norway! Norway and Sweden are now united, and the King of Sweden is also the King of Norway. In fact, we've completed a campaign in which we conquered Norway. And last evening I came here with Papa to Christiania, which is the capital of Norway.

"But I'd better tell you things in order. Papa's entry into Stockholm after the liberation of France was wonderful. The people in the streets, through which Papa's open carriage drove, were so excited and happy, and the crowds were so huge, that people didn't even notice when they got stepped on. His Majesty fell on Papa's neck and cried like a child for joy. Her Majesty wept, too, but more discreetly. The Swedes consider themselves a heroic nation again, as they were under Charles XII. But Papa was tired and sad. Do you know why, Mama?

"Although the Danes had ceded Norway to us, the Norwegian Parliament in Eidsvold, on May 17, declared that the country wanted to be independent. Imagine that, Mama! Papa told me that for years there's been a party in Christiania that calls itself the 'Scandinavia United,' working for a Scandinavian Republic. But the Norwegians haven't dared proclaim a Republic. Instead they quickly appointed a Danish prince as their Regent! Only to annoy us, Mama! Then they declared they'd defend their independence.

"So—I can't describe to you how enthusiastic our Swedish officers were about this war. His Majesty, whose health grows steadily worse, and who can hardly move for gout, wanted to go into battle himself. Or rather—sail into battle. He begged Papa for a man-of-war, and pointed out that since his birth he has been Admiral of the Swedish Fleet. Papa had confided to me that Sweden could afford only three months of war with Norway. Papa paid for the man-of-war the old King begged so hard for, out of his own pocket. The old gentleman has no inkling of that.

"I, of course, declared that if the old King was allowed to go, I should, too. Papa didn't object. He only said, 'Oscar, these Norwegians are a brave people, risking this war with Sweden with only half as many troops as we and no ammunition to speak of.' Papa was deeply moved. He then handed me a document and said, 'Read that carefully, Oscar. I'm giving the Norwegians the most liberal constitution in Europe.'

"Nevertheless, the brave people insisted on their independence, and Papa went to Stromstad with his general staff. We followed: both Majesties, the entire court, and I. In the harbour lay the promised man-of-war. She's called 'Gustaf den Store' (Gustavus the Great), and we all went on board. A few days later our troops stormed the first Norwegian islands. His Majesty watched from the deck through his field glasses. From time to time, Papa sent an aide on board to report to him that our troops were advancing according to plan. When the Fortress of Kongsten was taken, Papa was standing beside me at the railing. Marshals von Essen and Adlercreutz were with the troops. Finally, I couldn't bear the booming of the cannon and the firing of the guns any longer. I grabbed Papa's arm. 'Send an officer to the Norwegians and tell them, in God's name, they can be independent. Papa, don't let the cannon fire on them!'

"Papa smiled. 'Of course not, Oscar. We're using blanks as we do on manoeuvres. And the fires that worry you so are flares.' Papa quickly put his finger to his lips and motioned toward the old King and the Queen, who were excitedly snatching the field glasses out of each other's hands. 'Then—then it's not a real campaign,' I whispered.

" 'No, Oscar, merely—an excursion.'

" 'Why are the Norwegians falling back?'

" 'Because their officers have calculated the range of my cannon, and realize that I'll win this round. Besides, the Norwegians have no idea of holding these fortifications. Their real line of defence begins west of Glommen. But I think—' At that moment the Swedish guns ceased firing. There was dead silence. The Norwegians were evacuating the Fortress of Kongsten. Only then did Papa ask for field glasses.

"'And what happens if the Norwegians withdraw to their mountains? Can you pursue them over the glaciers, Papa?'

"'Indeed, I can! In every war college in the world, cadets are taught how General Bernadotte once led an army corps in a forced march across the Alps.' Suddenly Papa looked tired and sad again. 'At the time I was defending a young Republic, and today—I'm robbing a small freedom-loving people of their independence. Oscar, one grows old, and outlives oneself.'

"The whole campaign lasted only fourteen days. Then the Norwegians requested a cessation of hostilities. Their Parliament was to be convened on November 10 (today) and Papa was asked to appear personally in Christiania to confirm the union of Norway and Sweden. We all returned to Stockholm, and Papa persuaded the old King to drive through the streets in an open carriage. The people cheered, and tears ran down the old gentleman's cheeks. Outside of the Norwegians, only our artillerymen know that we fought with blanks.

"Four days later Papa and I travelled to Norway. Papa was accompanied by Count Brahe, and Marshals Adlercreutz and von Essen. I had to ride beside my inevitable Cederström. We spent the nights in tents, because Papa had decided not to be a burden on the peasants. Usually it was so cold we couldn't sleep. Finally we reached the little city of Fredrikshald, where we stayed with the mayor. At last Papa let us sleep in beds again. . . . Every day we took long rides out around Fredrikshald. Papa wanted to become familiar with the country. The peasants stared at us and didn't greet us.

"I enclose a little song, Mama, which I call 'Song of the Rain' and composed during these endless rides. I hope you don't think the melody too sad.

"We also rode around between the grey walls of the fortress of Fredriksten, where the Norwegians once defended themselves against the Swedish King, Charles XII. He wanted to transform Sweden into a great power and conquer Russia. But most of his troops froze to death in Russia. Thereupon he went to Turkey, to attack the Russians from there. Finally the Swedes could scrape up no more money for his wars. He decided to conquer Norway. A rifle bullet killed him at the siege of Fredrikshald. On our ride through rain and fog we suddenly came up on a large wooden cross: 'On this spot, Charles XII fell,' it said. We all dismounted, and Papa motioned me to him. 'Oscar,' he said. 'Here fell a great military amateur. Promise me that you'll never personally command the Swedes in any war!'

" 'But Papa, you did, you're supreme commander,' I ventured.

" 'I started as a sergeant and you as an Heir Apparent . . .' he began, but by then von Essen and Adlercreutz were already reciting the Lord's Prayer. Papa didn't pray with them, but kept watching me. (Papa never prays.) When the Marshals said, 'Amen,' Papa turned away quickly and we rode on.

" 'I'm of the opinion,' he said abruptly, 'that the shot which killed your hero-King came from his own ranks. I've studied all the documents I can find on it. The man was a curse upon Sweden, gentlemen. Forget him, I beg you to forget him.'

" 'Highness, views on this differ,' said Adlercreutz, offended. Mama, you must always speak very discreetly about Charles XII.

"Last evening, in a gala coach brought from Stockholm, we finally entered Christiania. I think Papa had expected bright lights and a cheering crowd. The streets were dark and deserted. Suddenly out of the darkness somewhere cannon thundered. Papa jumped. Only a salute, I thought immediately.

"The carriage stopped in front of the palace of the former Danish governor. A guard-of-honour presented arms. Papa was horrified by the soldiers' slovenly uniforms and by the way they marched out of step. He scrutinized the palace. That looked like an ordinary house. One-storied and very modest. He shook his head, and then strode with giant strides into the one large room of the house. Me behind him. The marshals and aides hurried to catch up with us. It must really have looked funny.

"The President of the Norwegian Parliament was waiting for us, with the members of the government. An enormous log fire threw red flickering lights over the gloomy gathering. Papa wore the violet dress cape, and the hat with the ostrich plumes.

"President of the Storting Christie welcomed Papa in excellent French. Papa put on his most captivating smile, shook the solemn gentlemen by the hand and extended the greetings of His Majesty, the King of Sweden and Norway. Whereupon the mournful ones tried hard not to laugh.

"I believe the Norwegians have a sense of humour. The old gentleman in Stockholm will have nothing to do with this union. It's all Papa's doing. Papa plunged into a resounding speech. 'Norway's new constitution, gentlemen, defends the Rights of Man, for which I fought as a fifteen-year-old in France. This union is more than a geographical necessity, it is my heart's desire.'

"But the Norwegians weren't impressed. They'll never forgive us the blanks and the flares. . . .

"I went with Papa to his bedroom, where he ripped off his decorations and disgustedly threw them on the dressing table. He said, 'Yesterday was your mama's birthday, I hope our letters got there in time.' Then he pulled the bed curtains together.

"Dear Mama, I feel terribly sorry for Papa, but one can't be a crown prince and a Republican at the same time. Please write him a gay, loving letter, we'll be in Stockholm again at the end of the month. And now my eyes are drooping with sleep, and the courier is waiting. With hugs and kisses,

"Your son Oscar"

"P.S. Could you possibly get hold of Herr van Beethoven's Seventh Symphony in Paris and send it to me?"

The courier also brought a letter from Count Brahe to Rosen. "From now on," it said, "on special occasions, the Norwegian flag is to be hoisted beside the Swedish above the house of Her Highness."

"We ought to have the Norwegian coat of arms painted on the carriage, too," Rosen said in great excitement. "His Highness, the Crown Prince, is greater than Charles XII."

I asked him for a map, to try to find the second country of which I'm now Crown Princess.

Paris, March 5, 1815

This afternoon began like many other afternoons. With the help of my nephew Marius, I was drafting a request to the eighteenth Louis to extend Julie's permit to remain in France as my guest. Julie was in the small salon writing a long letter saying nothing to Joseph in Switzerland. Then Count Rosen came in and announced a visitor: the Duke of Otranto, M. Fouché.

This man is incomprehensible to me. When, in the days of the Revolution, members of the National Assembly voted on the fate of Citizen Louis Capet, Representative Fouché spoke up loud and clear for *"la mort."* And now he's moving heaven and earth to persuade the executed man's brother to restore him to favour and give him a post. "Let him come in," I said disgustedly.

Joseph Fouché was in a state. His parchment-coloured face was flecked with red. I ordered tea. He stirred his cup amiably. "I hope I haven't interrupted Your Highness in some important business?"

"My sister has just drafted a request to His Majesty," Julie answered.

"To which Majesty?" Fouché inquired.

It was the silliest question in the world. "To King Louis, naturally," Julie said irritably. "To my knowledge no other majesty rules in France."

"This morning I might have had an opportunity to support your petition, madame." He sipped his tea and peered at Julie with amusement. "His Majesty offered me a post. In fact, a very influential one—Minister of Police."

"Impossible!" I burst out.

"And?" Julie asked wide-eyed.

"I refused." Joseph Fouché took a few more sips.

"If the King offered you the Ministry of Police," declared Marius, "he must feel insecure. And God knows he has no more reason to."

516

"Why not?" Fouché was surprised.

"The lists. The secret lists with the names not only of followers of the Republic, but also those of the Emperor. This secret, comprehensive list gives him absolute power," Marius asserted. "They say your name, Duke, is first on the list."

"The King has discontinued the compilation of this list," said Fouché, and put his teacup on the little table. "In his place, I'd feel insecure, too. After all, he's gaining ground."

"Tell me, just whom are you talking about?" I asked.

"The Emperor, of course."

The whole room began to spin, shadows danced before my eyes. I felt I was going to faint. Something I hadn't done since the days when I was expecting Oscar. . . .

As from afar, Fouché's voice reached me. "Eleven days ago the Emperor with his troops embarked at Elba, and on the first of March they landed at Golfe Juan."

And Marius, "That's fantastic, he has only four hundred men with him."

Fouché's answer: "—have gone over to him, kiss his coat and march with him in triumph to Paris."

"And abroad, Duke?" in a harsh French accent—Count Rosen, naturally. "The other countries will . . ."

"Désirée—you're awfully pale, aren't you well?" That was Julie.

And Fouché, "Quick, a glass of water for Her Highness—"

They held a glass to my lips. I drank. The salon stopped spinning. Fuzzy outlines came back into focus.

My nephew Marius' face beamed. "He'll have the entire army behind him. No one can cut in half the pay of French officers who have made this nation great. We're on the march—on the march once more."

"Against all of Europe?" asked Marcelline dryly. (Her husband didn't come home. He fell in the fighting near Paris—actually into the arms of a young girl who hid him.)

My glance fell on a lackey who wanted to say something and kept trying to be heard. I gave him a chance. A new visitor—the wife of Marshal Ney.

Mme Ney is as massive as a grenadier and as overwhelming as

an act of God. In she stormed, panting, and clasped me to her mighty bosom. "Well, what do you say to that, madame?" she boomed. "But he'll show him! He pounded the desk with his fist and swore that he would show him!"

"Do sit down, madame," I pleaded. "And tell me who will show what to whom?"

"My husband will show the Emperor!" she roared, and fell into the nearest chair. "He's just had orders to attack the Emperor at Besançon. And to take him prisoner. Do you know what my old Ney answered? He vowed he'd capture him like a mad bull, put him in a cage and exhibit him all over the country."

"Forgive me, madame," said Fouché. "I don't quite understand. Why is Marshal Ney so angry at his former commander in chief and Emperor?"

Not until that moment had Mme Ney noticed Fouché, and she was dreadfully embarrassed. "So—you're here, too," she said. "May I ask why? You're still in disfavour at court? You are still in retirement on your estates?"

Fouché cackled and shrugged his shoulders.

Mme Ney became uneasy. Very uneasy. "You don't seriously believe that the Emperor will succeed?" she asked in an unusually subdued voice.

"Yes." Marius was emphatic. "Yes, madame, he will succeed."

Julie rose. "I'll write my husband all about it. It will interest him very much."

Fouché shrugged. "Don't bother. The King's secret police would get your letter immediately. And I'm sure, madame, that the Emperor has for a long time been in cahoots with your husband. It's practically taken for granted that the Emperor informed all his brothers of his plans from Elba."

"You don't believe it's an organized plan?" Mme Ney snorted. "My husband would have known about that."

"That the Army is discontented because both officers and men are on half-pay, and the pensions of old soldiers and of the disabled have been reduced can hardly have escaped the notice of Marshal Ney," thundered my nephew Marius.

"Nor the Emperor's on Elba," was Fouché's parting shot.

A long pause ensued. Mme Ney turned to me abruptly, her chair creaked, her deep voice growled. "Madame, you, as the wife of a marshal, will see I'm right, it is . . ."

"You're wrong, madame. I'm no longer the wife of a marshal, but the Crown Princess of Sweden and Norway. Please excuse me, I have a headache."

I had such a headache as never before, Painful, pounding. I lay on my bed, and had nothing to say to anyone. Not even to myself. Especially not to myself. . . . One can hide from the family, one can escape from servants. But one can under no circumstances evade Hortense. At eight o'clock that evening Marie announced "the former Queen of Holland, now the Duchess of St. Leu." I pulled the covers up over my head. Five minutes later Marcelline was wailing at my door. "Aunt, you must come, Hortense is sitting in the small salon, and says she'll wait for you, even if it takes all night. She's brought her sons with her."

I never moved. Ten minutes later Julie leaned over my bed. "Désirée! Don't be so cruel. Poor Hortense implores you to receive her."

I resigned myself to my fate. "Let her come up, but only for a minute."

Hortense shoved her sons in first. "Don't deny my poor children your protection, take them until everything is over," she sobbed. Hortense has got very thin in the last year and her mourning makes her look very pale, her colourless hair is untidy and neglected.

"Your children aren't in danger," I said.

"Yes, they are," she whispered despairingly. "The King can have them arrested any moment and hold them as hostages against the Emperor. My children are still the heirs of the dynasty, madame."

"The heir to the dynasty is named Napoleon, like his father—and lives at present in Vienna," I said calmly.

"And if something happens to this child—while he's a prisoner—in Vienna?" she hissed.

"What then, madame?"

Hortense gazed lovingly at her two angular little boys. A slightly mad smile hovered around her lips as she brushed back a strand of hair from the younger child's forehead. "The King will not dare follow my children into the house of the Swedish Crown Princess. I implore you—"

"Of course, the children can stay here."

"Napoleon Louis, Charles Louis Napoleon—kiss your kind aunt's hand."

I hastily yanked the covers over my head again.

But I wasn't destined to rest that evening. I had hardly got to sleep when candlelight and rattling woke me up again. Someone was rummaging in my chest of drawers. I sat up.

"Julie! Are you searching for something?"

"My crown, Désirée. Do you know what's become of my little crown, the one I once forgot in your dressing room?"

"Yes, it knocked around for several days, and then I put it in the bottom drawer of the chest. Under the warm underwear from Sweden. But what do you want with a crown in the middle of the night, Julie?"

"I want to try it on," she said softly. "And perhaps polish it, so it shines again."

Paris, March 20, 1815

Last night Louis XVIII slunk out of the Tuileries through the back door. And now the Bourbons are back in their perennial exile. The rumour is they stopped at Ghent, so the old gentleman must have been very tired. . . . This morning, General Exelmans ordered the occupation of the deserted Tuileries and the Tricolour hoisted. In the streets broadsides with a proclamation by Napoleon are being distributed. And no one has ever worn a white cockade! Every lapel sports a blue-white-red ribbon. People's buttonholes and coat lapels must be stretched and worn out.

The lackeys and cleaning women in the Tuileries—always the same, of course—are once again working like people possessed. The new curtains and draperies have been torn down. And the dark-green ones with the bees taken out of storage and rehung. Hortense has taken charge. She's had all the gilded eagles hauled out of the cellar, and has dusted them personally.

At my house, too, everything is unfortunately at sixes and sevens. A courier from the Emperor informed Julie that His Majesty will reach the Tuileries at nine o'clock this evening. Good—Julie will be there swathed in purple, the crown of an Imperial princess on her head. (Probably crooked.) She is so excited and scatter-brained that she can't even fix her daughters' hair.

"The rest of the family are still on the way. Hortense and I have to receive him alone . . . Désirée, I'm so afraid of him!"

"Nonsense, Julie, he's the same Bonaparte he was in Marseilles. Your brother-in-law, Julie. What is there to be afraid of?"

"Is he really the same? This triumphal procession—from Elba to Golfe Juan, from Golfe Juan through Grenoble to Paris! Regiments falling on their knees before him, Marshal Ney . . ."

"Yes, the great rebel, Marshal Ney, went over to Napoleon with flags flying. The entire Army is convinced that now everything will be as it was in the old days. War-time bonuses, rapid advancements, marshals' batons, posts as governer, distribution of kingdoms . . . Julie, the Army cheers, but all the other people are silent!"

Uncomprehendingly, she stared at me. Then she borrowed the earrings of the Queen of Sweden and departed. I hope Joseph will bring back her jewels. . .

In the meantime, Marie filled my bathtub in the dressing room and scrubbed the Bonaparte boys. They are driving to the Tuileries later with Julie. I must, at Hortense's request, use the curling irons on their straight hair.

"Do you believe he's coming back, Aunt?" Louis Napoleon suddenly asked me.

"Of course, the Emperor's nearly in Paris."

"I mean his son, the little King of Rome," said Louis Napoleon hesitantly, avoiding my eyes. Silently I curled the last lock of Louis Napoleon's hair.

Then I got out my diary and began to write.

Late at night. At eight o'clock this evening a state carriage from the stables of the Tuileries arrived for Julie and the children. The carriage still carried the Bourbon coat of arms. My house became very quiet. I began to pace restlessly around the rooms. Count Rosen leaned out of an open window.

"I'd give a lot to be there," he admitted.

"Where?"

"In front of the Tuileries—I'd like to see the arrival."

"Put on a civilian suit, pin on a tricolour badge, and wait for me!" I exclaimed. He looked dazed. "Hurry," I urged. With which I slipped into a coat and grabbed a hat.

We had trouble getting to the Tuileries. First we hired a carriage, then we left it because one could get farther on foot. An impenetrably dense crowd pushed toward the Tuileries. Pushed and was pushed. I clung to my young Count's arm so as not to lose him in the throng. We tried to go forward but found ourselves hemmed in.

The Tuileries were brightly lighted as on the night of a great ball. But I knew that the great ballroom was practically empty. Julie, Hortense, two little girls, two little boys. The Duke of Vicenza and Marshal Davout, and perhaps a few generals. That was all. . . .

Suddenly mounted guards rode full tilt into the crowd. "Clear the way!" In the distance a storm seemed to have broken loose. The storm moved closer, roared nearer, was upon us. *"Vive l'Empereur! Vive l'Empereur!"* the mob bellowed and boomed. The faces of the people next to us seemed to be all mouths, yelling mouths. . . . The carriage came in sight, the horses galloping wildly toward the Tuileries. Officers of all ranks, from all regiments, galloped after it. Around us and over us reverberated one single shout.

On the open staircase, lackeys stood with torches. The carriage door was flung open. For a fraction of a second, I saw the figure of the Emperor. Then Marshal Ney climbed out of the carriage . . . The crowd surged forward, broke through the cordon of guards, lifted the Emperor to their shoulders. They carried him up the open staircase. They carried him back to the Tuileries. The torchlight flickered over his face, he was smiling, his eyes closed—greedy and pleasure-seeking, like one who is thirsty and at last gets something to drink.

Again we were thrown back. Again a carriage rolled up. Again all necks were craned. This time they murmured in disillusionment. Only Fouché, come to welcome the Emperor. Only Fouché, at his service. . . .

I'd had enough. Rosen had to beat a retreat through the mass of people. But when we reached the opposite bank of the Seine, we wandered through deserted streets. "One mustn't overestimate the importance of two, even three thousand enthusiasts, Your Highness." Our footsteps echoed. We were in sight of my house. Dark and without a flag it stood between its neighbours.

From every other roof waved the Tricolour.

Paris, June 18, 1815

Marie had just brought me my breakfast in bed, when the cannon boomed and the church bells began to ring. We hadn't expected a victory, and yet the guns in front of the Dômes des Invalides and the bells of Notre-Dame were proclaiming it. Just as in the old days. . . .

Julie is living with Joseph again in the Elysée Palace. Mme Letizia and all the Bonaparte brothers have returned. But in the Tuileries, Hortense is hostess. She dines with him, and arranges court balls to shorten his nights. For at night Napoleon wanders aimlessly through the empty apartments of the Empress and the deserted nursery of the little King of Rome. He's written one letter after another to Marie Louise. And bought the child a rocking horse. Marie Louise's dressing room has been repapered. Napoleon urged the workmen on. "Her Majesty may arrive at any moment from Vienna." But Marie Louise and the child have not come.

Immediately after his return Napoleon announced an election. This was to prove to foreign countries how hated the Bourbons were in France. These were the first free elections since the days of the

Republic. So France elected the new National Assembly. Carnot became a deputy and—Lafayette.

It can't be the same man, I thought, when I read the election returns in the *Moniteur*. But Marie said it was. The very same General Lafayette who first proclaimed the Rights of Man. How is it possible that, in all these years, no one has given a thought to Lafayette?

Papa often told us children about him. About the Marquis de Lafayette, who, at nineteen, outfitted his own ship and sailed with his Corps Lafayette to America to fight as a volunteer for the independence of the United States. In appreciation, the Continental Congress made him a major general. . . . No, Papa, I haven't forgotten what you told me. And this Corps Lafayette fought on foreign soil for liberty. One day, this young Marquis returned to France and, in a frayed American general's uniform, mounted the rostrum in the National Assembly in Paris, and read the Declaration of the Rights of Man. You brought home the newspaper that day, Papa, and read the Declaration to your small daughter. Word for word, so I'd never forget it. . . . Then Lafayette founded France's National Guard to defend our new Republic. But what happened to him after that?

I asked my nephew, Marius. But he neither knew nor cared. Jean-Baptiste could tell me. But Jean-Baptiste is in Stockholm. His ambassador has left Paris, all the foreign diplomats have gone. Foreign countries are maintaining no further diplomatic relations with Napoleon. They don't answer his letters either, but reply only with arms.

Day and night gendarmes ride through villages routing out peasant lads to turn into soldiers, and requisitioning horses. But the peasants go into hiding, and there are no more horses. The officers who once rode with Napoleon from victory to victory produce doctors' certificates. Napoleon has disillusioned them. The state treasury is empty, their pay hasn't been raised. Even my warlike Marius must suddenly take the cure. And the marshals? The marshals have country estates to which they have retired. Davout alone stands by Napoleon. And Ney, whose regiments went over to Napoleon and forced him willy-nilly to go, too. Napoleon quickly appointed a

General Grouchy a marshal. Then he marched at the head of his last army across the frontier to intercept the allies.

That was three days ago. His Order of the Day was published everywhere. We know it all by heart: "For every courageous Frenchman the time has come to conquer or to die." After this direful proclamation, stocks on the *Bourse* slumped still further. People hoarded foodstuffs. The theatres emptied, the restaurants were dark. With head bowed, Paris awaited the coup de grâce.

And then the miracle: victory bells rang out.

I dressed and went into the garden. A bee buzzed. At first I wandered aimlessly. Then I stopped and listened. Yes—it was all deathly still again. No bells. No cannon. Only the bee.

I was glad when I saw the stranger. Now I wasn't alone in that breathless silence. The stranger was in civilian clothes, narrow-shouldered, of uncertain age. I walked toward him. His thin face was crisscrossed witth many little wrinkles. Then I saw his near-sighted squint. It was Lucien Bonaparte.

Lucien, who went into exile when Napoleon became Emperor. Who has lived in England all these years. How strange he should have come back just now.

"Do you still remember me, Désirée? I was at your engagement party."

We sat down on a bench.

"Why have you come back, Lucien?"

"Yes—why? After the Restoration I was the one Bonaparte who could do what he wanted. I wanted to stay in England. But I heard of his return." Lucien leaned back and gazed dreamily at the garden. "How beautiful a little piece of turf can be. So quiet, so wonderfully quiet."

"Yes, the victory bells just stopped ringing."

"They were a mistake, Désirée." He watched the flight of a butterfly. "Good old Davout, whom Napoleon left in Paris to bolster morale on the so-called home front, had them rung too soon. Napoleon has won only a skirmish—the overture to a great battle. The village of Charleroi was taken. But the decision rests with Ligny and Waterloo. . . . Do you see how that blue butterfly . . ."

"Lucien, why have you come to see me?"

"To spend ten peaceful minutes somewhere. The Government is being kept fully informed. And the National Assembly is sitting continuously as in the days of the Revolution." He stood up. "Now I must go to wait for further couriers."

But I detained him. "This Lafayette. Lucien—is this Deputy Lafayette the same man who proclaimed the Rights of Man?"

"Of course."

"I thought Lafayette died ages ago. Why have we never heard more from him?"

"Because he was busy with his vegetable garden. On a small, very modest estate, Désirée. When the mob stormed the Tuileries and carried the bloody heads of the aristocrats around on pikes, Deputy Lafayette protested. An order for his arrest was issued. Lafayette had to flee. He was captured at Liége and was in Prussian and Austrian prisons for many years. Not until the days of the Consulate was he released. Then he returned to France."

"And then, Lucien?"

"Then he cultivated his vegetable garden, carrots, tomatoes and probably asparagus, too. The man had fought all his life for the Rights of Man—do you suppose he wanted anything to do with the First Consul? Or with the Emperor Napoleon?"

He took my arm in a friendly way. I walked to the garden gate with Lucien.

Paris, June 23, 1815

"If, for the first time after so many years, I raise my voice—" began Lafayette in that critical session of the National Assembly. The *Moniteur* printed the entire speech. I had read that far when the door to my dressing room flew open. Julie, screaming, staggered in, fell at my knees, and buried her tear-stained face in my lap.

The first halfway intelligible words she was able to get out were,

"He has abdicated." Then again nothing but sobs. And at last, "The Prussians may be in Paris any moment—" Marie came in, we stretched Julie out on the sofa, I sat beside her and she babbled incoherently like a drunkard.

"—and he came back—in the middle of the night. In an old post chaise—he requisitioned somewhere—his own carriage and all his belongings—fell into the hands of the Prussian general, Blücher —he drove right to us in the Elysée . . . He wanted to see all his brothers and the Ministers, but they stayed only five minutes, they wanted to hurry back to the National Assembly. The Emperor told them that he must call up a hundred thousand men at once—for a new army—and, yes, then he urged poor Lucien to go before the Deputies, in his name, and reproach the Nation for leaving him in the lurch."

"And did Lucien go?"

Julie nodded. "Yes, he went and came back barely twenty minutes later. When Lucien mounted the rostrum terrible invectives were hurled at him. Lucien stood up under it calmly, not a muscle in his white face twitched while the Deputies shouted, '*A bas Bonaparte, à bas Bonaparte!*' Only when they bombarded him with inkwells did he take off his glasses. Finally the chairman called for silence, the uproar ceased, and Lucien said in an unemotional voice that the Nation had deserted his brother. But at that point Lafayette jumped up. 'Have you forgotten where the bones of your sons and brothers whiten? In Africa, on the Tagus, on the Weichsel, in the ice of Russia; two million men have fallen for the sake of one who wished to fight all Europe! It is enough!' Without a word, Lucien left the rostrum.

"I heard this all from Fouché. Lucien himself told us nothing," Julie sobbed. "Joseph and Lucien talked with Napoleon all night. Until dawn—I had to keep serving coffee and brandy—the Emperor constantly paced up and down and pounded on the table and screamed. . . ." Julie covered her face with her thin hands.

"Could Joseph and Lucien talk him into abdicating?"

Julie shook her head and let her hands fall. "This morning Lafayette declared in the National Assembly, 'If General Bonaparte does not abdicate within the hour, I will demand his deposition.'

527

Fouché came to us with this threat. They allowed Napoleon only one hour."

"And all day yesterday and all last night," I pointed out.

"Finally the Emperor signed—Fouché stood beside him. He abdicated in favour of the King of Rome. But this didn't interest the ministers."

Marie began to massage Julie's ankles, as she had in the old days.

"And—I'm not going back to the Elysée," Julie whispered suddenly. "The children must come here, I want to stay here—" There was a wild look in her eyes. "They couldn't arrest me in your house, could they? Not here . . ."

"The allied troops aren't in Paris yet. Perhaps they'll never get here," I said.

Julie's lips trembled. "The Allies? No, our Government, Désirée—ours. A General Becker has already been assigned to watch the Emperor—by the Directorate."

"The Directorate?"

"The new government is called a directorate. They're negotiating now with the Allies. Carnot and Fouché are two of the five directors. And I'm so afraid of them—" She began to weep helplessly again. "And in the streets, they screamed at me, 'A bas les Bonapartes!' "

The door burst open—Joseph.

"Julie, you must pack. The Emperor wants to leave Paris immediately and move to Malmaison. The whole family is to go with him. Come, Julie, please hurry."

With a wild cry, Julie dug her fingers into my shoulders. Never, never in her life would she leave me. Joseph's eyes were inflamed, his face, with heavy bags under his eyes, was grey, one could see he hadn't slept for two days and nights. "The whole family is going to Malmaison, Julie," he repeated.

Julie relaxed her hold on my shoulder. "Julie—you must go with your husband."

She shook her head, her teeth were chattering. "In the streets they're still shouting, 'A bas les Bonapartes!' " she repeated.

"Even so, Julie," I said, and pulled her to her feet.

"I wanted to ask if Julie, the children and I might drive to Malmaison in your carriage," Joseph murmured, avoiding my eyes.

"I meant to lend Mme Letizia my carriage. But perhaps there'll be room for you all. The Swedish coat of arms is clearly visible."

"But you will help me, Désirée, you will, won't you?" cried Julie. Joseph went to her swiftly, put his arm around her, and led her to the door.

It's just a year since Josephine died. All the roses are blooming now at Malmaison.

Paris, during the night of June 29-30, 1815

His sword lies on my night table, his destiny has come full circle, and I was the instrument. They say I fulfilled a patriotic mission. But my heart is heavy. My only outward mark is an angry bruise. . . . Perhaps this night will be over sooner if I write in my diary. This morning, earlier than God, the Nation suddenly wanted to speak to me. It sounds crazy, but it's really true.

I had lain awake for two hours, turning and tossing in this summer heat. These days the sun beats down mercilessly on the women who are again lining up at the butchers and bakers. The last cannon rumble by, to be set up in front of the city gates. No one pays any particular attention. Paris may be attacked by the Prussians, the English, the Russians, the Saxons and the Austrians, but it doesn't seem to concern people while they wait for a piece of bread. . . . Unbelievably early, in rushed Yvette. Count Rosen had to speak to me right away. Even before she could finish, the Swede was at my bedside.

"Respectfully reporting, Your Highness. Representatives of the Nation wish to speak to Your Highness as soon as possible."

All the time, he was buttoning the tunic of his parade uniform. I had to laugh. "I'm no authority on questions of etiquette, but if you must storm into my bedroom at dawn, I think you should be fully dressed."

"Your pardon, Highness—the Nation," the Count stammered.

"Which nation?" My laughter died.

"The French Nation." Count Rosen had finally finished buttoning his parade uniform, and stood at attention.

"Coffee, Yvette," I said. "Strong coffee." I looked at the Count in bewilderment. "Until I have my coffee, one must speak to me very slowly, and explain everything clearly, or I don't get it. You say the French Nation wishes—well, what does it wish?"

"The Nation, or rather representatives of the Nation, request an audience. It is of the utmost importance, the courier assures me. That's why I put on my parade uniform."

"Yes, I see it."

Yvette brought my coffee. I burned my tongue on it.

"The courier is waiting for an answer," Count Rosen said.

"I can receive them in half an hour—the representatives of the Nation, that is. Not the whole Nation, Count!"

I was making silly remarks to calm my fear. What did they want of me? I was perspiring, but my hands were cold as ice. I slipped into a thin white muslin dress and white sandals. Yvette wanted to do my hair, but I couldn't sit still. While I was powdering my nose, someone announced that the gentlemen had arrived. The gentlemen —which gentlemen?

Because of the heat, all the shutters in the large salon had been closed. The dawn light blurred all the outlines. On the sofa under the portrait of the First Consul sat three gentlemen. They rose as I entered. They were the representatives of the Nation.

The Nation had as representatives Their Excellencies, Fouché and Talleyrand. I didn't recognize the man between them. He was short and very thin. Wore an old-fashioned white peruke and a faded foreign uniform. As I came nearer, I saw that his cheeks and his brow were wrinkled. The eyes in the old face shone with a curious brilliance.

"Your Highness, may we present General Lafayette?" said Talleyrand.

My heart skipped a beat. The Nation. The Nation had really come to me. . . . I curtsied deeply and as awkwardly as a schoolgirl.

Fouché's unemotional voice cut through the silence. "Highness, in the name of the French Government—"

"Have you really come to see me, General Lafayette?" I whispered. Lafayette smiled so simply, so sincerely, that I gathered courage.

"My papa never parted with his first printing of the Rights of Man. The broadside stayed in his room until he died. I never thought I'd have the honour of meeting Lafayette in person, and in my own salon." I stopped in embarrassment.

"Your Highness, on behalf of the French Government, which Foreign Minister Talleyrand and I represent, and in the name of the Nation, which General Lafayette represents, we turn to you in this solemn hour," Fouché began again.

Then I looked from one to the other of them. Fouché, one of the five directors at present governing France. Talleyrand who just yesterday returned from the Congress of Vienna, where he had all along represented the France of the Bourbons. Both ex-ministers of Napoleon, both hung with orders and decorations, both in gold-braided frock coats. And between them Lafayette in a shabby uniform without decorations.

"Can I do something for you, gentlemen?" I asked.

"I've seen a situation like this coming for a long time, Your Highness," Talleyrand said. He spoke very softly, very rapidly. "Perhaps Your Highness remembers, I once intimated that, one day, the Nation might very possibly ask a very great favour of you. Does Your Highness remember?"

I nodded.

"This situation has now arisen. The French Nation has a favour to ask of the Crown Princess of Sweden."

My hands were damp with fear.

"I'd like to give Her Highness a picture of the situation," Fouché said. "The allied troops are at the gates of Paris. The Prince of Bénévent, as Minister of Foreign Affairs, has communicated with the commanders in chief, Wellington and Blücher, to forestall an attack, and to prevent looting. We are naturally offering unconditional surrender."

"The commanders in chief of the allied troops have informed us that they will consider our proposals only under one condition," Talleyrand said quietly. "And that condition is . . ."

"General Bonaparte must leave France without delay," Fouché's voice broke.

A brief paused followed. What did they expect me to do? I turned to Talleyrand. But Fouché continued, "Although we informed General Napoleon that his departure is the wish of the French Government, a wish shared by the French Nation, he has not gone." Fouché's voice cracked again. "The General has replied with so incredible a suggestion that one can't escape the impression that Malmaison harbours a madman. Yesterday, General Bonaparte sent his aide-de-camp, Count Flahault, to Paris with a counteroffer that General Bonaparte command what remains of the Army, and beat back the enemy from the gates. In other words—a bloodbath for Paris!"

My mouth was very dry. I swallowed a few times. It didn't help.

"We firmly declined General Bonaparte's offer, and requested him to proceed at once to the port of Rochefort, to leave France," Fouché went on. "Whereupon, tonight, he sent General Becker to us. Becker, whom the French Government has assigned to General Bonaparte—as let's say, commissary, and who is responsible for the smooth carrying-out of his travel arrangements—delivered a new defiant demand. Bonaparte, a mere general, demands—demands, Your Highness—the supreme command of the remaining regiments in order to defend Paris. And not until after a defensive action in Paris—and he assumes, of course, that this will be successful and enable us to obtain favourable peace terms—will General Bonaparte agree to go abroad." Fouché snorted and mopped up the perspiration on his forehead. "What defiance, Your Highness, what defiance."

I was silent.

Talleyrand appealed to me. "We cannot capitulate nor protect Paris from destruction until General Bonaparte has left France. The allied troops have reached Versailles. We have no time to lose, Your Highness. General Bonaparte must leave Malmaison by this evening, and be on his way to Rochefort."

"Why Rochefort?"

"The Allies will, of course, demand the extradition of General Bonaparte." Talleyrand tried to conceal a yawn. "But when General Bonaparte abdicated, he insisted that two frigates of the French Navy be placed at his disposal so that he could go abroad. The frigates have been waiting for him in vain for two days in Rochefort harbour."

Fouché narrowed his eyes. "Besides, the English Navy has blockaded all our ports. I hear the English cruiser *Bellerophon* is lying at anchor at Rochefort beside the frigates."

Fouché consulted his watch.

Here it comes, I thought—now. . . . I swallowed and asked softly, "What have I to do with it?"

"You, dear Crown Princess, as a member of the Swedish Royal House, are in a position to talk to General Bonaparte in the name of the Allies." Talleyrand smiled, clearly amused.

"Your Highness can at the same time convey to General Bonaparte the French Government's answer to his impudent suggestion." As he spoke, Fouché extracted a sealed letter from his breast pocket.

"I'm afraid the French Government will have to ask one of its regular couriers to take this document to Malmaison," I said.

"And the request that he go abroad? Or surrender himself to the Allies, so that France can have peace at last?" Fouché trembled with fury.

Slowly I shook my head. "You are mistaken, gentlemen. I'm only a private person here."

"My child, you haven't been told the whole truth—"

I jumped. For the first time I heard Lafayette's voice. A deep, serene and kindly voice. "This General Bonaparte has assembled a few battalions in Malmaison, young men, ready for anything. . . . We're afraid the General might reach a decision which wouldn't affect the ultimate outcome, but would cost the lives of several hundred men. Several hundred human lives mean a great deal, my child."

I looked down at my feet.

"General Bonaparte's wars have already cost Europe millions of human lives," the quiet voice continued relentlessly.

I looked up and saw, over their shoulders, the portrait of the young Napoleon. From far away I heard my own voice. "I'll try, gentlemen."

After that, everything happened quickly.

Fouché pressed the sealed letter into my hand. "General Becker will accompany Your Highness," he said.

And I, "No, I'll take only my Swedish aide."

"A battalion of the guards is at your disposal," said Talleyrand impressively.

"I don't think I'll be in danger. Count Rosen—my carriage. We're driving at once to Malmaison."

My heart fluttered. Yvette gave me my gloves. "And which hat, Your Highness?"

Hat, which hat . . . Talleyrand was saying something. "—convinced that gratitude will be proved, and perhaps an exception will be made of Mme Julie Bonaparte." Why was he tormenting me?

I turned my back on him. General Lafayette stood near the door to the garden, peeking through the cracks in the closed shutters. I went over to him. "My child," he said, "with your permission I will sit in your garden and await your return."

"All day long?"

"All day long, and I'll be thinking of you all the time."

"Your Highness—the carriage." Count Rosen wore the formal blue-and-yellow sash over his parade uniform.

The drive to Malmaison seemed much shorter than usual. I had the carriage top put back because I could hardly breathe. But it didn't do any good. Close behind us galloped a lone rider. General Becker, the commissary, whose duty it was to watch over the former Emperor of the French on behalf of the French Government. From time to time, Count Rosen looked at me out of the corner of his eye. We spoke not a single word the whole way.

Near Malmaison the road was barricaded, and National Guardsmen stood watch. When they recognized General Becker, they quickly pushed the barricade aside. The entrance to the park was also guarded by heavily armed sentries. Becker sprang from his horse. My carriage was allowed to pass. My heart began to flutter again. In my distress, I tried to pretend that things were as they used to be. A visit to Malmaison, where I knew every bench and every rosebush. I'd see the little pond again, and . . .

The carriage stopped.

Count Rosen helped me out. Ménéval appeared on the open staircase, the Duke of Vicenza behind him. And then I was surrounded by familiar faces. Hortense ran to me—and Julie. I forced my quivering lips into a smile.

"How wonderful that you've come, dearest," Julie said.

"A delightful surprise," Joseph declared. Beside Joseph was Lucien. His near-sighted eyes searched my face. I smiled desperately. Mme Letizia waved to me from the open window of the white-and-gold salon. How glad they all were to see me.

"Joseph," I gulped, "I must—please, I must speak to your brother immediately."

"How kind of you, Désirée. But you must be patient. The Emperor is expecting an important communication from the Government in Paris, and is not to be disturbed until it comes."

My mouth was dry again. "Joseph—I'm bringing your brother this message."

"And?" they all asked in one breath: Joseph, Lucien, Hortense and Julie, Ménéval and Vicenza, General Bertrand and Jérôme Bonaparte. "And—?"

"I have to give it first to General Bonaparte."

Joseph's face went a shade paler when I said "General Bonaparte." "His Majesty," he said, "is on the bench in the maze. You remember the maze and his bench, Désirée?"

"I know this park very well," I whispered, and turned to go. Spurs jangled behind me. "Wait here, Count Rosen. I walk this path alone."

I knew the intricacies of the maze, so charmingly devised by Josephine. I knew how one turns so as not to run into the hedges, but come suddenly and surprisingly to the little white bench on which only two can sit very close together.

On this little bench sat Napoleon.

He wore the green chasseur uniform, his thin hair was carefully brushed back. His face, with the pale plump cheeks and the domineering chin, was cupped in his hand. Unseeingly he stared at the flowering hedge before him.

When I saw him, I suddenly became quite calm. And with my fear, the sweetness of all my memories vanished, too. I even wondered coolly how best to address him to attract his attention. Then it occurred to me that it didn't matter, we two were alone in the maze of fragrant hedges. . . . But before I spoke to him he turned his head a little and saw my white dress. "Josephine—" he murmured, "Josephine—"

When no answer came, he looked up. Reality returned. He saw the white dress, but he recognized me. He was surprised and very pleased. "Eugénie—are you really here?"

No one heard him call me Eugénie. No one saw him move over to one side of the little bench for two, who had to sit very close together. When I sat close beside him, he turned to me and smiled.

"It's been many long years since you and I looked at a flowering hedge together." And because I still said nothing, "You remember, don't you, Eugénie?" With which, still smiling, he moved his hand as though to sweep back a lock of hair, which had long since disappeared.

"One has time to remember while one waits. I'm waiting for a message from the Government. An extremely important message." He frowned, two deep furrows appeared at either side of his nose, his chin jutted out. "And I'm not used to waiting."

"You need wait no longer, General Bonaparte. I bring the Government's answer." I quickly pulled the letter out of my handbag. I heard him hastily break the seal. I didn't watch him while he read.

"How does it happen that you bring me this letter, madame? Did the Government not consider it sufficiently important to send me their answer by a minister or an officer? A casual guest, a lady, making a friendly call, chosen as messenger!"

"I'm not a casual visitor, General Bonaparte. Nor a lady making a friendly call," said I, and took a deep breath. "I am the Crown Princess of Sweden, General Bonaparte."

"And what has that to do with it?" he demanded.

"The French Government has asked me to inform you that the Allies will consider the surrender of Paris only after you have left

France. To save Paris from destruction, it is imperative that you leave today."

"I make an offer to repulse the enemy at the gates of Paris, and they reject it," he roared.

"The first allied troops have reached Versailles," I said quietly. "Do you want to be taken prisoner here at Malmaison?"

"Don't worry, madame, I know how to defend myself."

"That's just it, General. Unnecessary bloodshed must be avoided."

His eyes narrowed, only two slits. "So—must it? And if it's important to the honour of a nation?"

I could mention the millions, I thought, who have already died for the honour of this nation. But he knew these figures better than I. I clenched my teeth. I wouldn't give in. I'd sit on this bench, and not give in. But he had stood up. He probably wanted to pace up and down. But there was no room in the heart of the maze. Like a cage, I thought, and shrank from the idea.

"Madame." He was so close to me I had to lean back my head to see his face. "You say, the French Government wishes me to leave. And—the Allies?"

His face was contorted; in the corners of his mouth were tiny bubbles.

"The Allies insist on taking you prisoner, General."

For a long minute he looked at me steadily. Then turned his back on me and leaned against the hedge. "This scrap of paper from the so-called French Government, which you have just delivered to me, madame, refers again to frigates in Rochefort. I'm to embark for whatever destination I choose. . . . Madame, why doesn't the Government hand me over to the Allies?"

"I think . . . it would embarrass the gentlemen."

He wheeled around and looked at me again. "I must merely board one of the ships, name my destination, and . . ."

"The harbour of Rochefort, like all the other French ports, is patrolled by the English Navy. You wouldn't get far, General."

He didn't shout, he didn't bluster, he sat down very quietly beside me. We had so little room that I could hear every breath he drew. At first he breathed very heavily.

"When I saw you awhile ago, and recognized your face, madame,

I felt for a moment that my youth had come back. I was wrong—
Your Royal Highness."

"Why? I remember perfectly the evenings we raced each other.
You were already a general, a very young and handsome general."
I spoke as in a dream, the words came of themselves. It was hot and
still and the hedge smelled sweet. "Occasionally you even let me
win. But you've probably forgotten that long ago."

"No—Eugénie."

"And once—it was late in the evening, and the meadow beyond
our garden was all dark—you told me that you knew your destiny.
Your face was so white in the moonlight. That was the first time I
was afraid of you."

"And that was the first time I kissed you, Eugénie."

I smiled. "You were thinking about my dowry, General . . ."

"Not—entirely—Eugénie. Truly—not entirely. . . ."

Then we again sat beside each other in silence. I sensed he was
watching me sideways, that something had occurred to him that had
to do with me. I clasped my hands tightly together. A few hundred
men's lives mean a great deal, my child . . . If I could pray, I would
pray now.

"And if I don't let myself be taken prisoner, but give myself up
voluntarily as a prisoner of war—what then?"

"I don't know," I said unhappily.

"An island? Another island. Perhaps that rock in the ocean called
St. Helena they suggested at the Congress of Vienna?" Naked fear
showed in his eyes—his whole face. "Is it—St. Helena?"

"I honestly don't know. Where is St. Helena?"

"Beyond the Cape of Good Hope. Far beyond, Eugénie!"

"Nevertheless, General, I wouldn't let myself be taken prisoner.
Never, General, never. I'd much rather go voluntarily."

But he leaned forward again and put his hand over his eyes, which
still reflected his overwhelming fear. I stood up. He didn't move.

"I'm going now," I said. And stayed there, waiting.

He raised his head. "Where are you going?"

"Back to Paris. You have given neither the Crown Princess of
Sweden nor the French Government an answer. But you have until
—this evening."

With that he began to roar with laughter. It came so unexpectedly that it startled me.

"Shall I keep them from taking me prisoner? Here or in Rochefort? Shall I prevent it?" He felt for his sword. "Shall we cheat Blücher and Wellington of their sport?" He ripped the sword from its scabbard. "Take it, Eugénie, take the sword of Waterloo!"

Steel glinted in the sunlight.

Hesitantly I stretched out my hand. "Be careful, don't hold it by the blade." Awkwardly I clutched the hilt. Then I stared in dismay at the sword in my hand. Napoleon had stood up. "At this moment I surrender myself to the Allies. I consider myself a prisoner of war. It is customary to hand over one's sword to the officer who takes one prisoner. Bernadotte can explain this to you someday. I have handed over my sword to the Crown Princess of Sweden, because—" his words tumbled over each other—"because we've reached the hedge, Eugénie. And you have won."

"I can hardly explain about the hedge to the French Government," I said. "They're waiting for your answer at my house, General Bonaparte."

"Oh, they're waiting?" he jeered. "M. Talleyrand and Fouché are waiting in your house to deliver up France to the Bourbons again?"

"No, Lafayette is waiting."

He grimaced. "Eugénie, don't hold the sword like an umbrella."

"And your answer to the Government, General?"

"Show them my sword and say that I'm giving myself up to the Allies as a prisoner of war. In an hour—no, in two—I leave for Rochefort. From there I'll send a letter to my oldest and best enemy, the Prince Regent of England. My fate after that depends on the Allies." Napoleon paused and added hastily, "The frigates are, under all circumstances, to wait in Rochefort."

"They're lying at anchor besides the English cruiser *Bellerophon,*" I said. Then I waited for a word of farewell. No word came, and I turned to leave.

"Madame!"

I turned around quickly. "Madame, they say the climate on St.

Helena is very unhealthy. Can I count on any effort to persuade the English to change my destination?"

"You said yourself that St. Helena lies beyond the Cape of Good Hope."

He stared straight ahead. "After my first abdication I tried to commit suicide. In Fontainebleau . . . but my life was saved. I have not yet fulfilled my destiny. On St. Helena I will dictate my political testament. You've probably never been suspended between life and death, madame?"

"The evening you became engaged to Viscountess de Beauharnais, I tried to drown myself in the Seine."

His eyes bored through me. "You tried to . . . And how were you rescued, Eugénie?"

"Bernadotte pulled me back."

He shook his head, baffled. "How strange. Bernadotte pulled you back. You will be Queen of Sweden. I hand you the sword of Waterloo. . . . Do you believe in predestination?"

"No, only in curious coincidences." I held out my hand to him.

"Can you find your way back alone through the maze, Eugénie?" I nodded.

"Tell my brothers to prepare everything for my departure. Above all, my civilian clothes. I wish to be alone here for a while. And our engagement—long ago—it wasn't only the dowry. Now go, Eugénie—go very quickly. Before I repent."

I went very quickly. The paths in the maze seemed to have no end. The sun blazed down. Not a branch, not a leaf stirred, no bird sang. I have the sword, I thought, everything is over, I have the sword. . . . My white dress clung to me, my eyes were swimming. Roses in many colours, so many white, she had so loved white. I began to run. A window opened. Julie's voice, "That took you a long time." Yes, a lifetime. I ran on, they were waiting for me on the open staircase—the brothers, Rosen's gleaming sash, the dark uniform of the commissary. How odd that not one of them moved. Like wax figures, they stood and stared at me.

They weren't staring at me at all, but at the sword I clutched. . . .

I stopped running and took a deep breath. Count Rosen reached out his hand to take the sword. I shook my head. The others remained motionless. "General Becker."

"At your command, Highness?"

"General Bonaparte has decided to surrender to the Allies. The General handed over his sword to me, as Crown Princess of Sweden. In two hours, General Bonaparte leaves for Rochefort."

Footsteps on the stairs. The women of the Bonaparte family joined the men. "Napoleon—" Mme Letizia whispered, and began to cry softly. "In just two hours. . . ."

Joseph's fingers closed firmly around Julie's arm. "I will accompany my brother to Rochefort, General Becker," he said calmly. He hates him, I thought again, or he wouldn't go with him.

General Bertrand said something to Joseph in a low voice. "Two regiments are ready, at the command of His Majesty."

"General Bonaparte wants to spare France this—this civil war," I exclaimed. "Don't rob him of this opportunity."

Then I began to shiver and my eyes swam again. Close beside me, Julie was sobbing. "Has Napoleone had anything to eat?" Mme Letizia demanded. "Is he going far?" And then I heard nothing more, the roaring in my ears was so loud. I'm drowning in this uproar, I thought, and said, "The General wants his civilian clothes to be got ready. He wishes to be alone a little longer."

Somehow I must have climbed into my carriage. The wheels rolled. When I opened my eyes again, I saw the road, the meadows, trees and bushes all unchanged. How strange, I thought in amazement. A light breeze had come up. It smelled sweet as the roses at Malmaison. Count Rosen took the sword from my cramped fingers and leaned it in the corner of the carriage next to me. Then it happened. I don't know why I ducked back my head at the right moment. But I did, and I heard my own scream. The stone struck my knee. It was a very sharp stone. . . .

Rosen shouted in Swedish to Johansson, and Johansson lashed the horses. The next stone hit only a rear wheel. Rosen's face was deathly pale. "Your Highness—I swear—the would-be assassin will be caught!"

"Why? He's done nothing."

"Nothing? If someone throws stones at the Crown Princess of Sweden?"

"The stone wasn't aimed at the Crown Princess of Sweden. Only at Marshal Bernadotte's wife. And she no longer exists."

It was dusk, the sweet breeze was cooler, I could breathe again. A horseman overtook us. Probably a courier from General Becker to inform the Government that it was all over. I leaned back and looked at the evening sky. The first stars gleamed. Over—yes, all over. . . . I couldn't imagine ever leaving this carriage again, seeing people, thinking, acting.

"It's not quite proper, but perhaps you would hold my hand, Count—I'm so tired and so alone."

Shyly he put his hand over mine.

When we reached the outskirts of the city, darkness had fallen. In front of every house, whispering groups had gathered. Now Napoleon has put on his civilian clothes, he's driving to the coast, his mother has given him some food, he has started on his long journey, Paris is saved—

Near the rue d'Anjou we came upon a crowd of people surging forward. We had to stop. From the rue d'Anjou came muffled shouting. All at once someone called, "The Crown Princess of Sweden!" Others took up the cry. In the rue d'Anjou it sounded like a storm. Gendarmes appeared, pushed back the crowd, our horses started forward. In front of my house, torches burned high. The gate was wide open, we drove right on. Then the gates were closed quickly behind us. The storm outside subsided into a sound like the distant roaring of the sea.

When I alighted from the carriage I felt an agonizing pain in my knee. I clenched my teeth and reached for the sword. Then I limped into the house. The hall was brightly lighted, the doors were open. Startled, I blinked in the sudden brightness. At many strangers. . . .

"I thank you in the name of France—citizeness."

Lafayette had come to meet me. His eyes smiled out of a hundred wrinkles. His hand lay protectingly under my arm to lead me into the room. "Who are all these people?" I whispered dumfounded.

"Representatives of the Nation, my child," Lafayette said kindly.

"And—this great Nation, Highness, has many representatives."

542

Talleyrand had joined us. Behind him stood Fouché with a white cockade on his coat lapel. The many representatives of the Nation bowed. Suddenly there was a dead silence. Only the roaring of the sea in the street penetrated the closed shutters.

"And all those people in the street? What are they waiting for?"

"A rumour has spread that Your Highness was trying to negotiate," said Fouché rapidly. "The people of Paris have been waiting for hours for the return of Your Highness."

"Tell the people that the Em—that General Bonaparte has surrendered to the Allies and has departed. Then they will go home."

"They want to see you, citizeness," Lafayette said.

"Me? See me?"

Lafayette nodded. "You bring us peace. Capitulation without civil war. You have fulfilled your mission, citizeness."

I shook my head in horror. No, no, not that . . . But Lafayette wouldn't let go my arm. "Show yourself to the people, citizeness. You have saved many lives. May I escort you to a window?"

Helplessly, I let him lead me into the dining room. A window overlooking the rue d'Anjou was opened. Shouts rose from the darkness. Lafayette went to the window. He flung wide his arms. The shouting ebbed away. The old man's voice rang like a trumpet: "Citizens and citizenesses—peace is assured. General Bonaparte has given himself up as a prisoner of war, and to a woman . . ."

"A footstool," I whispered.

"A—what?" asked Rosen.

"A footstool, I'm too short for a crown princess!" I told him, and thought—Josephine, Josephine. . . .

"—and to a woman, a citizeness, chosen by a freedom-loving people in the far north as their crown princess—Napoleon has surrendered his sword. The sword of Waterloo!"

Again shouts rose from the darkness. Lafayette stepped quickly aside. A footstool was placed in front of the window.

With both hands I held out the sword. Torches glowed, the darkness below me seethed. Then I made out the words. They kept shouting the same thing to me: *"Nôtre dame de la paix!"*—"Our Lady of Peace!" First exultantly, and finally in rhythm again and again. *"Nôtre dame de la paix! Nôtre dame de la paix!"*

I stood still and tears streamed down my cheeks. Lafayette went back and thrust young Count Rosen forward. The old man took up a candlestick and let the light play on the Swedish uniform and the blue-and-yellow sash. "Sweden, long live Sweden," the crowd cheered. The Swedish flag was run up the flagpole over the gate; the night breeze toyed with it and made it look enormous. *"Nôtre dame de la paix. . . .!"* They cheered long after I'd got down from the footstool, and the windows were closed. Then I stood, feeling strange and lonely in my own salon. The representatives of la Grande Nation formed excited little groups. I think they were quarrelling. Someone said, "Talleyrand has already started on the armistice negotiations." And another, "Fouché will send a secret courier to fat Louis!"

They unfortunately made no move to leave. I laid the sword on the table beneath the portrait of the First Consul. Marie put fresh candles in the candelabra. She was wearing her new blue silk. "Marie—I think we should offer them some refreshment. Perhaps the cherries we planned to preserve? And some wine?"

"I would have baked some cakes if I'd known all this earlier. This time we've managed to get a lot of flour."

Yes, the sacks of flour in the basement. I listened. In the street they were still shouting.

"Marie, those people down there have been hungry for days. Have the sacks of flour brought up from the cellar. The cook can dole it out in front of the house. The gendarmes will help. Each is to have as much as he can carry away in a handkerchief or scarf."

"Eugénie—you're crazy," Marie said tenderly.

Ten minutes later the representatives of the Nation rushed to the wine as though dying of thirst, and spat the cherry pips in all directions. My knee throbbed so painfully I could hardly think. I limped to the door. But Talleyrand stopped me. "Has Your Highness hurt her leg?"

"No, no—I'm only tired, Your Excellency."

He raised his lorgnon. "Our Republican friend, the Marquis de Lafayette, seems to be an old idol of Your Highness."

His tone of voice infuriated me. "He's the one man with clean hands in this room," I blurted out.

544

"Naturally, Your Highness. All these years he's devoted himself to his vegetable garden, and washed his hands in innocence. Now they're clean—those hands!"

"The silent ones in the country . . ." I began.

"Are always a dictator's most useful subjects."

We listened. Even through the closed shutters we heard the scraping of many feet, and the gendarmes' commands. "That's only the distribution of flour," I murmured.

"How kind you are, my child—first you bring peace of mind and then food for the hungry." Lafayette had joined me, his blue eyes looked at me affectionately.

"How kind and how wise." Talleyrand smiled as he took a glass of wine from a servant. "The little country with the big future—first negotiates and later distributes food." He handed me the glass. "To Sweden, Your Highness."

It occurred to me that I had eaten nothing all day, and I dared not drink on an empty stomach. I noticed, too, that Fouché wanted to snatch the sword. "No, you don't," I cried, limping quickly over.

"But the French government—" he protested. For the first time I saw the gleam in his small eyes. A very greedy gleam.

"The sword has been surrendered to the Allies and not to the French government. I will keep it until General Blücher and General Wellington decide about it."

I held the sword of Waterloo again like an umbrella and supported myself with it. Perhaps cold compresses will help my poor knee, I thought, and looked at the portrait. The First Consul stared scornfully into space.

The silent ones of the country were quarrelling again with the traitors to the Republic. I heard them all the way up to my bedroom. My knee was blue and very swollen. Shaking her head, Marie peeled off my rumpled dress. The street was quiet. I began to write in my diary. . . . And now at last it's down. Papa, Lafayette has become an old man. And your broadside of the Rights of Man is probably in Sweden. . . .

Since Napoleon's return from Elba no more than ninety, ninety-five—no—a hundred days have passed. A hundred days and a hundred eternities—am I actually only thirty-five years old? Jean-Baptiste died one death in the Battle of Leipzig, and the young Désirée in the maze at Malmaison. How can two such strangers ever live together again?

I don't believe I'll ever write in my diary again, Papa.

Part Four

THE QUEEN OF SWEDEN

Paris, February, 1818

Now it has actually happened to me.

Although I've known for years that one day it would, I couldn't really imagine it. But now it's come. And nothing, nothing can undo it.

I was at the piano trying to play a new melody Oscar had composed. A shame that Jean-Baptiste wasted so much money on my piano and deportment lessons, I thought once again as I pecked at the keys. At which point the Swedish Ambassador was announced. There was nothing unusual in this, he called frequently, and the afternoon was grey and rainy—just right for a cup of tea.

But the moment he entered the room, I understood. He just stood there. The door closed behind him. We were alone. Yet he stood motionless at the door and didn't move. The whole room lay between us. I wanted to hurry to him. Then he bowed. We were both most uneasy. His bow was so deep, so—solemn. I saw the mourning band on his arm, and felt as though all the blood had left my face.

"Your Majesty—" He slowly stood erect. "Your Majesty, I come with sad news. King Charles passed away on the fifth of February."

I might have been turned to stone. People I've loved have died. The trembling little old king I'd hardly known at all. But his death meant . . .

"His Majesty has delegated me to inform Your Highness of all the circumstances, and to give you this letter."

I didn't stir. The Ambassador came to me, and held out a sealed letter to me. "Your Majesty, please—" he implored. I reached out a trembling hand and took the letter.

"Sit down, Baron," I murmured, and sank into the nearest chair. My hands shook while I broke the heavy seal. It was a large sheet of paper, on which Jean-Baptiste had scribbled in great haste:

Dearest, you are now Queen of Sweden. Please behave accordingly. In haste, Your J-B.

And below, a postscript,

Don't forget to destroy this letter at once.

Behave accordingly: I let the letter fall and smiled. I knew the Ambassador was watching me. The Ambassador with his band of mourning. I quickly tried to assume a sad and dignified expression. "My husband writes me that I'm now Queen of Sweden," I said earnestly.

At that the Ambassador began to smile. "On February 6, His Majesty was proclaimed by the Royal Heralds King Charles XIV John of Sweden and Norway, and the wife of His Majesty was proclaimed Queen Desideria."

"Jean-Baptiste should never have permitted that! I mean, to call me Desideria," I murmured. To that the Ambassador had no answer. "How—how did it happen?" I asked at last.

"The old gentleman passed away peacefully. He had a stroke on the first of February, and two days later we knew the end was near. His Majesty and His Highness, the Crown Prince, were in the sickroom."

I tried to imagine the scene. The Stockholm Palace, the overcrowded sickroom, Jean-Baptiste, and His Highness, the Crown Prince. Oscar—Crown Prince Oscar . . .

"My friend, Solomon Brelin, has written me exactly what happened. In the antechamber outside the sickroom the members of the court and the Government had assembled. The connecting door was open. At about seven o'clock, on February the fifth, the King's breathing became quieter. We realized he had regained consciousness. The Queen fell on her knees at his bedside, Princess Sofia began to pray half out loud. Suddenly the old gentleman opened his eyes and stared fixedly in the direction of the Crown Prince—I mean His Majesty. And His Majesty steadily returned his look. He moved only once, to ask the Crown Prince to bring him a coat. My friend writes that His Majesty was very pale and seemed cold. Although the heat in the small room was almost unbearable. . . .

"The longer the dying man gazed at the Crown Prince—I mean at His Majesty—the quieter and easier became his breathing. At a quarter to eleven it was all over."

I bowed my head. I, too, was suddenly cold. "And then?"

"The Dowager Queen and Princess Sofia Albertina left the death room, and the others, too, withdrew. Only His Majesty remained. He expressly wished to be left alone with the dead King."

The Ambassador shivered a little, but went on quickly. "At midnight His Majesty received members of the Government, representatives of the Army, and the senior civil servants, who swore the oath of allegiance to him. This ceremony is required by the Constitution. Early in the morning His Majesty was proclaimed by the Royal Heralds King of Sweden and Norway. After that, His Majesty attended the service of mourning. And after this, His Majesty mounted his horse, and received the oath of allegiance from the troops of the Stockholm garrison. Meanwhile, the citizens of Stockholm had gathered at the Palace gates to do homage to their sovereign. The next day His Majesty, for the first time, ascended his throne in Parliament, and took the royal oath. As His Majesty laid his hand on the Bible, Crown Prince Oscar knelt before his father. . . . Your Majesty cannot imagine the rejoicing in Sweden. The coronation ceremony at the request of His Majesty will not be held until the eleventh of May."

"Really—the eleventh of May?"

"Has His Majesty a special reason to choose this date?"

"On the eleventh of May, it will be just twenty-five years since the soldier Jean-Baptiste Bernadotte became a sergeant in the Army of the French Republic. It was a great day in my husband's life, Your Excellency."

"Yes, yes, of course, Your Majesty."

I rang for tea. Marcelline came in to help me serve it. We drank our first cups in silence.

"More tea, Your Excellency?"

"You're very kind, Your Majesty."

Poor Marcelline was so shocked she dropped a cup, with a crash. Soon afterward the Ambassador took his leave. "The French King will undoubtedly pay Your Majesty a visit of condolence," he assured me.

"Broken china means good luck," whispered Marcelline and looked at me in awe.

"Perhaps— Why are you staring at me like that?"

"Her Majesty, Queen of Sweden and Norway!" She rolled out the words impressively.

"I must order some mourning tomorrow," I said.

I walked slowly over to the piano. Looked at the music Oscar, Crown Prince of Sweden and Norway, had written. I riffled the keys. Then I closed up the keyboard. "I'll never play the piano again, Marcelline."

"Why not, Aunt?"

"Because I play too badly. Too badly for a queen."

"Now we can't go to see Aunt Julie. You'll go to Stockholm, naturally. Aunt Julie will be all upset. She counted so much on your visit."

"She can still count on it," I said, and went up to my bedroom. I simply threw myself on the bed, and stared into the darkness.

Julie Bonaparte—exiled from France like all the others with the name Bonaparte. They allowed her to stay in my house for one week after Napoleon's departure. But then I had to pack her boxes, and take her and the children across the Belgian frontier.

Since that time I've written a request every month to the eighteenth Louis asking him to authorize Julie's return. And every other month I've received a courteous, very courteous, refusal. And after every refusal, I've gone to Brussels to comfort Julie and take care of her. Every time I come, she complains of some new symptoms, and swallows so much medicine it makes me sick even to watch her. Brother-in-law Joseph didn't stay around long. He took the title of Count de Survilliers and sailed to America. There he bought a farm near New York. His letters sound contented. His present life reminds him of his youth on his mother's farm. Thin and embittered, Julie drags herself from her sofa to her bed, from her bed to her sofa. How can he have imagined that she'd ever be well enough to follow him to America? I stroke her hands, and put compresses on her forehead. Julie, for years, we were together every day— Tell me, when did you stop loving Joseph?

That first week after the Hundred Days. . . . Hortense came for her sons. Count Flahault accompanied her. They were on their way to Switzerland. Hortense was quiet and sensible, she seemed almost happy. Beyond the Cape of Good Hope there are no women. Her lifelong jealousy is over. Only at the very last—I was helping her younger child into the carriage—her eyes flashed again.

"But one will come back and be the third," she whispered.

"Who, and third what?" I demanded.

"One of my sons, madame," she smiled craftily, "Napoleon the Third."

Hortense succeeded in reaching Switzerland. But not all were so lucky. Not Marshal Ney. . . . For after the Hundred Days, the eighteenth Louis ceased to believe he had gained the throne through chance, but by his own proprietary right. While he laboriously climbed the front stairs to the Tuileries, he remembered bitterly his flight out of the back door. The Tuileries courtyard was deserted, and all over Paris people had hung banners of the Republic from their windows. Louis sat down at his desk and demanded the lists. But the lists of Republicans and Bonapartists had vanished during the Hundred Days. Then Fouché was announced. He brought not only the lists but he had also added new names. With them Fouché handed over to Louis—France. A Republican government wouldn't have kept Fouché long as a minister. So he bargained with the Bourbons. He welcomed them as a representative of the Provisional Government, and they appointed him Minister of Police. The eighteenth Louis was thinking primarily of the lists.

Marshal Ney, in the meantime, had assembled what was left of the Army, and was leading them from Waterloo back to France. His name was also on the lists—hadn't he promised to take Napoleon prisoner and to exhibit him in a cage? Ney tried to escape to

Switzerland, but was captured in flight. King Louis first had him brought before a court martial, but the court martial acquitted him. So Louis called the Upper House together, an assembly of the old nobility and of repatriated exiles. Marshal Ney, the son of a cooper, was sentenced to die for high treason.

That's when I wrote my first petition to King Louis. I wrote clumsily, with trembling fingers, while, beside me, Mme Ney knelt and prayed. But while I was still writing, the entire quarter around the Jardin de Luxembourg was cordoned off by Fouché's gendarmes. In the park cracked a volley of shots. We didn't know about this until Rosen came in, saw what I was writing, and told me it was too late. Mme Ney screamed. She screamed until she could scream no more. I often meet her, she has become taciturn and suspicious. But her screams still echo through my house. . . .

How many faces seem to haunt me from the darkness. Shot, imprisoned, exiled—Louis struck one name after another from the lists. Finally only one single name remained. Then he struck this one off, too, and sent his Minister of Police, the Duke of Otranto, into exile.

Julie in Brussels, Joseph in America. The other Bonapartes in Italy. But I was still here, and King Louis would call on me. Suddenly I was dreadfully frightened, because I didn't know what had become of Jean-Baptiste's letter. Perhaps I'd left it lying in the salon —and he said that I was to behave "accordingly."

Accordingly.

I was relieved to feel the letter under my pillow. Marie came in and lighted the candles.

She'll scold me for lying on the silk bedspread with my shoes on, I thought. But Marie didn't scold me at all. She shone a light on my face, and looked at me respectfully, just like Marcelline.

"Don't be angry, I'll take off my shoes." I sat up, embarrassed.

"Your niece told me about it. You might have told me yourself," Marie grumbled.

"I know what you're thinking. That my papa wouldn't have approved. I know it myself. You don't have to tell me."

"Hold up your arms, Eugénie, and let me take off your dress."

I raised my arms. She slipped off my dress. "There—now sit up straight, Eugénie, and lift your head. It doesn't matter what one is, but how one acts. If you're a queen, then at least be a good one. When do we leave for Stockholm?"

I picked up the letter and reread the casual scrawl. Written in such haste, so full of anxiety that I might be unworthy of him. I reached for a candle and held the letter to the flame.

"Well, when do we go, Eugénie?"

"In three days. Then I won't have time to receive King Louis. By the way—we're going to Brussels, Marie. Julie needs me, and in Stockholm I'm superfluous."

"But they can't have a coronation without us!" Marie protested.

"Apparently they can. Or they would have invited us to it." The last corner of the letter crumbled into ashes. I got out my diary, and began, for the first time in ages, to write it all down. Now it has really happened to me—I am Queen of Sweden.

Paris, June, 1821

The letter lay among many others on my breakfast table. The dark-green seal showed clearly the coat of arms forbidden all over the world. At first I thought I must be dreaming. I examined the seal from all sides. It actually was a letter with the crest of the Emperor. And addressed to Her Majesty, Queen Desideria of Sweden and Norway. I finally opened this unexpected communication.

Madame, I have been informed that my son, the Emperor of the French, died on May the fifth of this year on the island of St. Helena . . .

I looked up. The chest of drawers, the night table, the mirror in its gilt frame. Nothing had changed. Oscar's picture as a child, and Jean-Baptiste's portrait. Everything looked as usual. I couldn't take it in. After a while I read the letter to the end.

... on the island of St. Helena. His earthly remains at the order of the governor of the island will be buried with the military honours due a general. The English Government has forbidden the erection of a tombstone with the name "Napoleon." Only the inscription "General N. Bonaparte" has been allowed. Therefore I have decided that the grave will remain unmarked. I am dictating these lines to my son Lucien who frequently stays with me in Rome. My eyesight has been failing for years, and unfortunately I am now blind. Lucien has begun to read aloud to me my son's memoirs, which he dictated to Count de Montholon on St. Helena. They contain the sentence, "Désirée Clary was Napoleon's first love." This proves, madame, that my son never stopped thinking of his first love. Since they tell me the manuscript is soon to be printed, please let me know whether this sentence should be omitted. We understand you must consider your exalted position, and will gladly comply with your wishes. I send you my son Lucien's kind regard, and remain as always your devoted ...

The blind old woman had signed the letter herself. It was barely legible and in Italian: *"Laetizia, madre di Napoleone."*

In the course of the day I asked my nephew Marius how the letter with the green coat of arms had come to my house. Since I've appointed Marius my Court Chamberlain, he's supposed to know about these things.

"An attaché to the Swedish Embassy brought it. The letter was delivered to the Swedish Chargé d'Affaires in Rome."

"Did you see the crest?"

"No. Was it an important letter?"

"It was the last letter I shall ever receive with the Emperor's crest on it. I want you to send some money to the English Ambassador asking that in my name a wreath be laid on the grave at St. Helena. On the nameless grave, you'd better add."

"Aunt, your wish cannot be granted. There are no flowers on St. Helena. The terrible climate of the island kills all plant life."

"Do you think Marie Louise will marry Count von Neipperg now, Aunt? They say she already has three children by him," said Marcelline.

"She was as good as married to him long ago, my child."

"And what about the son of her first marriage? The King of

Rome was referred to as Napoleon II in all official French documents for several days during the second abdication negotiations," Marius declared vehemently.

"The King of Rome, also known as l'Aiglon, is now called François Joseph Charles, Duke of Reichstadt, son of Marie Louise, Duchess of Parma. Talleyrand showed me a copy of the letters patent making him a duke."

"And his father isn't mentioned at all?"

"No. As far as the document goes, his father is—unknown."

"If Napoleon had foreseen his future—" Marcelline began.

"He knew," I said. Then I sat down at my desk. An island without flowers. An island on which nothing survived. Our garden in Marseilles, the meadow—yes, the meadow. I began my letter to his mother.

"Aunt Julie once intimated that you—" Marcelline stammered. "Or rather, that he once—I mean that . . ."

"You can read about it in his memoirs." I sealed my letter. "Nothing will be left out."

In a hotel room in Aix-la-Chapelle, June, 1822

That I could once again experience all the sweetness, the anxiety, the impatience of a first rendezvous, I thought this morning, in front of my mirror. My fingers shook as I put on my rouge. Not too much, I told myself, I'm forty-two years old, he must not think I'm trying to seem younger. But I want him to find me attractive. . . .

"And when will I see him?" I asked for about the hundredth time.

"At half-past twelve, Aunt. In your salon," Marcelline answered patiently.

"But he gets here early in the morning, doesn't he?"

"No one knows the exact hour of his arrival, so the appointment was made for half-past twelve, Aunt."

"And will he dine with me?"

"Of course. Accompanied by his chamberlain, Karl Gustaf Löwenhjelm."

"My Löwenhjelm's uncle." My Löwenhjelm is Gustaf, too. He has recently been sent me from Stockholm to replace Count Rosen, who went back home. But he's so pompous and distant I hardly dare speak to him.

"Otherwise, Aunt, only Marius and I will be there. So you'll be able to talk to him freely."

My Löwenhjelm, his Löwenhjelm, Marcelline and Marius. No. And again, no. I made up my mind. "Marcelline, be sweet and send me Count Löwenhjelm."

He'll arrive, I thought, and need to wash, and, after the long drive, he'll want exercise. Besides, he's never been in Aix, the hotel is near the Cathedral. Like any tourist, he'll want to see the Cathedral. . . .

I said to Löwenhjelm, "You must be sure your uncle understands. Your uncle is to leave as soon as he sees me. Promise me that?"

My Löwenhjelm was horrified. "The advantage of ceremonial protocol is that surprises cannot possibly occur," he explained. I refused to give in. "As Your Majesty commands," he sighed.

So I put on my hat with the travelling veil. The veil came down over my cheeks. I tied the ribbons tightly under my chin. Besides, I thought, it's dark in the Cathedral. I left the hotel by myself. This is the last, the decisive surprise of my life, I thought on the way to the Cathedral. The first rendezvous with a new man can mean anything—or nothing. In half an hour I'll know.

I sat on a choir bench and folded my hands. Eleven years is a long time. Perhaps, without realizing it, I've changed into an old lady. In any case, he has grown up. A young man sent abroad to find a bride in the courts of Europe. Reliable Karl Gustaf Löwenhjelm has been assigned to accompany him, so he won't stray.

The same reliable Löwenhjelm who, years ago, awaited his father's arrival in Sweden, to initiate him into Swedish court ceremonial. But I will disregard this ceremonial. . . .

That morning countless tourists visited the Cathedral. They surged around the tomb of Charlemagne. I followed every one with my eyes. Him? asked my heart. Or the little man with flat feet over there?

I don't know how a mother feels who's seen her son grow up. Who tells him good night and kisses his cheek with its first stubbly beard, and knows when he first falls in love. Because then he suddenly pays attention to how he looks. All that, I've missed. I'm now looking for a man, of whom I've dreamed all my life but never met. Great presence, irresistible charm, everything—I expect it all from an unknown son.

I recognized him immediately. Not because he was with Löwenhjelm, who hasn't changed since my long-ago Stockholm days. But by his carriage, his walk, the slight turn of his head when he whispered something to Löwenhjelm. He wore a dark civilian suit, he is almost as big as his father. Only slender—yes, much slenderer. I stood up and went up to him. As in a dream, without thinking how I'd speak to him. He stood before the tomb of Charlemagne, and leaned a little forward to read the inscription. I plucked at his companion's arm. Löwenhjelm looked up, and silently moved away.

"Is that Charlemagne's tomb?" I heard myself ask in French. It was the silliest question in the world, it said so on the tomb.

"As you see, madame," he said, without looking up.

"I know that my behaviour is unseemly, but—but I'd like very much to meet Your Highness," I whispered.

He turned to me. "You know who I am, madame?"

The dark fearless eyes of his childhood. And the same thick hair. My hair . . . But a strange little moustache, which he had twirled up ridiculously.

"Your Highness is the Crown Prince of Sweden. And I—I'm a sort of compatriot. My husband lives in Stockholm . . ." I hesitated. He looked at me steadily. "I wanted to ask Your Highness something, but it will take a little time."

"Yes?" He looked around. "I don't know why my companion has suddenly deserted us," he murmured. "But I have an hour. If you'll permit me, madame, I'll gladly accompany you." He smiled into my eyes. "May I, madame?"

I nodded. There was a lump in my throat. While we walked to the exit, I saw Oscar's Löwenhjelm hiding behind a pillar. Oscar didn't see him. Without speaking to each other, we strolled through the fish market in front of the Cathedral, across a wide road, and finally into a narrow street. I pulled my veil over my face because I felt Oscar looking at me out of the corner of his eye. He stopped at a small café with a few miserable little tables and two dusty palms in flowerpots.

"May I offer my charming compatriot a glass of wine?"

I looked in horror at the hideous potted plants. It wouldn't be proper, I thought, and blushed. Didn't he realize I was an elderly woman? Or was Oscar trained to be attentive to just any woman?

It's only because he's finally skipped out on his frightful Löwenhjelm, I comforted myself—and accepted. "It's not very grand here, but we can at least talk undisturbed, madame," he said amiably. Then, to my horror, he asked, "Waiter, have you any champagne?"

"Not so early in the morning!" I objected.

"Why not? Anytime. If there's something to celebrate."

"But there's nothing to celebrate," I protested.

"Yes. Knowing you, madame. Can't you push that ugly veil aside, so I can see your face, and not just the tip of your nose?"

"My nose is a great misfortune," I said. "When I was young, I was sick about it. Strange, but no one has the kind of nose he likes."

"My father has a fantastic nose. It juts out like an eagle's beak. His face is all nose and eyes."

The waiter brought champagne and filled our glasses.

"*Skål*—unknown countrywoman! French and Swedish both, aren't you?"

"Like Your Highness," I said. The champagne was much too sweet.

"No, madame, I'm only Swedish now," he said quickly, "and Norwegian. This champagne tastes awful, doesn't it?"

"Too sweet, Your Highness."

"We seem to have the same tastes, madame; I'm glad. Most women prefer sugary-sweet wine. Our Koskull, for instance . . ."

I caught my breath sharply. "What do you mean—'our Koskull'?"

"The lady-in-waiting, Mariana von Koskull. First, the late King's ray of sunshine. Then Papa's favourite, and, if I'd followed his wishes, my mistress. What surprises you, madame?"

"That you—tell all this to a stranger," I said sternly.

"A countrywoman, madame. The late Queen Hedwig Elisabeth had little use for her husband's primitive urges. Mlle von Koskull used to read aloud to him, and he was happy if he could stroke her arm as she read. Papa accepted the etiquette of the Swedish Court as it was. He didn't want to upset anything or change anything. He took over the Koskull, too."

I stared at him, fascinated. "Are you serious?"

"Madame, my father is the loneliest man I know. My mother hasn't come to see him for years. Papa works sixteen hours a day, and spends the late evening hours with a few friends he made while he was Crown Prince. For instance, Count Brahe, if this name means anything to you. Mlle von Koskull often joins them. With a guitar. She sings Swedish drinking songs for Papa. The songs are wonderful, but unfortunately he can't understand the words."

"And the court balls, the receptions? One can't have a court without them?"

"Papa can. Don't forget, madame, we have no queen at our court."

I sipped my champagne slowly. He promptly refilled my glass. "Everything will be different when Your Highness marries."

"Do you think a young princess would be happy in an immense ice-cold palace, madame, in which the King refuses to receive any-one but his councillors of state and his old friends? My father has become very odd. A king who doesn't understand the language of his country, and is beset by a sickening neurotic fear of being de-posed. Do you know what it's come to now? My father absolutely forbids newspapers to publish any article personally displeasing to him. Although the Swedish Constitution guarantees freedom of the press. Madame, the King himself violates the Constitution, do you realize what that means?"

Oscar's face was pale with misery. I asked tonelessly, "Your Highness, you're not set against your father?"

"No. Or it wouldn't upset me so. . . . Madame, my father's for-

560

eign policy has secured for Sweden a position in Europe no one would have believed possible. His trade policy turned this bankrupt state into a prosperous country. Sweden has him to thank for her independence. Yet today he opposes with all his strength every liberal tendency in Parliament. And why? Because His Majesty thinks liberalism might lead to revolution, and the revolution would cost him his crown. In Scandinavia, revolution isn't the problem at all. But only a healthy evolution. But that a former Jacobin can not grasp. Am I boring you, madame?"

I shook my head.

"Things have gone so far that some people—individuals, madame, not any party—talk of forcing the King to abdicate—in my favour."

"That—you mustn't even think of it, much less talk about it, Highness," I whispered through quivering lips.

His thin shoulders slumped forward. "I'm tired, madame. I wanted to be a composer, but what came of it? A few songs, a few military marches. I began an opera, but haven't time to finish it, because I must not only devote myself to my duties as Crown Prince and as artillery general, but also as a go-between. I, madame, I must make my father realize that the French Revolution also brought about changes in Sweden. Papa should receive commoners instead of having only the old nobility at court functions. Papa must refrain, in every speech before a new session of Parliament, from talking about his achievements as a military commander, and about the large sums from his private fortune he has sacrificed for Sweden. Papa must . . ."

I couldn't bear it any longer. I had to interrupt him. "And this Koskull?"

"I don't think she's ever done any more than sing songs for him. Though—of course, Papa was a man in the prime of life when his loneliness began, wasn't he? Besides, he had the antedeluvian notion that mistresses, whose talents had been proved for a couple of generations, should teach Crown Princes in the art of love. Madame, he recently sent Mlle von Koskull to my room in the middle of the night—armed with her guitar."

"Your papa meant well, Highness!"

"My father locks himself in his study, and is out of touch with

561

reality. He needs—" He broke off and refilled the glasses again. The deep furrows in his forehead reminded me of Jean-Baptiste. The champagne tasted flat. "When I was a child, madame, I wanted more than anything to see Napoleon's coronation. I wasn't allowed to. I can't remember why, but I remember my mother, who was with me in the nursery, saying, 'We'll go to another coronation, Oscar. You and I. Mama promises. And it will be a much more beautiful coronation than tomorrow's, believe me, much more beautiful. . . .' Yes, madame, I went to another coronation. But my mother didn't come. Why are you crying into your champagne glass?"

"Your mother's name is Desideria—the desired one. Perhaps, at the time, her presence was not desired."

"Not desired? My father had her proclaimed queen in two marvellous countries and she—she never came to either. Do you think a man like my father would beg her to?"

"Perhaps your mother isn't suited to be a queen, Highness."

"The people of Paris shouted *Nôtre dame de la paix* up at my mother's window, because she prevented a civil war. My mother wrested Napoleon's sword from him . . ."

"No, he gave it to her."

"Madame, my mother is a wonderful woman. But she is at least as stubborn as my father. I assure you that the Queen's presence in Sweden is not only desirable, but a necessity."

"If that is so, the Queen will come, of course," I said softly.

"Mama. Thank God, Mama! And now take off the veil, so I can see you, really see you. Yes—you haven't changed. You're even more beautiful. Your eyes are larger, your face is fuller, and your forehead . . . Why are you crying, Mama?"

"When did you recognize me, Oscar?"

"Recognize? I only stationed myself at Charlemagne's tomb to wait for you. Moreover, I was delighted to learn how you speak to strange gentlemen."

"I was sure your Löwenhjelm would keep his mouth shut!"

"My Löwenhjelm had nothing to do with it. From the beginning I meant to see you again without witnesses. The Count knew how

I'd racked my brain to arrange it. So he tipped me off that you had beaten me to it."

"Oscar—is everything you told me about Papa true?"

"Of course. I only exaggerated a little to speed your homecoming. When are you coming?"

He took my hand and pressed it to his cheek. Homecoming—homecoming to a foreign land in which I had once been so cold. He rubbed his cheek against my hand. "Oscar, you have whiskers, like a real man. . . . And you don't know how deeply they hurt me in Stockholm."

"Mama, little Mama—who hurt you? The weird widow of the murdered Vasa? She's been dead for years. The old gentleman's widow? Hedwig Elisabeth died a few months after her husband. Or old Princess Sofia Albertina? Don't be ridiculous, Mama, who could hurt you now? Don't forget, now you're the Queen."

"No, no, I'm not forgetting. I think of it every minute, it haunts me, I'm afraid of it . . ."

"Mama, back there in the Cathedral, you murmured something about a favour from His Highness. Did you say that only to start a conversation?"

"No, I do want to ask you something. It's about my daughter-in-law."

"There's no such person. Papa has compiled a long list of princesses I'm to see. Oranienburg princesses, and above all, Prussian princesses. One more hideous than the other. Papa got their portraits."

"I'd so much like to have you marry for love, Oscar."

"Believe me, I'd rather, too. When you come home, I'll secretly show you my little daughter! Her name is Oscara, Mama!"

I'm a grandmother . . . And grandmothers are old ladies! And I had hastened to my last rendezvous without apprehension.

"Mama, Oscara has inherited your dimple."

Oscara. My granddaughter Oscara. . . . "Tell me, have these dimples a mother?"

"A charming mother—Jaquette Gyldenstolpe."

"Does Papa know?"

"What are you thinking of, Mama! Promise me you'll never mention it?"

"But shouldn't you . . ."

"Marry her? Mama, you forget who I am."

This gave me a turn. I don't know why. Oscar continued rapidly, "Papa first decided on a union with the House of Hanover. But to the English the Bernadotte Dynasty isn't elegant enough. I suppose I'll have to marry a Prussian princess."

"Listen, Oscar. It has been arranged that from here you travel with me to Brussels for the wedding."

"I've forgotten—who is marrying whom?"

"Aunt Julie's daughter Zenaïde is marrying a son of Lucien Bonaparte. Joseph Bonaparte is returning from America for the occasion. Perhaps he'll stay in Europe with Julie."

"I hope so, then we'll finally be rid of her and her frail health."

"Aunt Julie is very delicate."

"Forgive me, Mama, but all the Bonapartes are unattractive to me."

Like his father. Practically the same words. . . .

"Aunt Julie is a Clary, remember that."

"All right. We'll go to the wedding, Mama. And what then?"

"From Brussels I'm going to Switzerland to visit Hortense, the Duchess of St. Leu, at Castle Arenenberg. She was a Beauharnais, the daughter of the beautiful Josephine. I want you to go with me."

"Mama, I really have no desire to see these Bonapartes."

"I want you to meet Hortense's niece, the little Shooting Star."

"The little—what?"

"Her father is Eugène, the former Viceroy of Italy. Now he's called the Duke of Leuchtenberg, he married a daughter of the King of Bavaria. And the child is the most beautiful little Josephine you could ever imagine."

"No matter how beautiful she is, I still couldn't marry her."

"Why not?"

"You keep forgetting who I am! An obscure little Leuchtenberg isn't a suitable match for the Crown Prince of Sweden—for a Bernadotte, Mama!"

"No? Well, let me tell you something, Oscar. But first pour me some more champagne, I'm beginning to enjoy it. So—and now listen to me! Her paternal grandfather was Viscount de Beauharnais, a general in the French Army. And her grandmother was Viscountess de Beauharnais, born Tascher de la Pagerie, the most beautiful woman of her time, the toast of Paris, and one of the great courtesans. By her second marriage she became Empress of the French. Your paternal grandfather was an honourable lawyer's clerk in Pau, and I know nothing at all about your papa's mother."

"But Mama . . ."

"Let me finish! Her maternal grandfather is the King of Bavaria. The Bavarian dynasty is one of the oldest royal families in Europe. Your maternal grandfather, on the other hand, was the silk merchant François Clary from Marseilles."

He beat his brow. "The granddaughter of a courtesan!"

"Yes—and an enchanting one at that. I've seen little Josephine only once, as a child, but—the same smile, the same charm as the older Josephine."

Oscar sighed. "Mama, on dynastic grounds . . ."

"Exactly, on dynastic grounds. I want to be the ancestress of a beautiful dynasty."

"Papa will never consent."

"No one succeeded in forcing him to marry a homely woman. I'll talk to Papa. All you have to do is see the Shooting Star."

"Waiter, the bill."

Arm in arm we walked to our hotel. My heart beat fast from happiness and too much bad champagne.

"How old is she, Mama?"

"Just fifteen. But I'd already been kissed at that age."

"You were a precocious child, Mama. Why do you call her a shooting star?"

I wanted to explain it to him. But the hotel was in sight, and he turned suddenly serious, his hand firmly encircled my wrist. "Mama, promise me you'll come with my bride on her journey to Stockholm?"

"Yes, I promise."

"And that you'll stay?"

I hesitated. "That depends."

"On what, Mama?"

"On myself, Oscar. I can only stay if I succeed in being a good queen. I take it very seriously."

"All you need is practice, Mama. . . . There they are—your Löwenhjelm and my Löwenhjelm—prancing with excitement."

"I'll carry out several reforms at the Swedish court," I whispered in his ear.

He smiled into my eyes. "Let's let the evening sun go down before the Shooting Star falls from heaven."

I nodded. "Let's retire Mlle Koskull to a well-earned rest," I suggested.

"Mama, we're both a little drunk," Oscar declared uneasily. We began to laugh and couldn't stop.

Does this seem proper for an illegitimate grandmother?

In the Royal Palace, Stockholm
Spring, 1823

"How beautiful our country is," whispered my daughter-in-law, Crown Princess Josefina of Sweden, deeply moved. We stood side by side at the railing of an imposing cruiser which had awaited us in the port of Lübeck, and was taking us to Stockholm.

"Is it much farther? Should Pierre put on his wooden leg?" Marie asked every few minutes.

Oscar and the Shooting Star were married in Munich. But Oscar wasn't there. The Catholic Shooting Star naturally wanted to be married in a Catholic Church, and Oscar is a Protestant. He, therefore, was married by proxy in Munich. The official wedding celebration will begin after we reach Stockholm. I don't know whose brilliant idea it was to spare us the interminable journey through Denmark and southern Sweden by sending us this cruiser which passes the many small islands around Stockholm. Nor do I understand why Jean-Baptiste had me sail on a warship with eighty-four guns.

The sky was pale blue, and the islands rose craggy and steep from the waves. On every cliff and meadow there were birches—many thousands of birches with every variation of yellow in their spring foliage. "Our beautiful country," the granddaughter of Josephine repeated beside me, her eyes shining as she drank in the view of the birch forests.

"Should Pierre put on his wooden leg yet?" asked Marie again. Pierre sat beside his mother on deck and wanted to stand close behind me when we arrived—on his crutches and his wooden leg.

"We are nearing Vaxholm, Your Majesty," Chamberlain Count Gustaf Löwenhjelm told me, and handed me a field glass. "Vaxholm is one of our strongest fortifications." But I was thinking I'd never in all my life seen so many birch trees all at once. "Our country," the Shooting Star had said—our country?

Marcelline and Marius accompanied me. Etienne wrote me gratefully because I'd appointed his daughter chief stewardess of my household. And Marius will continue to administer my finances, and become a Swedish court official instead of a senior partner in the firm of Clary. Marius, Marcelline, Marie and Pierre—little bits of France I've brought with me. And Yvette, of course, the one person except Julie who can cope with my unruly hair.

Julie . . . How strong are the weak. How tenaciously her transparent, bloodless fingers clung to my arm, and for how many years she implored me, "Don't leave me, Désirée, write another petition to the King of France. I want to live in Paris, stay with me, help me, help me. . . ." My petitions were of no avail, but I'd always stayed near her. Until, at her daughter's wedding, she said, "Zenaïde and her husband will live in Florence. Italy reminds me of Marseilles. I'll move to Florence with the young couple." And Joseph, who had discoursed volubly about his herd of cattle and his railway shares in the state of New Jersey, said unexpectedly, "When I was born, Corsica was still Italian. When I am old, I'll join you in Italy." Julie slipped her arm under his. "So everything will be for the best," she said, indifferently but with satisfaction. She'd entirely forgotten about me. . . .

"I'm so happy, Mama," the Shooting Star beside me whispered. "From the very first moment, at Aunt Hortense's, Oscar and I felt we were made for each other. But I was sure neither you nor His Majesty would ever consent."

"Why not, my child?"

"Because—Mama, I'm only the daughter of a Duke of Leuchtenberg. Oscar could have made a much better match. You'd expected a princess from a royal family, hadn't you, Mama?"

Birches in yellow-green spring veils, waves as blue as the sky. The child had asked me something, and held her curly head a little sideways, like the dead Josephine.

"Expected, Josefina? One counts on nothing, one only hopes—when a son's happiness is at stake."

A salute of guns boomed out. I drew back in fear. The fortress of Vaxholm was welcoming us. So I knew I had no more time. Count on nothing, only hope, with all one's heart. . . .

"Remember that, Josefina, when your children fall in love . . . Why do you blush? Because I'm talking about your children? Darling, as a little girl you wouldn't believe me when I said ducks lay eggs. Now don't tell me you still believe in the stork. I don't know if, in the years to come, we'll often have a chance to talk entre nous. That's why I urge you now to let your children marry for love. You will promise me?"

"But the succession to the throne, Mama?"

"You must have several children. One of your sons is bound to fall in love with a princess, leave that to fate. But teach all the Bernadottes that one marries only for love."

Her long lashes fluttered in dismay. "But if she's a commoner. Think of that, Mama!"

"What is there to think about, Josefina? We're of middle-class stock—we Bernadottes."

The salutes thundered again. A small boat steered toward us. I raised the field glasses to my eyes. "Josefina, powder your nose quickly. Oscar is coming on board."

I hardly heard the roar of cannon. The coast was black with waiting people, the wind carried their cheers through the blue air, and more and more little boats, with garlands of flowers, danced around our ship. Oscar and Josefina stood close together and waved. Josefina wore a gay blue dress, and an ermine stole, now slightly yellow with age. It once belonged to Josephine, a present from Napoleon. Hortense gave it to the child many years ago as a remembrance of her beautiful grandmama.

"The port of Djurgaarden, Your Majesty. We'll soon land," announced Löwenhjelm.

I turned around. "Marie, it's time for Pierre to put on his wooden leg." I clenched my fists, my palms were wringing wet.

"Aunt—they've made a triumphal arch of birch branches," cried Marcelline. The guns boomed. Yyette rushed up and held a mirror in front of my face. Powder, rouge, a little silver on my eyelids. Marie put the heavy sable stole over my shoulders. Silver-grey velvet and sables seemed suitable for a mother-in-law.

Marie's work-worn hand covered my tense fingers. Her face has grown old and wrinkled. "We've reached our goal, Eugénie."

"No, Marie, we're just beginning."

The cannon were silent. And music resounded, an exultant fanfare. "I composed that for you," said Oscar. He said it to the Shooting Star. Löwenhjelm again handed me the field glasses.

A violet velvet cape. White plumes on the hat.

Suddenly everyone whisked away. Even Oscar and the Shooting Star. All alone I stood on the ship's bridge. The Swedish National Anthem burst forth. The thousands on the quay turned into statues. Only the delicate birch boughs on the triumphal arch quivered lightly.

Then two gentlemen, who'd been standing close beside the violet velvet cape, strode together up to the bridge to escort me to land. Count Brahe smiled and Count Rosen went deathly pale with excitement. But a hand in a white glove motioned them both aside, the violet velvet cape came forward, the ship's narrow bridge swayed, and on my arm I felt a strong, very familiar hand.

The crowd yelled, the cannons thundered, the orchestra rejoiced. Oscar escorted his Crown Princess ashore. Under the triumphal arch, a little girl in a white dress was thrust before me. The child, practically invisible behind a huge bouquet of blue lilies and yellow tulips, had to recite a poem. Then, obviously relieved, she thrust

the blue and yellow flowers at me. No one expected me to thank
her. But when I opened my mouth there was a sudden hush. I was
stiff with fear, but my voice was loud and calm. I began with the
words:

"Jag har varit länge borte—"

They held their breaths. Swedish—the Queen speaks Swedish.
I'd composed my little speech myself and Count Löwenhjelm had
translated it. Then I had learned it by heart. Word for word—it
was hard to do. My eyes filled and I concluded with: *"Länge leve
Sverige!"*

We drove through the streets in an open festive coach. The
Shooting Star beside me bowed graciously, to right and left. Jean-
Baptiste and Oscar sat opposite us. I held myself very erect and
smiled at the crowds until the muscles of my mouth ached. And
even then I smiled. "I can't get over it, Mama, you made a speech
in Swedish," said Oscar. "I'm terribly proud of you."

I felt Jean-Baptiste look at me, yet I dared not meet his eyes. Because we were in an open coach, and I had made a dreadful discovery!
I'm in love with him still.

Or perhaps again—I don't really know myself.

P.S. He's a grandfather. (But he doesn't suspect it.)

Drottningholm Castle in Sweden
August 16, 1823

Today at midnight I was for the first time a ghost. In my white
dressing gown I haunted the Palace as "the white lady."

The light summer nights are to blame; the sky is never completely dark. During my first visit to Drottningholm, I cried through
them. And now—twelve years later—I have to dance through them.
Oscar and the Shooting Star of course whirl from one party to an-

other. And I'm forcing Jean-Baptiste to go, too. Naturally, he makes a hundred excuses. Work and more work. Even his age is dragged in. Jean-Baptiste is sixty years old, it's true, but he couldn't be healthier. I've laughed him out of it and transformed the lonely bachelor quarters in the Stockholm Palace and in Drottningholm into fine court households.

A regiment of ladies-in-waiting and chamberlains were appointed. The lackeys were dressed in brand-new liveries. Paperhangers and carpenters, tailors, dressmakers and hairdressers had their hands full. They all profited and they were all happy. And last but not least my dear silk merchants. . . .

Oscar suggested holding large-scale manoeuvres in south Sweden and travelling to Skaane with the entire court. "Why?" asked Jean-Baptiste, and dug in his heels. Naturally, without avail. Oscar and I had our way, and south Sweden welcomed the royal family. Evenings we danced in the castles of the landed gentry, mornings I stood for hours watching parades, afternoons I received one deputation of citizens after another. Marie—so good and so tired herself—massaged my poor legs. And the new Swedish ladies-in-waiting helped me with my Swedish vocabulary. It was an awful trip but I, in the literal sense of the word, stood it.

Now we're in Drottningholm and supposedly resting. Yesterday I went to bed early, but I couldn't sleep. The clock struck midnight. The sixteenth of August, I thought. The sixteenth of August is dawning. I slipped into a dressing gown and began to wander around. I wanted to go to Jean-Baptiste. Everything was unearthly quiet except that the parquet floors creaked. How I hate these palaces . . . In Jean-Baptiste's study I almost collided with the marble bust of Moreau that Jean-Baptiste always keeps with him. Finally I groped my way through his dressing room, walked in—and nearly got shot.

Quick as a flash a pistol was aimed at me, and someone shouted in French, "Who's there?"

"A ghost, Fernand!" I laughed. "Only a ghost."

"Your Majesty frightened me," declared Fernand, offended. Then he got up from his camp cot and bowed. He wore a long nightshirt and still held the pistol in his hand. The camp cot barred the way to Jean-Baptiste's bedroom.

"Do you always sleep in front of His Majesty's door?" I demanded.

"Always," Fernand assured me. "Because the Marshal is afraid."

At that the door was flung open. Jean-Baptiste was still dressed. The green eyeshade he wears in secret when he works on his papers was rakishly askew.

"What does this disturbance mean?" he roared.

I dipped into a court curtsy. "Your Majesty, a ghost requests an audience."

"Shove the bed aside so Her Majesty can come in," Jean-Baptiste mumbled as he hastily removed the eyeshade. Somewhat embarrassed, Fernand pushed aside the camp cot, clutching his nightshirt tightly around him.

And then for the first time since my arrival in Drottningholm I entered Jean-Baptiste's bedroom. On the desk, documents were piled high. On the floor lay leather volumes in confusion. He's still studying, I thought. As he did in Hanover. As he did in Marienburg. . . . Jean-Baptiste stretched wearily. His voice was tender. "What does the ghost want?"

"The ghost is only reporting," I said, and sat down comfortably in an armchair. "It's the ghost of a young girl, who once married a young general, and lay on a bridal bed full of roses and thorns."

Jean-Baptiste sat on the arm of my chair and put his arm around me. "And why does the ghost walk tonight?"

"Because that happened twenty-five years ago," I said softly.

"My God," he shouted. "It's our silver wedding anniversary."

I crept closer to him. "Yes—and in the whole kingdom of Sweden no one but us will remember it. No cannons, no schoolchildren reciting poems, not even a regimental band playing a march composed by Oscar for this occasion. How lovely, Jean-Baptiste."

"We have both come a long way," he murmured, and he held me tighter. "And yet in the end you came to me." He closed his eyes.

"You have reached your goal, Jean-Baptiste," I whispered. "And nevertheless, you're afraid—of ghosts."

He didn't answer. He felt heavy against me. He seemed tired, very tired.

"You have Fernand sleep outside your door with a pistol. What are the names of the ghosts you fear?"

"Vasa," he groaned. "At the Congress of Vienna, the last Vasa king—the exiled one—presented his and his son's claims to the throne."

"That was eight years ago. Besides, the Swedes deposed him because he was crazy. Is he really crazy?"

"I don't know. His policies were. Sweden was at the brink of ruin—The Allies naturally brushed aside his claims. And finally, they're indebted to me. After all, I conducted that gruesome campaign . . ."

"Don't talk about it, Jean-Baptiste, don't torture yourself with those memories," I said quickly. A shudder ran through him. I felt it with every fibre of my being. "Jean-Baptiste, the Swedes know very well what you have done for them. Aren't there figures that prove to you that through you Sweden has become a sound and prosperous country?"

"Yes, yes—I have figures," he murmured. "But the opposition in Parliament . . ."

"Do they speak of the Vasas?"

"No, never. But it's enough that this opposition, which calls itself Liberal, exists. That its newspapers always harp on the fact that I wasn't born here."

I straightened up. "Jean-Baptiste, if anyone reproaches because you weren't born here, and don't speak the language, it's a far cry from *lèse-majesté*. It's simply the truth."

"From opposition to revolution is a short step," he muttered stubbornly.

"Nonsense! The Swedes know what they want—you were proclaimed and crowned King."

"And I can be murdered or deposed to make room for the last of the Vasas. He's an officer in the Austrian Army."

At that I decided to lay the ghost of the Vasas once and for all. I would have to hurt and frighten him, I thought sadly. But from now on he could sleep in peace.

573

"Jean-Baptiste—in Sweden the Bernadotte Dynasty rules, and you are the only one who seems not to realize it."

He only shrugged his shoulders.

"But, unfortunately, there are people who feel that, in your fear of the opposition, you disregard the Constitution." I didn't look at him. "The Swedes put great stock in the freedom of their press, dearest. And every time you suppress a newspaper, someone or other suggests you should be forced to abdicate."

He recoiled as though I'd hit him. "So? Look, I'm not afraid of shadows. My ghosts are very real. The Prince of Vasa . . ."

"Jean-Baptiste, no one mentions the Prince of Vasa."

"Who then? Whom do the Liberals want as my successor?"

"Oscar, of course. The Crown Prince."

A deep sigh of relief. "Is that true?" he whispered. "Look me in the eye—is that really true?"

"No one is dissatisfied with the Bernadotte Dynasty. It's established, Jean-Baptiste, established. You must tell Fernand to sleep in his own room. And not with firearms. And why should I run into Fernand in his nightshirt outside your door when I want to visit you late at night?"

Gold epaulettes scratched my cheeks, the candles had burned low.

"My darling, you shouldn't visit me late at night. Queens don't creep around their palaces in their dressing gowns. You're supposed to wait in your apartments with true feminine restraint until I come to you!" Later—much later—we drew back the curtains from the windows.

The sun had risen. The Drottningholm park was bathed in golden light. I stood close to Jean-Baptiste. "As for Oscar—" I began, but he stopped me. Very gently, he kissed me on the top of the head.

"I gave Oscar what I lacked—an education. An education suitable for a sovereign. Sometimes I regret I'll never see him king."

"That's the way it goes, you won't live to see it," I said impressively.

He laughed. "No, I'm not afraid of our young rascal."

I took his arm. "Come with me. We'll have breakfast together just as we did twenty-five years ago."

When we came out of Jean-Baptiste's bedroom Fernand had vanished. "Fernand knows I can lay ghosts," I boasted. In the study we stopped suddenly, silently. "Comrade Moreau," murmured Jean-Baptiste thoughtfully. I ran my finger lightly over the marble cheek, and discovered how badly things are dusted in royal palaces. Then, close together, we strolled on again.

"I'm glad I gave in to you and let Oscar marry Josefina," Jean-Baptiste said unexpectedly.

"If he'd followed your wishes he'd have some hideous royal princess as a wife and run to Mlle von Koskull for consolation—you unnatural father, you!"

"Nevertheless—the granddaughter of our Josephine on the Swedish throne—" Jean-Baptiste looked at me reproachfully.

"But wasn't she enchanting—our Josephine?"

"Much too enchanting. I only hope people here in Scandinavia don't know the details."

We had reached my dressing room, and there we found a great surprise. On the breakfast table, set for two, was a huge bouquet of fragrant roses. Red, white, yellow, and pink roses. Propped against the vase was a note.

"To Their Majesties, our Marshal J.-B. Bernadotte and his wife, with best wishes—Marie and Fernand."

Jean-Baptiste began to laugh—and I to cry. We're so very different, and yet . . .

Yes—and yet.

Royal Palace in Stockholm
February, 1829

I really feel sorry for the old Princess Sofia Albertina. From such a fine family—the last Vasa in Sweden. And now she lies dying, with a silk merchant's daughter holding her hand.

I've been leafing through the pages of this diary. I see I once called her an old goat. She was one of those who ridiculed me. Strange, that her bleating once hurt me so. . . . Since her brother's death, the old Princess has been living in the so-called Heir Apparent's Palace in the Gustavus Adolphus market place. Jean-Baptiste has always seen to it that she dined at court from time to time. But only Oscar ever paid any real attention to her. He calls her Aunt, and says when he was a child she smuggled him sweet coughdrops. Yesterday he noticed she was suffering greatly and was very weak. This morning she unexpectedly sent one of her ancient ladies-in-waiting: it was the last wish of Her Highness, Princess Sofia Albertina, to speak to me—to me—alone!

Poor old thing, I thought on the way to her. Now the last of the Vasas has also gone crazy. . . . In my honour the old Princess had got all dressed up. She lay on a sofa and as I entered she tried to rise. "Please don't, Highness," I exclaimed, shocked by her appearance. She looked more like a goat than ever. Her skin stretched taut over her sunken cheeks and was as transparent and wrinkled as tissue paper. Her lifeless eyes were deep-sunk in their sockets. But her scraggly white hair was tied with girlish rose-coloured ribbons. Her salon overflowed with embroidery—red roses on violet backgrounds on cushions, chairs, and on the bell pull. The poor creature had embroidered nothing but roses all her life long, and always in the same pattern! The old face forced a smile. I sat down beside her and she dismissed her ladies-in-waiting.

"I'm very grateful to Your Majesty for coming. I hear Your Majesty is very busy."

"Yes, we have a great deal to do. Jean-Baptiste with affairs of state and Oscar with his new duties. Oscar is now Admiral of the Swedish Fleet, Your Highness."

She nodded. "I know about that. Oscar often calls on me."

"Has he also told you about his plans for reform? He's working now on a book about prisons. He wants to improve prison conditions and set up a new kind of penal institution," I said enthusiastically.

She looked at me in astonishment. No, Oscar hadn't spoken of that. "A peculiar occupation for an admiral," she remarked sharply.

"And for a composer," I added. She nodded, already bored. Somewhere a clock ticked. . . .

"Your Majesty visits many hospitals?" she suddenly demanded.

"Of course, that's part of my job. Besides, I want to improve them. In France, we invariably have nuns as nurses. Does Your Highness know who takes care of the sick in Swedish hospitals?"

"Worthy devout souls, I suppose?" she asked sharply.

"No—former prostitutes, Your Highness."

She recoiled. Never before in her life had she heard this word straight out. She was speechless.

"I've been to see these nurses. Old beggar women hoping to earn a bowl of soup. Without training, without interest in their calling. Without the slightest conception of cleanliness. I'll change all this, Your Highness."

The clock ticked. . . .

"I'm told you speak some Swedish, madame," she said next.

"I try, Highness. Jean-Baptiste hasn't time for lessons. The plain people don't blame him for that. They take it for granted that a man knows only his native tongue. But—"

"Our aristocrats speak excellent French."

"But commoners, too, study foreign languages, and I have a feeling they expect the same of us. That's why I speak Swedish when I receive deputations of citizens—as well as I can, Highness."

She seemed to have fallen asleep, and her face was as white as her powdered hair. The clock ticked on, and I was afraid it might suddenly stop. I began to feel terribly sorry for the dying Princess. No member of her family at her side, her favourite brother murdered at a masquerade, her nephew declared insane, and banished. And now the poor creature had to see someone like me on the throne of her forefathers.

"You're a good queen," she said unexpectedly.

"We do our best—Jean-Baptiste, Oscar and I."

A shadow of her former malicious smile flitted over her wrinkled face. "You're a very clever woman." That floored me.

"Once—when Hedwig Elisabeth reproached you for being only a silk merchant's daughter, you flounced out of the room, and shortly afterward left Sweden. Until you came back as Queen. People here never forgave Hedwig Elisabeth for that. A court without a young crown princess—" She giggled shamelessly. "So the late Queen had to play the part of a wicked stepmother until her death—hee-hee-hee." This memory seemed to revive her.

"Oscar has brought the children to see me—little Charles, and the new baby."

"The new baby is called Oscar, too," I said proudly.

"Charles takes after you, madame," she assured me.

Children are a real pleasure when you don't have to be waked up by them at six o'clock in the morning, I thought. Then it occurred to me that even Josefina probably sleeps as late as she wants to. My grandchildren have a whole retinue of governesses and nurses. While Oscar's cradle was beside my bed his entire first year.

"I would like to have had children, but no suitable husband for me was ever found," lamented the dying Princess. "Oscar says you wouldn't mind if his children married commoners. How could you suggest such a thing, madame?"

"I haven't thought much about it. But princes can renounce their titles, can't they?"

"Of course. One need only find new names for them—" She mulled it over. "Count Upsala or Baron Drottningholm or . . ."

"But why? We have a good bourgeois name—Bernadotte."

At the words "good bourgeois" her face contracted with misery. "But the future Bernadottes will, I hope, be a family of composers, arists, or writers," I quickly comforted her. "Oscar is very musical. And Josefina's aunt Hortense paints and writes poetry. In my family, too—" I stopped, she had dozed off and wasn't listening to me at all.

To my great surprise she spoke again.

"I wanted to talk to you about the crown, madame."

She's delirious, I thought, her mind is wandering as the end draws near.

"Which crown?" I asked out of politeness.

"The crown of the Queen of Sweden."

I suddenly felt very hot. In the middle of the Stockholm winter, when I'm usually half-frozen, I was hot. Her eyes were wide open, her voice was calm and clear.

"You weren't crowned with His Majesty, madame. Perhaps you don't even know that we also have a crown for our queens. A very ancient crown—not large but very heavy. I've held it in my hands several times. You are the mother of the Bernadotte Dynasty, madame. Why won't you be crowned?"

"Until now no one has thought of it," I said softly.

"But I have thought of it. I am the last Vasa in Sweden, and I ask the first Bernadotte to accept the ancient crown. Madame, promise me you will be crowned?"

"I care very little for these ceremonies," I murmured. "I'm too small for them, I don't look the least regal."

Her bloodless fingers reached out for my hand. "I no longer have time to plead with you. . . ."

I laid my hand in hers.

Once at a coronation I had to carry a lace handkerchief on a velvet cushion, the bells of Notre-Dame had pealed . . . Could she read my thoughts?

"I've had them read aloud to me the memoirs of this Napoleon Bonaparte. How strange—" She examined me critically. "How strange, madame, that the two outstanding men of our times have been in love with you. You're really no beauty."

Then she sighed—softly, so softly. "A pity I'm a Vasa. I'd much rather have been a Bernadotte and married a commoner—and been less bored."

When I left, I bowed deeply and kissed the withered hand. The dying Princess smiled, first in surprise and a little maliciously. For I really am no beauty.

Royal Palace in Stockholm
May, 1829

"His Royal Highness regrets, but it is impossible for His Royal Highness to arrange a free hour any afternoon this week. The Crown Prince is engaged for every minute," Oscar's chamberlain announced to me.

"Inform His Royal Highness that it's to fulfill a wish of his mother's." Oscar's chamberlain hesitated, wanted to refuse me. I looked at him sternly. And he vanished.

"Aunt, you know Oscar has endless obligations. His responsibilities as High Admiral, the reception and audiences he must hold. And since His Majesty has two ministers who speak horrible French, Oscar must also attend all the Councils of State." Marcelline interferes in matters that are none of her business.

Oscar's chamberlain returned. "His Royal Highness' regrets, but it is out of the question this week."

"Then tell His Royal Highness I'll expect him this afternoon at four o'clock. The Crown Prince will accompany me on an errand."

"Your Majesty, His Royal Highness regrets . . ."

"I know, my dear Count, my son regrets that he cannot fulfill my wish. Therefore inform the Crown Prince that this is no longer the wish of his mother, but an order of the Queen."

Oscar was announced at the stroke of four. Escorted by two adjutants and his chamberlain. Around the sleeve of his blue admiral's uniform he wore a mourning band. I myself was in black. The entire court wore mourning for Prince Sofia Albertina, who died on March 17, and was laid to rest in the Vasa tomb in Riddarholm Church. Her state funeral startled the populace. They thought she'd died long ago, and had completely forgotten her.

"At your command, Majesty," Oscar greeted me formally, and clicked his heels together. Then he tried to look off into space above my head to show me how furious he was.

"Please dismiss your gentlemen, I want to go with you alone." I straightened my hat with its mourning veil. "Come, Oscar."

Without a word we left my apartments. Without a word we descended the stairs. He kept a pace behind me. When we got to the side door through which we usually leave the Palace so as not to excite notice, he asked, "Where is your carriage?"

"We're walking," I replied. "It's such lovely weather."

The sky was pale blue, the Mälar gurgled green, in the mountains the snow is beginning to melt.

"We're going to Västra Långgatan," I informed him.

Oscar took the lead, and I tramped after him through the narrow alleys behind the Palace. Although he was inwardly boiling with rage, he continually smiled and saluted. Because all the passers-by recognized him and bowed. I pulled my mourning veil over my face, but it was wholly unnecessary. I was very simply dressed, and looked so uninteresting that no one had any idea I could be with His Royal Highness.

Oscar stopped. "Here, Your Majesty, is the Västra Långgatan. May I ask where we go from here?"

"To a silk shop. It belongs to a certain Persson. I've never been there, but it won't be hard to find."

At that Oscar lost his patience. "Mama! I cancelled two appointments and postponed an audience to obey your orders. And where are you taking me? To a silk shop. Why don't you have the court purveyors come to you?"

"Persson is not a court purveyor. And besides—I want to see his shop."

"May I ask why you need me for this?"

"You can help me pick out the material. For my coronation robe, Oscar. . . . And I'd also like to introduce you to this M. Persson."

Oscar was speechless. "To a silk merchant, Mama?"

My spirits sank. Perhaps it was a bad idea to bring Oscar with me. Sometimes I forget my son is a Crown Prince. How they all stare at him.

"Persson was an apprentice for your grandfather Clary in Marseilles. He even lived in our villa." I swallowed desperately.

"Oscar—he's the one person in Stockholm who knew my papa and my home."

At that Oscar quickly unbent and tenderly took my arm. Then we looked hopefully around. Finally Oscar stopped an elderly gentleman to ask for Persson's shop. Unfortunately the old gentleman bowed so respectfully, almost down to the ground, that Oscar, too, had to bend practically double to hear what he said. At last they both straightened up.

"Over there," Oscar said triumphantly.

It was a relatively small shop. But displayed in the window I saw fine quality silk and velvet in rolls. Oscar pushed open the door. In front of the counter ranged a crowd of customers. No well-turned-out court ladies, but rather middle-class women in good dark street dresses and tight velvet jackets. Their unrouged faces were framed in heavy curls. This hairdress is frightfully modern, and I realized that Persson's customers knew what was what. The ladies fingered the various materials with such concentration that they didn't even notice Oscar's uniform, and we were elbowed this way and that until our turn came. Behind the counter were three young men. One of them had a horseface and blond hair, and reminded me of the erstwhile young Persson. Finally he asked me, "May I serve you?"

"I'd like to see your silk," said I, in my broken Swedish. At first he didn't understand me, and I repeated it in French.

"I'd better call my father. My father speaks very good French," said young Horseface eagerly, and disappeared through a side door. Suddenly, to my surprise, I realized that we had plenty of room and were actually entirely alone at the counter. All the other customers stood back against the wall, gaping at us. They were whispering a single word, "Drottningen." I pushed back my veil to see the material better.

At that moment the side door opened, and Persson came in. Persson from Marseilles. Our Persson. He hadn't changed very much, his blond hair had gone a colourless grey. His blue eyes weren't shy any more but calm and self-sufficient. And he smiled encouragingly as one always smiles at customers, and thereby showed his long yellow teeth.

"Madame wishes to see some silk?" he asked in French.

"Your French if possible is worse than ever, M. Persson," I declared. "And I once took so much trouble with your accent."

A shudder went through the tall gaunt figure. He opened his mouth to say something, but his underlip began to quiver, and he couldn't get out a word. There was dead silence in the shop.

"Had you forgotten me, M. Persson?"

He shook his head. Slowly as in a dream. I tried to help him and leaned across the counter. "M. Persson, I want to see your silk," I said clearly.

Confused, he mopped his brow and mumbled in his atrocious French, "Now you've really come to me, Mlle Clary."

That was too much for Oscar. The crowded shop, the eavesdropping ladies, and Persson stuttering in French . . .

"Perhaps you'd be good enough to take Her Majesty and me to your office and show us the silk there," he said in Swedish.

Young Persson raised the connecting flap between the counter and the space beyond, and took us through a side door into a small office. The high desk with the firm's books and a hundred swatches of silk everywhere reminded me vividly of Papa's holy of holies. Over the desk hung a framed broadside. It had turned very yellow, but I recognized it immediately.

"Well, here I am, Persson," I murmured, and sat down on the chair beside the high desk. I felt completely at home.

"I'd like to present my son. Oscar, M. Persson was apprenticed to your grandfather in Marseilles."

"Then it surprises me, M. Persson, that you have not long ago been appointed purveyor to the court," Oscar remarked amiably.

"I never applied for it," said Persson slowly. "Besides, I've had rather a bad name in certain circles since my return from France." He indicated the framed broadside. "Because of that."

"What's that in the frame?" Oscar inquired.

Persson took it down from the wall and handed it to Oscar.

"Oscar," I said, "that's the first printing of the Rights of Man. Papa—your grandfather—brought it home. And M. Persson and I learned the Rights of Man together by heart. Before his return to Sweden, M. Persson asked me for this broadside as a remembrance."

Oscar didn't answer. He went to the window, wiped off the glass with the sleeve of his admiral's uniform, and began to read. Persson and I looked at each other. He'd stopped trembling, his eyes were wet. "And the Mälar is really as green as you told me. Once I couldn't imagine it. Now it flows in front of my windows. . . ."

"To think you remember all that, mademoi—I mean Your Majesty," said Persson hoarsely.

"Naturally— That's why, that's why it took me so long to come to see you. I was afraid you might take offense, that . . ."

"Take offense? How could I ever take offense at you?" Persson asked in dismay.

"That I'm now Queen. You and I were always Republicans." I smiled. Persson sneaked a horrified look at Oscar. But Oscar wasn't listening. He was too engrossed in the Rights of Man.

At that Persson lost his shyness completely and whispered, "That was in France, Mlle Clary. But in Sweden we're both—Monarchists." He glanced at Oscar again and added, "Provided, of course—that—"

I nodded. "Yes, provided that— But you have a son yourself, Persson. It all ultimately depends on the training of the children."

"Of course. And His Royal Highness is, after all, a grandson of François Clary," he reassured me. We were silent and thought of the villa, and the shop.

"The sword of this General Bonaparte," Persson said suddenly. "The sword stood in the hall nearly every evening at the house in Marseilles. I—was very annoyed about it." Persson's colorless face was quite pink.

I looked at him out of the corner of my eye. "Persson—were you jealous?"

He turned away. "If I had ever imagined that a daughter of François Clary would have been happy in Stockholm, I would have—" He stopped.

I was speechless. He would have offered me a home and a shop —quite close to the Royal Palace. Close to—

"I need a new dress, Persson," I said softly.

He turned to me again, his face colourless again and very dignified.

"An evening dress, or one Your Majesty wishes to wear in the daytime?"

"An evening dress, which I must wear by day. Perhaps you've read in the paper that I'm to be crowned August 21. Have you any material that—well, that's suitable for a coronation robe?"

"Of course." Persson nodded. "The white brocade."

He opened the door. "François," he called. "Bring me the white brocade from Marseilles. You know which one." And to me, "I've taken the liberty of calling my son 'François' in memory of your papa."

I held the heavy roll of brocade on my knees. Oscar laid aside the framed broadside, and examined the material. "Wonderful— Mama, the real thing." I stroked the stiff silk, felt the woven threads of genuine gold. "Isn't it heavy, Mama?"

"Dreadfully heavy, Oscar. I carried the package myself to the travelling coach. M. Persson had so much luggage I had to help him."

"And Your Majesty's papa said that this brocade was suitable only for a queen's robe of state," Persson added.

"Why have you never offered it to anyone at the court?" I asked. "The late Queen would have loved it."

"I've kept the brocade in memory of your papa and the firm of Clary, Your Majesty. Besides—" His horseface assumed a superior air. "Besides, I am not a court purveyor. The brocade is not for sale."

"Not even today?" Oscar asked.

"Not even today, Your Highness."

I sat very still while Persson summoned his son. "François, wrap up the brocade from the firm of Clary." And bowing before me, "May I have the honour of presenting the brocade to Your Majesty?"

My head dropped, I couldn't speak.

"I'll send the material to the Palace immediately, Your Majesty," Persson said, and I stood up. On the wallpaper over the high desk there was a light spot where the broadside had hung. "If Your Majesty will wait a moment—" Persson rummaged in the waste-basket, found a discarded newspaper and wrapped it around the frame.

"May I ask Your Majesty to accept this, too. Many years ago I promised to cherish this broadside, and throughout my life it has been sacred to me." The long teeth protruded as he smiled ironically. "I've wrapped it up so that Your Majesty won't be embarrassed carrying it. I myself have had several unpleasant experiences because of it."

Arm in arm like a pair of lovers Oscar and I walked back. The Palace came in sight, and I still hadn't told him. Desperately I searched for the right words. "Oscar, perhaps you feel you've wasted an afternoon because of me, but—" The first sentries presented arms.

"Come along, Oscar, I want to talk to you." I felt how impatient he was, but I had to stop on the bridge. The Mälar frothed beneath us. My heart contracted. At this hour, the lights of Paris begin to dance in the silent Seine.

"I've always secretly hoped that Persson would give me back Papa's broadside. And that's why I took you with me, Oscar."

"Are you going to discuss the Rights of Man with me now?"

"Only that, Oscar. " But he had no more time and was extremely irritable.

"Mama, for me the Rights of Man are no longer a revelation. Here every educated person has heard of them."

"Then we must see that the uneducated also learn them by heart," I said. "I still want to tell you that . . ."

"That I must fight for them? Shall I solemnly promise you that?"

"Fight. The Rights of Man have long since been proclaimed. You must only—defend them." I stared into the shimmering water. A childhood memory cropped up—a severed head rolling in bloody sawdust.

"Before and after their proclamation, much blood was shed. Napoleon degraded them by quoting them in his orders of the day. Others desecrated them, Oscar—over and again. But my son should stand up for them, and teach his children to."

Oscar was silent. He was silent for a long time, then took the package, took off the wrappings and let them flutter into the Mälar.

Just as we were against our side door he suddenly laughed. "Mama, your old admirer's declaration of love was priceless—if Papa only knew."

My coronation day
(*August 21, 1829*)

"Désirée, I implore you, don't be late for your own coronation!"

This sentence will pursue me to the end of my days. Jean-Baptiste shouted it at me continually while I desperately searched through all my bureau drawers. Marie helped me. And Marcelline and Yvette. Betweentimes I marvelled at Jean-Baptiste who today wore his own coronation panoply. Gold chains around his neck and the comic boots with the ermine braid which up to now I'd seen only in portraits. The heavy coronation robe he would don later. When he put on his crown.

"Désirée, won't you ever be ready?"

"Jean-Baptiste, I can't find them, I can't."

"What are you looking for now?"

"My sins, Jean-Baptiste. I wrote them all down and the list has disappeared."

"My God, can't you remember them?"

"No, there are so many of them, all too insignificant to remember. That's why I wrote them all down. Yvette, look in the laundry again."

Before the coronation, the Shooting Star and I were to go to confession. We're the only Catholic members of the Protestant Bernadotte royal family in Lutheran Sweden. So the clergy—the Protestant clergy of Sweden and the Catholic priest who looks after the welfare of my soul—decided that I must make my confession quietly in the Palace chapel. Oscar had this chapel built on the top floor of the Palace for the devout young granddaughter of the somewhat less pious older Josephine. Right after the absolution of my sins I was quickly to put on my coronation robes and drive in the state procession to the Storkyrka. Everything had been arranged. On the bed lay the white-gold dress made of the brocade Papa once held in his hand. Beside it the purple robe of the queens of Sweden, which had been shortened somewhat for me, and the small crown, freshly polished. I had not dared try it on.

"Mama, it's high time." Josefina had come in.

"But I can't find my list of sins," I moaned. "Could you lend me yours?"

The Shooting Star was indignant. "Mama, I have no list! One should remember one's sins."

"The sins are not in Your Majesty's laundry," Yvette announced.

We departed for the small salon. Oscar, in his gala uniform, was waiting there.

"I never realized your mama's coronation would arouse so much enthusiasm. Even in the small village people are celebrating. Look down below, Oscar, it's black with people," Jean-Baptiste said to him. They were both hidden behind the curtains so they couldn't be seen from the street.

"Mama is tremendously popular," Oscar answered. "You don't know what Mama means to . . ."

Jean-Baptiste smiled at me. "Really?" he said to Oscar, but he was annoyed.

"You must hurry, you and Josefina. Have you your sins or haven't you, Désirée?"

"I haven't them," I said, and sank down exhausted on the sofa. "And Josefina won't lend me hers. What are your sins, Josefina?"

"Those I tell only the father-confessor." The Shooting Star smiled with tight-closed lips and her head a little to one side.

"What are your sins, Jean-Baptiste?" I inquired.

"I am a member of the Protestant Church. . . . Perhaps Josefina can help you out with a few sins on the way. You must go now!"

Yvette handed me my veil and gloves.

"One should never expect help from one's family," I remarked bitterly.

"I know a confession for you, Mama. You've lived in sin for years with a man!" Oscar declared.

"This jest goes too far," Jean-Baptiste exclaimed. But I quieted him.

"Let him finish, Jean-Baptiste. What do you mean, darling?"

"The Catholic Church doesn't recognize civil marriages. Did you marry Papa in a church or in a registry office?"

"In a registry office, only in a registry office," I assured him.

"There's your sin, Mama, a great sin of long standing. There— and now you must hurry."

We got there in time for confession, and dashed back breathless. In my salon the entire court had assembled. I took a quick look and rushed by the line of court curtsies. "Aunt, you haven't much time," Marcelline said in my dressing room. And my Marie—old, bent, but determined—ripped the clothes off my back. Yvette wrapped me in a hairdresser's cape.

"Leave me alone," I begged, "please leave me alone a moment."

"Aunt, the archbishop is waiting in front of the church," Marcelline warned me. Then she finally disappeared.

If a woman is vain and studies her face every day in the mirror, then it's no shock to find it older. It happens so gradually. I am forty-nine years old, and I've laughed so much and wept so much that I have many little wrinkles around my eyes, and two lines down to the corners of my mouth, dating to the time that Jean-Baptiste was fighting the battle of Leipzig. . . . I rubbed some rose cream on my forehead and cheeks, stroked a tiny brush across my eyebrows, which Yvette keeps well plucked. Then silver paint on my eyelids. Just as la grande Josephine taught me. . . .

How many letters and deputations from all parts of the country are here today. As if Sweden had been waiting for years for my coronation. Jean-Baptiste can't understand it. Does he honestly be- lieve that it's enough to be married to him to become a queen? Doesn't he realize that this coronation signifies my final acceptance? Jean-Baptiste, it is a bride's promise. This time I'll even go to church and swear before an altar to be loyal and serve you for better or worse. . . . And because a bride should be young and beautiful, I'll be generous with the rouge.

The crowds in the streets began to gather at five o'clock this morning to see me drive past. I mustn't disappoint them. Most women don't have to look young when they are forty-nine. Their children are grown or their husbands have arrived. They belong to themselves again. But not me. I'm only beginning. But it's not my fault I founded a dynasty. . . . I took some delicate brown powder and powdered my nose as thickly as possible. When the organ plays I'll weep. Organ music always makes me weep. And my nose will turn red. If only, once in my life—if only today I could look like a queen. I am so frightened. . . .

"How young you are, Désirée—not a single grey hair!" Jean-Baptiste stood behind me. He kissed my hair.

I had to laugh. "Lots of grey hairs, Jean-Baptiste, but dyed for the first time. Do you like it?"

No answer. I looked around. Jean-Baptiste was wearing the heavy ermine cape, and on his forehead the crown of the kings of Sweden. He seemed suddenly very strange and very large—no longer my Jean-Baptiste, but King Charles XIV John, the King.

The King stared at the yellowed broadside on the wall. He hadn't seen it before, it had been a long time since he'd been in my dressing room.

"What's that, little one?"

"An old broadside, Jean-Baptiste. The first printing of the Rights of Man."

Steep furrows between his eyebrows.

"My father bought it many years ago. When it was still damp from the press. I had to learn it by heart. Now this yellowing paper gives me strength. And I need strength, you know, I—" Tears streamed over my fresh make-up. "I wasn't born to be a queen."

Then I had to powder over the traces of my tears. "Yvette."

Jean-Baptiste asked, "May I stay here?" and sat down beside the dressing table. Yvette brought the curling iron, and began to roll up the little side curls.

"Don't forget Her Majesty's hair must lie flat on top or the crown won't sit right," Jean-Baptiste warned. He took out a paper and studied it.

"Your sins, Jean-Baptiste? What a long list!"

"No, notes for the coronation ceremony. Shall I read them to you once more?"

I nodded.

"Listen carefully. The coronation procession opens with pages and heralds in the costumes that were made for my coronation. Very pretty costumes, you'll be impressed. . . . The heralds have fanfares. After them come members of the Government, then the deputies. Finally a delegation from Norway. You will, of course, be crowned also as Queen of Norway. I'd rather thought that perhaps you ought to have another coronation in Norway. In Christiania. The overwhelming and really touching joy with which all Sweden is celebrating your coronation makes me consider . . ."

"No," I said. "Not in Christiania. Under no circumstances!"

"Why not?"

"Desideria—the desired one. Here, but not in Norway. Never forget that you forced Norway into this union."

"It was necessary, Désirée."

"Perhaps it will last Oscar's lifetime. But not much longer. Anyway, then it won't matter . . ."

"Ten minutes before your coronation do you realize that you're talking treason?"

"In a hundred years we'll both be sitting on a comfortable cloud in heaven and we can discuss it again. By that time the Norwegians will again have declared their independence and, to annoy Sweden, have elected a Danish prince as their King. You and I, on our cloud, will have a good laugh. For this Dane will surely have a drop of Bernadotte blood in his veins, marriages between neighbours' children are so frequent. . . . Yvette, call Marie, she must help me put on my coronation dress."

Marcelline and Marie rushed in at the same time. I slipped off the cape. Marie stood before me, with the coronation costume. The gold threads in the white material had in the passage of time acquired a silvery shimmer. And when I had put on the dress, I took a deep breath. It was the most beautiful thing I had ever seen.

"What happens next, Jean-Baptiste? Who will march behind the Norwegian delegation?"

"Your two Counts with the royal insignia. On blue velvet cushions."

"Can you still remember how I carried Josephine's lace handkerchief, through all of Notre-Dame? And the crisis because they couldn't find twelve virgins?"

"The royal insignia should have been carried by the highest officials in the state," Jean-Baptiste said, "but you insisted . . ."

"Yes, I insisted that Count Brahe and Count Rosen carry them. When other Swedes had not yet become accustomed to a silk merchant's daughter, they were her knights."

"Behind them will come the lady you selected with the crown. The crown will lie on a red cushion."

"Aren't you satisfied with my choice? It doesn't say anywhere that she has to be a virgin. Only a lady from a distinguished aristocratic family. I therefore decided to award this honour to Mlle Mariana von Koskull, the former lady-in-waiting." I winked at Jean-Baptiste. "In appreciation of her services to the royal houses of Vasa and Bernadotte."

But Jean-Baptiste was suddenly concentrating on the crown jewels. I slipped on the large rings. Finally I clasped the big diamond necklace. It scratched and felt cold and strange around my neck.

"Marcelline, you can tell them in the salon that I'm ready."

Marie was about to adjust my purple robe, but Jean-Baptiste took it from her. Tenderly, very tenderly, he laid it over my shoulders. We stood side by side in front of the big mirror.

"It's like a fairy tale," I whispered. "Once upon a time there was a tall king and a tiny queen." Then I turned around quickly. "Jean-Baptiste—the broadside!"

Calmly he took the frame from the wall. And stood before me in his coronation robe, with Sweden's crown on his anointed head, and held out the broadside to me. I bowed my head and kissed the glass over the faded text of the Rights of Man. When I looked up, Jean-Baptiste's face was white with emotion.

The folding doors to the salon were flung open. Josefina had brought the children. Three-year-old Charles rushed to me, then stopped in fright. "That isn't Grandmama," he said, shying away. "That's a queen." Josefina, in rose-coloured shimmering velvet, held up the infant Oscar to me. I took the child in my arms, he was wonderfully warm, had astonishingly blue eyes, and practically no hair.

For your sake, too, for you, too, I'm being crowned, you second Oscar. . . .

The distant roar of cheering in front of the closed windows reminded me of the night in which the many torches had burned bright in the rue d'Anjou. I heard Jean-Baptiste ask, "Why doesn't someone open the windows?" And, "What are they shouting? What are they crying down there?"

But I already knew. It was in French, my Swedes wanted me to understand. They remembered what they'd once read about that night. They cheered: *"Nôtre dame de la paix!"* I quickly handed Josefina the infant, because I'd begun to tremble.

What happened next was like a dream. Probably the pages and heralds had already left the Palace. Probably behind them marched the ministers and the Norwegian delegates. As we descended the marble staircase we caught a glimpse of Count Brahe and Count Rosen with the royal insignia. Rosen tried to catch my eye. I nodded almost imperceptibly, and thought about the drive from Malmaison to Paris, and about Villatte— The two counts slowly, solemnly left the Palace. For the fraction of a second I saw Mlle von Koskull in blue, with the crown sparkling on the velvet cushion. The Koskull looked very happy and proud because she hadn't been forgotten, and had no idea how faded she looked. Then Josefina and Oscar climbed into an open carriage. And at last came the gilded coach for Their Majesties.

"I'll be the last to arrive at the church, like a bride," I remarked. Then from all sides rose cheers. I saw Jean-Baptiste smile and wave and wanted to smile and wave myself but I was numb. For they were shouting at me, to me alone: *"Länge leve Drottningen— Drottningen—"* and I realized I was going to cry. I couldn't help myself.

At the church, Jean-Baptiste himself arranged the folds of my purple robe and escorted me to the portals. There I was met by the archbishop with all the other bishops of Sweden. "Blessed be they who come in the name of the Lord," the bishop said. Then the music of the organ rose triumphantly, and I couldn't think clearly again until the archbishop placed the crown on my head. . . .

It is late night, and everyone thinks I've gone to bed to rest up for the festivities tomorrow and the day after tomorrow in honour of Queen Desideria of Sweden and Norway. But I wanted, once more, to write in my diary. How odd that this happens to be the last page. Once it was all empty white pages, and lay on my birthday table. I was then just going on fourteen years old and asked what I should write in it. And Papa answered, "The story of French Citizeness Bernardine Eugénie Désirée Clary."

Papa, I've written the whole story and have nothing more to add. For the story of this citizeness is finished, and that of the Queen begins. I'll never comprehend how this all came about. But I promise you, Papa, to do all I can so as not to disgrace you, and never to forget that, all your life long, you were a highly respected silk merchant.

AUTHOR'S NOTE

This book is based on history, but like every novel it has its own reality. In a few incidents I have departed from history because I am persuaded that history is not always recorded to the last detail. In the light of my own interpretation of the characters and of their reactions I, for one, have chosen to believe that what might have happened did happen.

A.S.

594